Buffy the vampire slayer™
OMNIBUS

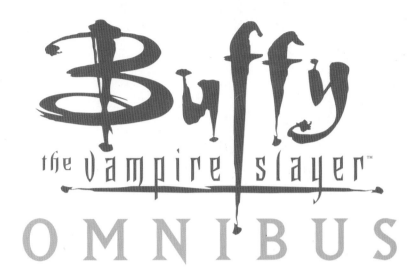

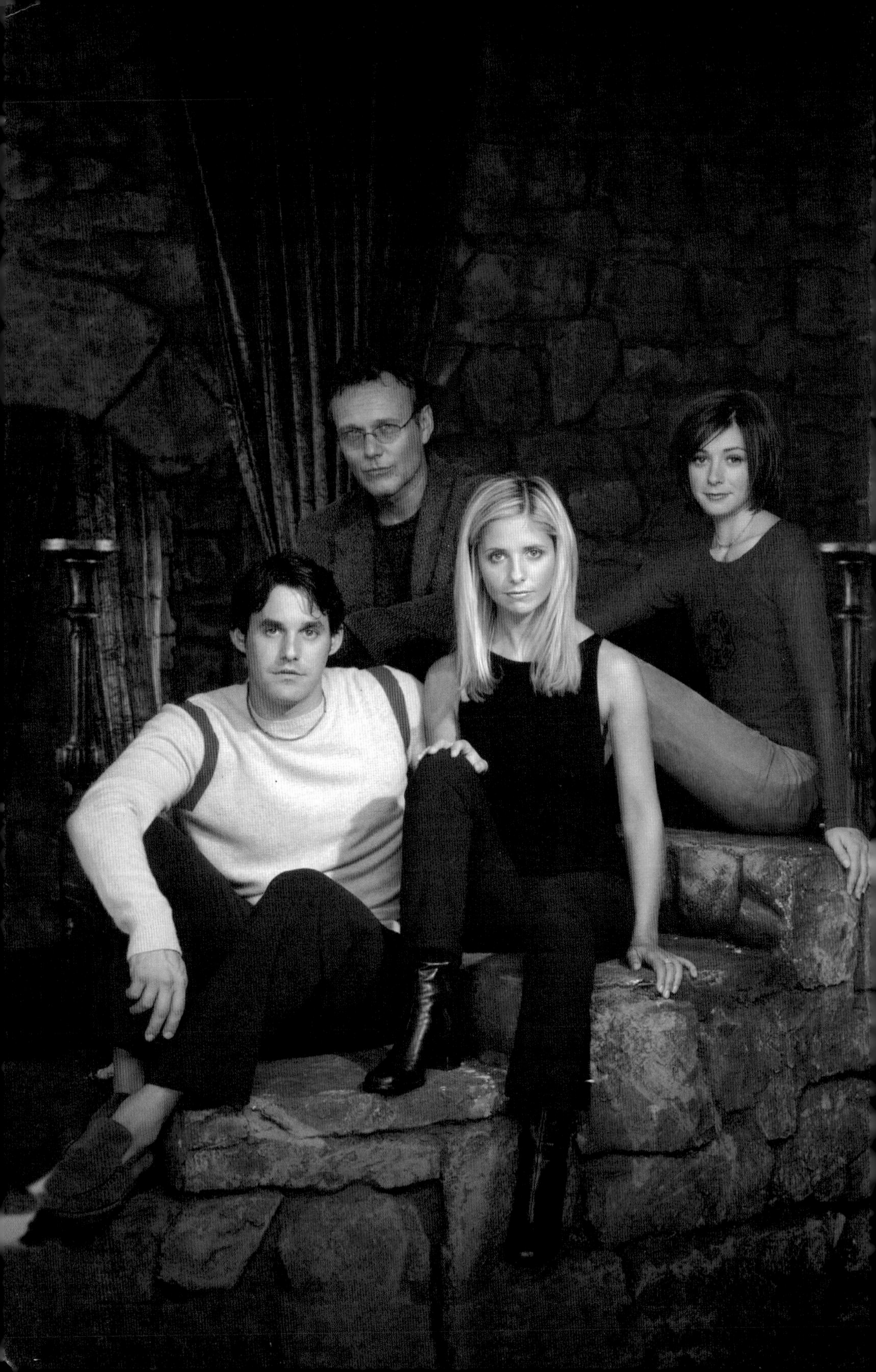

Buffy the Vampire Slayer™

OMNIBUS

VOLUME 5

CHRIS BOAL
CHYNNA CLUGSTON
JANE ESPENSON
TOM FASSBENDER
CHRISTOPHER GOLDEN
BRIAN HORTON
PAUL LEE
LOGAN LUBERA
JIM PASCOE
DOUG PETRIE
CLIFF RICHARDS

Based on the television series created by Joss Whedon.

These stories take place during Buffy the Vampire Slayer *Season Four.*

DARK HORSE BOOKS®

Publisher MIKE RICHARDSON
Editors SCOTT ALLIE & SIERRA HAHN
Assistant Editors on Original Series MATT DRYER, BEN ABERNATHY, MIKE CARRIGLITTO & ADAM GALLARDO
Collection Designers LIA RIBACCHI & HEIDI WHITCOMB
Cover Illustration PAUL LEE & BRIAN HORTON

Special thanks to Debbie Olshan at Twentieth Century Fox, David Campiti at Glass House Graphics, Caroline Kallas, and George Snyder.

BUFFY THE VAMPIRE SLAYER™ OMNIBUS VOLUME FIVE

This volume reprints
Buffy the Vampire Slayer: Haunted #1–4, originally published December 2001 through March 2002;
Buffy the Vampire Slayer: "Take Back the Night," originally published in *Dark Horse Presents Annual 2000,* June 2000;
Buffy the Vampire Slayer: "Killing Time," originally published in *Dark Horse Presents* 150, January 2000;
Buffy the Vampire Slayer #21–28, originally published May through December 2000; and
Buffy the Vampire Slayer: Oz #1–3, originally published July through September 2001,
all from Dark Horse Comics.

Published by Dark Horse Books
A division of Dark Horse Comics, Inc.
10956 SE Main Street
Milwaukie, OR 97222

darkhorse.com

To find a comics shop in your area, call the Comic Shop Locator Service toll-free at (888) 266-4226.

First edition: September 2008
ISBN 978-1-59582-225-3

10 9 8 7 6 5 4 3 2 1
Printed in Hong Kong

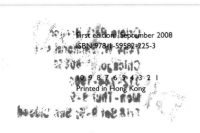

INTRODUCTION

One of the things I was most often accused of overlooking, in editing the old run of *Buffy* comics, was what a great character Faith was. She had very little presence in the comics, a fact that fans complained about constantly. Frankly, I agree with them.

The reason she was left out was precisely the reason why she was such a great character on the show. With the old comic we were always trying to keep up with television continuity. We had to portray the characters in a generalized way—how does Xander act this season of the show? What's his *general* m.o.? When Willow hooked up with Tara, I asked Joss if it was going to stick, and when he told me yes, I had Tara brought into the cast of the comic—by the time she appeared in an issue, she'd been on the show nearly a year. As I may have mentioned, it takes a lot longer to make a comic than a TV show—we didn't want to write a script about a charac-ter that would be out of date by the time the comic was published.

No one changed more quickly, in more different directions, than Faith. It's one of the reasons she was so fun to watch, and the reason we couldn't do much with her in the monthly comic. We couldn't trust her to act the same way for more than a couple months. In a show where all the characters grew and evolved, Faith made them all look like they were standing still.

After writing a couple of short stories, Jane Espenson asked about doing something substantial. Jane chose a character she'd loved writing—the Mayor, the Big Bad from her first season with the show. I shared with her a trick the *Buffy* comics writers and I had figured out—Joss always left the summers between television seasons a mystery, leaving room for us to decide what happened. So Jane, who teamed with artist Cliff Richards, was able to deal with the aftermath of "Graduation Day." With the Mayor, we got our first Faith comics story.

In late 1999, Cliff teamed with Doug Petrie for the short story "Killing Time," and a few months later he joined Tom Fassbender and Jim Pascoe for their first *Buffy* story, which sets up the longer story "Out of the Woodwork," to be featured in *Omnibus* Volume 6.

Buffy novelist Christopher Golden teamed with Cliff for *The Blood of Carthage*. They were joined by Chynna Clugston, whose manga-influenced style suited the flashbacks to pre–Season One Willow and Xander. Paul Lee and Brian Horton provided flash-backs focused on Spike and Drusilla. I used Paul and Brian on this section because I didn't know if they'd be right for Buffy and her inner circle—ironically, they went on to become two of the best artists at capturing the likenesses of the cast.

Immediately after *Blood of Carthage*, Cliff teamed with Chris Boal, a writer whom Joss introduced me to. Cliff's final story in this volume was the first issue of the monthly series written by Fassbender and Pascoe, whose work will come to dominate the next two volumes in the *Omnibus* series.

The only story in this volume not drawn by Cliff sees Golden again focusing on a supporting character. *Buffy* fans love Oz; his departure from the show, and the unlikelihood of his return, made a comics series almost a necessity. Oz's werewolf appearance needed an overhaul, though, so I called in one of my favorite artists from the world of horror comics. John Totleben provided covers in which he designed and defined the supernatural characters in the series, including the werewolf. He wasn't interested in drawing actor likenesses, so Seth Green did not appear on any of the art covers for the miniseries.

But I was always more interested in the monsters anyway.

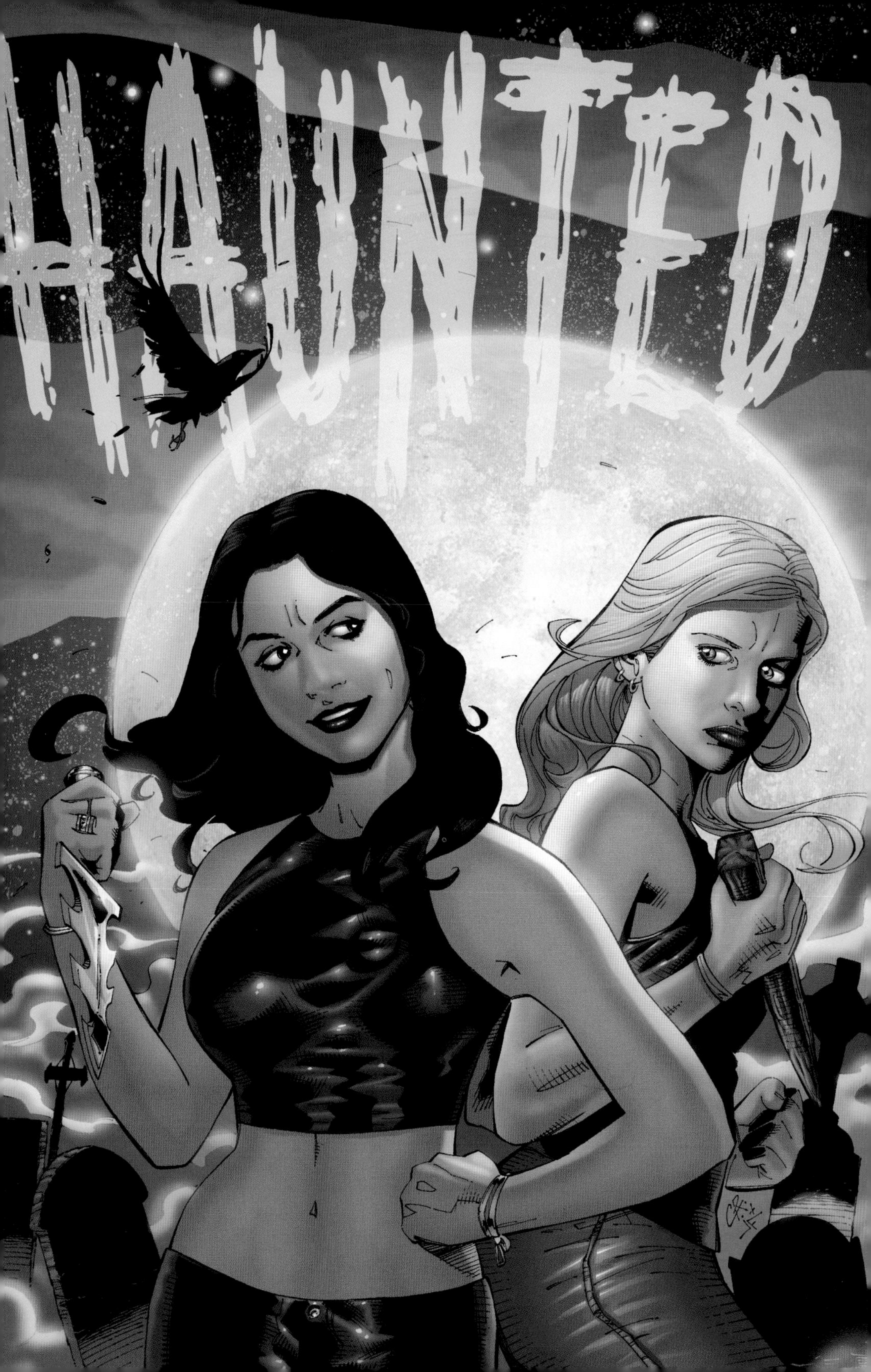
HAUNTED

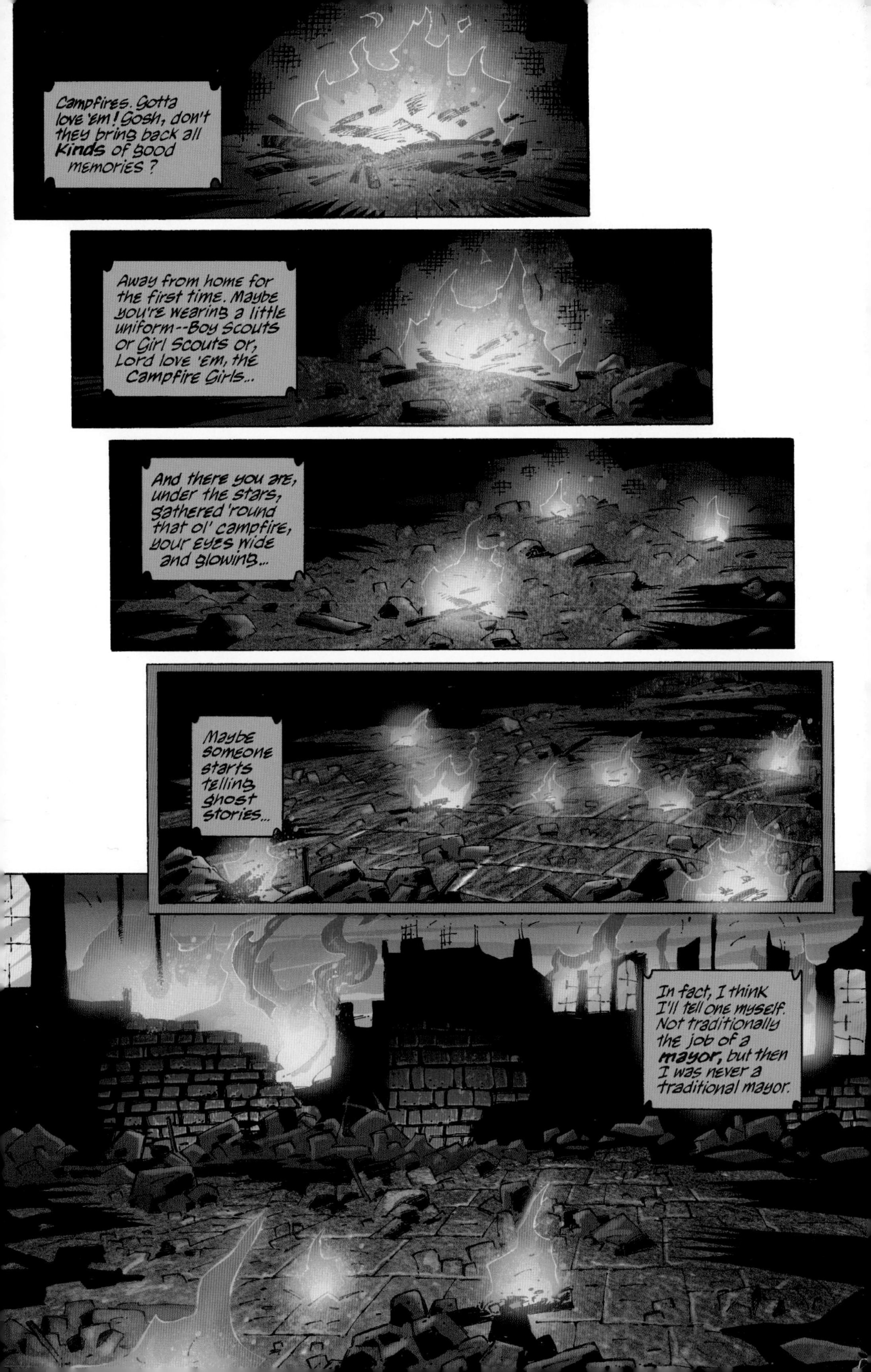

Campfires. Gotta love 'em! Gosh, don't they bring back all **kinds** of good memories?
Away from home for the first time. Maybe you're wearing a little uniform--Boy Scouts or Girl Scouts or, Lord love 'em, the Campfire Girls...
And there you are, under the stars, gathered 'round that ol' campfire, your eyes wide and glowing...
Maybe someone starts telling ghost stories...
In fact, I think I'll tell one myself. Not traditionally the job of a **mayor,** but then I was never a traditional mayor.

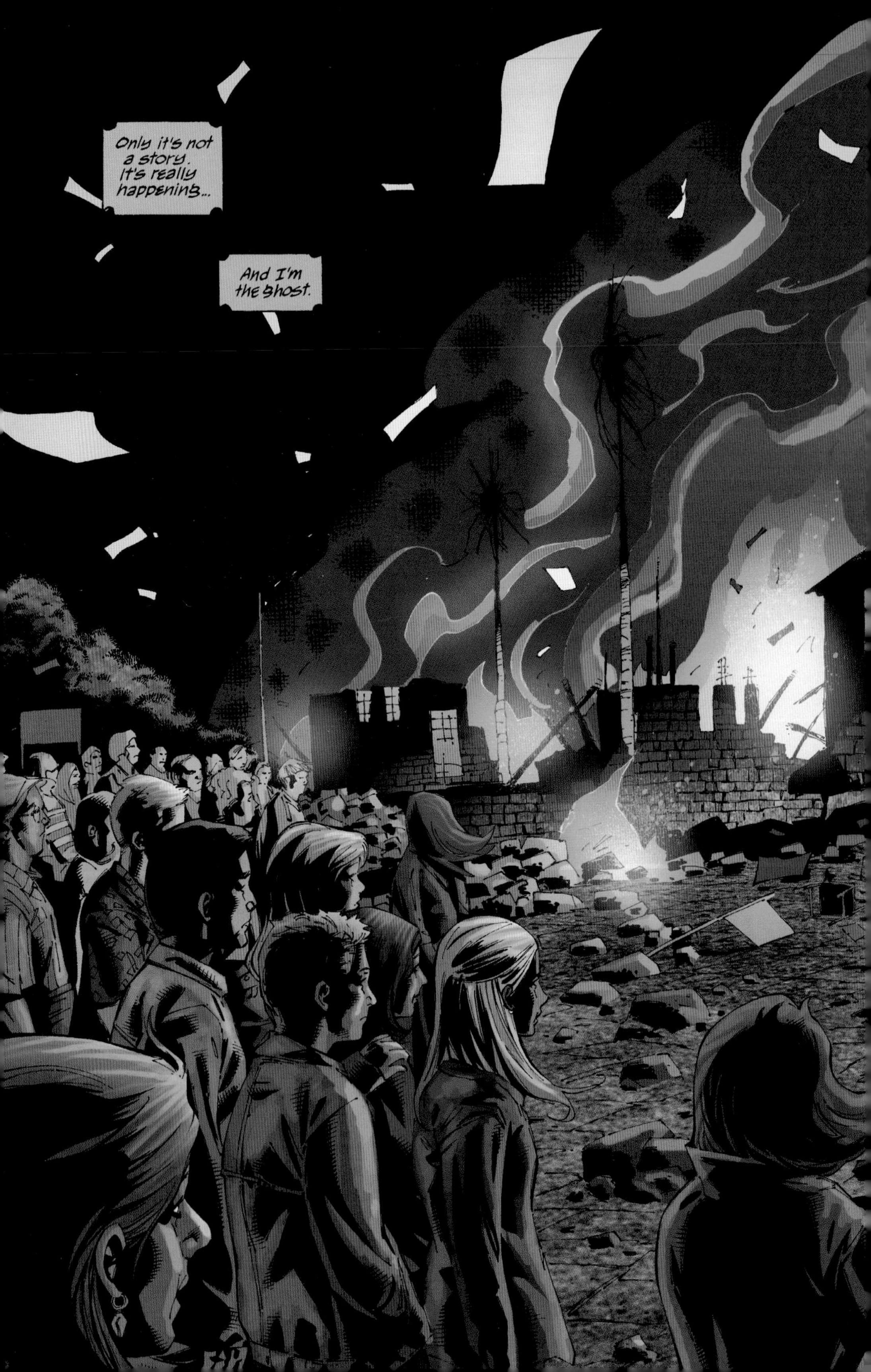
Only it's not a story. It's really happening...
And I'm the ghost.

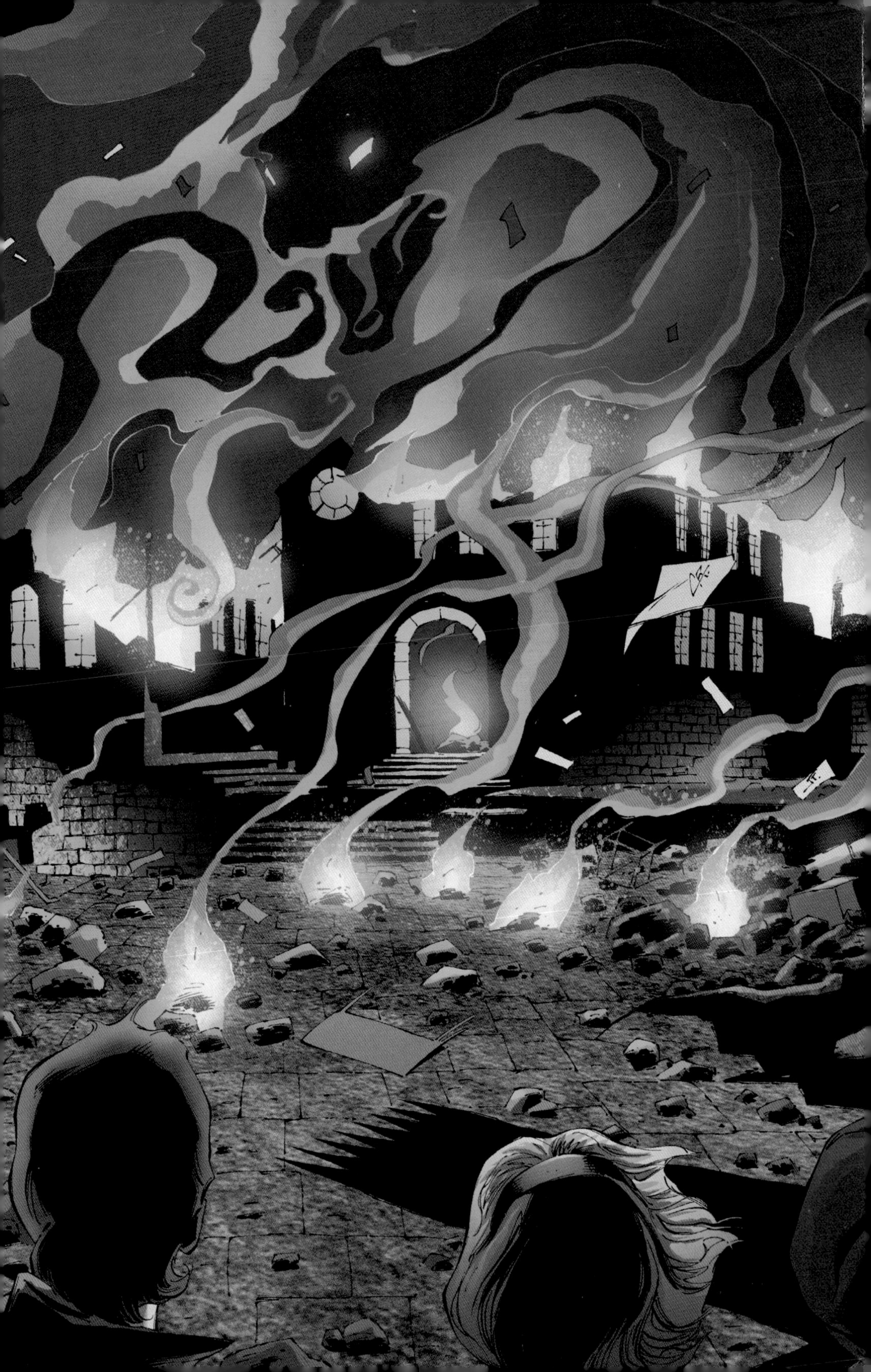

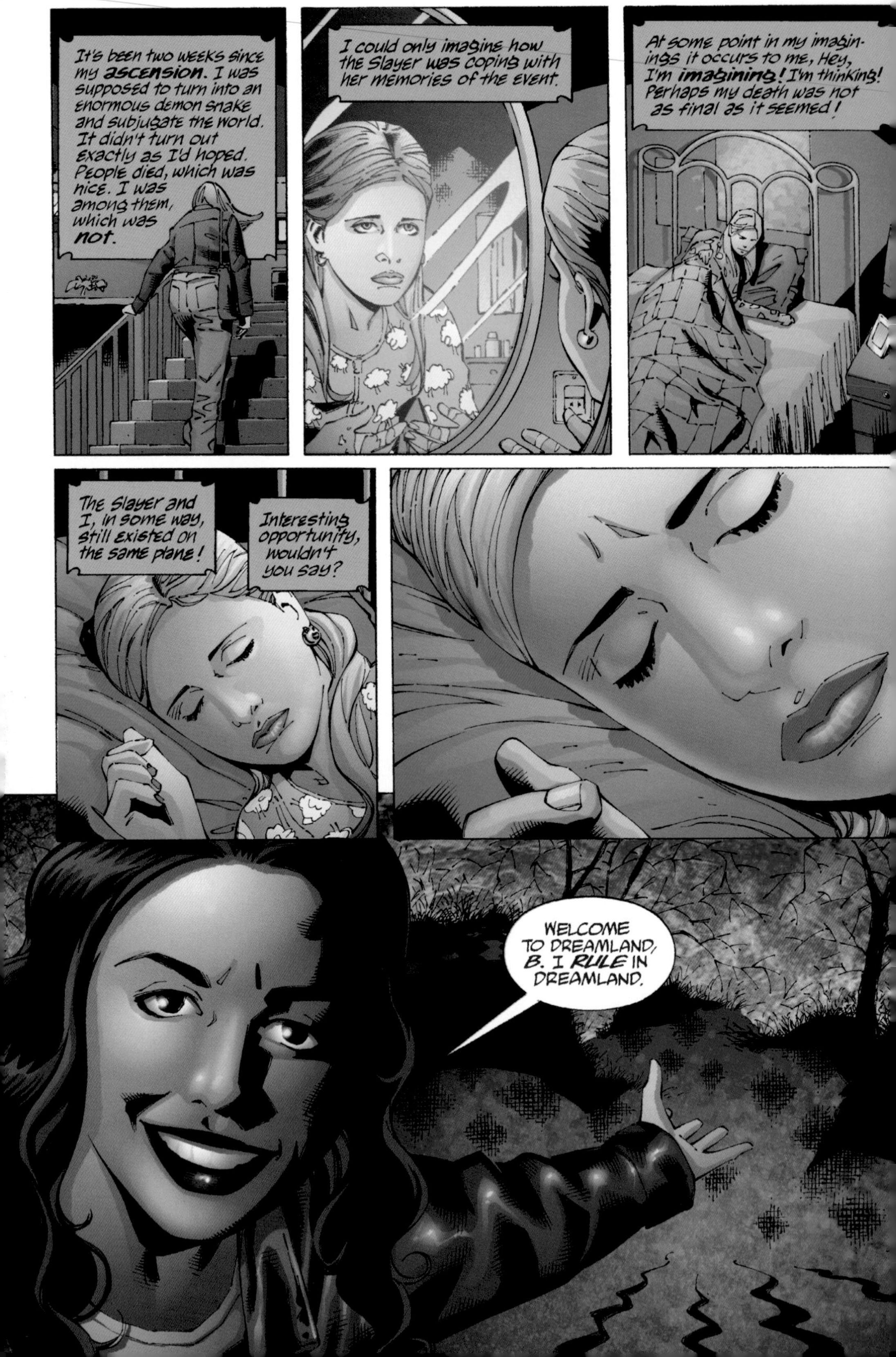

It's been two weeks since my ascension. I was supposed to turn into an enormous demon snake and subjugate the world. It didn't turn out exactly as I'd hoped. People died, which was nice. I was among them, which was not.
I could only imagine how the Slayer was coping with her memories of the event.
At some point in my imaginings it occurs to me, Hey, I'm imagining! I'm thinking! Perhaps my death was not as final as it seemed!
The Slayer and I, in some way, still existed on the same plane!
Interesting opportunity, wouldn't you say?
WELCOME TO DREAMLAND, B. I RULE IN DREAMLAND.

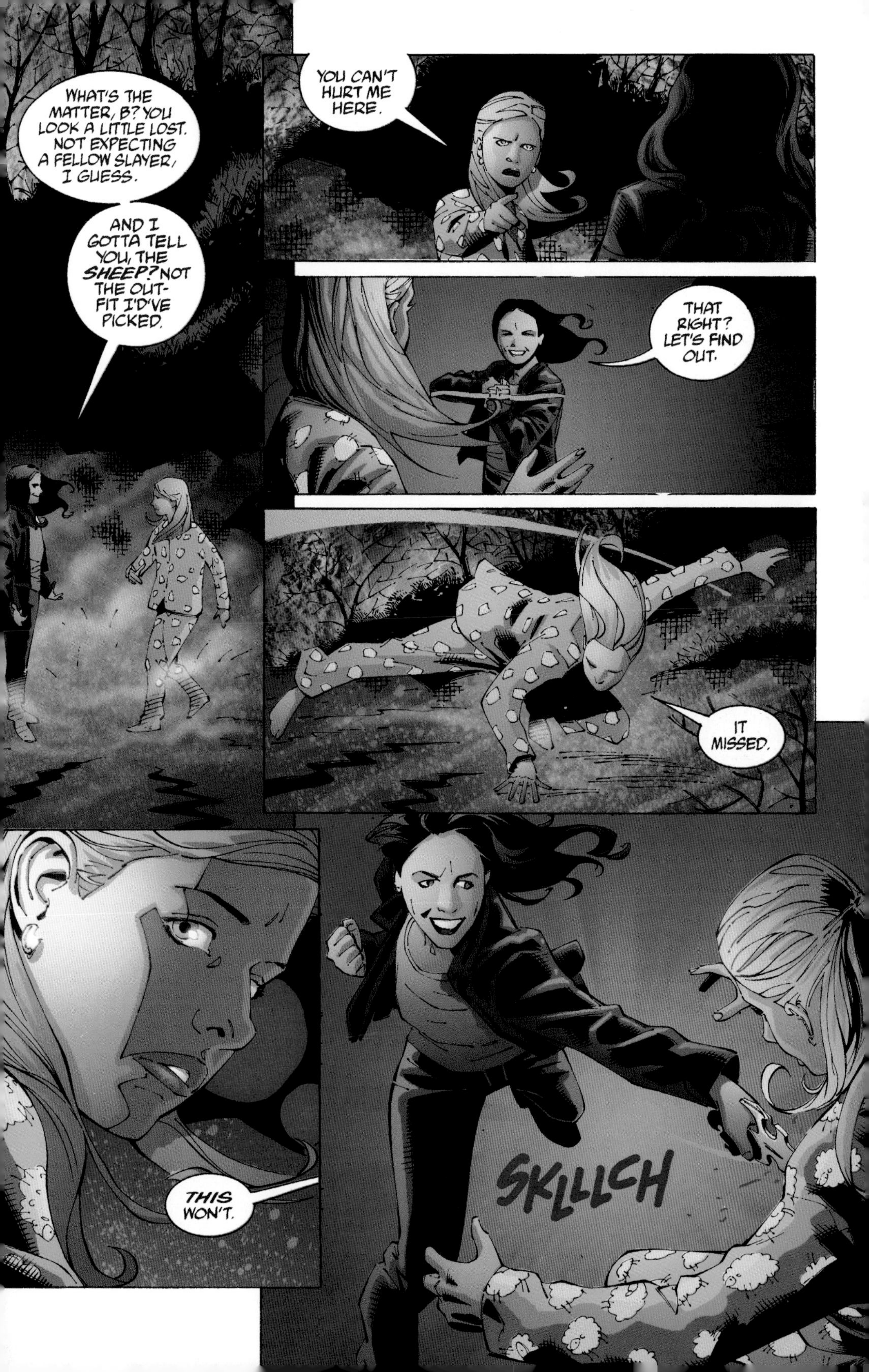

WHAT'S THE MATTER, B? YOU LOOK A LITTLE LOST. NOT EXPECTING A FELLOW SLAYER, I GUESS.
AND I GOTTA TELL YOU, THE SHEEP? NOT THE OUT-FIT I'D'VE PICKED.
YOU CAN'T HURT ME HERE.
THAT RIGHT? LET'S FIND OUT.
IT MISSED.
THIS WON'T.
SKLLLCH

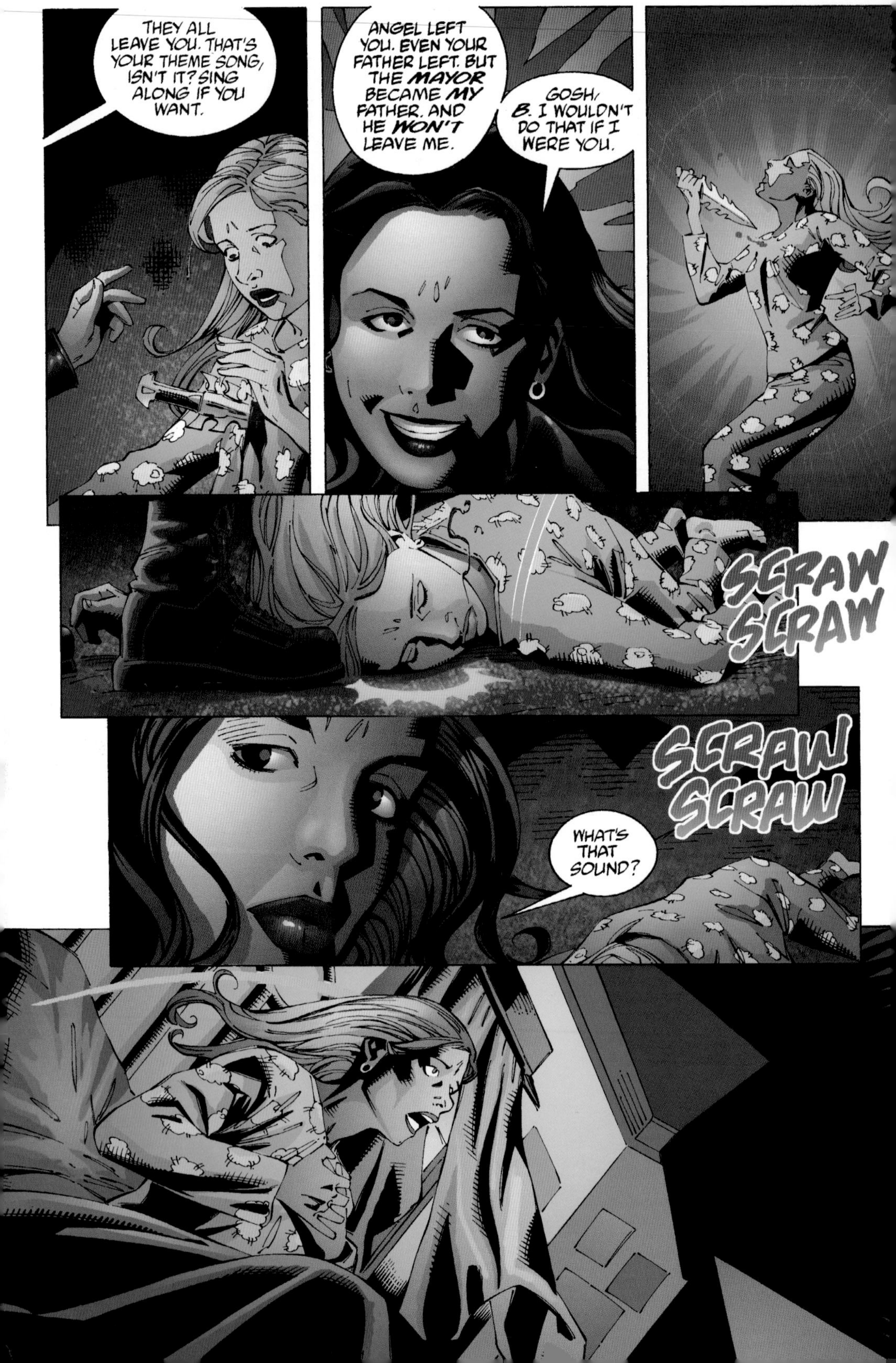
THEY ALL LEAVE YOU. THAT'S YOUR THEME SONG, ISN'T IT? SING ALONG IF YOU WANT.
ANGEL LEFT YOU. EVEN YOUR FATHER LEFT. BUT THE MAYOR BECAME MY FATHER. AND HE WON'T LEAVE ME.
GOSH, B. I WOULDN'T DO THAT IF I WERE YOU.
SCRAW SCRAW
SCRAW SCRAW
WHAT'S THAT SOUND?

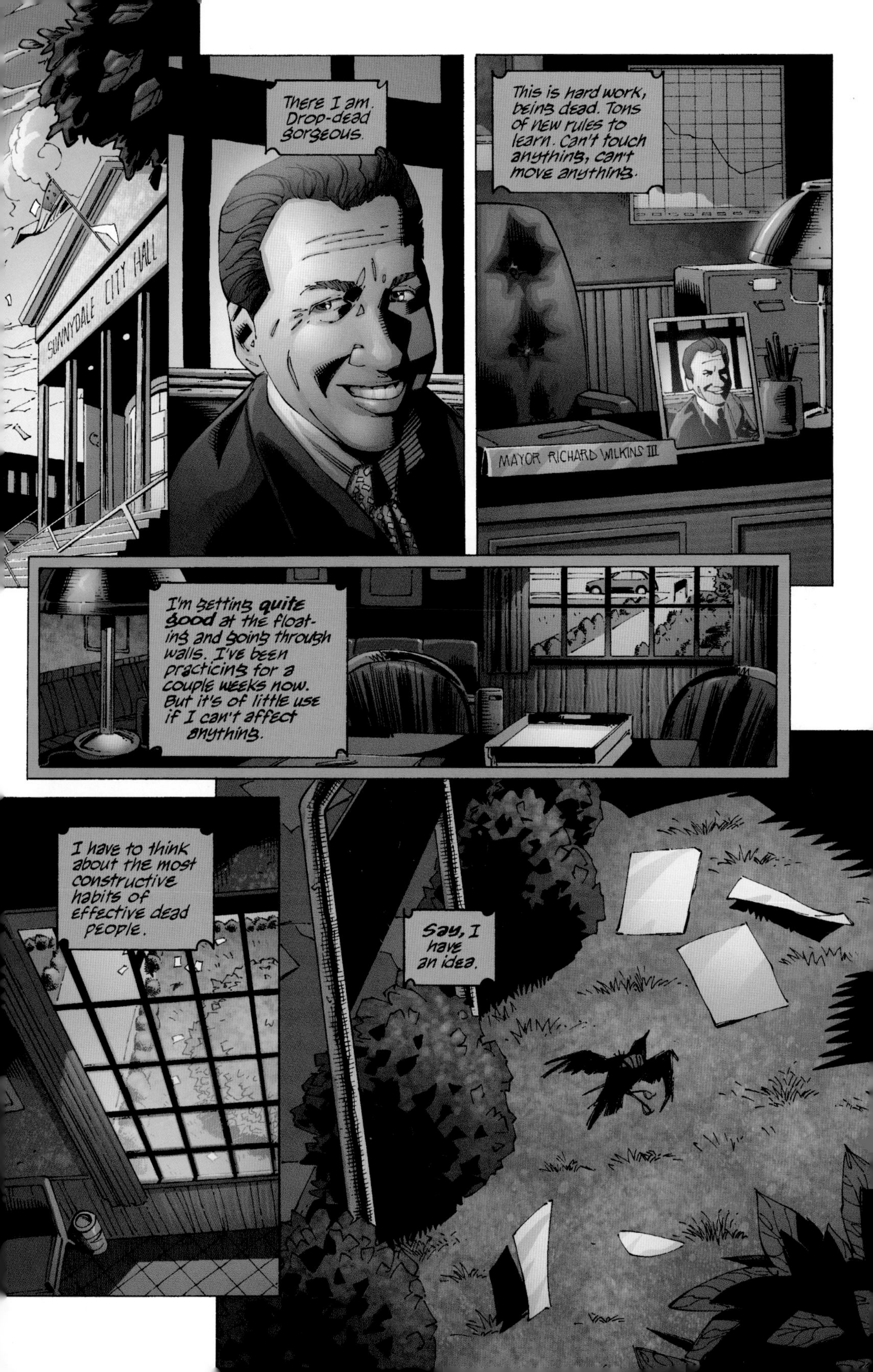

SUNNYDALE CITY HALL
There I am. Drop-dead gorgeous.
This is hard work, being dead. Tons of new rules to learn. Can't touch anything, can't move anything.
MAYOR RICHARD WILKINS III
I'm getting **quite good** at the floating and going through walls. I've been practicing for a couple weeks now. But it's of little use if I can't affect anything.
I have to think about the most constructive habits of effective dead people.
Say, I have an idea.

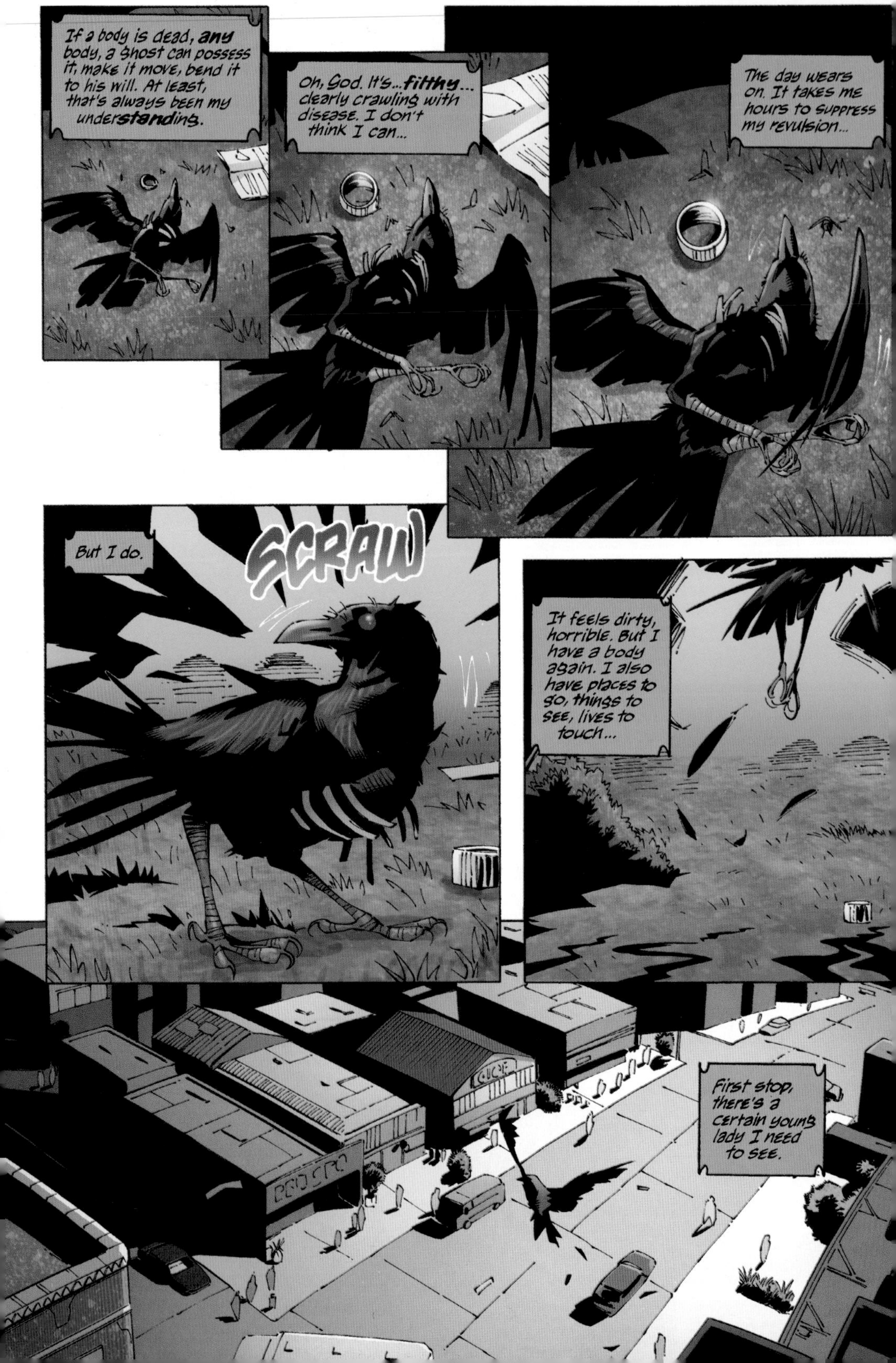
If a body is dead, **any** body, a ghost can possess it, make it move, bend it to his will. At least, that's always been my under**standing**.
Oh, God. It's... **filthy**... clearly crawling with disease. I don't think I can...
The day wears on. It takes me hours to suppress my revulsion...
But I do.
SCRAW
It feels dirty, horrible. But I have a body again. I also have places to go, things to see, lives to touch...
First stop, there's a certain young lady I need to see.

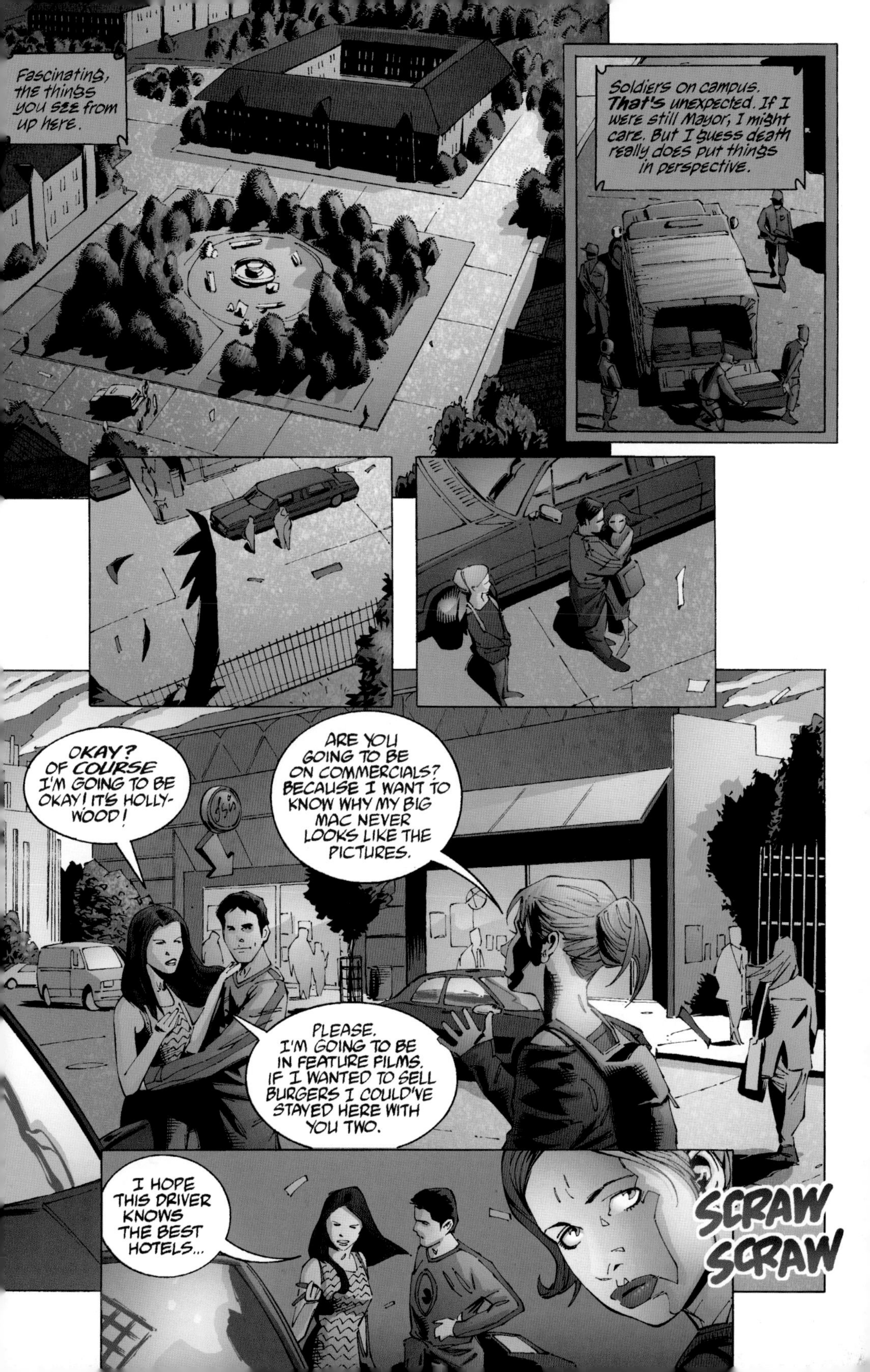
Fascinating, the things you see from up here.
Soldiers on campus. That's unexpected. If I were still Mayor, I might care. But I guess death really does put things in perspective.
OKAY? OF COURSE I'M GOING TO BE OKAY! IT'S HOLLY-WOOD!
ARE YOU GOING TO BE ON COMMERCIALS? BECAUSE I WANT TO KNOW WHY MY BIG MAC NEVER LOOKS LIKE THE PICTURES.
PLEASE. I'M GOING TO BE IN FEATURE FILMS. IF I WANTED TO SELL BURGERS I COULD'VE STAYED HERE WITH YOU TWO.
I HOPE THIS DRIVER KNOWS THE BEST HOTELS...
SCRAW SCRAW

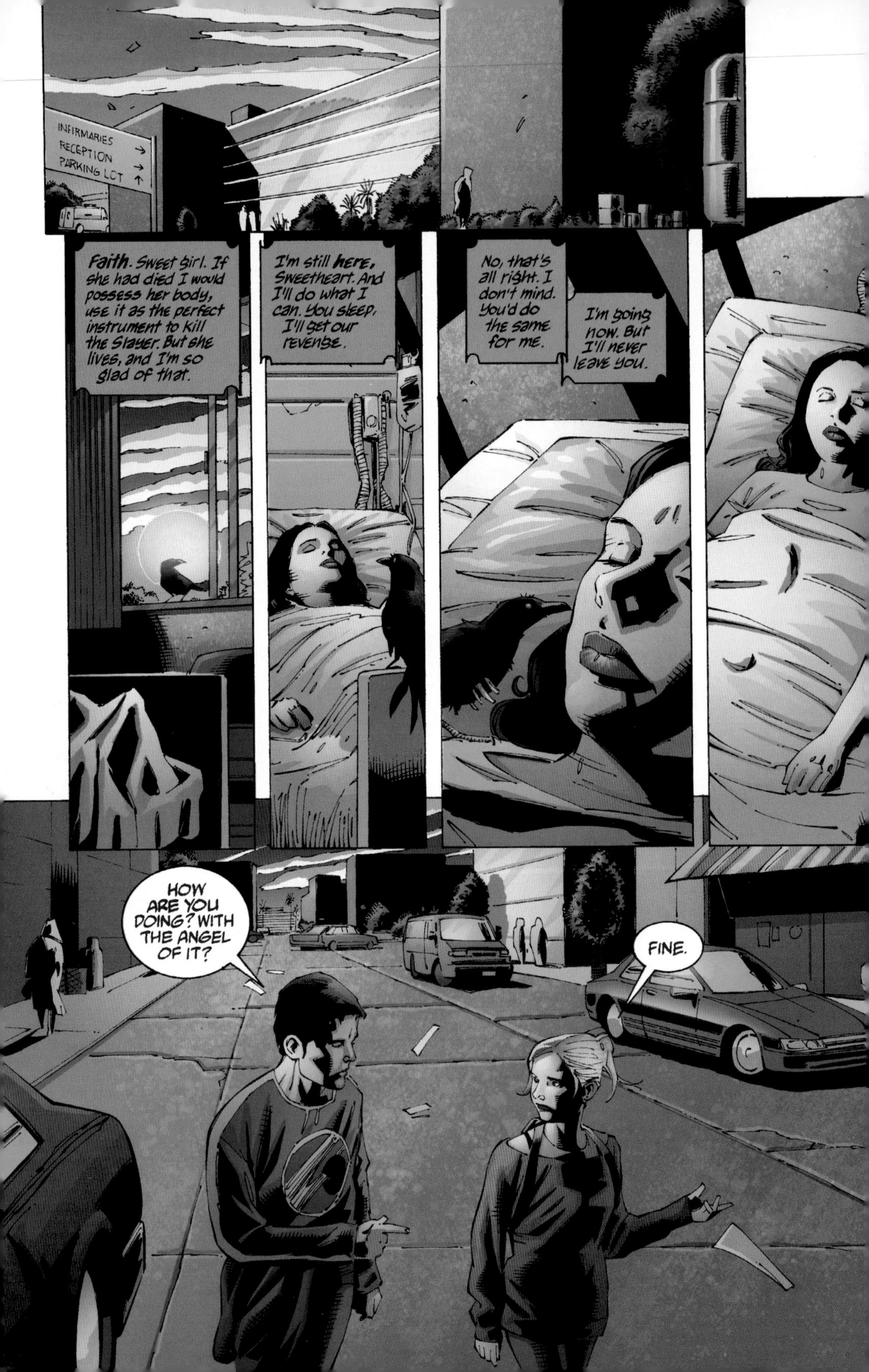
INFIRMARIES
RECEPTION
PARKING LOT
Faith. Sweet girl. If she had died I would possess her body, use it as the perfect instrument to kill the Slayer. But she lives, and I'm so glad of that.
I'm still here, Sweetheart. And I'll do what I can. You sleep, I'll get our revenge.
No, that's all right. I don't mind. You'd do the same for me.
I'm going now. But I'll never leave you.
HOW ARE YOU DOING? WITH THE ANGEL OF IT?
FINE.

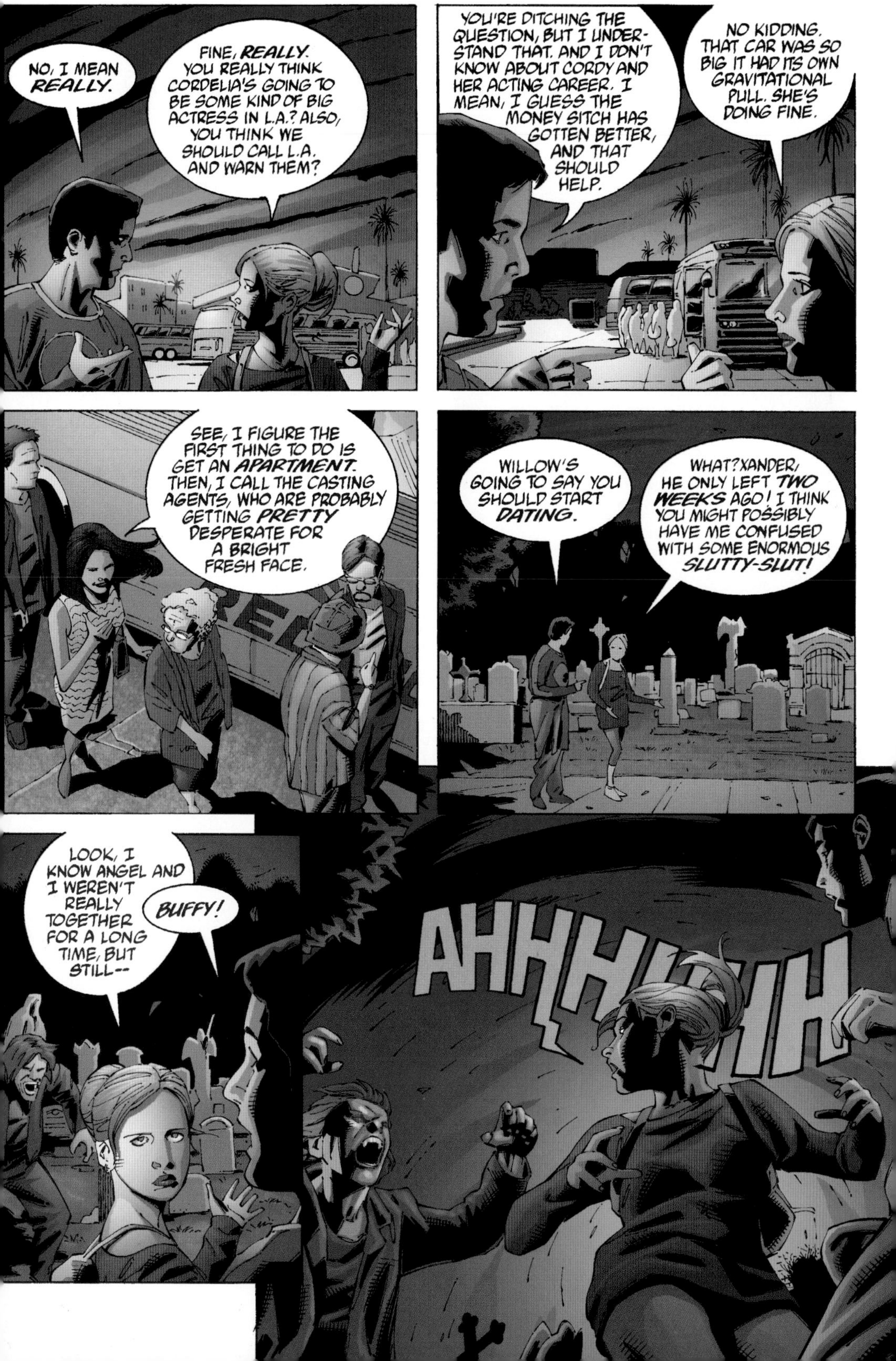
NO, I MEAN *REALLY*.
FINE, *REALLY*. YOU REALLY THINK CORDELIA'S GOING TO BE SOME KIND OF BIG ACTRESS IN L.A.? ALSO, YOU THINK WE SHOULD CALL L.A. AND WARN THEM?
YOU'RE DITCHING THE QUESTION, BUT I UNDERSTAND THAT. AND I DON'T KNOW ABOUT CORDY AND HER ACTING CAREER. I MEAN, I GUESS THE MONEY SITCH HAS GOTTEN BETTER, AND THAT SHOULD HELP.
NO KIDDING. THAT CAR WAS SO BIG IT HAD ITS OWN GRAVITATIONAL PULL. SHE'S DOING FINE.
SEE, I FIGURE THE FIRST THING TO DO IS GET AN *APARTMENT*. THEN, I CALL THE CASTING AGENTS, WHO ARE PROBABLY GETTING *PRETTY* DESPERATE FOR A BRIGHT FRESH FACE.
WILLOW'S GOING TO SAY YOU SHOULD START *DATING*.
WHAT? XANDER, HE ONLY LEFT *TWO WEEKS* AGO! I THINK YOU MIGHT POSSIBLY HAVE ME CONFUSED WITH SOME ENORMOUS *SLUTTY-SLUT*!
LOOK, I KNOW ANGEL AND I WEREN'T REALLY TOGETHER FOR A LONG TIME, BUT STILL--
BUFFY!
AHHHHHH

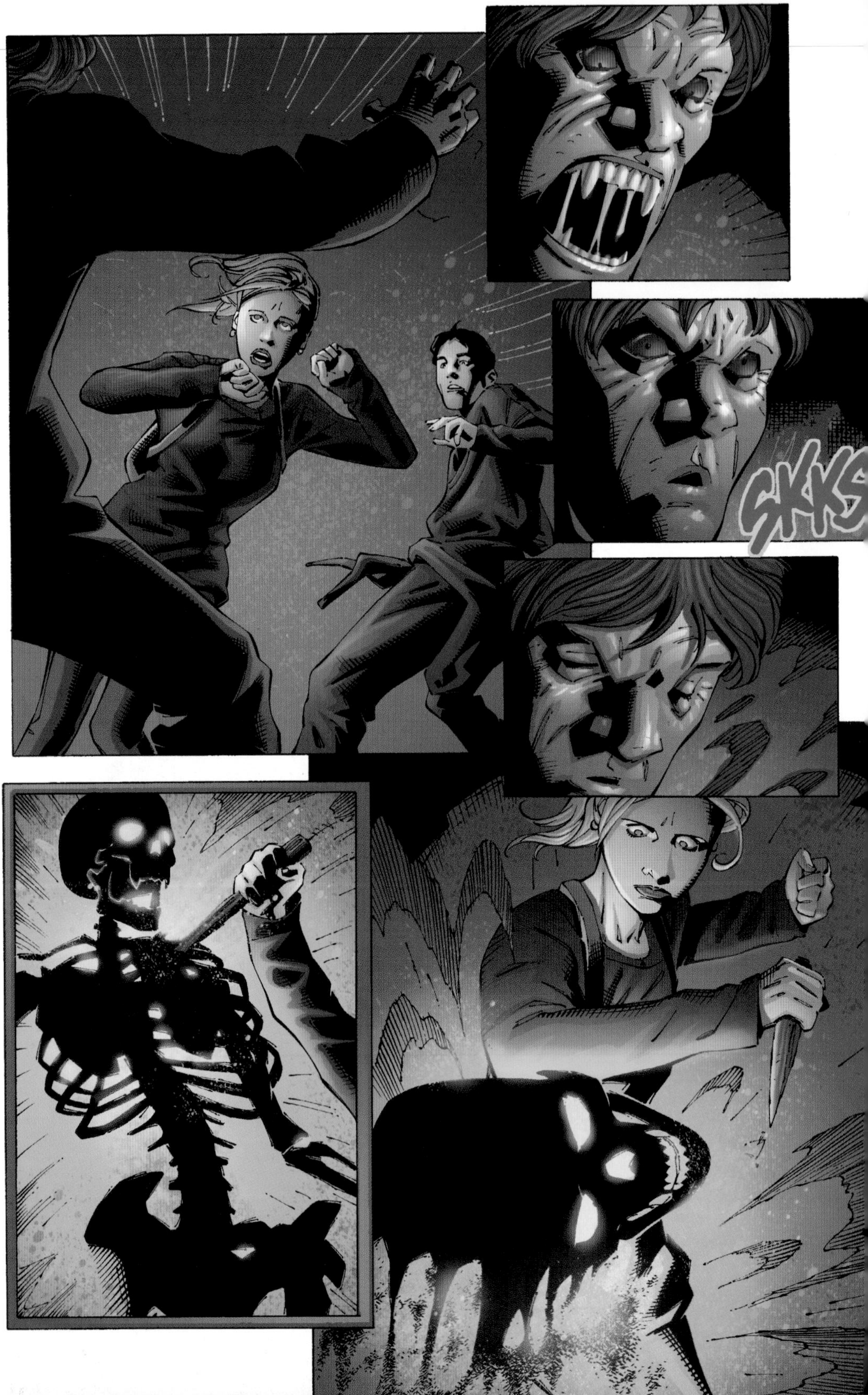
SKKS

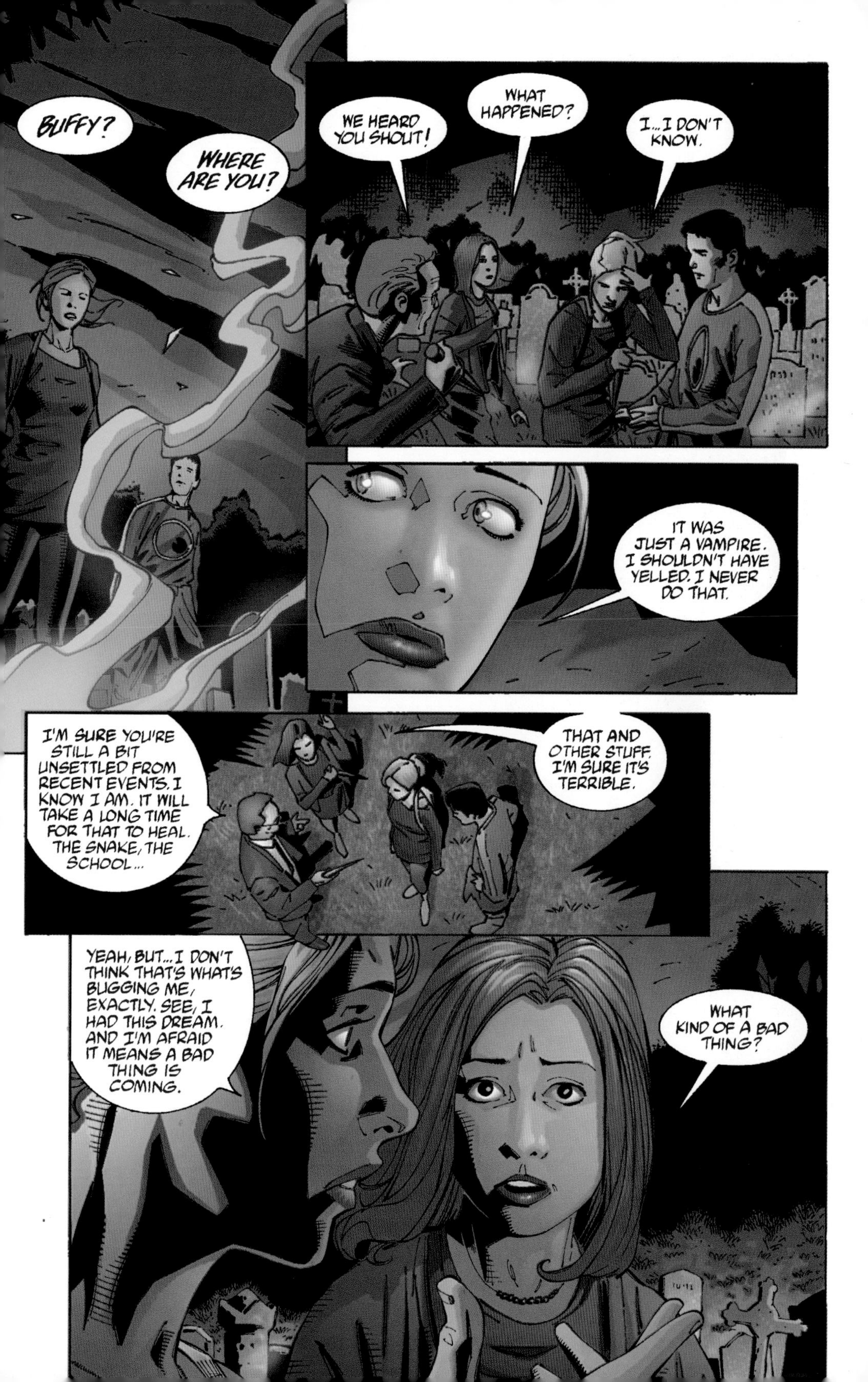
BUFFY?
WHERE ARE YOU?
WE HEARD YOU SHOUT!
WHAT HAPPENED?
I... I DON'T KNOW.
IT WAS JUST A VAMPIRE. I SHOULDN'T HAVE YELLED. I NEVER DO THAT.
I'M SURE YOU'RE STILL A BIT UNSETTLED FROM RECENT EVENTS. I KNOW I AM. IT WILL TAKE A LONG TIME FOR THAT TO HEAL. THE SNAKE, THE SCHOOL...
THAT AND OTHER STUFF. I'M SURE IT'S TERRIBLE.
YEAH, BUT... I DON'T THINK THAT'S WHAT'S BUGGING ME, EXACTLY. SEE, I HAD THIS DREAM. AND I'M AFRAID IT MEANS A BAD THING IS COMING.
WHAT KIND OF A BAD THING?

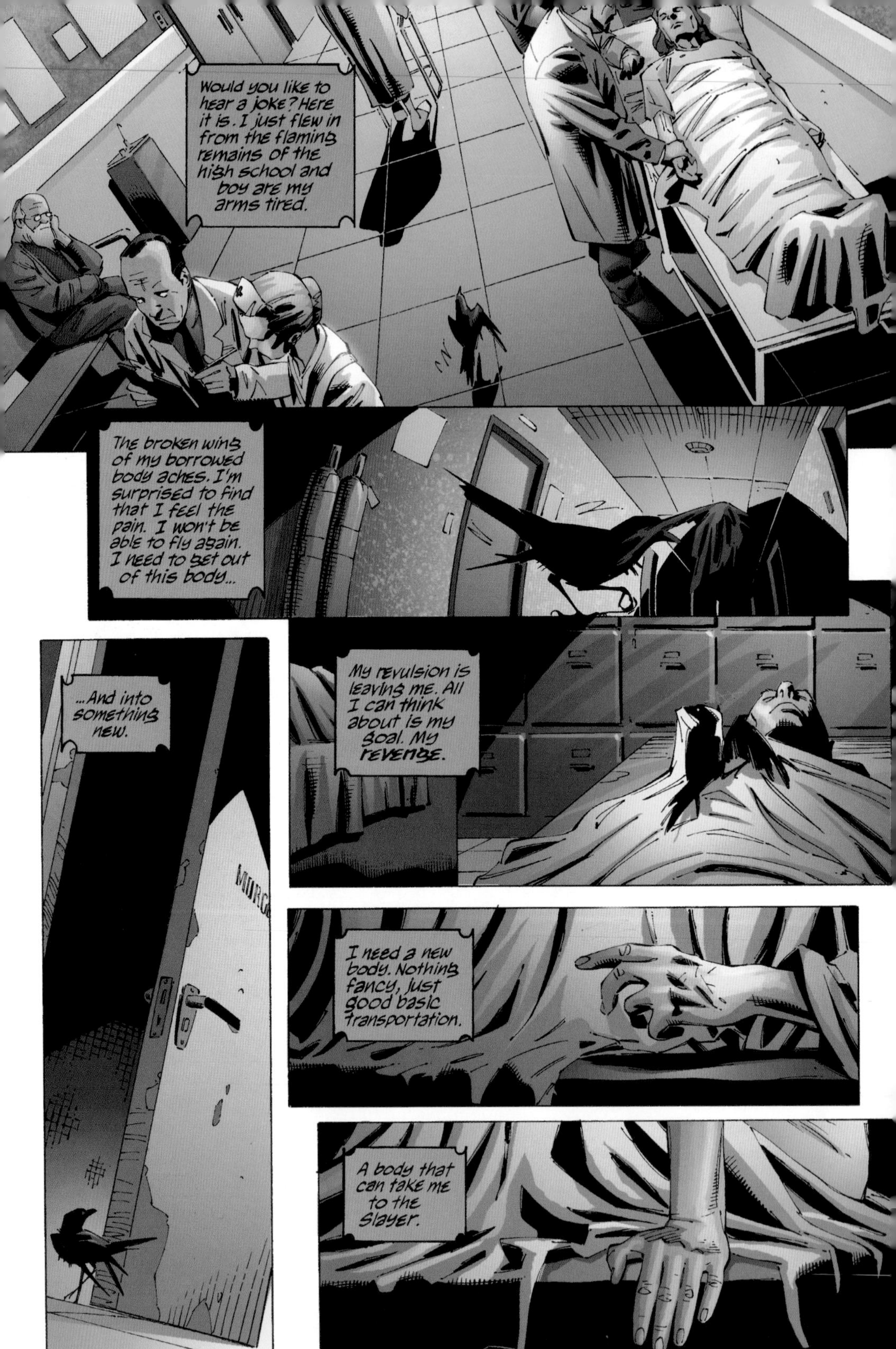
Would you like to hear a joke? Here it is. I just flew in from the flaming remains of the high school and boy are my arms tired.
The broken wing of my borrowed body aches. I'm surprised to find that I feel the pain. I won't be able to fly again. I need to get out of this body...
...And into something new.
My revulsion is leaving me. All I can think about is my goal. My revenge.
I need a new body. Nothing fancy, just good basic transportation.
A body that can take me to the Slayer.

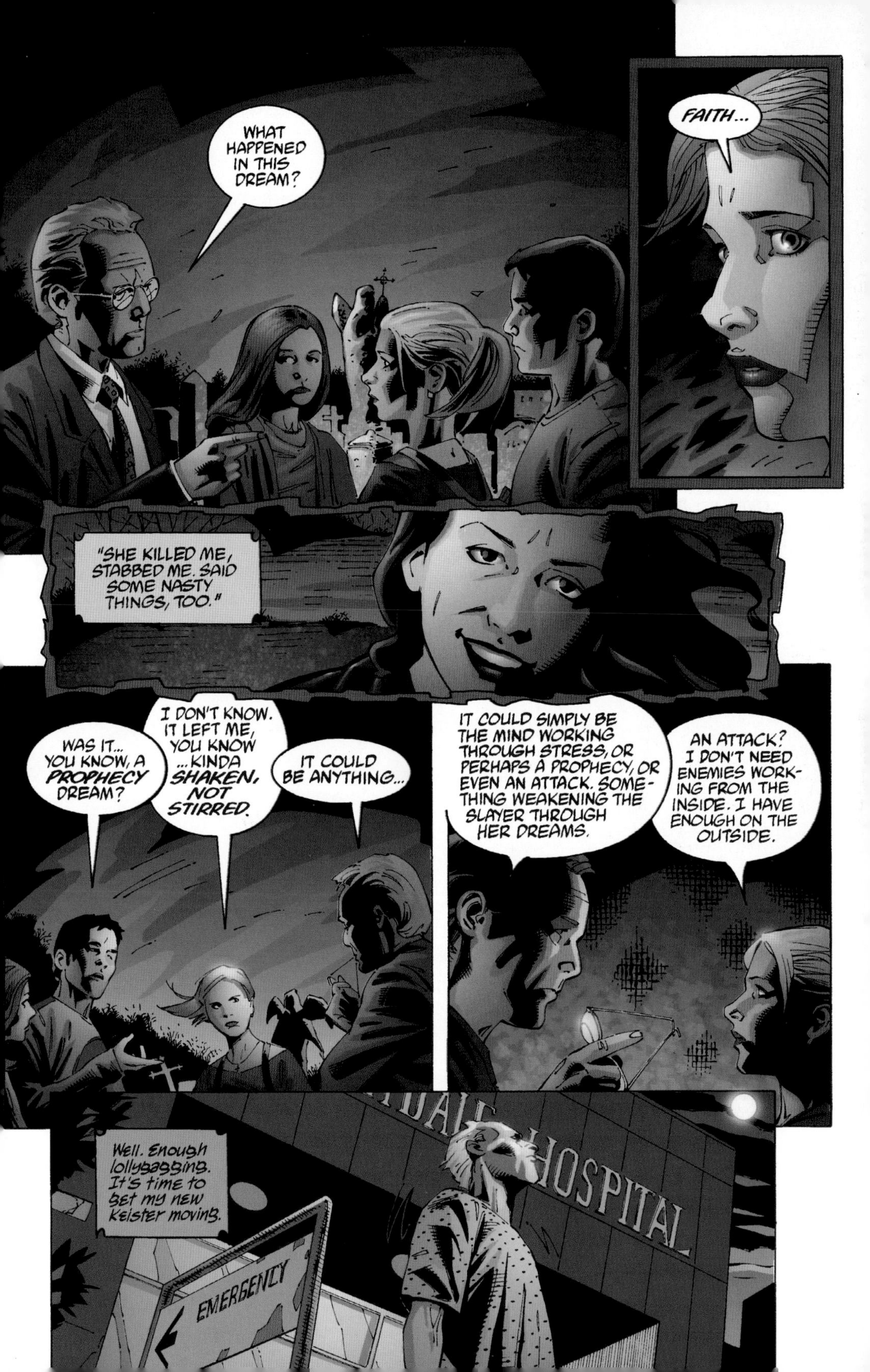
WHAT HAPPENED IN THIS DREAM?
FAITH...
"SHE KILLED ME, STABBED ME. SAID SOME NASTY THINGS, TOO."
WAS IT... YOU KNOW, A *PROPHECY* DREAM?
I DON'T KNOW. IT LEFT ME, YOU KNOW ...KINDA *SHAKEN, NOT STIRRED.*
IT COULD BE ANYTHING...
IT COULD SIMPLY BE THE MIND WORKING THROUGH STRESS, OR PERHAPS A PROPHECY, OR EVEN AN ATTACK. SOMETHING WEAKENING THE SLAYER THROUGH HER DREAMS.
AN ATTACK? I DON'T NEED ENEMIES WORKING FROM THE INSIDE. I HAVE ENOUGH ON THE OUTSIDE.
Well. Enough lollygagging. It's time to get my new keister moving.
HOSPITAL
EMERGENCY

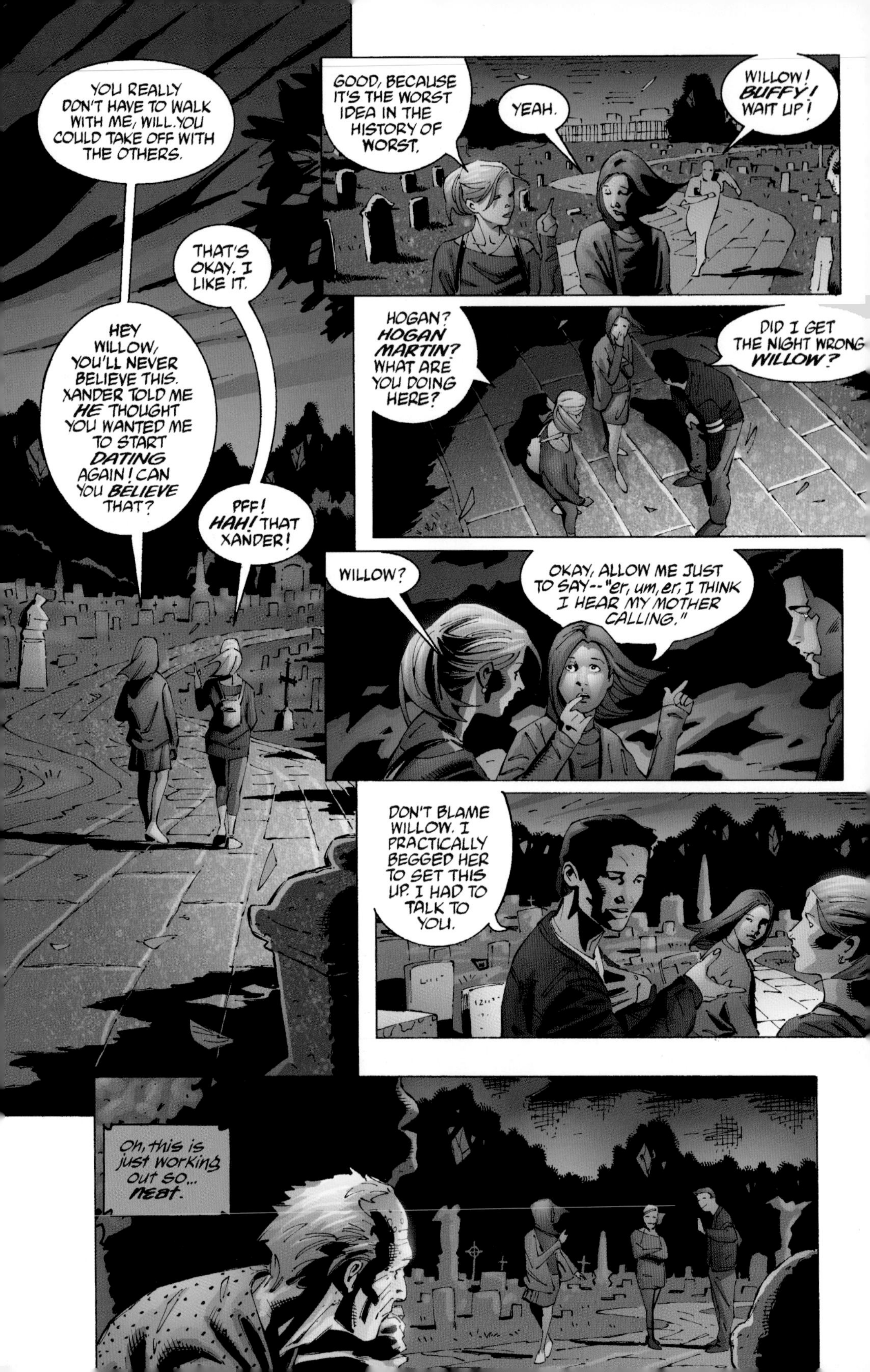
YOU REALLY DON'T HAVE TO WALK WITH ME, WILL. YOU COULD TAKE OFF WITH THE OTHERS.
THAT'S OKAY. I LIKE IT.
HEY WILLOW, YOU'LL NEVER BELIEVE THIS. XANDER TOLD ME HE THOUGHT YOU WANTED ME TO START DATING AGAIN! CAN YOU BELIEVE THAT?
PFF! HAH! THAT XANDER!
GOOD, BECAUSE IT'S THE WORST IDEA IN THE HISTORY OF WORST.
YEAH.
WILLOW! BUFFY! WAIT UP!
HOGAN? HOGAN MARTIN? WHAT ARE YOU DOING HERE?
DID I GET THE NIGHT WRONG WILLOW?
WILLOW?
OKAY, ALLOW ME JUST TO SAY-- "er, um, er, I THINK I HEAR MY MOTHER CALLING."
DON'T BLAME WILLOW. I PRACTICALLY BEGGED HER TO SET THIS UP. I HAD TO TALK TO YOU.
Oh, this is just working out so... neat.

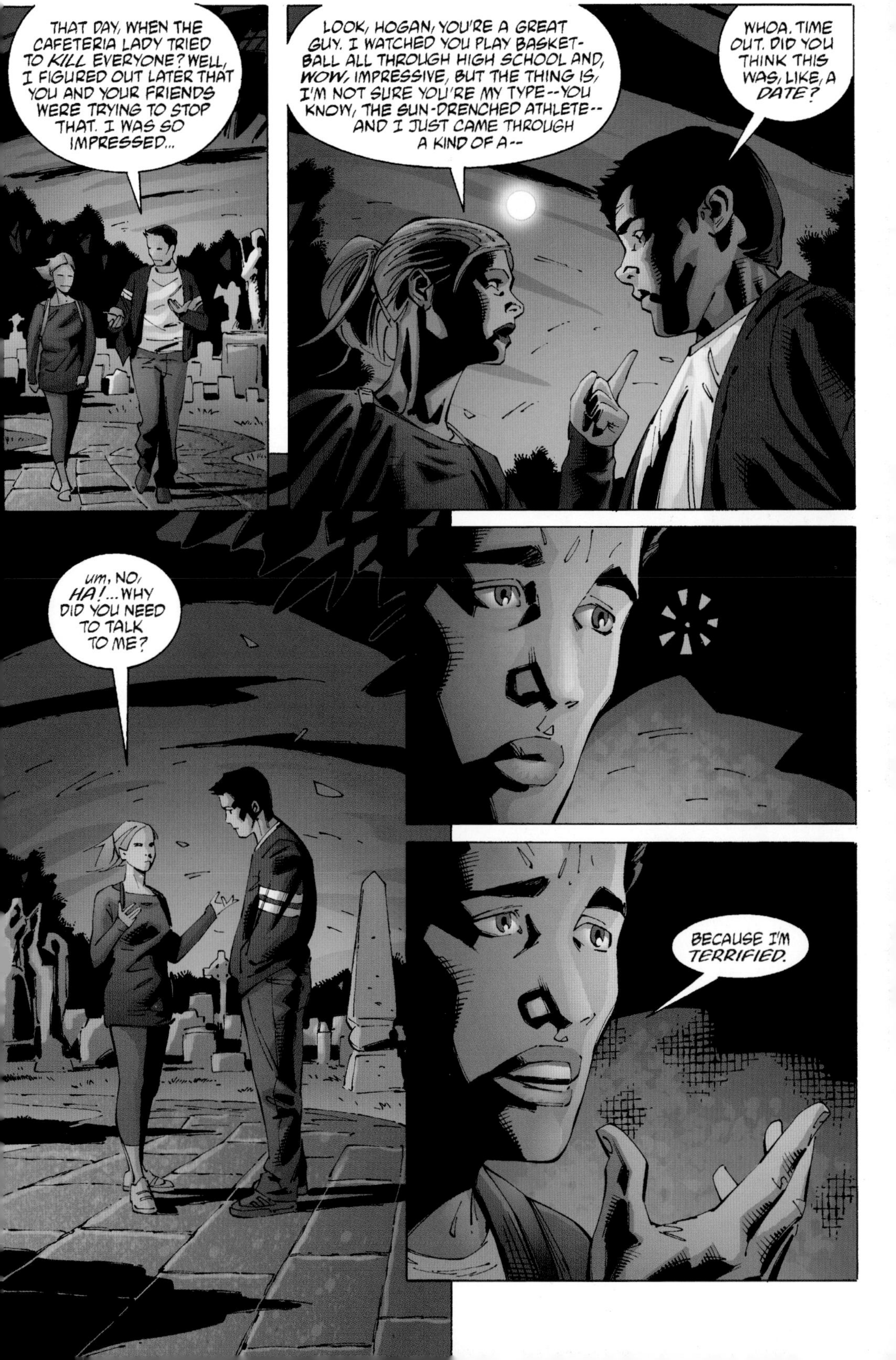
THAT DAY, WHEN THE CAFETERIA LADY TRIED TO KILL EVERYONE? WELL, I FIGURED OUT LATER THAT YOU AND YOUR FRIENDS WERE TRYING TO STOP THAT. I WAS SO IMPRESSED...
LOOK, HOGAN, YOU'RE A GREAT GUY. I WATCHED YOU PLAY BASKET-BALL ALL THROUGH HIGH SCHOOL AND, WOW, IMPRESSIVE, BUT THE THING IS, I'M NOT SURE YOU'RE MY TYPE--YOU KNOW, THE SUN-DRENCHED ATHLETE--AND I JUST CAME THROUGH A KIND OF A--
WHOA. TIME OUT. DID YOU THINK THIS WAS, LIKE, A DATE?
um, NO, HA!...WHY DID YOU NEED TO TALK TO ME?
BECAUSE I'M TERRIFIED.

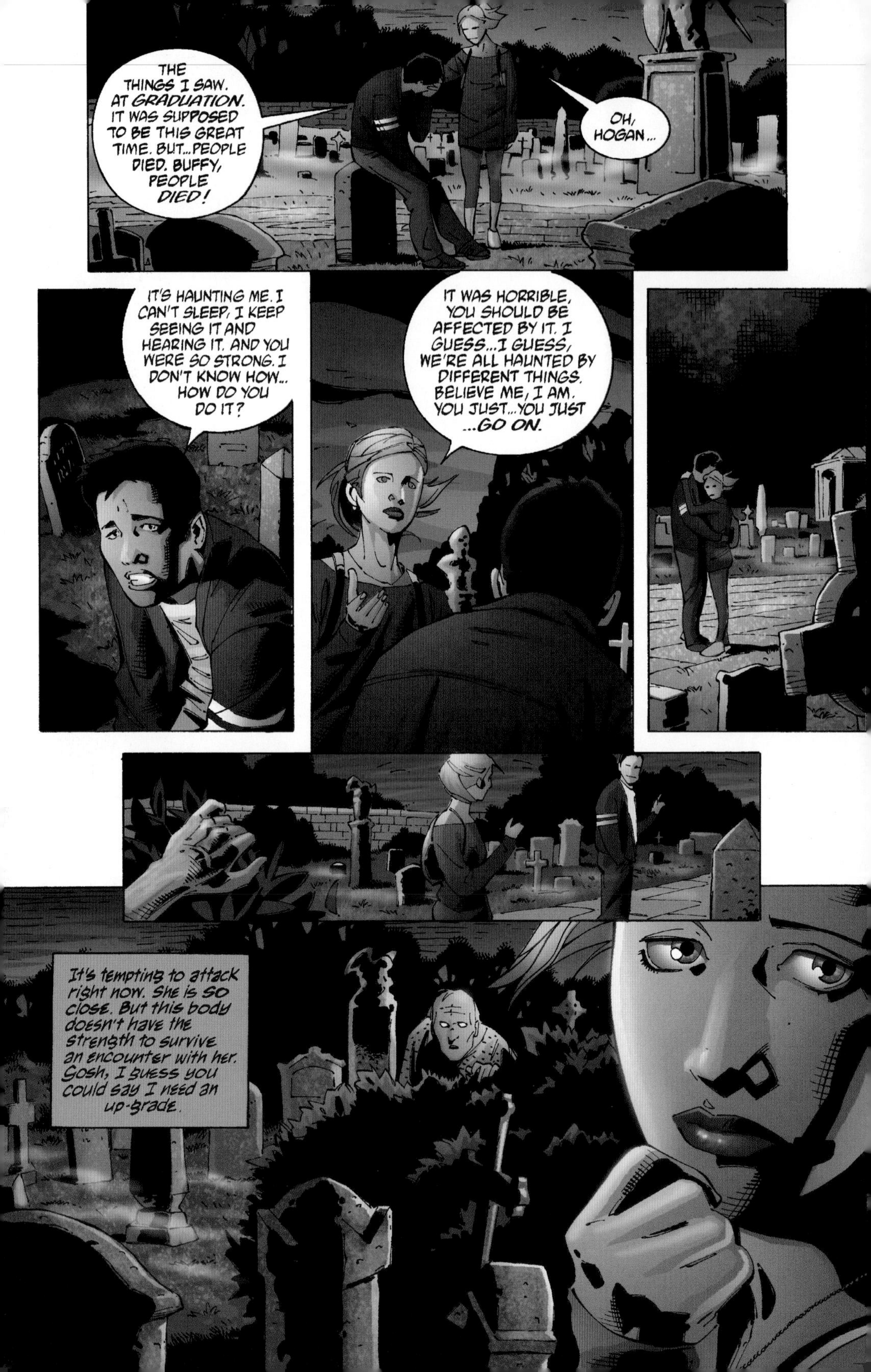
THE THINGS I SAW. AT GRADUATION. IT WAS SUPPOSED TO BE THIS GREAT TIME. BUT...PEOPLE DIED. BUFFY, PEOPLE DIED!
OH, HOGAN...
IT'S HAUNTING ME. I CAN'T SLEEP, I KEEP SEEING IT AND HEARING IT. AND YOU WERE SO STRONG. I DON'T KNOW HOW... HOW DO YOU DO IT?
IT WAS HORRIBLE, YOU SHOULD BE AFFECTED BY IT. I GUESS...I GUESS, WE'RE ALL HAUNTED BY DIFFERENT THINGS. BELIEVE ME, I AM. YOU JUST...YOU JUST ...GO ON.
It's tempting to attack right now. She is so close. But this body doesn't have the strength to survive an encounter with her. Gosh, I guess you could say I need an up-grade.

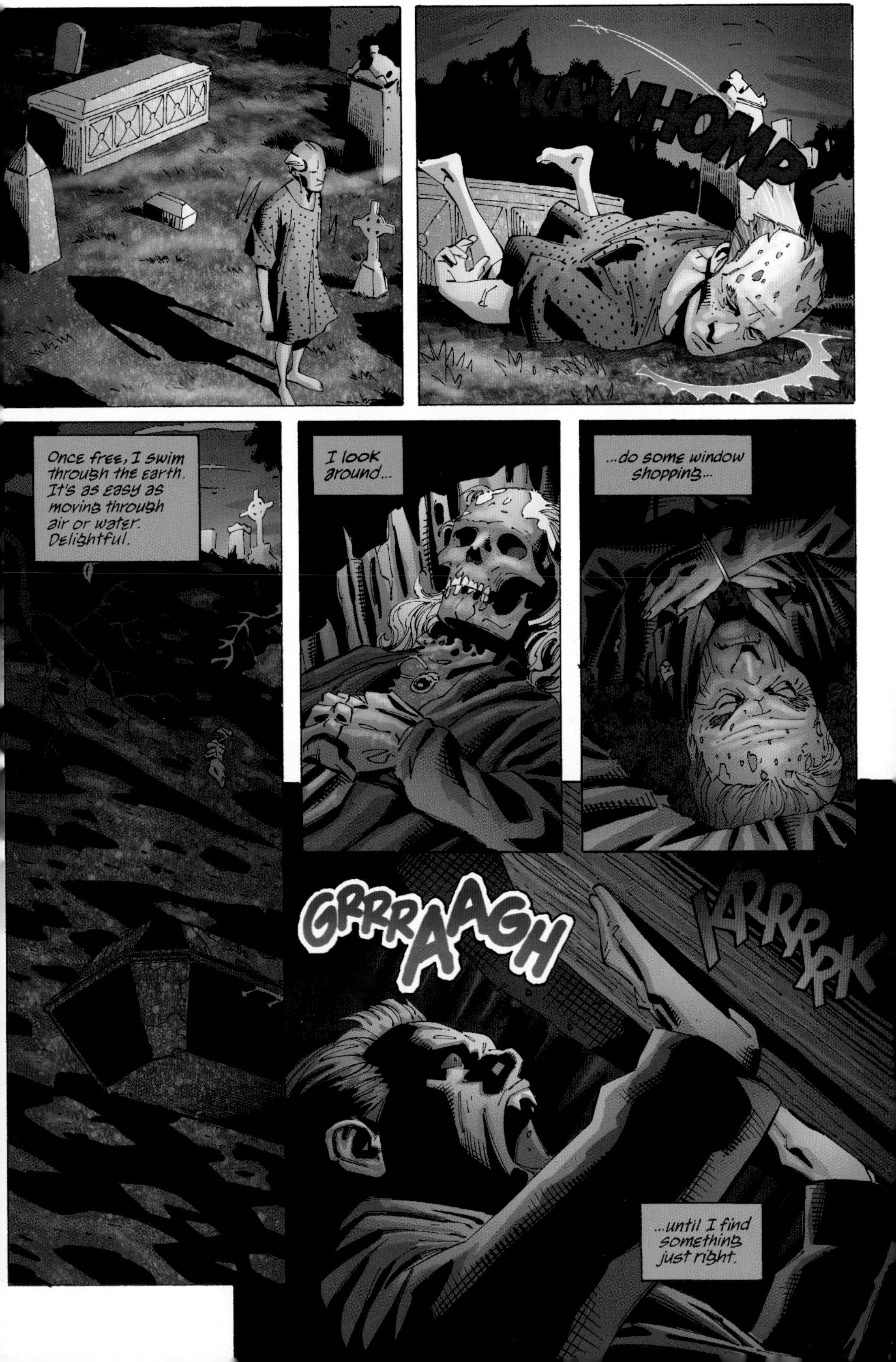
KA-WHOMP
Once free, I swim through the earth. It's as easy as moving through air or water. Delightful.
I look around...
...do some window shopping...
GRRRAAGH
KRRRRK
...until I find something just right.

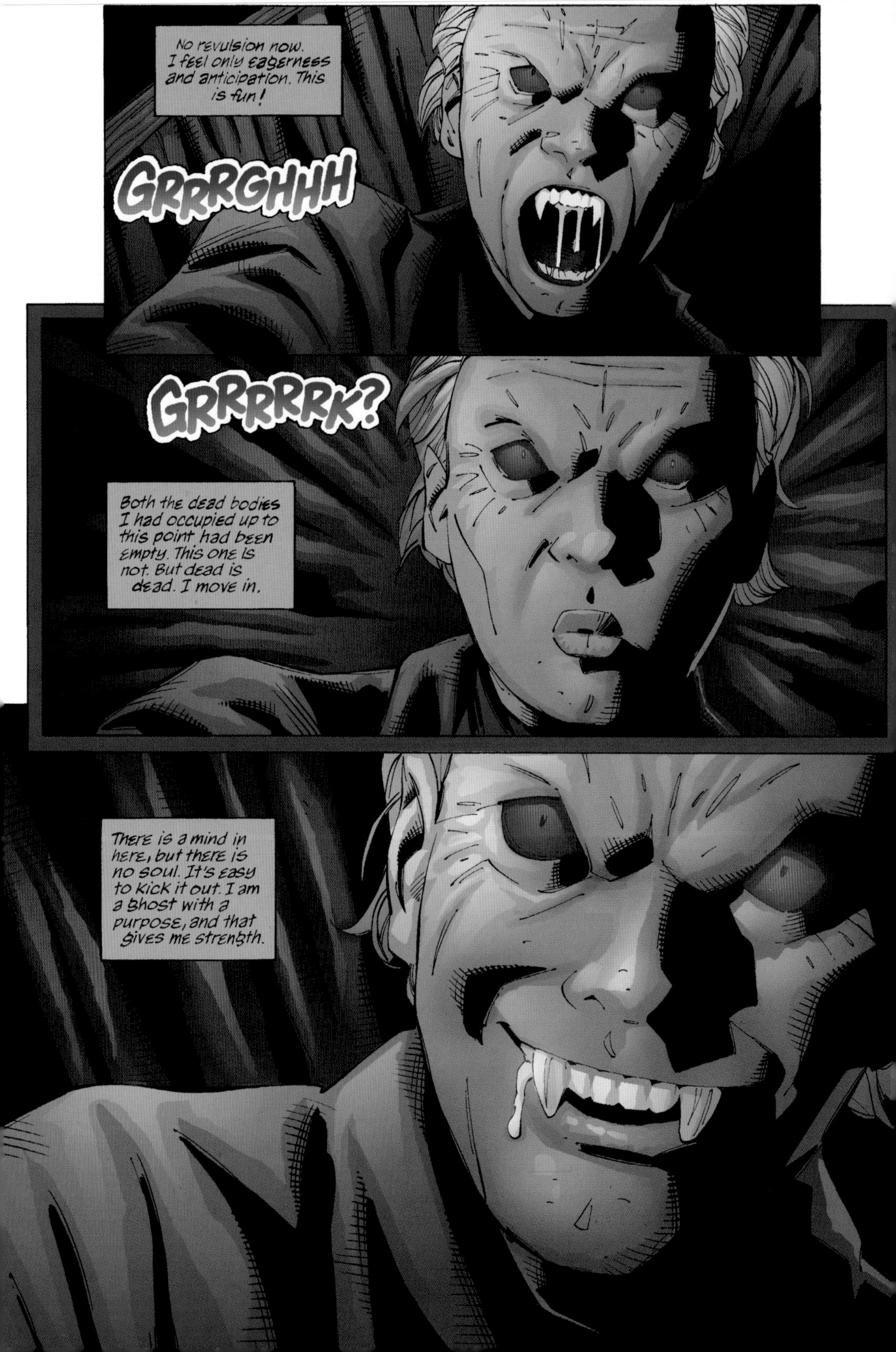
No revulsion now. I feel only eagerness and anticipation. This is fun!
GRRRGHHH
GRRRRRK?
Both the dead bodies I had occupied up to this point had been empty. This one is not. But dead is dead. I move in.
There is a mind in here, but there is no soul. It's easy to kick it out. I am a ghost with a purpose, and that gives me strength.

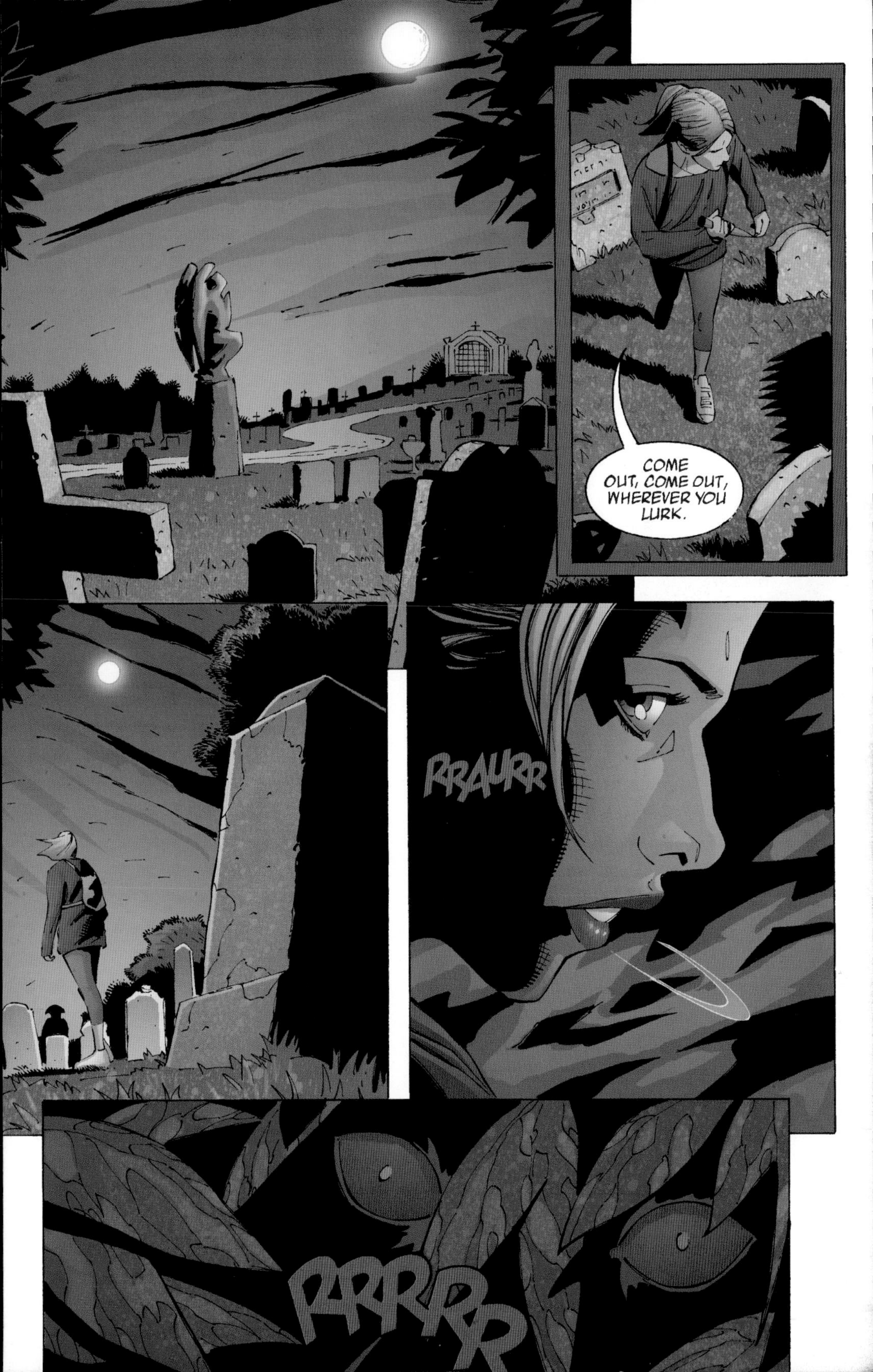
COME OUT, COME OUT, WHEREVER YOU LURK.
RRAURR
RRRRR

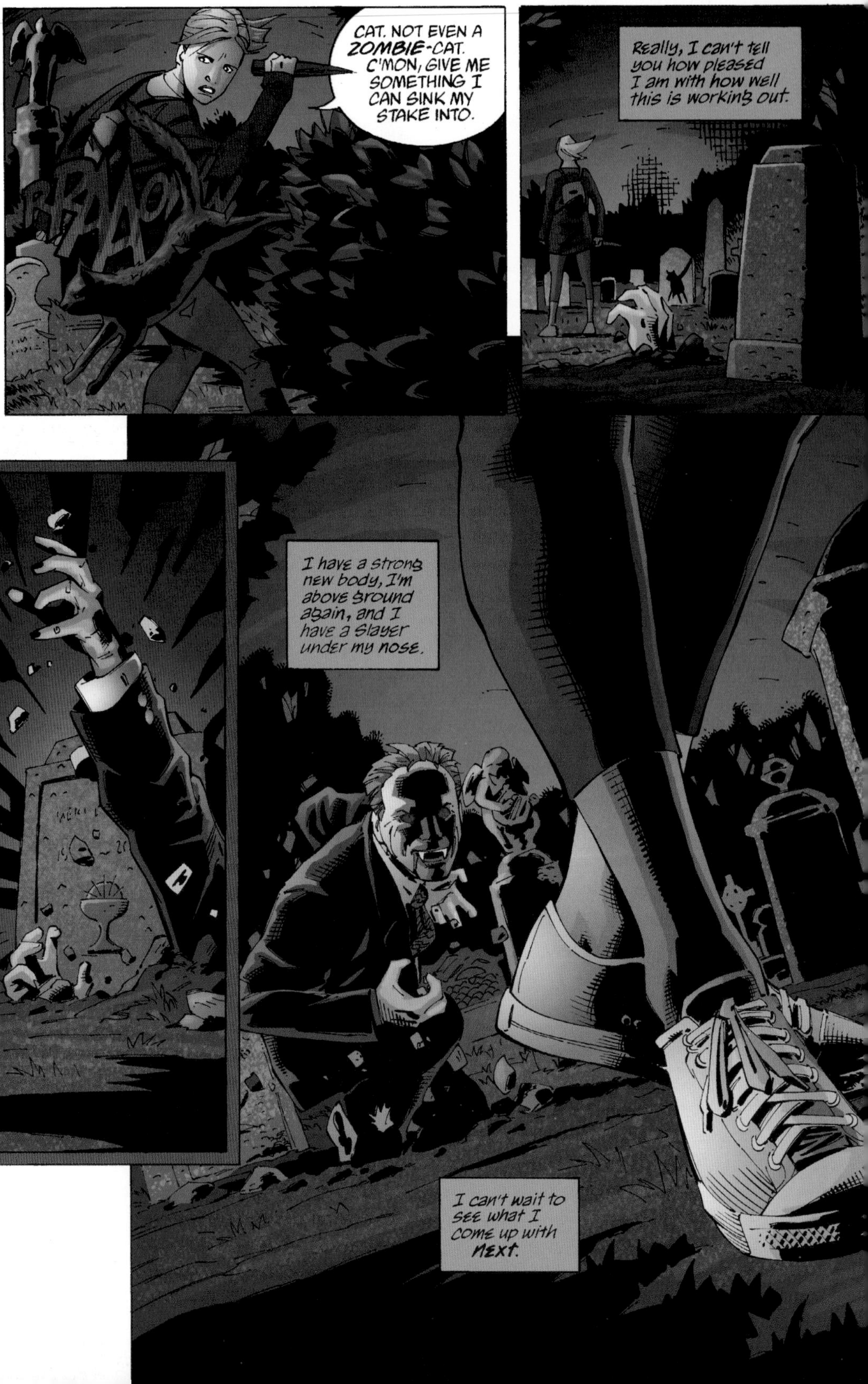
CAT. NOT EVEN A ZOMBIE-CAT. C'MON, GIVE ME SOMETHING I CAN SINK MY STAKE INTO.
BRAOW
Really, I can't tell you how pleased I am with how well this is working out.
I have a strong new body, I'm above ground again, and I have a Slayer under my nose.
I can't wait to see what I come up with next.

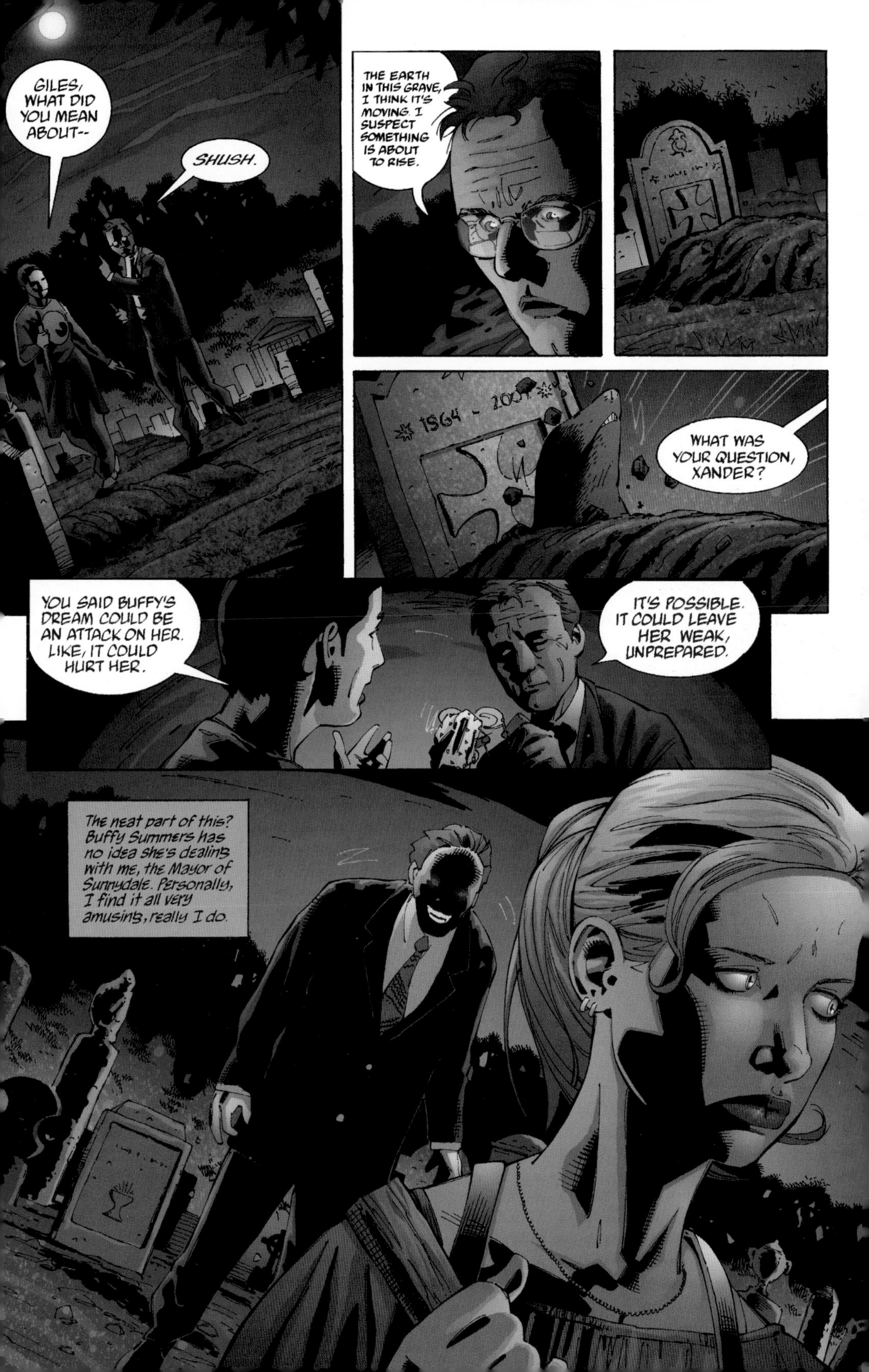

GILES, WHAT DID YOU MEAN ABOUT--
SHUSH.
THE EARTH IN THIS GRAVE, I THINK IT'S MOVING. I SUSPECT SOMETHING IS ABOUT TO RISE.
1864 - 2001
WHAT WAS YOUR QUESTION, XANDER?
YOU SAID BUFFY'S DREAM COULD BE AN ATTACK ON HER. LIKE, IT COULD HURT HER.
IT'S POSSIBLE. IT COULD LEAVE HER WEAK, UNPREPARED.
The neat part of this? Buffy Summers has no idea she's dealing with me, the Mayor of Sunnydale. Personally, I find it all very amusing, really I do.

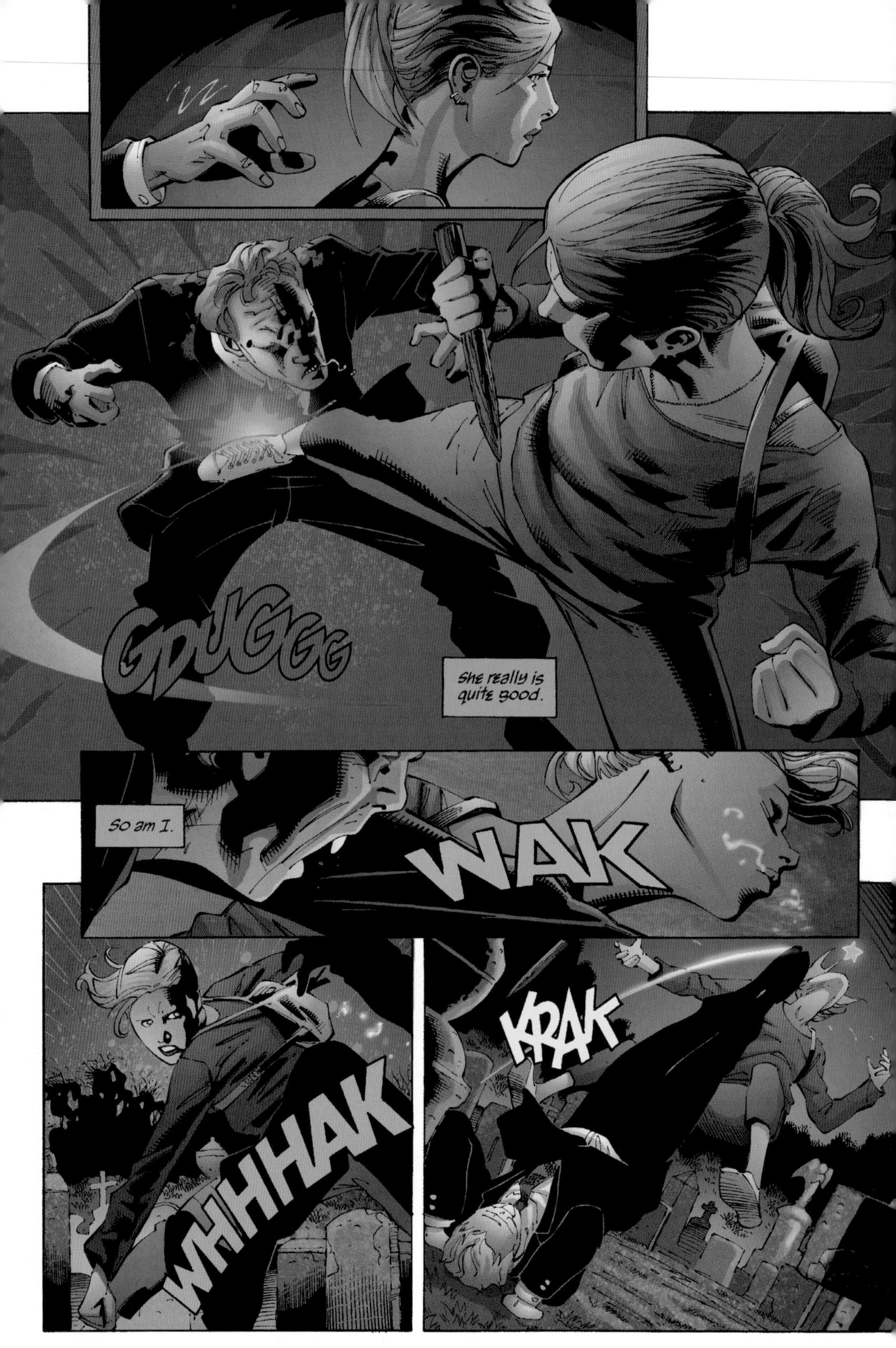
GDUGGG
She really is
quite good.
So am I.
WAK
WHHHAK
KRAK

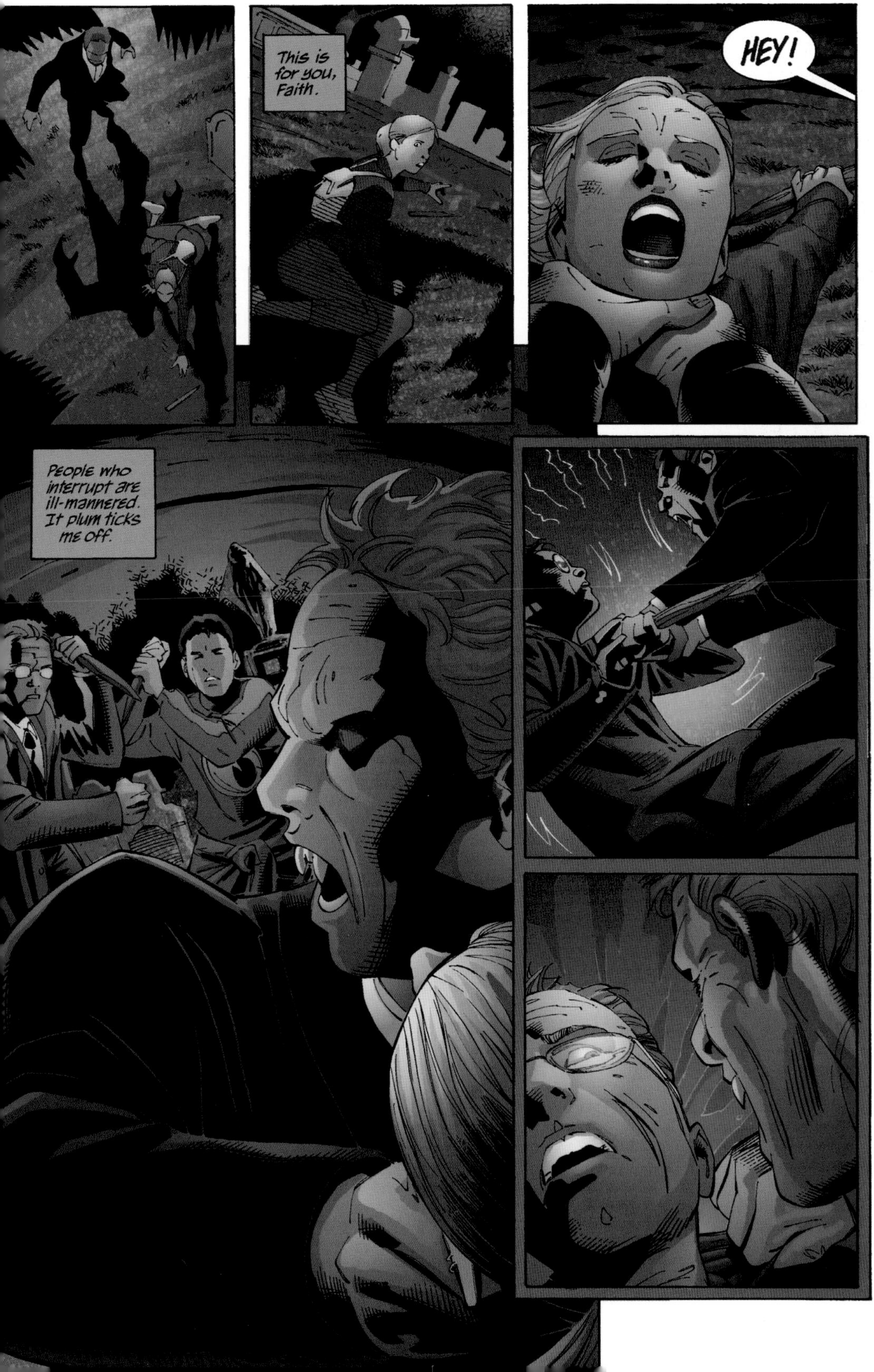
This is for you, Faith.
HEY!
People who interrupt are ill-mannered. It plum ticks me off.

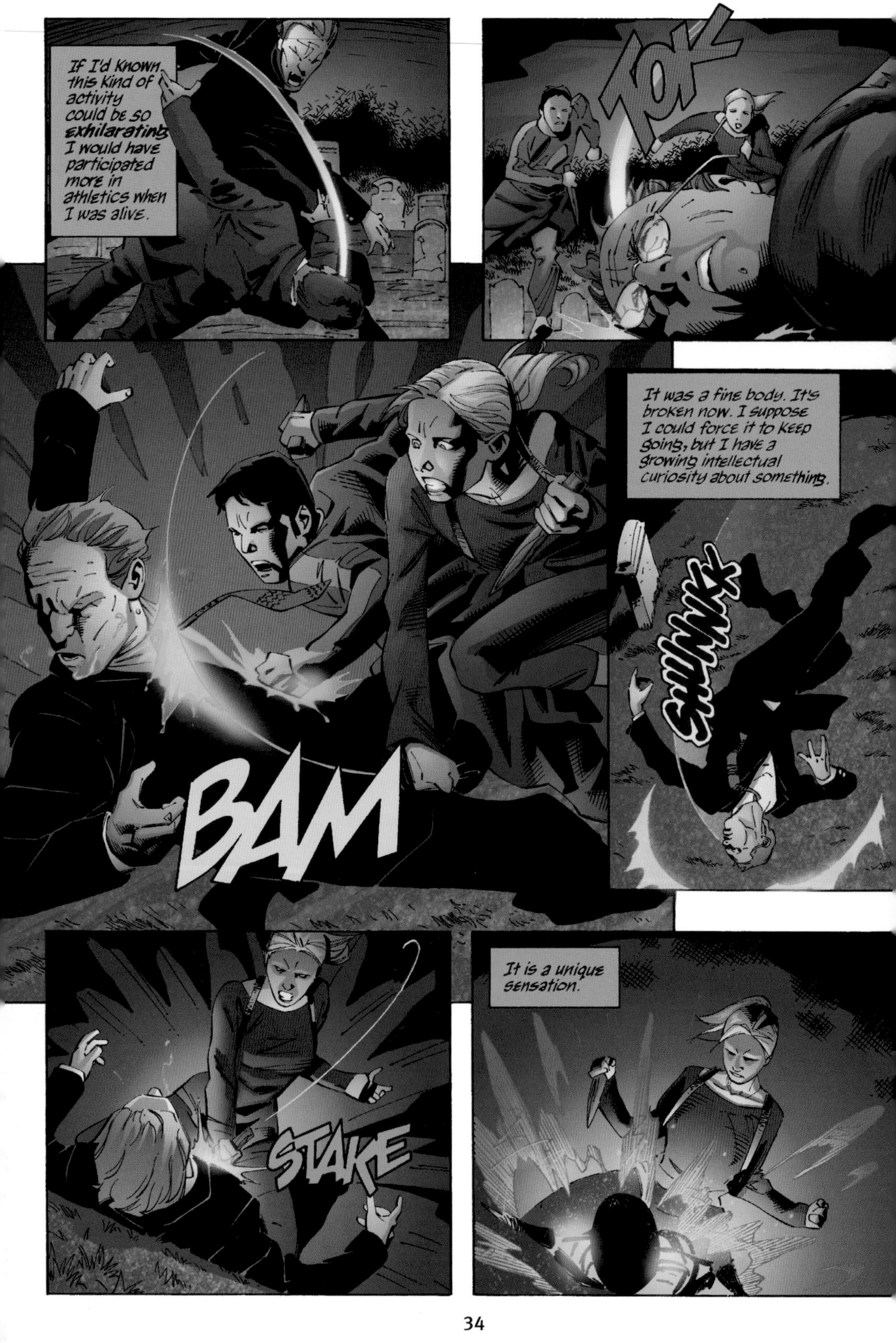
If I'd known this kind of activity could be so exhilarating I would have participated more in athletics when I was alive.
TOK
It was a fine body. It's broken now. I suppose I could force it to keep going, but I have a growing intellectual curiosity about something.
SHUNNK
BAM
STAKE
It is a unique sensation.

HE DIDN'T WAKE UP. THE WHOLE WAY OVER HERE, HE DIDN'T WAKE UP.

HE'LL BE FINE. GILES PATCHES UP GREAT. A LITTLE *DRY WALL*, SOME *SPACKLE*...

NO. IT SHOULDN'T HAVE HAPPENED. SOMETHING'S WRONG--

OH!

WHAT?

I JUST REMEMBERED. A *BODY*. IN A HOSPITAL GOWN JUST LIKE THAT ONE. GILES AND I FOUND IT IN THE CEMETERY. WE WERE LOOKING FOR YOU, TO SHOW IT TO YOU!

SOMEONE *DIED* WHILE I WAS PATROLLING?

NO. SEE, IT WAS STONE COLD. I THINK IT WAS DEAD FOR DAYS.

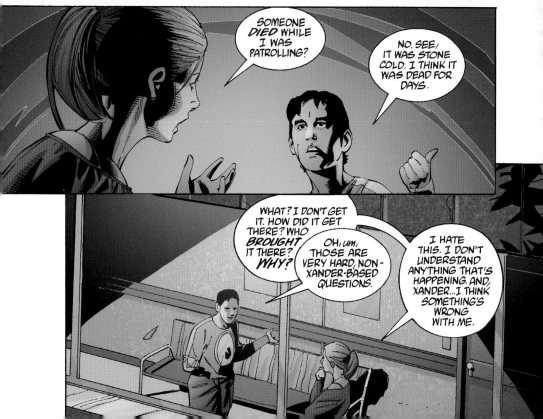

WHAT? I DON'T GET IT. HOW DID IT GET THERE? WHO *BROUGHT* IT THERE? *WHY?*

OH, UM, THOSE ARE VERY HARD, NON-XANDER-BASED QUESTIONS.

I HATE THIS. I DON'T UNDERSTAND ANYTHING THAT'S HAPPENING. AND, XANDER...I THINK SOMETHING'S WRONG WITH ME.

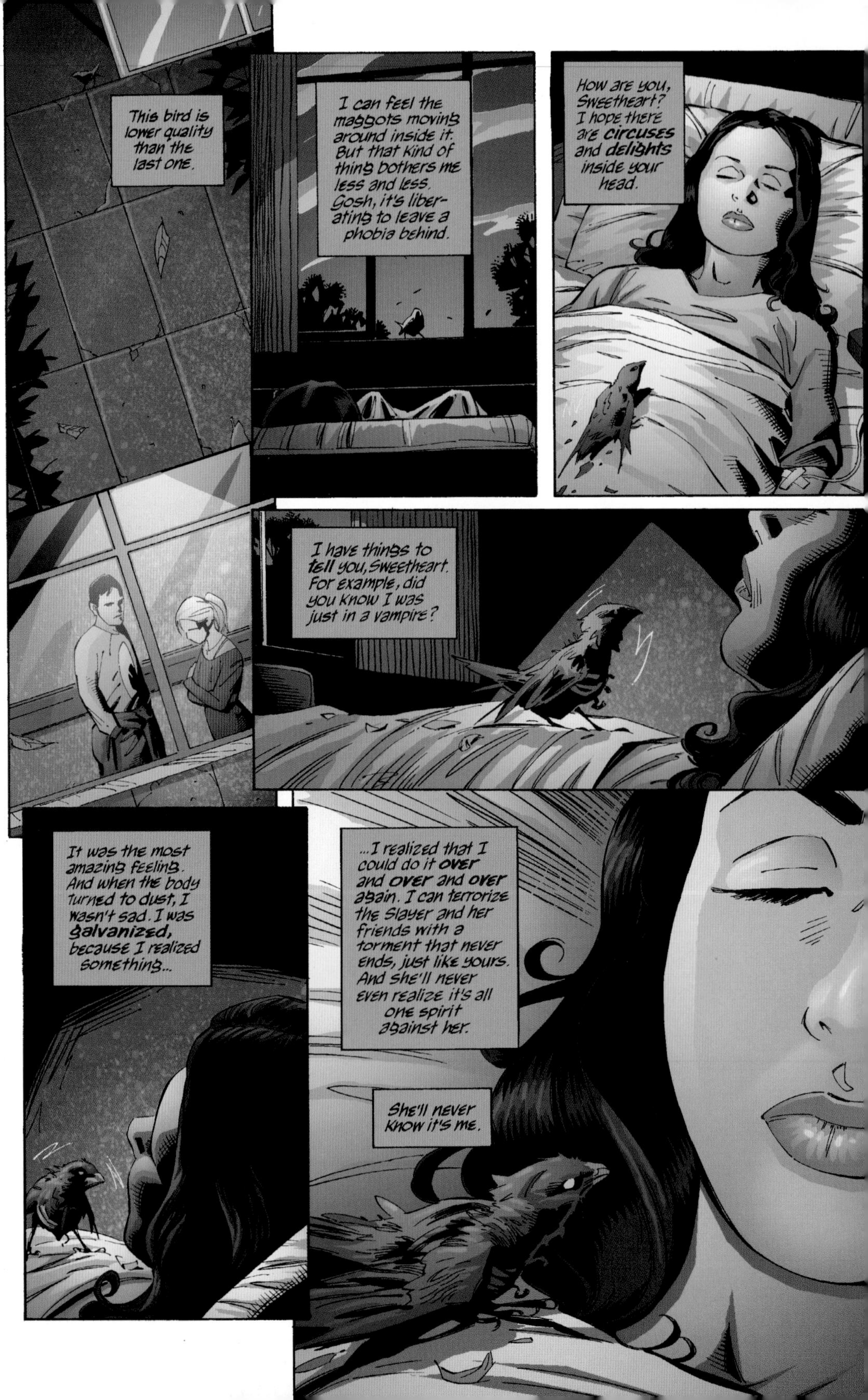
This bird is lower quality than the last one.
I can feel the maggots moving around inside it. But that kind of thing bothers me less and less. Gosh, it's liberating to leave a phobia behind.
How are you, Sweetheart? I hope there are circuses and delights inside your head.
I have things to tell you, Sweetheart. For example, did you know I was just in a vampire?
It was the most amazing feeling. And when the body turned to dust, I wasn't sad. I was galvanized, because I realized something...
...I realized that I could do it over and over and over again. I can terrorize the Slayer and her friends with a torment that never ends, just like yours. And she'll never even realize it's all one spirit against her.
She'll never know it's me.

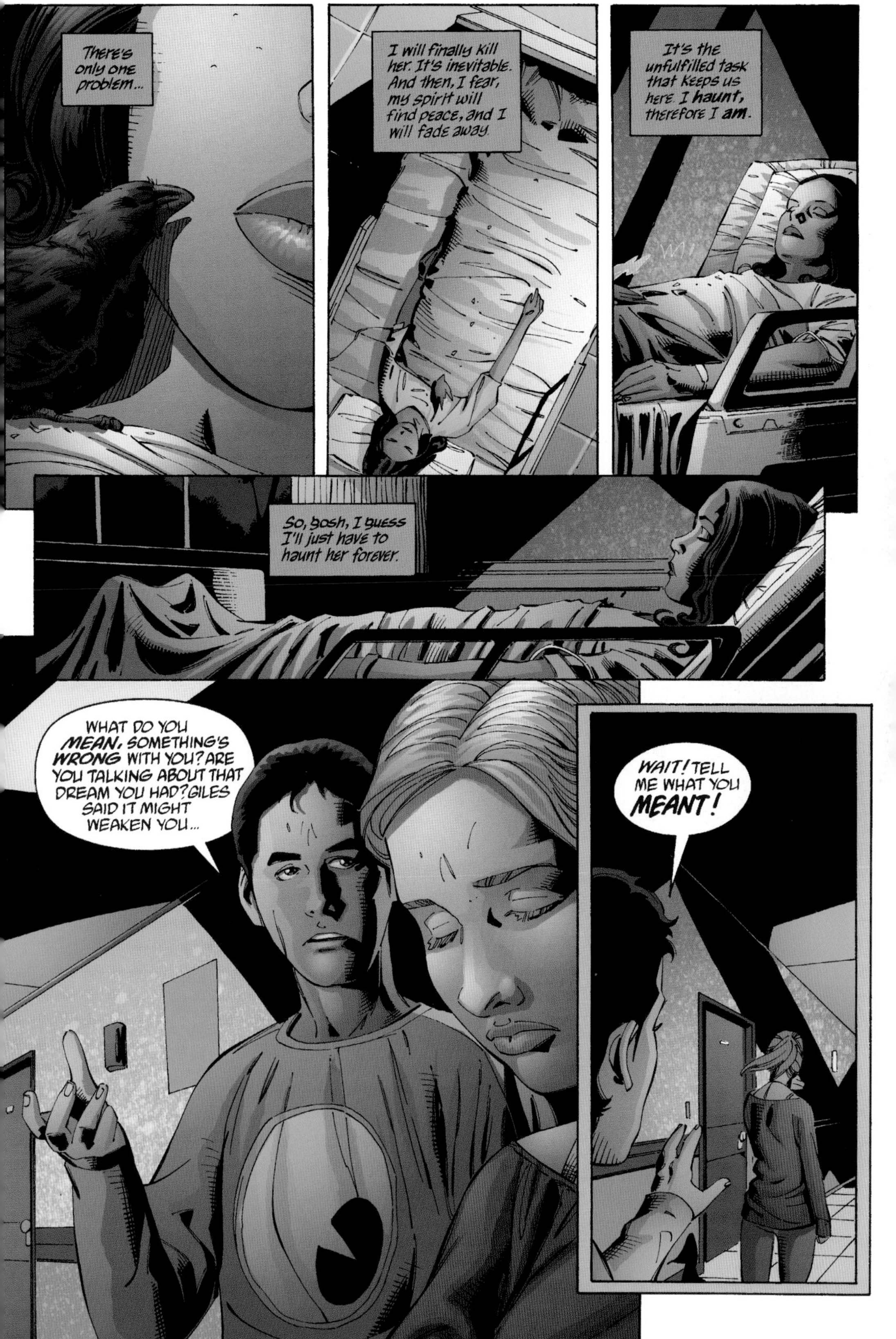
There's only one problem...
I will finally kill her. It's inevitable. And then, I fear, my spirit will find peace, and I will fade away.
It's the unfulfilled task that keeps us here. I haunt, therefore I am.
So, gosh, I guess I'll just have to haunt her forever.
WHAT DO YOU MEAN, SOMETHING'S WRONG WITH YOU? ARE YOU TALKING ABOUT THAT DREAM YOU HAD? GILES SAID IT MIGHT WEAKEN YOU...
WAIT! TELL ME WHAT YOU MEANT!

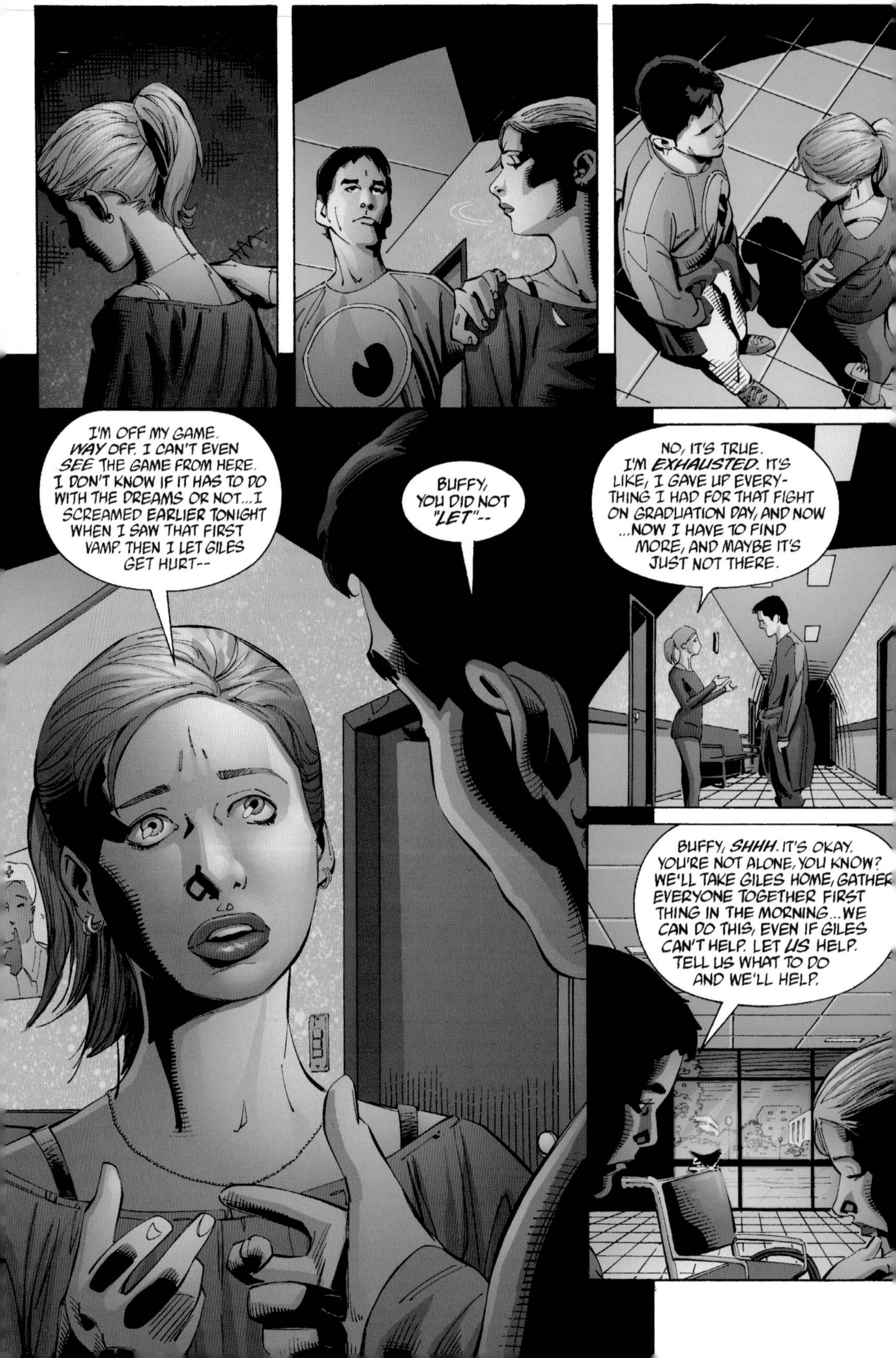

I'M OFF MY GAME. WAY OFF. I CAN'T EVEN SEE THE GAME FROM HERE. I DON'T KNOW IF IT HAS TO DO WITH THE DREAMS OR NOT... I SCREAMED EARLIER TONIGHT WHEN I SAW THAT FIRST VAMP. THEN I LET GILES GET HURT--
BUFFY, YOU DID NOT "LET"--
NO, IT'S TRUE. I'M EXHAUSTED. IT'S LIKE, I GAVE UP EVERYTHING I HAD FOR THAT FIGHT ON GRADUATION DAY, AND NOW ...NOW I HAVE TO FIND MORE, AND MAYBE IT'S JUST NOT THERE.
BUFFY, SHHH. IT'S OKAY. YOU'RE NOT ALONE, YOU KNOW? WE'LL TAKE GILES HOME, GATHER EVERYONE TOGETHER FIRST THING IN THE MORNING... WE CAN DO THIS, EVEN IF GILES CAN'T HELP. LET US HELP. TELL US WHAT TO DO AND WE'LL HELP.

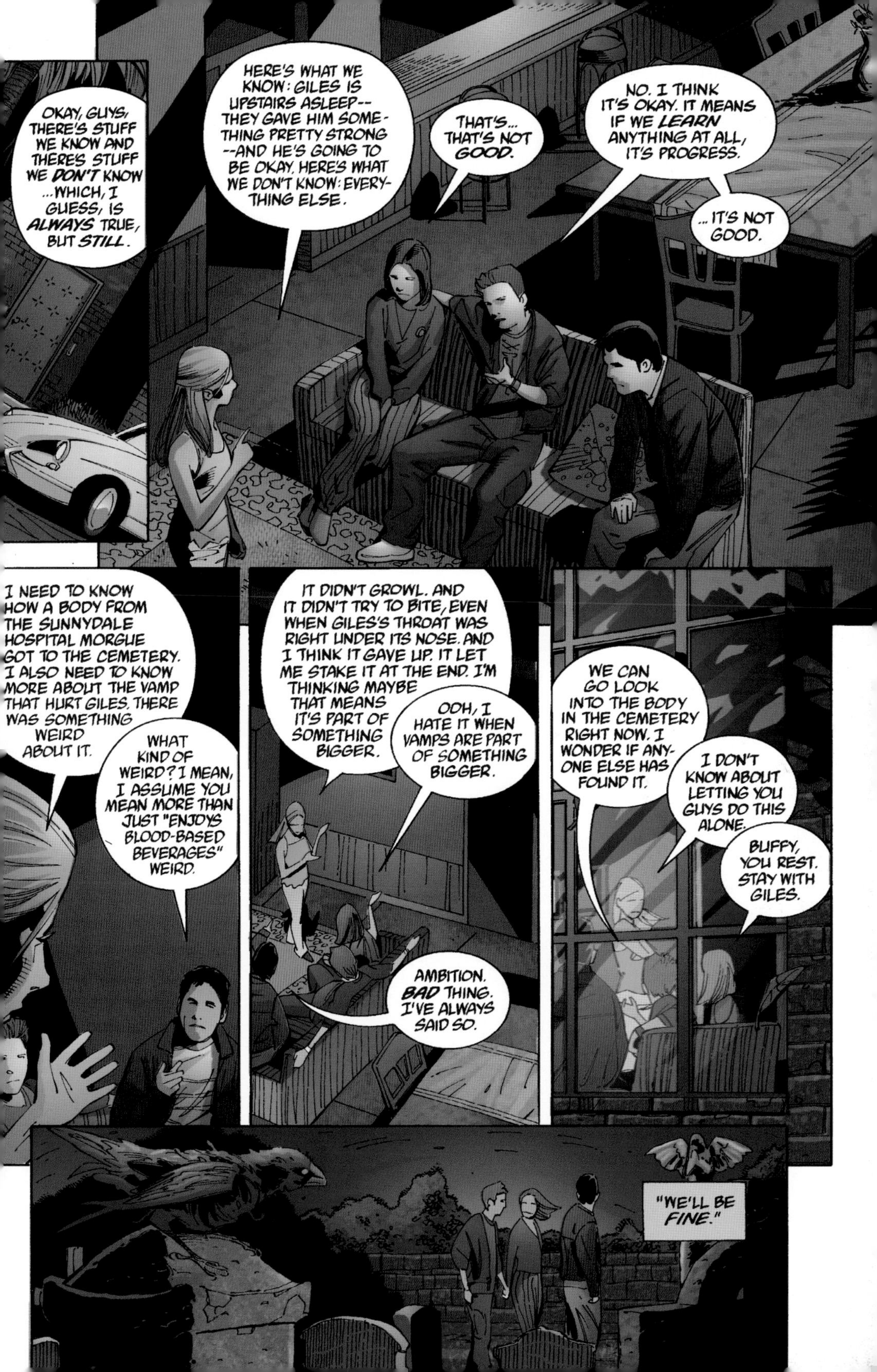
OKAY, GUYS, THERE'S STUFF WE KNOW AND THERE'S STUFF WE DON'T KNOW ...WHICH, I GUESS, IS ALWAYS TRUE, BUT STILL.
HERE'S WHAT WE KNOW: GILES IS UPSTAIRS ASLEEP-- THEY GAVE HIM SOMETHING PRETTY STRONG --AND HE'S GOING TO BE OKAY. HERE'S WHAT WE DON'T KNOW: EVERYTHING ELSE.
THAT'S... THAT'S NOT GOOD.
NO. I THINK IT'S OKAY. IT MEANS IF WE LEARN ANYTHING AT ALL, IT'S PROGRESS.
...IT'S NOT GOOD.
I NEED TO KNOW HOW A BODY FROM THE SUNNYDALE HOSPITAL MORGUE GOT TO THE CEMETERY. I ALSO NEED TO KNOW MORE ABOUT THE VAMP THAT HURT GILES. THERE WAS SOMETHING WEIRD ABOUT IT.
WHAT KIND OF WEIRD? I MEAN, I ASSUME YOU MEAN MORE THAN JUST "ENJOYS BLOOD-BASED BEVERAGES" WEIRD.
IT DIDN'T GROWL. AND IT DIDN'T TRY TO BITE, EVEN WHEN GILES'S THROAT WAS RIGHT UNDER ITS NOSE. AND I THINK IT GAVE UP. IT LET ME STAKE IT AT THE END. I'M THINKING MAYBE THAT MEANS IT'S PART OF SOMETHING BIGGER.
OOH, I HATE IT WHEN VAMPS ARE PART OF SOMETHING BIGGER.
AMBITION. BAD THING. I'VE ALWAYS SAID SO.
WE CAN GO LOOK INTO THE BODY IN THE CEMETERY RIGHT NOW. I WONDER IF ANYONE ELSE HAS FOUND IT.
I DON'T KNOW ABOUT LETTING YOU GUYS DO THIS ALONE.
BUFFY, YOU REST. STAY WITH GILES.
"WE'LL BE FINE."

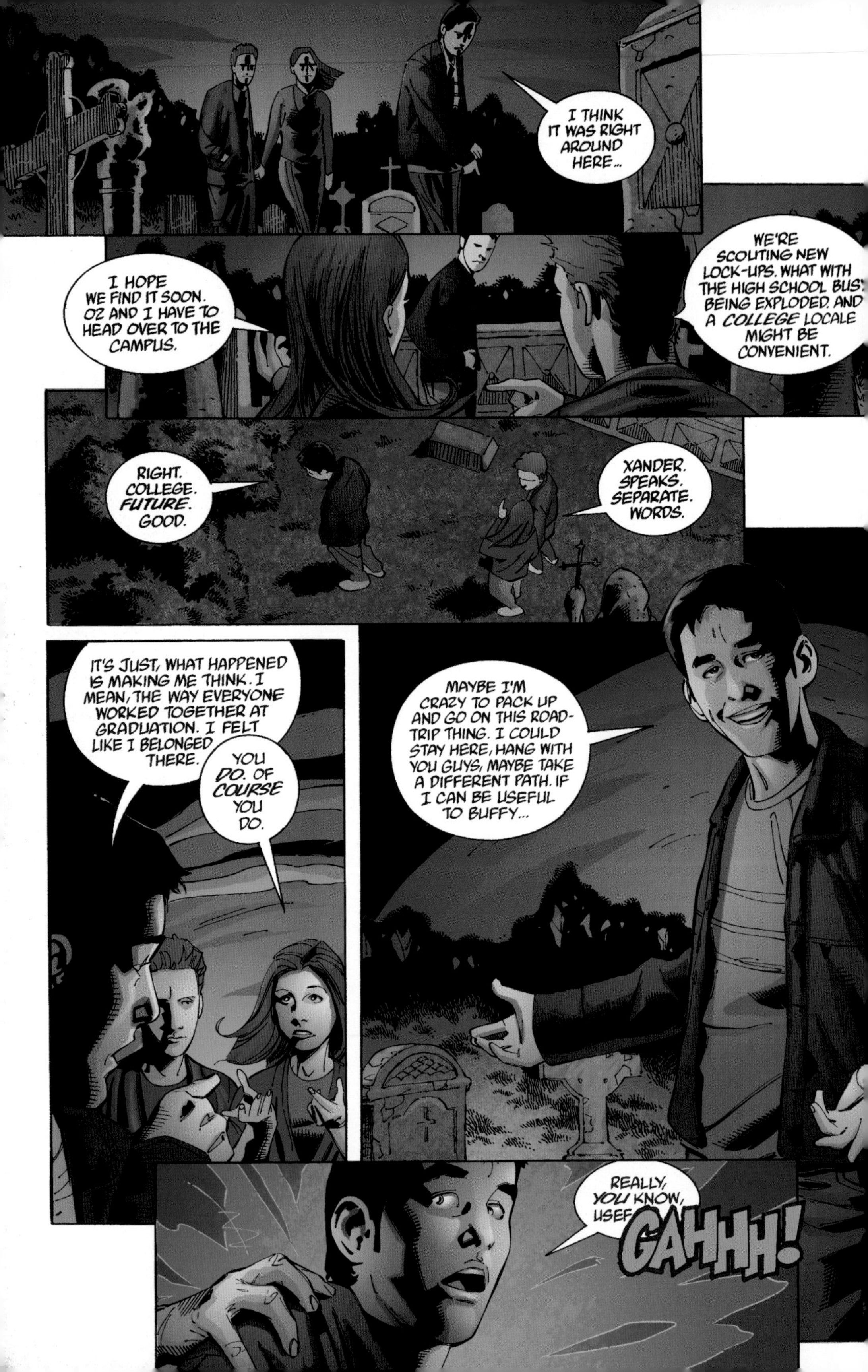
I THINK IT WAS RIGHT AROUND HERE...
I HOPE WE FIND IT SOON. OZ AND I HAVE TO HEAD OVER TO THE CAMPUS.
WE'RE SCOUTING NEW LOCK-UPS. WHAT WITH THE HIGH SCHOOL BUSY BEING EXPLODED. AND A COLLEGE LOCALE MIGHT BE CONVENIENT.
RIGHT. COLLEGE. FUTURE. GOOD.
XANDER. SPEAKS. SEPARATE. WORDS.
IT'S JUST, WHAT HAPPENED IS MAKING ME THINK. I MEAN, THE WAY EVERYONE WORKED TOGETHER AT GRADUATION. I FELT LIKE I BELONGED THERE.
YOU DO. OF COURSE YOU DO.
MAYBE I'M CRAZY TO PACK UP AND GO ON THIS ROAD-TRIP THING. I COULD STAY HERE, HANG WITH YOU GUYS, MAYBE TAKE A DIFFERENT PATH. IF I CAN BE USEFUL TO BUFFY...
REALLY, YOU KNOW, USEF
GAHHH!

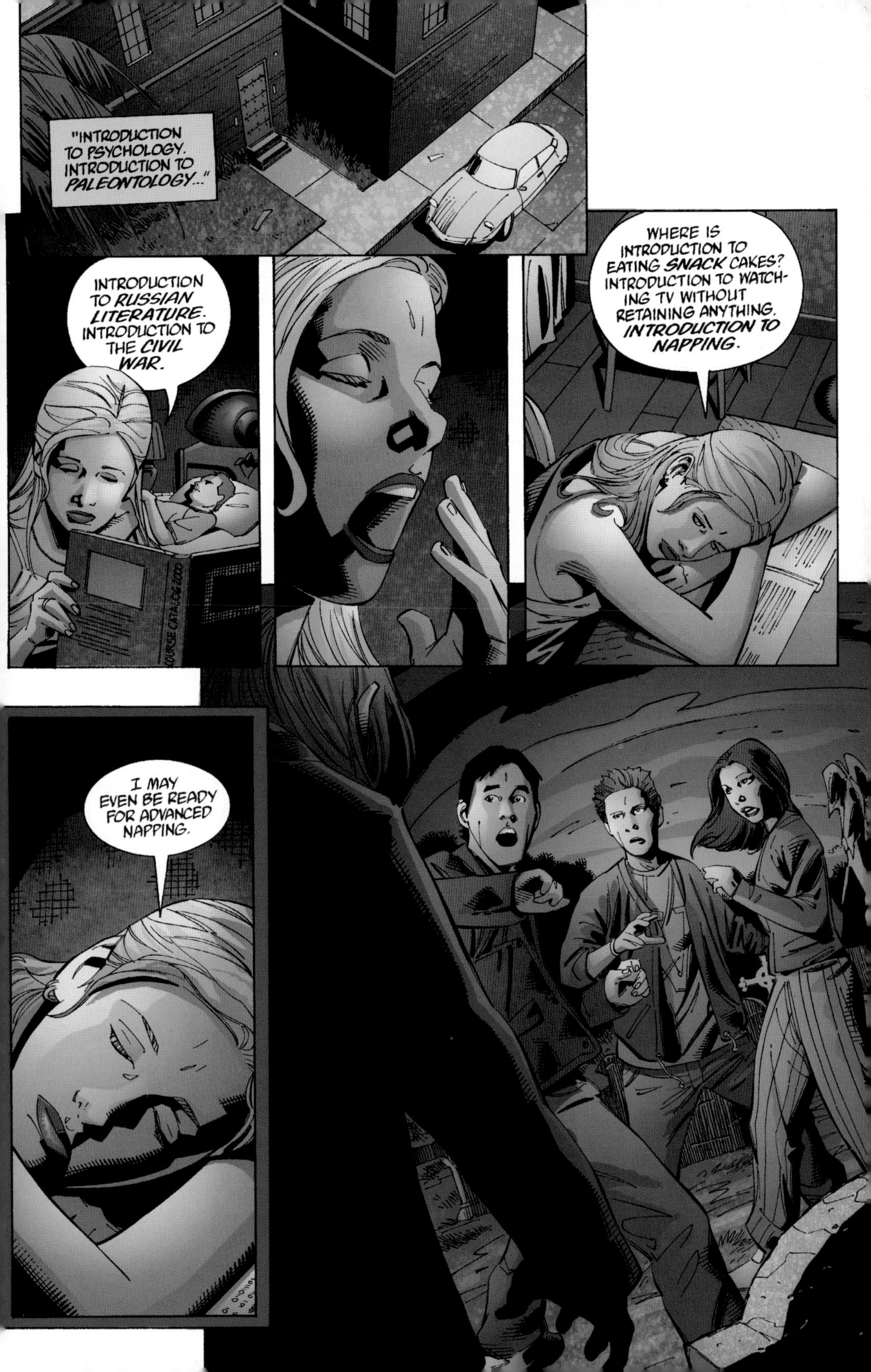
"INTRODUCTION TO PSYCHOLOGY. INTRODUCTION TO PALEONTOLOGY..."
INTRODUCTION TO RUSSIAN LITERATURE. INTRODUCTION TO THE CIVIL WAR.
COURSE CATALOG 2000
WHERE IS INTRODUCTION TO EATING SNACK CAKES? INTRODUCTION TO WATCHING TV WITHOUT RETAINING ANYTHING. INTRODUCTION TO NAPPING.
I MAY EVEN BE READY FOR ADVANCED NAPPING.

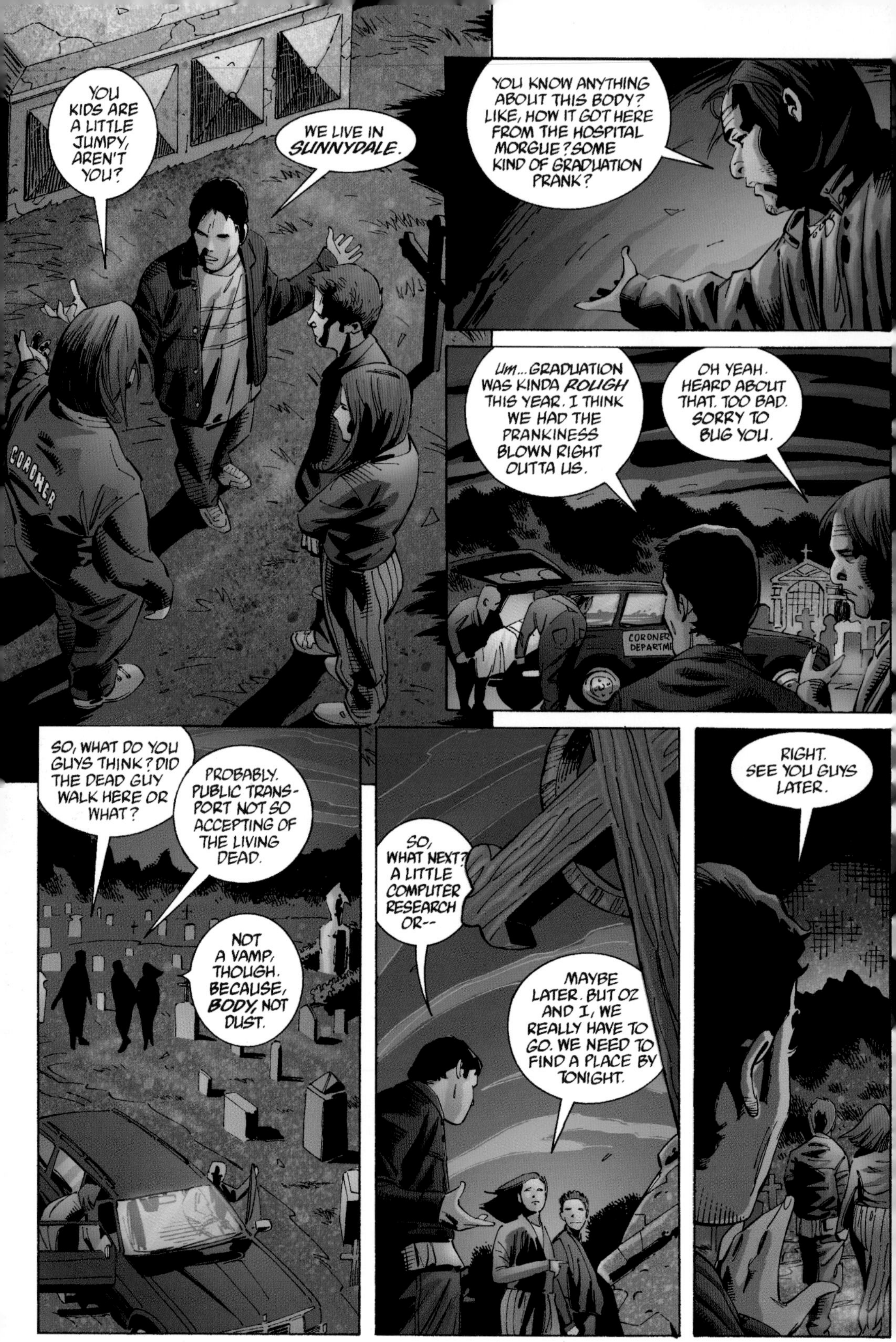
YOU KIDS ARE A LITTLE JUMPY, AREN'T YOU?
WE LIVE IN *SUNNYDALE*.
CORONER
YOU KNOW ANYTHING ABOUT THIS BODY? LIKE, HOW IT GOT HERE FROM THE HOSPITAL MORGUE? SOME KIND OF GRADUATION PRANK?
Um... GRADUATION WAS KINDA *ROUGH* THIS YEAR. I THINK WE HAD THE PRANKINESS BLOWN RIGHT OUTTA US.
OH YEAH. HEARD ABOUT THAT. TOO BAD. SORRY TO BUG YOU.
CORONER DEPARTME
SO, WHAT DO YOU GUYS THINK? DID THE DEAD GUY WALK HERE OR WHAT?
PROBABLY. PUBLIC TRANS-PORT NOT SO ACCEPTING OF THE LIVING DEAD.
NOT A VAMP, THOUGH. BECAUSE, *BODY*, NOT DUST.
SO, WHAT NEXT? A LITTLE COMPUTER RESEARCH OR--
MAYBE LATER. BUT OZ AND I, WE REALLY HAVE TO GO. WE NEED TO FIND A PLACE BY TONIGHT.
RIGHT. SEE YOU GUYS LATER.

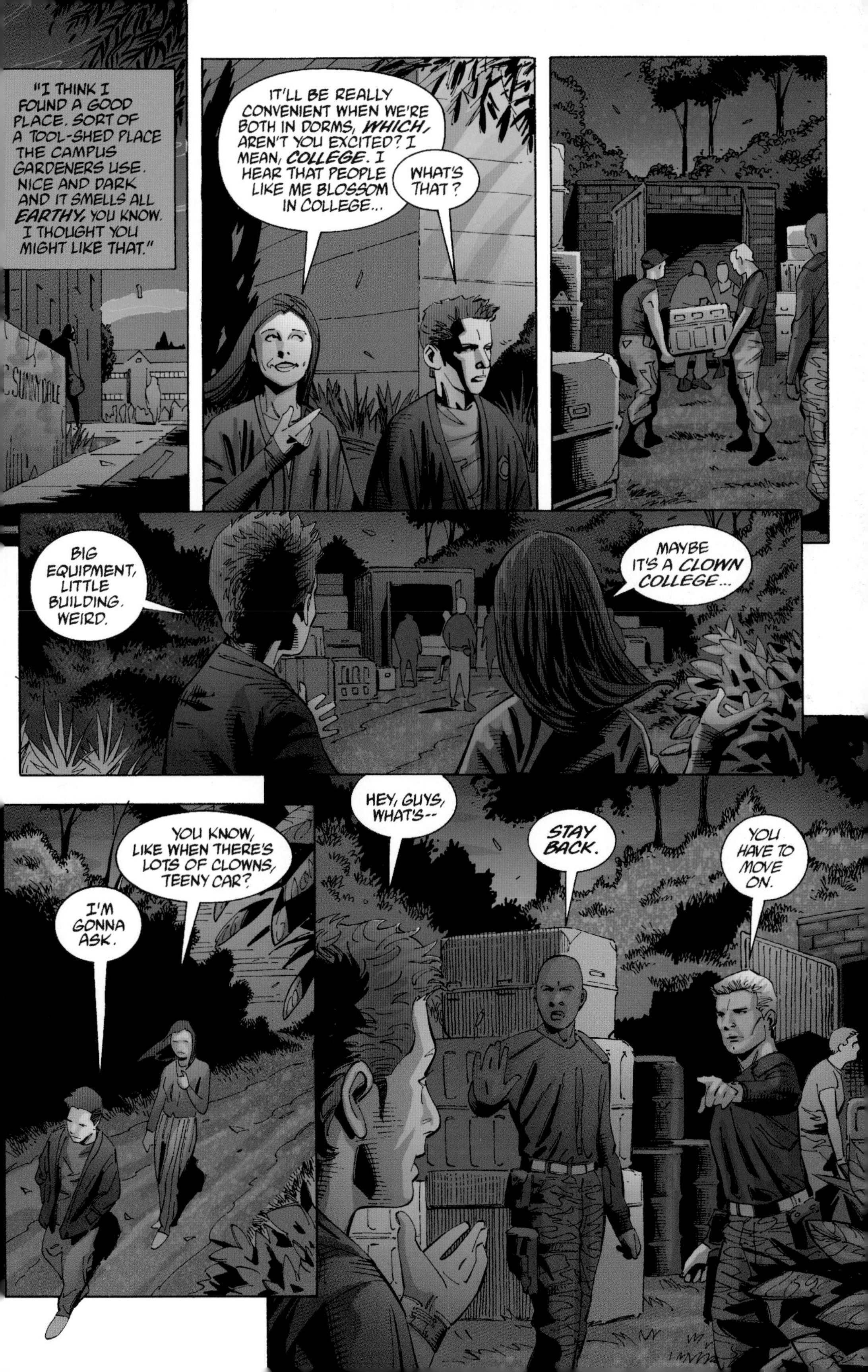
"I THINK I FOUND A GOOD PLACE. SORT OF A TOOL-SHED PLACE THE CAMPUS GARDENERS USE. NICE AND DARK AND IT SMELLS ALL EARTHY, YOU KNOW. I THOUGHT YOU MIGHT LIKE THAT."
IT'LL BE REALLY CONVENIENT WHEN WE'RE BOTH IN DORMS, WHICH, AREN'T YOU EXCITED? I MEAN, COLLEGE. I HEAR THAT PEOPLE LIKE ME BLOSSOM IN COLLEGE...
WHAT'S THAT?
BIG EQUIPMENT, LITTLE BUILDING. WEIRD.
MAYBE IT'S A CLOWN COLLEGE...
YOU KNOW, LIKE WHEN THERE'S LOTS OF CLOWNS, TEENY CAR?
I'M GONNA ASK.
HEY, GUYS, WHAT'S--
STAY BACK.
YOU HAVE TO MOVE ON.

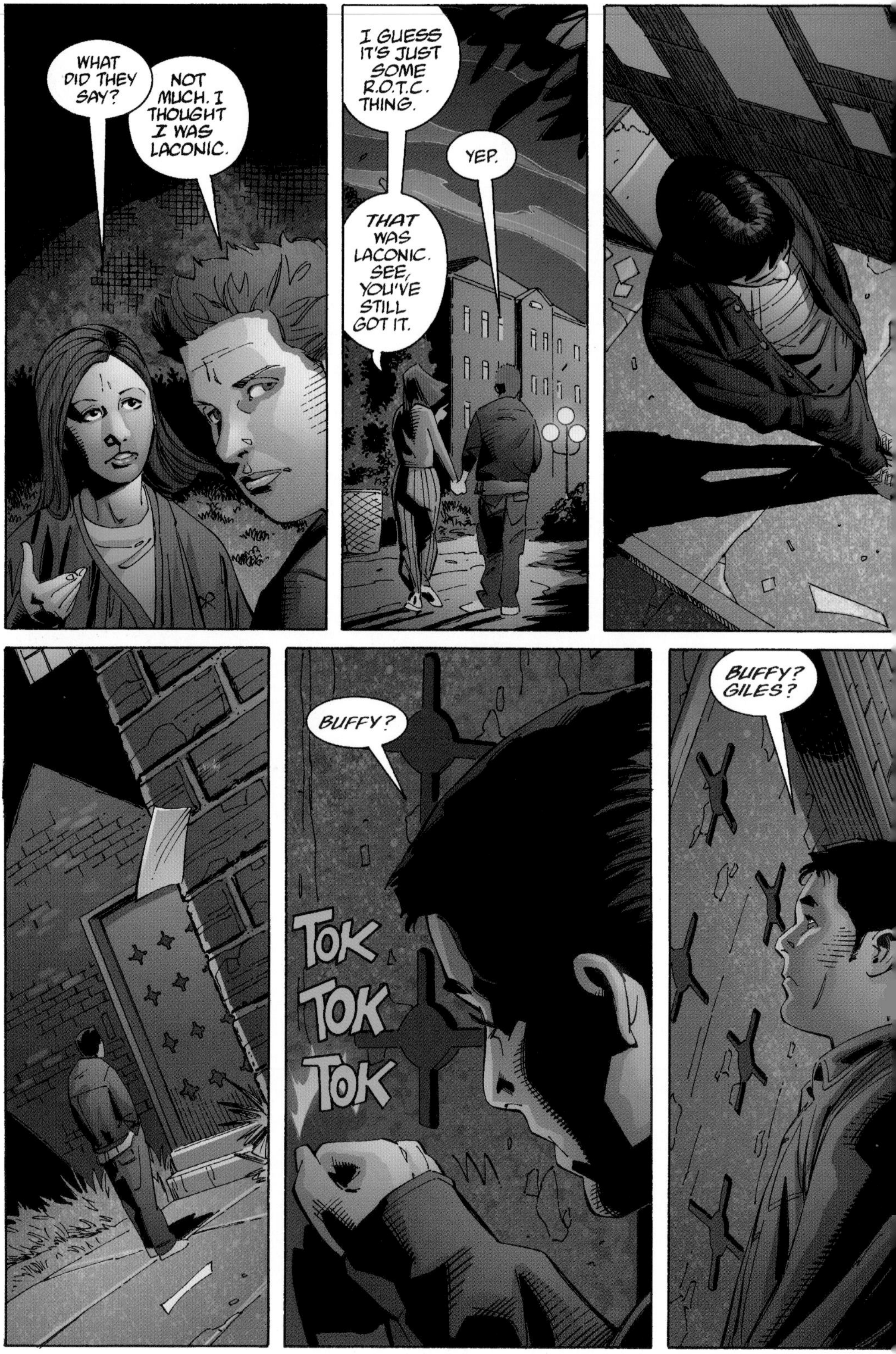
WHAT DID THEY SAY?
NOT MUCH. I THOUGHT I WAS LACONIC.
I GUESS IT'S JUST SOME R.O.T.C. THING.
YEP.
THAT WAS LACONIC. SEE, YOU'VE STILL GOT IT.
BUFFY?
TOK TOK TOK
BUFFY? GILES?

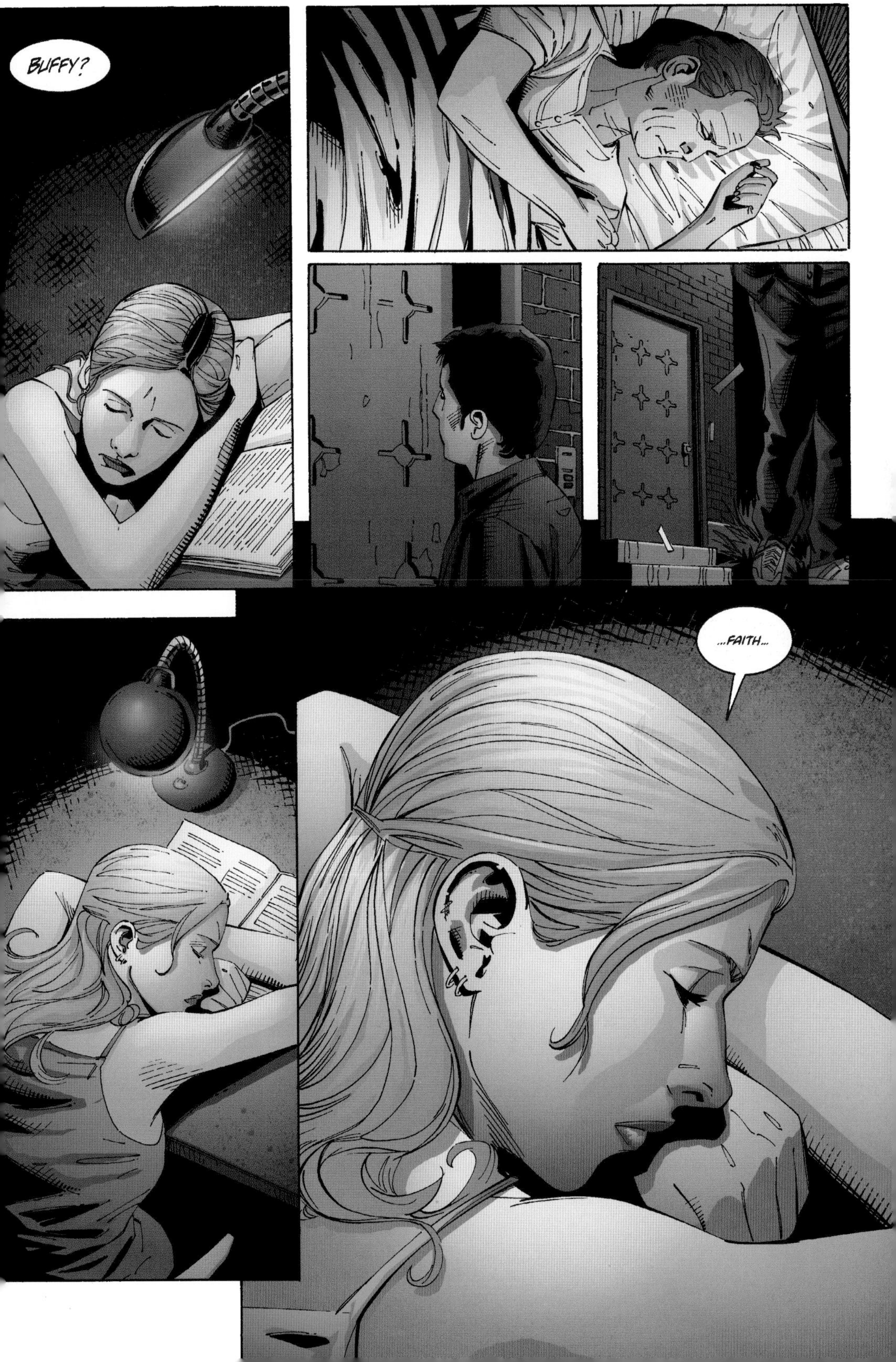
BUFFY?
...FAITH...

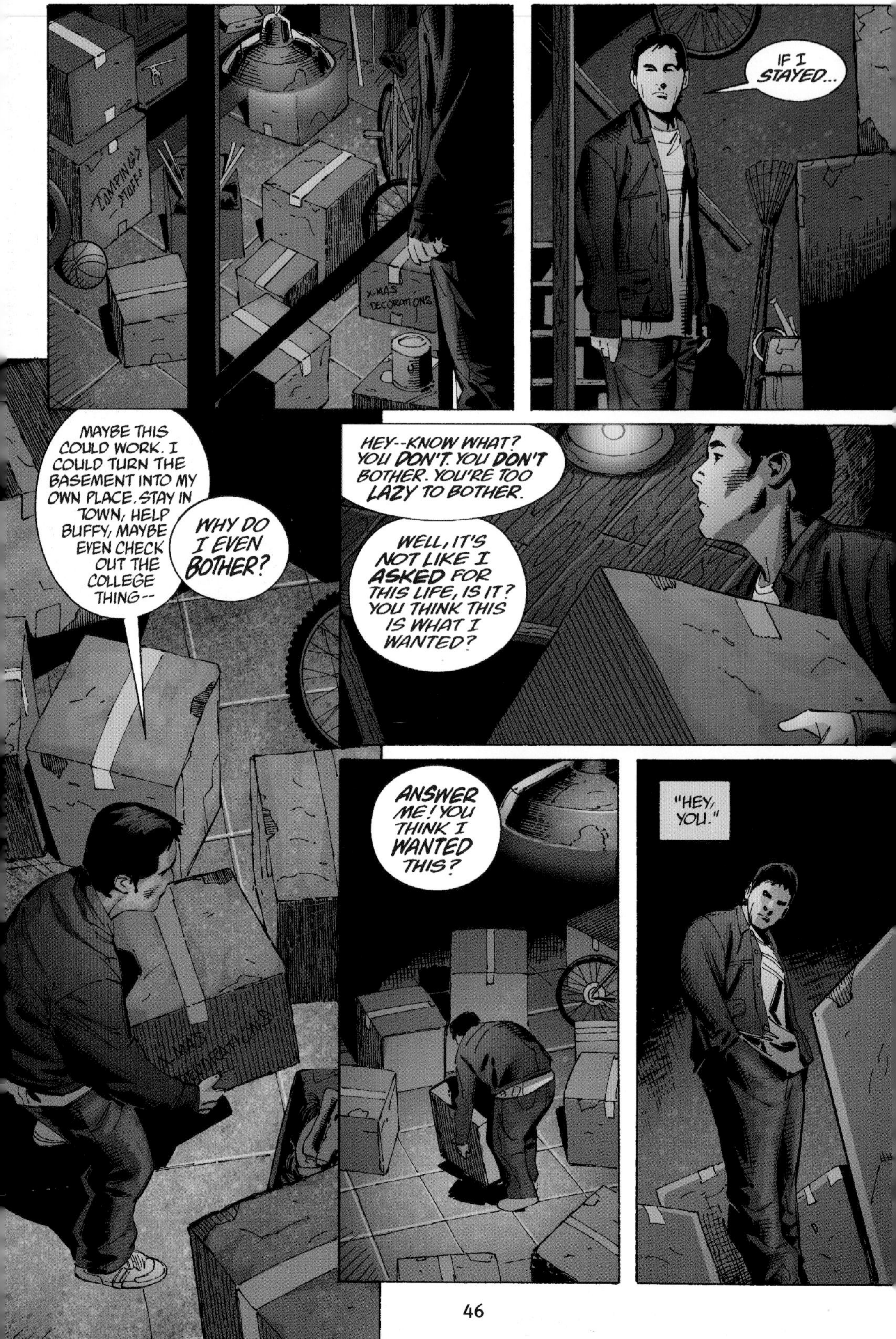
CAMPING STUFF
X-MAS DECORATIONS
IF I STAYED...
MAYBE THIS COULD WORK. I COULD TURN THE BASEMENT INTO MY OWN PLACE. STAY IN TOWN, HELP BUFFY, MAYBE EVEN CHECK OUT THE COLLEGE THING--
WHY DO I EVEN BOTHER?
HEY--KNOW WHAT? YOU DON'T. YOU DON'T BOTHER. YOU'RE TOO LAZY TO BOTHER.
WELL, IT'S NOT LIKE I ASKED FOR THIS LIFE, IS IT? YOU THINK THIS IS WHAT I WANTED?
X-MAS DECORATIONS
ANSWER ME! YOU THINK I WANTED THIS?
"HEY, YOU."

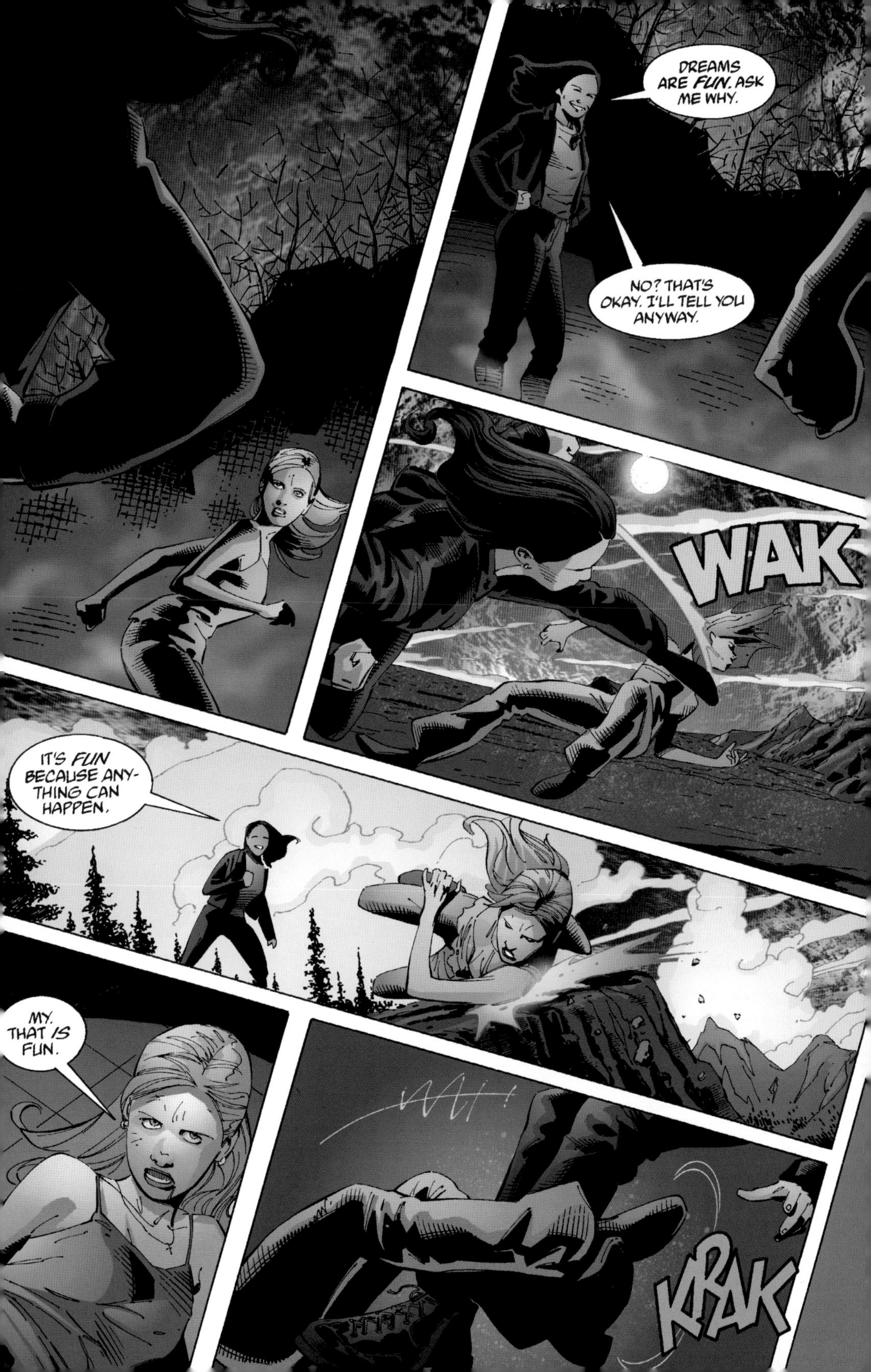
DREAMS ARE FUN. ASK ME WHY.
NO? THAT'S OKAY. I'LL TELL YOU ANYWAY.
WAK
IT'S FUN BECAUSE ANY-THING CAN HAPPEN.
MY. THAT IS FUN.
KRAK

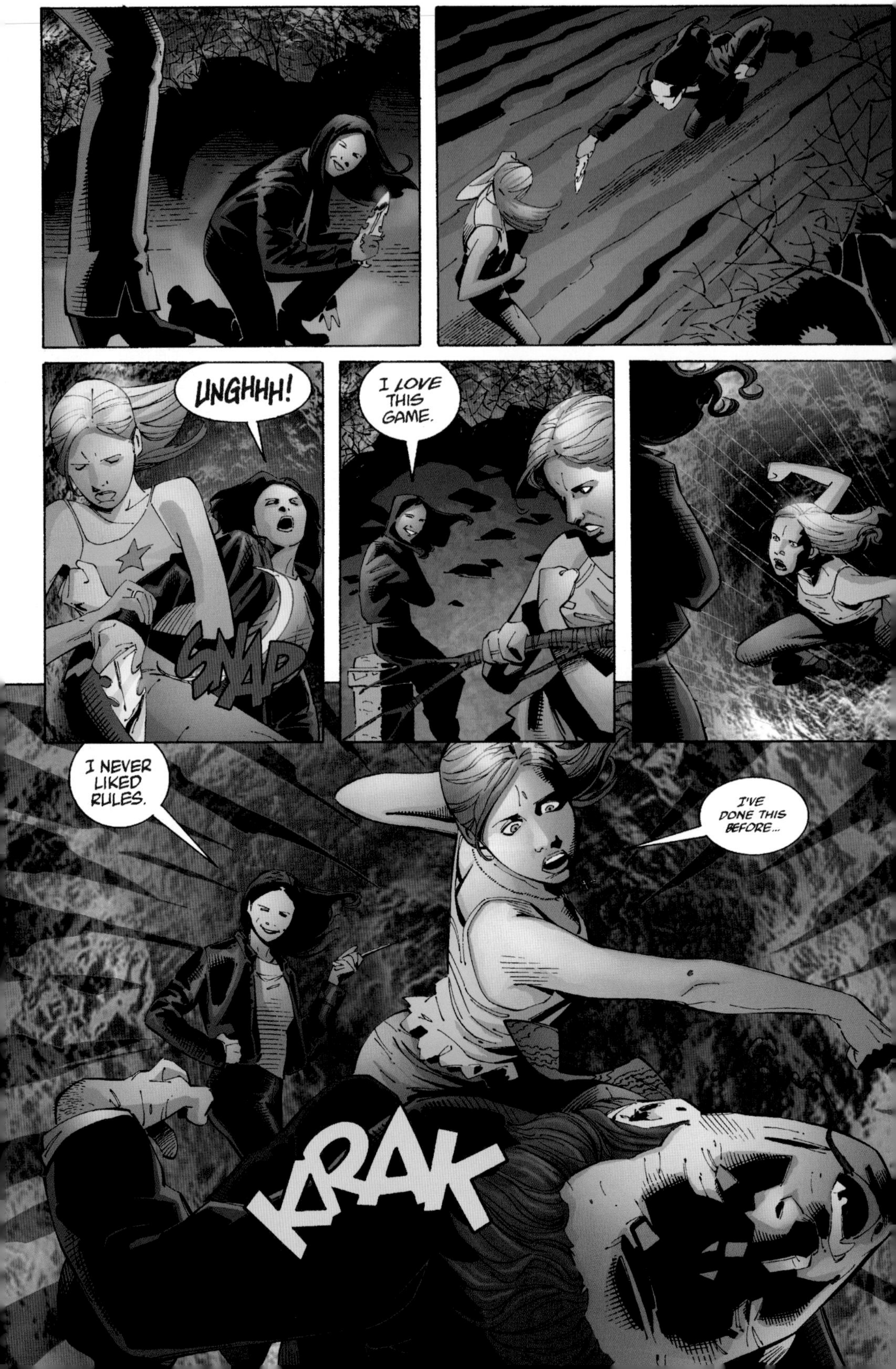
UNGHHH!
SNAP
I LOVE THIS GAME.
I NEVER LIKED RULES.
I'VE DONE THIS BEFORE...
KRAK

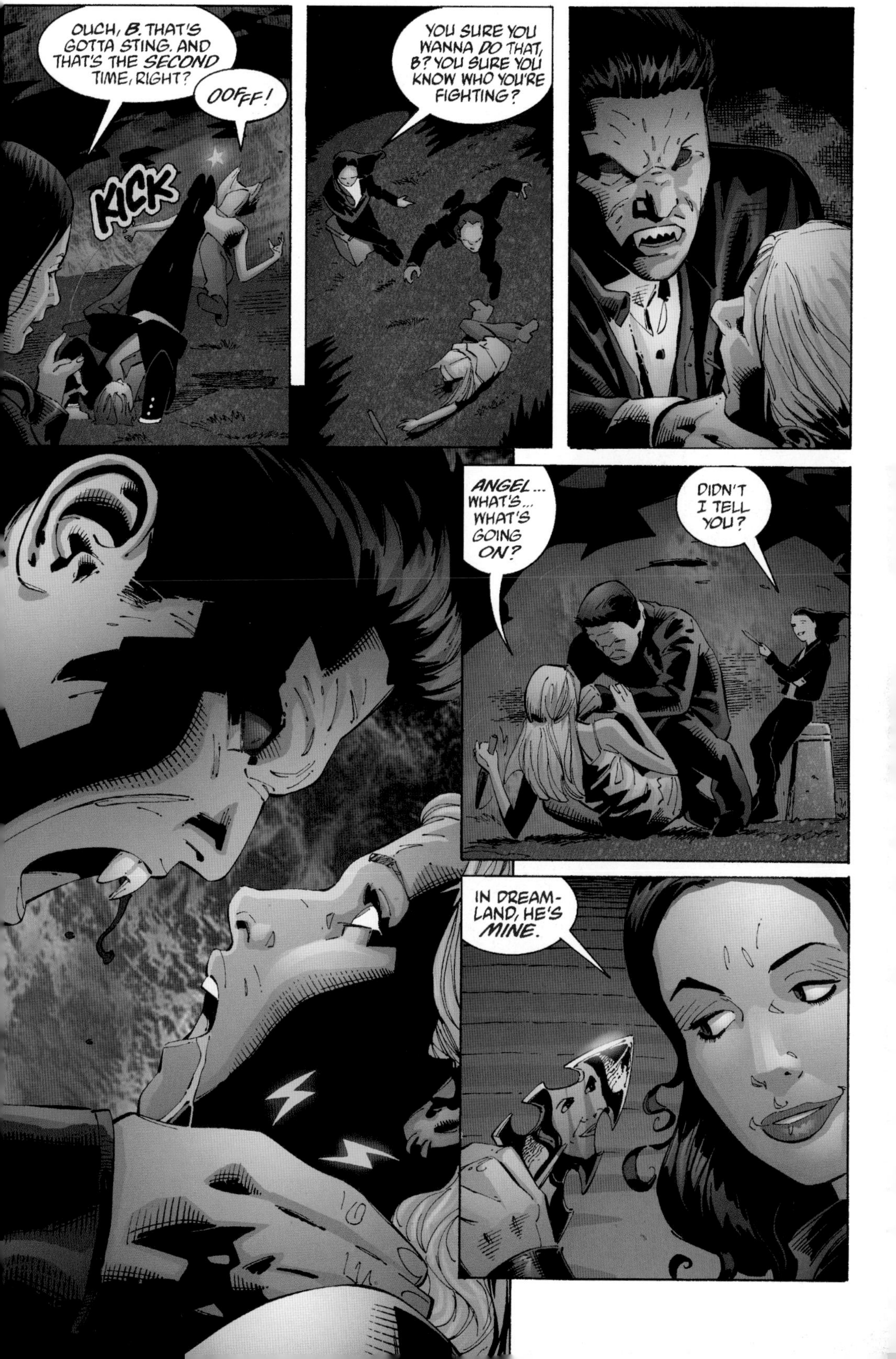
OUCH, B. THAT'S GOTTA STING. AND THAT'S THE SECOND TIME, RIGHT?
OOFFF!
KICK
YOU SURE YOU WANNA DO THAT, B? YOU SURE YOU KNOW WHO YOU'RE FIGHTING?
ANGEL... WHAT'S... WHAT'S GOING ON?
DIDN'T I TELL YOU?
IN DREAM-LAND, HE'S MINE.

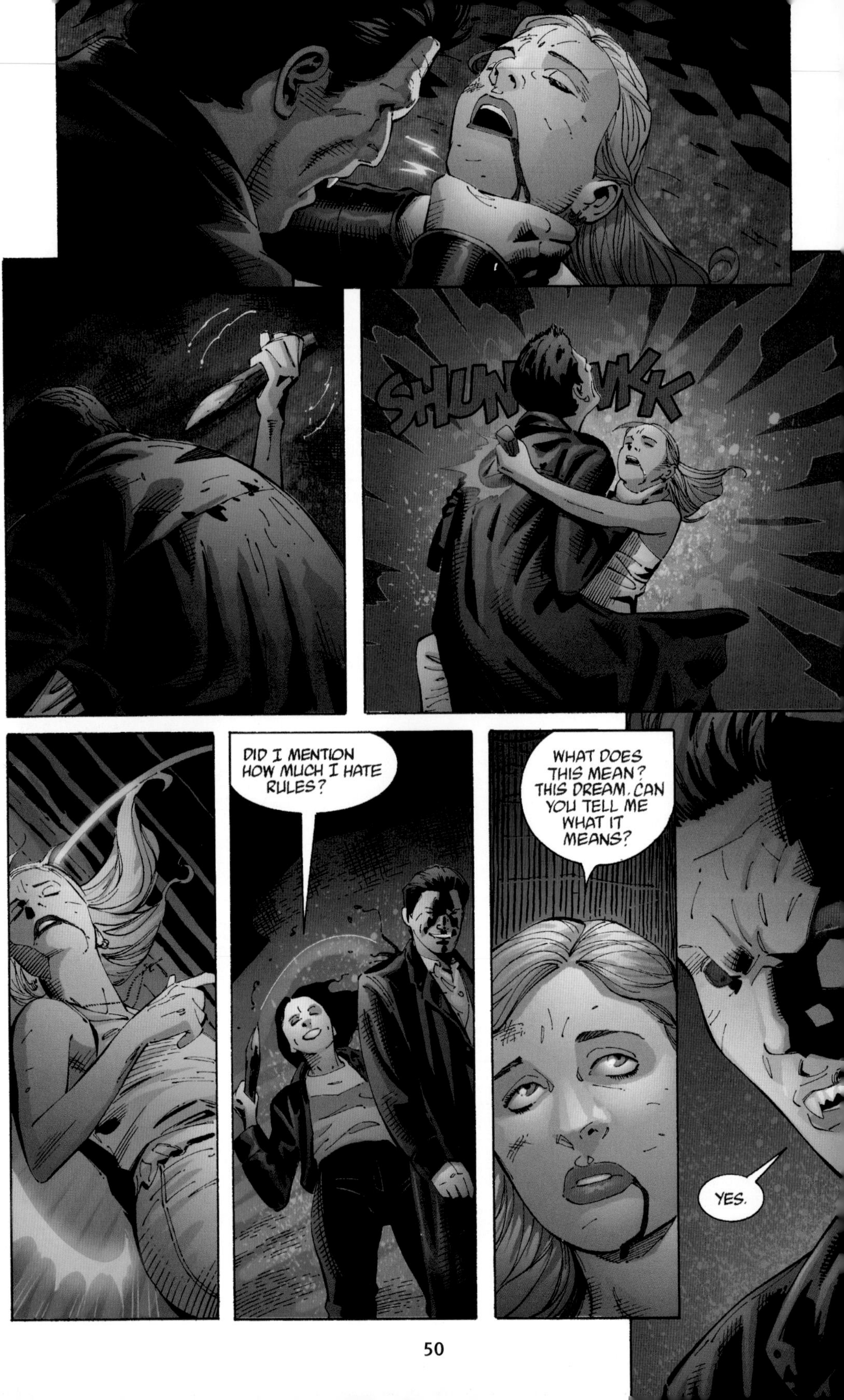
SHUNKK
DID I MENTION HOW MUCH I HATE RULES?
WHAT DOES THIS MEAN? THIS DREAM. CAN YOU TELL ME WHAT IT MEANS?
YES.

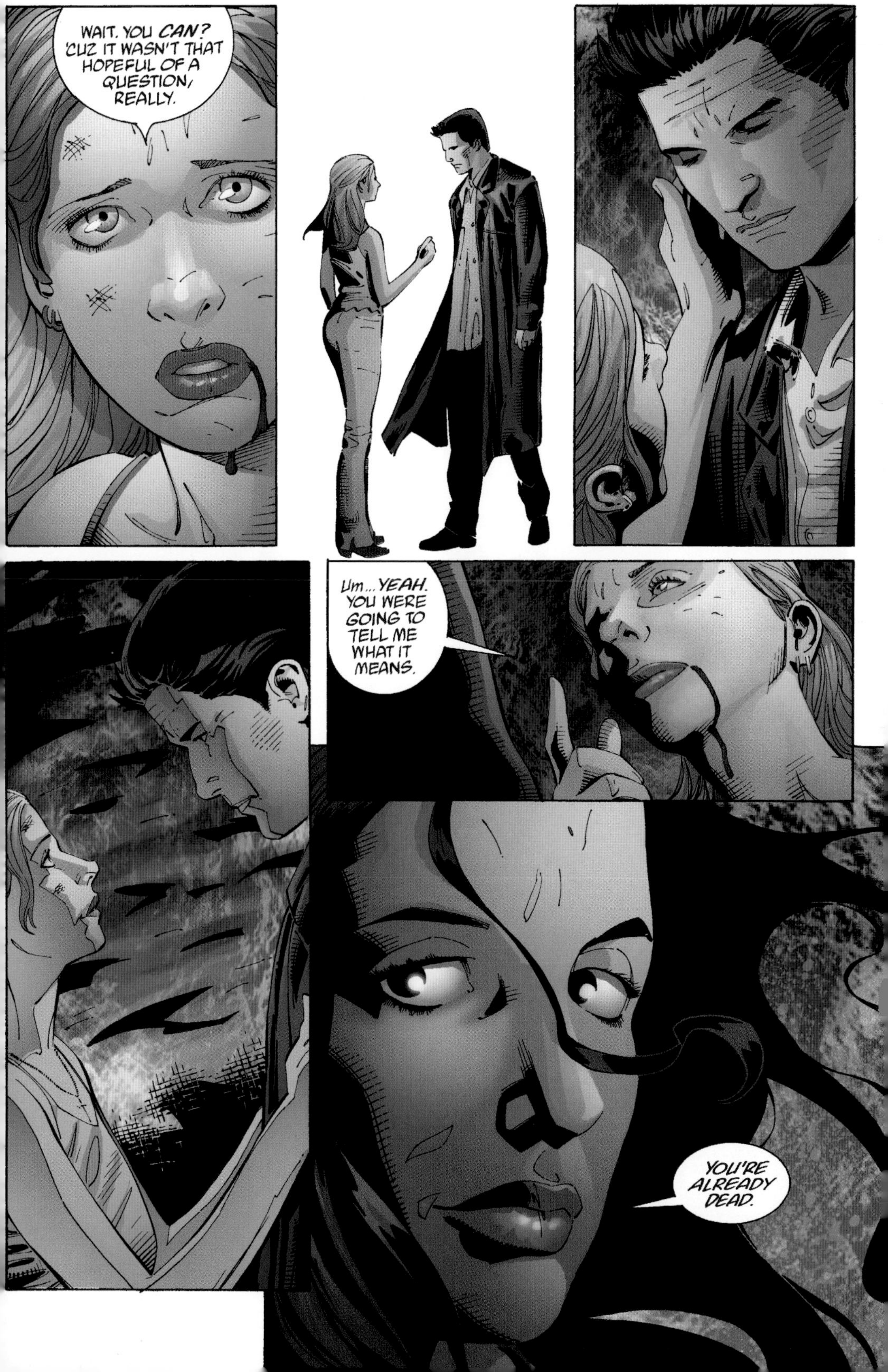
WAIT. YOU CAN? 'CUZ IT WASN'T THAT HOPEFUL OF A QUESTION, REALLY.
Um... YEAH. YOU WERE GOING TO TELL ME WHAT IT MEANS.
YOU'RE ALREADY DEAD.

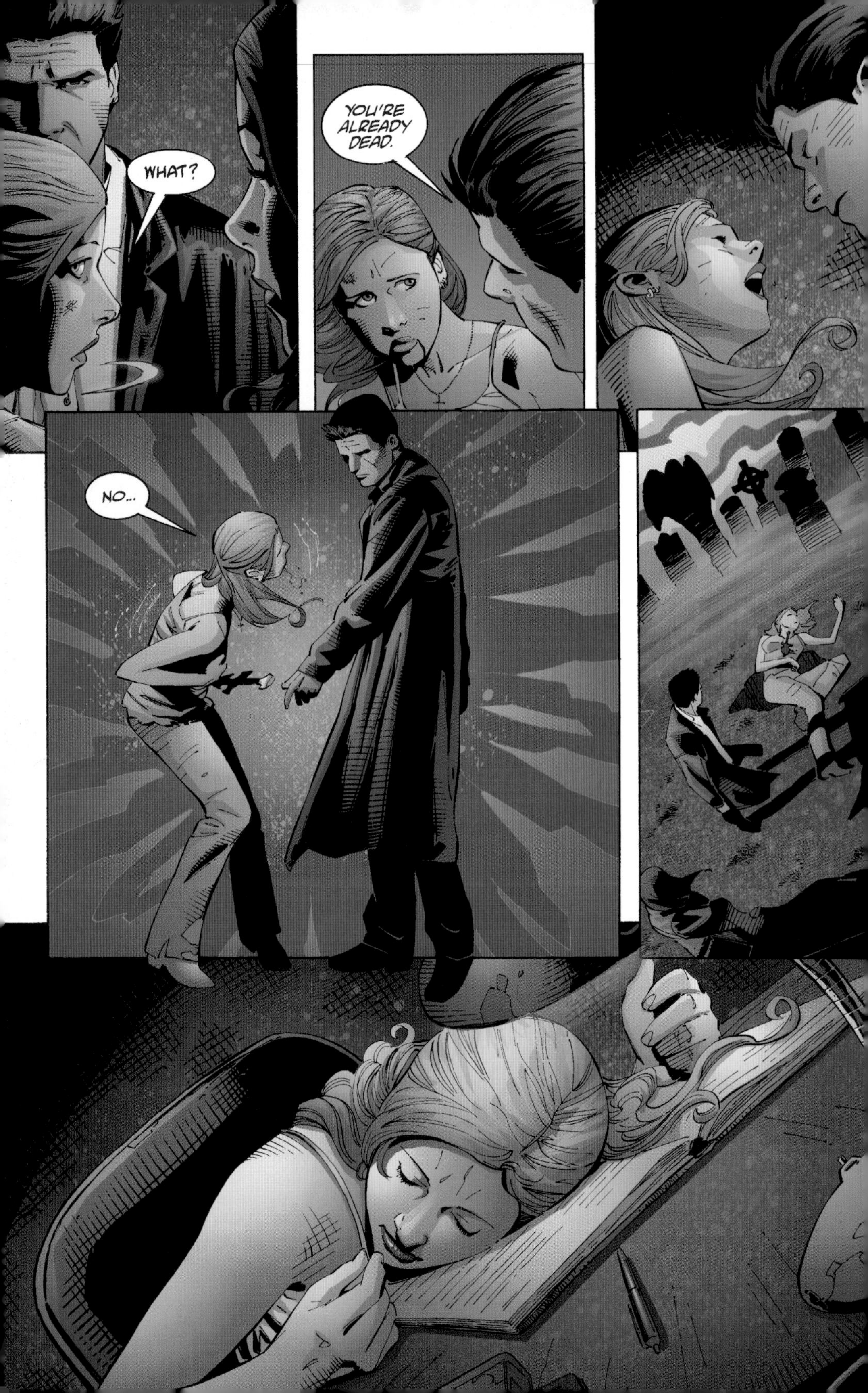
WHAT?
YOU'RE ALREADY DEAD.
NO...

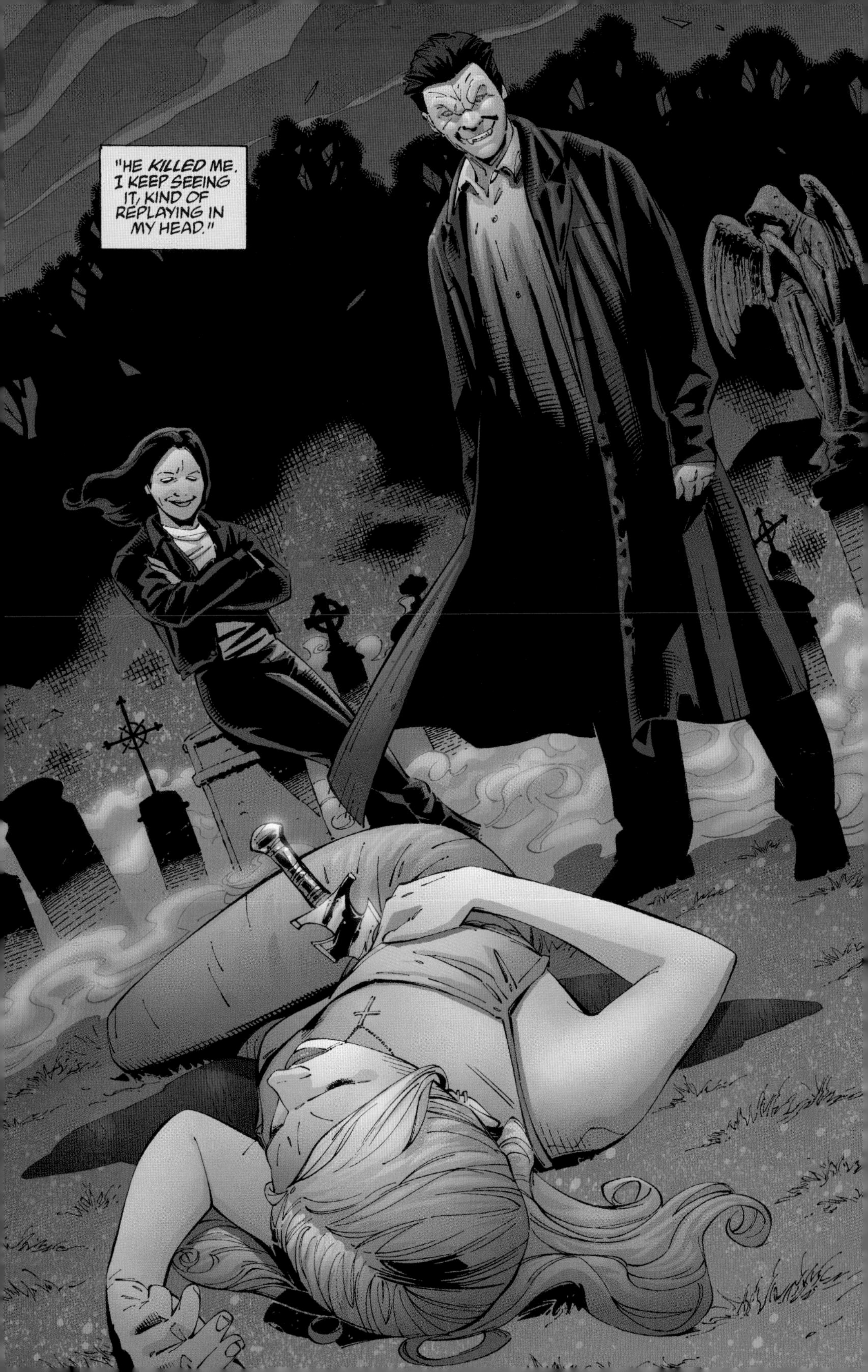
"HE KILLED ME. I KEEP SEEING IT, KIND OF REPLAYING IN MY HEAD."

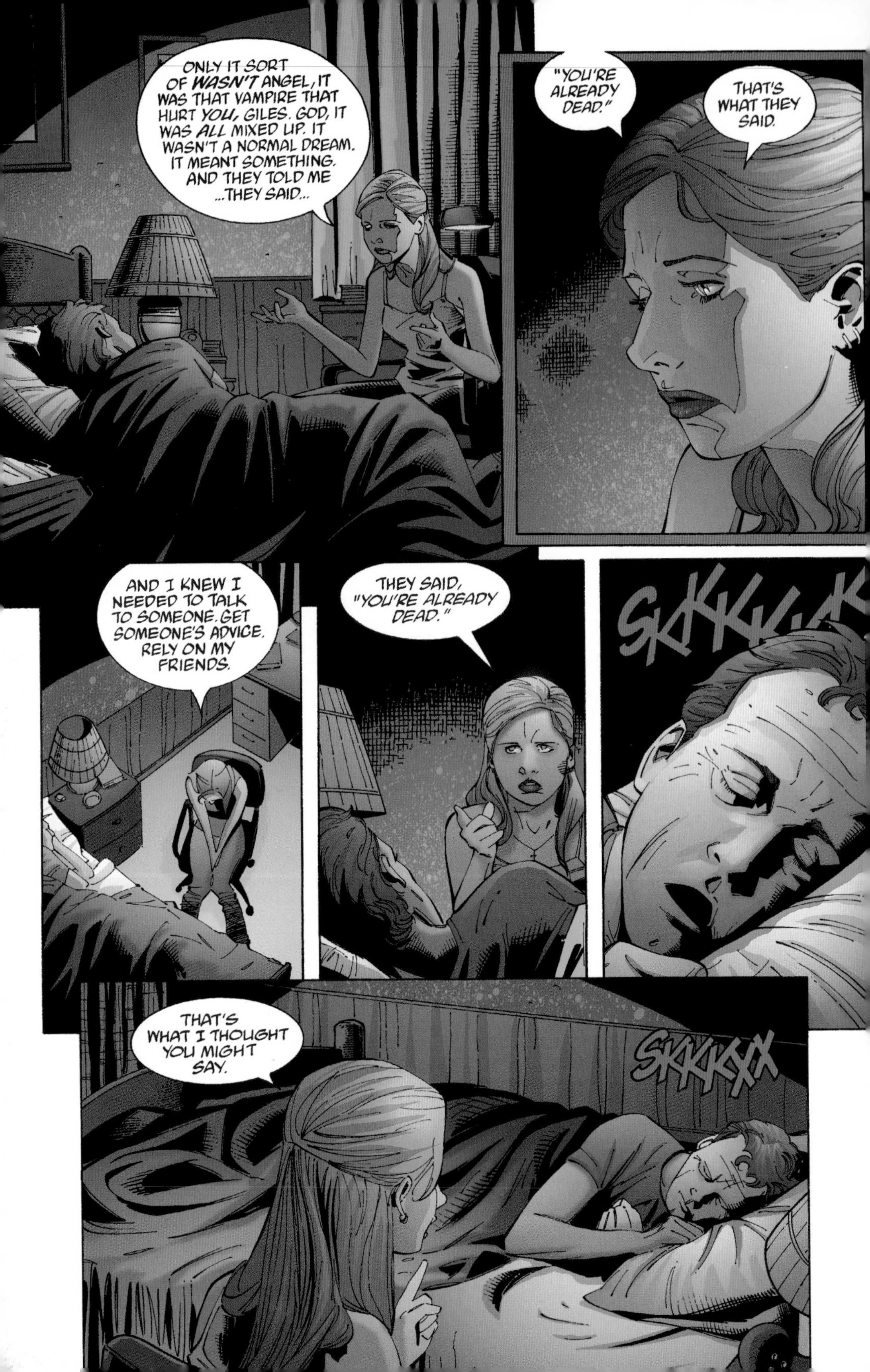
ONLY IT SORT OF WASN'T ANGEL, IT WAS THAT VAMPIRE THAT HURT YOU, GILES. GOD, IT WAS ALL MIXED UP. IT WASN'T A NORMAL DREAM. IT MEANT SOMETHING. AND THEY TOLD ME ...THEY SAID...
"YOU'RE ALREADY DEAD."
THAT'S WHAT THEY SAID.
AND I KNEW I NEEDED TO TALK TO SOMEONE. GET SOMEONE'S ADVICE. RELY ON MY FRIENDS.
THEY SAID, "YOU'RE ALREADY DEAD."
SKKKKK
THAT'S WHAT I THOUGHT YOU MIGHT SAY.
SKKKXX

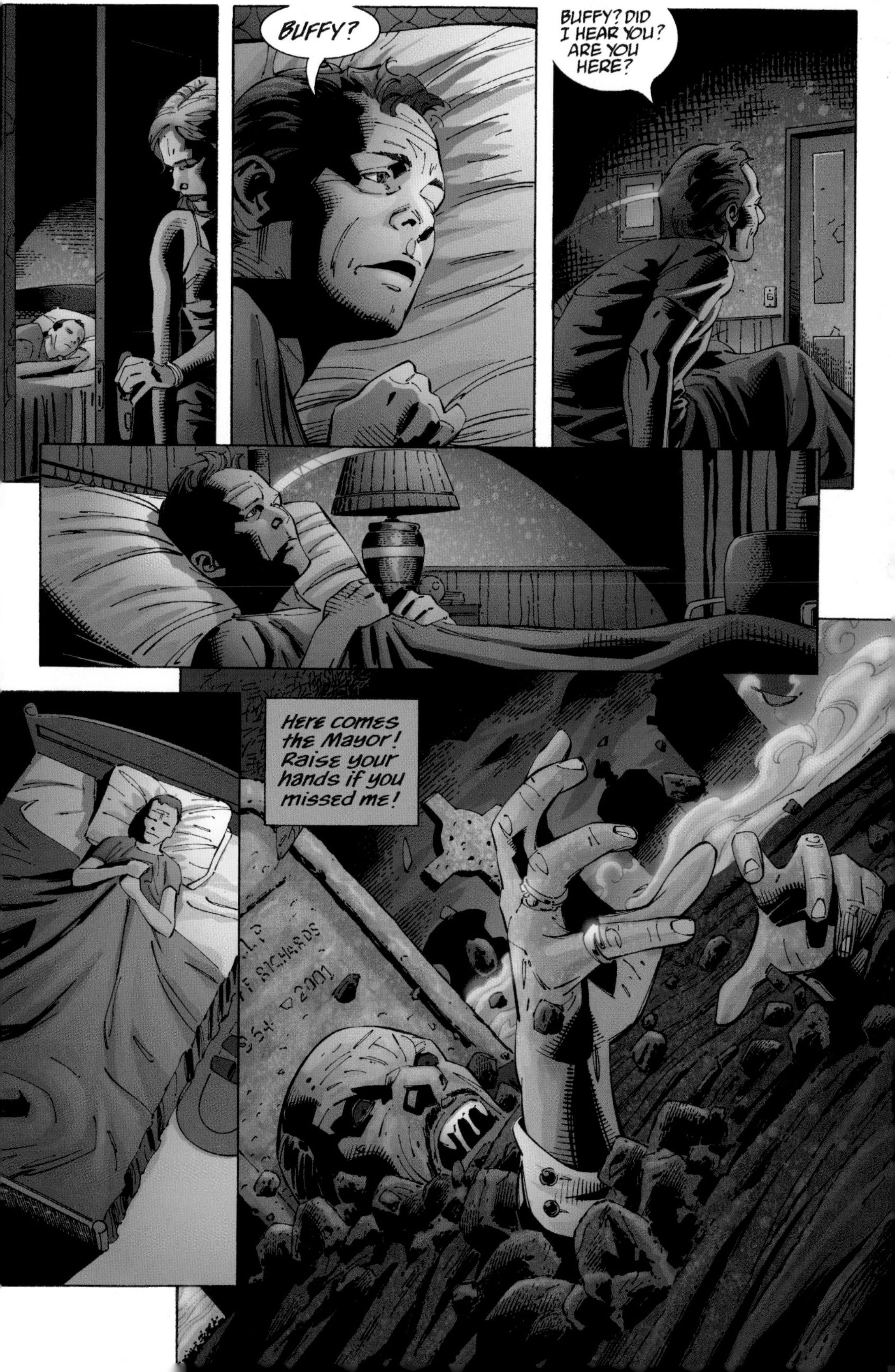
BUFFY?
BUFFY? DID I HEAR YOU? ARE YOU HERE?
Here comes the Mayor! Raise your hands if you missed me!

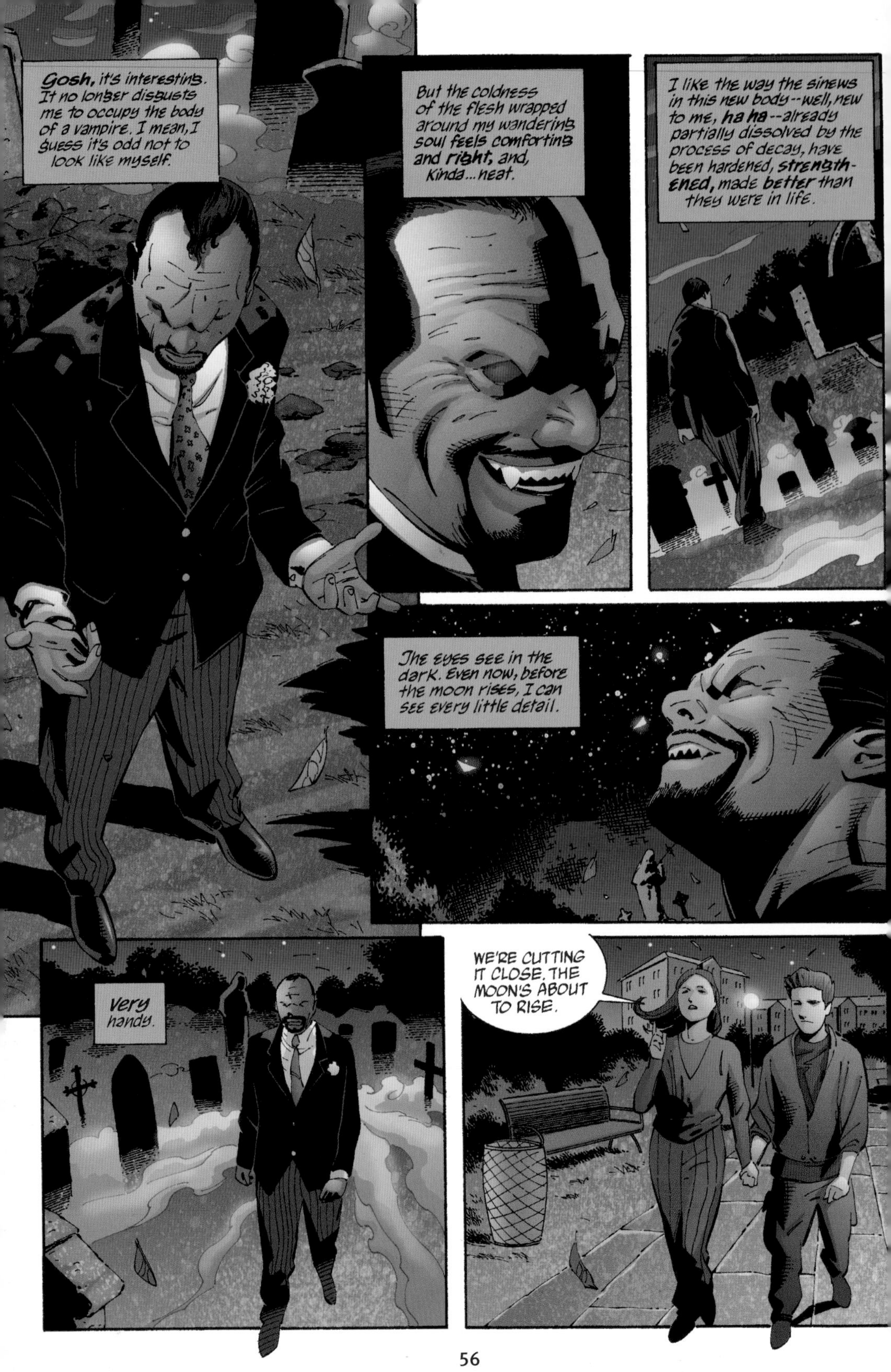
Gosh, it's interesting. It no longer disgusts me to occupy the body of a vampire. I mean, I guess it's odd not to look like myself.
But the coldness of the flesh wrapped around my wandering soul feels comforting and right, and, kinda... neat.
I like the way the sinews in this new body--well, new to me, ha ha--already partially dissolved by the process of decay, have been hardened, strength-ened, made better than they were in life.
The eyes see in the dark. Even now, before the moon rises, I can see every little detail.
Very handy.
WE'RE CUTTING IT CLOSE. THE MOON'S ABOUT TO RISE.

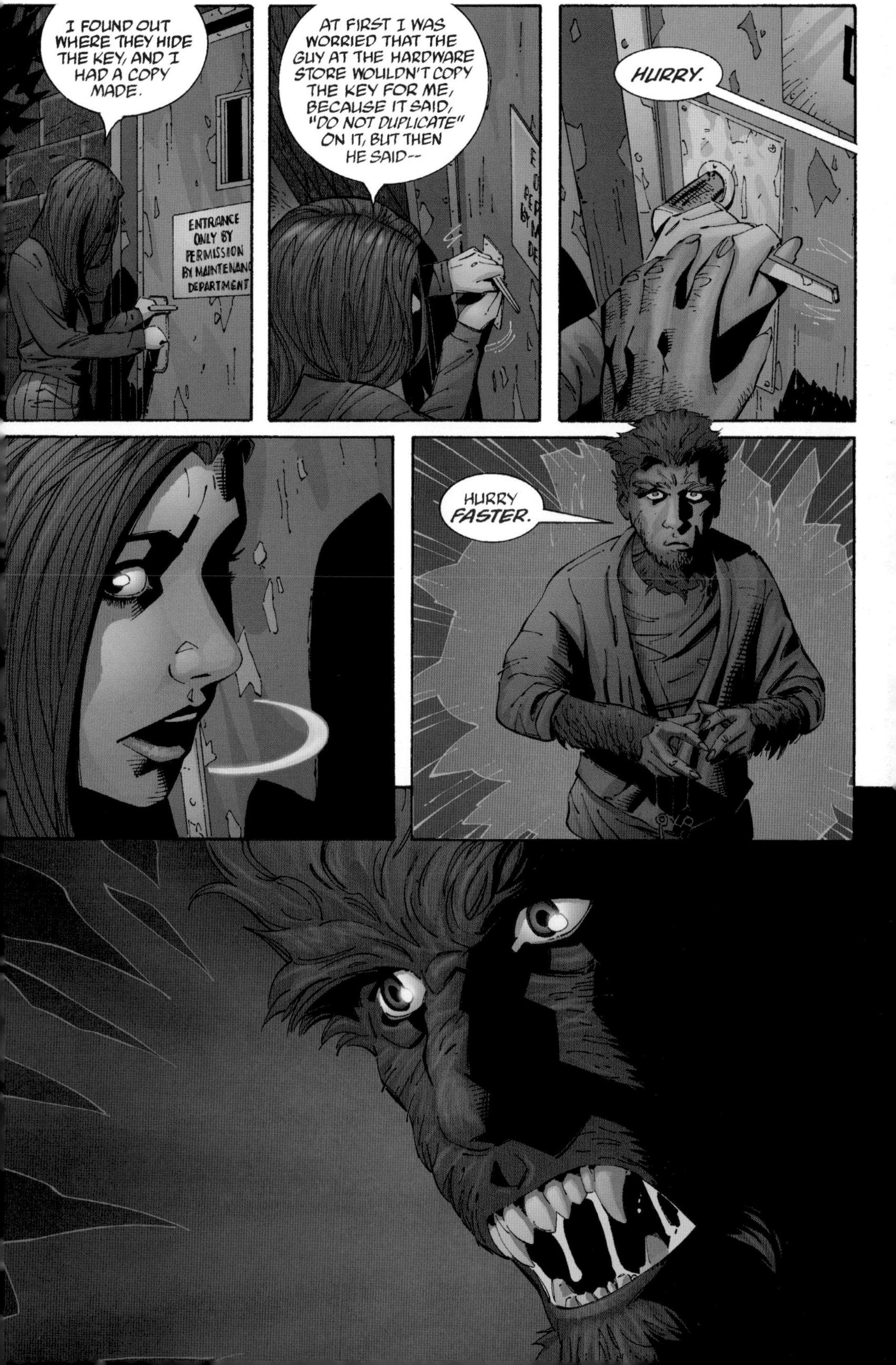
I FOUND OUT WHERE THEY HIDE THE KEY, AND I HAD A COPY MADE.
ENTRANCE ONLY BY PERMISSION BY MAINTENANC DEPARTMENT
AT FIRST I WAS WORRIED THAT THE GUY AT THE HARDWARE STORE WOULDN'T COPY THE KEY FOR ME, BECAUSE IT SAID, "DO NOT DUPLICATE" ON IT, BUT THEN HE SAID--
HURRY.
HURRY FASTER.

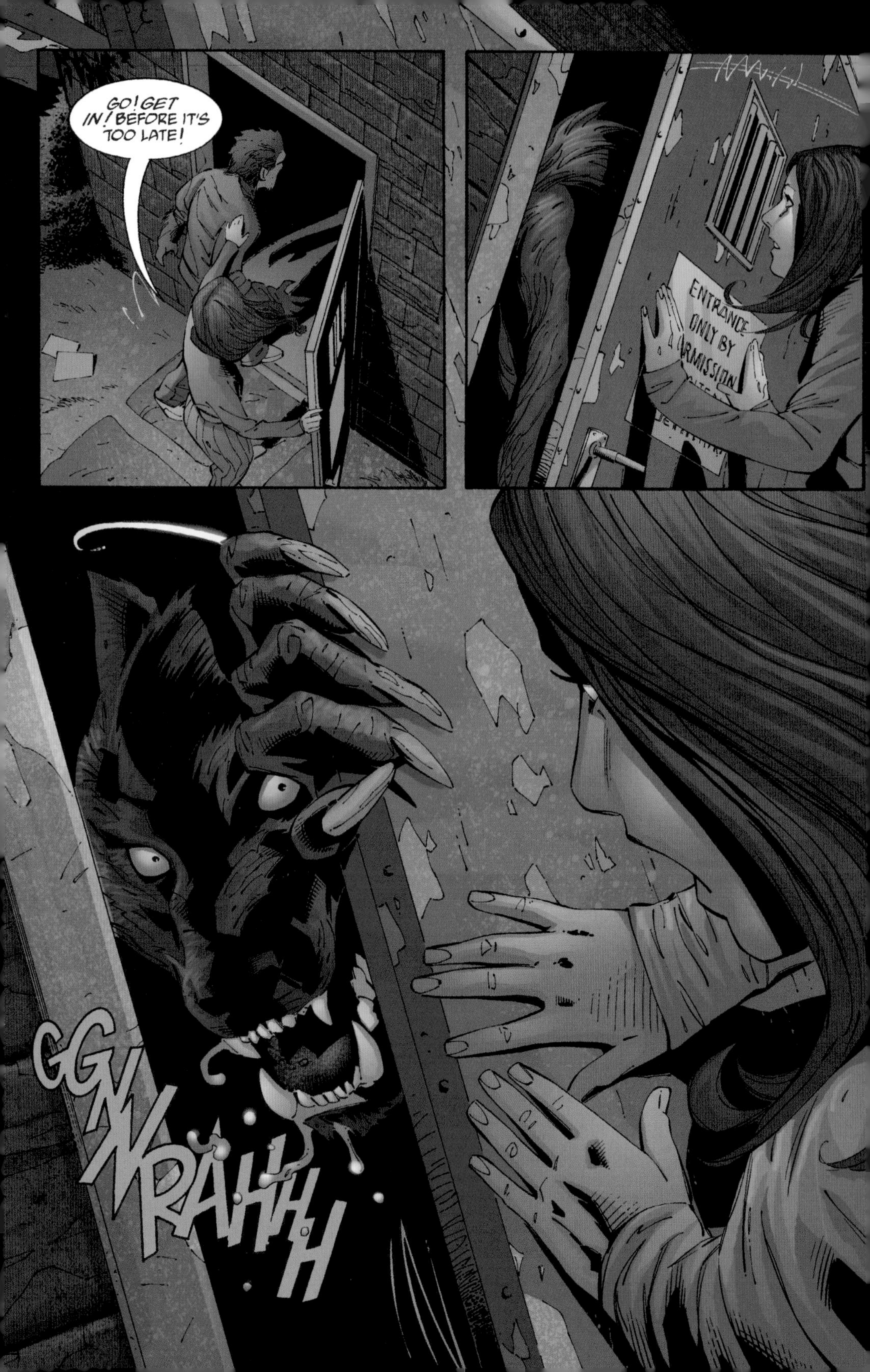
GO! GET IN! BEFORE IT'S TOO LATE!
ENTRANCE ONLY BY PERMISSION
GGNRAHHH

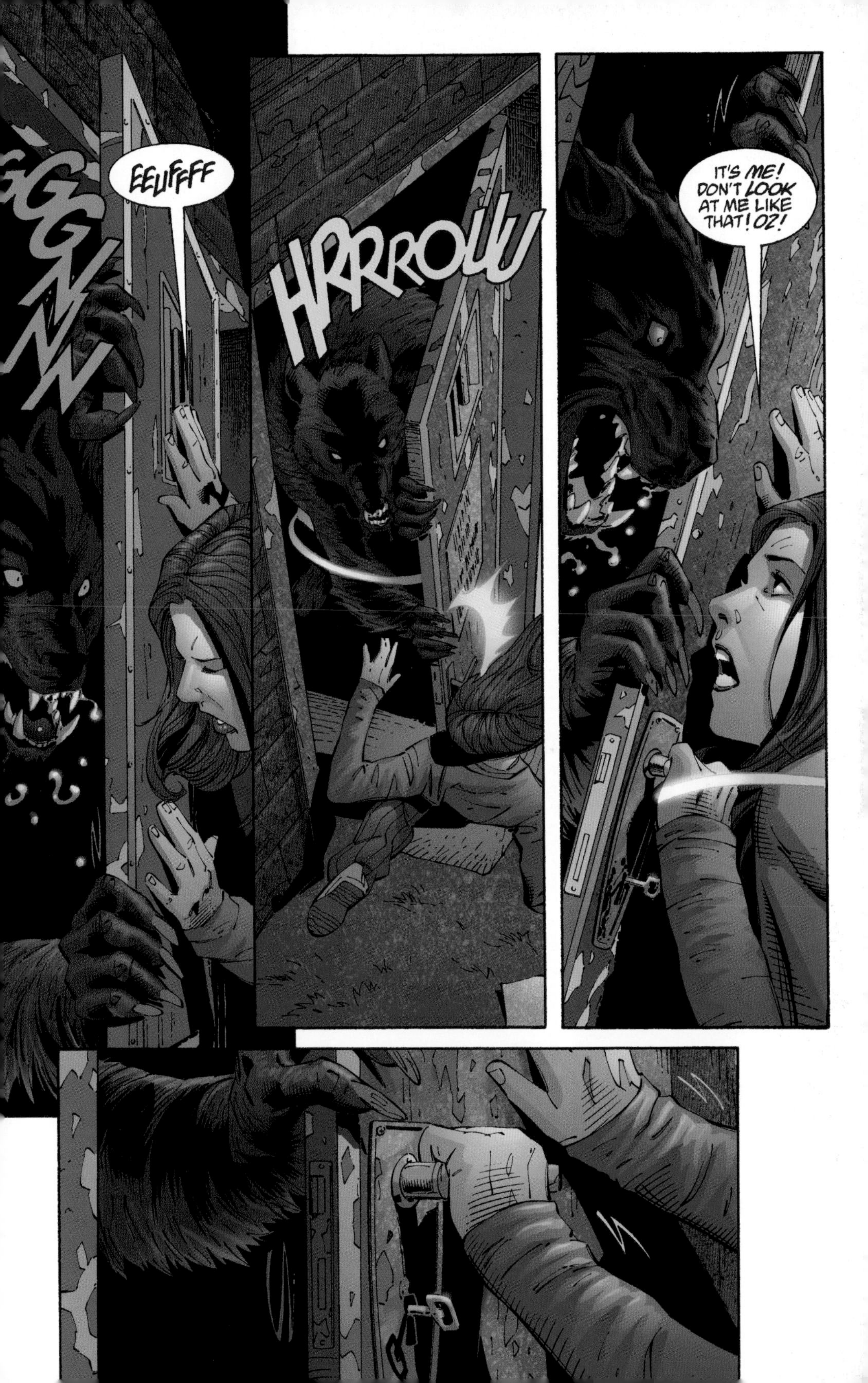
GGGNN
EEUFFFF
HRRROUU
IT'S ME! DON'T LOOK AT ME LIKE THAT! OZ!

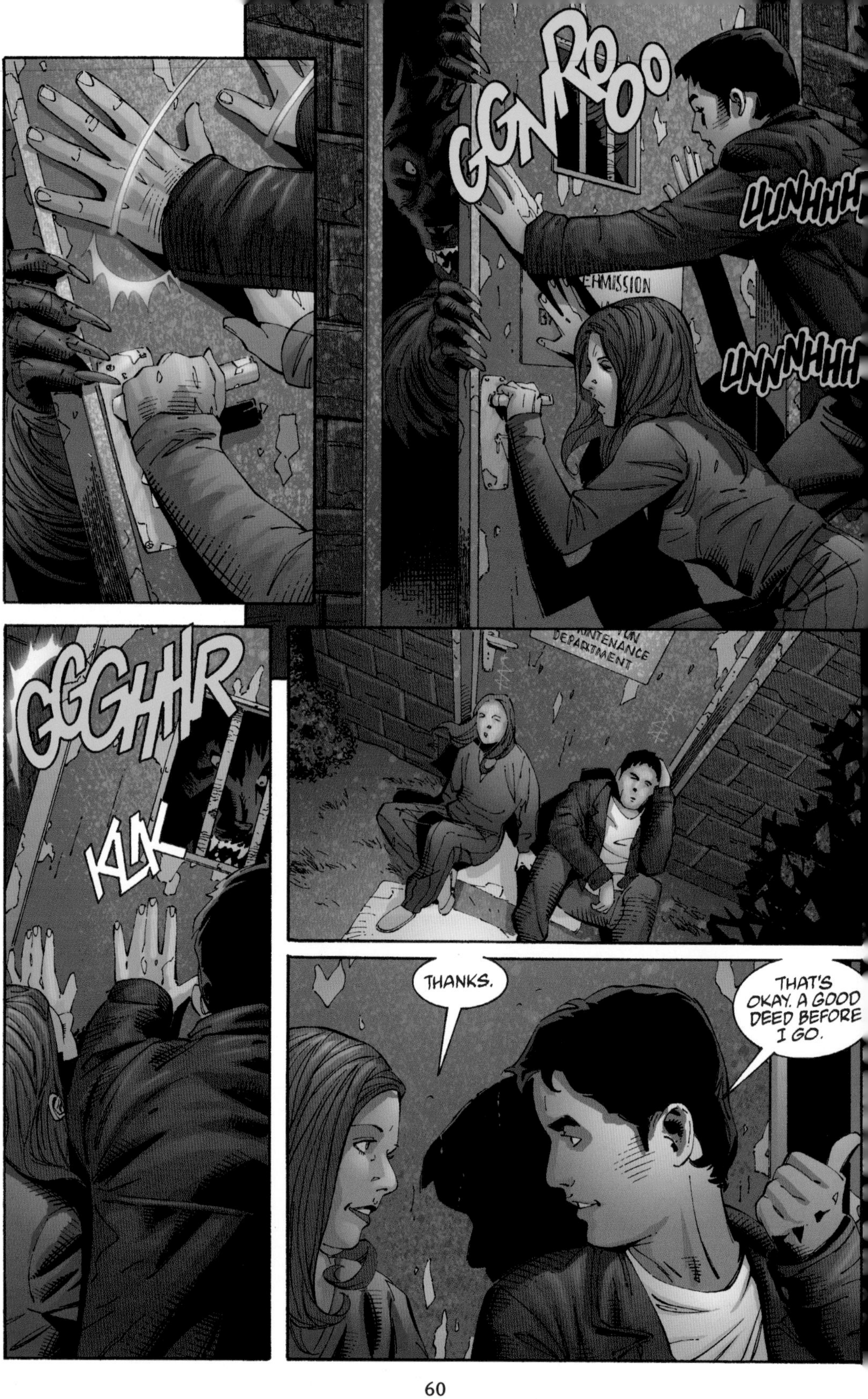

GGNROOO
UUNHHH
PERMISSION
UNNNHHH
GGGHR
KLIK
MAINTENANCE DEPARTMENT
THANKS.
THAT'S OKAY. A GOOD DEED BEFORE I GO.

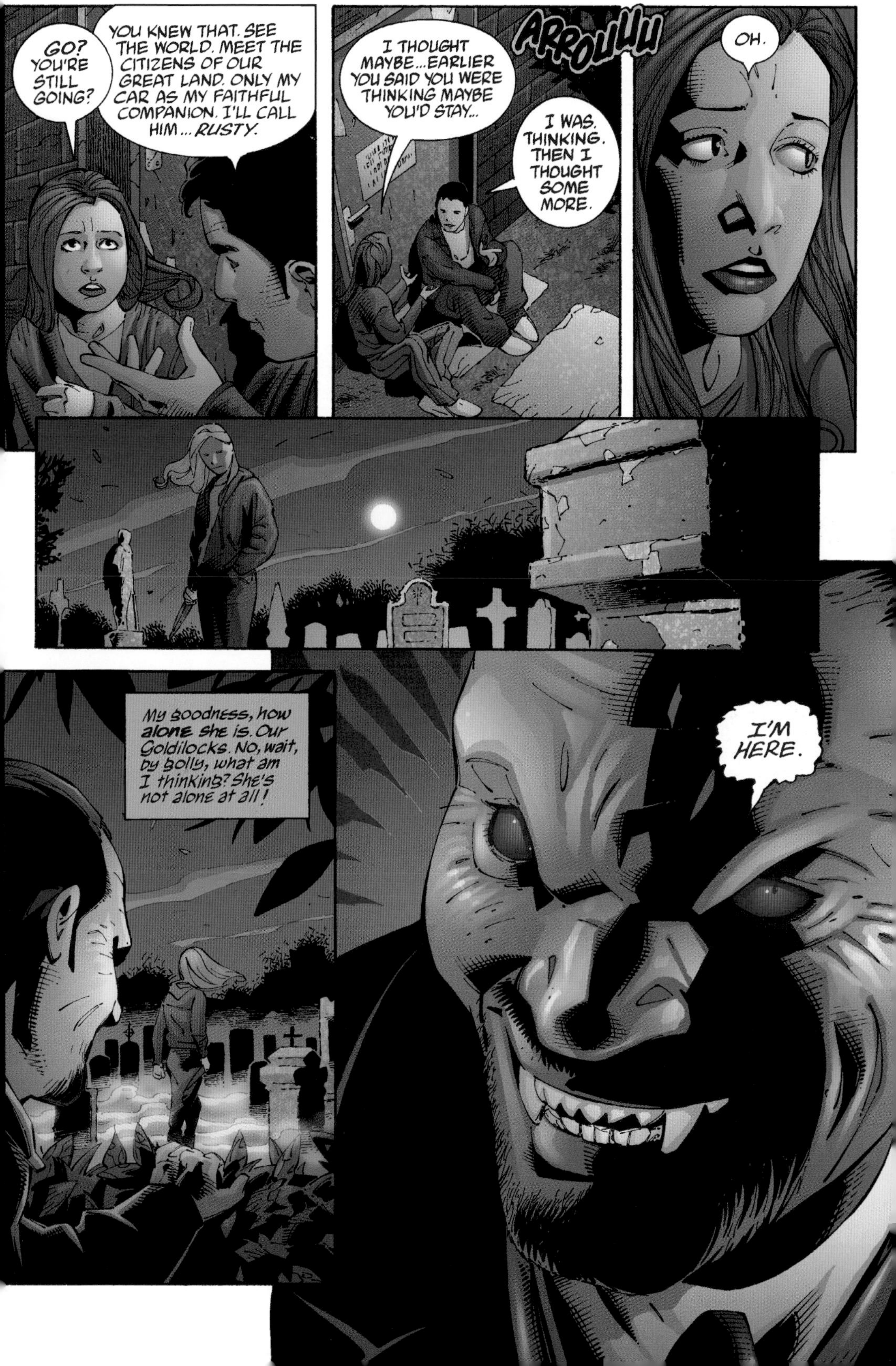
GO? YOU'RE STILL GOING?
YOU KNEW THAT. SEE THE WORLD. MEET THE CITIZENS OF OUR GREAT LAND. ONLY MY CAR AS MY FAITHFUL COMPANION. I'LL CALL HIM... RUSTY.
I THOUGHT MAYBE... EARLIER YOU SAID YOU WERE THINKING MAYBE YOU'D STAY...
I WAS. THINKING. THEN I THOUGHT SOME MORE.
ARROUUUU
OH.
My goodness, how alone she is. Our Goldilocks. No, wait, by golly, what am I thinking? She's not alone at all!
I'M HERE.

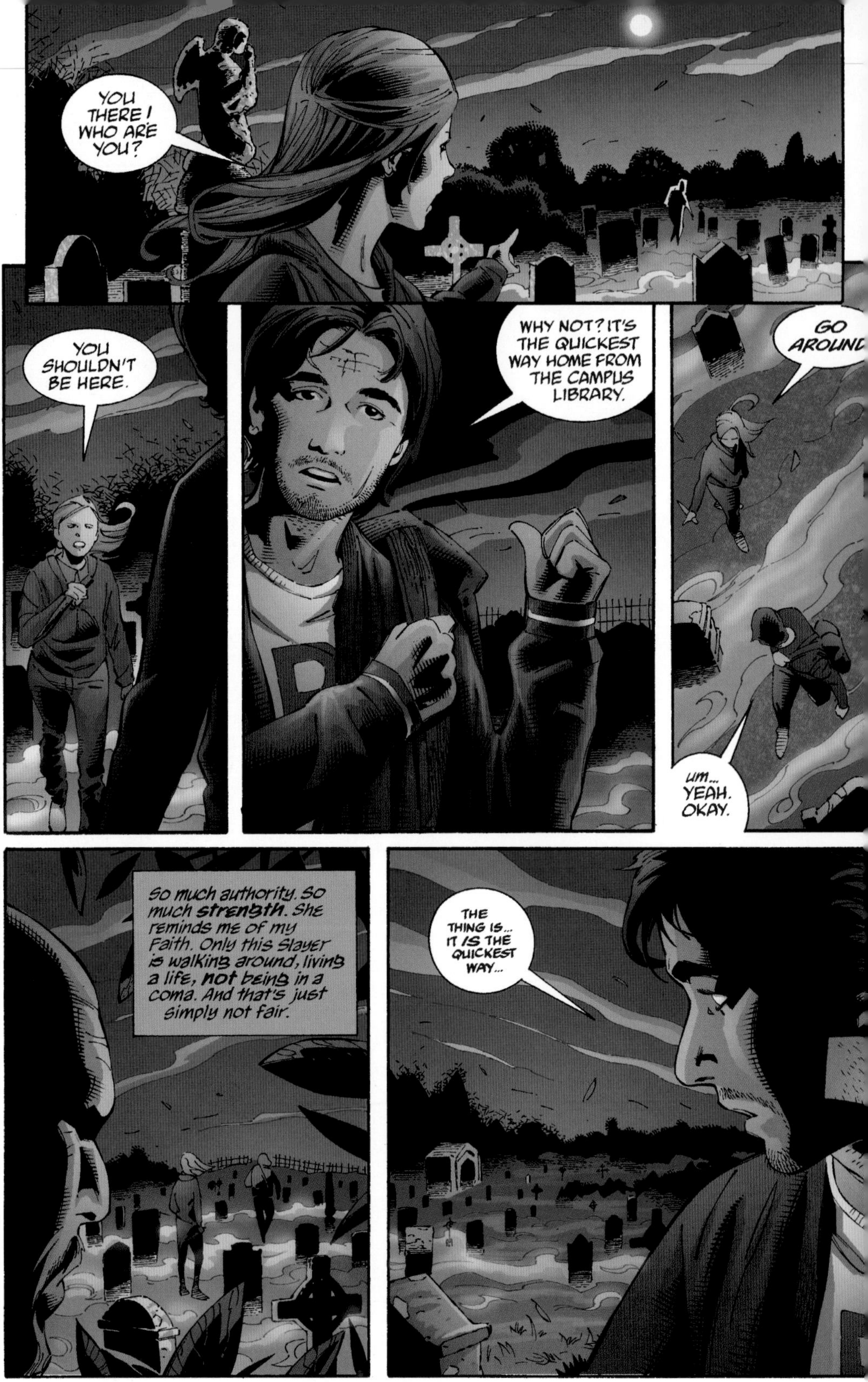
YOU THERE! WHO ARE YOU?
YOU SHOULDN'T BE HERE.
WHY NOT? IT'S THE QUICKEST WAY HOME FROM THE CAMPUS LIBRARY.
GO AROUND
UM... YEAH. OKAY.
So much authority. So much strength. She reminds me of my Faith. Only this Slayer is walking around, living a life, not being in a coma. And that's just simply not fair.
THE THING IS... IT IS THE QUICKEST WAY...

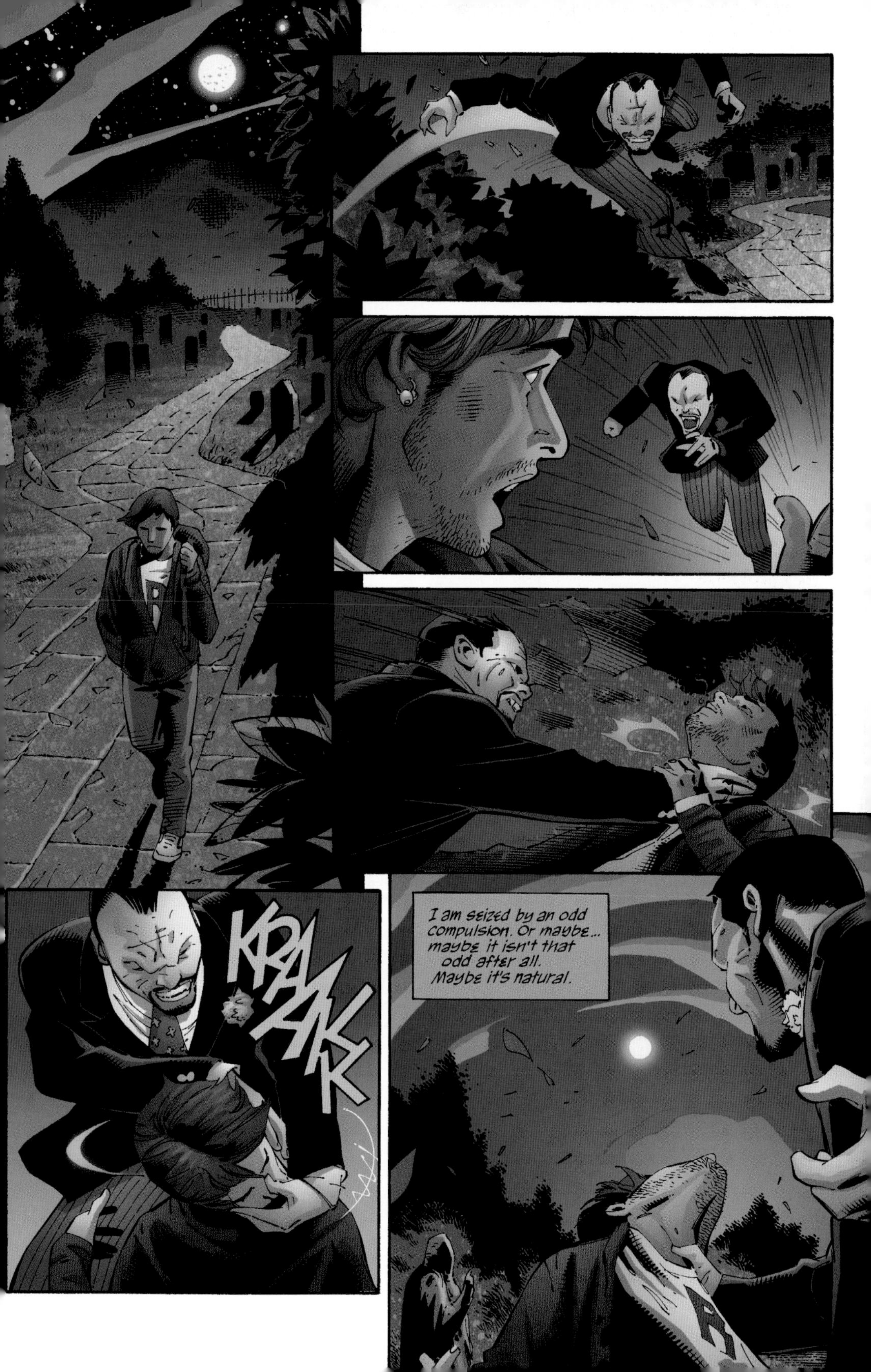
KRAKAKK
I am seized by an odd compulsion. Or maybe... maybe it isn't that odd after all. Maybe it's natural.

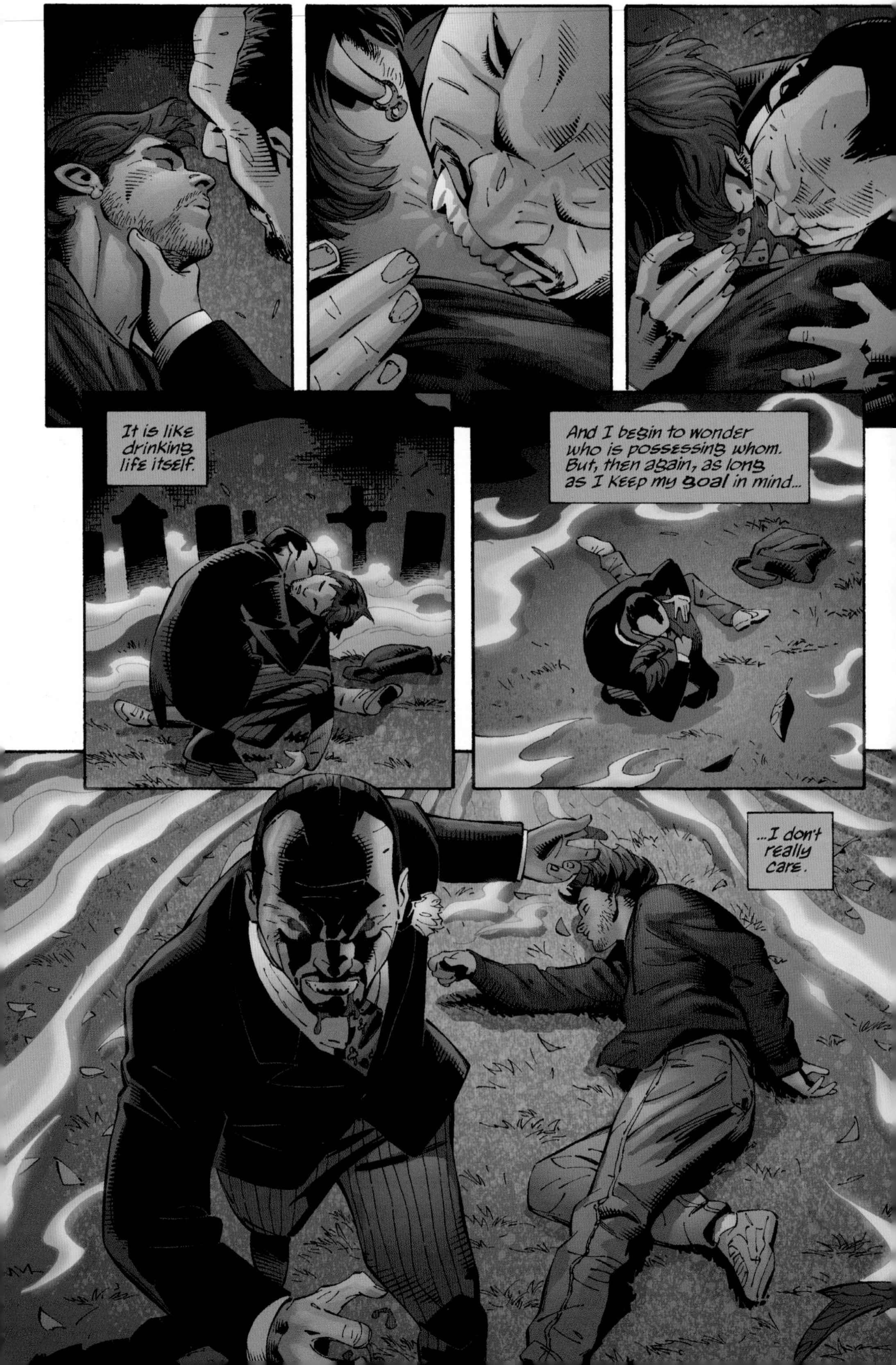
It is like drinking life itself.
And I begin to wonder who is possessing whom. But, then again, as long as I keep my goal in mind...
...I don't really care.

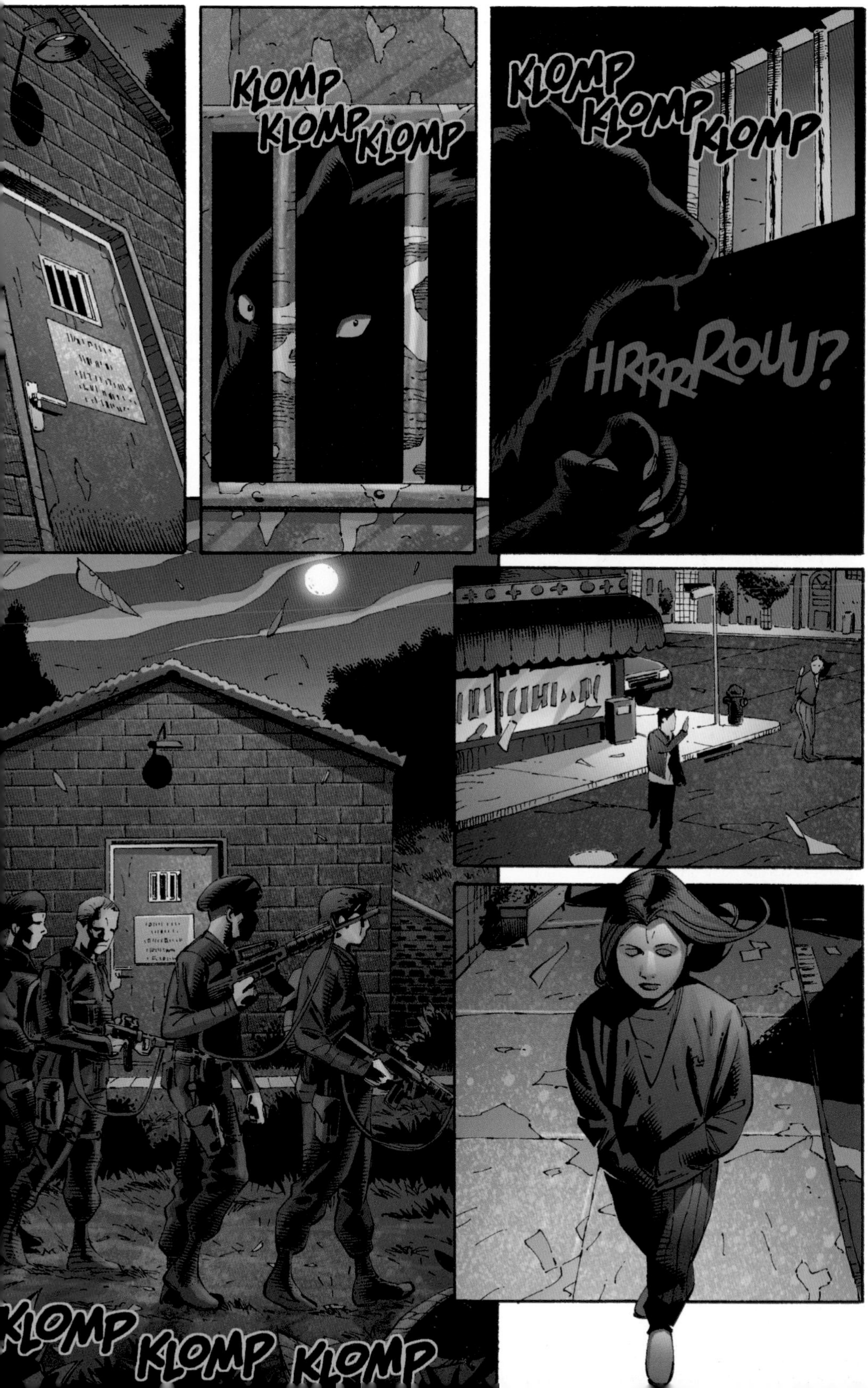
KLOMP
KLOMP KLOMP
KLOMP
KLOMP KLOMP
HRRRRROUU?
KLOMP KLOMP KLOMP

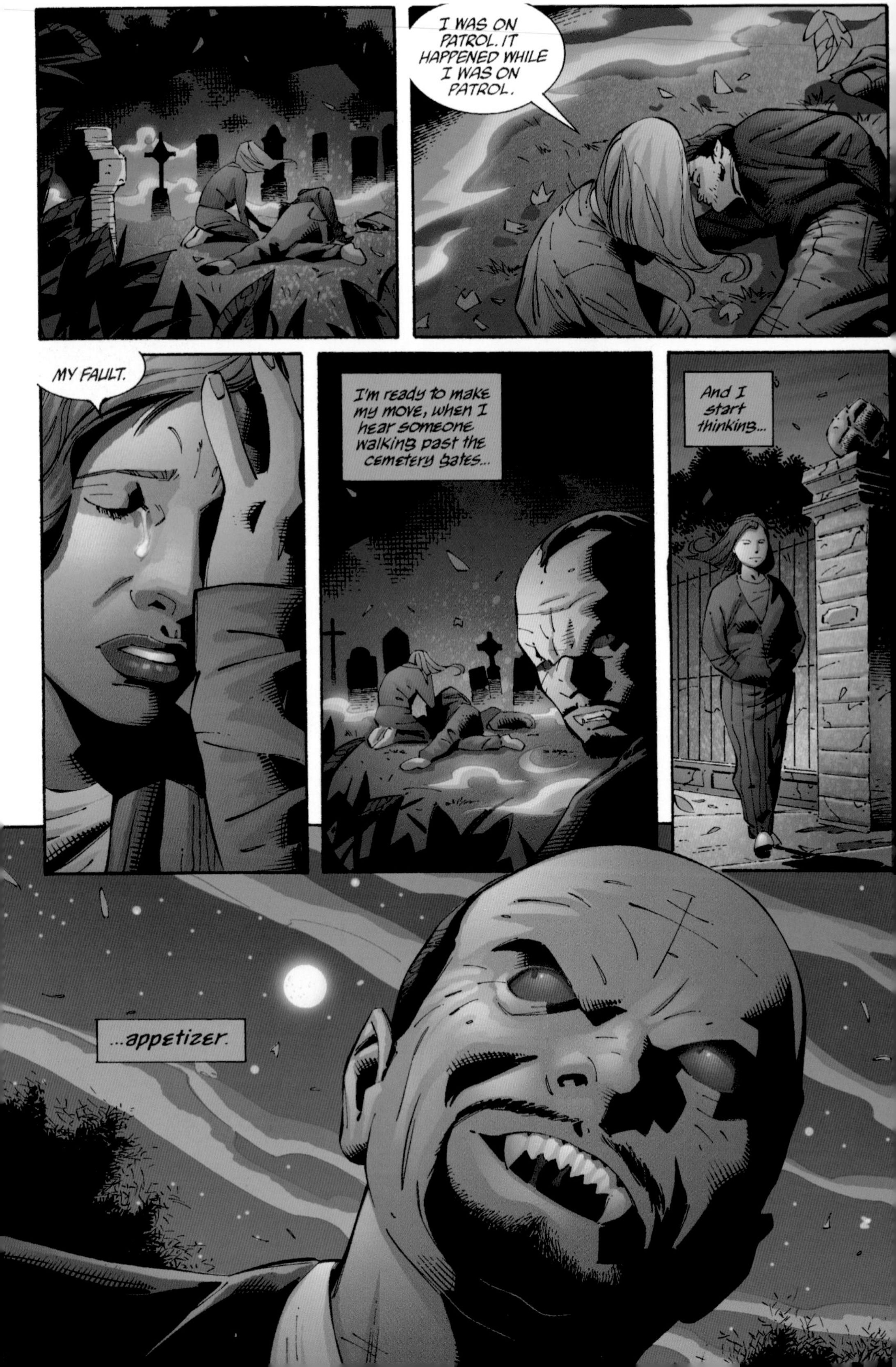
I WAS ON PATROL. IT HAPPENED WHILE I WAS ON PATROL.
MY FAULT.
I'm ready to make my move, when I hear someone walking past the cemetery gates...
And I start thinking...
...appetizer.

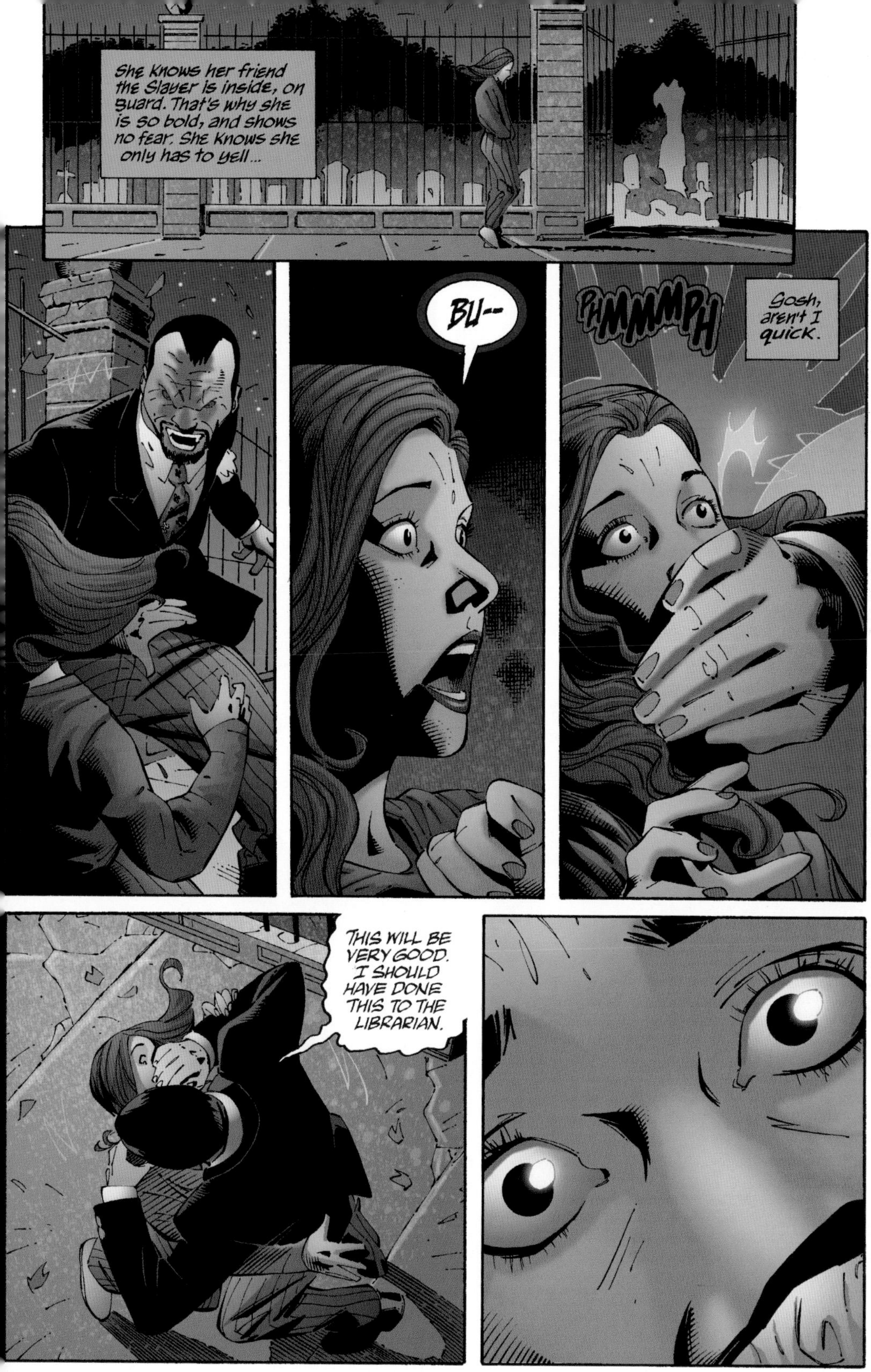
She knows her friend the Slayer is inside, on guard. That's why she is so bold, and shows no fear. She knows she only has to yell...
BU--
PHMMMPH
Gosh, aren't I quick.
THIS WILL BE VERY GOOD. I SHOULD HAVE DONE THIS TO THE LIBRARIAN.

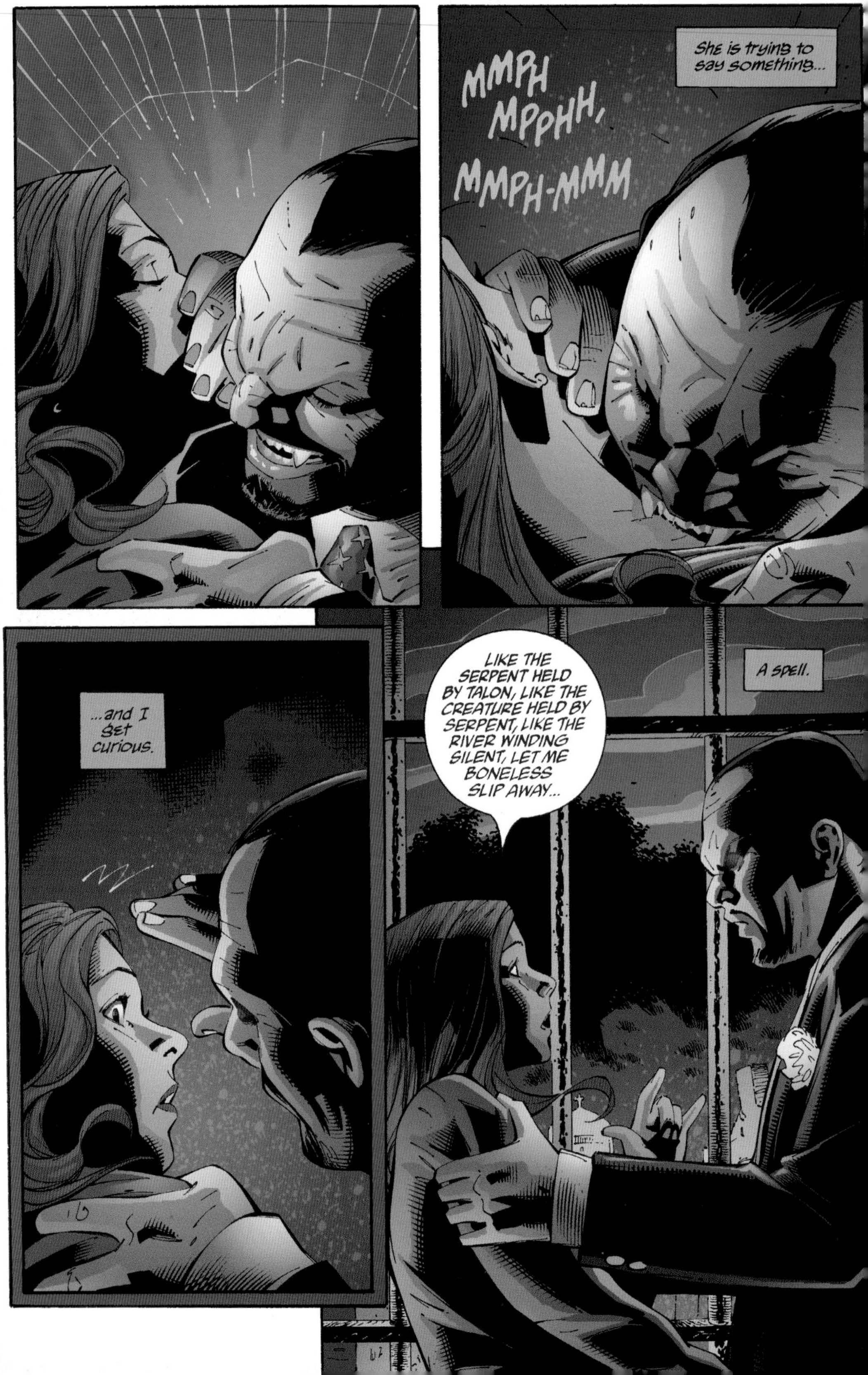
She is trying to say something...
MMPH MPPHH, MMPH-MMM
...and I get curious.
A spell.
LIKE THE SERPENT HELD BY TALON, LIKE THE CREATURE HELD BY SERPENT, LIKE THE RIVER WINDING SILENT, LET ME BONELESS SLIP AWAY...

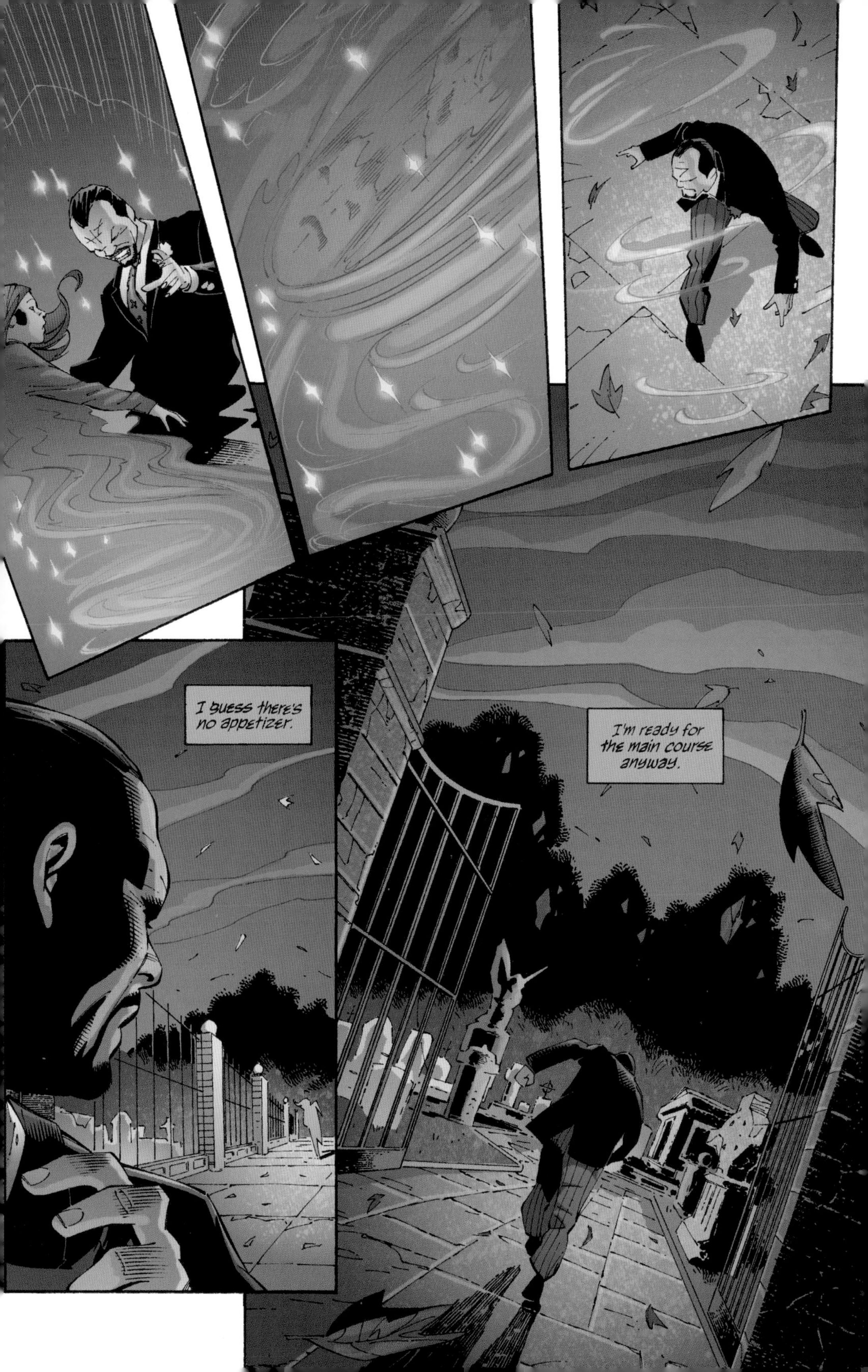
I guess there's no appetizer.
I'm ready for the main course anyway.

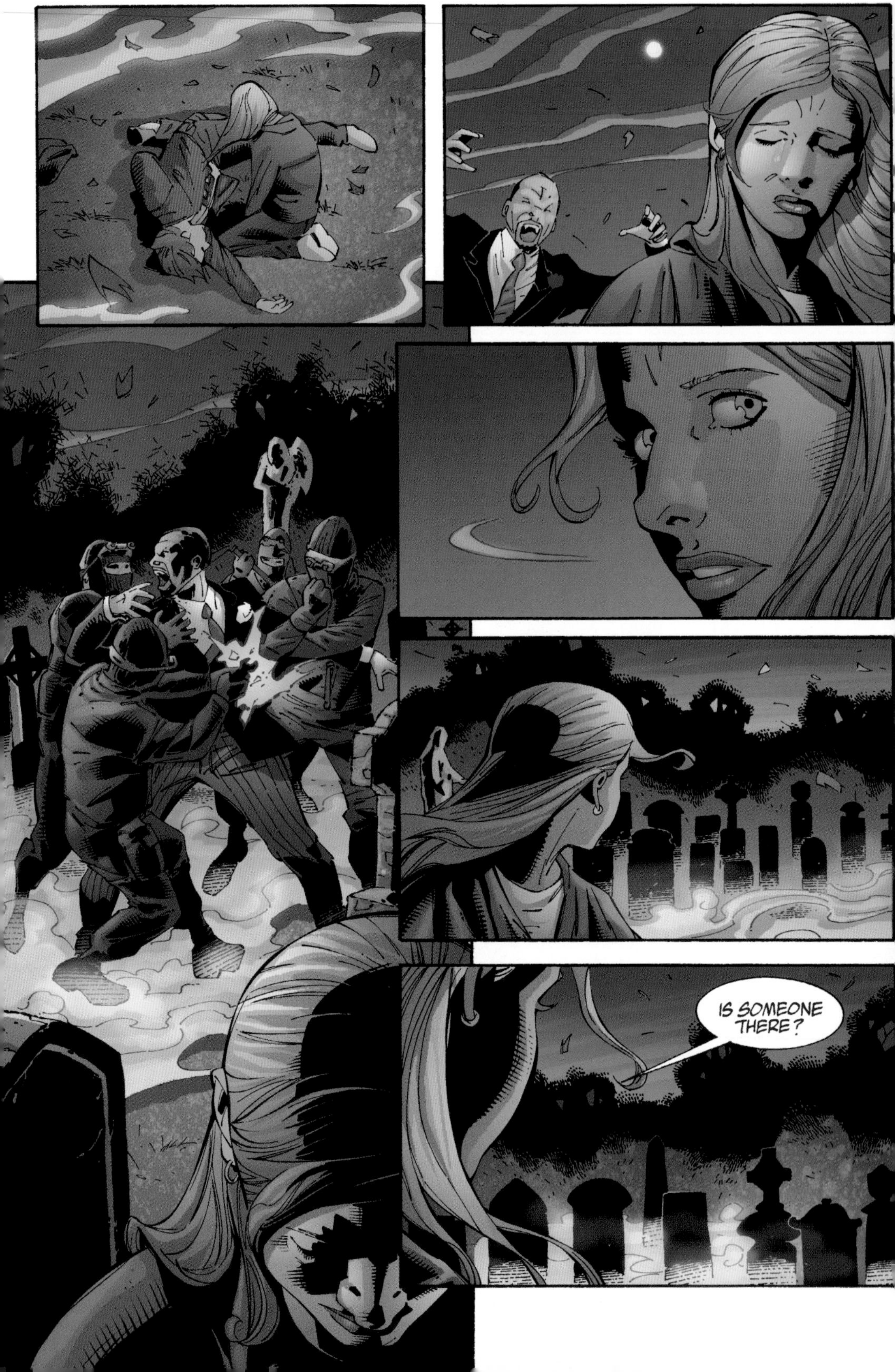
IS SOMEONE THERE?

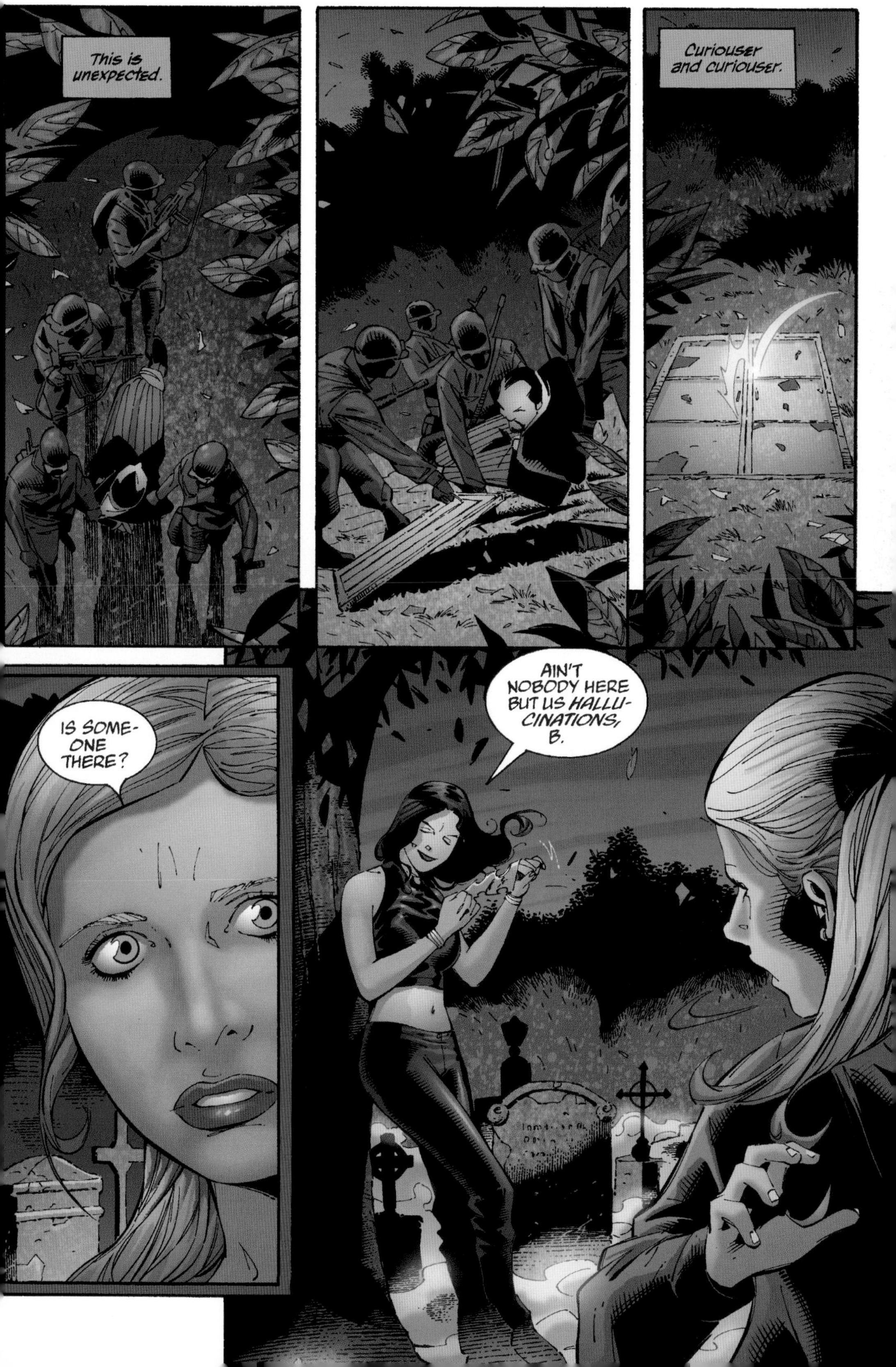
This is unexpected.
Curiouser and curiouser.
IS SOME-ONE THERE?
AIN'T NOBODY HERE BUT US HALLU-CINATIONS, B.

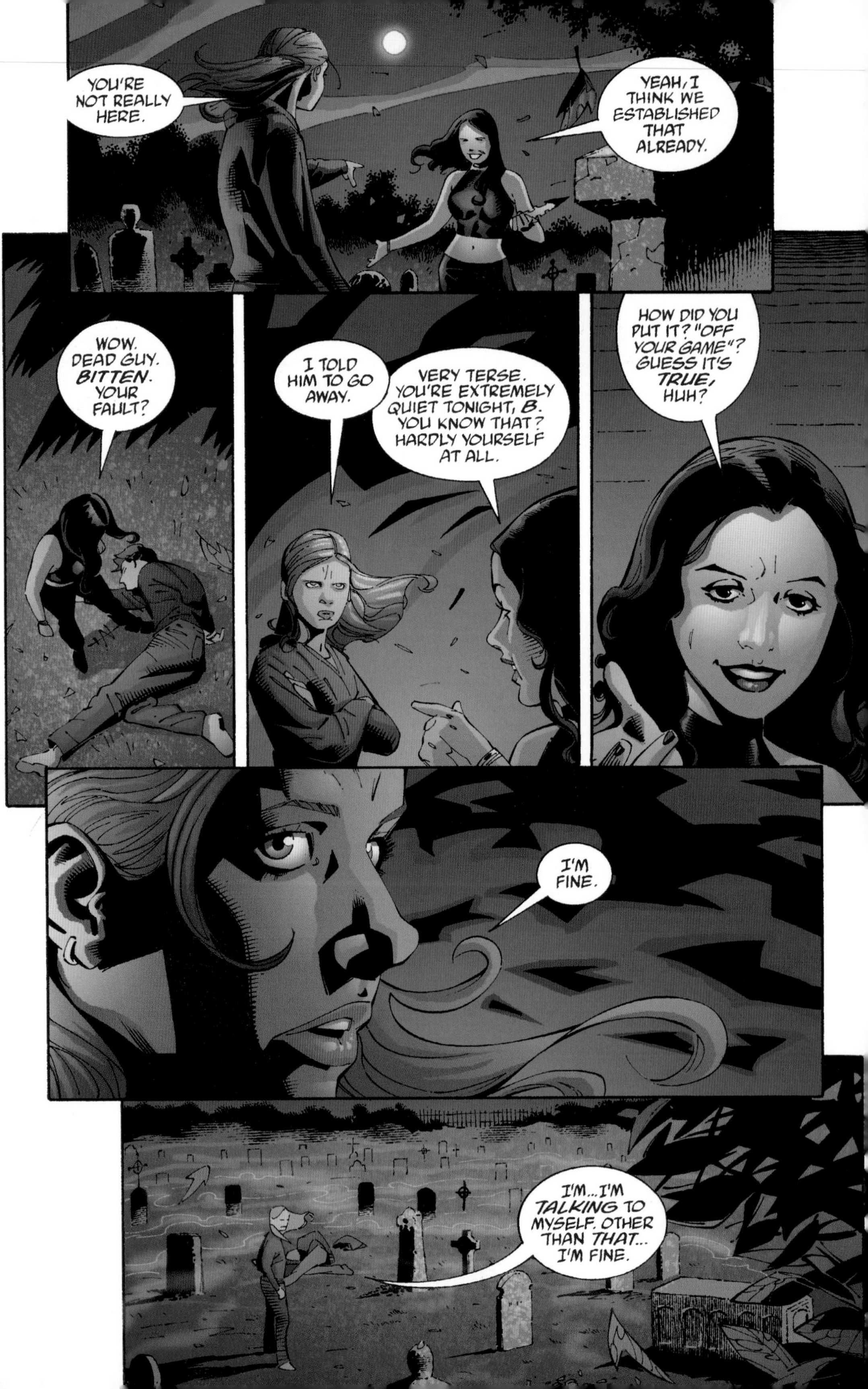
YOU'RE NOT REALLY HERE.
YEAH, I THINK WE ESTABLISHED THAT ALREADY.
WOW. DEAD GUY. *BITTEN*. YOUR FAULT?
I TOLD HIM TO GO AWAY.
VERY TERSE. YOU'RE EXTREMELY QUIET TONIGHT, *B*. YOU KNOW THAT? HARDLY YOURSELF AT ALL.
HOW DID YOU PUT IT? "OFF YOUR GAME"? GUESS IT'S *TRUE*, HUH?
I'M FINE.
I'M...I'M *TALKING* TO MYSELF. OTHER THAN *THAT*... I'M FINE.

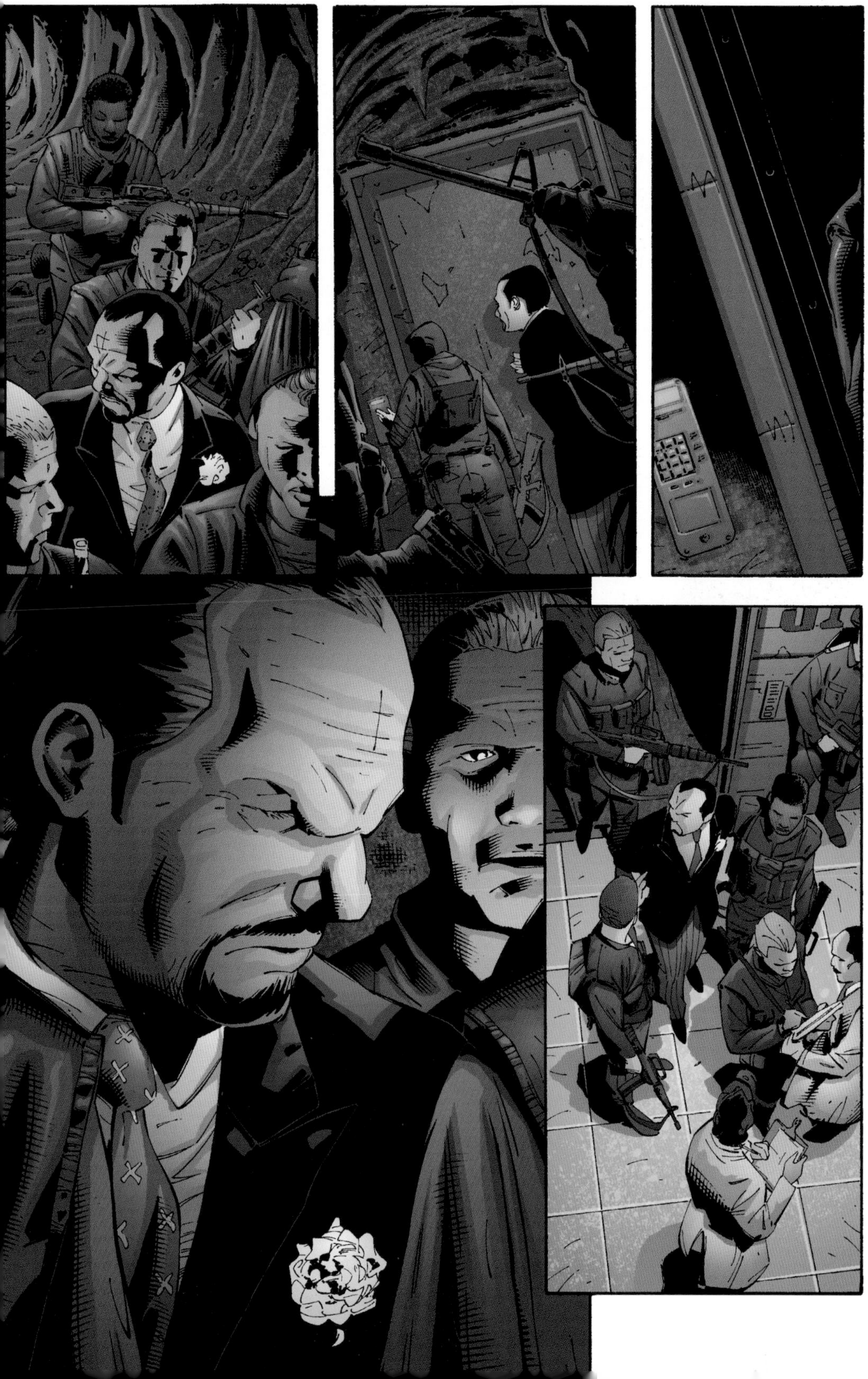

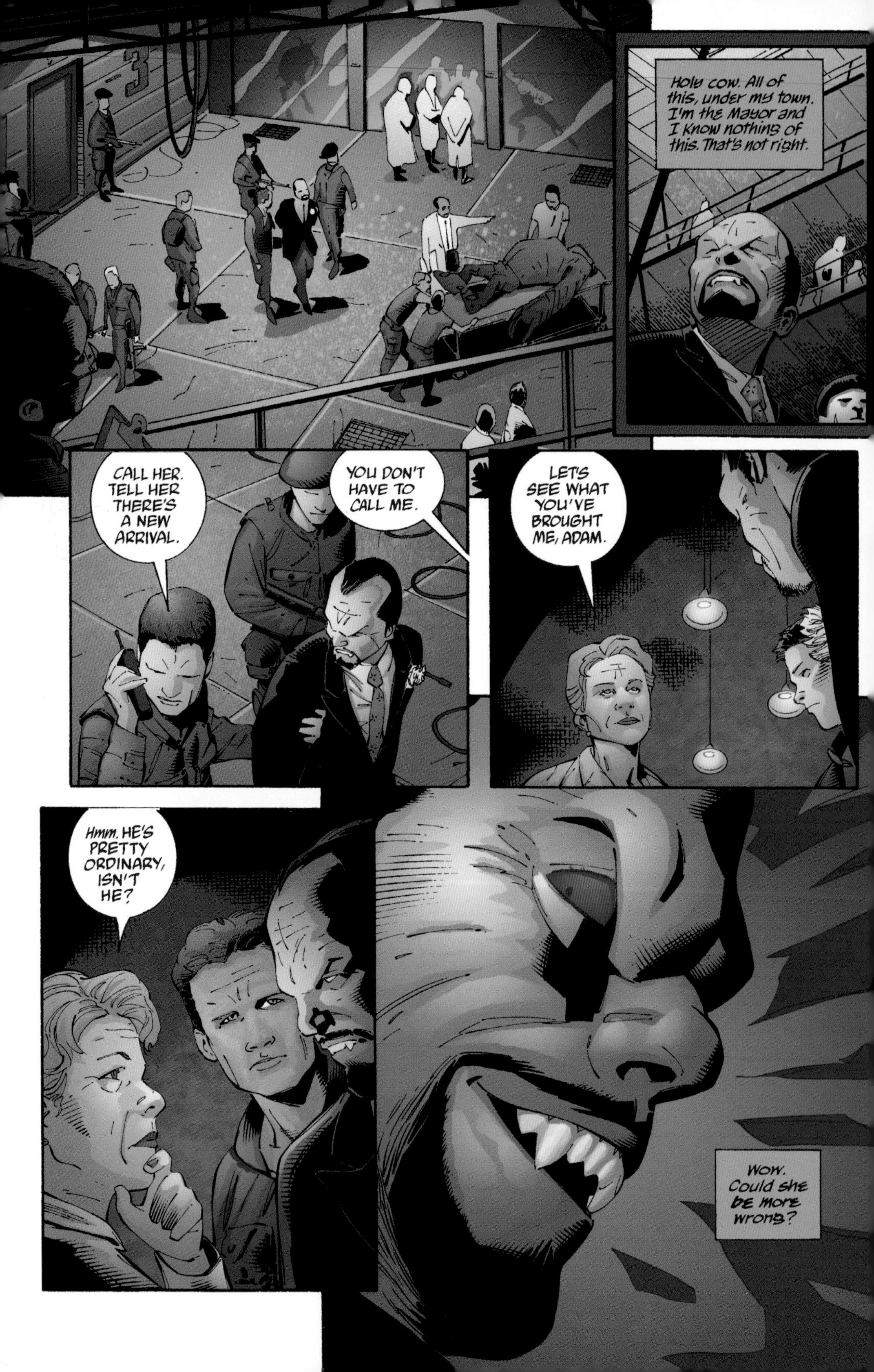
Holy cow. All of this, under my town. I'm the Mayor and I know nothing of this. That's not right.
CALL HER. TELL HER THERE'S A NEW ARRIVAL.
YOU DON'T HAVE TO CALL ME.
LET'S SEE WHAT YOU'VE BROUGHT ME, ADAM.
Hmm. HE'S PRETTY ORDINARY, ISN'T HE?
Wow. Could she be more wrong?

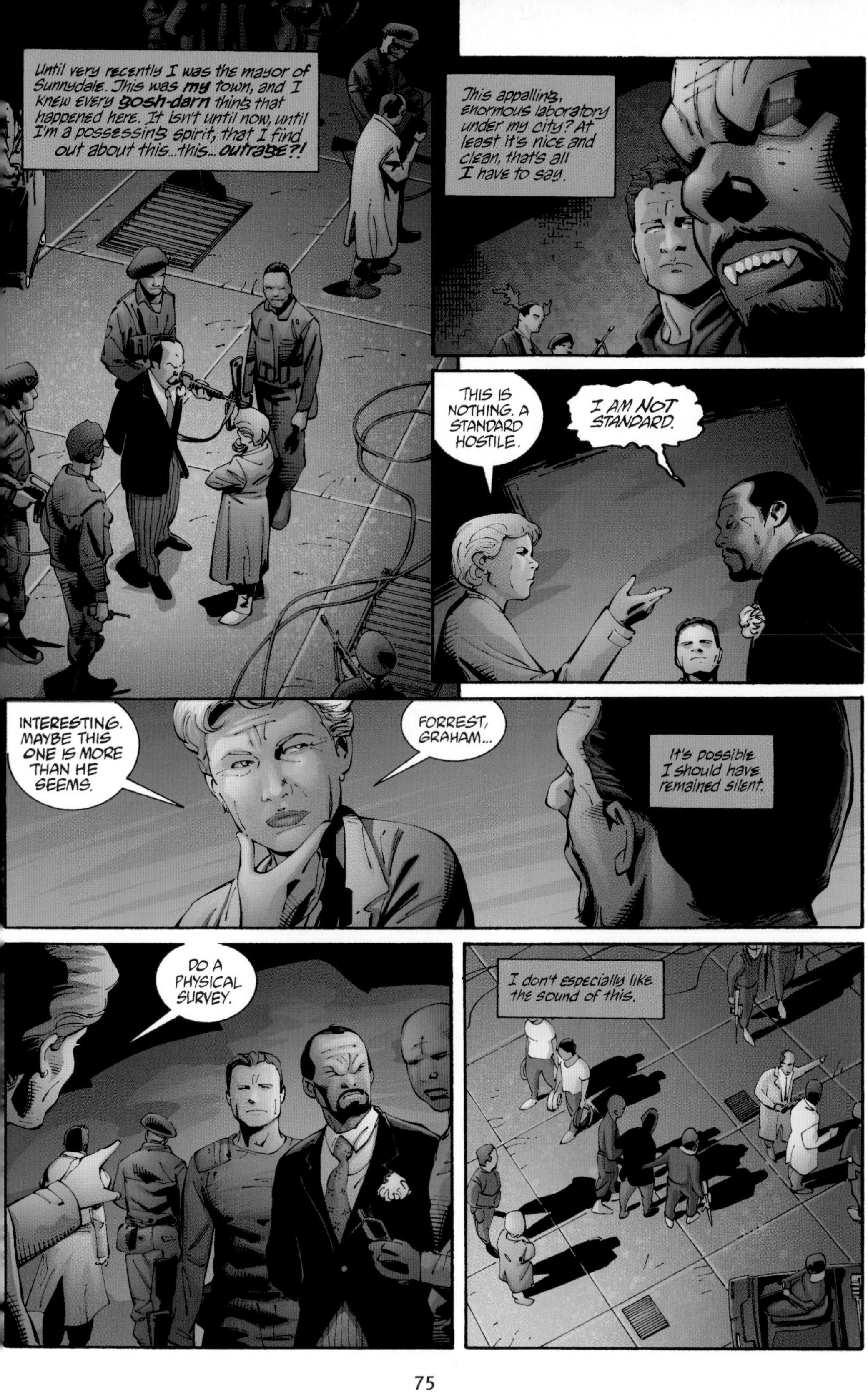
Until very recently I was the mayor of Sunnydale. This was my town, and I knew every gosh-darn thing that happened here. It isn't until now, until I'm a possessing spirit, that I find out about this...this...outrage?!
This appalling, enormous laboratory under my city? At least it's nice and clean, that's all I have to say.
THIS IS NOTHING. A STANDARD HOSTILE.
I AM NOT STANDARD.
INTERESTING. MAYBE THIS ONE IS MORE THAN HE SEEMS.
FORREST, GRAHAM...
It's possible I should have remained silent.
DO A PHYSICAL SURVEY.
I don't especially like the sound of this.

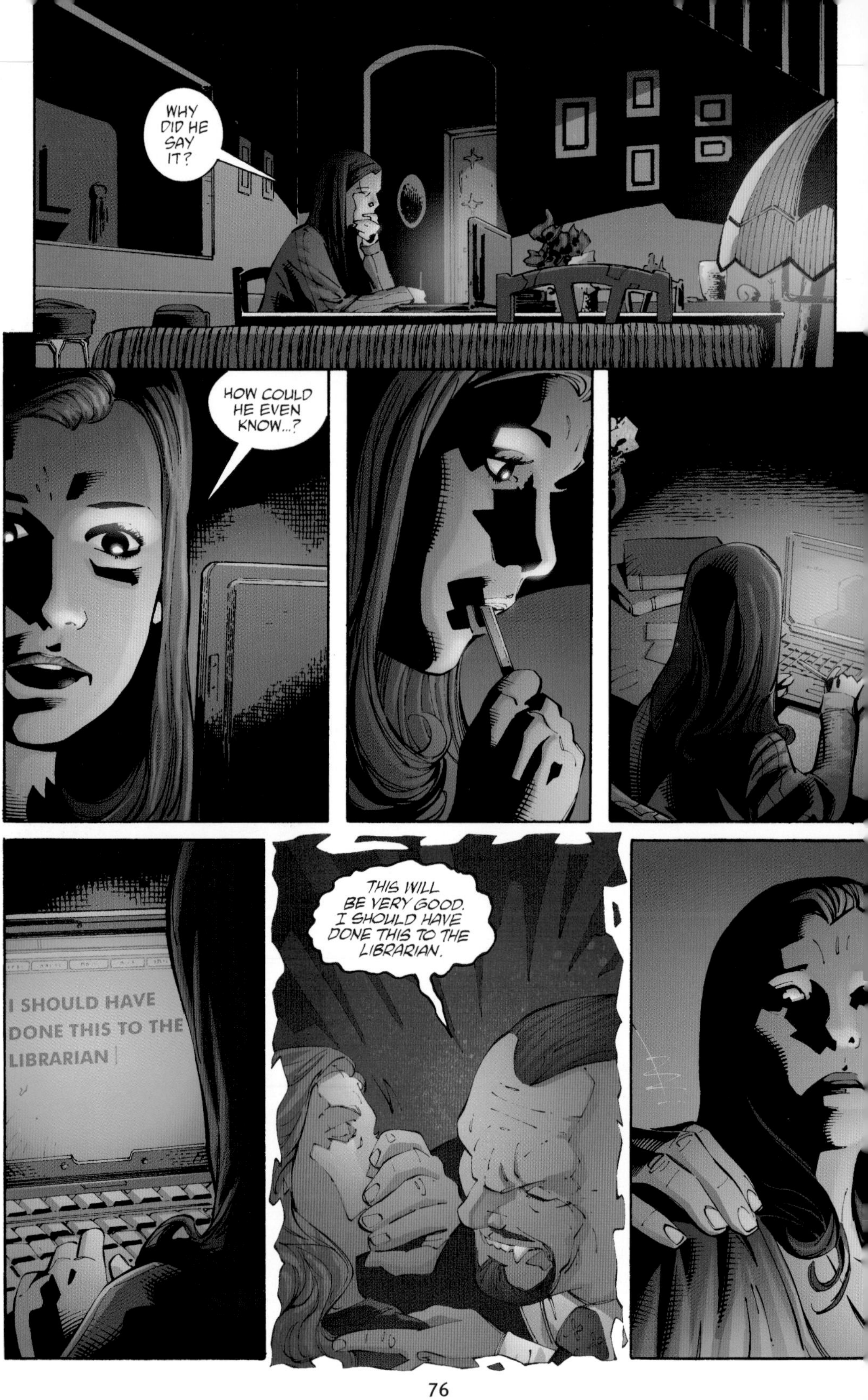
WHY DID HE SAY IT?
HOW COULD HE EVEN KNOW...?
I SHOULD HAVE DONE THIS TO THE LIBRARIAN
THIS WILL BE VERY GOOD. I SHOULD HAVE DONE THIS TO THE LIBRARIAN.

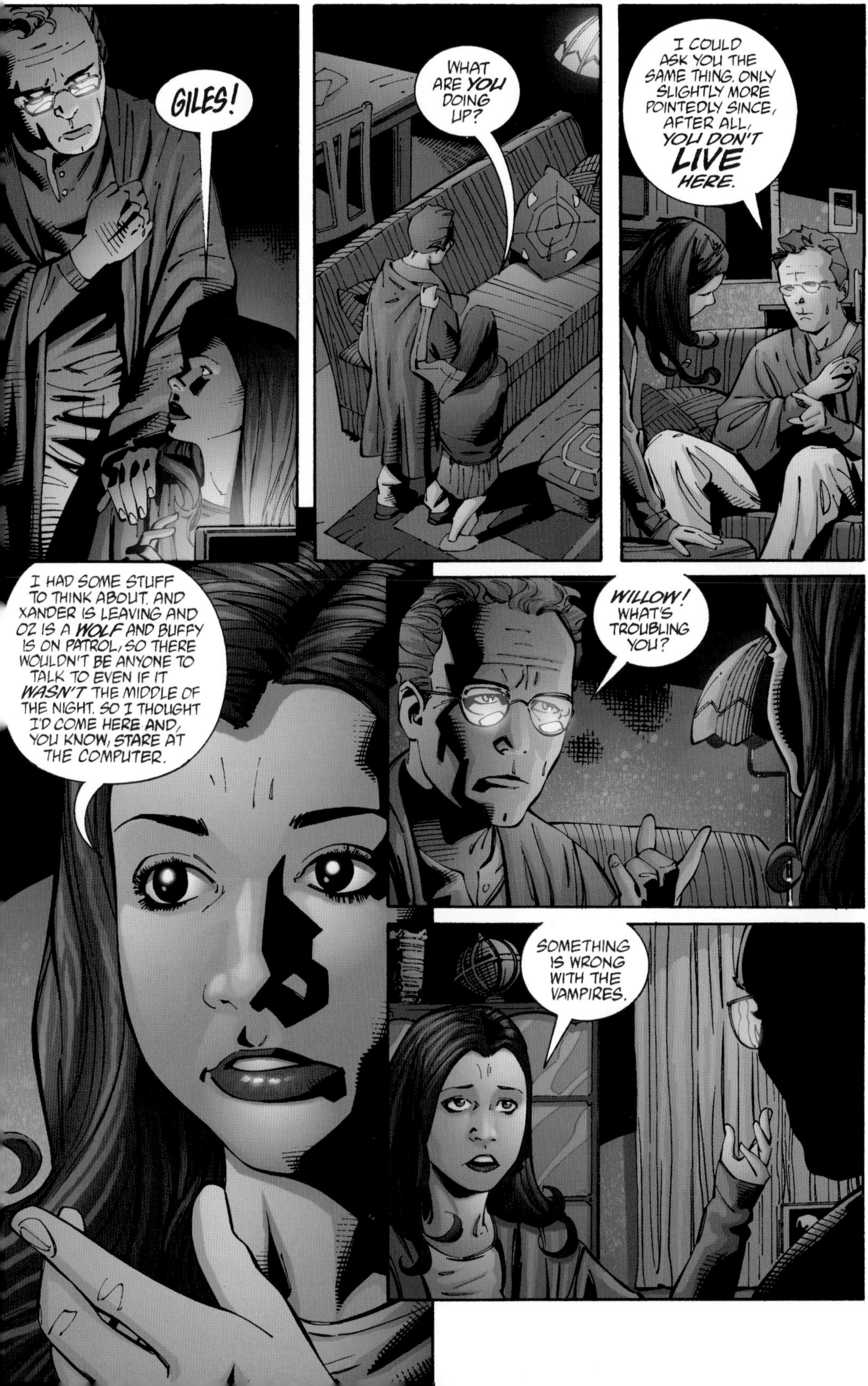
GILES!
WHAT ARE YOU DOING UP?
I COULD ASK YOU THE SAME THING. ONLY SLIGHTLY MORE POINTEDLY SINCE, AFTER ALL, YOU DON'T LIVE HERE.
I HAD SOME STUFF TO THINK ABOUT. AND XANDER IS LEAVING AND OZ IS A WOLF AND BUFFY IS ON PATROL, SO THERE WOULDN'T BE ANYONE TO TALK TO EVEN IF IT WASN'T THE MIDDLE OF THE NIGHT. SO I THOUGHT I'D COME HERE AND, YOU KNOW, STARE AT THE COMPUTER.
WILLOW! WHAT'S TROUBLING YOU?
SOMETHING IS WRONG WITH THE VAMPIRES.

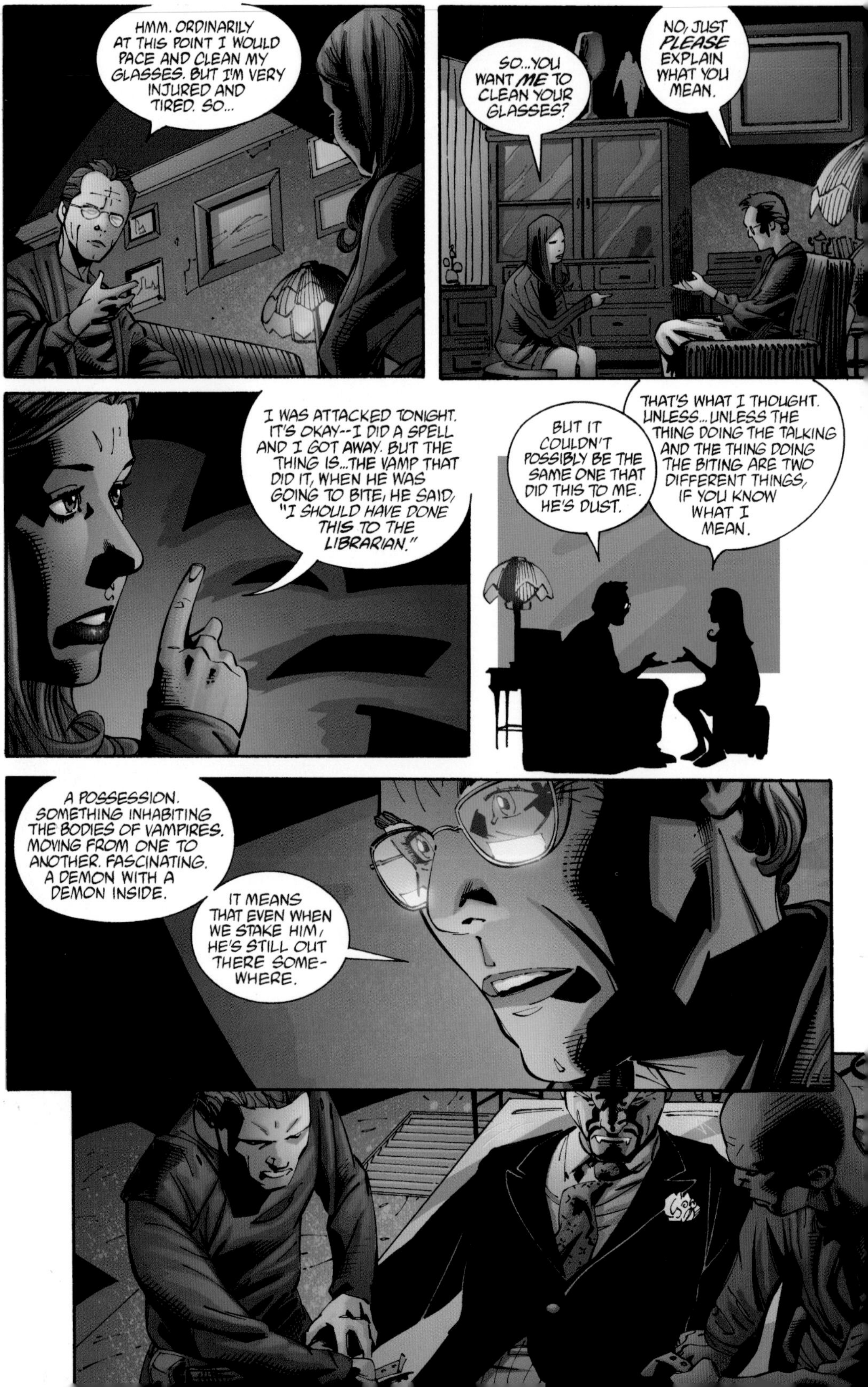
HMM. ORDINARILY AT THIS POINT I WOULD PACE AND CLEAN MY GLASSES. BUT I'M VERY INJURED AND TIRED. SO...
SO...YOU WANT ME TO CLEAN YOUR GLASSES?
NO, JUST PLEASE EXPLAIN WHAT YOU MEAN.
I WAS ATTACKED TONIGHT. IT'S OKAY--I DID A SPELL AND I GOT AWAY. BUT THE THING IS...THE VAMP THAT DID IT, WHEN HE WAS GOING TO BITE, HE SAID, "I SHOULD HAVE DONE THIS TO THE LIBRARIAN."
BUT IT COULDN'T POSSIBLY BE THE SAME ONE THAT DID THIS TO ME. HE'S DUST.
THAT'S WHAT I THOUGHT. UNLESS... UNLESS THE THING DOING THE TALKING AND THE THING DOING THE BITING ARE TWO DIFFERENT THINGS, IF YOU KNOW WHAT I MEAN.
A POSSESSION. SOMETHING INHABITING THE BODIES OF VAMPIRES. MOVING FROM ONE TO ANOTHER. FASCINATING. A DEMON WITH A DEMON INSIDE.
IT MEANS THAT EVEN WHEN WE STAKE HIM, HE'S STILL OUT THERE SOME-WHERE.

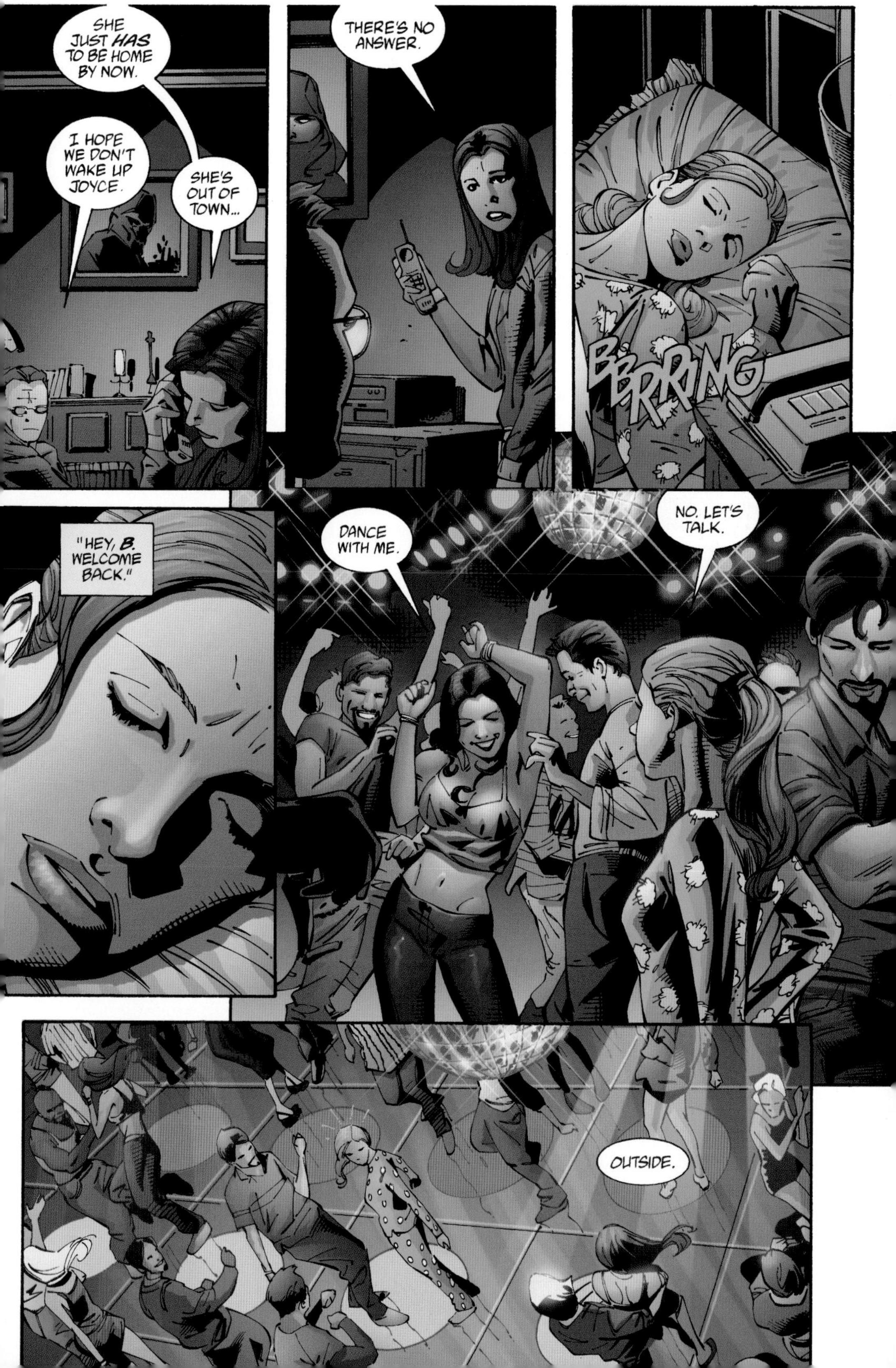
SHE JUST HAS TO BE HOME BY NOW.
I HOPE WE DON'T WAKE UP JOYCE.
SHE'S OUT OF TOWN...
THERE'S NO ANSWER.
BBRRRING
"HEY, B. WELCOME BACK."
DANCE WITH ME.
NO. LET'S TALK.
OUTSIDE.

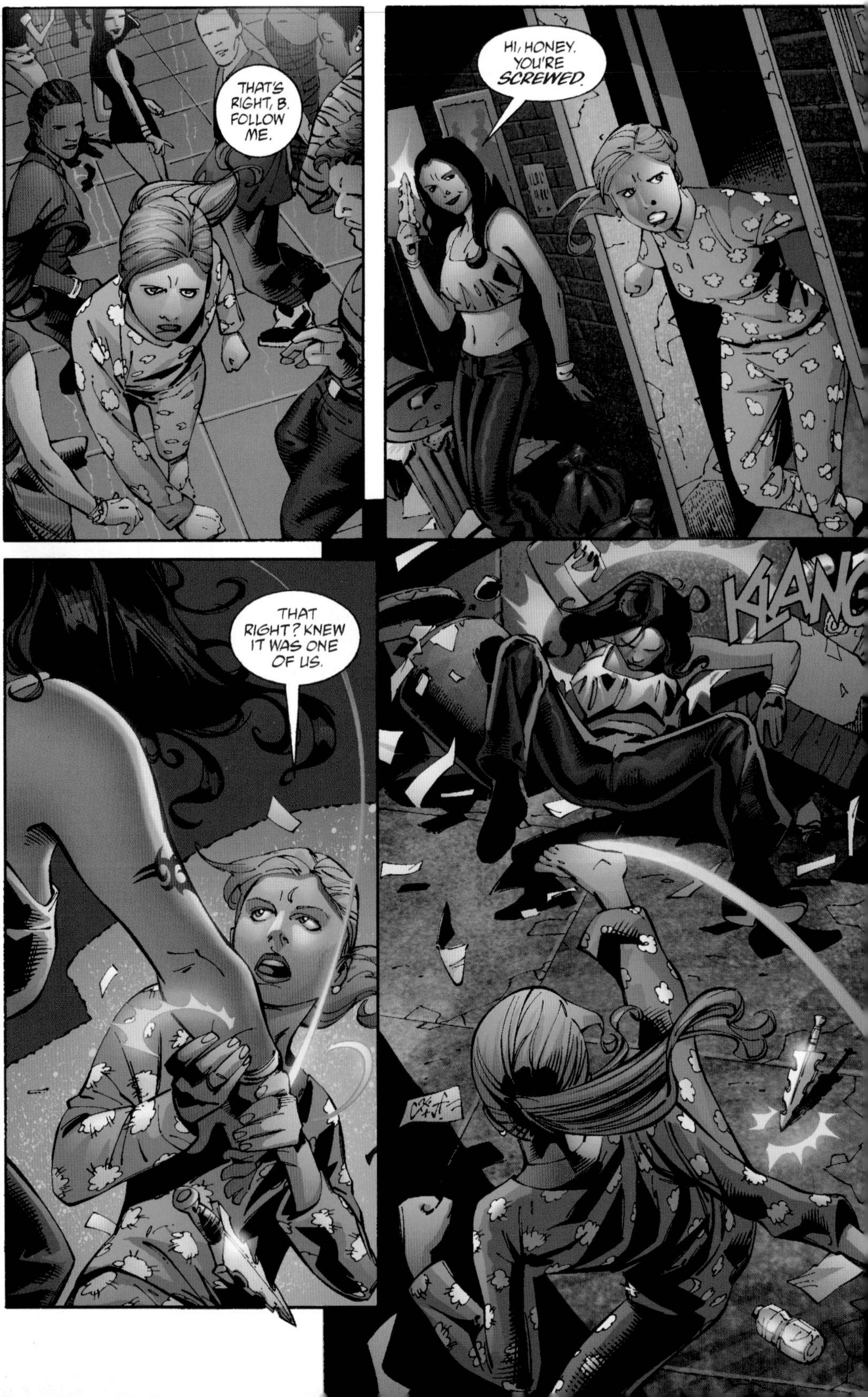
THAT'S RIGHT, B. FOLLOW ME.
HI, HONEY. YOU'RE SCREWED.
THAT RIGHT? KNEW IT WAS ONE OF US.
KLANG

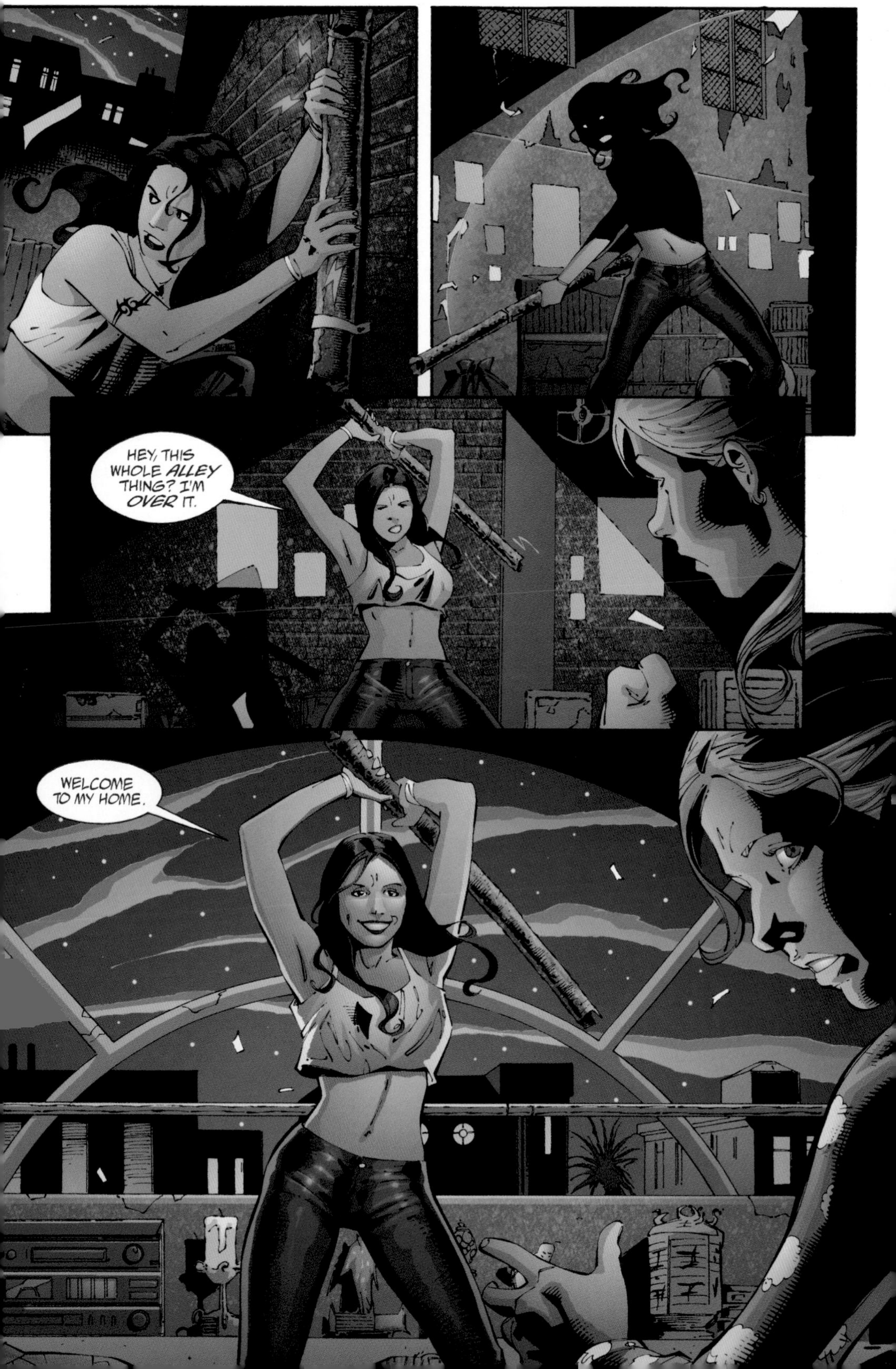
HEY, THIS WHOLE ALLEY THING? I'M OVER IT.
WELCOME TO MY HOME.

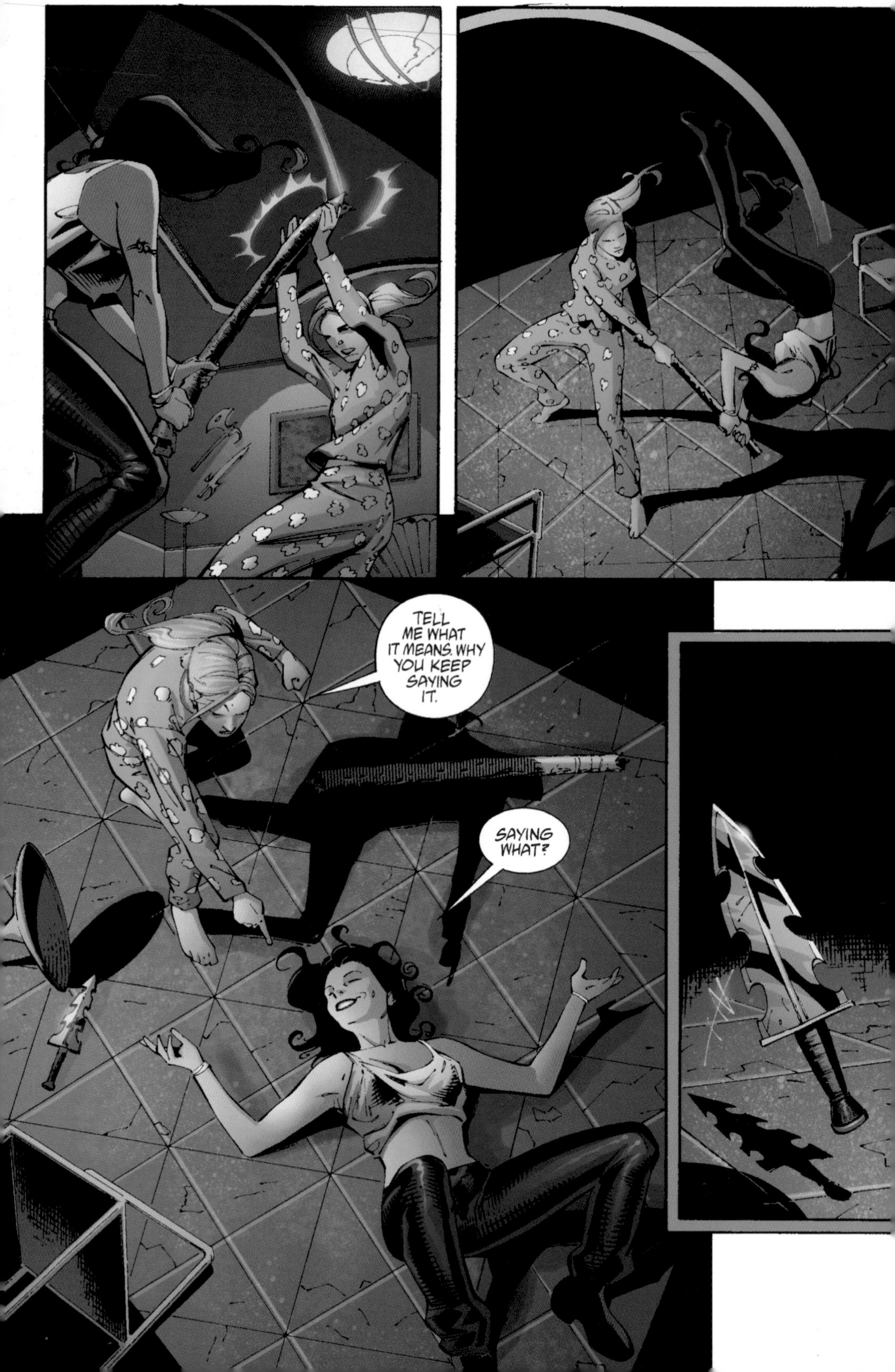
TELL ME WHAT IT MEANS. WHY YOU KEEP SAYING IT.
SAYING WHAT?

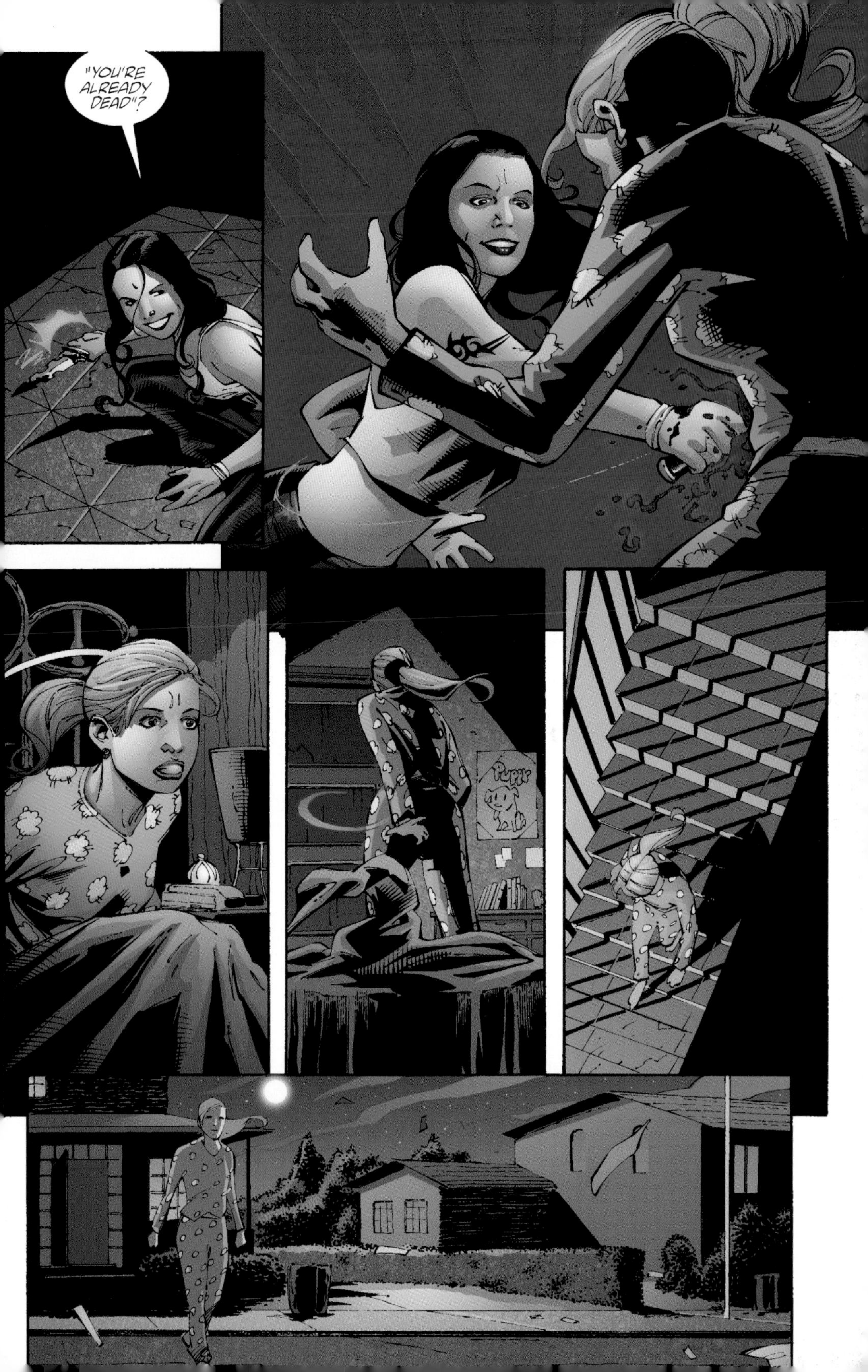
"YOU'RE ALREADY DEAD"?
PUPPY

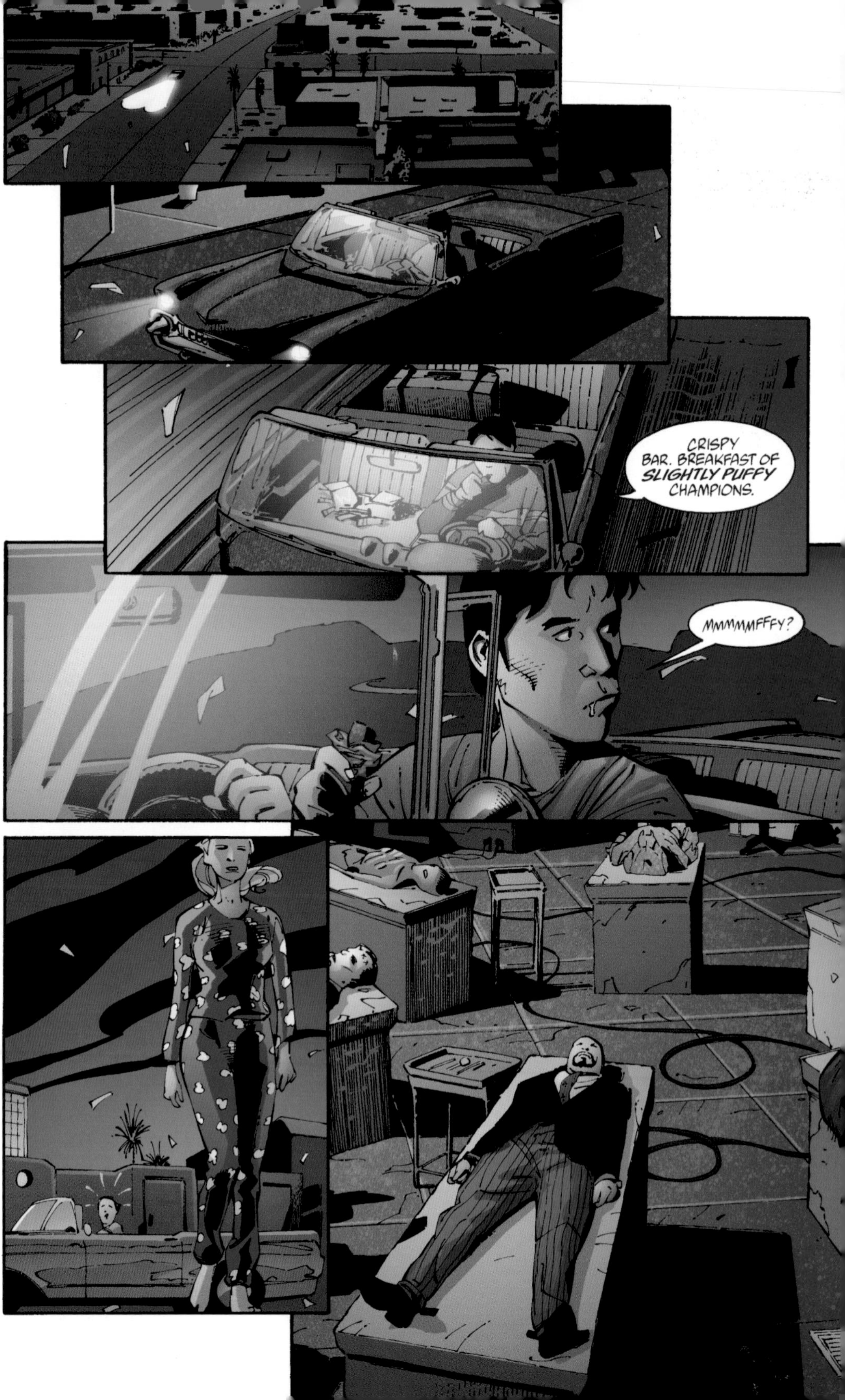
CRISPY BAR. BREAKFAST OF SLIGHTLY PUFFY CHAMPIONS.
MMMMMFFFY?

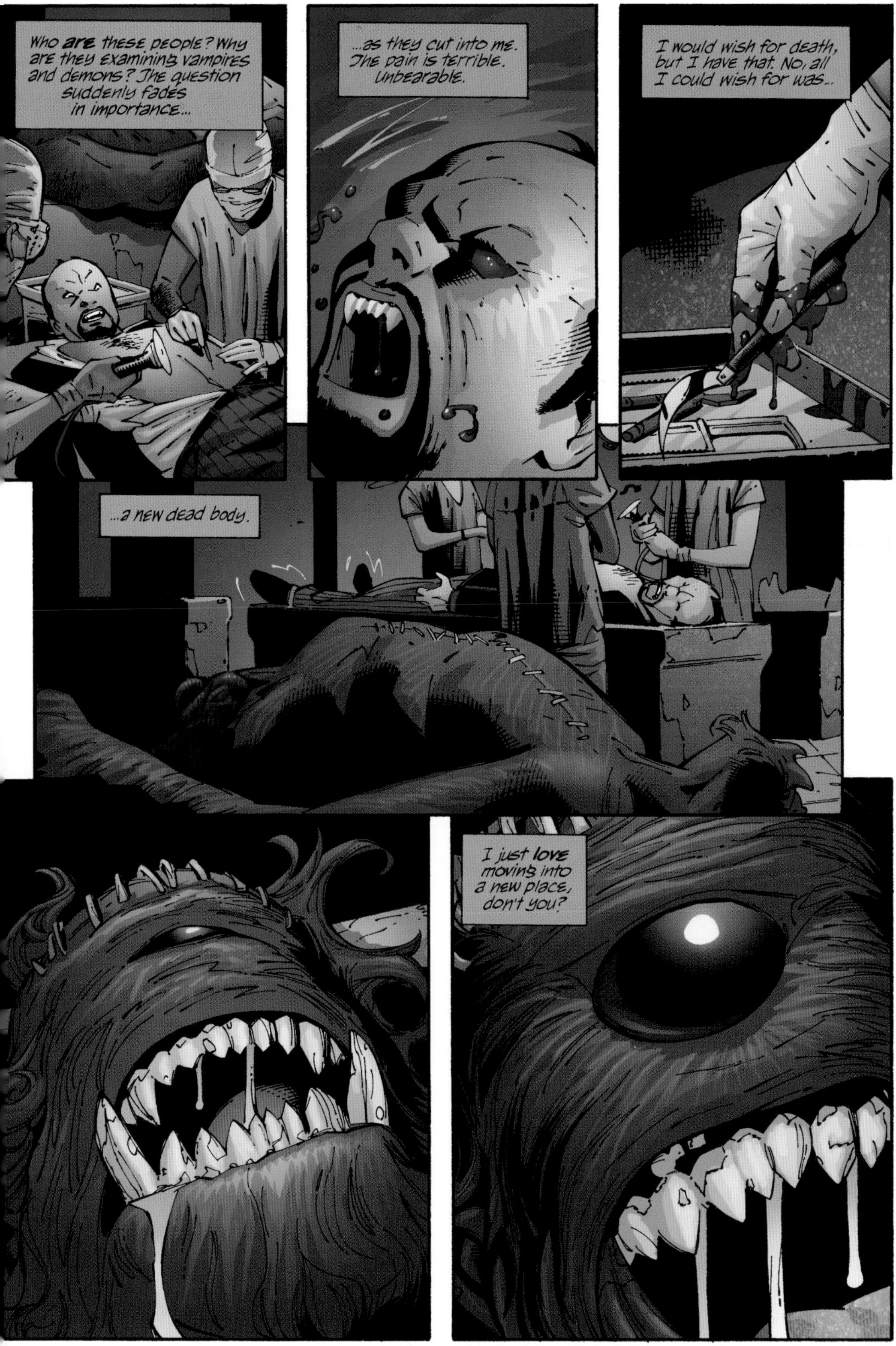
Who are these people? Why are they examining vampires and demons? The question suddenly fades in importance...
...as they cut into me. The pain is terrible. Unbearable.
I would wish for death, but I have that. No, all I could wish for was...
...a new dead body.
I just love moving into a new place, don't you?

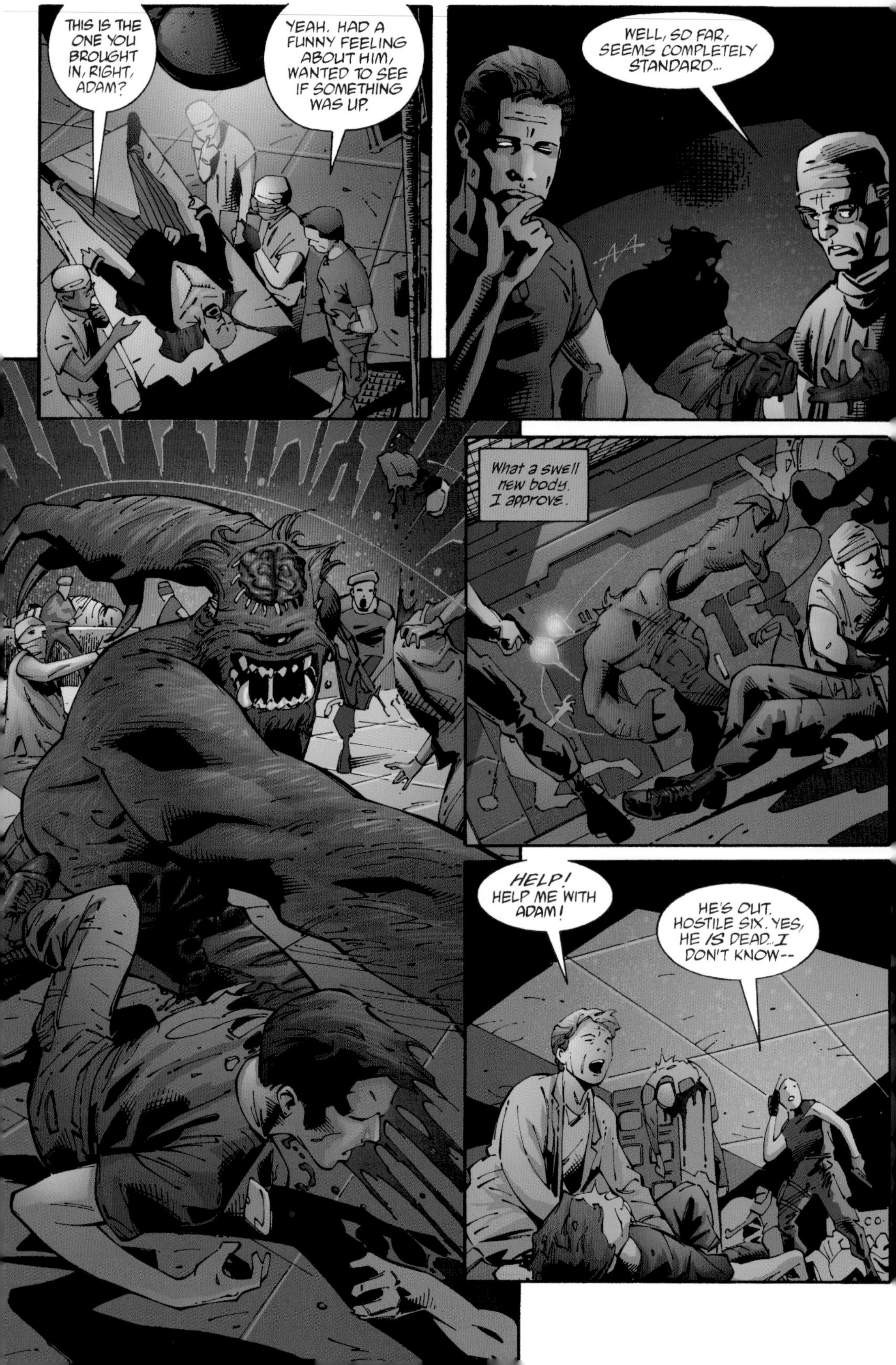
THIS IS THE ONE YOU BROUGHT IN, RIGHT, ADAM?
YEAH. HAD A FUNNY FEELING ABOUT HIM, WANTED TO SEE IF SOMETHING WAS UP.
WELL, SO FAR, SEEMS COMPLETELY STANDARD...
What a swell new body. I approve.
HELP! HELP ME WITH ADAM!
HE'S OUT. HOSTILE SIX. YES, HE IS DEAD... I DON'T KNOW--

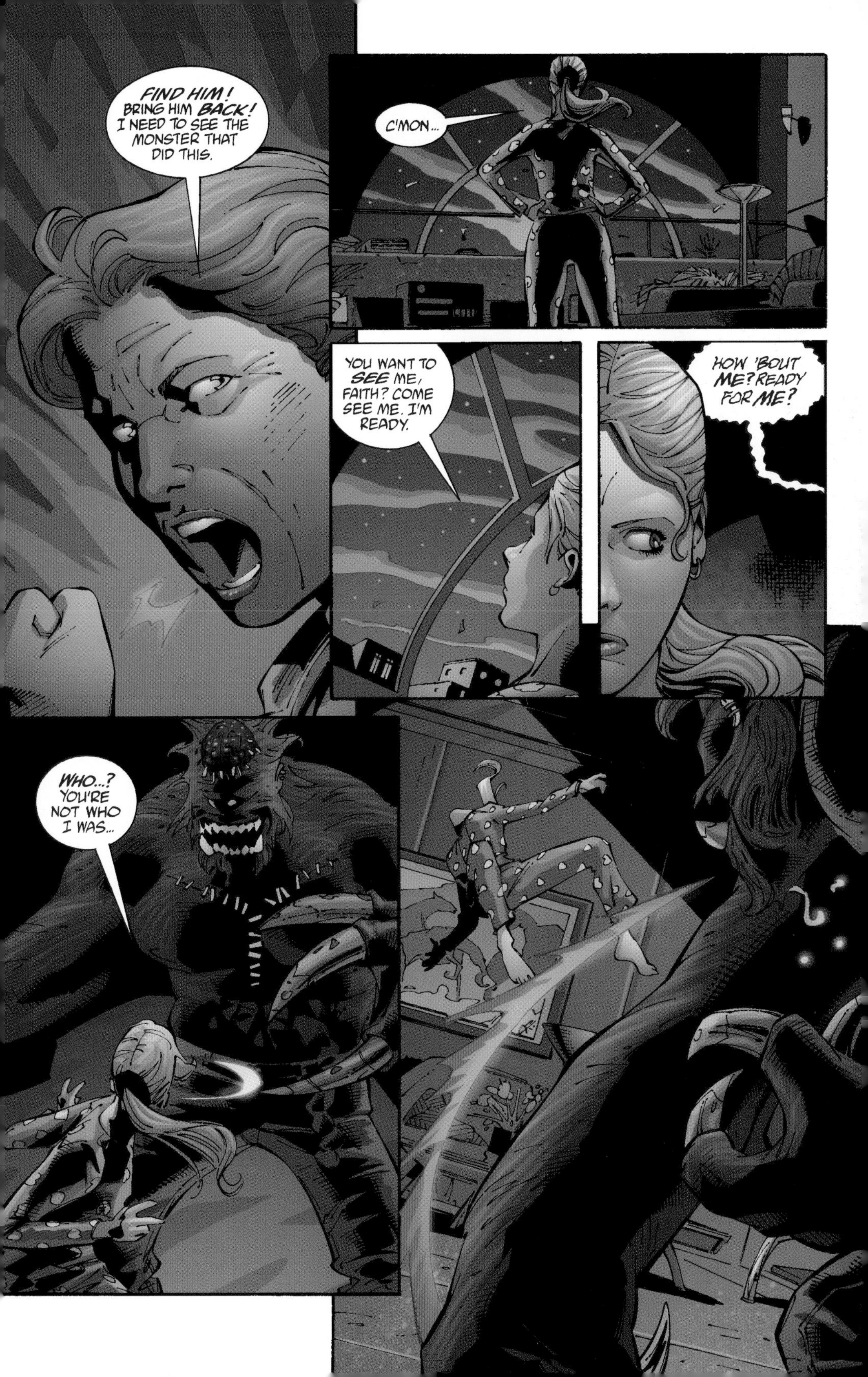
FIND HIM! BRING HIM BACK! I NEED TO SEE THE MONSTER THAT DID THIS.
C'MON...
YOU WANT TO SEE ME, FAITH? COME SEE ME. I'M READY.
HOW 'BOUT ME? READY FOR ME?
WHO...? YOU'RE NOT WHO I WAS...

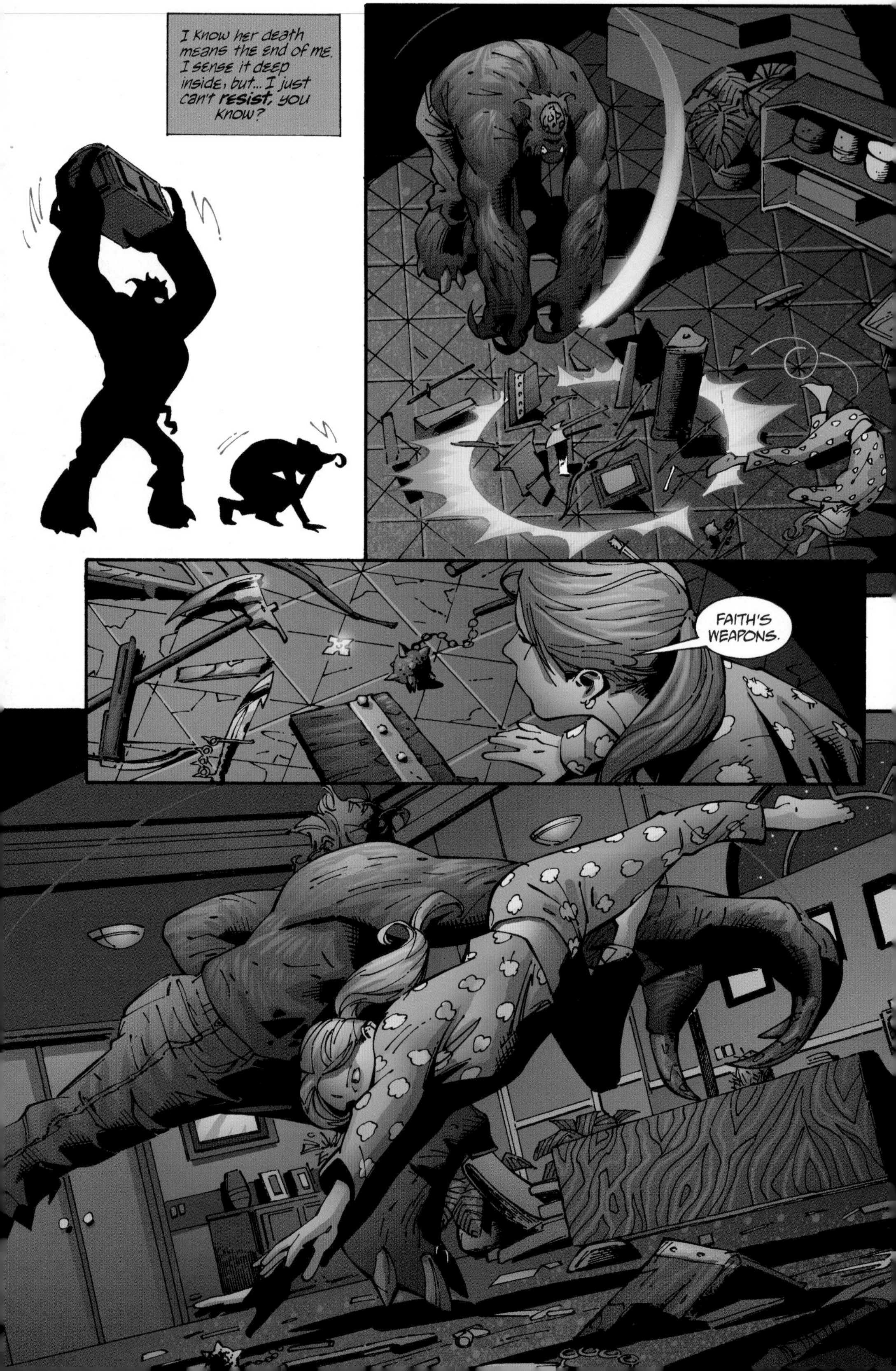
I know her death means the end of me. I sense it deep inside, but... I just can't **resist,** you know?
FAITH'S WEAPONS.

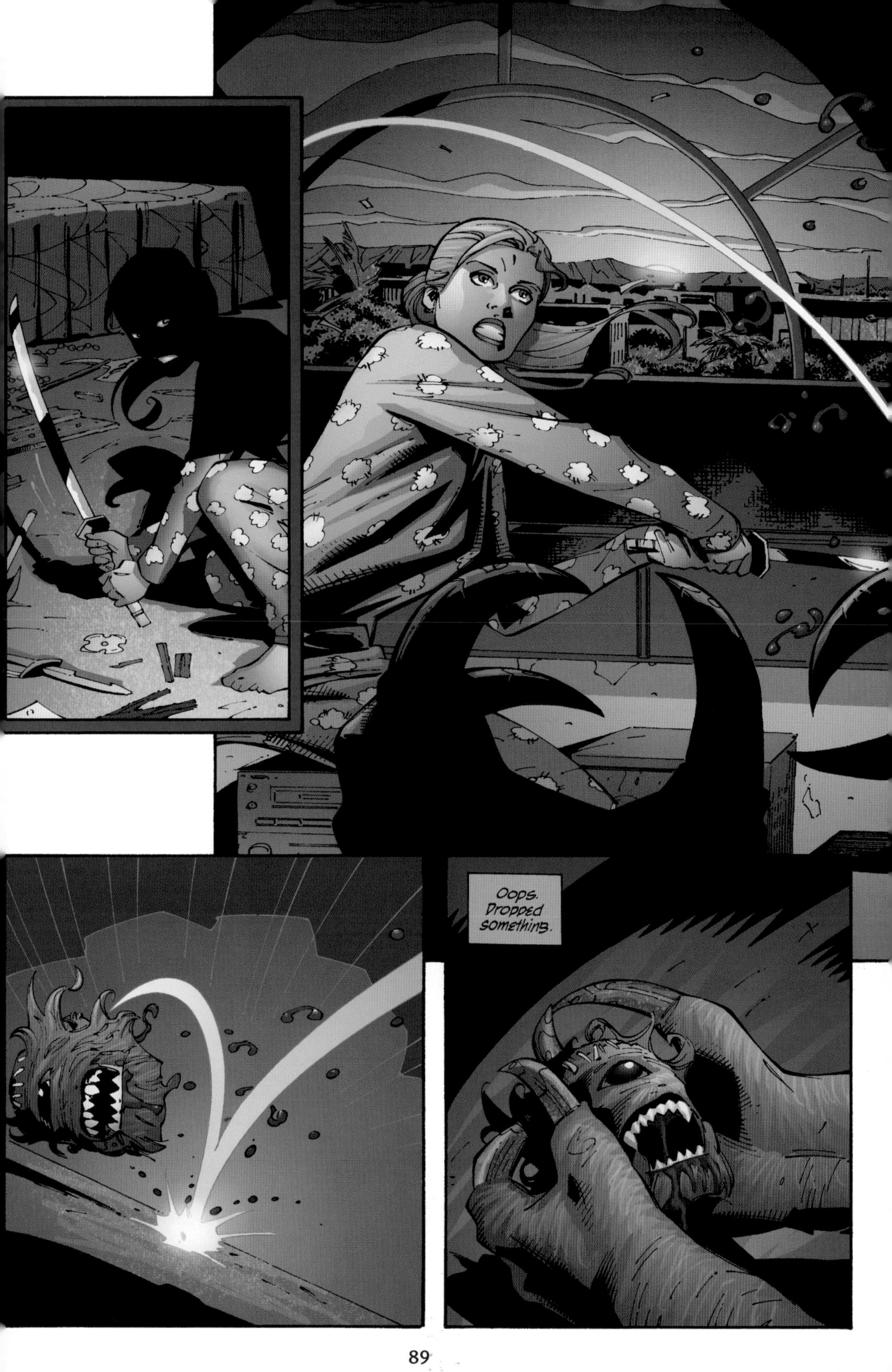
Oops. Dropped something.

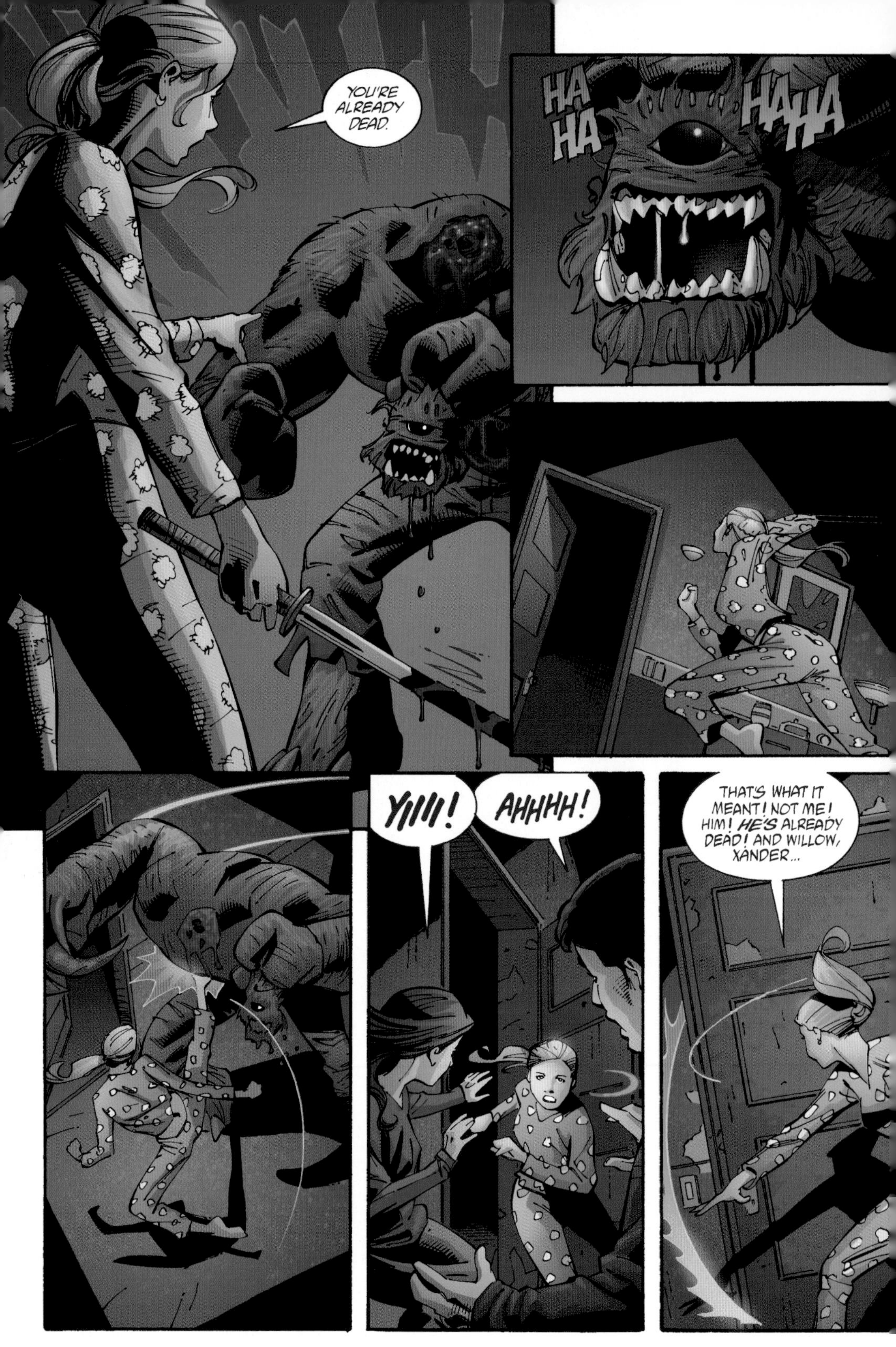
YOU'RE ALREADY DEAD.
HA HA
HAHA
YIIII!
AHHHH!
THAT'S WHAT IT MEANT! NOT ME! HIM! HE'S ALREADY DEAD! AND WILLOW, XANDER...

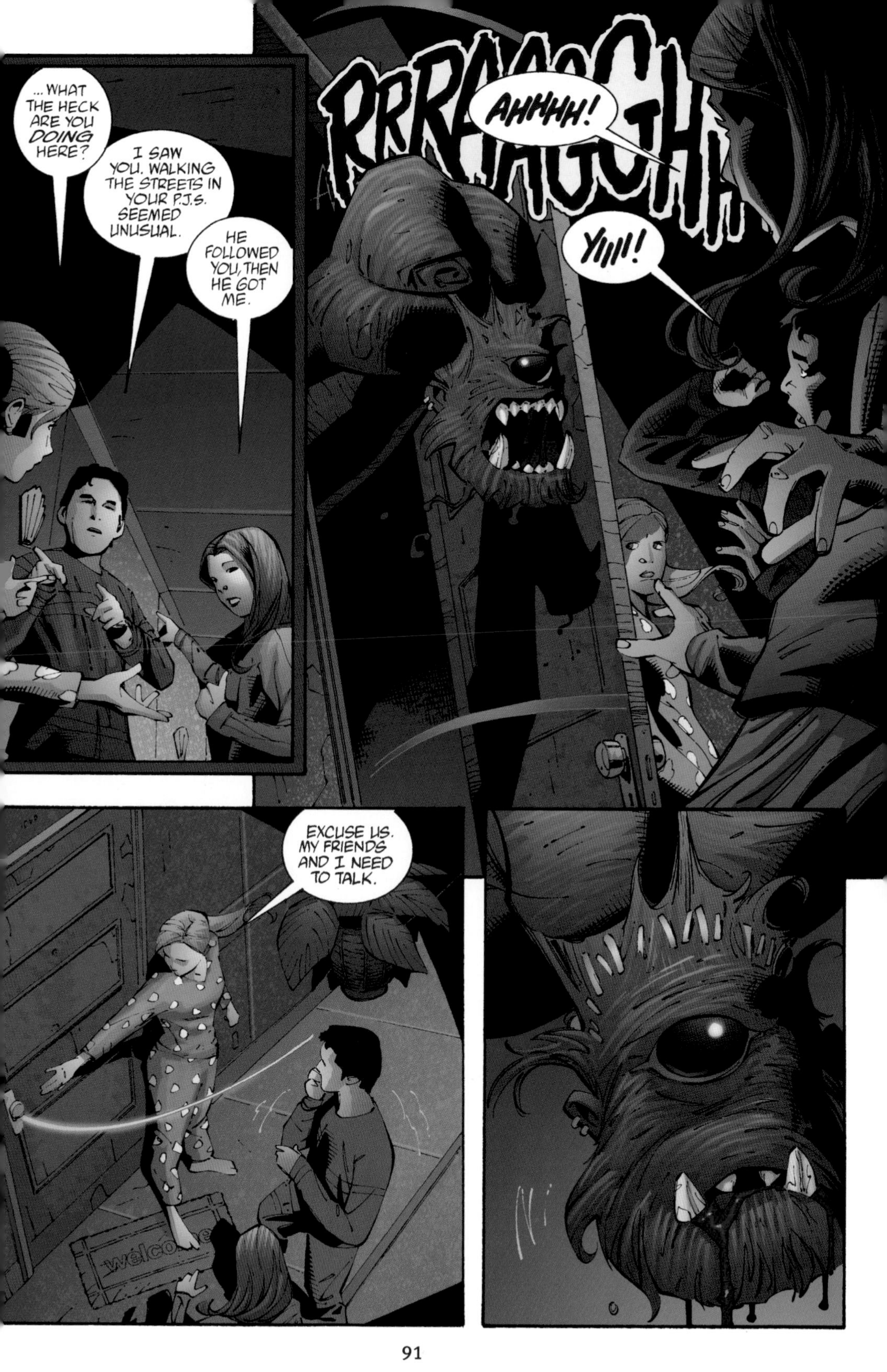
...WHAT THE HECK ARE YOU *DOING* HERE?
I SAW YOU. WALKING THE STREETS IN YOUR P.J.S. SEEMED UNUSUAL.
HE FOLLOWED YOU, THEN HE GOT ME.
RRRAAGGH
AHHHH!
YIII!
EXCUSE US. MY FRIENDS AND I NEED TO TALK.
welcome

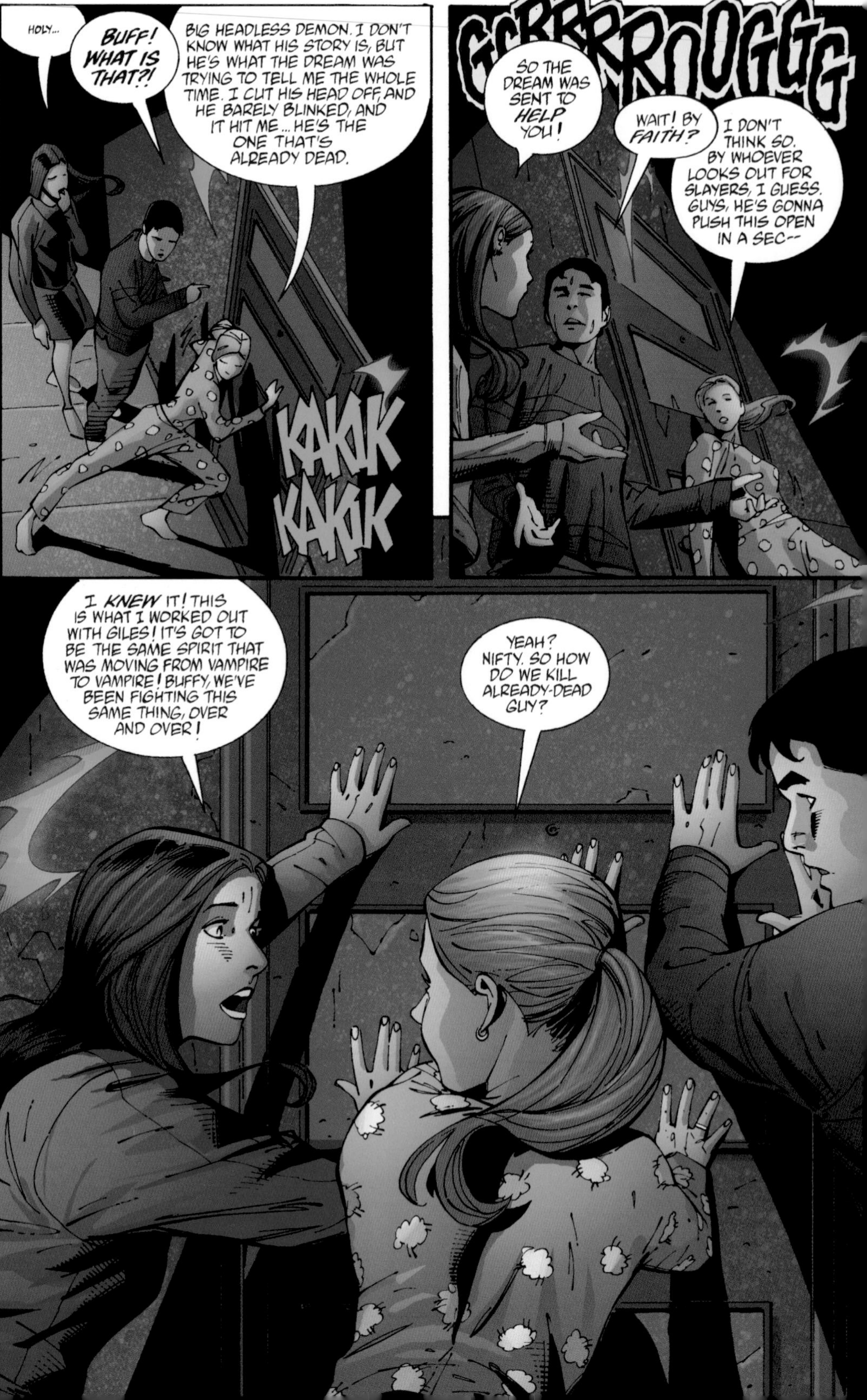
HOLY...
BUFF! WHAT IS THAT?!
BIG HEADLESS DEMON. I DON'T KNOW WHAT HIS STORY IS, BUT HE'S WHAT THE DREAM WAS TRYING TO TELL ME THE WHOLE TIME. I CUT HIS HEAD OFF, AND HE BARELY BLINKED, AND IT HIT ME ... HE'S THE ONE THAT'S ALREADY DEAD.
KAKAK KAKAK
GRRRRRROGGG
SO THE DREAM WAS SENT TO HELP YOU!
WAIT! BY FAITH?
I DON'T THINK SO. BY WHOEVER LOOKS OUT FOR SLAYERS, I GUESS. GUYS, HE'S GONNA PUSH THIS OPEN IN A SEC--
I KNEW IT! THIS IS WHAT I WORKED OUT WITH GILES! IT'S GOT TO BE THE SAME SPIRIT THAT WAS MOVING FROM VAMPIRE TO VAMPIRE! BUFFY, WE'VE BEEN FIGHTING THIS SAME THING, OVER AND OVER!
YEAH? NIFTY. SO HOW DO WE KILL ALREADY-DEAD GUY?

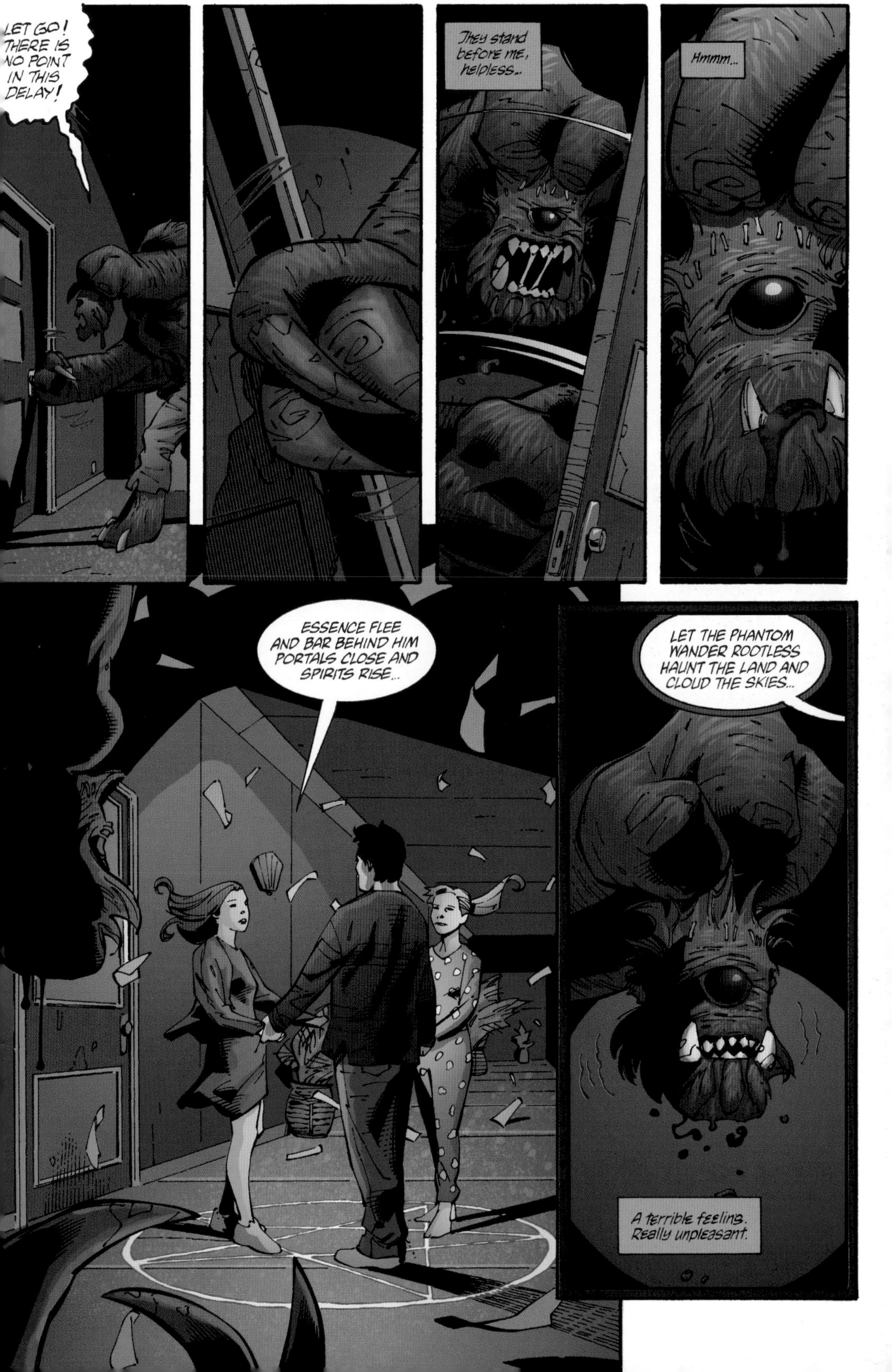
LET GO! THERE IS NO POINT IN THIS DELAY!
They stand before me, helpless...
Hmmm...
ESSENCE FLEE AND BAR BEHIND HIM PORTALS CLOSE AND SPIRITS RISE...
LET THE PHANTOM WANDER ROOTLESS HAUNT THE LAND AND CLOUD THE SKIES...
A terrible feeling. Really unpleasant.

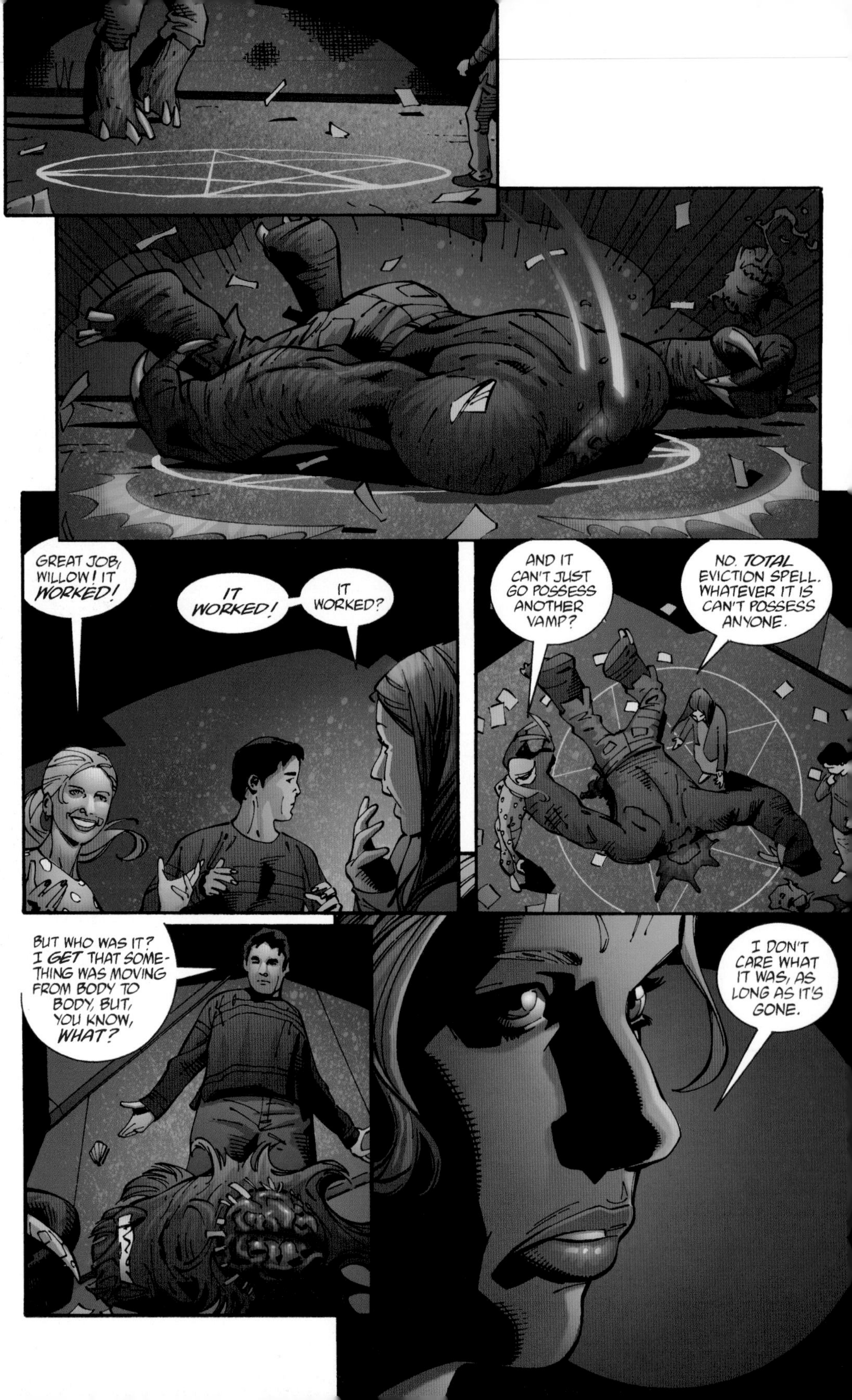
GREAT JOB, WILLOW! IT WORKED!
IT WORKED!
IT WORKED?
AND IT CAN'T JUST GO POSSESS ANOTHER VAMP?
NO. TOTAL EVICTION SPELL. WHATEVER IT IS CAN'T POSSESS ANYONE.
BUT WHO WAS IT? I GET THAT SOMETHING WAS MOVING FROM BODY TO BODY, BUT, YOU KNOW, WHAT?
I DON'T CARE WHAT IT WAS, AS LONG AS IT'S GONE.

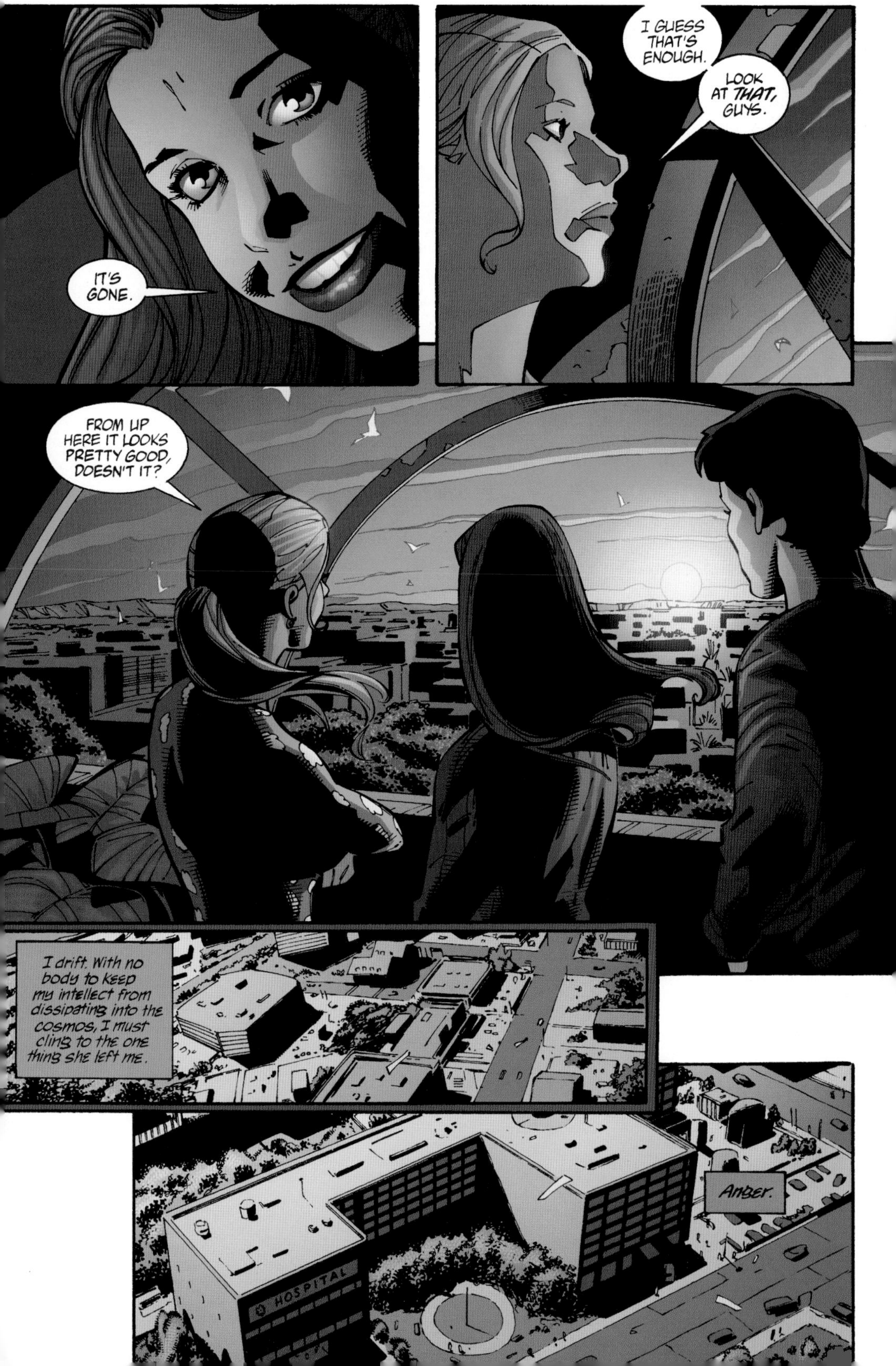
IT'S GONE.
I GUESS THAT'S ENOUGH.
LOOK AT *THAT*, GUYS.
FROM UP HERE IT LOOKS PRETTY GOOD, DOESN'T IT?
I drift. With no body to keep my intellect from dissipating into the cosmos, I must cling to the one thing she left me.
Amber.
HOSPITAL

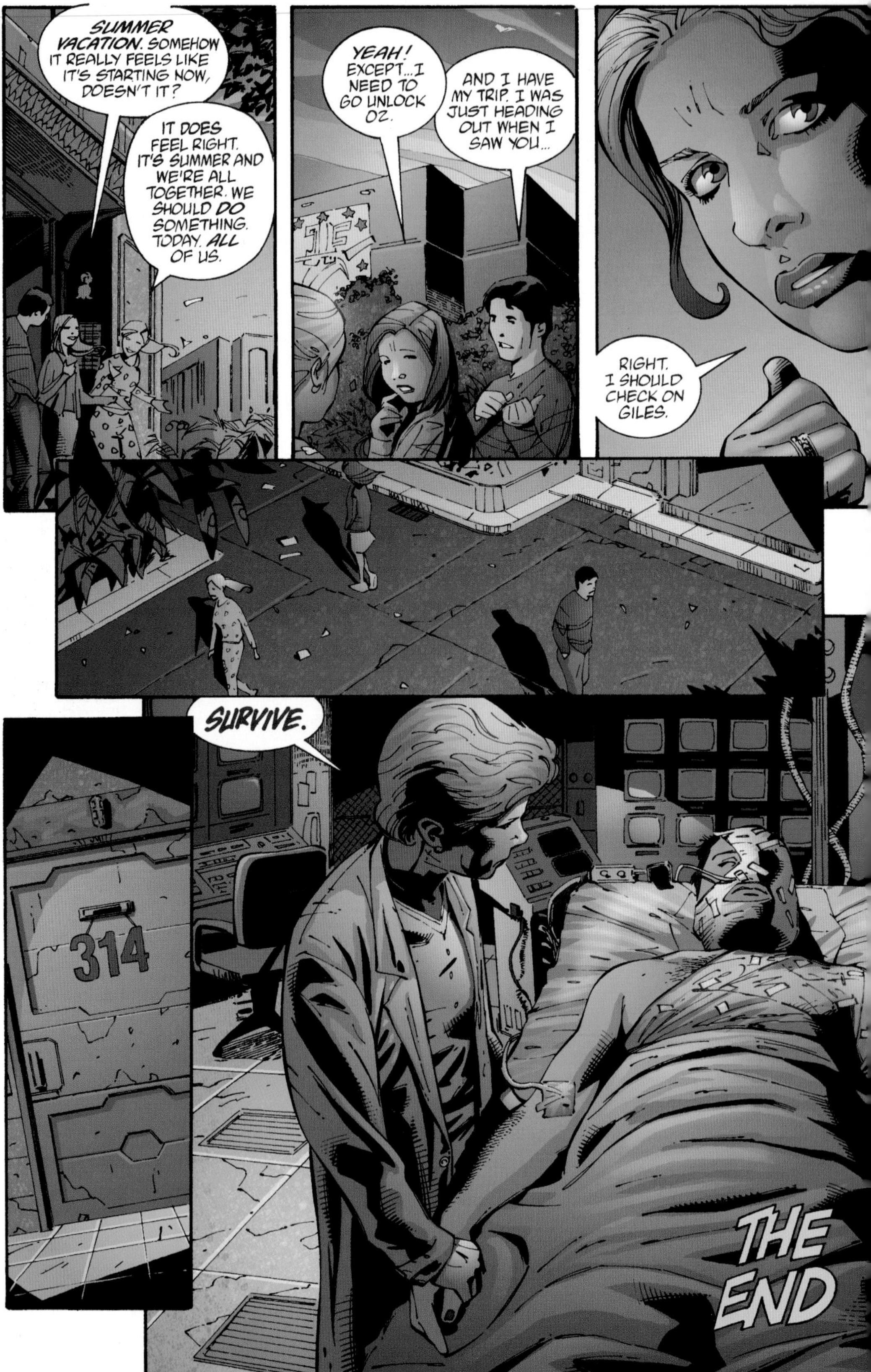
SUMMER VACATION. SOMEHOW IT REALLY FEELS LIKE IT'S STARTING NOW, DOESN'T IT?
IT DOES FEEL RIGHT. IT'S SUMMER AND WE'RE ALL TOGETHER. WE SHOULD DO SOMETHING. TODAY. ALL OF US.
YEAH! EXCEPT...I NEED TO GO UNLOCK OZ.
AND I HAVE MY TRIP. I WAS JUST HEADING OUT WHEN I SAW YOU...
RIGHT. I SHOULD CHECK ON GILES.
SURVIVE.
314
THE END

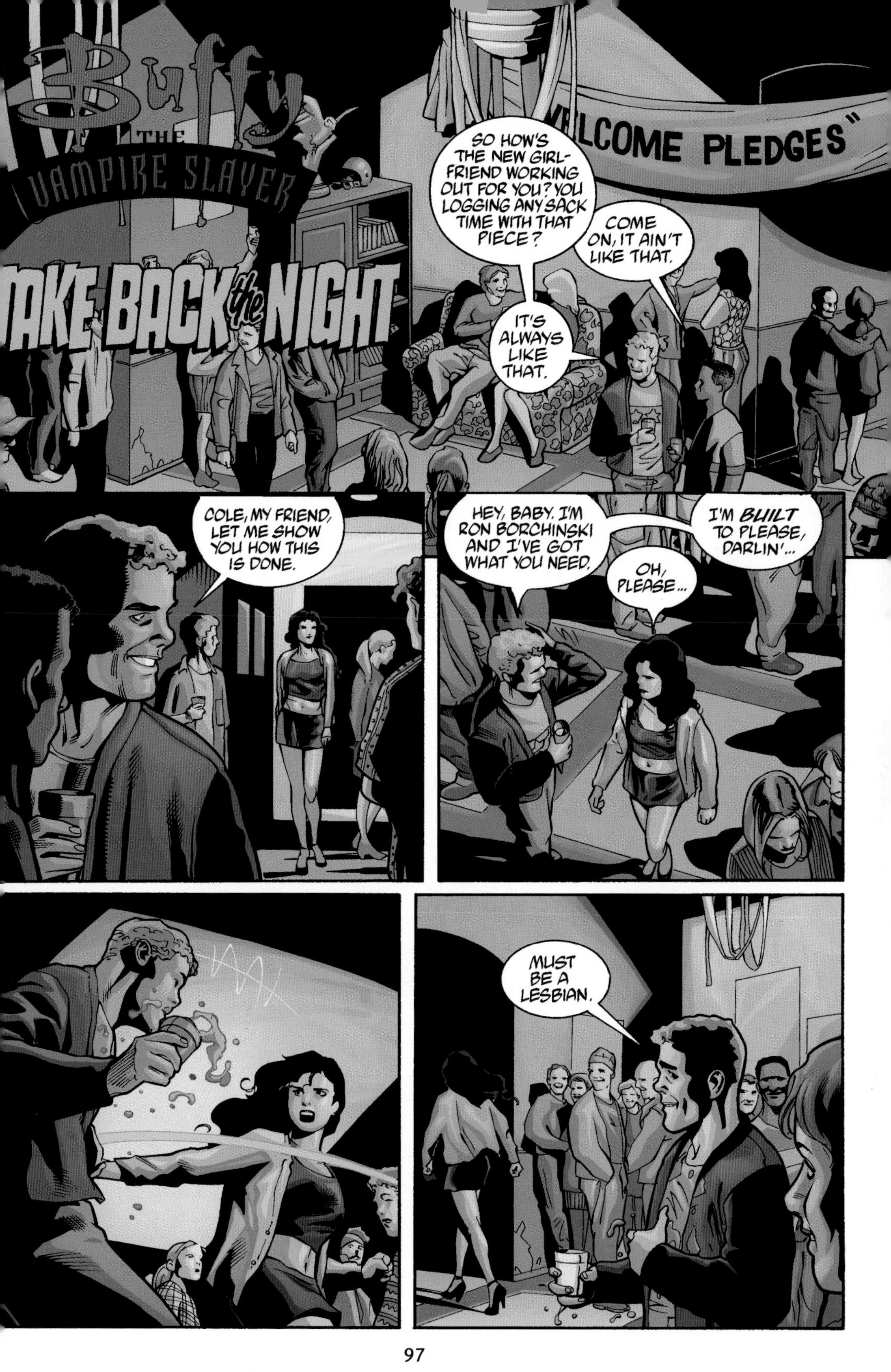
Buffy THE VAMPIRE SLAYER
TAKE BACK the NIGHT
"WELCOME PLEDGES"
SO HOW'S THE NEW GIRL-FRIEND WORKING OUT FOR YOU? YOU LOGGING ANY SACK TIME WITH THAT PIECE?
COME ON, IT AIN'T LIKE THAT.
IT'S ALWAYS LIKE THAT.
COLE, MY FRIEND, LET ME SHOW YOU HOW THIS IS DONE.
HEY, BABY. I'M RON BORCHINSKI AND I'VE GOT WHAT YOU NEED.
I'M BUILT TO PLEASE, DARLIN'...
OH, PLEASE...
MUST BE A LESBIAN.

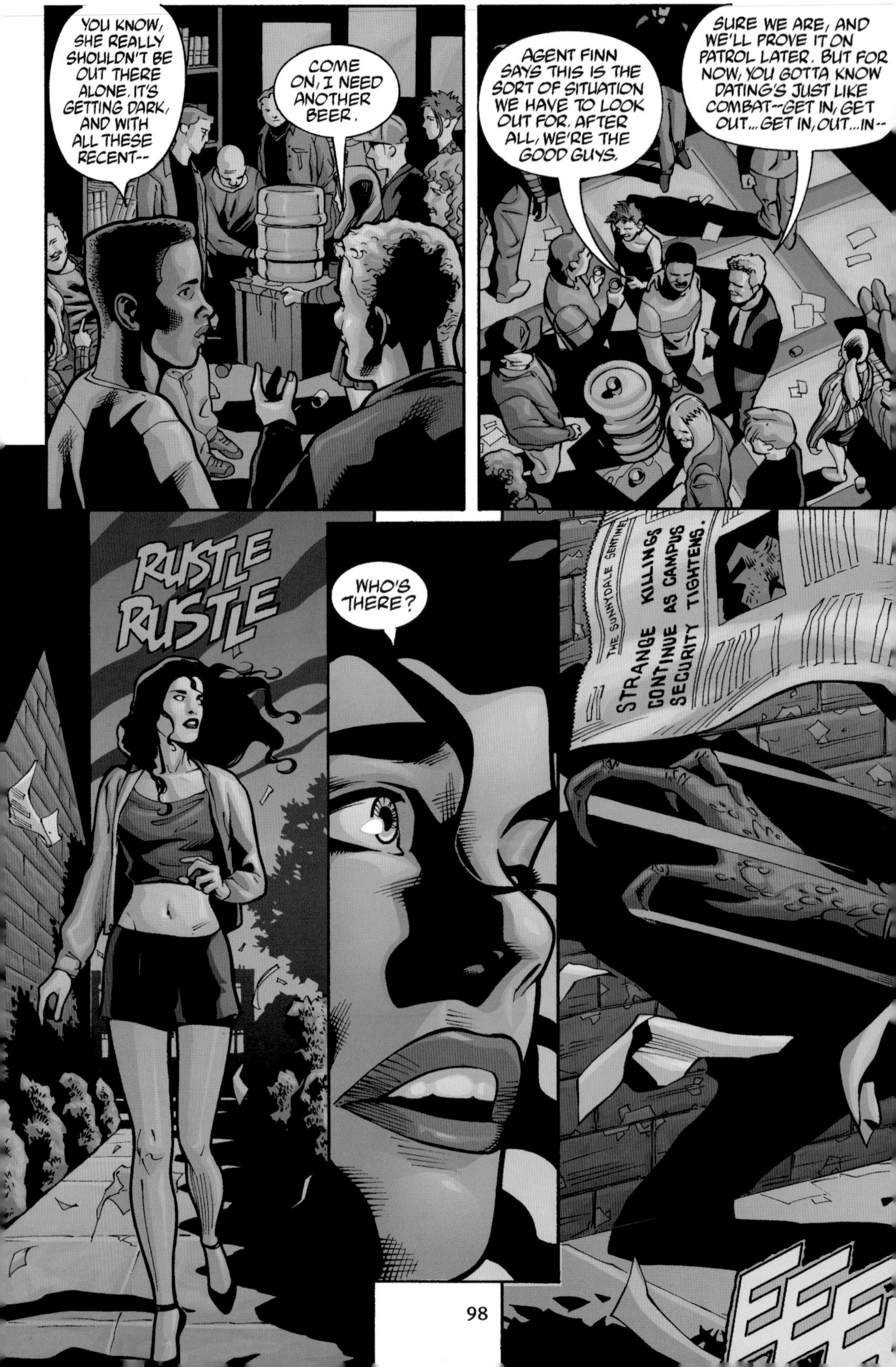
YOU KNOW, SHE REALLY SHOULDN'T BE OUT THERE ALONE. IT'S GETTING DARK, AND WITH ALL THESE RECENT--
COME ON, I NEED ANOTHER BEER.
AGENT FINN SAYS THIS IS THE SORT OF SITUATION WE HAVE TO LOOK OUT FOR. AFTER ALL, WE'RE THE GOOD GUYS.
SURE WE ARE, AND WE'LL PROVE IT ON PATROL LATER. BUT FOR NOW, YOU GOTTA KNOW DATING'S JUST LIKE COMBAT--GET IN, GET OUT... GET IN, OUT... IN--
RUSTLE RUSTLE
WHO'S THERE?
THE SUNNYDALE SENTINEL
STRANGE KILLINGS CONTINUE AS CAMPUS SECURITY TIGHTENS.

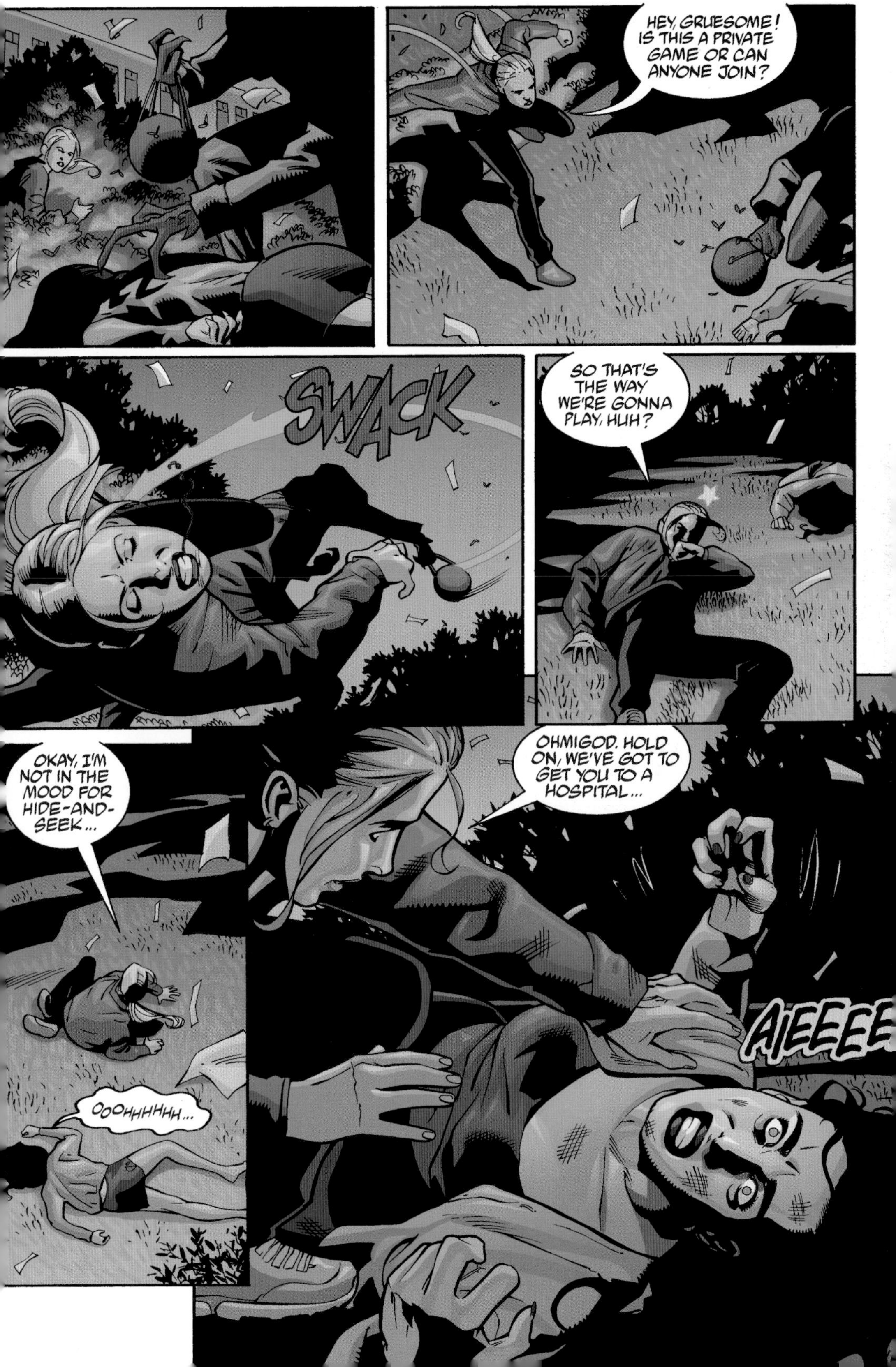
HEY, GRUESOME! IS THIS A PRIVATE GAME OR CAN ANYONE JOIN?
SWACK
SO THAT'S THE WAY WE'RE GONNA PLAY, HUH?
OKAY, I'M NOT IN THE MOOD FOR HIDE-AND-SEEK...
OHMIGOD. HOLD ON, WE'VE GOT TO GET YOU TO A HOSPITAL...
AIEEEE
OOOHHHHHH...

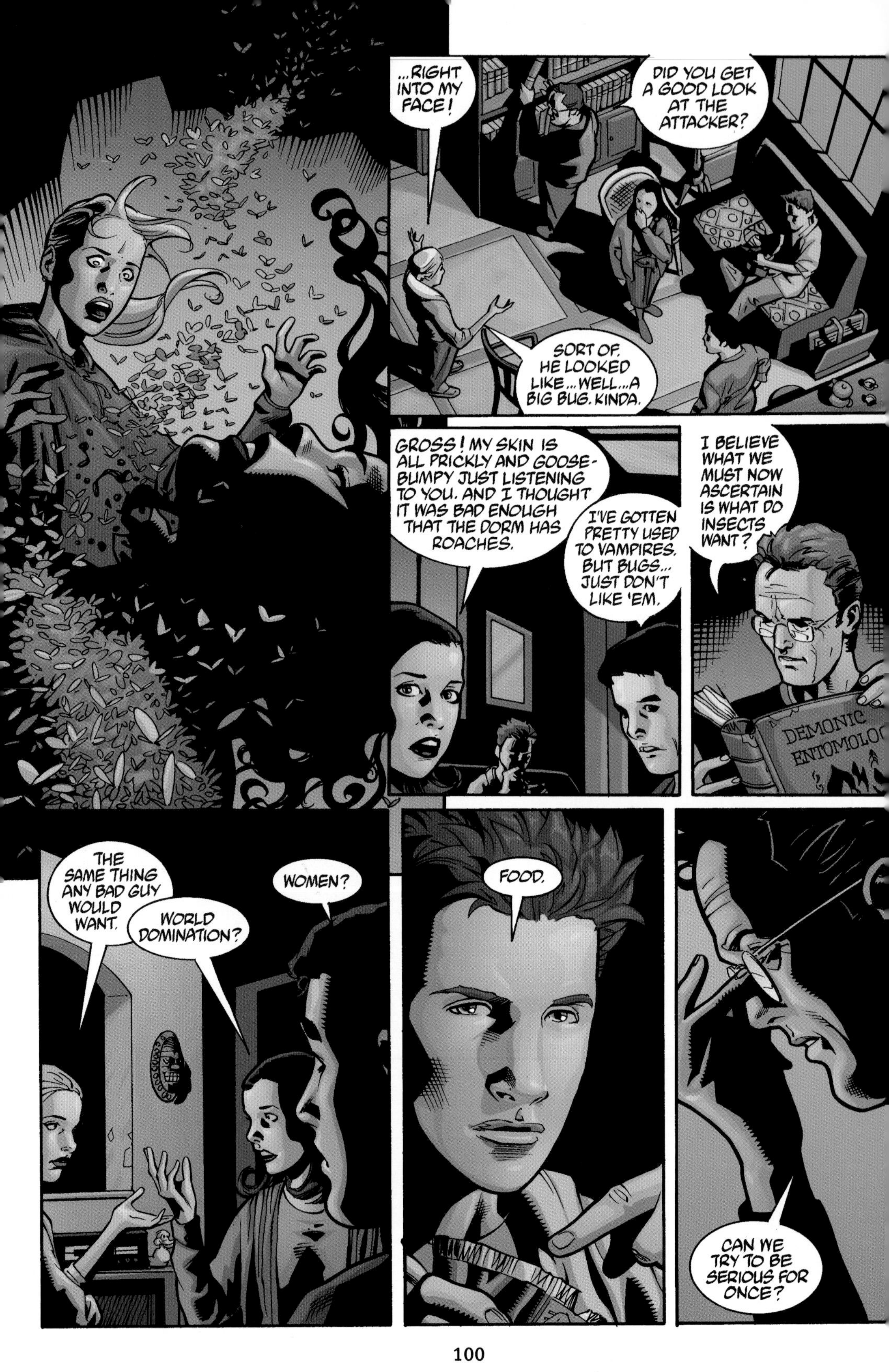
...RIGHT INTO MY FACE!
DID YOU GET A GOOD LOOK AT THE ATTACKER?
SORT OF. HE LOOKED LIKE... WELL... A BIG BUG. KINDA.
GROSS! MY SKIN IS ALL PRICKLY AND GOOSE-BUMPY JUST LISTENING TO YOU. AND I THOUGHT IT WAS BAD ENOUGH THAT THE DORM HAS ROACHES.
I'VE GOTTEN PRETTY USED TO VAMPIRES. BUT BUGS... JUST DON'T LIKE 'EM.
I BELIEVE WHAT WE MUST NOW ASCERTAIN IS WHAT DO INSECTS WANT?
DEMONIC ENTOMOLOG
THE SAME THING ANY BAD GUY WOULD WANT.
WORLD DOMINATION?
WOMEN?
FOOD.
CAN WE TRY TO BE SERIOUS FOR ONCE?

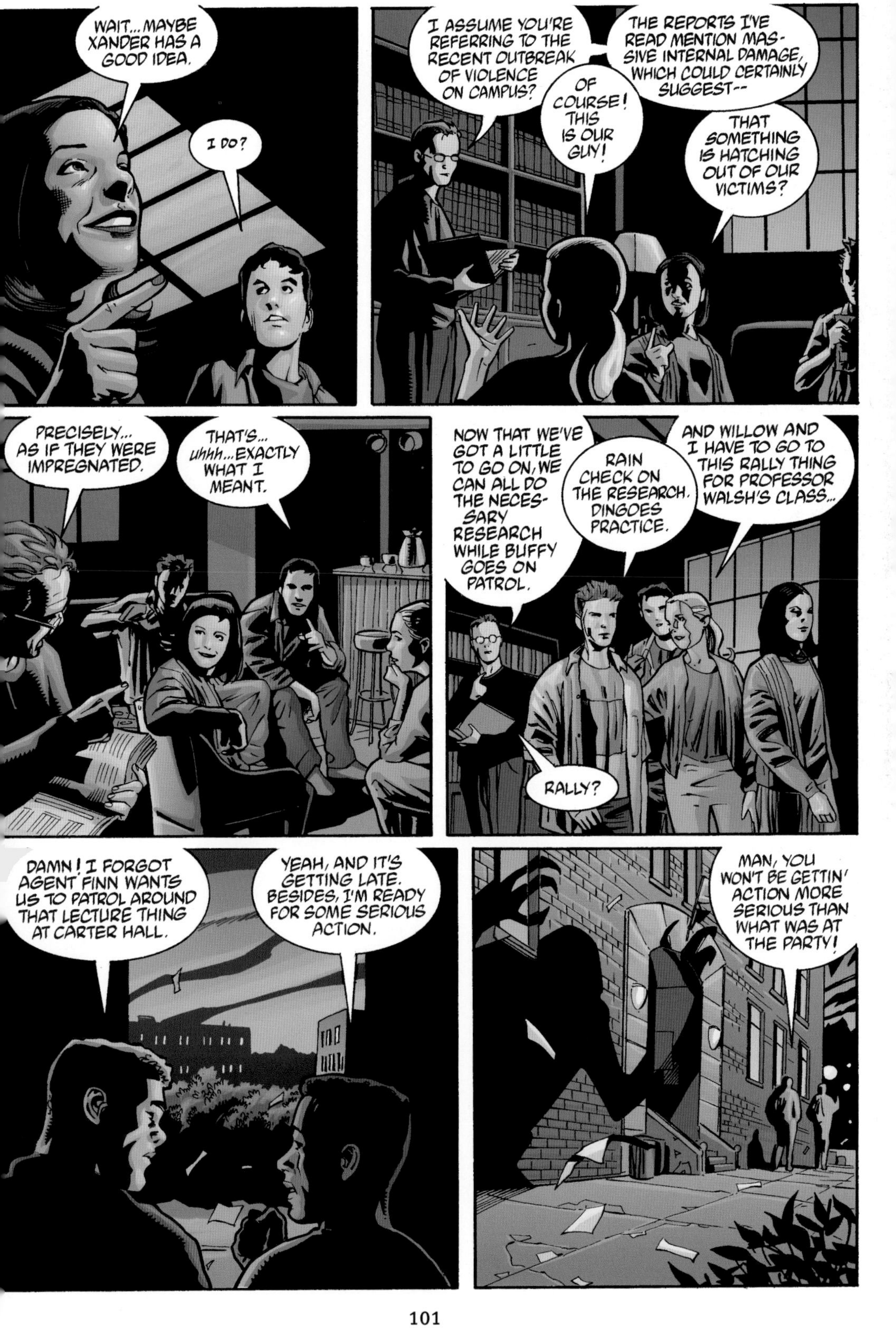
WAIT... MAYBE XANDER HAS A GOOD IDEA.
I DO?
I ASSUME YOU'RE REFERRING TO THE RECENT OUTBREAK OF VIOLENCE ON CAMPUS?
THE REPORTS I'VE READ MENTION MASSIVE INTERNAL DAMAGE, WHICH COULD CERTAINLY SUGGEST--
OF COURSE! THIS IS OUR GUY!
THAT SOMETHING IS HATCHING OUT OF OUR VICTIMS?
PRECISELY... AS IF THEY WERE IMPREGNATED.
THAT'S... uhhh... EXACTLY WHAT I MEANT.
NOW THAT WE'VE GOT A LITTLE TO GO ON, WE CAN ALL DO THE NECESSARY RESEARCH WHILE BUFFY GOES ON PATROL.
RAIN CHECK ON THE RESEARCH. DINGOES PRACTICE.
AND WILLOW AND I HAVE TO GO TO THIS RALLY THING FOR PROFESSOR WALSH'S CLASS...
RALLY?
DAMN! I FORGOT AGENT FINN WANTS US TO PATROL AROUND THAT LECTURE THING AT CARTER HALL.
YEAH, AND IT'S GETTING LATE. BESIDES, I'M READY FOR SOME SERIOUS ACTION.
MAN, YOU WON'T BE GETTIN' ACTION MORE SERIOUS THAN WHAT WAS AT THE PARTY!

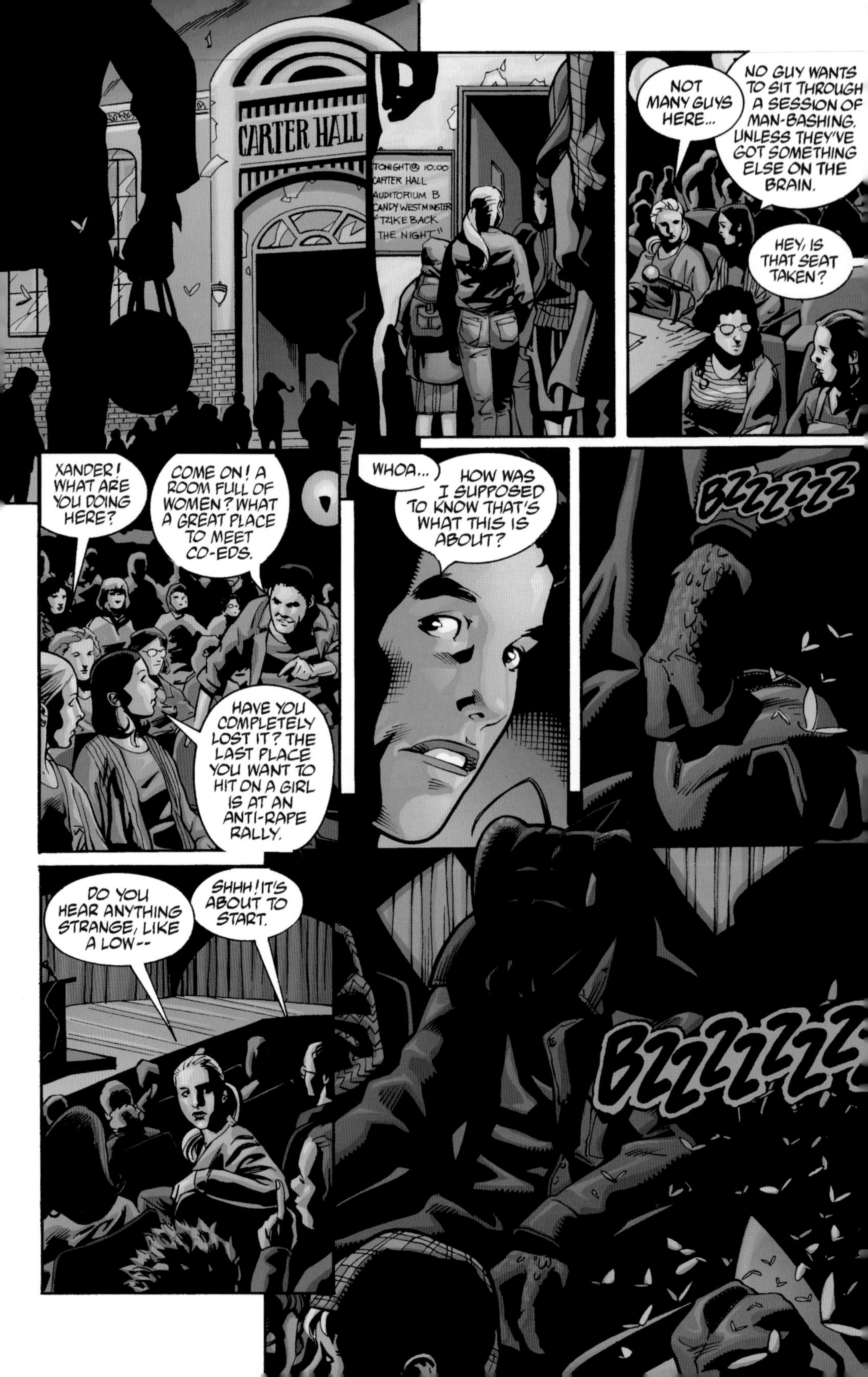
CARTER HALL
TONIGHT@ 10:00 CARTER HALL AUDITORIUM B CANDY WESTMINSTER "TAKE BACK THE NIGHT"
NOT MANY GUYS HERE...
NO GUY WANTS TO SIT THROUGH A SESSION OF MAN-BASHING. UNLESS THEY'VE GOT SOMETHING ELSE ON THE BRAIN.
HEY, IS THAT SEAT TAKEN?
XANDER! WHAT ARE YOU DOING HERE?
COME ON! A ROOM FULL OF WOMEN? WHAT A GREAT PLACE TO MEET CO-EDS.
HAVE YOU COMPLETELY LOST IT? THE LAST PLACE YOU WANT TO HIT ON A GIRL IS AT AN ANTI-RAPE RALLY.
WHOA...
HOW WAS I SUPPOSED TO KNOW THAT'S WHAT THIS IS ABOUT?
BZZZZZZ
DO YOU HEAR ANYTHING STRANGE, LIKE A LOW--
SHHH! IT'S ABOUT TO START.
BZZZZZZ

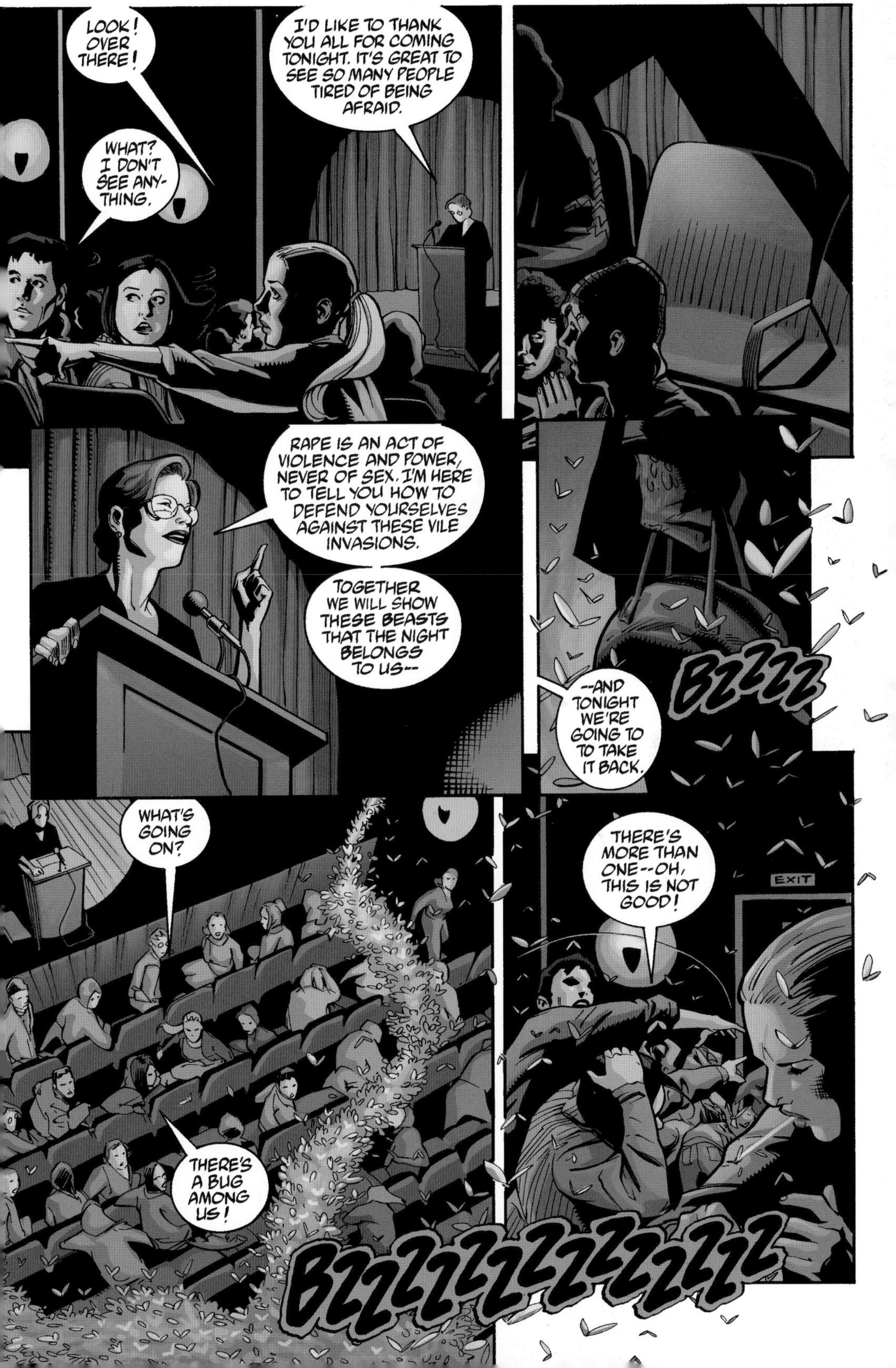
LOOK! OVER THERE!
I'D LIKE TO THANK YOU ALL FOR COMING TONIGHT. IT'S GREAT TO SEE SO MANY PEOPLE TIRED OF BEING AFRAID.
WHAT? I DON'T SEE ANY-THING.
RAPE IS AN ACT OF VIOLENCE AND POWER, NEVER OF SEX. I'M HERE TO TELL YOU HOW TO DEFEND YOURSELVES AGAINST THESE VILE INVASIONS.
TOGETHER WE WILL SHOW THESE BEASTS THAT THE NIGHT BELONGS TO US--
--AND TONIGHT WE'RE GOING TO TO TAKE IT BACK.
BZZZZ
WHAT'S GOING ON?
THERE'S A BUG AMONG US!
THERE'S MORE THAN ONE--OH, THIS IS NOT GOOD!
EXIT
BZZZZZZZZZZZZZ

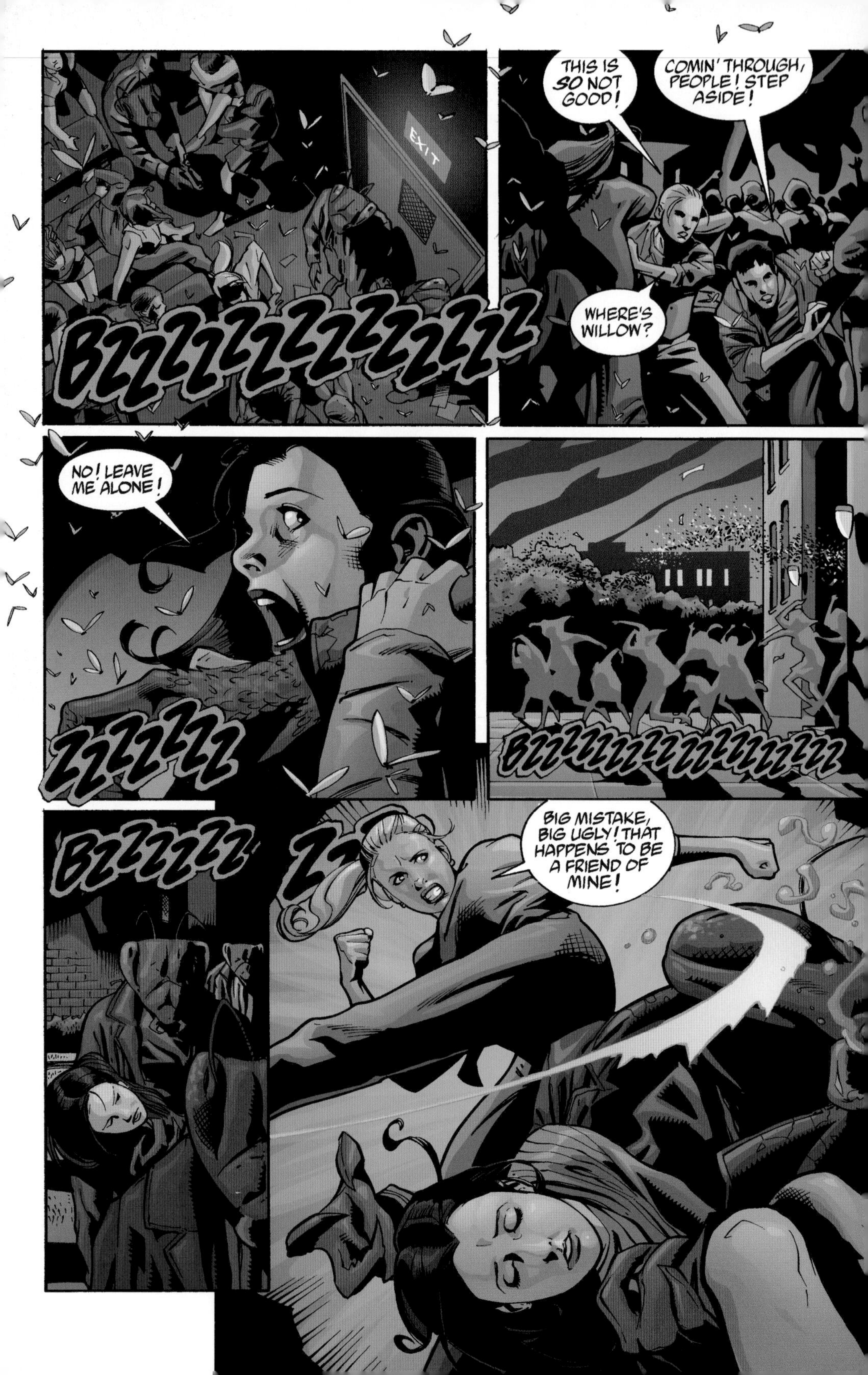
BZZZZZZZZZZZZZZZZ
THIS IS SO NOT GOOD!
COMIN' THROUGH, PEOPLE! STEP ASIDE!
WHERE'S WILLOW?
NO! LEAVE ME ALONE!
ZZZZZZZ
BZZZZZZZZZZZZZZZZZZZZZZ
BZZZZZZZ
BIG MISTAKE, BIG UGLY! THAT HAPPENS TO BE A FRIEND OF MINE!

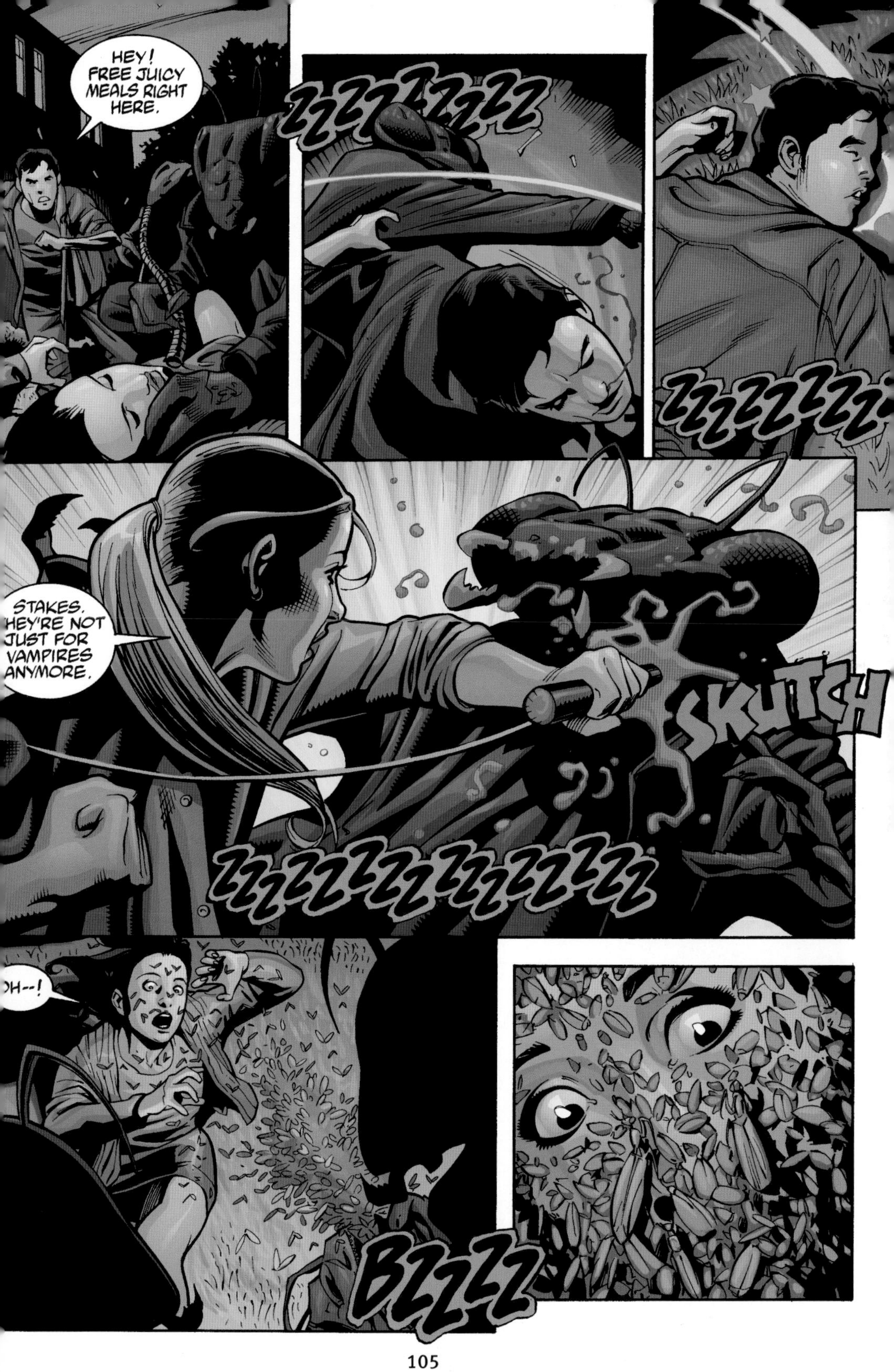
HEY! FREE JUICY MEALS RIGHT HERE.
ZZZZZZZZZZZ
ZZZZZZZZZ
STAKES. HEY'RE NOT JUST FOR VAMPIRES ANYMORE.
SKUTCH
ZZZZZZZZZZZZZZZZZZ
OH--!
BZZZZ

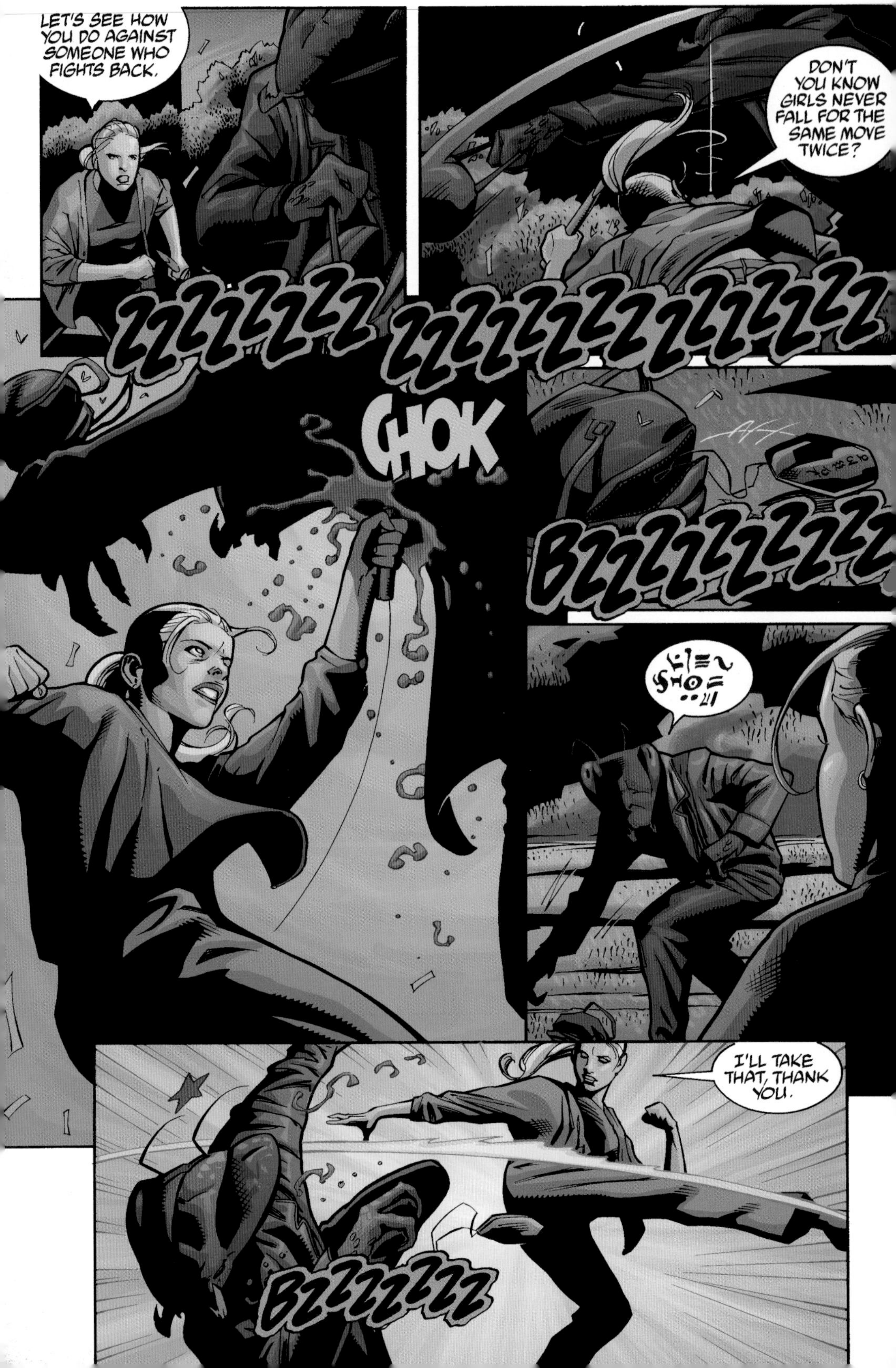

LET'S SEE HOW YOU DO AGAINST SOMEONE WHO FIGHTS BACK.
DON'T YOU KNOW GIRLS NEVER FALL FOR THE SAME MOVE TWICE?
ZZZZZZZZ
ZZZZZZZZZZZZZZZZZZ
CHOK
BZZZZZZZZZ
I'LL TAKE THAT, THANK YOU.
BZZZZZZZ

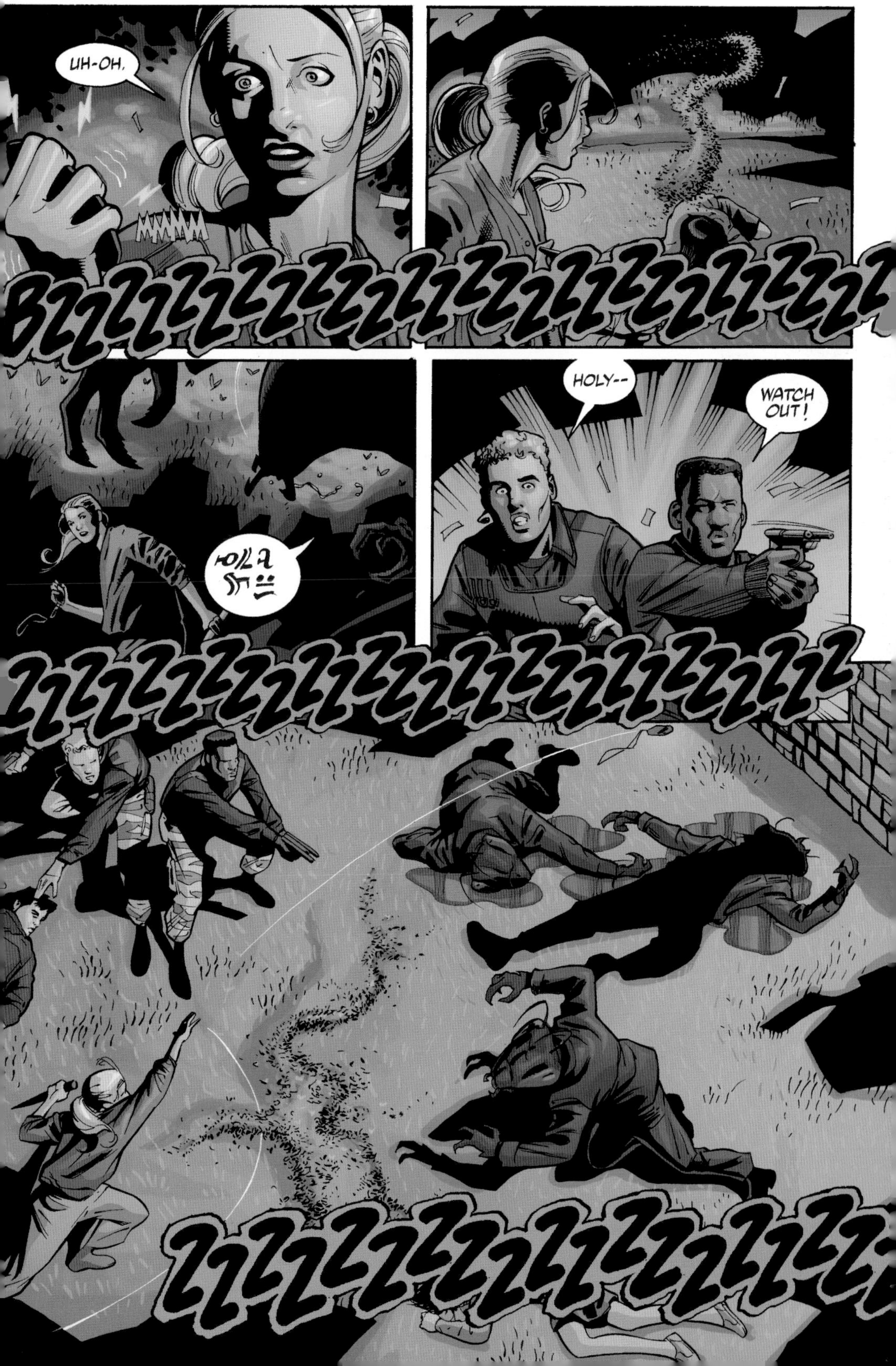
UH-OH.
MMMM
BZZZZZZZZZZZZZZZZZZZ
HOLY--
WATCH OUT!
ZZZZZZZZZZZZZZZZZZZZ
ZZZZZZZZZZZZZZZZZ

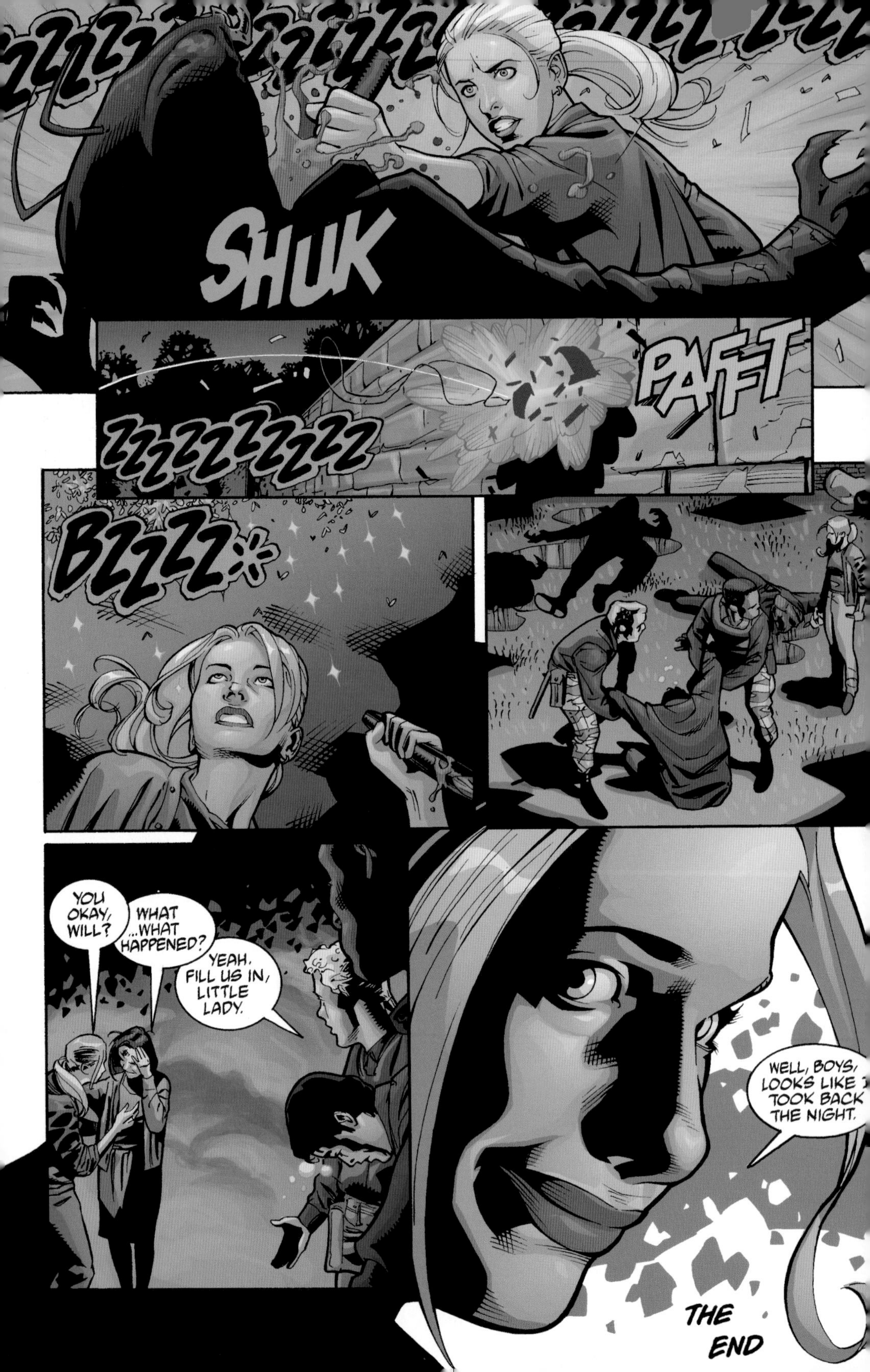
ZZZZZZZZZZZZZZZZZZ
SHUK
PAFFT
ZZZZZZZZZZZ
BZZZZ
YOU OKAY, WILL?
WHAT ...WHAT HAPPENED?
YEAH. FILL US IN, LITTLE LADY.
WELL, BOYS, LOOKS LIKE TOOK BACK THE NIGHT.
THE END

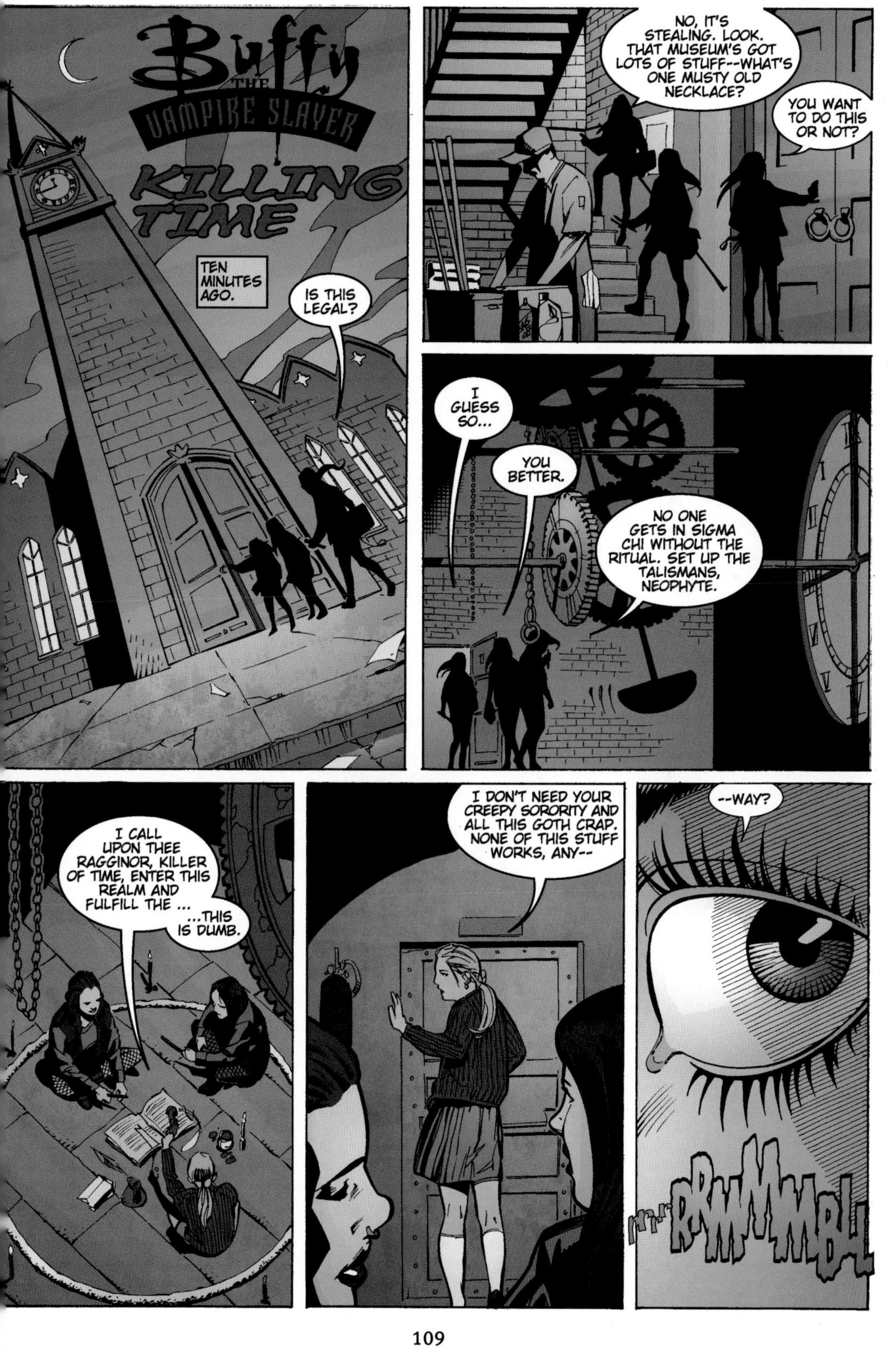
Buffy the Vampire Slayer
KILLING TIME
TEN MINUTES AGO.
IS THIS LEGAL?
NO, IT'S STEALING. LOOK. THAT MUSEUM'S GOT LOTS OF STUFF--WHAT'S ONE MUSTY OLD NECKLACE?
YOU WANT TO DO THIS OR NOT?
I GUESS SO...
YOU BETTER.
NO ONE GETS IN SIGMA CHI WITHOUT THE RITUAL. SET UP THE TALISMANS, NEOPHYTE.
I CALL UPON THEE RAGGINOR, KILLER OF TIME, ENTER THIS REALM AND FULFILL THE ...
...THIS IS DUMB.
I DON'T NEED YOUR CREEPY SORORITY AND ALL THIS GOTH CRAP. NONE OF THIS STUFF WORKS, ANY--
--WAY?
rrrRRMMMBL

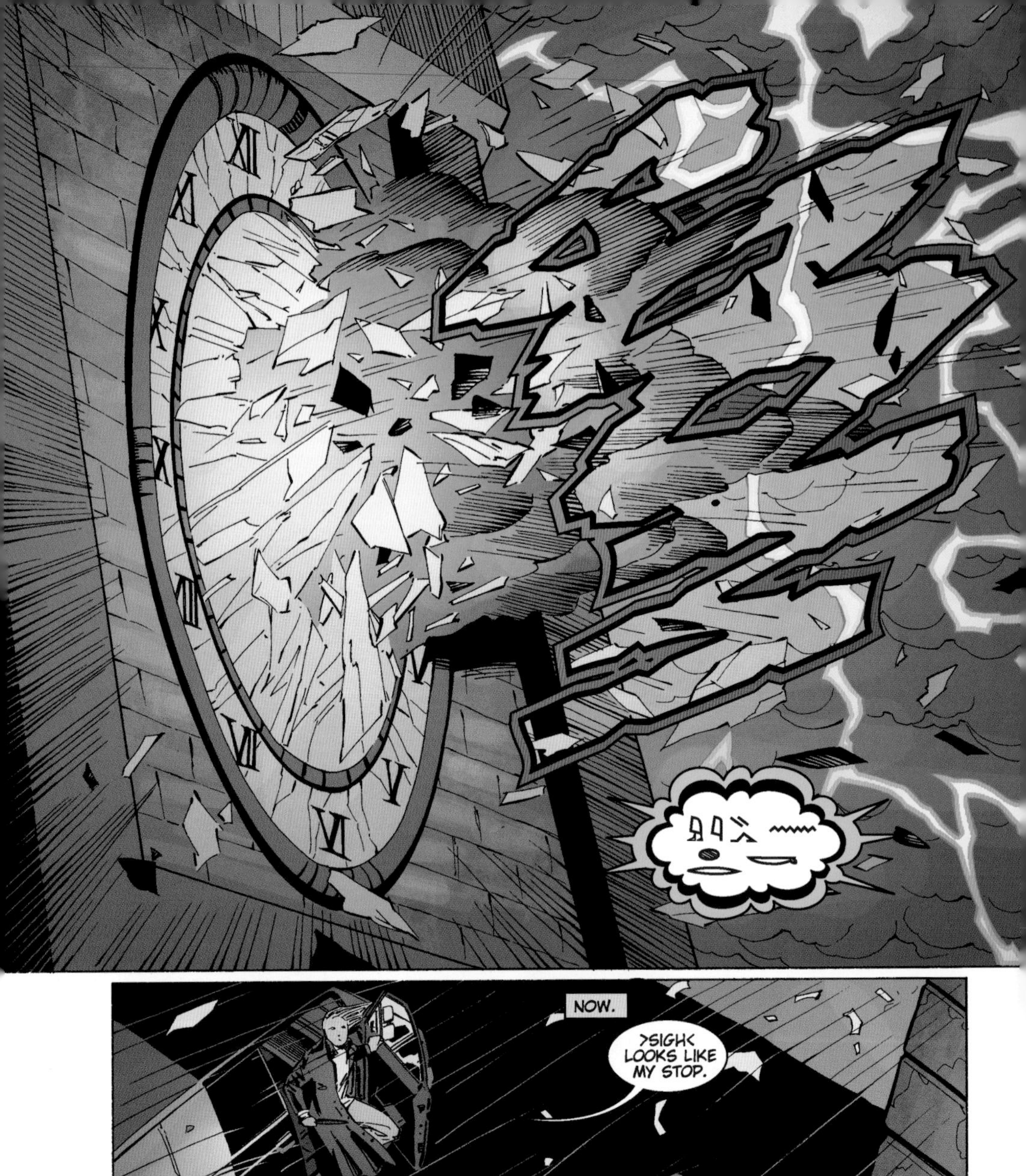

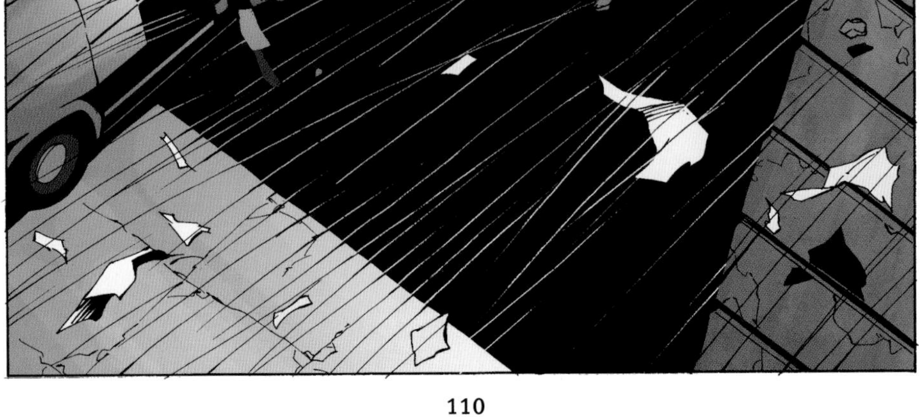
NOW.
>SIGH< LOOKS LIKE MY STOP.

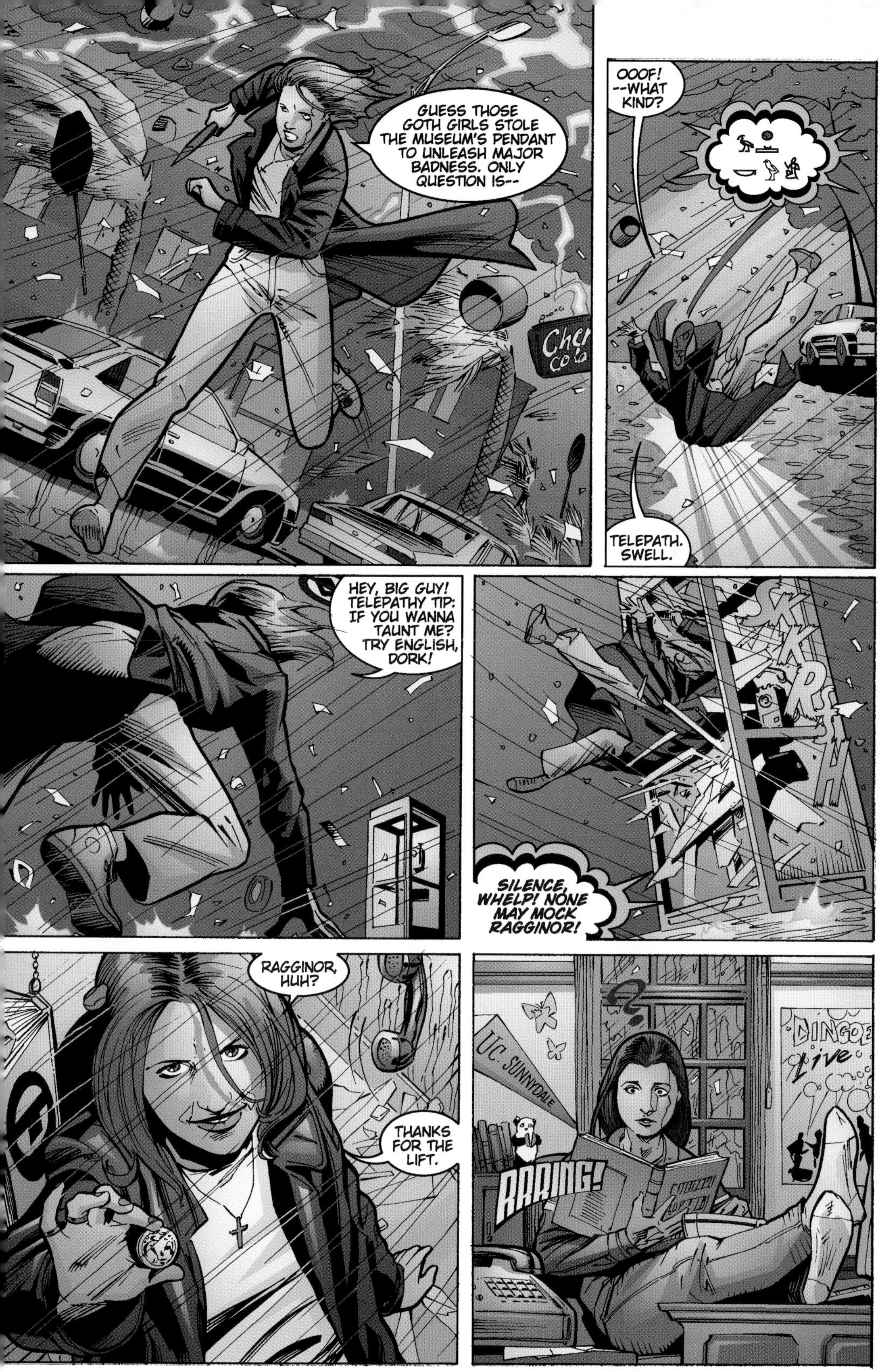
GUESS THOSE GOTH GIRLS STOLE THE MUSEUM'S PENDANT TO UNLEASH MAJOR BADNESS. ONLY QUESTION IS--
OOOF! --WHAT KIND?
TELEPATH. SWELL.
HEY, BIG GUY! TELEPATHY TIP: IF YOU WANNA TAUNT ME? TRY ENGLISH, DORK!
SKRASH
SILENCE, WHELP! NONE MAY MOCK RAGGINOR!
RAGGINOR, HUH?
THANKS FOR THE LIFT.
U.C. SUNNYDALE
DINGOES live
RRRING!

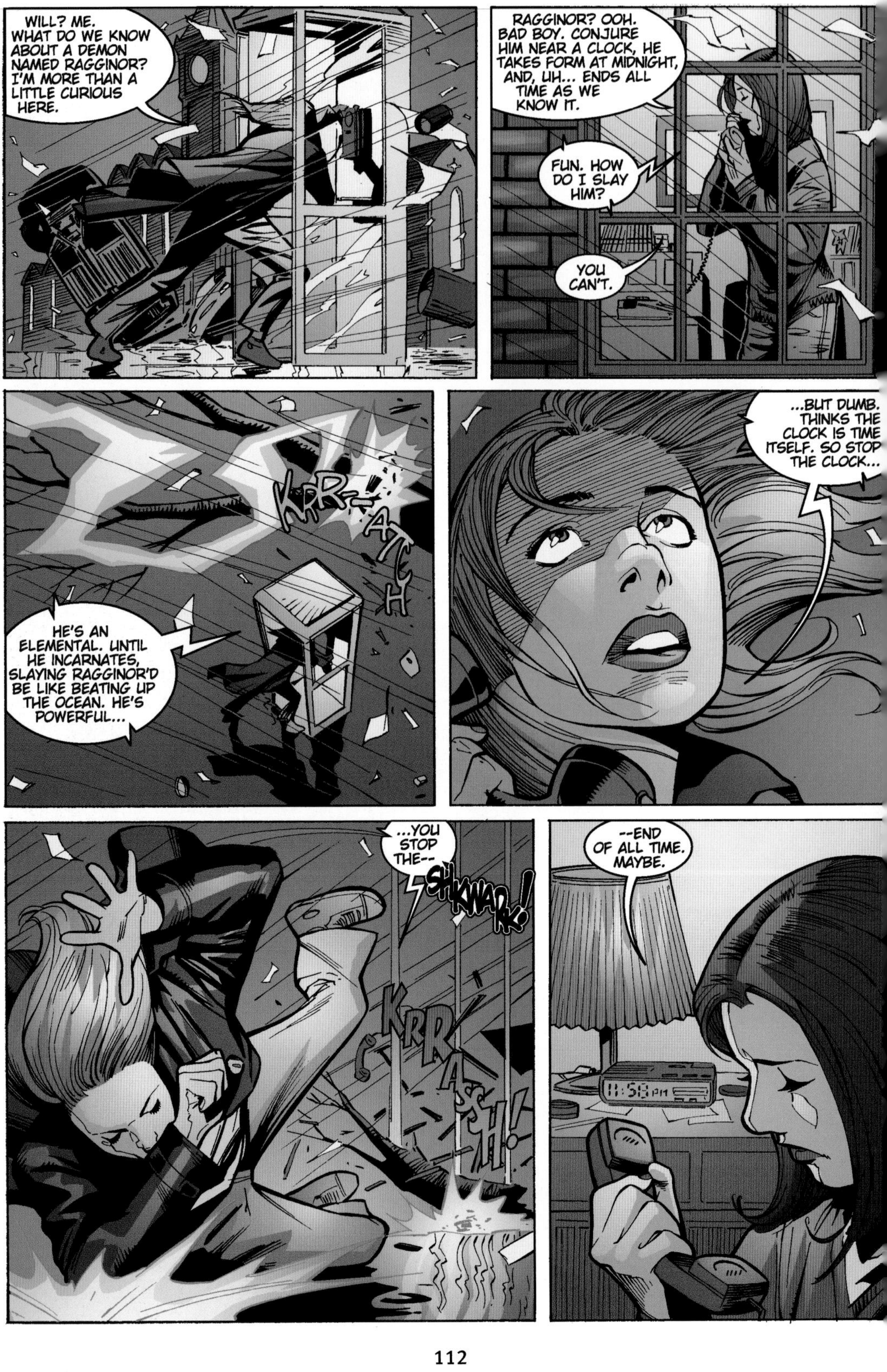
WILL? ME. WHAT DO WE KNOW ABOUT A DEMON NAMED RAGGINOR? I'M MORE THAN A LITTLE CURIOUS HERE.
RAGGINOR? OOH. BAD BOY. CONJURE HIM NEAR A CLOCK, HE TAKES FORM AT MIDNIGHT, AND, UH... ENDS ALL TIME AS WE KNOW IT.
FUN. HOW DO I SLAY HIM?
YOU CAN'T.
KRR--ATCH
HE'S AN ELEMENTAL. UNTIL HE INCARNATES, SLAYING RAGGINOR'D BE LIKE BEATING UP THE OCEAN. HE'S POWERFUL...
...BUT DUMB. THINKS THE CLOCK IS TIME ITSELF. SO STOP THE CLOCK...
...YOU STOP THE--
SHKWARK!
KRRASH!
--END OF ALL TIME. MAYBE.

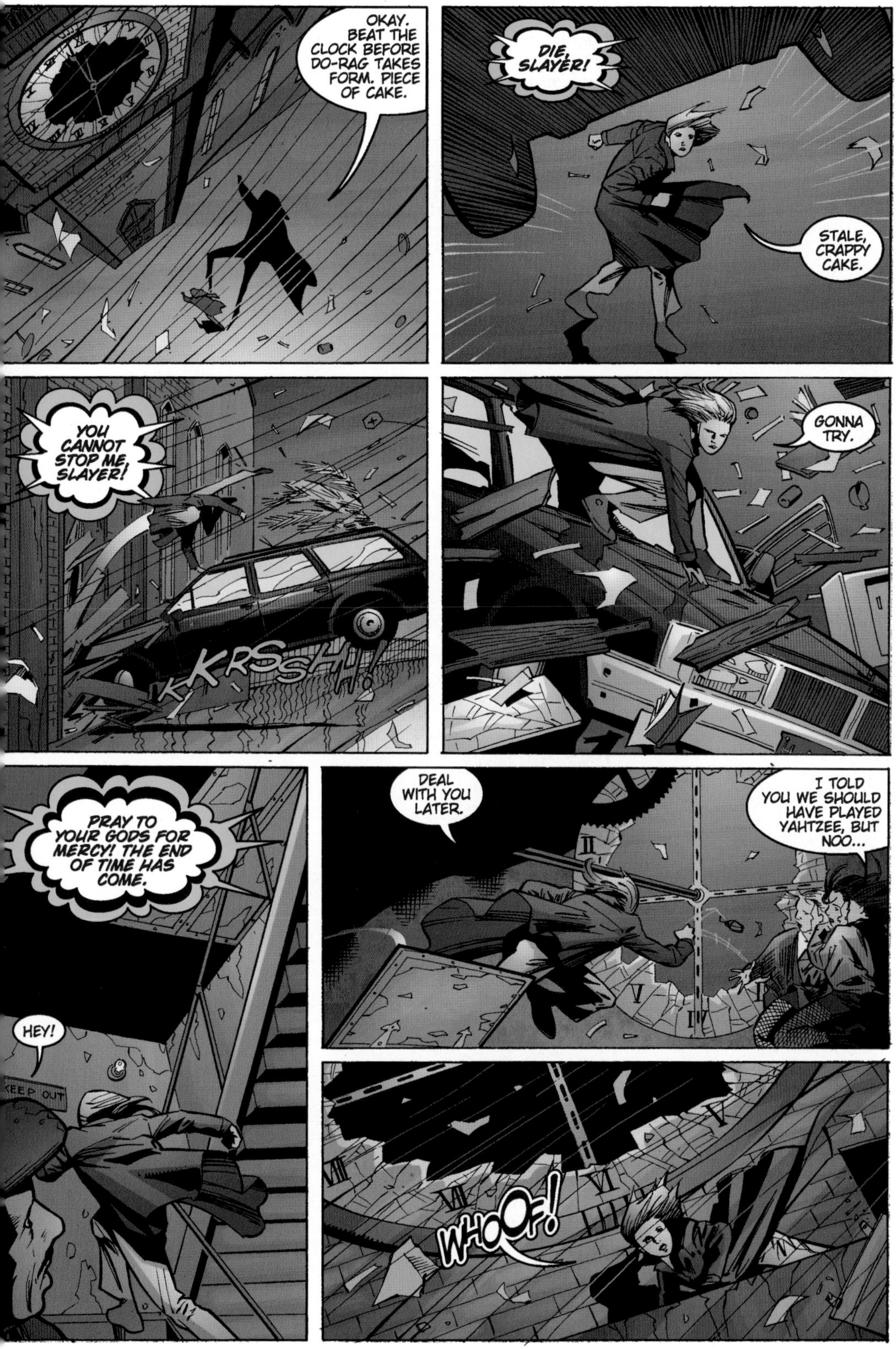
OKAY. BEAT THE CLOCK BEFORE DO-RAG TAKES FORM. PIECE OF CAKE.
DIE, SLAYER!
STALE, CRAPPY CAKE.
YOU CANNOT STOP ME, SLAYER!
KKRSSHH!
GONNA TRY.
PRAY TO YOUR GODS FOR MERCY! THE END OF TIME HAS COME.
HEY!
KEEP OUT
DEAL WITH YOU LATER.
I TOLD YOU WE SHOULD HAVE PLAYED YAHTZEE, BUT NOO...
WHOOF!

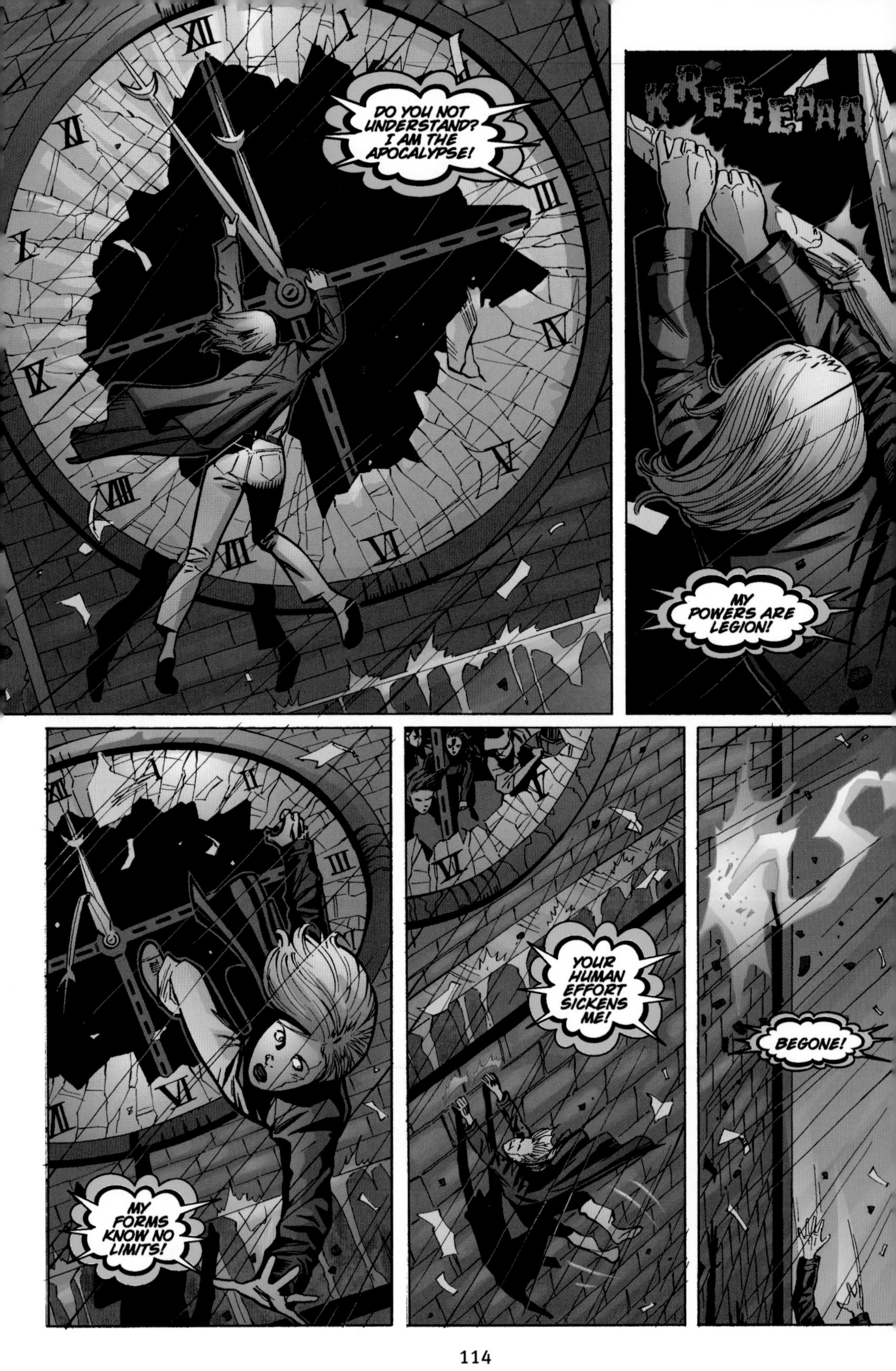
DO YOU NOT UNDERSTAND? I AM THE APOCALYPSE!
KREEEEAAA
MY POWERS ARE LEGION!
MY FORMS KNOW NO LIMITS!
YOUR HUMAN EFFORT SICKENS ME!
BEGONE!

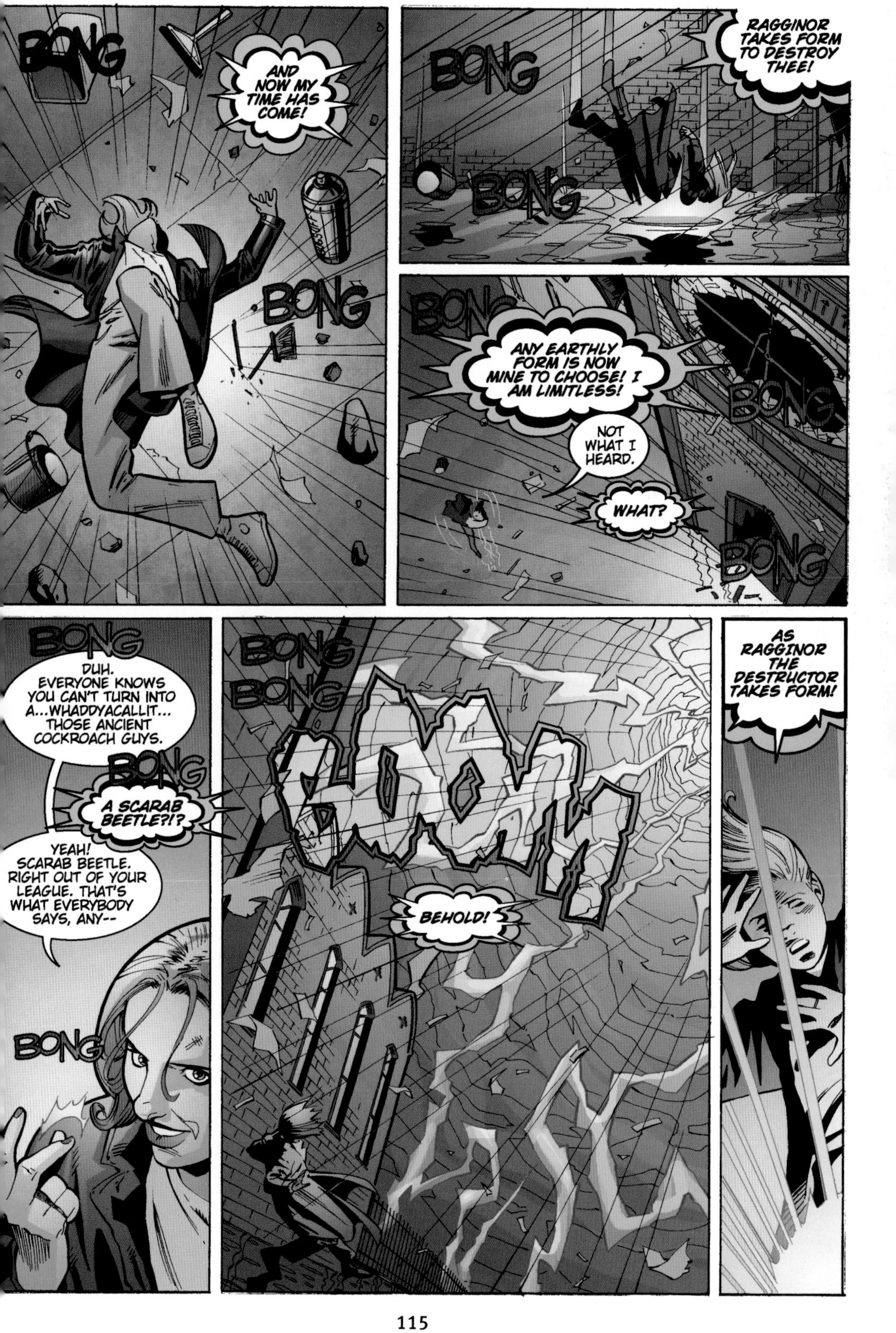
BONG
AND NOW MY TIME HAS COME!
BONG
BONG
BONG
BONG
RAGGINOR TAKES FORM TO DESTROY THEE!
BONG
ANY EARTHLY FORM IS NOW MINE TO CHOOSE! I AM LIMITLESS!
BONG
NOT WHAT I HEARD.
WHAT?
BONG
BONG
DUH. EVERYONE KNOWS YOU CAN'T TURN INTO A...WHADDYACALLIT... THOSE ANCIENT COCKROACH GUYS.
BONG
A SCARAB BEETLE?!?
YEAH! SCARAB BEETLE. RIGHT OUT OF YOUR LEAGUE. THAT'S WHAT EVERYBODY SAYS, ANY--
BONG
BONG
BONG
BOOM
BEHOLD!
AS RAGGINOR THE DESTRUCTOR TAKES FORM!

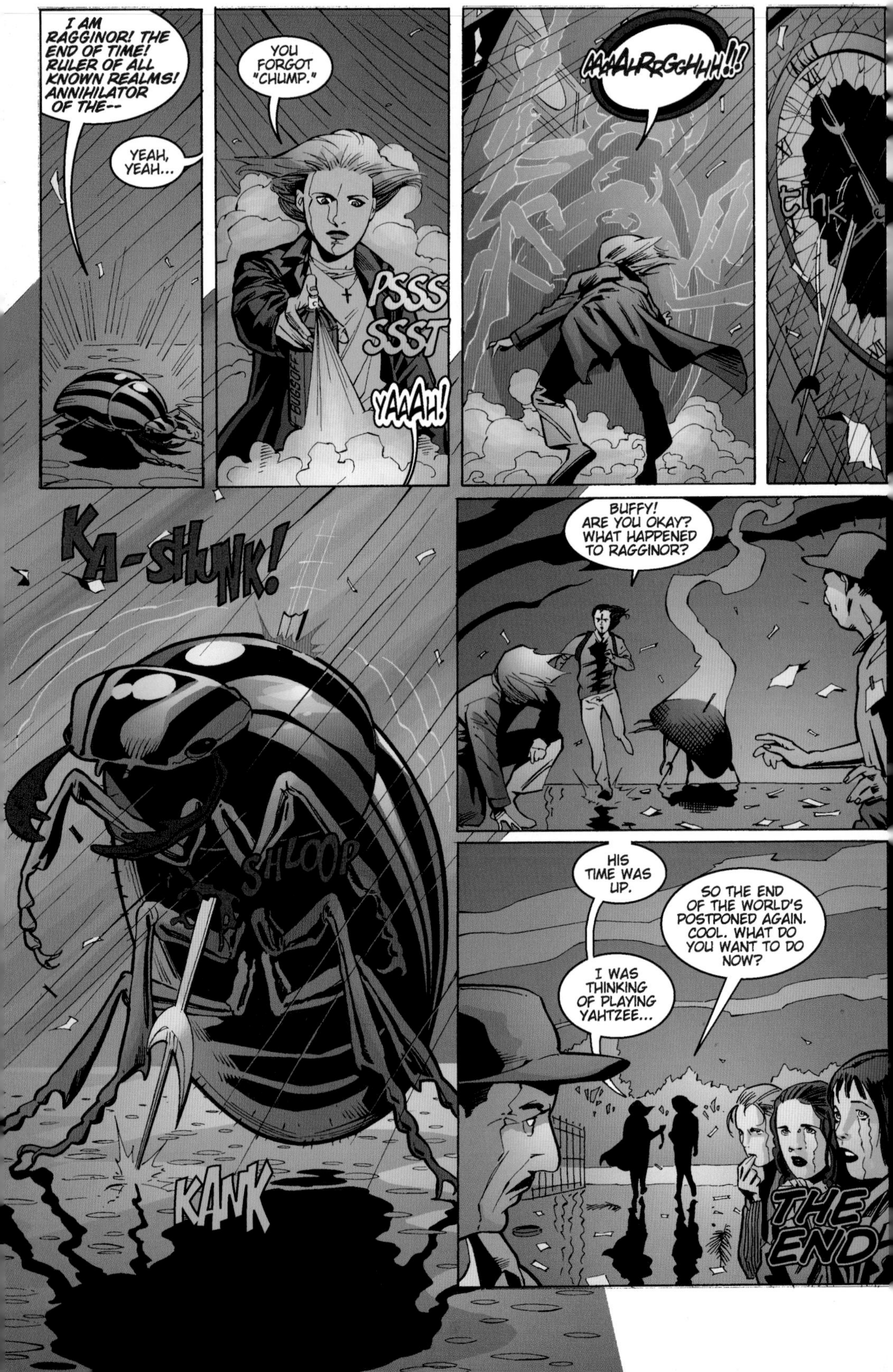
I AM RAGGINOR! THE END OF TIME! RULER OF ALL KNOWN REALMS! ANNIHILATOR OF THE--
YEAH, YEAH...
YOU FORGOT "CHUMP."
PSSSSSST
YAAAH!
BUGSOFF
AAAAHRRGGHHH!!!
tink
KA-SHUNK!
SHLOOP
KANK
BUFFY! ARE YOU OKAY? WHAT HAPPENED TO RAGGINOR?
HIS TIME WAS UP.
SO THE END OF THE WORLD'S POSTPONED AGAIN. COOL. WHAT DO YOU WANT TO DO NOW?
I WAS THINKING OF PLAYING YAHTZEE...
THE END

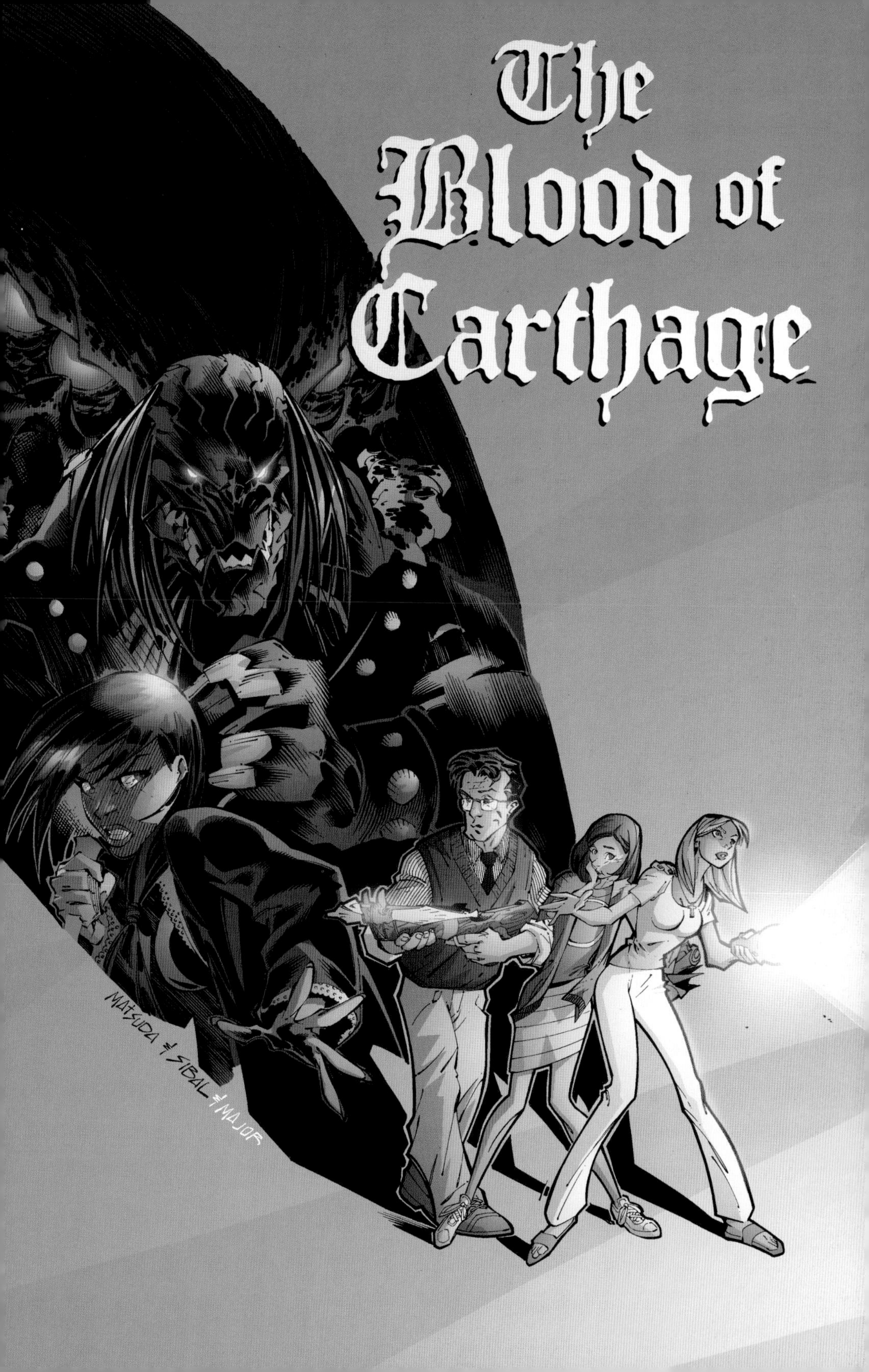
The Blood of Carthage
MATSUDA & SIBAL & MAJOR

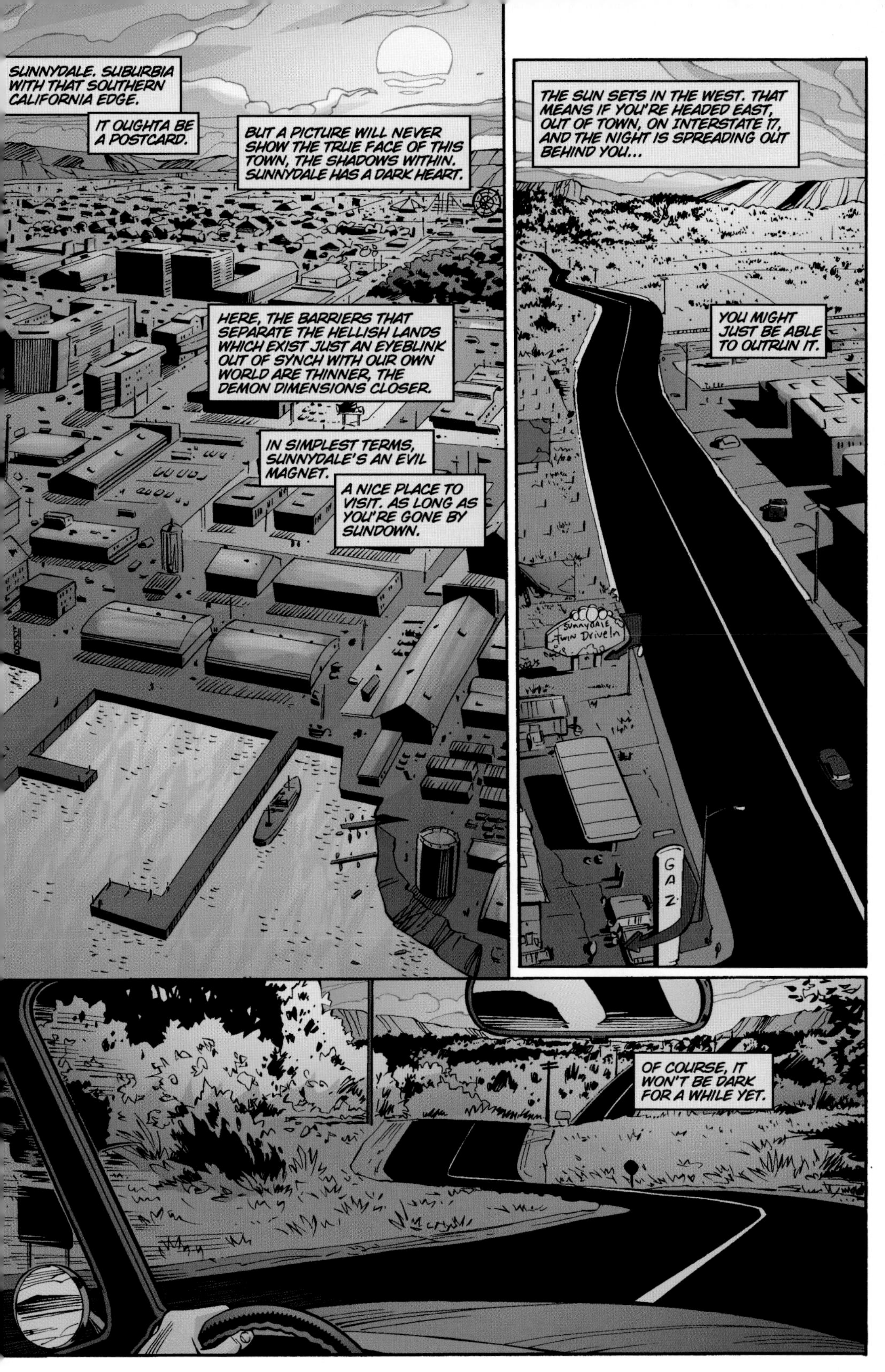
SUNNYDALE. SUBURBIA WITH THAT SOUTHERN CALIFORNIA EDGE.
IT OUGHTA BE A POSTCARD.
BUT A PICTURE WILL NEVER SHOW THE TRUE FACE OF THIS TOWN, THE SHADOWS WITHIN. SUNNYDALE HAS A DARK HEART.
HERE, THE BARRIERS THAT SEPARATE THE HELLISH LANDS WHICH EXIST JUST AN EYEBLINK OUT OF SYNCH WITH OUR OWN WORLD ARE THINNER, THE DEMON DIMENSIONS CLOSER.
IN SIMPLEST TERMS, SUNNYDALE'S AN EVIL MAGNET.
A NICE PLACE TO VISIT. AS LONG AS YOU'RE GONE BY SUNDOWN.
THE SUN SETS IN THE WEST. THAT MEANS IF YOU'RE HEADED EAST, OUT OF TOWN, ON INTERSTATE 17, AND THE NIGHT IS SPREADING OUT BEHIND YOU...
YOU MIGHT JUST BE ABLE TO OUTRUN IT.
SUNNYDALE Twin DriveIn
GAZ
OF COURSE, IT WON'T BE DARK FOR A WHILE YET.

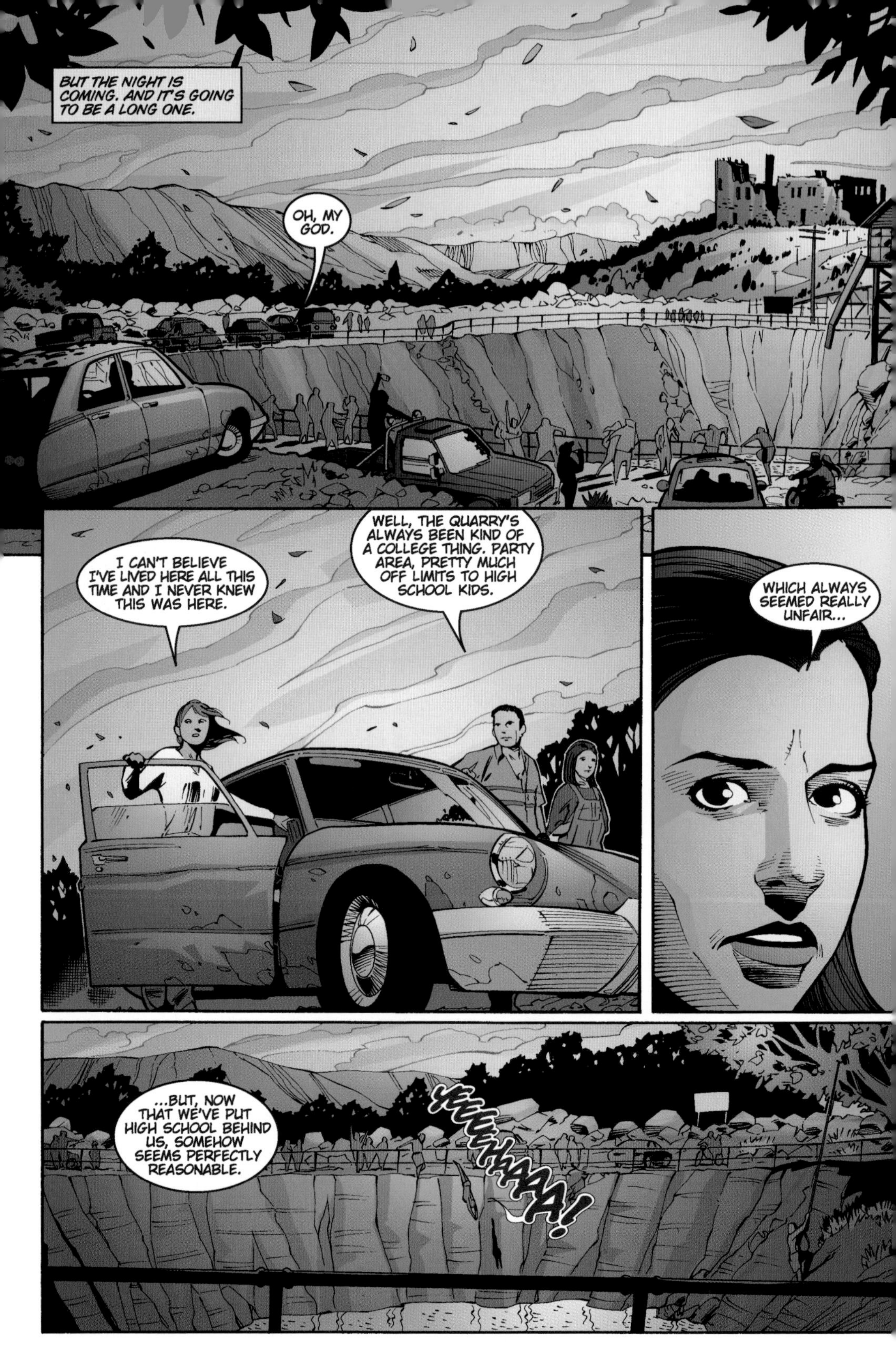
BUT THE NIGHT IS COMING. AND IT'S GOING TO BE A LONG ONE.
OH, MY GOD.
I CAN'T BELIEVE I'VE LIVED HERE ALL THIS TIME AND I NEVER KNEW THIS WAS HERE.
WELL, THE QUARRY'S ALWAYS BEEN KIND OF A COLLEGE THING. PARTY AREA, PRETTY MUCH OFF LIMITS TO HIGH SCHOOL KIDS.
WHICH ALWAYS SEEMED REALLY UNFAIR...
...BUT, NOW THAT WE'VE PUT HIGH SCHOOL BEHIND US, SOMEHOW SEEMS PERFECTLY REASONABLE.
YEEEEHAAAA!

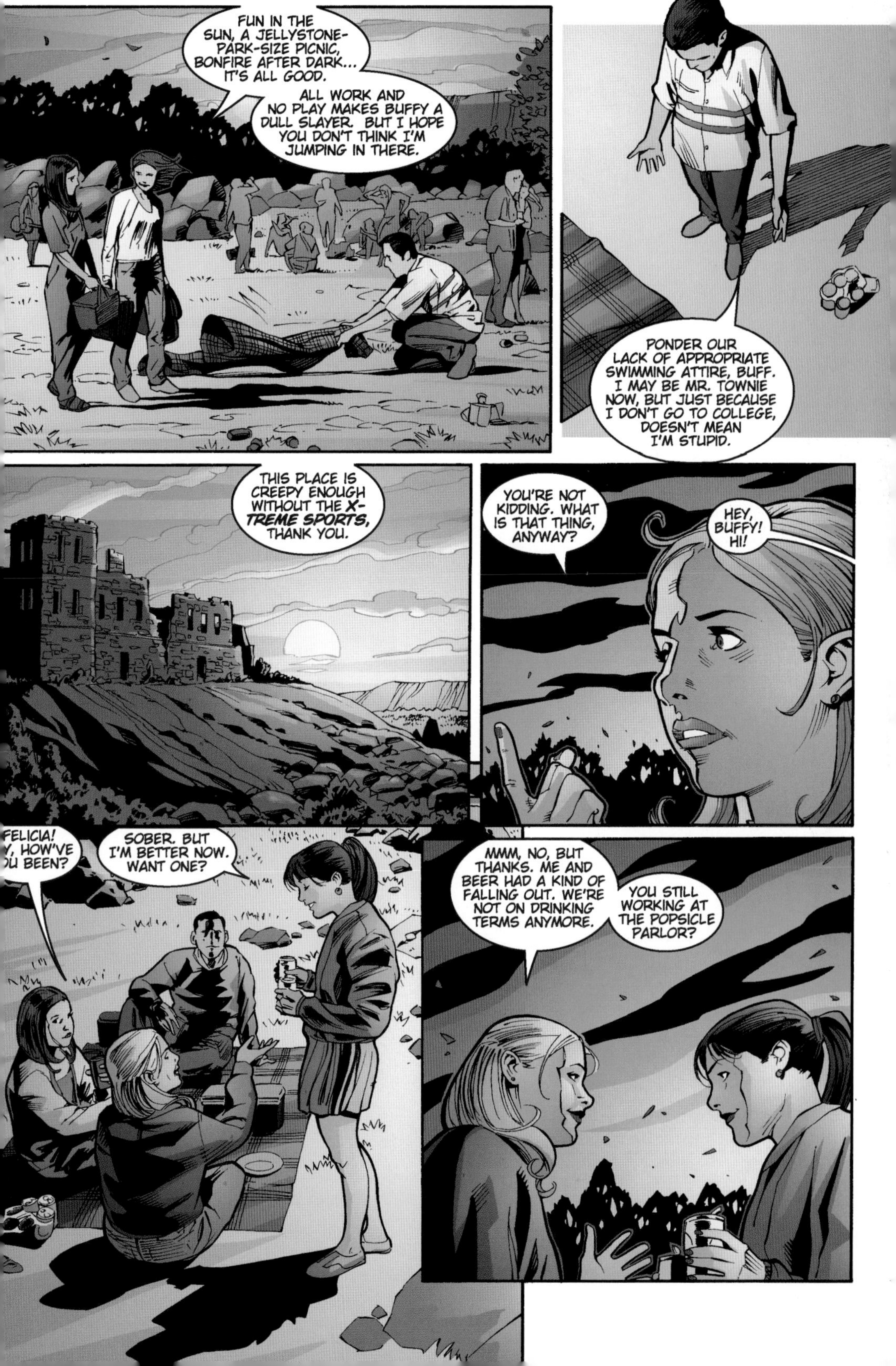
FUN IN THE SUN, A JELLYSTONE-PARK-SIZE PICNIC, BONFIRE AFTER DARK... IT'S ALL GOOD.
ALL WORK AND NO PLAY MAKES BUFFY A DULL SLAYER. BUT I HOPE YOU DON'T THINK I'M JUMPING IN THERE.
PONDER OUR LACK OF APPROPRIATE SWIMMING ATTIRE, BUFF. I MAY BE MR. TOWNIE NOW, BUT JUST BECAUSE I DON'T GO TO COLLEGE, DOESN'T MEAN I'M STUPID.
THIS PLACE IS CREEPY ENOUGH WITHOUT THE X-TREME SPORTS, THANK YOU.
YOU'RE NOT KIDDING. WHAT IS THAT THING, ANYWAY?
HEY, BUFFY! HI!
FELICIA! HOW'VE YOU BEEN?
SOBER. BUT I'M BETTER NOW. WANT ONE?
MMM, NO, BUT THANKS. ME AND BEER HAD A KIND OF FALLING OUT. WE'RE NOT ON DRINKING TERMS ANYMORE.
YOU STILL WORKING AT THE POPSICLE PARLOR?

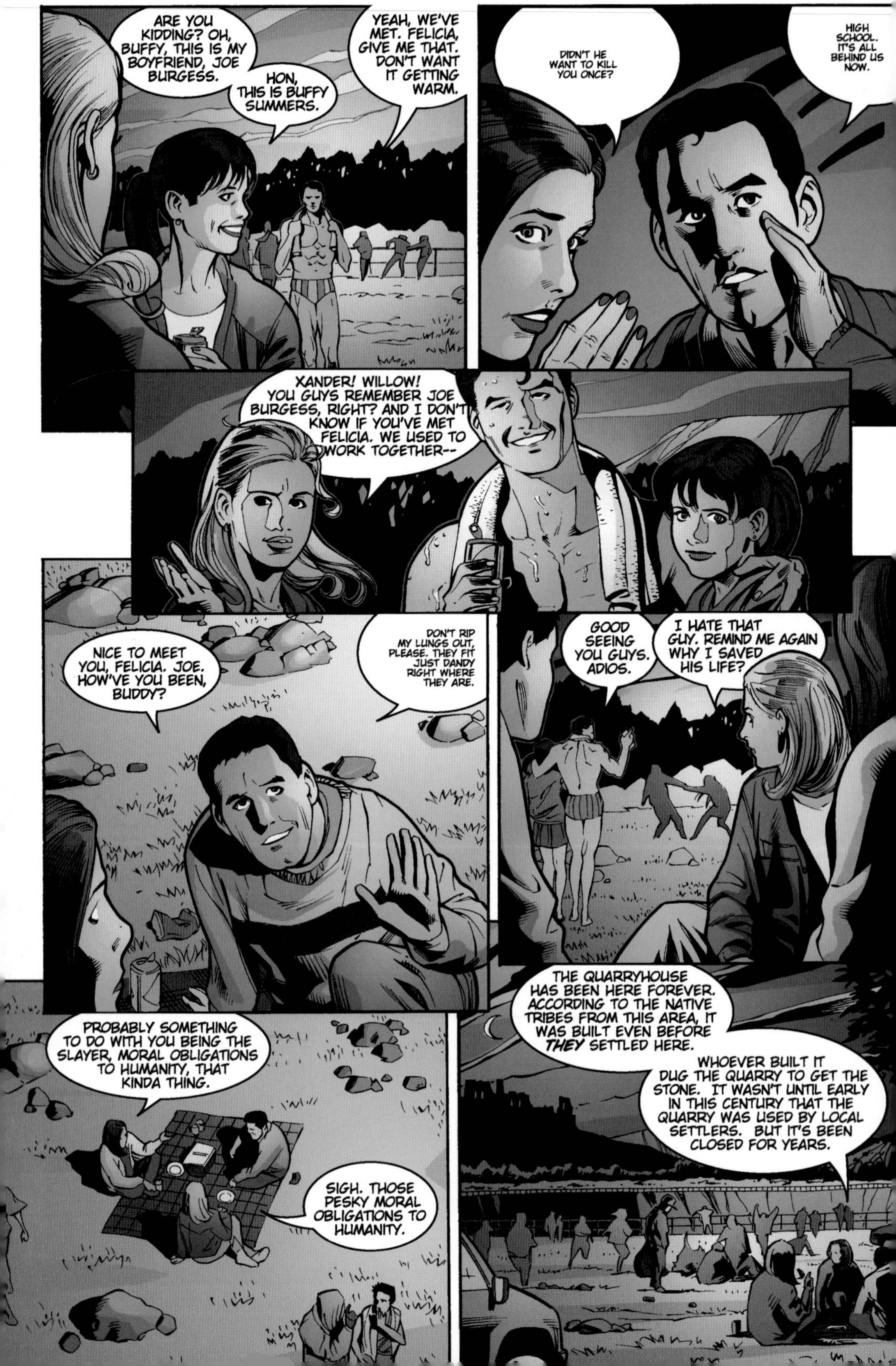
ARE YOU KIDDING? OH, BUFFY, THIS IS MY BOYFRIEND, JOE BURGESS.
HON, THIS IS BUFFY SUMMERS.
YEAH, WE'VE MET. FELICIA, GIVE ME THAT. DON'T WANT IT GETTING WARM.
DIDN'T HE WANT TO KILL YOU ONCE?
HIGH SCHOOL. IT'S ALL BEHIND US NOW.
XANDER! WILLOW! YOU GUYS REMEMBER JOE BURGESS, RIGHT? AND I DON'T KNOW IF YOU'VE MET FELICIA. WE USED TO WORK TOGETHER--
NICE TO MEET YOU, FELICIA. JOE. HOW'VE YOU BEEN, BUDDY?
DON'T RIP MY LUNGS OUT, PLEASE. THEY FIT JUST DANDY RIGHT WHERE THEY ARE.
GOOD SEEING YOU GUYS. ADIOS.
I HATE THAT GUY. REMIND ME AGAIN WHY I SAVED HIS LIFE?
PROBABLY SOMETHING TO DO WITH YOU BEING THE SLAYER, MORAL OBLIGATIONS TO HUMANITY, THAT KINDA THING.
SIGH. THOSE PESKY MORAL OBLIGATIONS TO HUMANITY.
THE QUARRYHOUSE HAS BEEN HERE FOREVER. ACCORDING TO THE NATIVE TRIBES FROM THIS AREA, IT WAS BUILT EVEN BEFORE *THEY* SETTLED HERE.
WHOEVER BUILT IT DUG THE QUARRY TO GET THE STONE. IT WASN'T UNTIL EARLY IN THIS CENTURY THAT THE QUARRY WAS USED BY LOCAL SETTLERS. BUT IT'S BEEN CLOSED FOR YEARS.

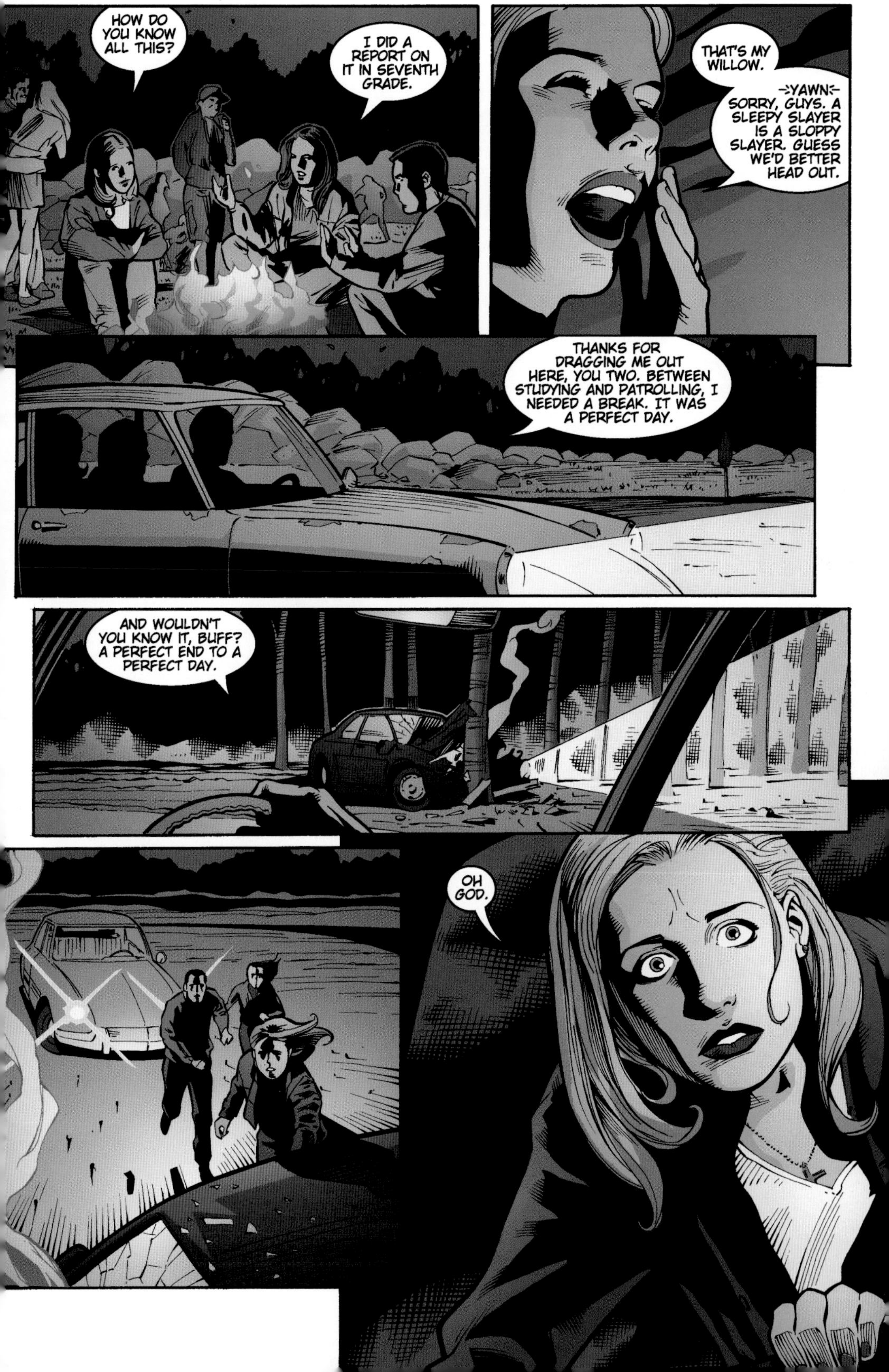
HOW DO YOU KNOW ALL THIS?
I DID A REPORT ON IT IN SEVENTH GRADE.
THAT'S MY WILLOW.
-YAWN-
SORRY, GUYS. A SLEEPY SLAYER IS A SLOPPY SLAYER. GUESS WE'D BETTER HEAD OUT.
THANKS FOR DRAGGING ME OUT HERE, YOU TWO. BETWEEN STUDYING AND PATROLLING, I NEEDED A BREAK. IT WAS A PERFECT DAY.
AND WOULDN'T YOU KNOW IT, BUFF? A PERFECT END TO A PERFECT DAY.
OH GOD.

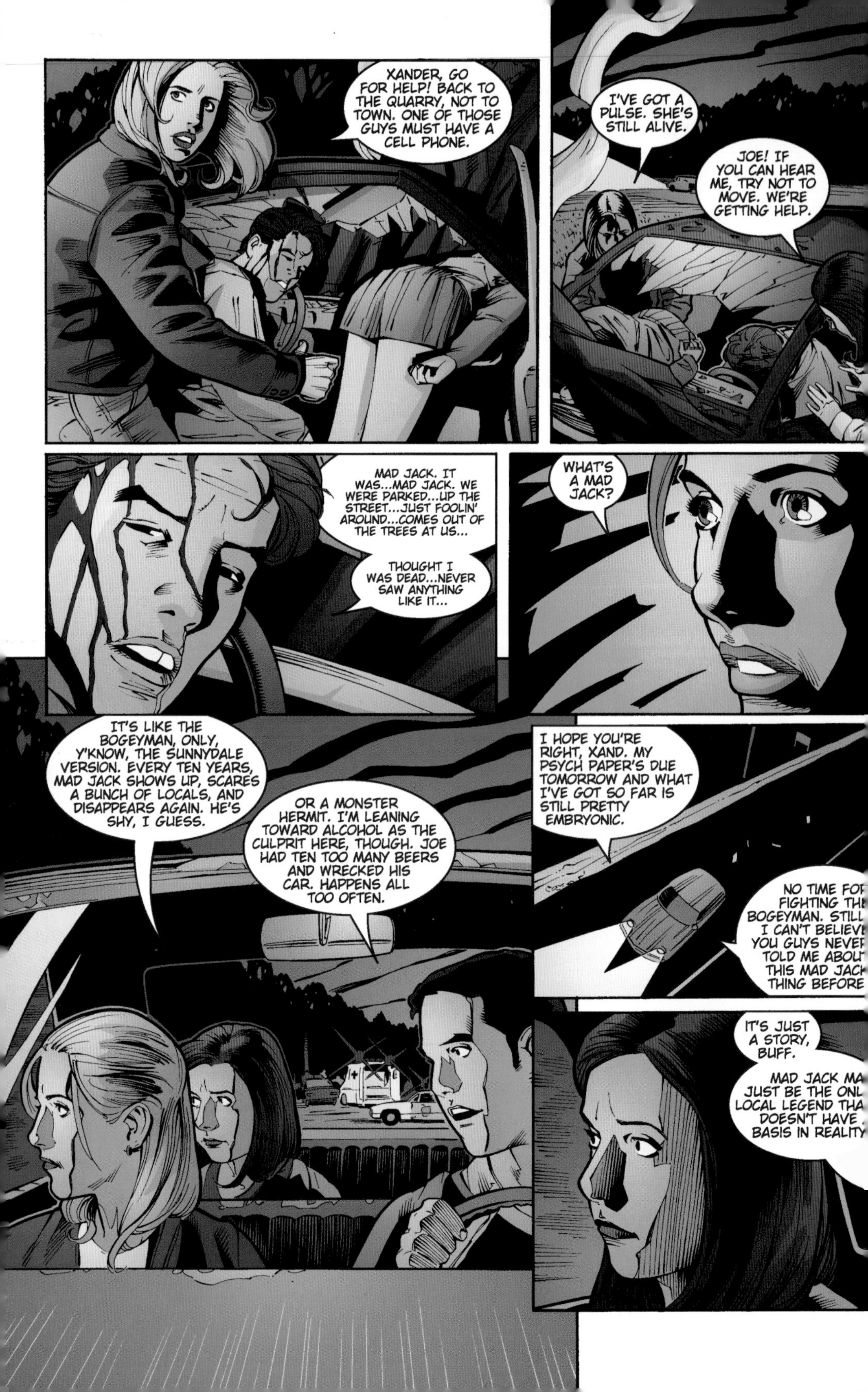

XANDER, GO FOR HELP! BACK TO THE QUARRY, NOT TO TOWN. ONE OF THOSE GUYS MUST HAVE A CELL PHONE.
I'VE GOT A PULSE. SHE'S STILL ALIVE.
JOE! IF YOU CAN HEAR ME, TRY NOT TO MOVE. WE'RE GETTING HELP.
MAD JACK. IT WAS...MAD JACK. WE WERE PARKED...UP THE STREET...JUST FOOLIN' AROUND...COMES OUT OF THE TREES AT US...
THOUGHT I WAS DEAD...NEVER SAW ANYTHING LIKE IT...
WHAT'S A MAD JACK?
IT'S LIKE THE BOGEYMAN, ONLY, Y'KNOW, THE SUNNYDALE VERSION. EVERY TEN YEARS, MAD JACK SHOWS UP, SCARES A BUNCH OF LOCALS, AND DISAPPEARS AGAIN. HE'S SHY, I GUESS.
OR A MONSTER HERMIT. I'M LEANING TOWARD ALCOHOL AS THE CULPRIT HERE, THOUGH. JOE HAD TEN TOO MANY BEERS AND WRECKED HIS CAR. HAPPENS ALL TOO OFTEN.
I HOPE YOU'RE RIGHT, XAND. MY PSYCH PAPER'S DUE TOMORROW AND WHAT I'VE GOT SO FAR IS STILL PRETTY EMBRYONIC.
IT'S JUST A STORY, BUFF.

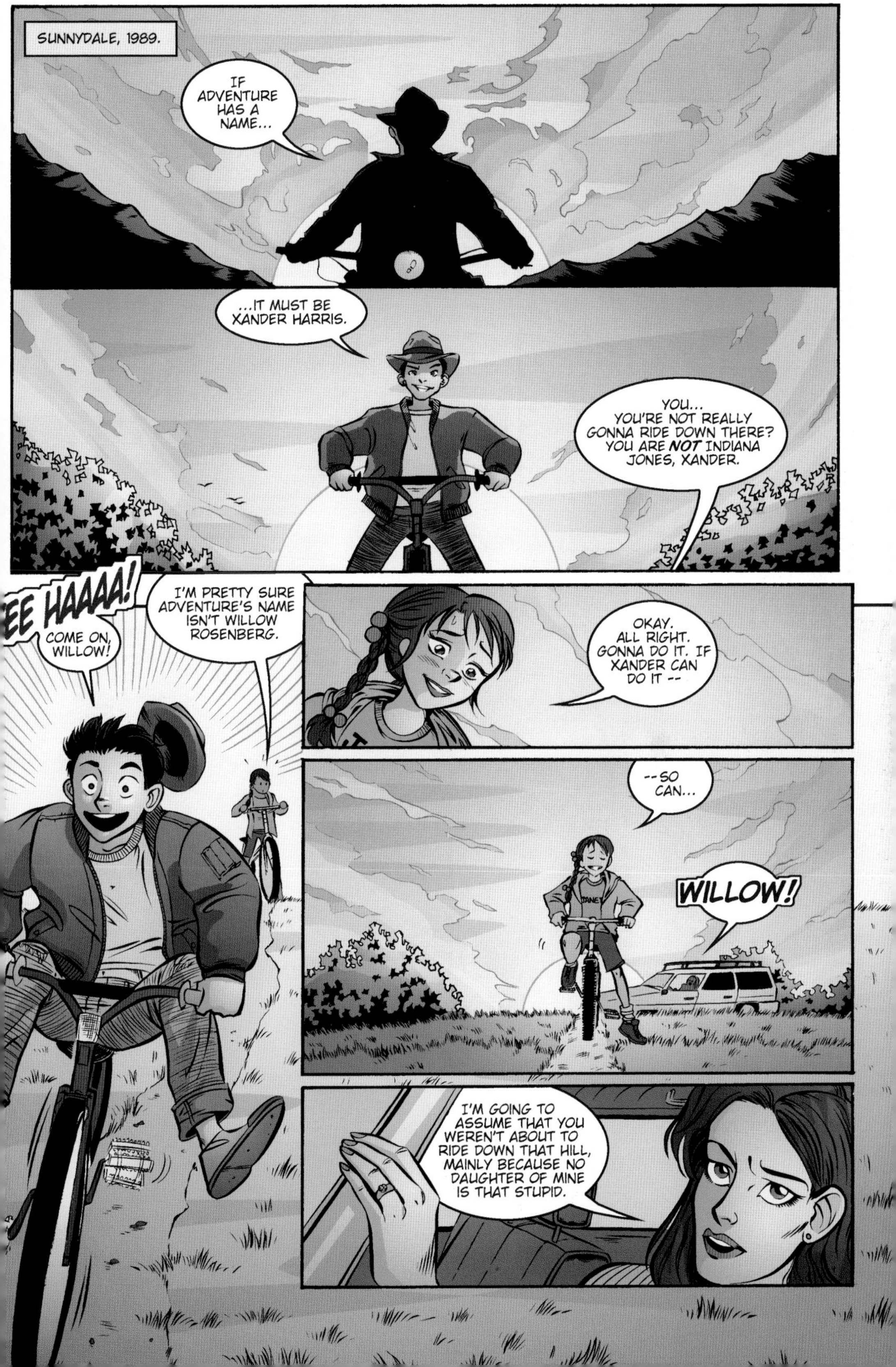
SUNNYDALE, 1989.
IF ADVENTURE HAS A NAME...
...IT MUST BE XANDER HARRIS.
YOU... YOU'RE NOT REALLY GONNA RIDE DOWN THERE? YOU ARE NOT INDIANA JONES, XANDER.
EE HAAAA!
COME ON, WILLOW!
I'M PRETTY SURE ADVENTURE'S NAME ISN'T WILLOW ROSENBERG.
OKAY. ALL RIGHT. GONNA DO IT. IF XANDER CAN DO IT --
--SO CAN...
WILLOW!
I'M GOING TO ASSUME THAT YOU WEREN'T ABOUT TO RIDE DOWN THAT HILL, MAINLY BECAUSE NO DAUGHTER OF MINE IS THAT STUPID.

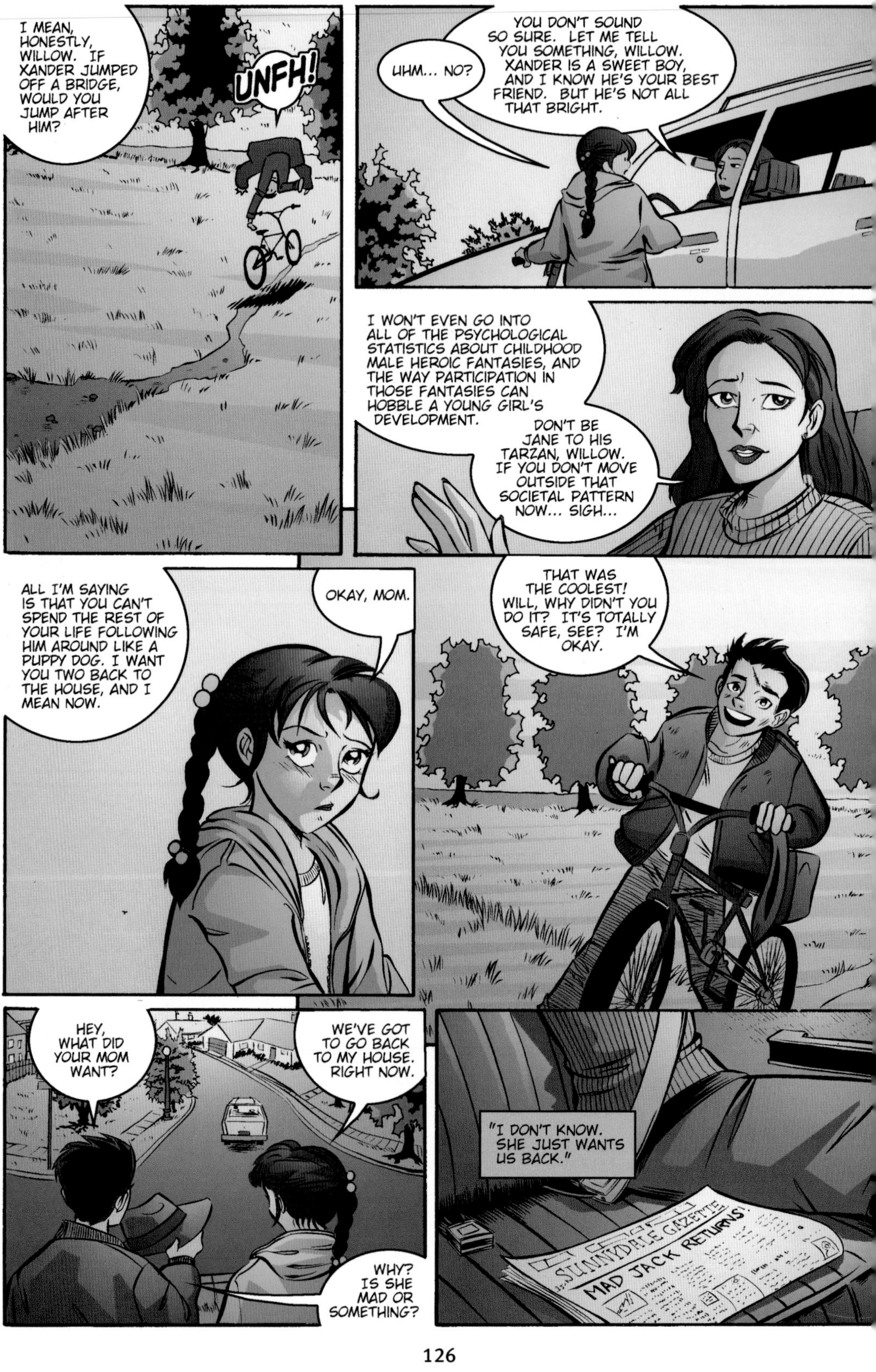
I MEAN, HONESTLY, WILLOW. IF XANDER JUMPED OFF A BRIDGE, WOULD YOU JUMP AFTER HIM?
UNFH!
UHM... NO?
YOU DON'T SOUND SO SURE. LET ME TELL YOU SOMETHING, WILLOW. XANDER IS A SWEET BOY, AND I KNOW HE'S YOUR BEST FRIEND. BUT HE'S NOT ALL THAT BRIGHT.
I WON'T EVEN GO INTO ALL OF THE PSYCHOLOGICAL STATISTICS ABOUT CHILDHOOD MALE HEROIC FANTASIES, AND THE WAY PARTICIPATION IN THOSE FANTASIES CAN HOBBLE A YOUNG GIRL'S DEVELOPMENT.
DON'T BE JANE TO HIS TARZAN, WILLOW. IF YOU DON'T MOVE OUTSIDE THAT SOCIETAL PATTERN NOW... SIGH...
ALL I'M SAYING IS THAT YOU CAN'T SPEND THE REST OF YOUR LIFE FOLLOWING HIM AROUND LIKE A PUPPY DOG. I WANT YOU TWO BACK TO THE HOUSE, AND I MEAN NOW.
OKAY, MOM.
THAT WAS THE COOLEST! WILL, WHY DIDN'T YOU DO IT? IT'S TOTALLY SAFE, SEE? I'M OKAY.
HEY, WHAT DID YOUR MOM WANT?
WE'VE GOT TO GO BACK TO MY HOUSE. RIGHT NOW.
WHY? IS SHE MAD OR SOMETHING?
"I DON'T KNOW. SHE JUST WANTS US BACK."
SUNNYDALE GAZETTE
MAD JACK RETURNS!

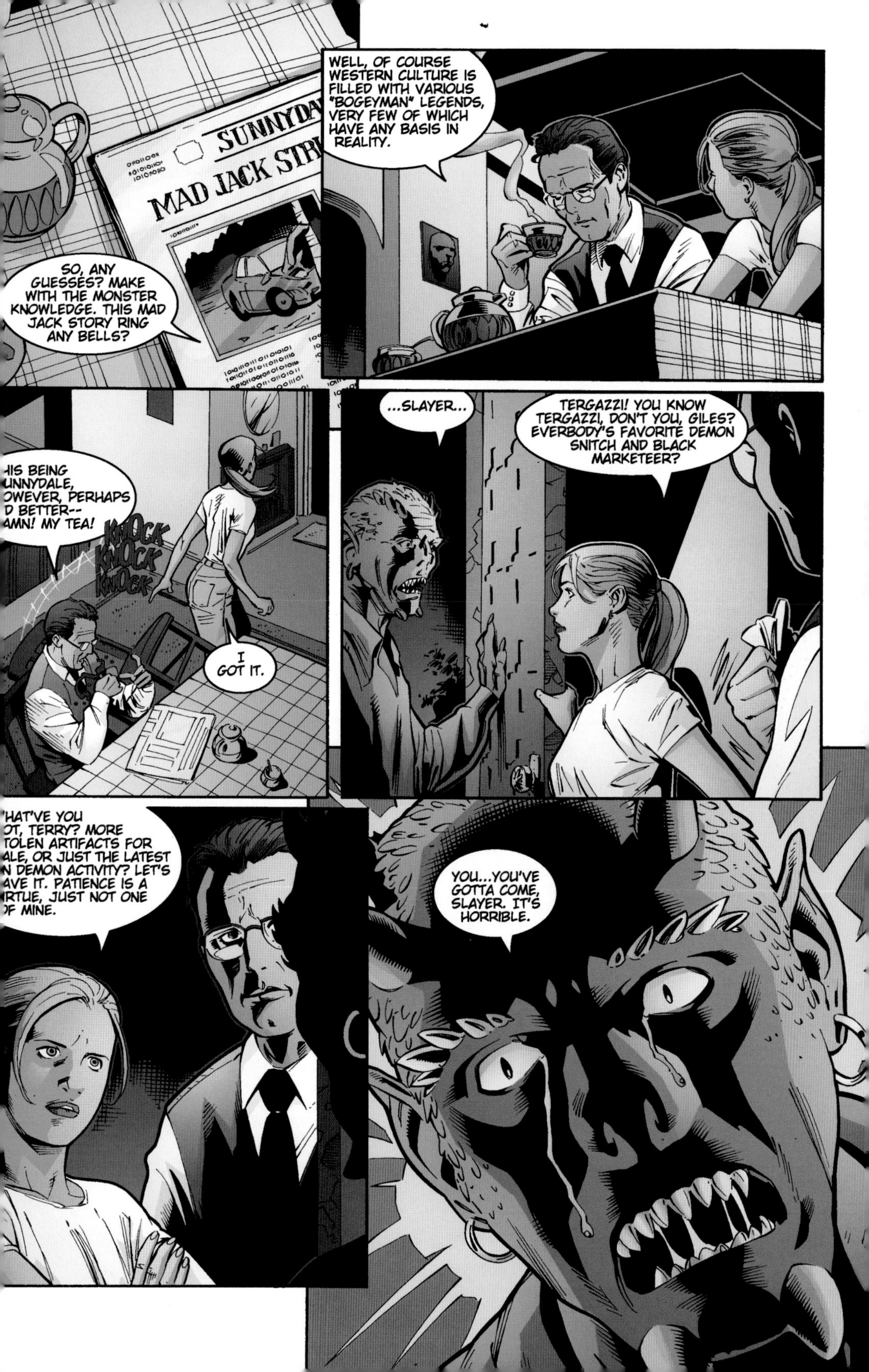
SUNNYDA
MAD JACK STR
SO, ANY GUESSES? MAKE WITH THE MONSTER KNOWLEDGE. THIS MAD JACK STORY RING ANY BELLS?
WELL, OF COURSE WESTERN CULTURE IS FILLED WITH VARIOUS "BOGEYMAN" LEGENDS, VERY FEW OF WHICH HAVE ANY BASIS IN REALITY.
HIS BEING SUNNYDALE, HOWEVER, PERHAPS D BETTER-- AMN! MY TEA!
KNOCK KNOCK KNOCK
I GOT IT.
...SLAYER...
TERGAZZI! YOU KNOW TERGAZZI, DON'T YOU, GILES? EVERBODY'S FAVORITE DEMON SNITCH AND BLACK MARKETEER?
HAT'VE YOU OT, TERRY? MORE TOLEN ARTIFACTS FOR ALE, OR JUST THE LATEST N DEMON ACTIVITY? LET'S AVE IT. PATIENCE IS A RTUE, JUST NOT ONE F MINE.
YOU...YOU'VE GOTTA COME, SLAYER. IT'S HORRIBLE.

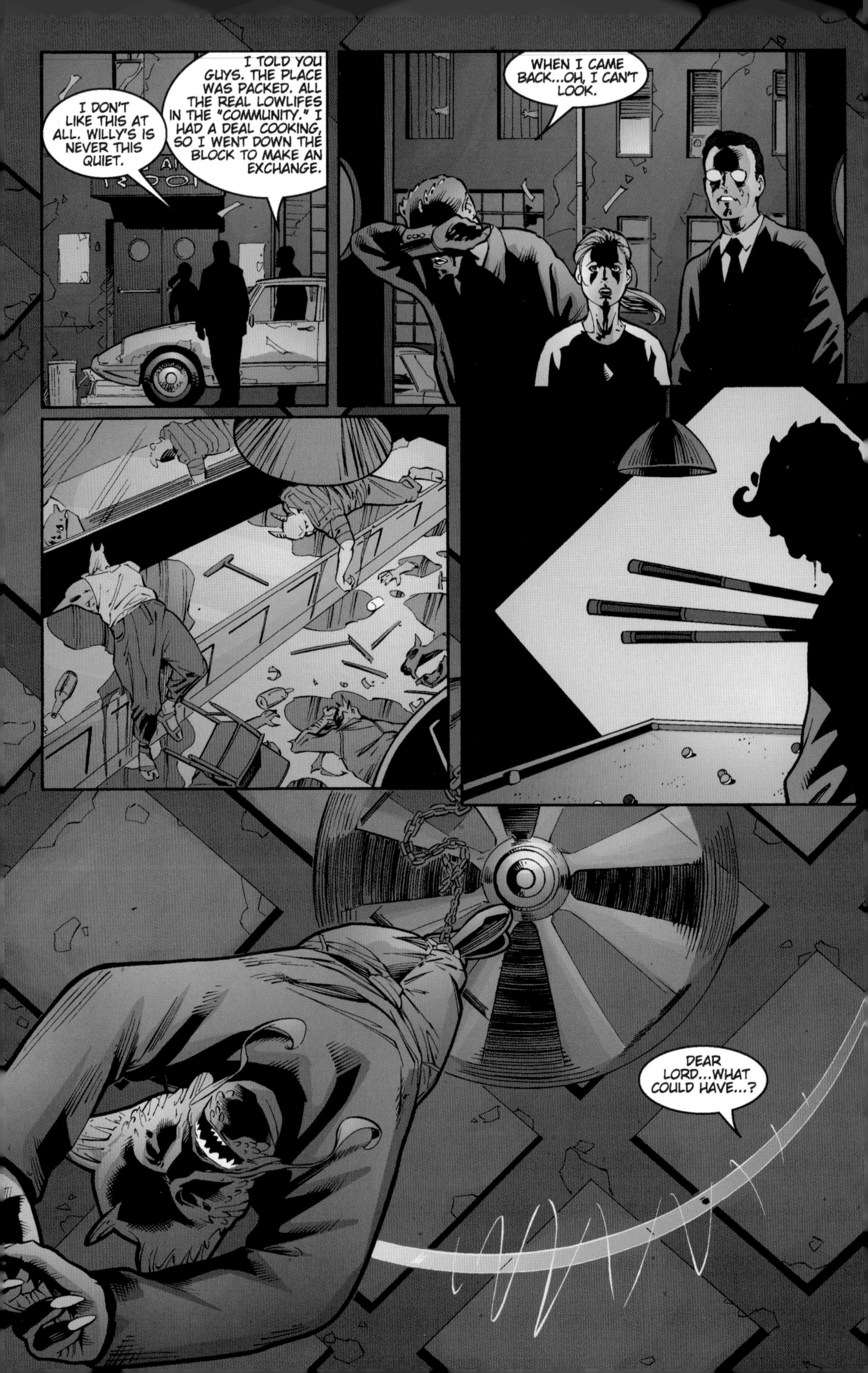
I DON'T LIKE THIS AT ALL. WILLY'S IS NEVER THIS QUIET.
I TOLD YOU GUYS. THE PLACE WAS PACKED. ALL THE REAL LOWLIFES IN THE "COMMUNITY." I HAD A DEAL COOKING, SO I WENT DOWN THE BLOCK TO MAKE AN EXCHANGE.
WHEN I CAME BACK...OH, I CAN'T LOOK.
DEAR LORD...WHAT COULD HAVE...?

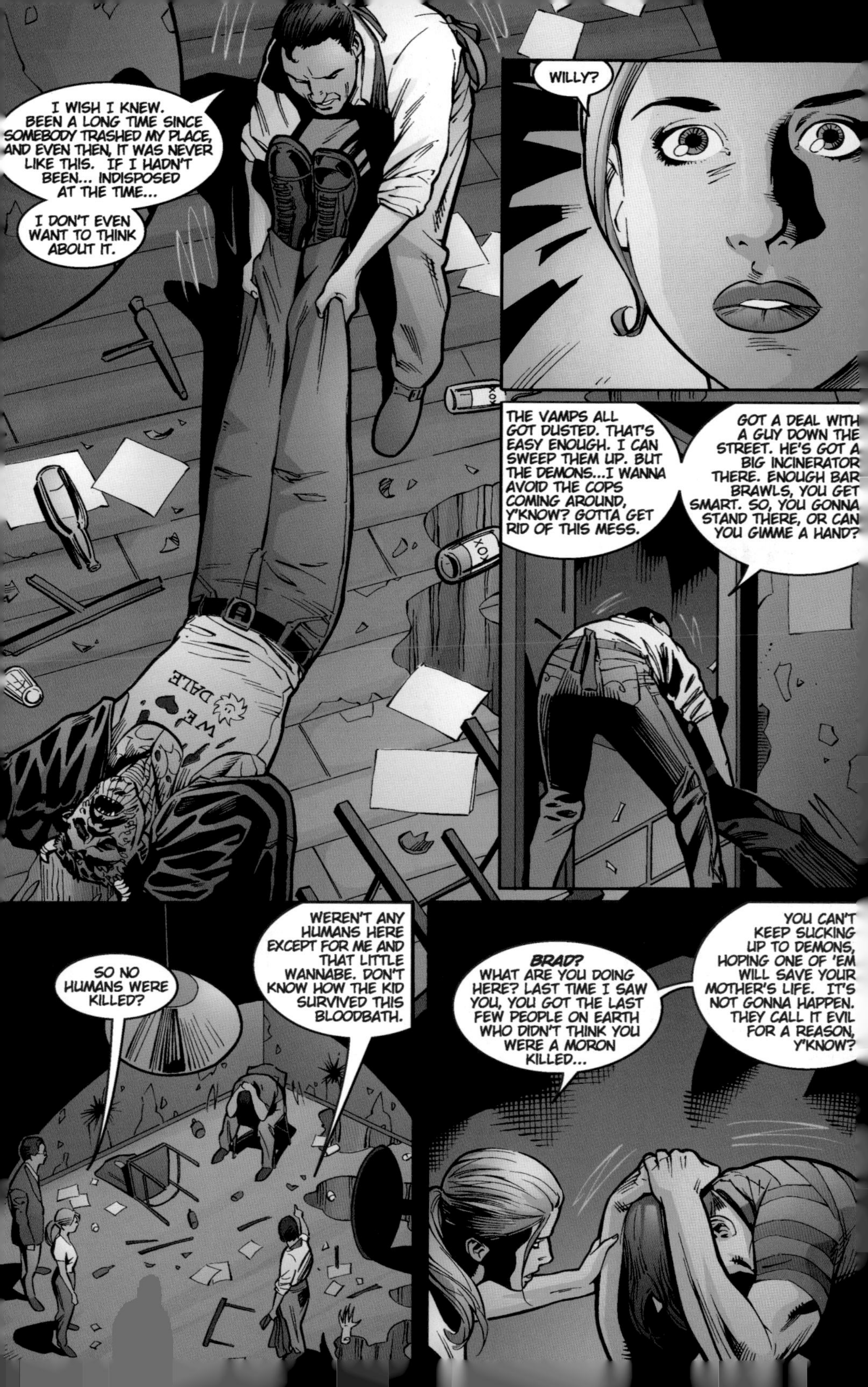
I WISH I KNEW. BEEN A LONG TIME SINCE SOMEBODY TRASHED MY PLACE, AND EVEN THEN, IT WAS NEVER LIKE THIS. IF I HADN'T BEEN... INDISPOSED AT THE TIME...
I DON'T EVEN WANT TO THINK ABOUT IT.
WE ♥ DALE
WILLY?
THE VAMPS ALL GOT DUSTED. THAT'S EASY ENOUGH. I CAN SWEEP THEM UP. BUT THE DEMONS...I WANNA AVOID THE COPS COMING AROUND, Y'KNOW? GOTTA GET RID OF THIS MESS.
GOT A DEAL WITH A GUY DOWN THE STREET. HE'S GOT A BIG INCINERATOR THERE. ENOUGH BAR BRAWLS, YOU GET SMART. SO, YOU GONNA STAND THERE, OR CAN YOU GIMME A HAND?
SO NO HUMANS WERE KILLED?
WEREN'T ANY HUMANS HERE EXCEPT FOR ME AND THAT LITTLE WANNABE. DON'T KNOW HOW THE KID SURVIVED THIS BLOODBATH.
BRAD? WHAT ARE YOU DOING HERE? LAST TIME I SAW YOU, YOU GOT THE LAST FEW PEOPLE ON EARTH WHO DIDN'T THINK YOU WERE A MORON KILLED...
YOU CAN'T KEEP SUCKING UP TO DEMONS, HOPING ONE OF 'EM WILL SAVE YOUR MOTHER'S LIFE. IT'S NOT GONNA HAPPEN. THEY CALL IT EVIL FOR A REASON, Y'KNOW?

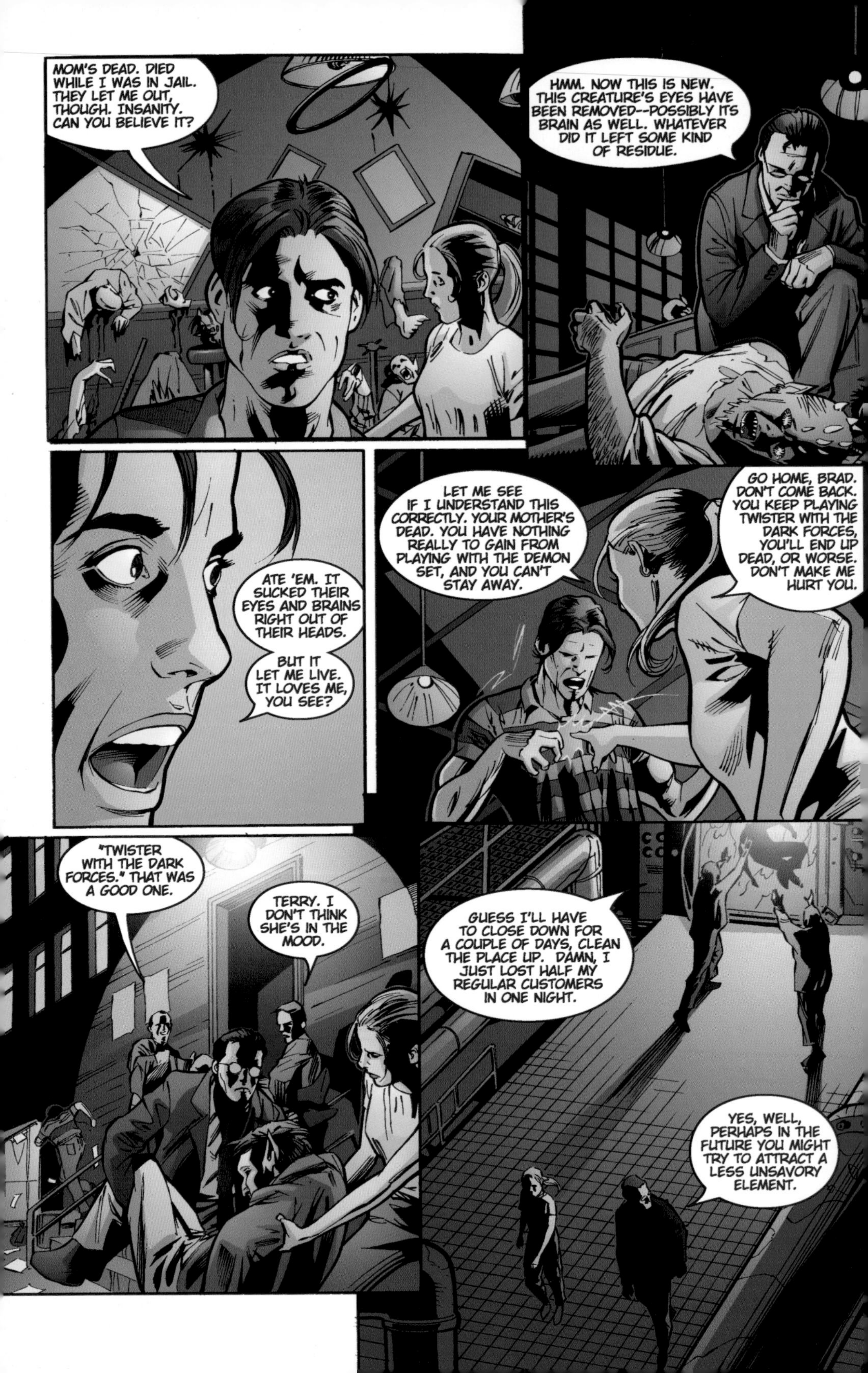
MOM'S DEAD. DIED WHILE I WAS IN JAIL. THEY LET ME OUT, THOUGH. INSANITY. CAN YOU BELIEVE IT?
HMM. NOW THIS IS NEW. THIS CREATURE'S EYES HAVE BEEN REMOVED--POSSIBLY ITS BRAIN AS WELL. WHATEVER DID IT LEFT SOME KIND OF RESIDUE.
ATE 'EM. IT SUCKED THEIR EYES AND BRAINS RIGHT OUT OF THEIR HEADS.
BUT IT LET ME LIVE. IT LOVES ME, YOU SEE?
LET ME SEE IF I UNDERSTAND THIS CORRECTLY. YOUR MOTHER'S DEAD. YOU HAVE NOTHING REALLY TO GAIN FROM PLAYING WITH THE DEMON SET, AND YOU CAN'T STAY AWAY.
GO HOME, BRAD. DON'T COME BACK. YOU KEEP PLAYING TWISTER WITH THE DARK FORCES, YOU'LL END UP DEAD, OR WORSE. DON'T MAKE ME HURT YOU.
"TWISTER WITH THE DARK FORCES." THAT WAS A GOOD ONE.
TERRY. I DON'T THINK SHE'S IN THE MOOD.
GUESS I'LL HAVE TO CLOSE DOWN FOR A COUPLE OF DAYS, CLEAN THE PLACE UP. DAMN, I JUST LOST HALF MY REGULAR CUSTOMERS IN ONE NIGHT.
YES, WELL, PERHAPS IN THE FUTURE YOU MIGHT TRY TO ATTRACT A LESS UNSAVORY ELEMENT.

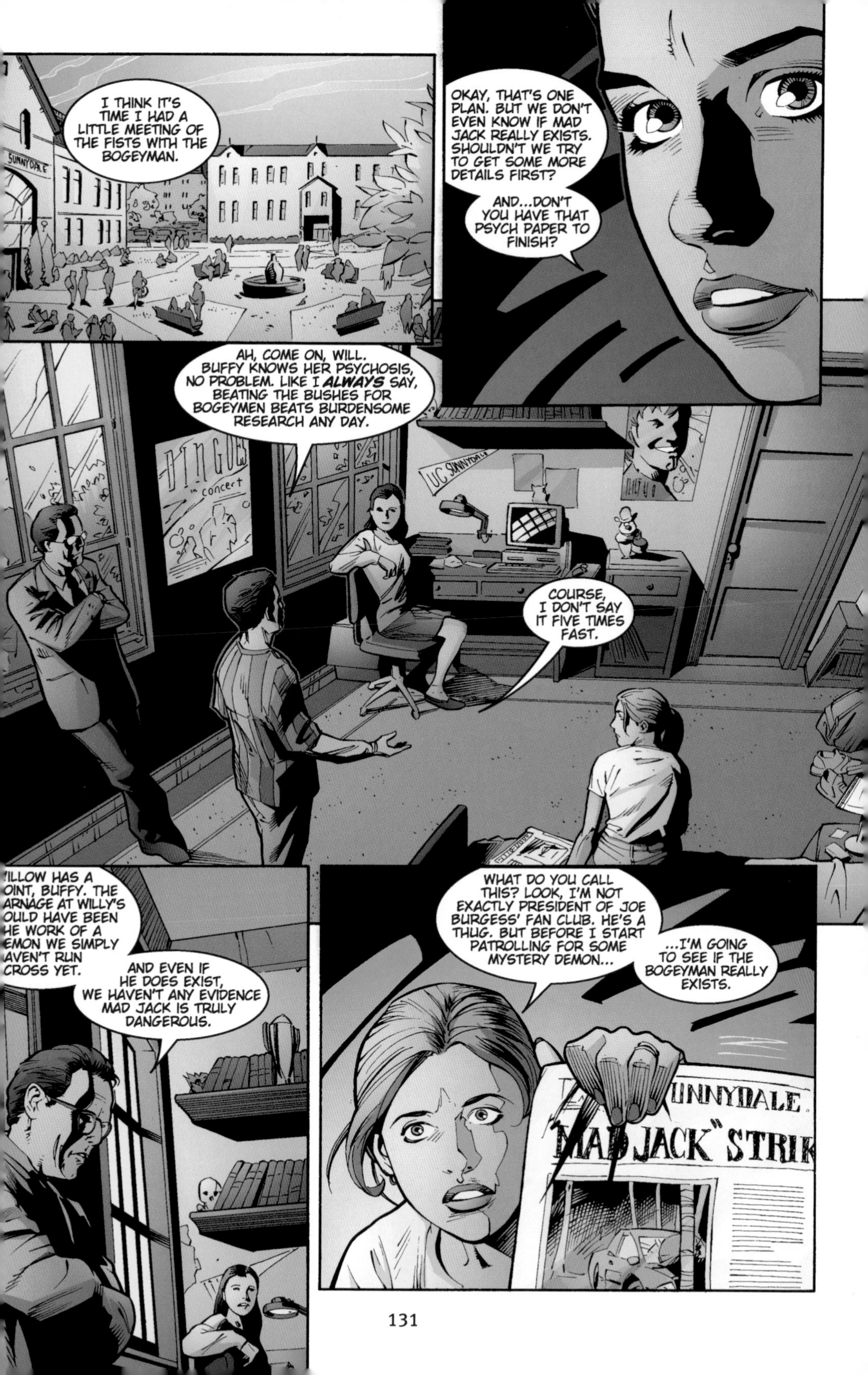
I THINK IT'S TIME I HAD A LITTLE MEETING OF THE FISTS WITH THE BOGEYMAN.
SUNNYDALE
OKAY, THAT'S ONE PLAN. BUT WE DON'T EVEN KNOW IF MAD JACK REALLY EXISTS. SHOULDN'T WE TRY TO GET SOME MORE DETAILS FIRST?
AND...DON'T YOU HAVE THAT PSYCH PAPER TO FINISH?
AH, COME ON, WILL. BUFFY KNOWS HER PSYCHOSIS, NO PROBLEM. LIKE I *ALWAYS* SAY, BEATING THE BUSHES FOR BOGEYMEN BEATS BURDENSOME RESEARCH ANY DAY.
DINGOES in concert
UC SUNNYDALE
COURSE, I DON'T SAY IT FIVE TIMES FAST.
ILLOW HAS A OINT, BUFFY. THE ARNAGE AT WILLY'S OULD HAVE BEEN HE WORK OF A EMON WE SIMPLY AVEN'T RUN CROSS YET.
AND EVEN IF HE DOES EXIST, WE HAVEN'T ANY EVIDENCE MAD JACK IS TRULY DANGEROUS.
WHAT DO YOU CALL THIS? LOOK, I'M NOT EXACTLY PRESIDENT OF JOE BURGESS' FAN CLUB. HE'S A THUG. BUT BEFORE I START PATROLLING FOR SOME MYSTERY DEMON...
...I'M GOING TO SEE IF THE BOGEYMAN REALLY EXISTS.
UNNYDALE
"MAD JACK" STRIK

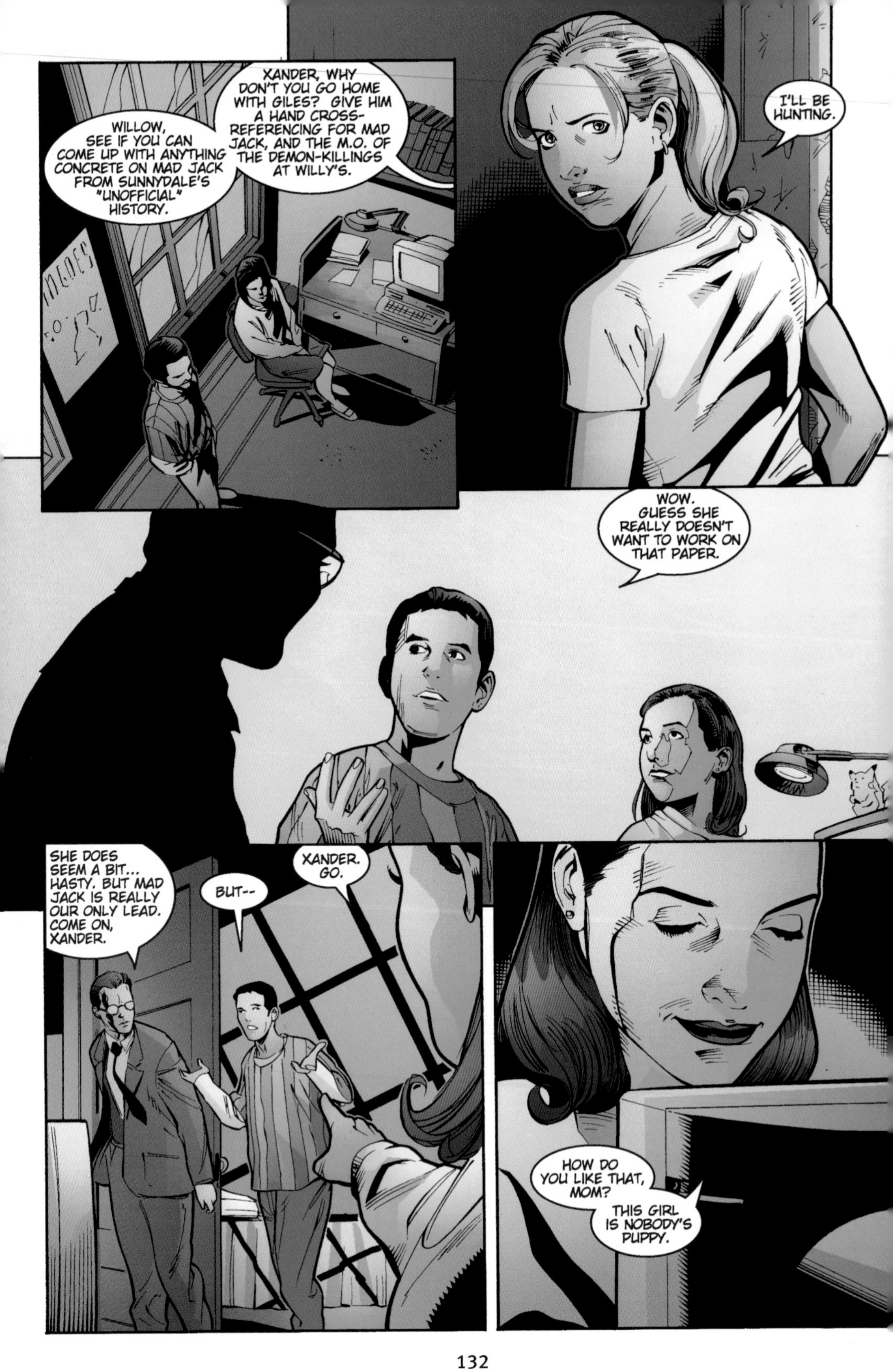

WILLOW, SEE IF YOU CAN COME UP WITH ANYTHING CONCRETE ON MAD JACK FROM SUNNYDALE'S "UNOFFICIAL" HISTORY.
XANDER, WHY DON'T YOU GO HOME WITH GILES? GIVE HIM A HAND CROSS-REFERENCING FOR MAD JACK, AND THE M.O. OF THE DEMON-KILLINGS AT WILLY'S.
I'LL BE HUNTING.
WOW. GUESS SHE REALLY DOESN'T WANT TO WORK ON THAT PAPER.
SHE DOES SEEM A BIT... HASTY. BUT MAD JACK IS REALLY OUR ONLY LEAD. COME ON, XANDER.
BUT--
XANDER. GO.
HOW DO YOU LIKE THAT, MOM?
THIS GIRL IS NOBODY'S PUPPY.

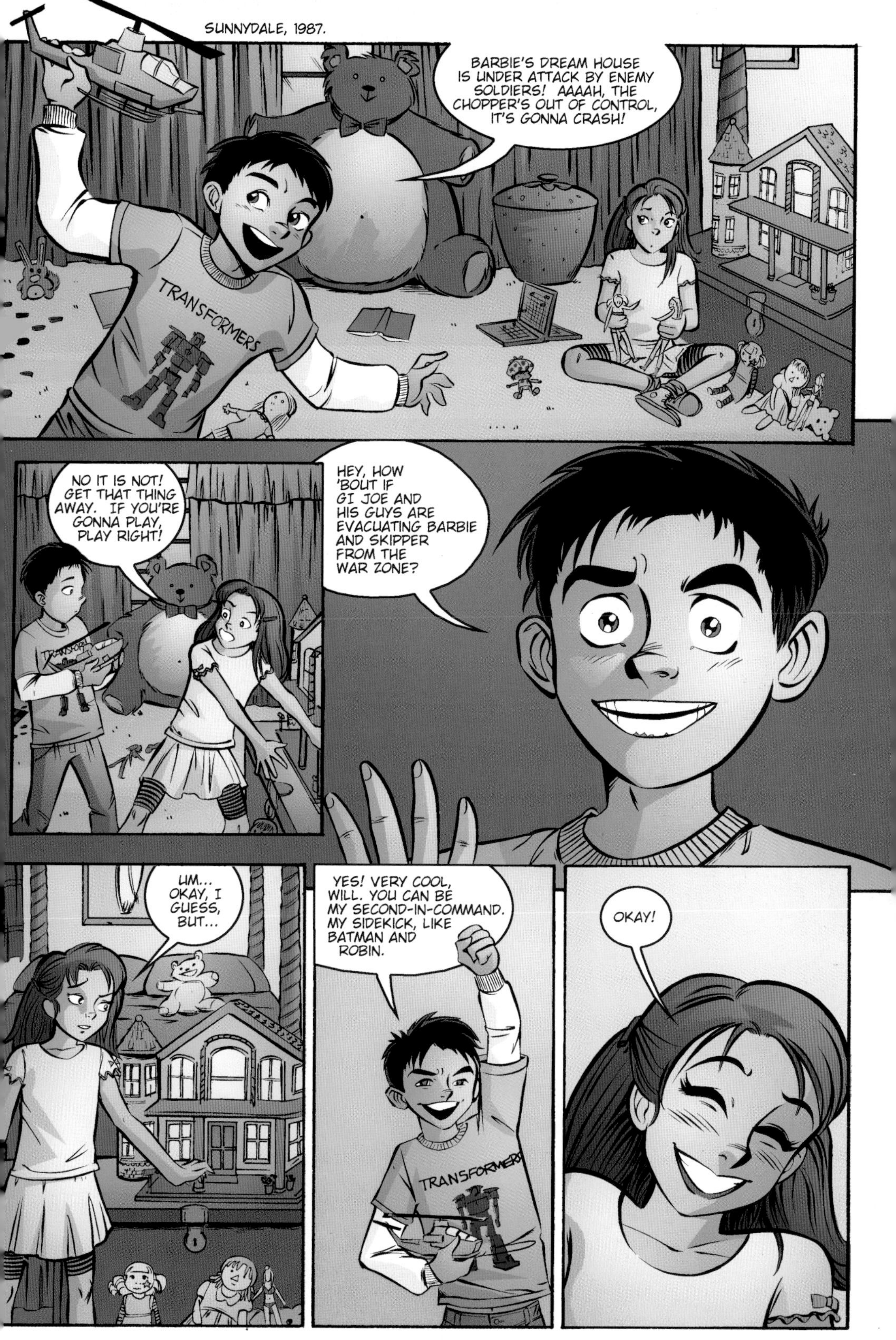
SUNNYDALE, 1987.
BARBIE'S DREAM HOUSE IS UNDER ATTACK BY ENEMY SOLDIERS! AAAAH, THE CHOPPER'S OUT OF CONTROL, IT'S GONNA CRASH!
TRANSFORMERS
NO IT IS NOT! GET THAT THING AWAY. IF YOU'RE GONNA PLAY, PLAY RIGHT!
HEY, HOW 'BOUT IF GI JOE AND HIS GUYS ARE EVACUATING BARBIE AND SKIPPER FROM THE WAR ZONE?
UM... OKAY, I GUESS, BUT...
YES! VERY COOL, WILL. YOU CAN BE MY SECOND-IN-COMMAND. MY SIDEKICK, LIKE BATMAN AND ROBIN.
TRANSFORMERS
OKAY!

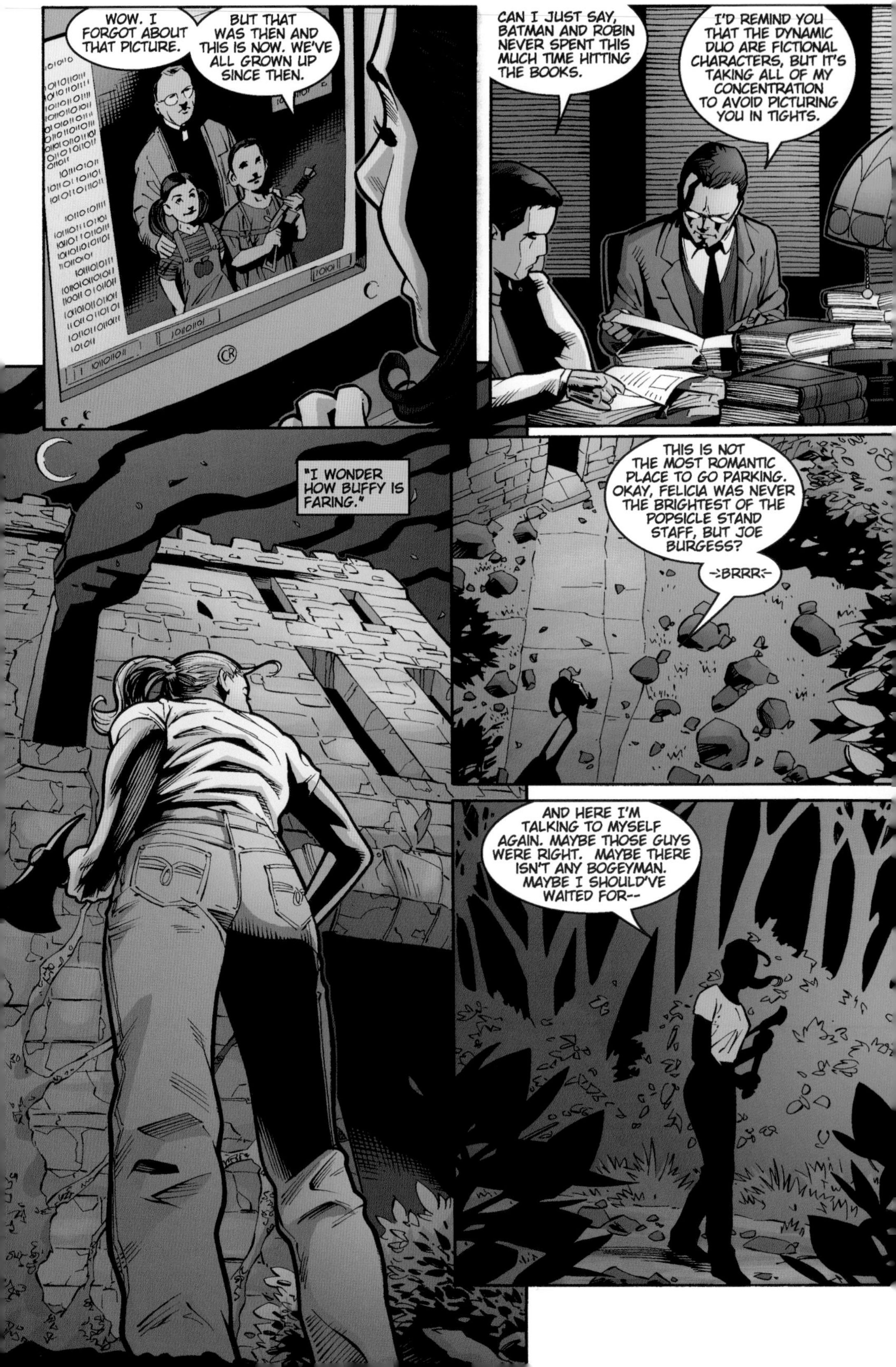

WOW. I FORGOT ABOUT THAT PICTURE.
BUT THAT WAS THEN AND THIS IS NOW. WE'VE ALL GROWN UP SINCE THEN.
CAN I JUST SAY, BATMAN AND ROBIN NEVER SPENT THIS MUCH TIME HITTING THE BOOKS.
I'D REMIND YOU THAT THE DYNAMIC DUO ARE FICTIONAL CHARACTERS, BUT IT'S TAKING ALL OF MY CONCENTRATION TO AVOID PICTURING YOU IN TIGHTS.
"I WONDER HOW BUFFY IS FARING."
THIS IS NOT THE MOST ROMANTIC PLACE TO GO PARKING. OKAY, FELICIA WAS NEVER THE BRIGHTEST OF THE POPSICLE STAND STAFF, BUT JOE BURGESS?
-BRRR-
AND HERE I'M TALKING TO MYSELF AGAIN. MAYBE THOSE GUYS WERE RIGHT. MAYBE THERE ISN'T ANY BOGEYMAN. MAYBE I SHOULD'VE WAITED FOR--

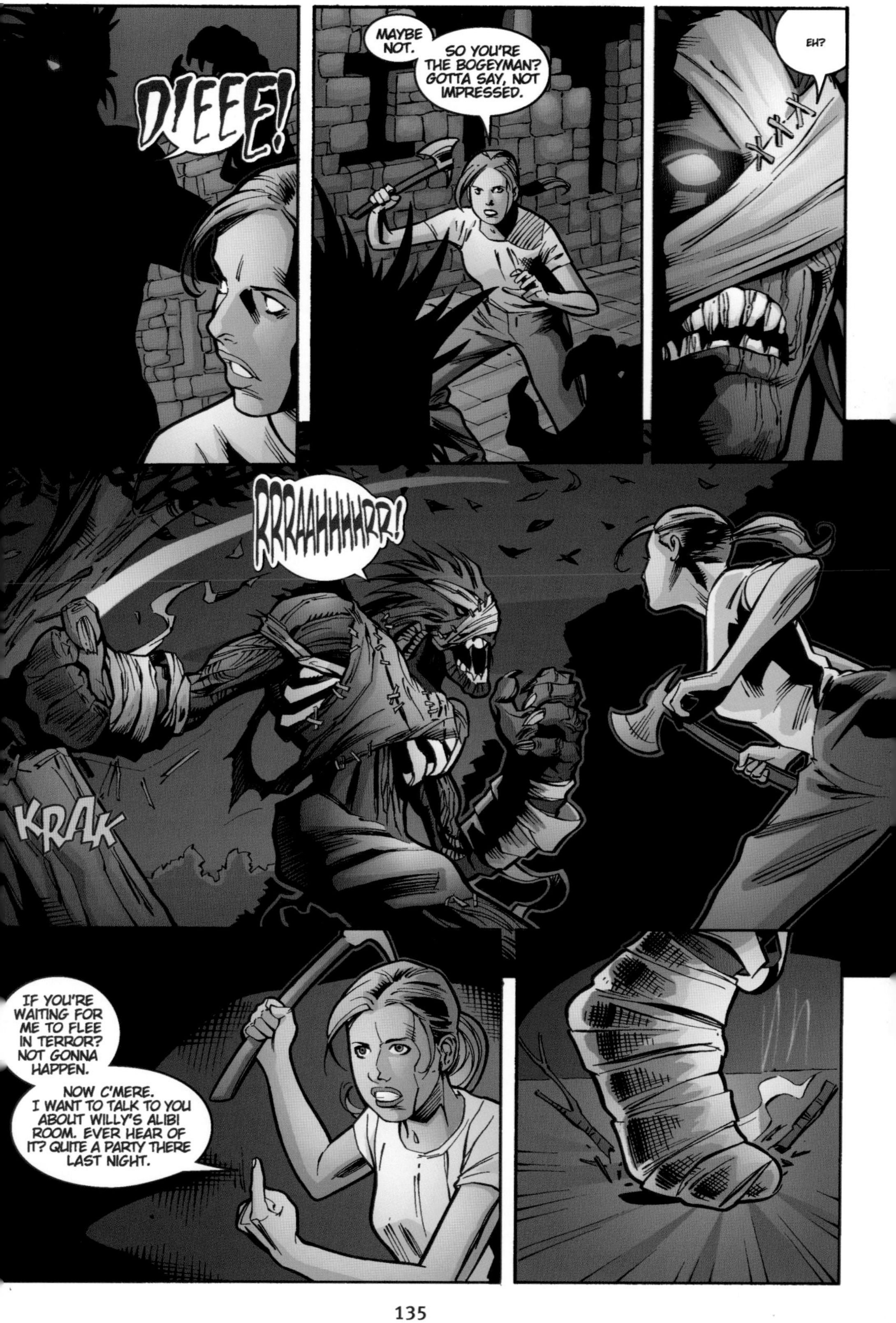
DIEEE!
MAYBE NOT.
SO YOU'RE THE BOGEYMAN? GOTTA SAY, NOT IMPRESSED.
EH?
RRRAAHHHHRR!
KRAK
IF YOU'RE WAITING FOR ME TO FLEE IN TERROR? NOT GONNA HAPPEN.
NOW C'MERE. I WANT TO TALK TO YOU ABOUT WILLY'S ALIBI ROOM. EVER HEAR OF IT? QUITE A PARTY THERE LAST NIGHT.

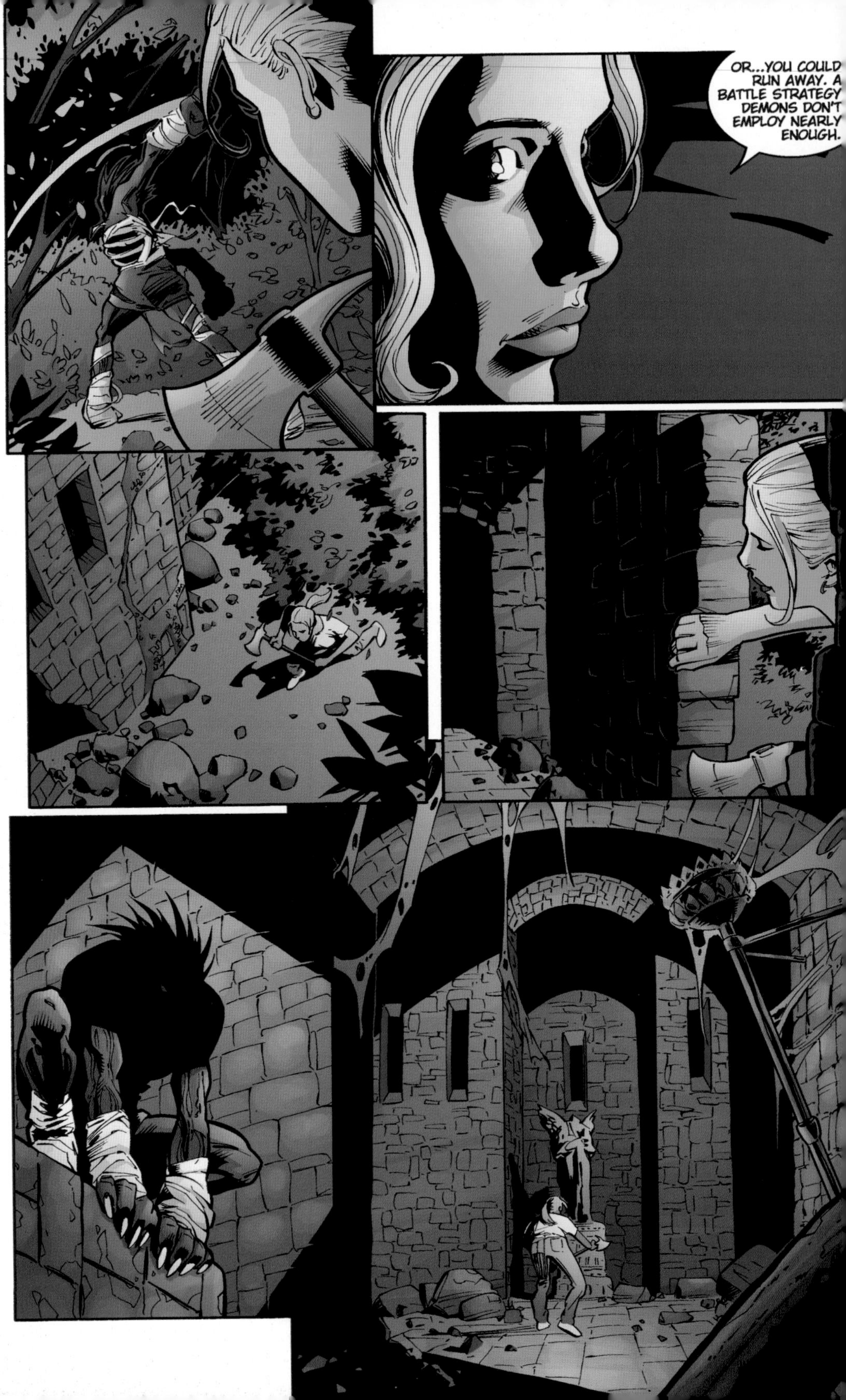
OR...YOU COULD RUN AWAY. A BATTLE STRATEGY DEMONS DON'T EMPLOY NEARLY ENOUGH.

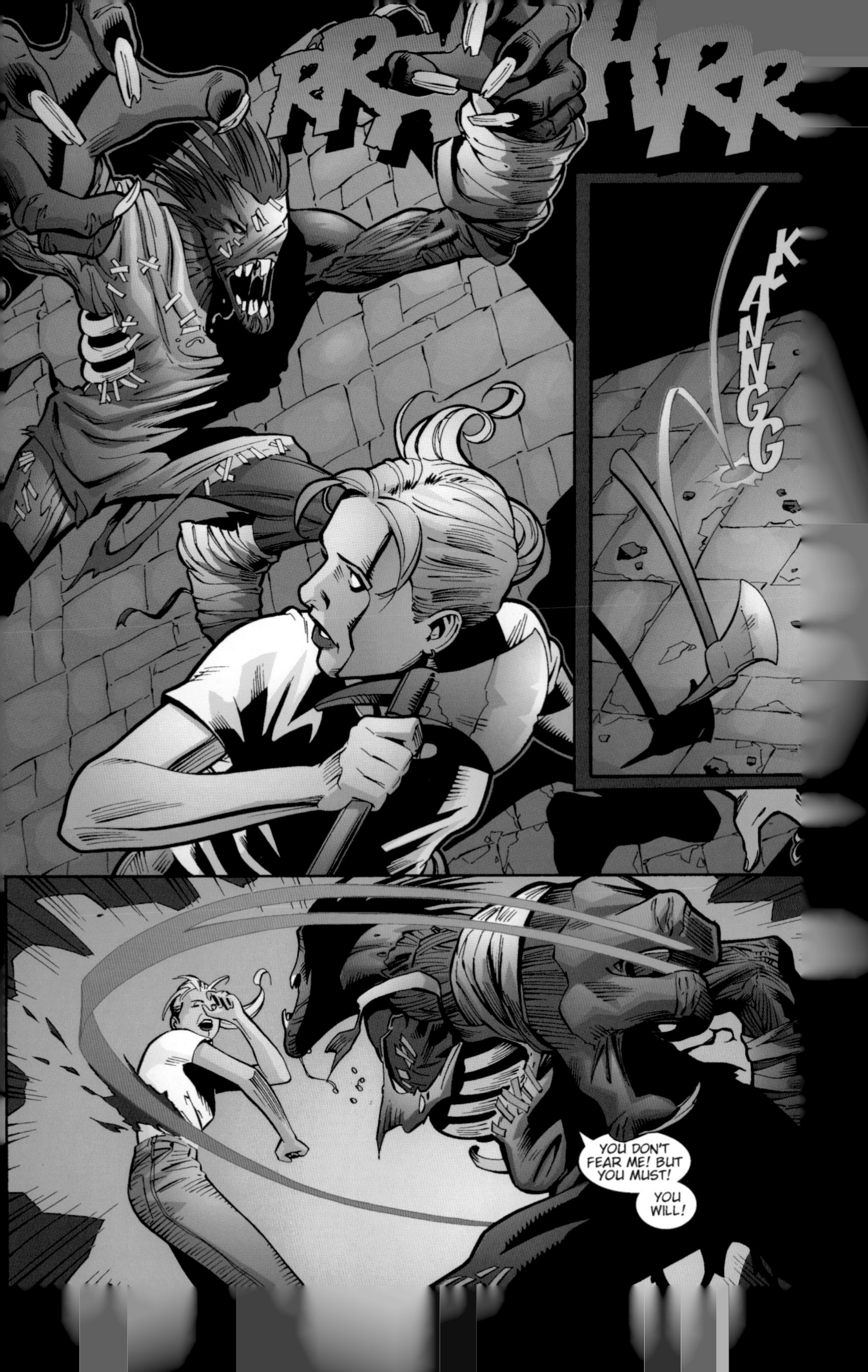
RRRAHRR
KKANGG
YOU DON'T FEAR ME! BUT YOU MUST!
YOU WILL!

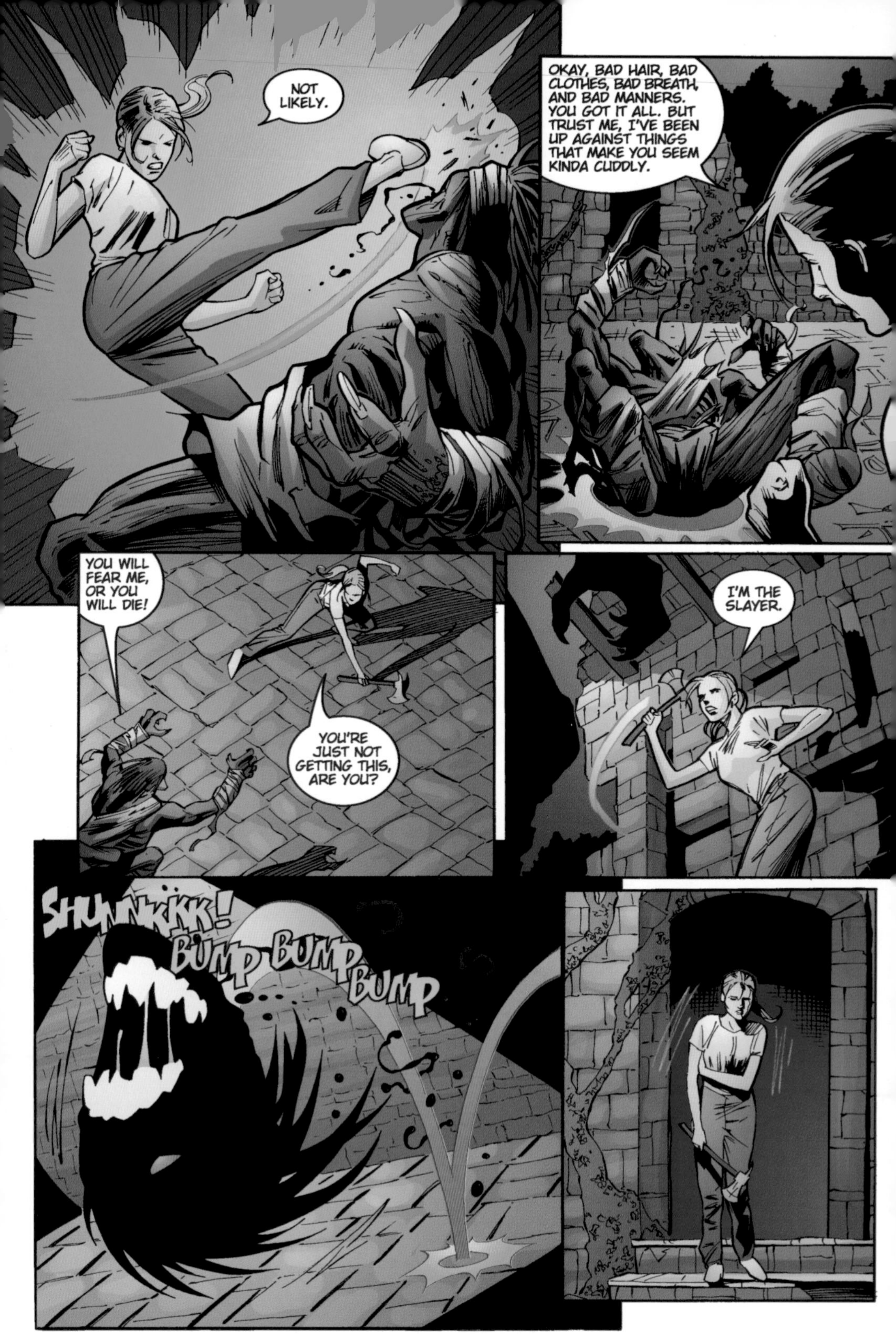
NOT LIKELY.
OKAY, BAD HAIR, BAD CLOTHES, BAD BREATH, AND BAD MANNERS. YOU GOT IT ALL. BUT TRUST ME, I'VE BEEN UP AGAINST THINGS THAT MAKE YOU SEEM KINDA CUDDLY.
YOU WILL FEAR ME, OR YOU WILL DIE!
YOU'RE JUST NOT GETTING THIS, ARE YOU?
I'M THE SLAYER.
SHUNNKKK!
BUMP BUMP BUMP

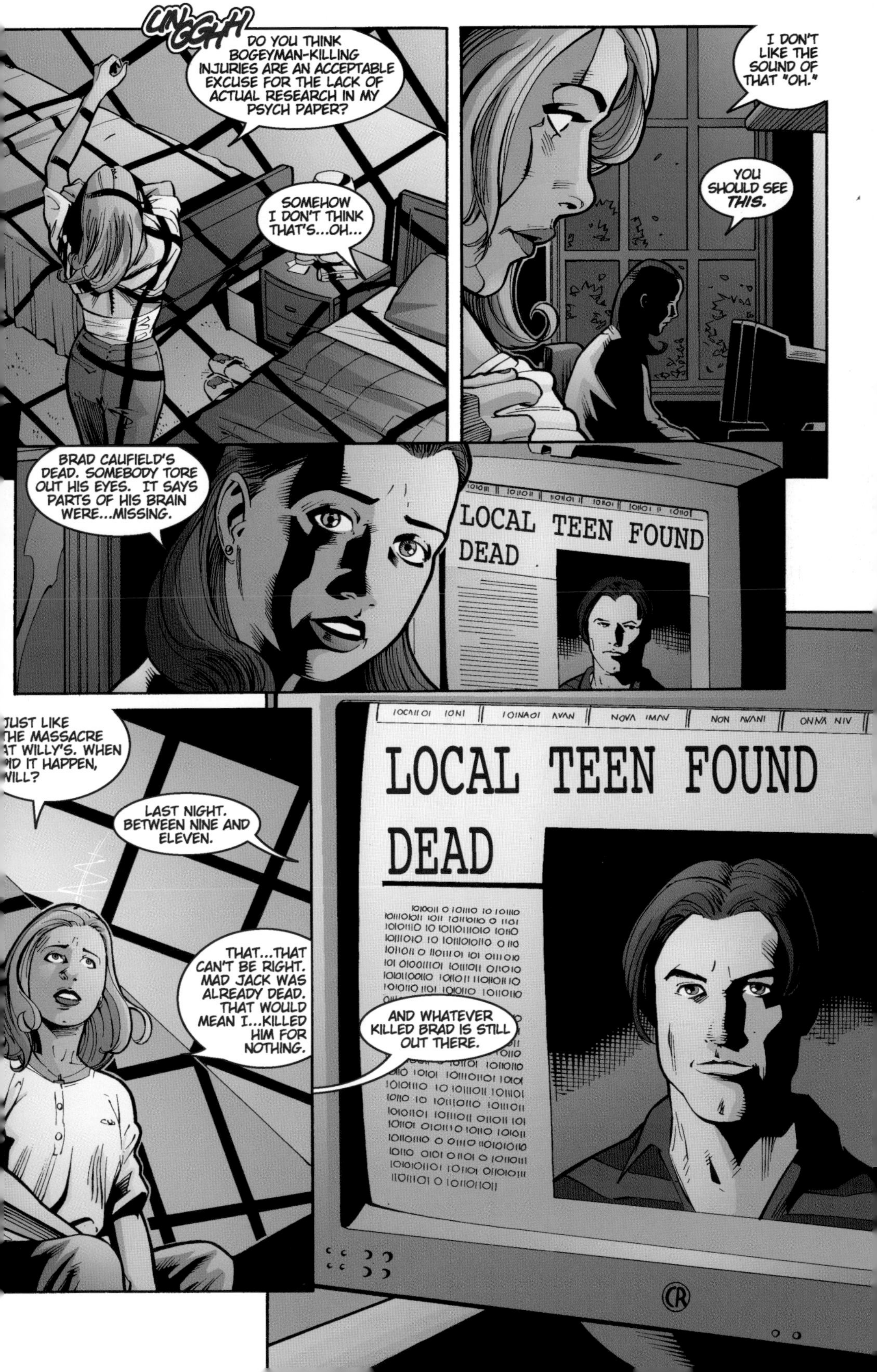
UNGGH!
DO YOU THINK BOGEYMAN-KILLING INJURIES ARE AN ACCEPTABLE EXCUSE FOR THE LACK OF ACTUAL RESEARCH IN MY PSYCH PAPER?
SOMEHOW I DON'T THINK THAT'S...OH...
I DON'T LIKE THE SOUND OF THAT "OH."
YOU SHOULD SEE *THIS.*
BRAD CAUFIELD'S DEAD. SOMEBODY TORE OUT HIS EYES. IT SAYS PARTS OF HIS BRAIN WERE...MISSING.
LOCAL TEEN FOUND DEAD
JUST LIKE THE MASSACRE AT WILLY'S. WHEN DID IT HAPPEN, WILL?
LAST NIGHT. BETWEEN NINE AND ELEVEN.
LOCAL TEEN FOUND DEAD
THAT...THAT CAN'T BE RIGHT. MAD JACK WAS ALREADY DEAD. THAT WOULD MEAN I...KILLED HIM FOR NOTHING.
AND WHATEVER KILLED BRAD IS STILL OUT THERE.

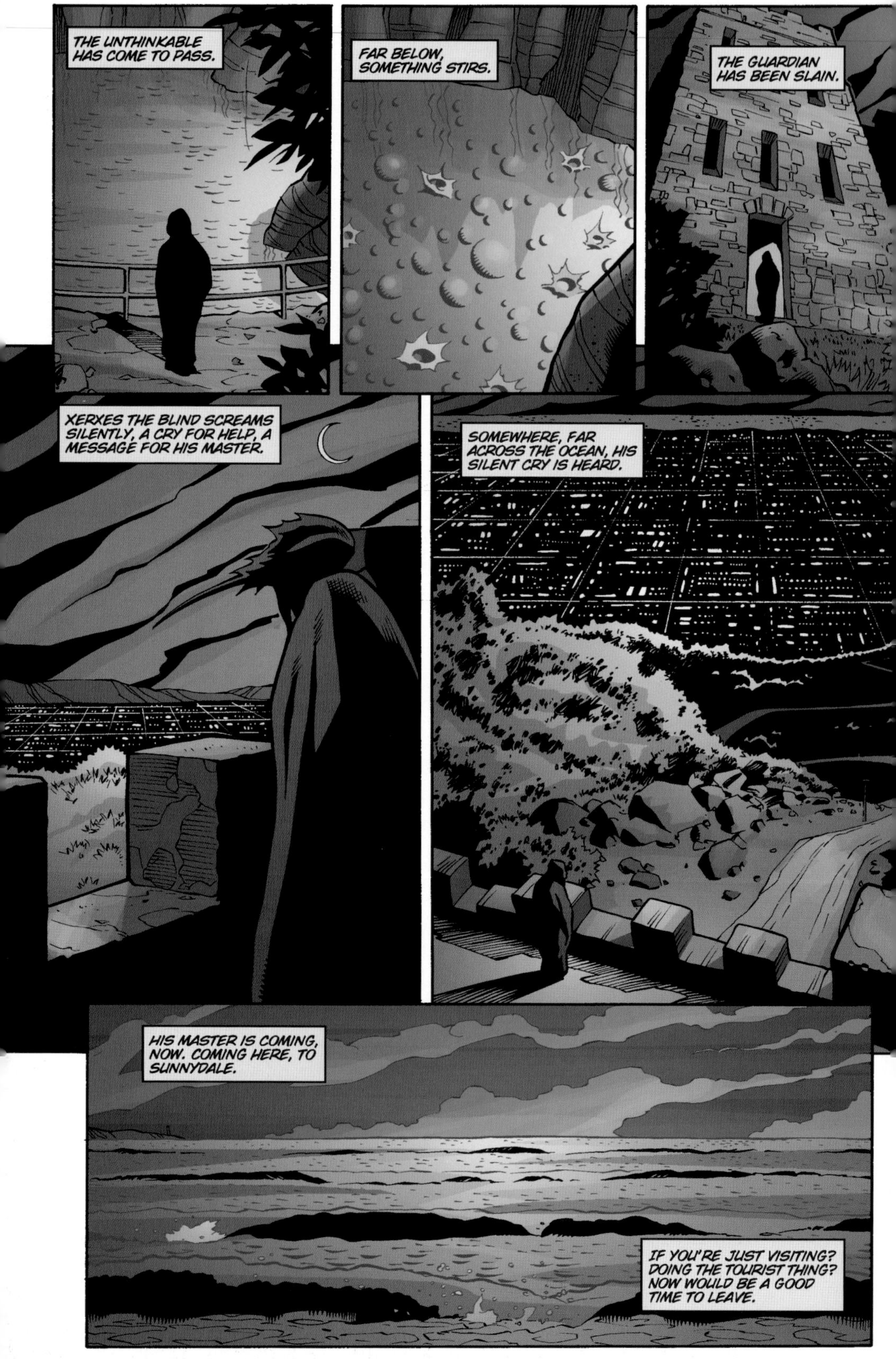
THE UNTHINKABLE HAS COME TO PASS.
FAR BELOW, SOMETHING STIRS.
THE GUARDIAN HAS BEEN SLAIN.
XERXES THE BLIND SCREAMS SILENTLY, A CRY FOR HELP, A MESSAGE FOR HIS MASTER.
SOMEWHERE, FAR ACROSS THE OCEAN, HIS SILENT CRY IS HEARD.
HIS MASTER IS COMING, NOW. COMING HERE, TO SUNNYDALE.
IF YOU'RE JUST VISITING? DOING THE TOURIST THING? NOW WOULD BE A GOOD TIME TO LEAVE.

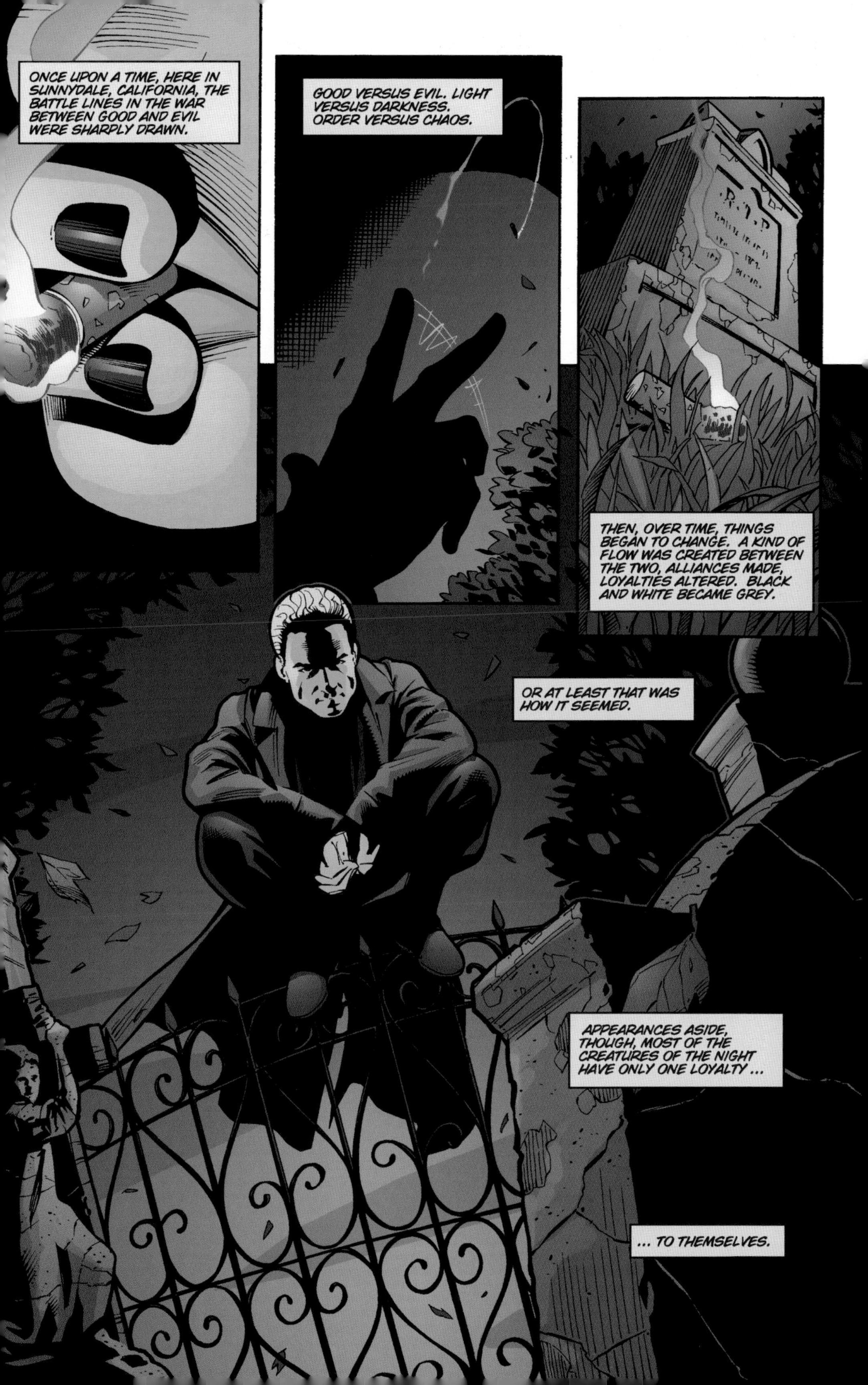
ONCE UPON A TIME, HERE IN SUNNYDALE, CALIFORNIA, THE BATTLE LINES IN THE WAR BETWEEN GOOD AND EVIL WERE SHARPLY DRAWN.
GOOD VERSUS EVIL. LIGHT VERSUS DARKNESS. ORDER VERSUS CHAOS.
R.I.P.
THEN, OVER TIME, THINGS BEGAN TO CHANGE. A KIND OF FLOW WAS CREATED BETWEEN THE TWO, ALLIANCES MADE, LOYALTIES ALTERED. BLACK AND WHITE BECAME GREY.
OR AT LEAST THAT WAS HOW IT SEEMED.
APPEARANCES ASIDE, THOUGH, MOST OF THE CREATURES OF THE NIGHT HAVE ONLY ONE LOYALTY ...
... TO THEMSELVES.

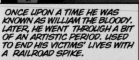

ONCE UPON A TIME HE WAS KNOWN AS WILLIAM THE BLOODY. LATER, HE WENT THROUGH A BIT OF AN ARTISTIC PERIOD. USED TO END HIS VICTIMS' LIVES WITH A RAILROAD SPIKE.

THOUGHT IT WAS COLORFUL, HAVING A SORT OF SIGNATURE LIKE THAT. SPIKE--THAT'S WHAT THEY CALL HIM NOW. HE LIKES THE NAME.

SOMETIMES HE FORGETS HE EVER HAD ANOTHER.

RECENTLY, SOMEONE TINKERED WITH HIS BRAIN. HE CAN'T KILL HUMANS ANYMORE. OF LATE, HE'S BEEN HANGING OUT WITH THE SLAYER AND HER CREW.

IT MAKES HIM FEEL LIKE A PET.

WHICH PUTS HIM IN A HELL OF A MOOD.

WELL, WELL, JAX. YOU PAID OFF THE CARETAKER TO LET YOU PARK HERE, AND STILL HAD ENOUGH LEFT OVER T' HIRE YOURSELF A BIT OF SWEET N' LOVELY.

COME ON, THEN. YOU'VE GOT ALL NIGHT FOR THAT. OL' SPIKE'S IN THE MOOD FOR SOME FUN. LET'S SEE WHAT NIFTY TOYS YOU'VE GOT WITH YOU THIS TIME.

JAX? DON'T KNOW IF YOU REMEMBER, MATE, BUT I'M NOT THE MOST PATIENT--

WHAMMM!

UHNFFF!

YOU HAVE GOT TO BE JOKING.

XERXES THE BLIND. IN SUNNYDALE.

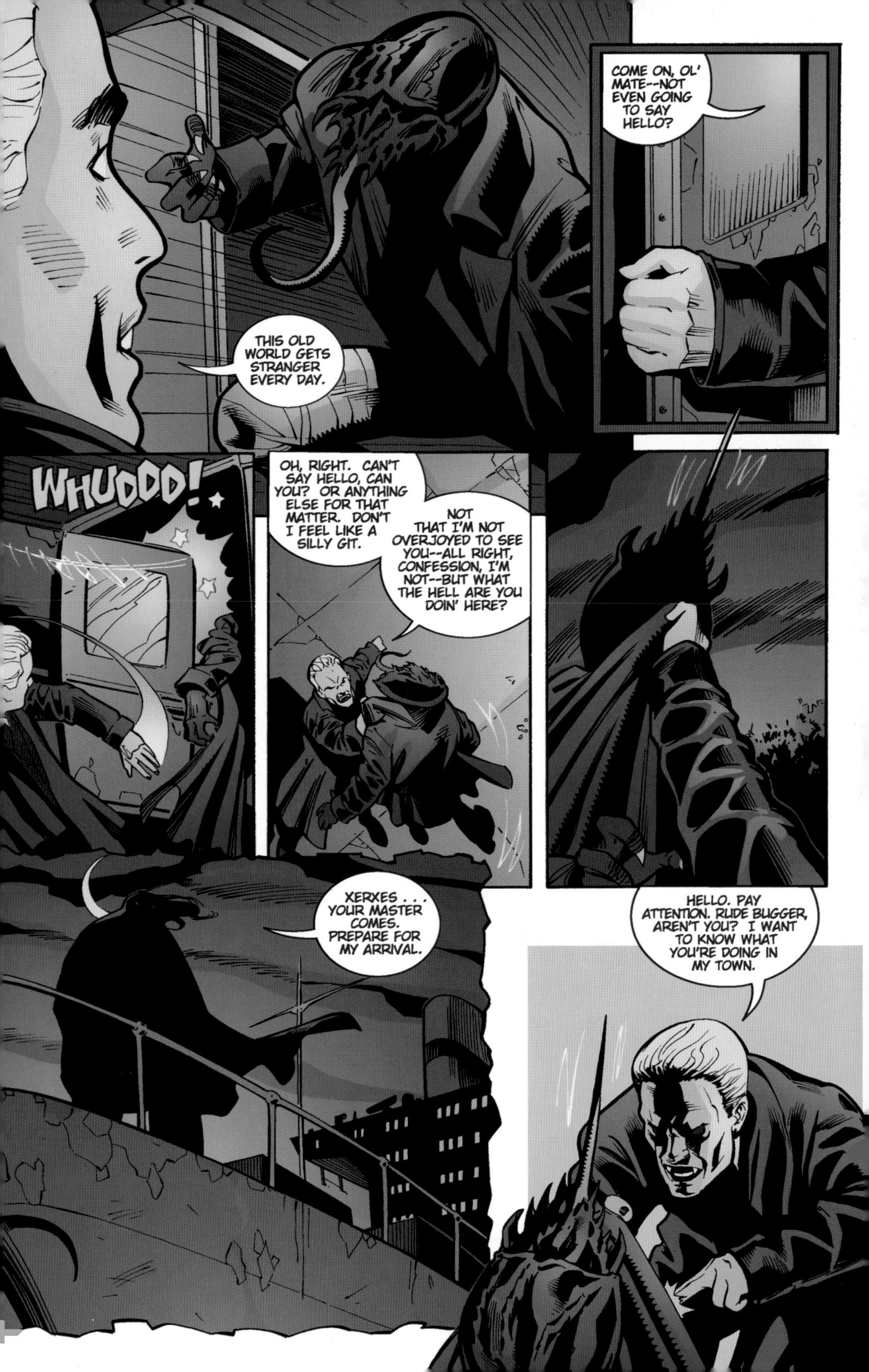
THIS OLD WORLD GETS STRANGER EVERY DAY.
COME ON, OL' MATE--NOT EVEN GOING TO SAY HELLO?
WHUDDD!
OH, RIGHT. CAN'T SAY HELLO, CAN YOU? OR ANYTHING ELSE FOR THAT MATTER. DON'T I FEEL LIKE A SILLY GIT.
NOT THAT I'M NOT OVERJOYED TO SEE YOU--ALL RIGHT, CONFESSION, I'M NOT--BUT WHAT THE HELL ARE YOU DOIN' HERE?
XERXES . . . YOUR MASTER COMES. PREPARE FOR MY ARRIVAL.
HELLO. PAY ATTENTION. RUDE BUGGER, AREN'T YOU? I WANT TO KNOW WHAT YOU'RE DOING IN MY TOWN.

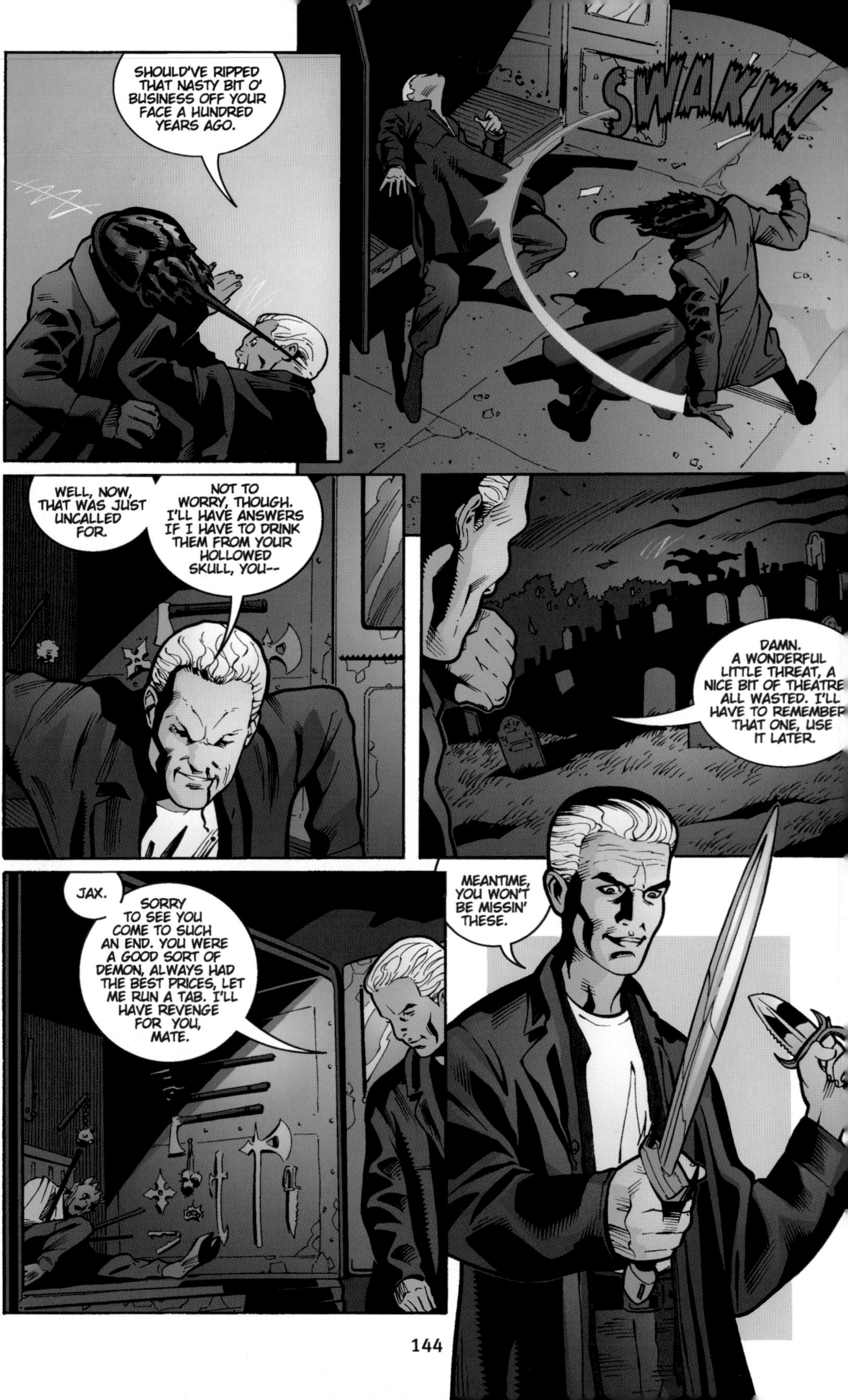
SHOULD'VE RIPPED THAT NASTY BIT O' BUSINESS OFF YOUR FACE A HUNDRED YEARS AGO.
SWAKK!
WELL, NOW, THAT WAS JUST UNCALLED FOR.
NOT TO WORRY, THOUGH. I'LL HAVE ANSWERS IF I HAVE TO DRINK THEM FROM YOUR HOLLOWED SKULL, YOU--
DAMN. A WONDERFUL LITTLE THREAT, A NICE BIT OF THEATRE ALL WASTED. I'LL HAVE TO REMEMBER THAT ONE, USE IT LATER.
JAX.
SORRY TO SEE YOU COME TO SUCH AN END. YOU WERE A GOOD SORT OF DEMON, ALWAYS HAD THE BEST PRICES, LET ME RUN A TAB. I'LL HAVE REVENGE FOR YOU, MATE.
MEANTIME, YOU WON'T BE MISSIN' THESE.

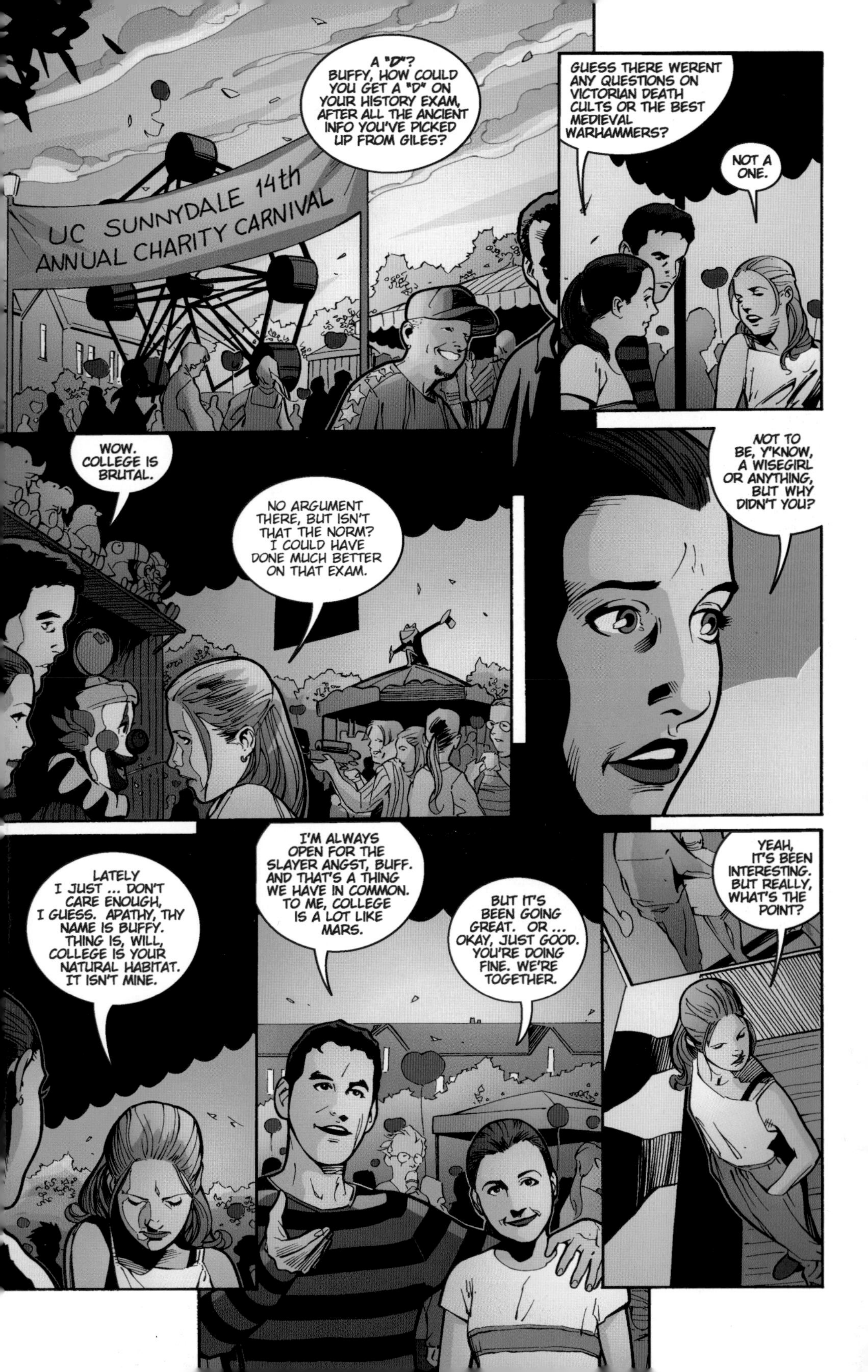
UC SUNNYDALE 14th ANNUAL CHARITY CARNIVAL
A "D"? BUFFY, HOW COULD YOU GET A "D" ON YOUR HISTORY EXAM, AFTER ALL THE ANCIENT INFO YOU'VE PICKED UP FROM GILES?
GUESS THERE WERENT ANY QUESTIONS ON VICTORIAN DEATH CULTS OR THE BEST MEDIEVAL WARHAMMERS?
NOT A ONE.
WOW. COLLEGE IS BRUTAL.
NO ARGUMENT THERE, BUT ISN'T THAT THE NORM? I COULD HAVE DONE MUCH BETTER ON THAT EXAM.
NOT TO BE, Y'KNOW, A WISEGIRL OR ANYTHING, BUT WHY DIDN'T YOU?
LATELY I JUST ... DON'T CARE ENOUGH, I GUESS. APATHY, THY NAME IS BUFFY. THING IS, WILL, COLLEGE IS YOUR NATURAL HABITAT. IT ISN'T MINE.
I'M ALWAYS OPEN FOR THE SLAYER ANGST, BUFF. AND THAT'S A THING WE HAVE IN COMMON. TO ME, COLLEGE IS A LOT LIKE MARS.
BUT IT'S BEEN GOING GREAT. OR ... OKAY, JUST GOOD. YOU'RE DOING FINE. WE'RE TOGETHER.
YEAH, IT'S BEEN INTERESTING. BUT REALLY, WHAT'S THE POINT?

WHAT'S THE POINT? BUFFY, WHAT YOU DO ON THIS CAMPUS COULD LAY THE GROUNDWORK FOR YOUR WHOLE LIFE.

UH-UH, WILL. ALL THAT DARWIN-Y SURVIVAL-OF-THE-CUTTHROATIEST DOESN'T INCLUDE ME, REMEMBER?

OOO-KAY. I SEE WHERE THIS IS GOING. WHAT'S THE POINT OF PLANNING FOR A FUTURE YOU'LL NEVER HAVE, RIGHT? IS THAT WHY YOU'VE BEEN SO EXTRA GUNG-HO WITH THE SLAYING LATELY?

A LITTLE LOUDER, XAND. I DON'T THINK ALL OF THE LITTLE SADISTS PLAYING MAKE-THE-CLOWN'S-HEAD-EXPLODE HEARD YOU.

THAT'S WHY YOU'VE BEEN LETTING YOUR CLASSWORK SLIDE THE LAST COUPLE OF WEEKS?

IT WAS MORE OF A SIDE EFFECT. I'VE BEEN FRUSTRATED, AND PUTTING ALL MY ENERGY INTO PATROLLING. I GUESS THAT'S WHY I JUMPED THE GUN ON THE MAD JACK THING.

BUFFY, I THOUGHT HALF THE POINT OF YOU GOING TO COLLEGE WAS TO PROVE THAT THERE IS SOMETHING TO LIFE BESIDES BEING THE SLAYER. THAT YOU CAN HAVE MORE.

IT WAS. BUT I'M NOT SURE THAT'S TRUE ANYMORE. THIS *IS* MY CAREER, GUYS. IT DOESN'T COME WITH A RETIREMENT PLAN 'CAUSE THERE IS NO RETIREMENT.

I HAVEN'T FELT THIS LOST ... THIS SCATTERED IN A LONG TIME. NOT SINCE ... ANGEL LEFT.

WE COULD MAINLINE SOME MOCHACCINOS. THAT ALWAYS MAKES YOU FEEL BETTER.

THAT MAKES ME HYPER, WILL. IT'S NOT THE SAME.

I HAVE TO FOCUS AGAIN. GET BACK ON TRACK WITH CLASSES AND EVERYTHING. I JUST HAVE TO FIGURE OUT HOW TO DO THAT BEFORE I REALLY SCREW SOMETHING UP.

146

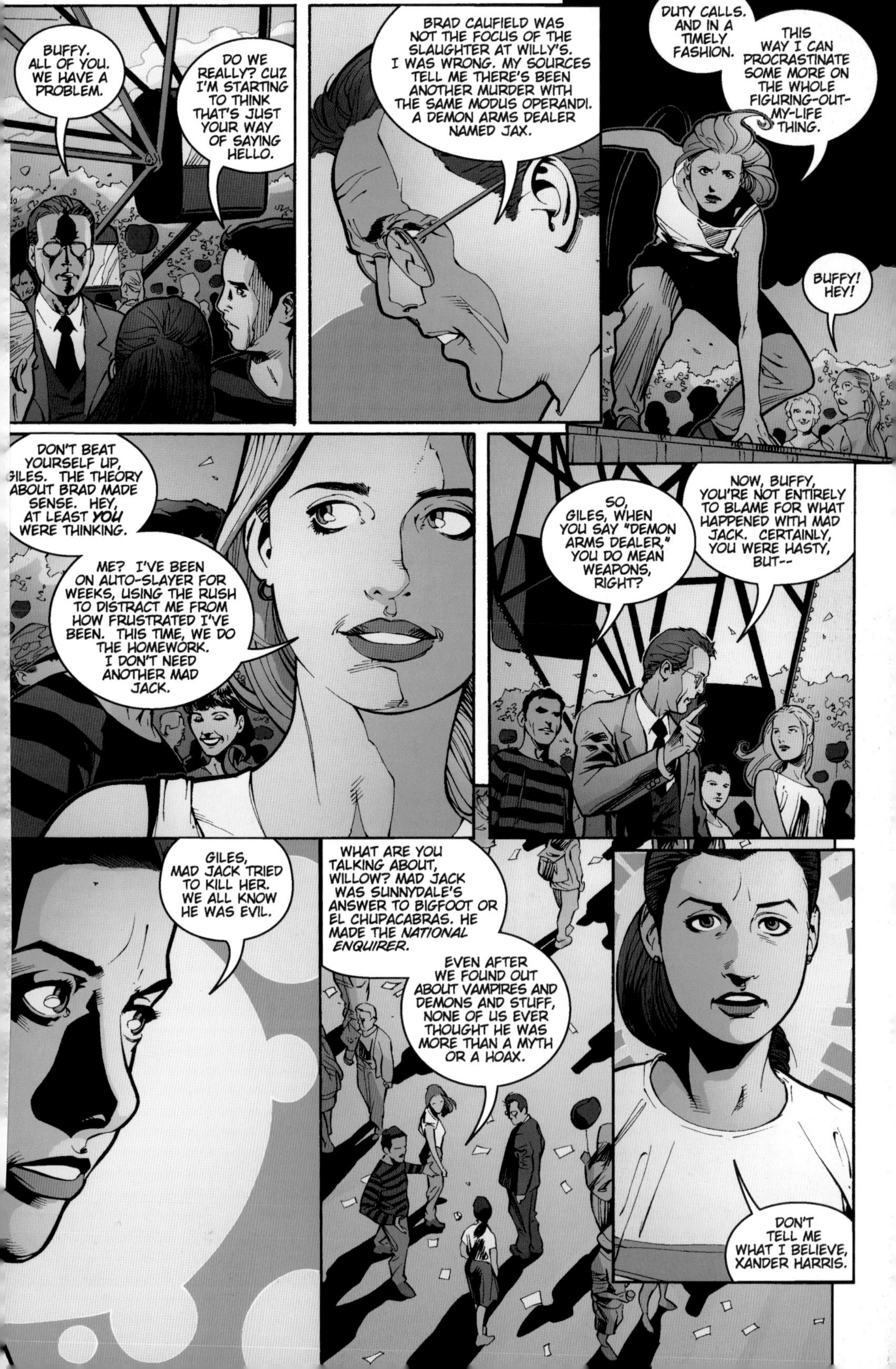
BUFFY. ALL OF YOU. WE HAVE A PROBLEM.
DO WE REALLY? CUZ I'M STARTING TO THINK THAT'S JUST YOUR WAY OF SAYING HELLO.
BRAD CAUFIELD WAS NOT THE FOCUS OF THE SLAUGHTER AT WILLY'S. I WAS WRONG. MY SOURCES TELL ME THERE'S BEEN ANOTHER MURDER WITH THE SAME MODUS OPERANDI. A DEMON ARMS DEALER NAMED JAX.
DUTY CALLS. AND IN A TIMELY FASHION.
THIS WAY I CAN PROCRASTINATE SOME MORE ON THE WHOLE FIGURING-OUT-MY-LIFE THING.
BUFFY! HEY!
DON'T BEAT YOURSELF UP, GILES. THE THEORY ABOUT BRAD MADE SENSE. HEY, AT LEAST *YOU* WERE THINKING.
ME? I'VE BEEN ON AUTO-SLAYER FOR WEEKS, USING THE RUSH TO DISTRACT ME FROM HOW FRUSTRATED I'VE BEEN. THIS TIME, WE DO THE HOMEWORK. I DON'T NEED ANOTHER MAD JACK.
SO, GILES, WHEN YOU SAY "DEMON ARMS DEALER," YOU DO MEAN WEAPONS, RIGHT?
NOW, BUFFY, YOU'RE NOT ENTIRELY TO BLAME FOR WHAT HAPPENED WITH MAD JACK. CERTAINLY, YOU WERE HASTY, BUT--
GILES, MAD JACK TRIED TO KILL HER. WE ALL KNOW HE WAS EVIL.
WHAT ARE YOU TALKING ABOUT, WILLOW? MAD JACK WAS SUNNYDALE'S ANSWER TO BIGFOOT OR EL CHUPACABRAS. HE MADE THE *NATIONAL ENQUIRER*.
EVEN AFTER WE FOUND OUT ABOUT VAMPIRES AND DEMONS AND STUFF, NONE OF US EVER THOUGHT HE WAS MORE THAN A MYTH OR A HOAX.
DON'T TELL ME WHAT I BELIEVE, XANDER HARRIS.

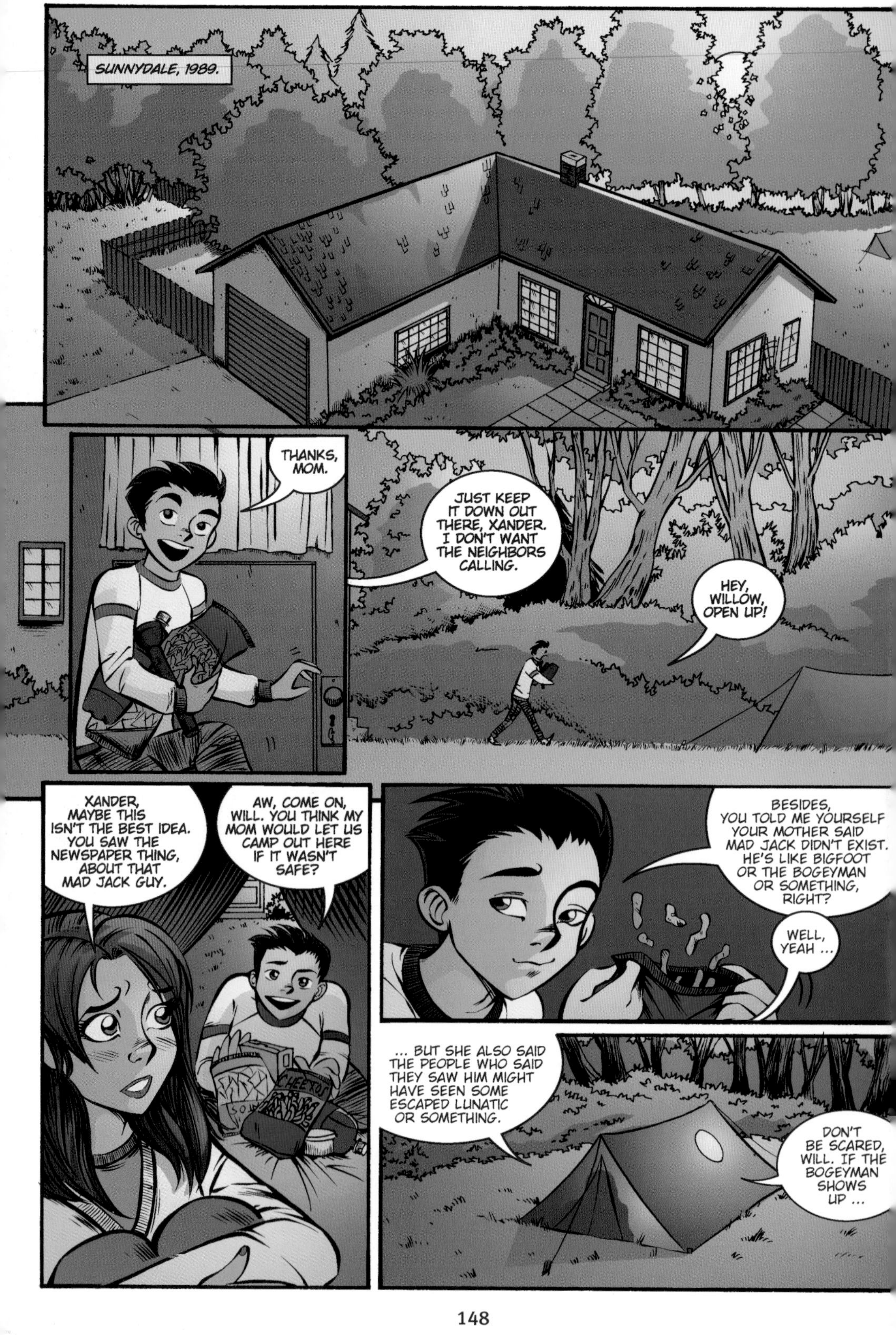
SUNNYDALE, 1989.
THANKS, MOM.
JUST KEEP IT DOWN OUT THERE, XANDER. I DON'T WANT THE NEIGHBORS CALLING.
HEY, WILLOW, OPEN UP!
XANDER, MAYBE THIS ISN'T THE BEST IDEA. YOU SAW THE NEWSPAPER THING, ABOUT THAT MAD JACK GUY.
AW, COME ON, WILL. YOU THINK MY MOM WOULD LET US CAMP OUT HERE IF IT WASN'T SAFE?
CHEETOS
BESIDES, YOU TOLD ME YOURSELF YOUR MOTHER SAID MAD JACK DIDN'T EXIST. HE'S LIKE BIGFOOT OR THE BOGEYMAN OR SOMETHING, RIGHT?
WELL, YEAH ...
... BUT SHE ALSO SAID THE PEOPLE WHO SAID THEY SAW HIM MIGHT HAVE SEEN SOME ESCAPED LUNATIC OR SOMETHING.
DON'T BE SCARED, WILL. IF THE BOGEYMAN SHOWS UP ...

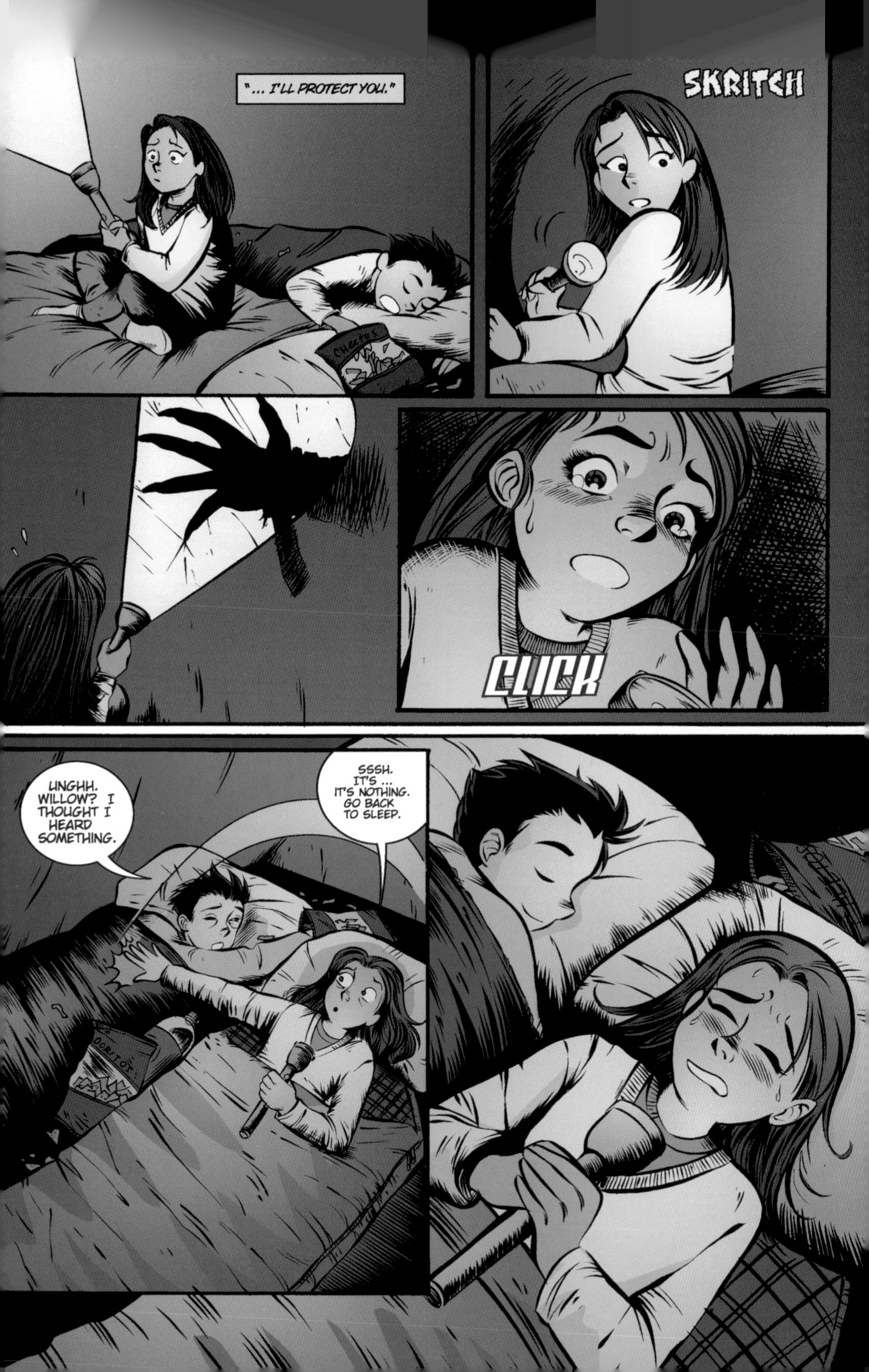
"... I'LL PROTECT YOU."
SKRITCH
CLICK
UNGHH. WILLOW? I THOUGHT I HEARD SOMETHING.
SSSH. IT'S ... IT'S NOTHING. GO BACK TO SLEEP.

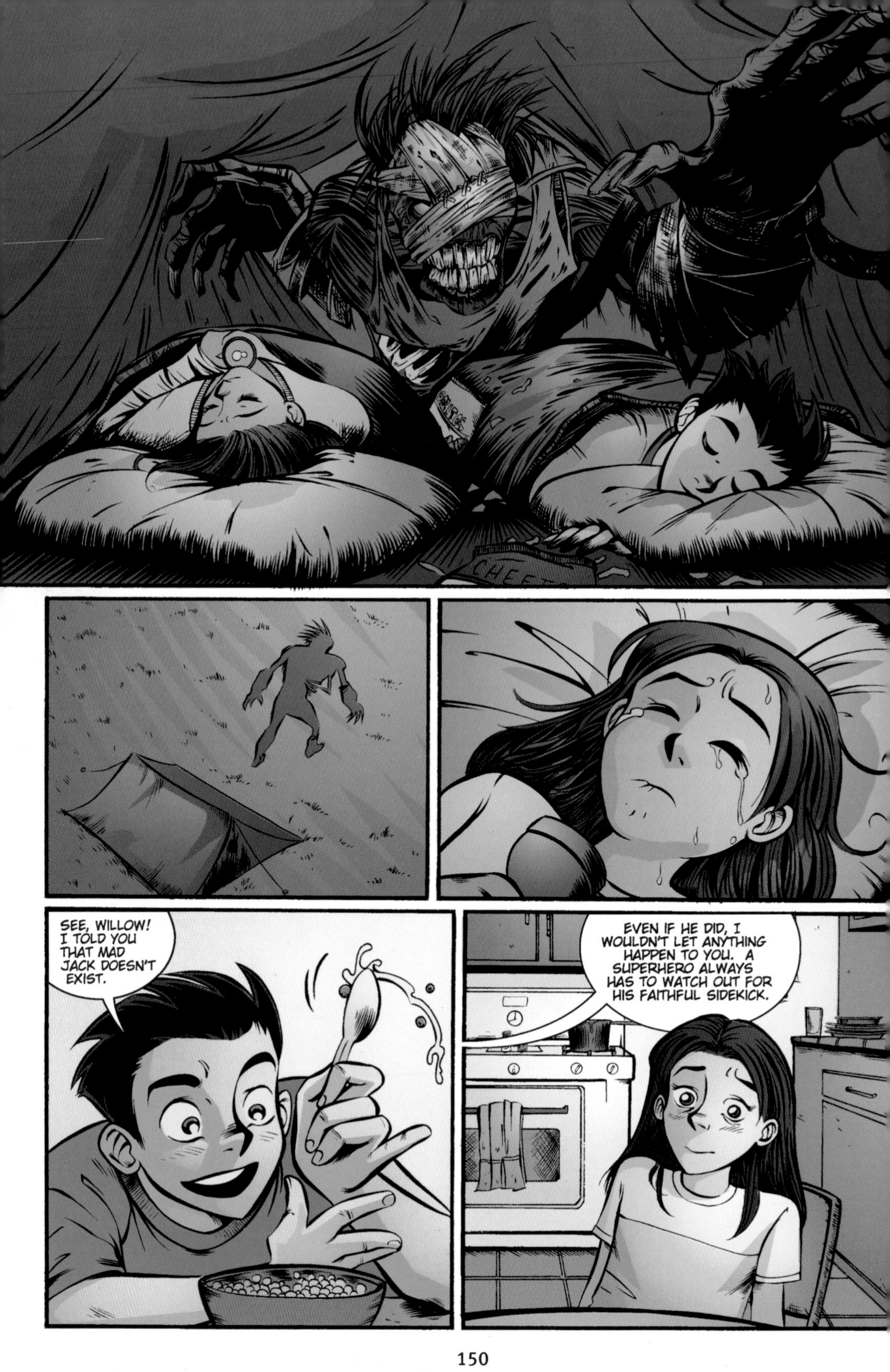
CHEET
SEE, WILLOW! I TOLD YOU THAT MAD JACK DOESN'T EXIST.
EVEN IF HE DID, I WOULDN'T LET ANYTHING HAPPEN TO YOU. A SUPERHERO ALWAYS HAS TO WATCH OUT FOR HIS FAITHFUL SIDEKICK.

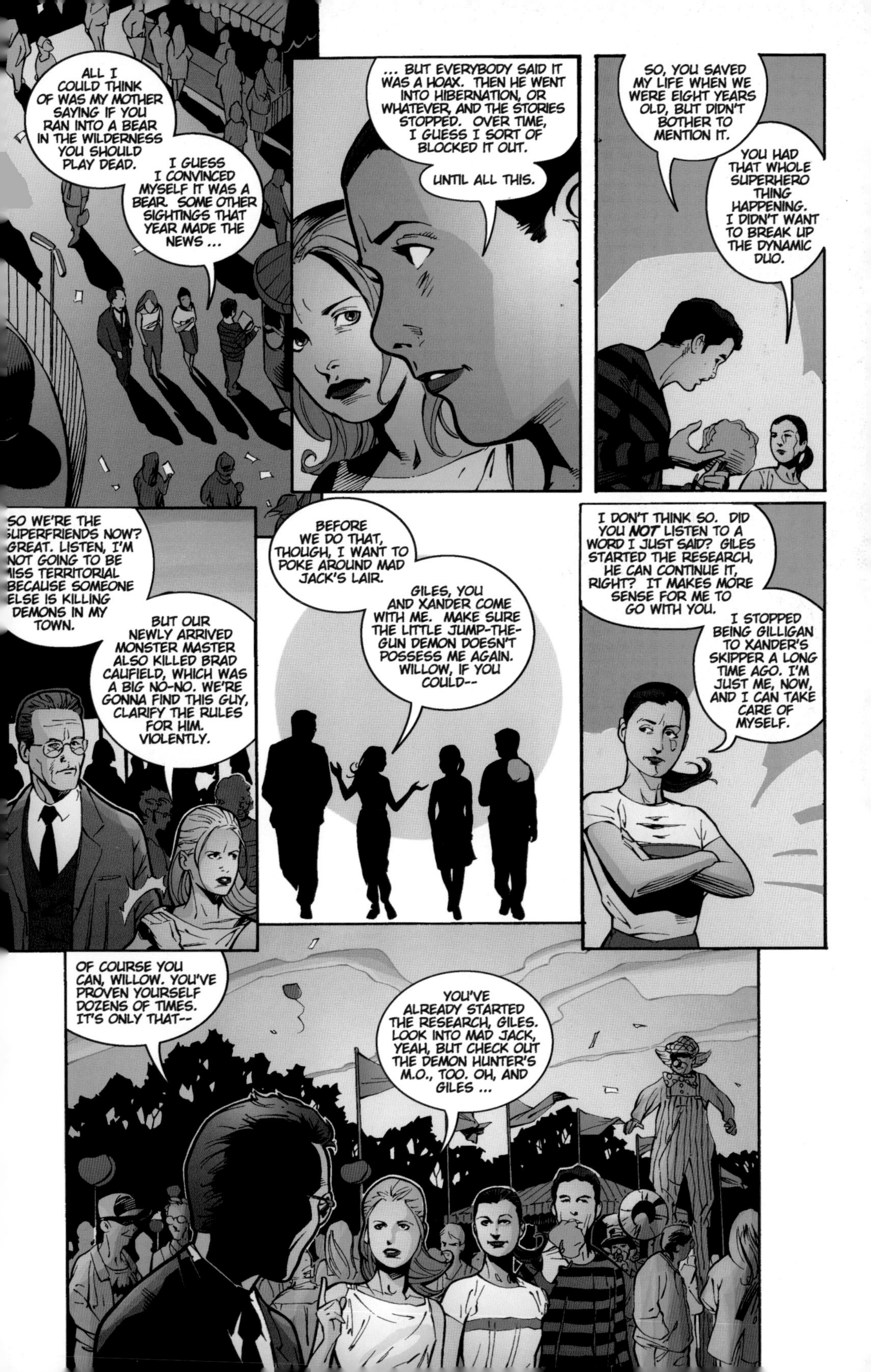
ALL I COULD THINK OF WAS MY MOTHER SAYING IF YOU RAN INTO A BEAR IN THE WILDERNESS YOU SHOULD PLAY DEAD.
I GUESS I CONVINCED MYSELF IT WAS A BEAR. SOME OTHER SIGHTINGS THAT YEAR MADE THE NEWS ...
... BUT EVERYBODY SAID IT WAS A HOAX. THEN HE WENT INTO HIBERNATION, OR WHATEVER, AND THE STORIES STOPPED. OVER TIME, I GUESS I SORT OF BLOCKED IT OUT.
UNTIL ALL THIS.
SO, YOU SAVED MY LIFE WHEN WE WERE EIGHT YEARS OLD, BUT DIDN'T BOTHER TO MENTION IT.
YOU HAD THAT WHOLE SUPERHERO THING HAPPENING. I DIDN'T WANT TO BREAK UP THE DYNAMIC DUO.
SO WE'RE THE SUPERFRIENDS NOW? GREAT. LISTEN, I'M NOT GOING TO BE MISS TERRITORIAL BECAUSE SOMEONE ELSE IS KILLING DEMONS IN MY TOWN.
BUT OUR NEWLY ARRIVED MONSTER MASTER ALSO KILLED BRAD CAUFIELD, WHICH WAS A BIG NO-NO. WE'RE GONNA FIND THIS GUY, CLARIFY THE RULES FOR HIM. VIOLENTLY.
BEFORE WE DO THAT, THOUGH, I WANT TO POKE AROUND MAD JACK'S LAIR.
GILES, YOU AND XANDER COME WITH ME. MAKE SURE THE LITTLE JUMP-THE-GUN DEMON DOESN'T POSSESS ME AGAIN. WILLOW, IF YOU COULD--
I DON'T THINK SO. DID YOU ***NOT*** LISTEN TO A WORD I JUST SAID? GILES STARTED THE RESEARCH, HE CAN CONTINUE IT, RIGHT? IT MAKES MORE SENSE FOR ME TO GO WITH YOU.
I STOPPED BEING GILLIGAN TO XANDER'S SKIPPER A LONG TIME AGO. I'M JUST ME, NOW, AND I CAN TAKE CARE OF MYSELF.
OF COURSE YOU CAN, WILLOW. YOU'VE PROVEN YOURSELF DOZENS OF TIMES. IT'S ONLY THAT--
YOU'VE ALREADY STARTED THE RESEARCH, GILES. LOOK INTO MAD JACK, YEAH, BUT CHECK OUT THE DEMON HUNTER'S M.O., TOO. OH, AND GILES ...

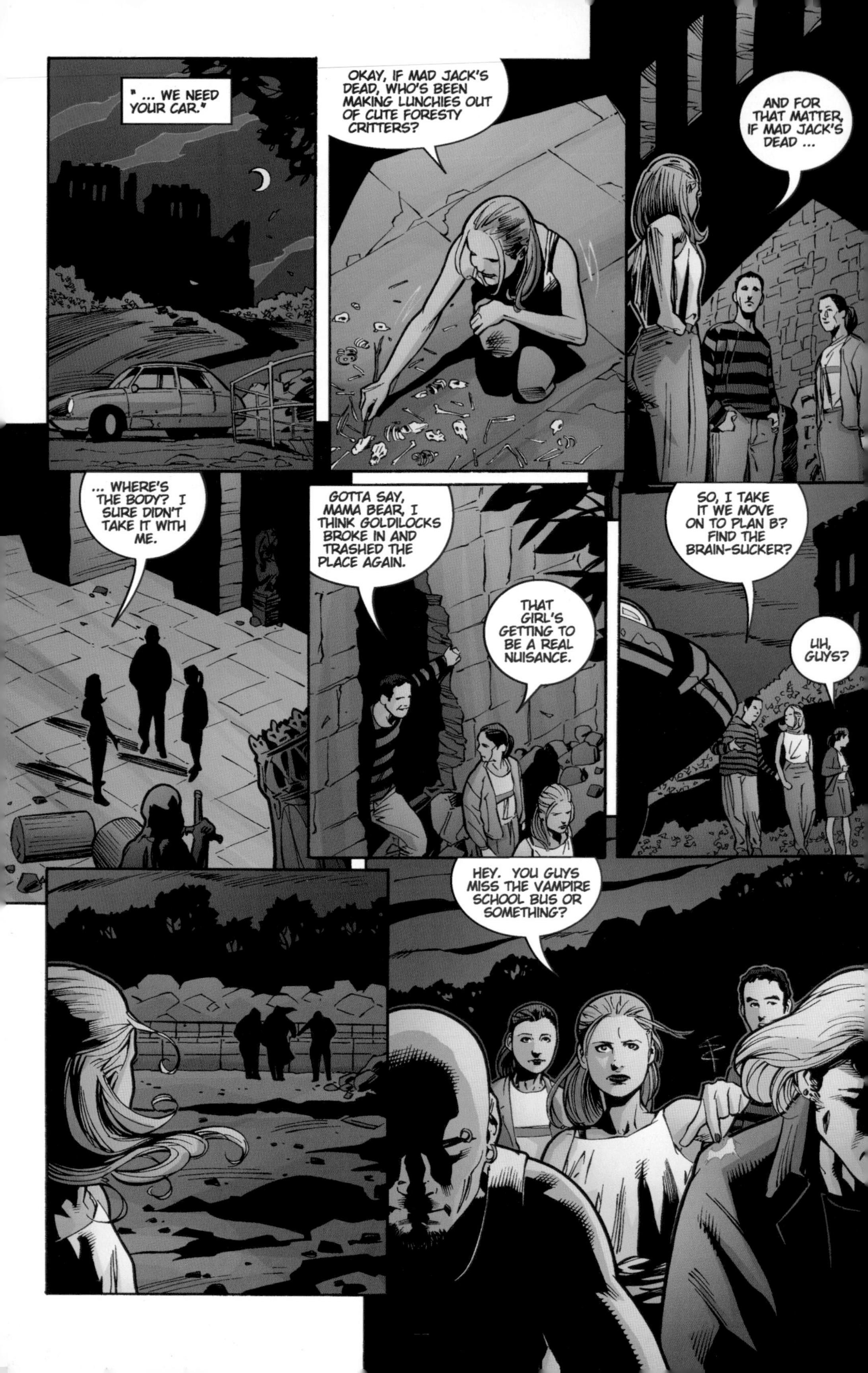
"... WE NEED YOUR CAR."
OKAY, IF MAD JACK'S DEAD, WHO'S BEEN MAKING LUNCHIES OUT OF CUTE FORESTY CRITTERS?
AND FOR THAT MATTER, IF MAD JACK'S DEAD ...
... WHERE'S THE BODY? I SURE DIDN'T TAKE IT WITH ME.
GOTTA SAY, MAMA BEAR, I THINK GOLDILOCKS BROKE IN AND TRASHED THE PLACE AGAIN.
THAT GIRL'S GETTING TO BE A REAL NUISANCE.
SO, I TAKE IT WE MOVE ON TO PLAN B? FIND THE BRAIN-SUCKER?
UH, GUYS?
HEY. YOU GUYS MISS THE VAMPIRE SCHOOL BUS OR SOMETHING?

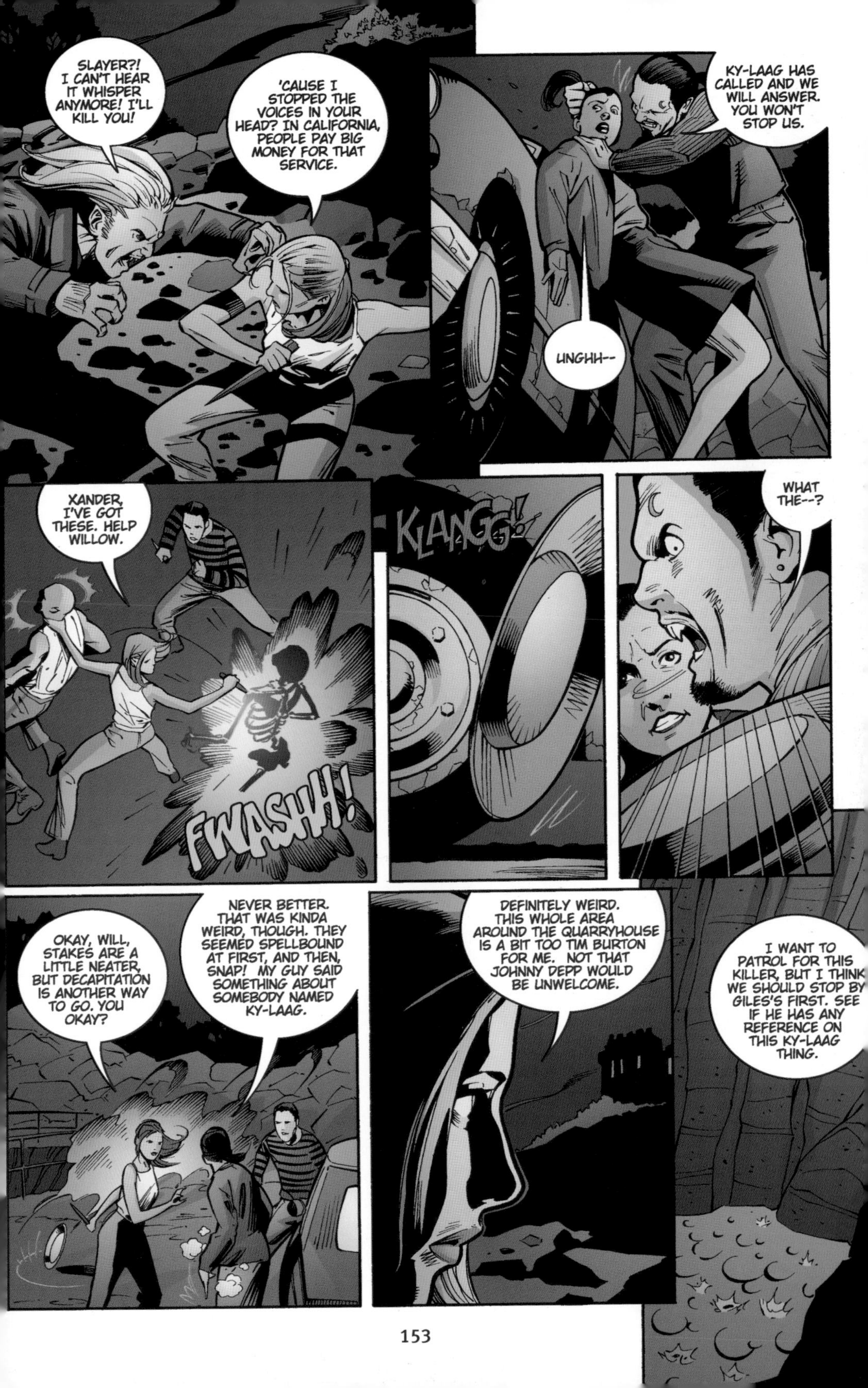
SLAYER?! I CAN'T HEAR IT WHISPER ANYMORE! I'LL KILL YOU!
'CAUSE I STOPPED THE VOICES IN YOUR HEAD? IN CALIFORNIA, PEOPLE PAY BIG MONEY FOR THAT SERVICE.
KY-LAAG HAS CALLED AND WE WILL ANSWER. YOU WON'T STOP US.
UNGHH--
XANDER, I'VE GOT THESE. HELP WILLOW.
FWASHH!
KLANGG!
WHAT THE--?
OKAY, WILL, STAKES ARE A LITTLE NEATER, BUT DECAPITATION IS ANOTHER WAY TO GO. YOU OKAY?
NEVER BETTER. THAT WAS KINDA WEIRD, THOUGH. THEY SEEMED SPELLBOUND AT FIRST, AND THEN, SNAP! MY GUY SAID SOMETHING ABOUT SOMEBODY NAMED KY-LAAG.
DEFINITELY WEIRD. THIS WHOLE AREA AROUND THE QUARRYHOUSE IS A BIT TOO TIM BURTON FOR ME. NOT THAT JOHNNY DEPP WOULD BE UNWELCOME.
I WANT TO PATROL FOR THIS KILLER, BUT I THINK WE SHOULD STOP BY GILES'S FIRST. SEE IF HE HAS ANY REFERENCE ON THIS KY-LAAG THING.

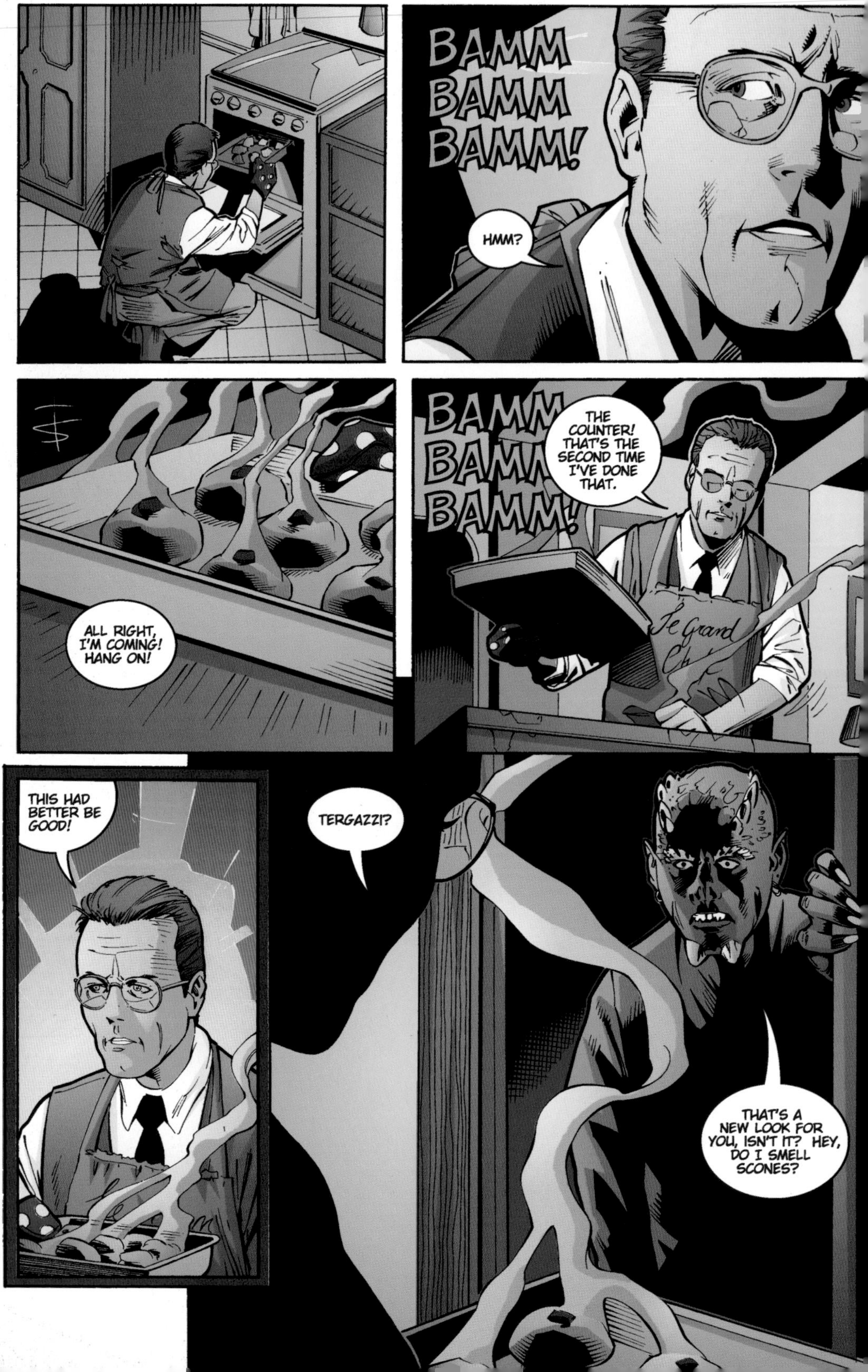
BAMM
BAMM
BAMM!
HMM?
ALL RIGHT, I'M COMING! HANG ON!
BAMM
BAMM
BAMM!
THE COUNTER! THAT'S THE SECOND TIME I'VE DONE THAT.
THIS HAD BETTER BE GOOD!
TERGAZZI?
THAT'S A NEW LOOK FOR YOU, ISN'T IT? HEY, DO I SMELL SCONES?

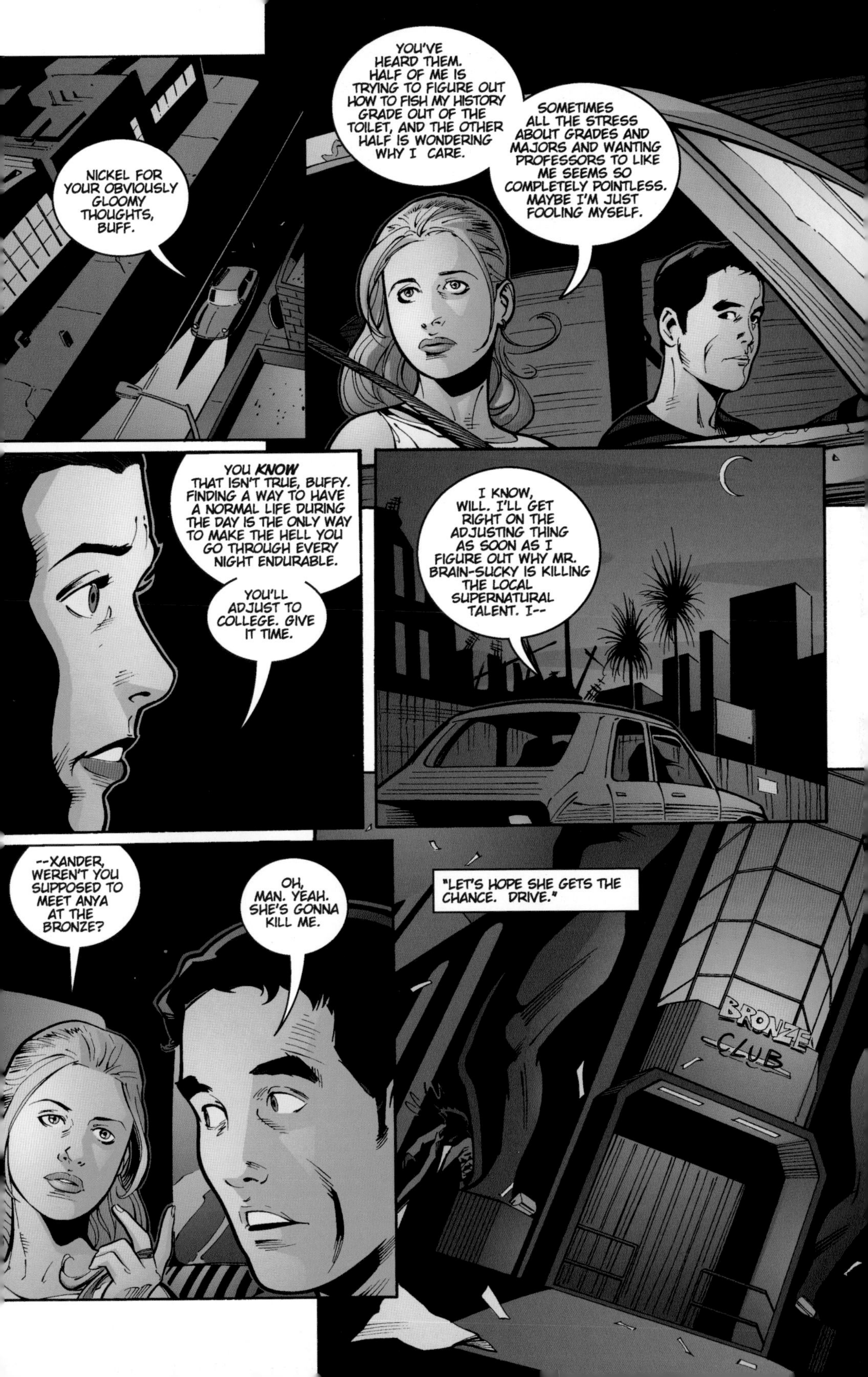
NICKEL FOR YOUR OBVIOUSLY GLOOMY THOUGHTS, BUFF.
YOU'VE HEARD THEM. HALF OF ME IS TRYING TO FIGURE OUT HOW TO FISH MY HISTORY GRADE OUT OF THE TOILET, AND THE OTHER HALF IS WONDERING WHY I CARE.
SOMETIMES ALL THE STRESS ABOUT GRADES AND MAJORS AND WANTING PROFESSORS TO LIKE ME SEEMS SO COMPLETELY POINTLESS. MAYBE I'M JUST FOOLING MYSELF.
YOU *KNOW* THAT ISN'T TRUE, BUFFY. FINDING A WAY TO HAVE A NORMAL LIFE DURING THE DAY IS THE ONLY WAY TO MAKE THE HELL YOU GO THROUGH EVERY NIGHT ENDURABLE.
YOU'LL ADJUST TO COLLEGE. GIVE IT TIME.
I KNOW, WILL. I'LL GET RIGHT ON THE ADJUSTING THING AS SOON AS I FIGURE OUT WHY MR. BRAIN-SUCKY IS KILLING THE LOCAL SUPERNATURAL TALENT. I--
--XANDER, WEREN'T YOU SUPPOSED TO MEET ANYA AT THE BRONZE?
OH, MAN. YEAH. SHE'S GONNA KILL ME.
"LET'S HOPE SHE GETS THE CHANCE. DRIVE."
BRONZE
CLUB

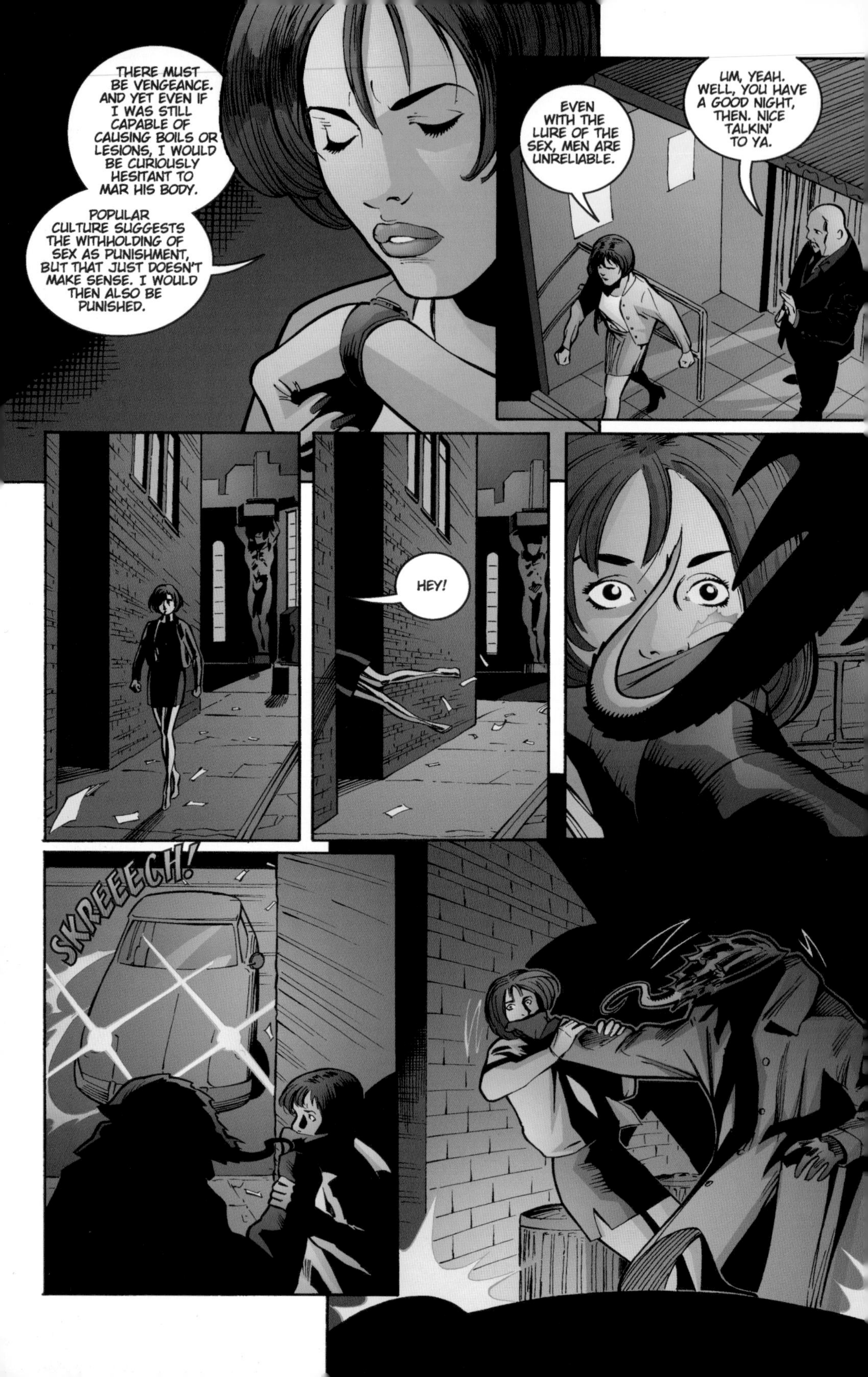
THERE MUST BE VENGEANCE. AND YET EVEN IF I WAS STILL CAPABLE OF CAUSING BOILS OR LESIONS, I WOULD BE CURIOUSLY HESITANT TO MAR HIS BODY.
POPULAR CULTURE SUGGESTS THE WITHHOLDING OF SEX AS PUNISHMENT, BUT THAT JUST DOESN'T MAKE SENSE. I WOULD THEN ALSO BE PUNISHED.
EVEN WITH THE LURE OF THE SEX, MEN ARE UNRELIABLE.
UM, YEAH. WELL, YOU HAVE A GOOD NIGHT, THEN. NICE TALKIN' TO YA.
HEY!
SKREEECH!

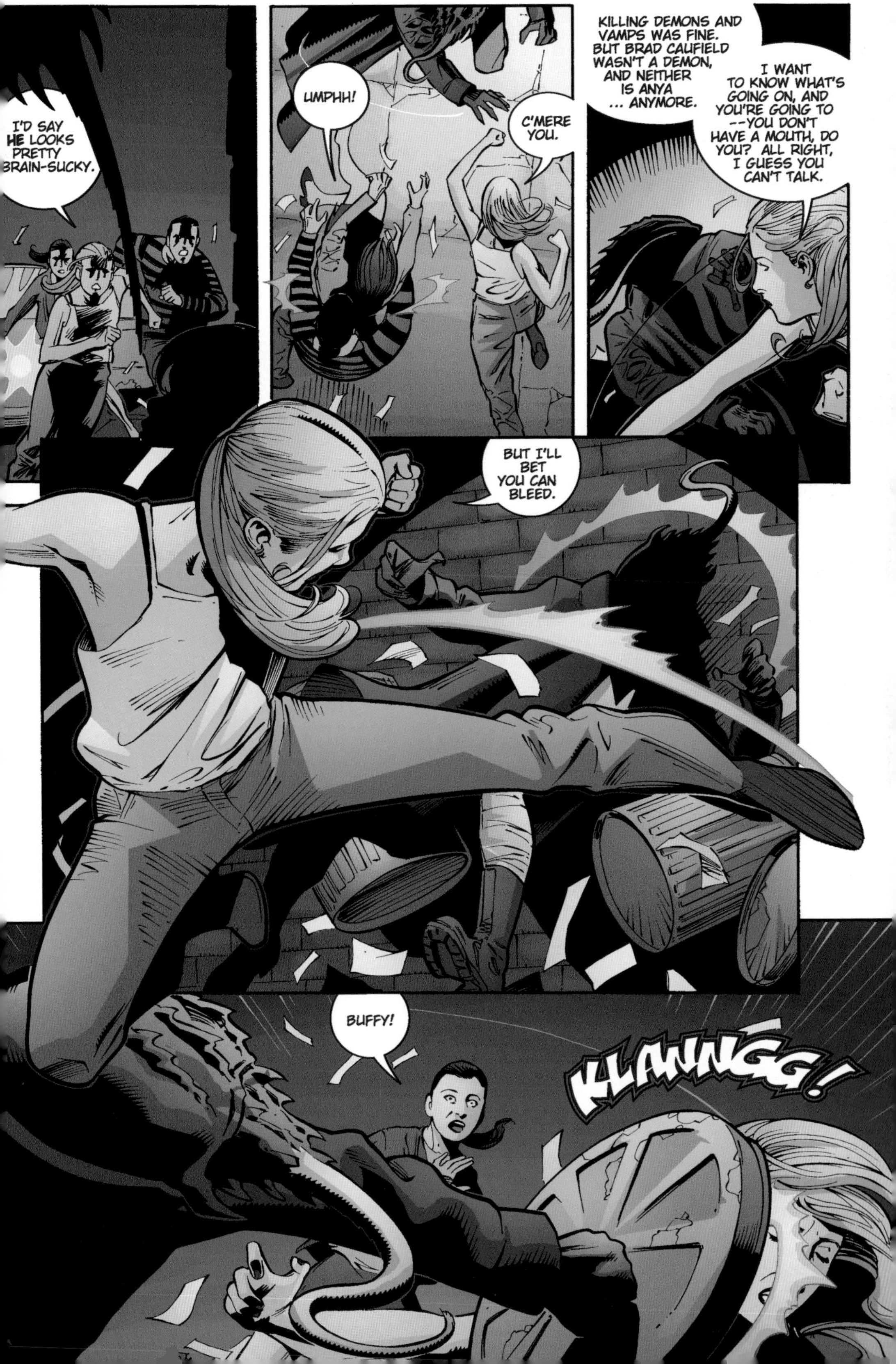

I'D SAY HE LOOKS PRETTY BRAIN-SUCKY.
UMPHH!
C'MERE YOU.
KILLING DEMONS AND VAMPS WAS FINE. BUT BRAD CAUFIELD WASN'T A DEMON, AND NEITHER IS ANYA ... ANYMORE.
I WANT TO KNOW WHAT'S GOING ON, AND YOU'RE GOING TO --YOU DON'T HAVE A MOUTH, DO YOU? ALL RIGHT, I GUESS YOU CAN'T TALK.
BUT I'LL BET YOU CAN BLEED.
BUFFY!
KLANNGG!

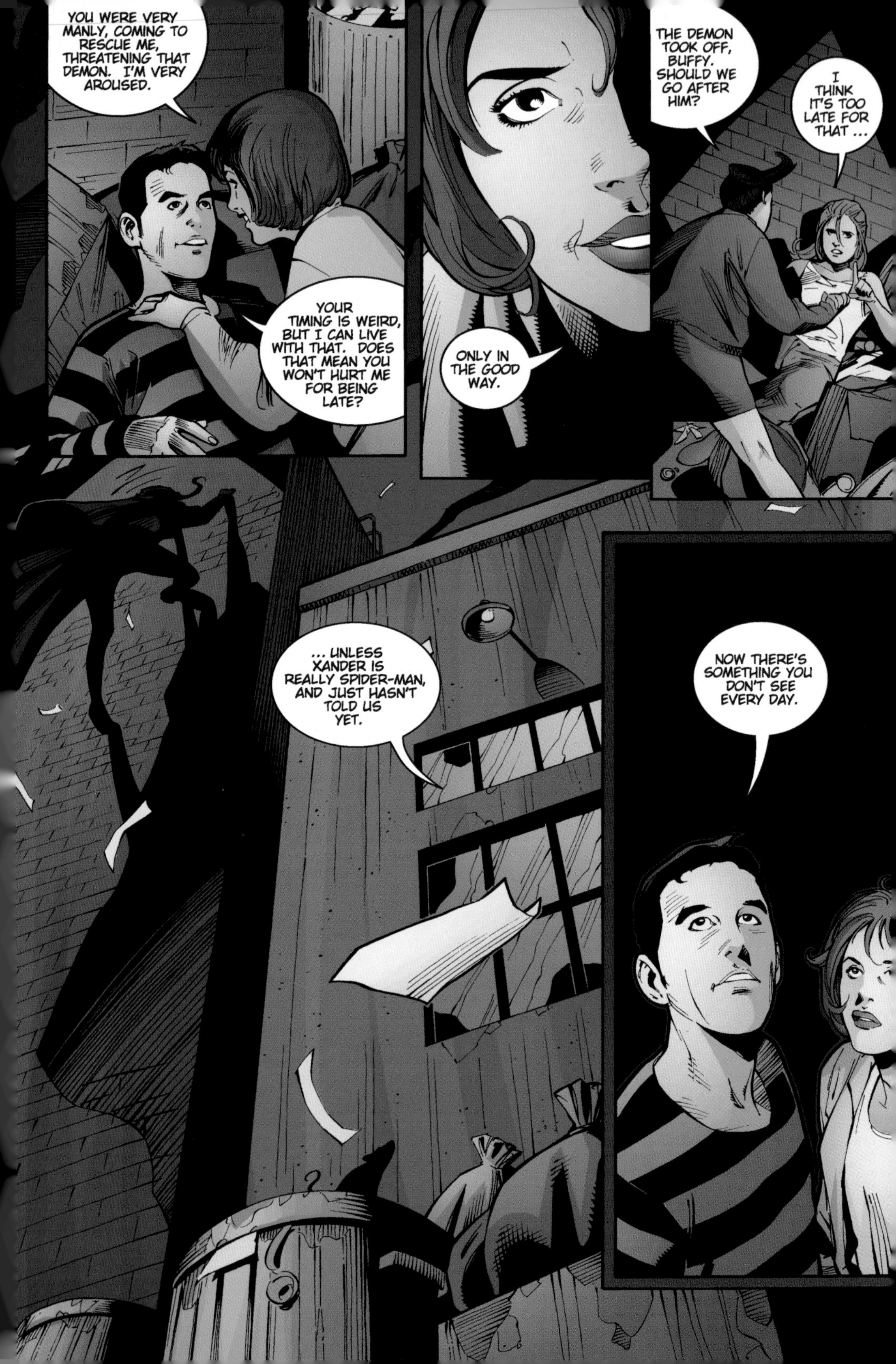
YOU WERE VERY MANLY, COMING TO RESCUE ME, THREATENING THAT DEMON. I'M VERY AROUSED.
YOUR TIMING IS WEIRD, BUT I CAN LIVE WITH THAT. DOES THAT MEAN YOU WON'T HURT ME FOR BEING LATE?
ONLY IN THE GOOD WAY.
THE DEMON TOOK OFF, BUFFY. SHOULD WE GO AFTER HIM?
I THINK IT'S TOO LATE FOR THAT ...
... UNLESS XANDER IS REALLY SPIDER-MAN, AND JUST HASN'T TOLD US YET.
NOW THERE'S SOMETHING YOU DON'T SEE EVERY DAY.

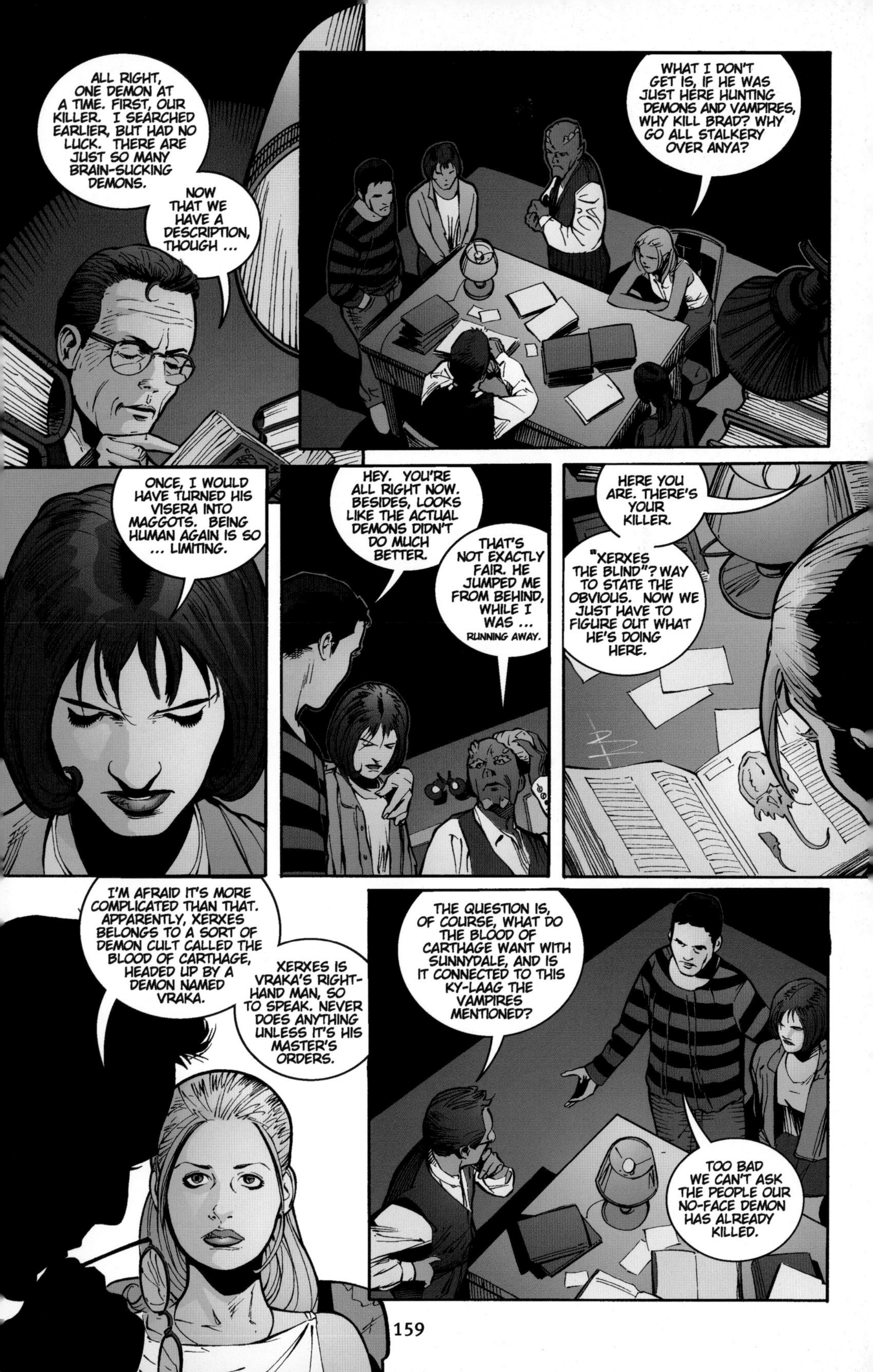
ALL RIGHT, ONE DEMON AT A TIME. FIRST, OUR KILLER. I SEARCHED EARLIER, BUT HAD NO LUCK. THERE ARE JUST SO MANY BRAIN-SUCKING DEMONS.
NOW THAT WE HAVE A DESCRIPTION, THOUGH ...
WHAT I DON'T GET IS, IF HE WAS JUST HERE HUNTING DEMONS AND VAMPIRES, WHY KILL BRAD? WHY GO ALL STALKERY OVER ANYA?
ONCE, I WOULD HAVE TURNED HIS VISERA INTO MAGGOTS. BEING HUMAN AGAIN IS SO ... LIMITING.
HEY. YOU'RE ALL RIGHT NOW. BESIDES, LOOKS LIKE THE ACTUAL DEMONS DIDN'T DO MUCH BETTER.
THAT'S NOT EXACTLY FAIR. HE JUMPED ME FROM BEHIND, WHILE I WAS ... RUNNING AWAY.
HERE YOU ARE. THERE'S YOUR KILLER.
"XERXES THE BLIND"? WAY TO STATE THE OBVIOUS. NOW WE JUST HAVE TO FIGURE OUT WHAT HE'S DOING HERE.
I'M AFRAID IT'S MORE COMPLICATED THAN THAT. APPARENTLY, XERXES BELONGS TO A SORT OF DEMON CULT CALLED THE BLOOD OF CARTHAGE, HEADED UP BY A DEMON NAMED VRAKA.
XERXES IS VRAKA'S RIGHT-HAND MAN, SO TO SPEAK. NEVER DOES ANYTHING UNLESS IT'S HIS MASTER'S ORDERS.
THE QUESTION IS, OF COURSE, WHAT DO THE BLOOD OF CARTHAGE WANT WITH SUNNYDALE, AND IS IT CONNECTED TO THIS KY-LAAG THE VAMPIRES MENTIONED?
TOO BAD WE CAN'T ASK THE PEOPLE OUR NO-FACE DEMON HAS ALREADY KILLED.

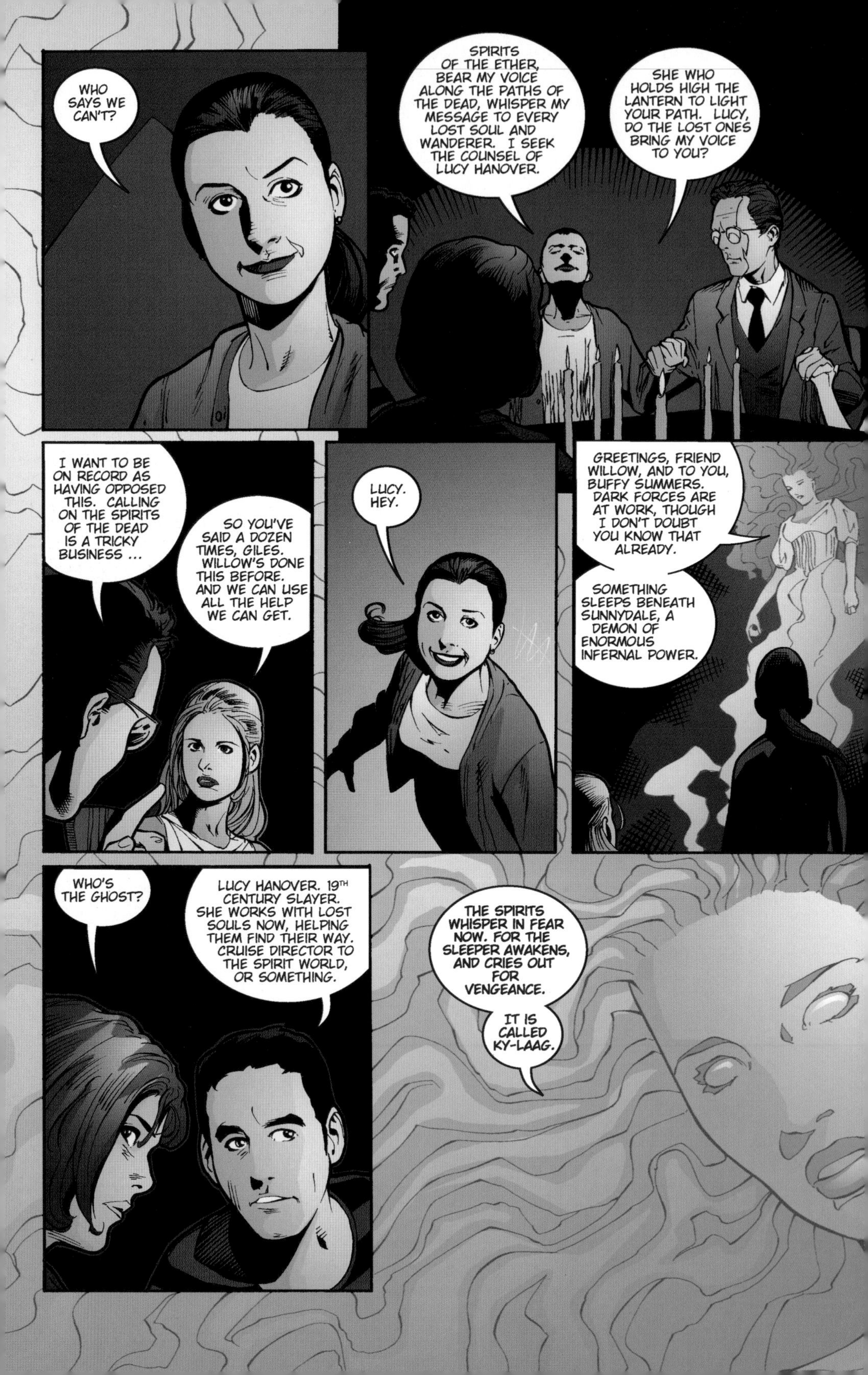

WHO SAYS WE CAN'T?
SPIRITS OF THE ETHER, BEAR MY VOICE ALONG THE PATHS OF THE DEAD, WHISPER MY MESSAGE TO EVERY LOST SOUL AND WANDERER. I SEEK THE COUNSEL OF LUCY HANOVER.
SHE WHO HOLDS HIGH THE LANTERN TO LIGHT YOUR PATH. LUCY, DO THE LOST ONES BRING MY VOICE TO YOU?
I WANT TO BE ON RECORD AS HAVING OPPOSED THIS. CALLING ON THE SPIRITS OF THE DEAD IS A TRICKY BUSINESS ...
SO YOU'VE SAID A DOZEN TIMES, GILES. WILLOW'S DONE THIS BEFORE. AND WE CAN USE ALL THE HELP WE CAN GET.
LUCY. HEY.
GREETINGS, FRIEND WILLOW, AND TO YOU, BUFFY SUMMERS. DARK FORCES ARE AT WORK, THOUGH I DON'T DOUBT YOU KNOW THAT ALREADY.
SOMETHING SLEEPS BENEATH SUNNYDALE, A DEMON OF ENORMOUS INFERNAL POWER.
WHO'S THE GHOST?
LUCY HANOVER. 19TH CENTURY SLAYER. SHE WORKS WITH LOST SOULS NOW, HELPING THEM FIND THEIR WAY. CRUISE DIRECTOR TO THE SPIRIT WORLD, OR SOMETHING.
THE SPIRITS WHISPER IN FEAR NOW. FOR THE SLEEPER AWAKENS, AND CRIES OUT FOR VENGEANCE.
IT IS CALLED KY-LAAG.

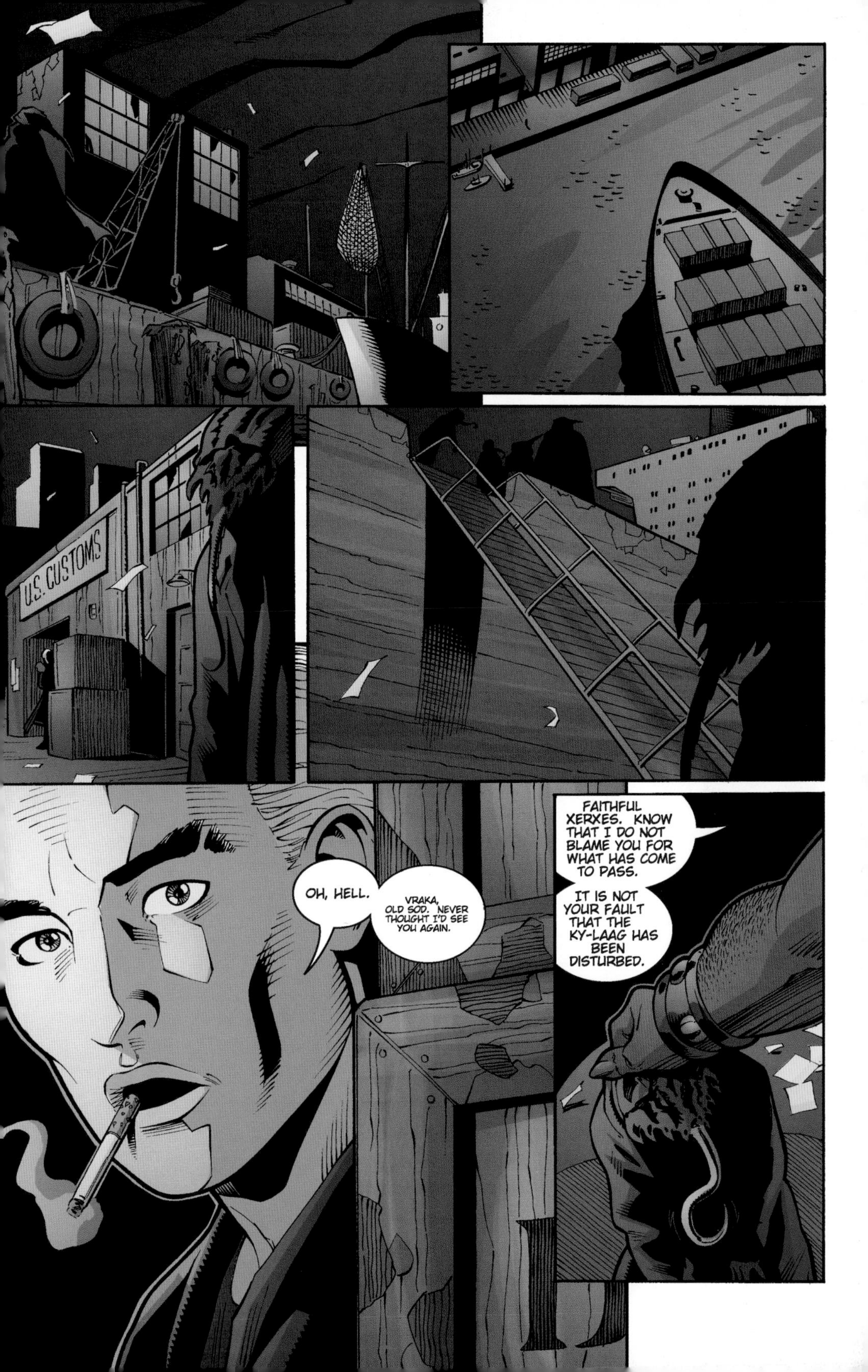
U.S. CUSTOMS
OH, HELL.
VRAKA, OLD SOD. NEVER THOUGHT I'D SEE YOU AGAIN.
FAITHFUL XERXES. KNOW THAT I DO NOT BLAME YOU FOR WHAT HAS COME TO PASS.
IT IS NOT YOUR FAULT THAT THE KY-LAAG HAS BEEN DISTURBED.

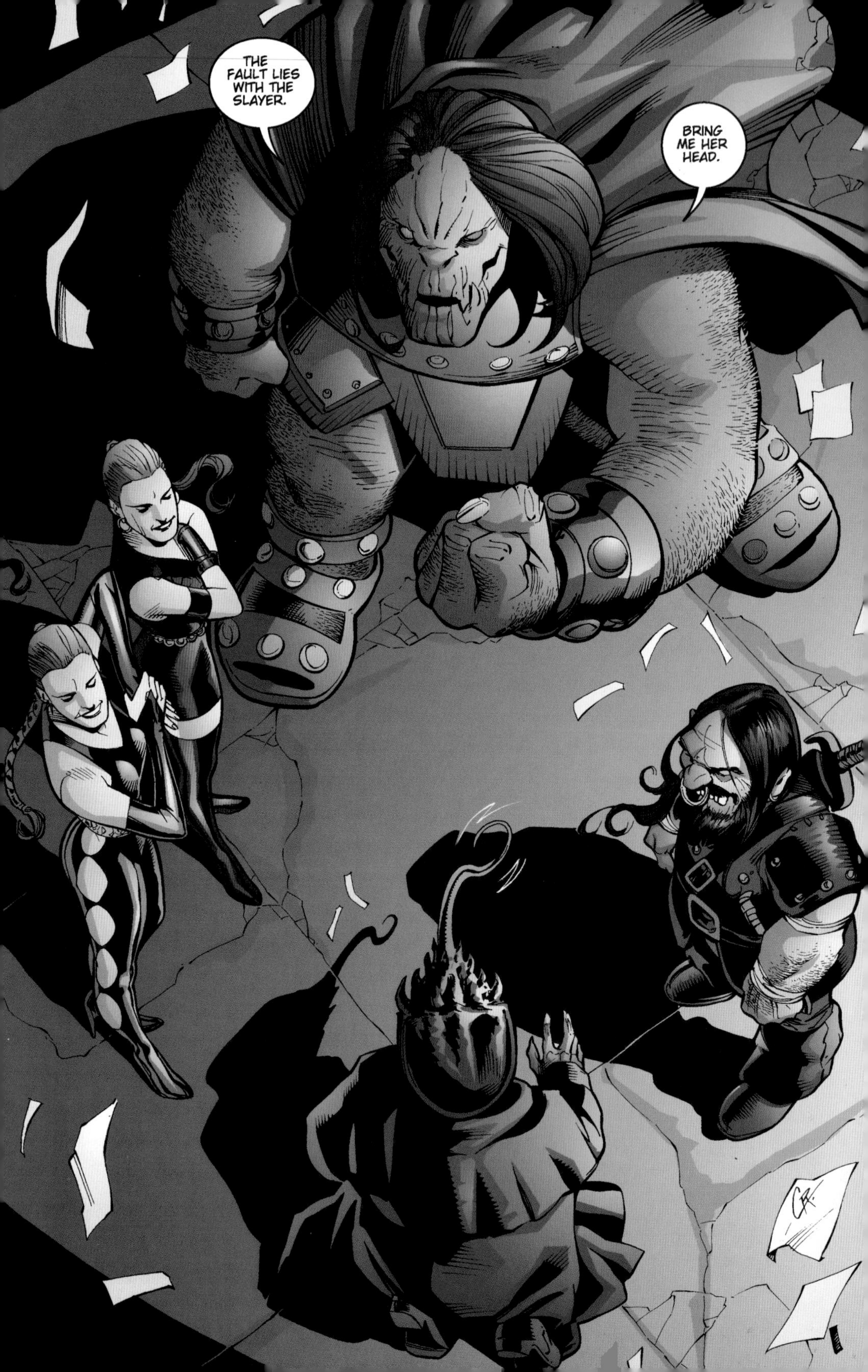
THE FAULT LIES WITH THE SLAYER.
BRING ME HER HEAD.

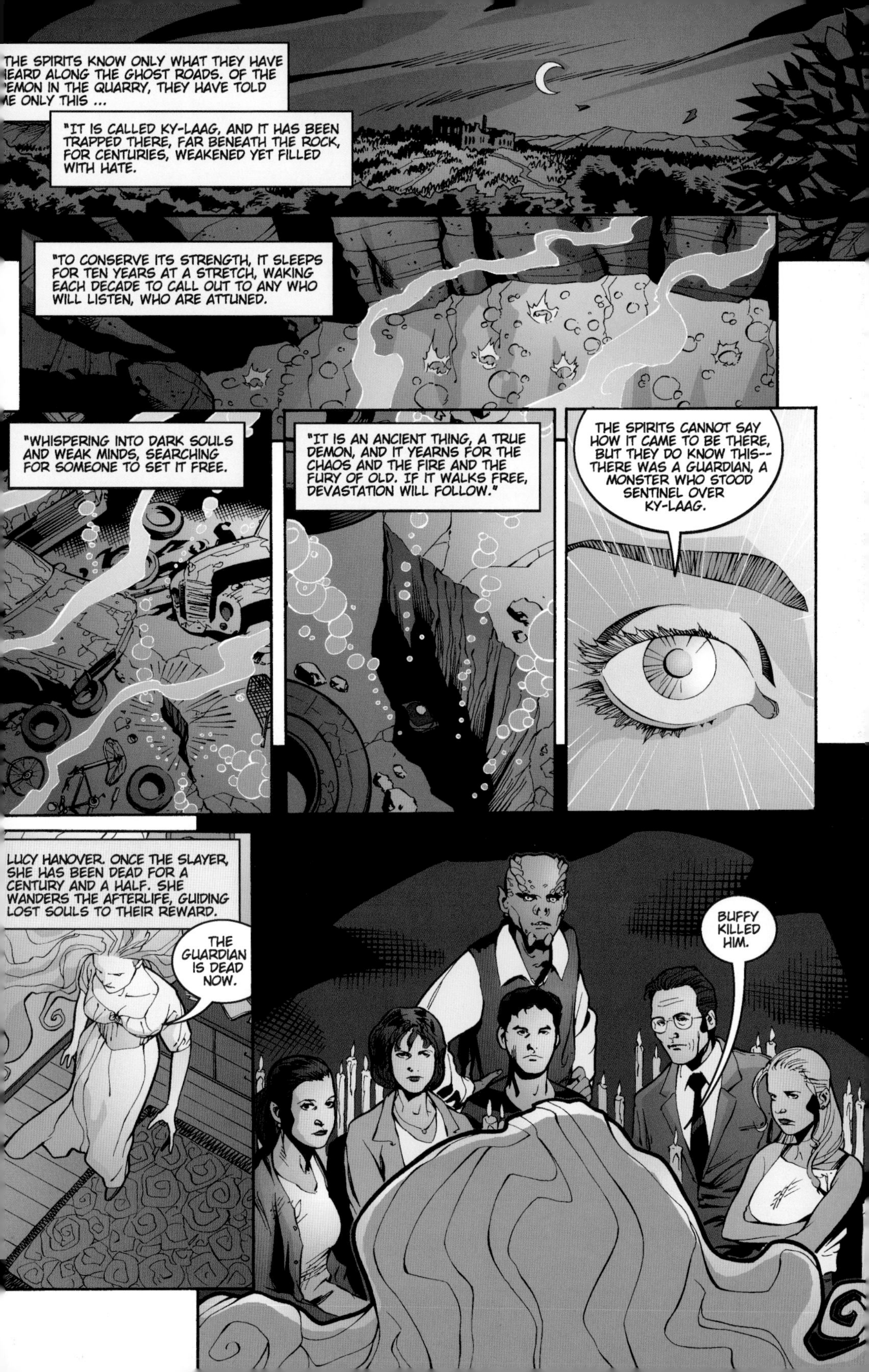
THE SPIRITS KNOW ONLY WHAT THEY HAVE HEARD ALONG THE GHOST ROADS. OF THE DEMON IN THE QUARRY, THEY HAVE TOLD ME ONLY THIS ...
"IT IS CALLED KY-LAAG, AND IT HAS BEEN TRAPPED THERE, FAR BENEATH THE ROCK, FOR CENTURIES, WEAKENED YET FILLED WITH HATE.
"TO CONSERVE ITS STRENGTH, IT SLEEPS FOR TEN YEARS AT A STRETCH, WAKING EACH DECADE TO CALL OUT TO ANY WHO WILL LISTEN, WHO ARE ATTUNED.
"WHISPERING INTO DARK SOULS AND WEAK MINDS, SEARCHING FOR SOMEONE TO SET IT FREE.
"IT IS AN ANCIENT THING, A TRUE DEMON, AND IT YEARNS FOR THE CHAOS AND THE FIRE AND THE FURY OF OLD. IF IT WALKS FREE, DEVASTATION WILL FOLLOW."
THE SPIRITS CANNOT SAY HOW IT CAME TO BE THERE, BUT THEY DO KNOW THIS-- THERE WAS A GUARDIAN, A MONSTER WHO STOOD SENTINEL OVER KY-LAAG.
LUCY HANOVER. ONCE THE SLAYER, SHE HAS BEEN DEAD FOR A CENTURY AND A HALF. SHE WANDERS THE AFTERLIFE, GUIDING LOST SOULS TO THEIR REWARD.
THE GUARDIAN IS DEAD NOW.
BUFFY KILLED HIM.

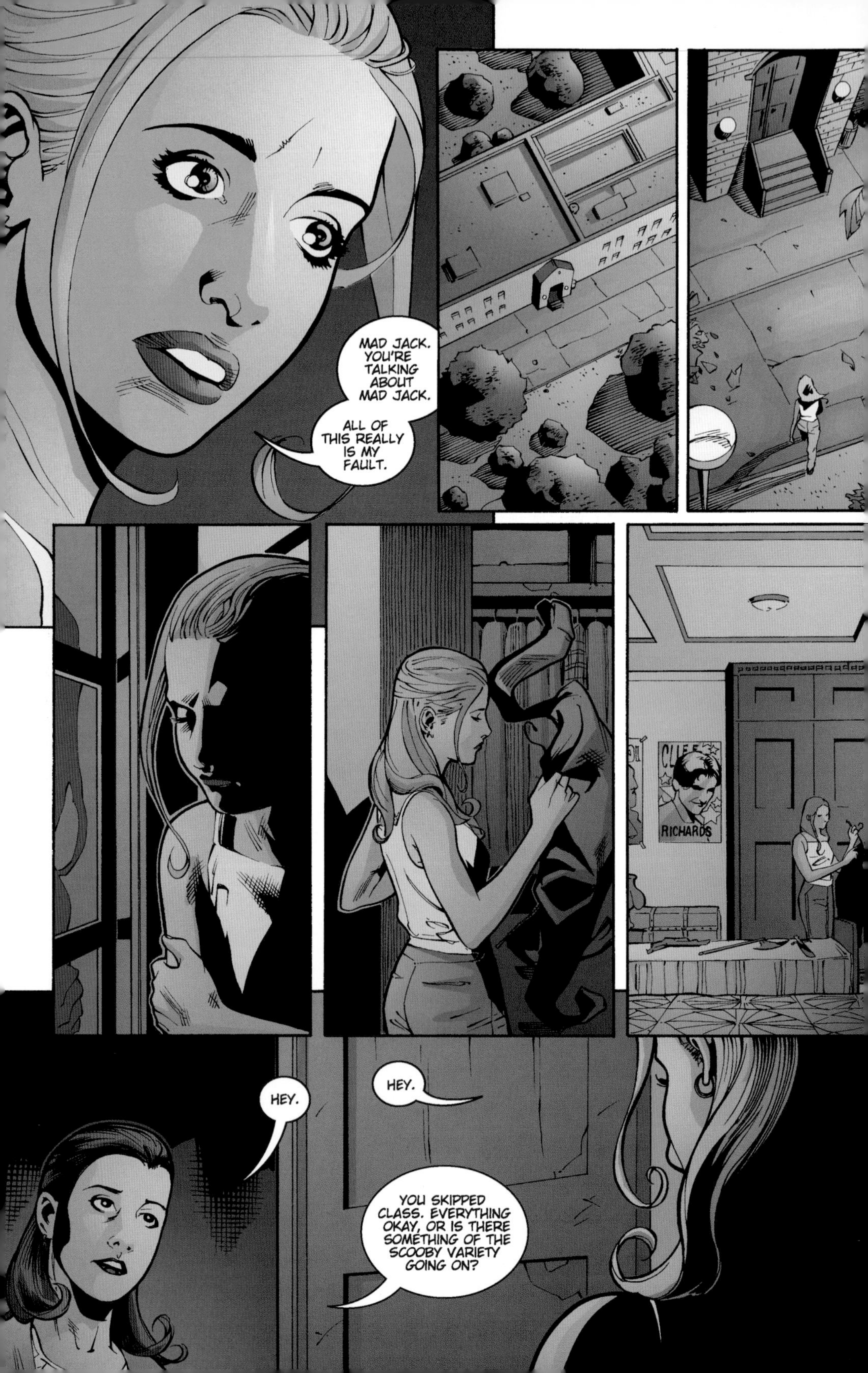
MAD JACK. YOU'RE TALKING ABOUT MAD JACK.
ALL OF THIS REALLY IS MY FAULT.
CLIFF RICHARDS
HEY.
HEY.
YOU SKIPPED CLASS. EVERYTHING OKAY, OR IS THERE SOMETHING OF THE SCOOBY VARIETY GOING ON?

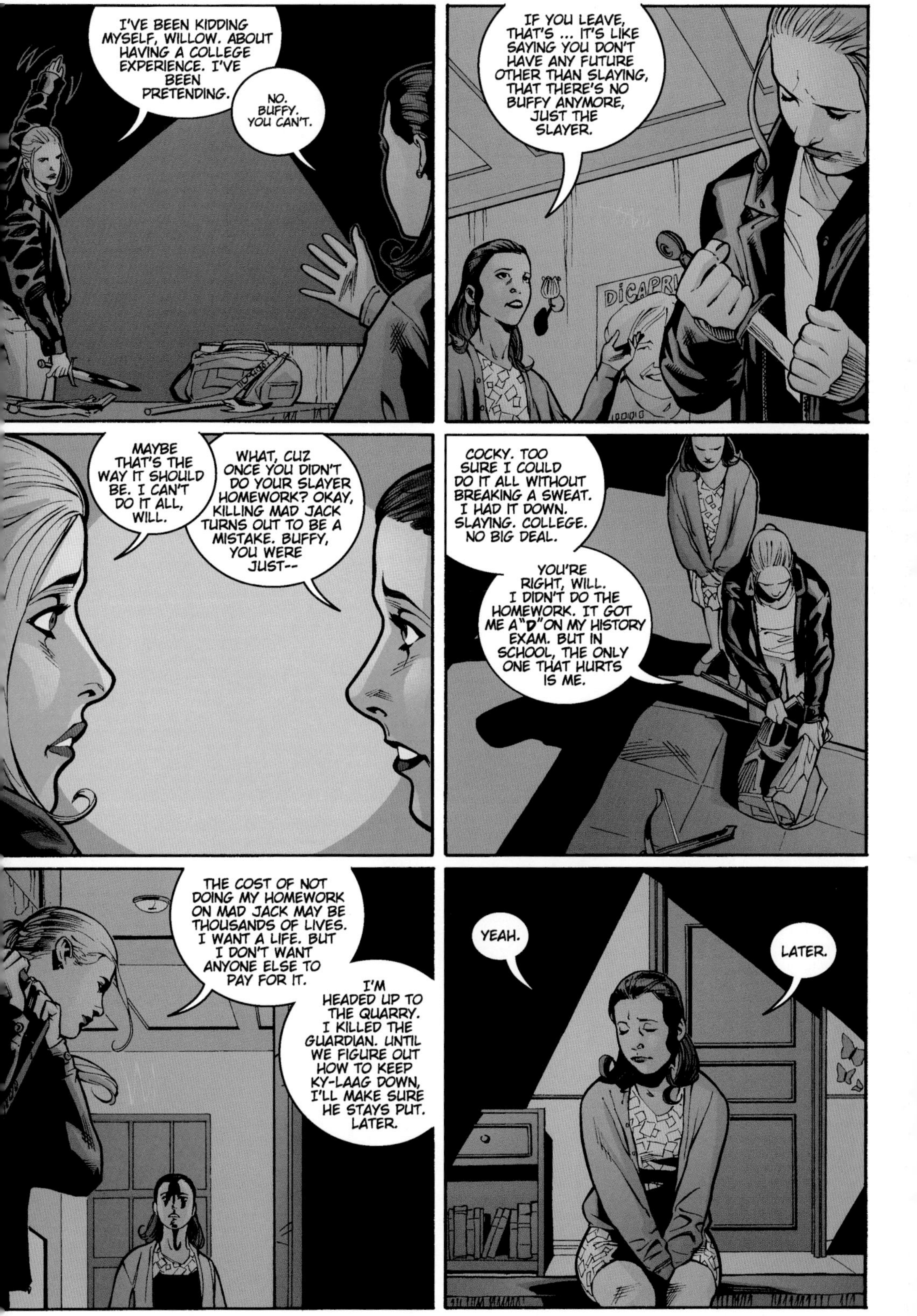
I'VE BEEN KIDDING MYSELF, WILLOW. ABOUT HAVING A COLLEGE EXPERIENCE. I'VE BEEN PRETENDING.
NO. BUFFY. YOU CAN'T.
IF YOU LEAVE, THAT'S ... IT'S LIKE SAYING YOU DON'T HAVE ANY FUTURE OTHER THAN SLAYING, THAT THERE'S NO BUFFY ANYMORE, JUST THE SLAYER.
MAYBE THAT'S THE WAY IT SHOULD BE. I CAN'T DO IT ALL, WILL.
WHAT, CUZ ONCE YOU DIDN'T DO YOUR SLAYER HOMEWORK? OKAY, KILLING MAD JACK TURNS OUT TO BE A MISTAKE. BUFFY, YOU WERE JUST--
COCKY. TOO SURE I COULD DO IT ALL WITHOUT BREAKING A SWEAT. I HAD IT DOWN. SLAYING. COLLEGE. NO BIG DEAL.
YOU'RE RIGHT, WILL. I DIDN'T DO THE HOMEWORK. IT GOT ME A "D" ON MY HISTORY EXAM. BUT IN SCHOOL, THE ONLY ONE THAT HURTS IS ME.
THE COST OF NOT DOING MY HOMEWORK ON MAD JACK MAY BE THOUSANDS OF LIVES. I WANT A LIFE. BUT I DON'T WANT ANYONE ELSE TO PAY FOR IT.
I'M HEADED UP TO THE QUARRY. I KILLED THE GUARDIAN. UNTIL WE FIGURE OUT HOW TO KEEP KY-LAAG DOWN, I'LL MAKE SURE HE STAYS PUT. LATER.
YEAH.
LATER.

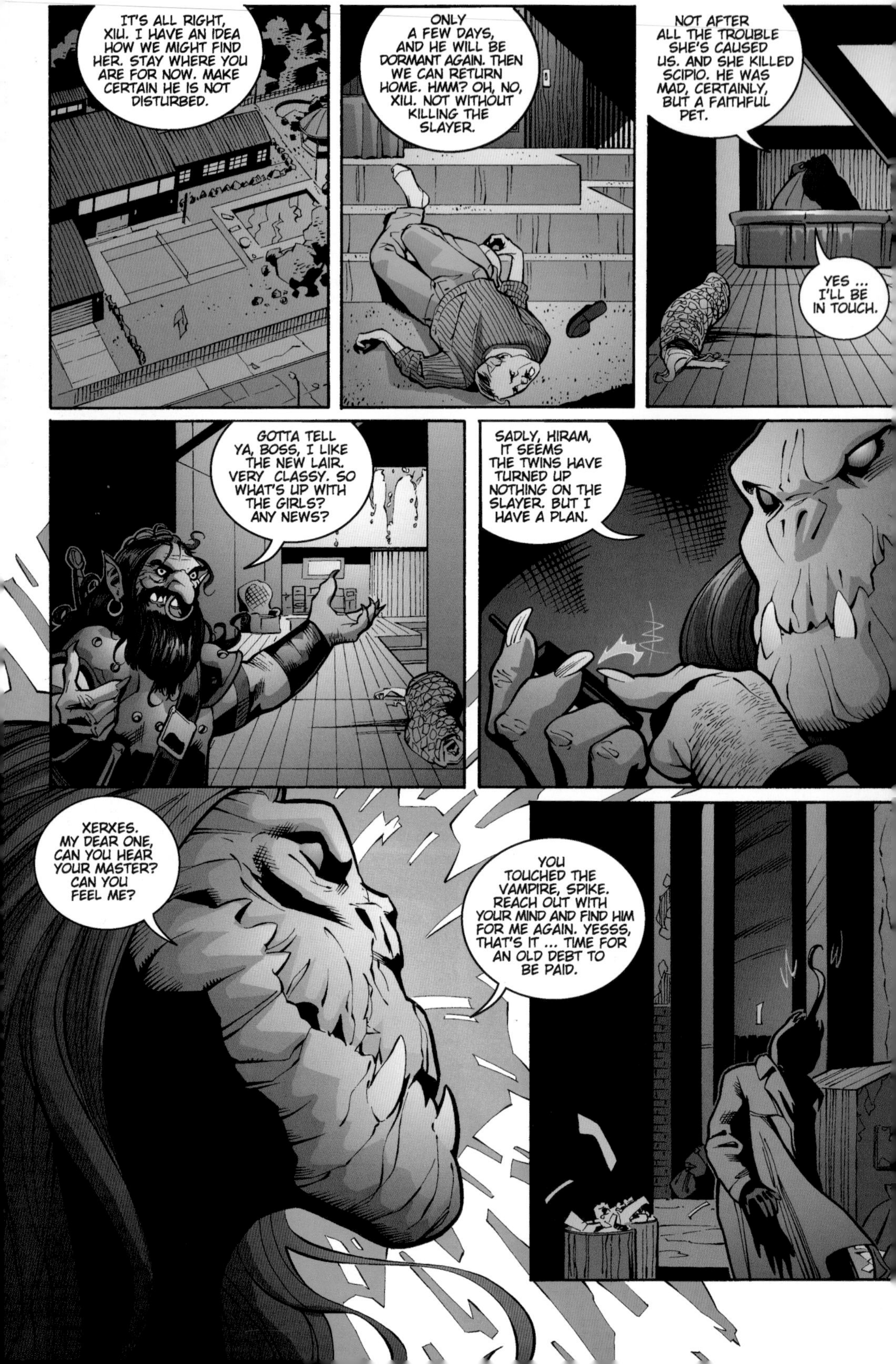
IT'S ALL RIGHT, XIU. I HAVE AN IDEA HOW WE MIGHT FIND HER. STAY WHERE YOU ARE FOR NOW. MAKE CERTAIN HE IS NOT DISTURBED.
ONLY A FEW DAYS, AND HE WILL BE DORMANT AGAIN. THEN WE CAN RETURN HOME. HMM? OH, NO, XIU. NOT WITHOUT KILLING THE SLAYER.
NOT AFTER ALL THE TROUBLE SHE'S CAUSED US. AND SHE KILLED SCIPIO. HE WAS MAD, CERTAINLY, BUT A FAITHFUL PET.
YES ... I'LL BE IN TOUCH.
GOTTA TELL YA, BOSS, I LIKE THE NEW LAIR. VERY CLASSY. SO WHAT'S UP WITH THE GIRLS? ANY NEWS?
SADLY, HIRAM, IT SEEMS THE TWINS HAVE TURNED UP NOTHING ON THE SLAYER. BUT I HAVE A PLAN.
XERXES. MY DEAR ONE, CAN YOU HEAR YOUR MASTER? CAN YOU FEEL ME?
YOU TOUCHED THE VAMPIRE, SPIKE. REACH OUT WITH YOUR MIND AND FIND HIM FOR ME AGAIN. YESSS, THAT'S IT ... TIME FOR AN OLD DEBT TO BE PAID.

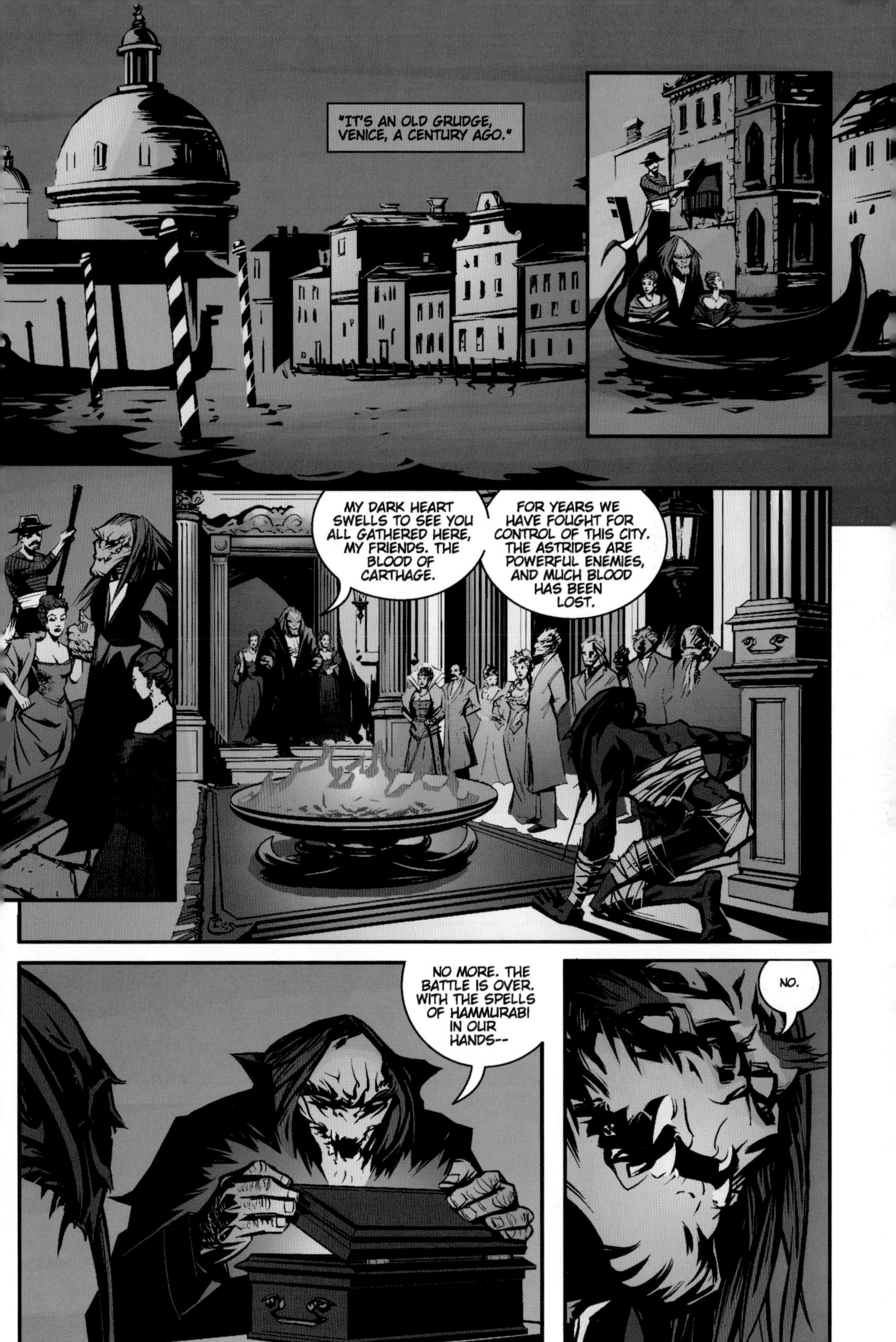
"IT'S AN OLD GRUDGE, VENICE, A CENTURY AGO."
MY DARK HEART SWELLS TO SEE YOU ALL GATHERED HERE, MY FRIENDS. THE BLOOD OF CARTHAGE.
FOR YEARS WE HAVE FOUGHT FOR CONTROL OF THIS CITY. THE ASTRIDES ARE POWERFUL ENEMIES, AND MUCH BLOOD HAS BEEN LOST.
NO MORE. THE BATTLE IS OVER. WITH THE SPELLS OF HAMMURABI IN OUR HANDS--
NO.

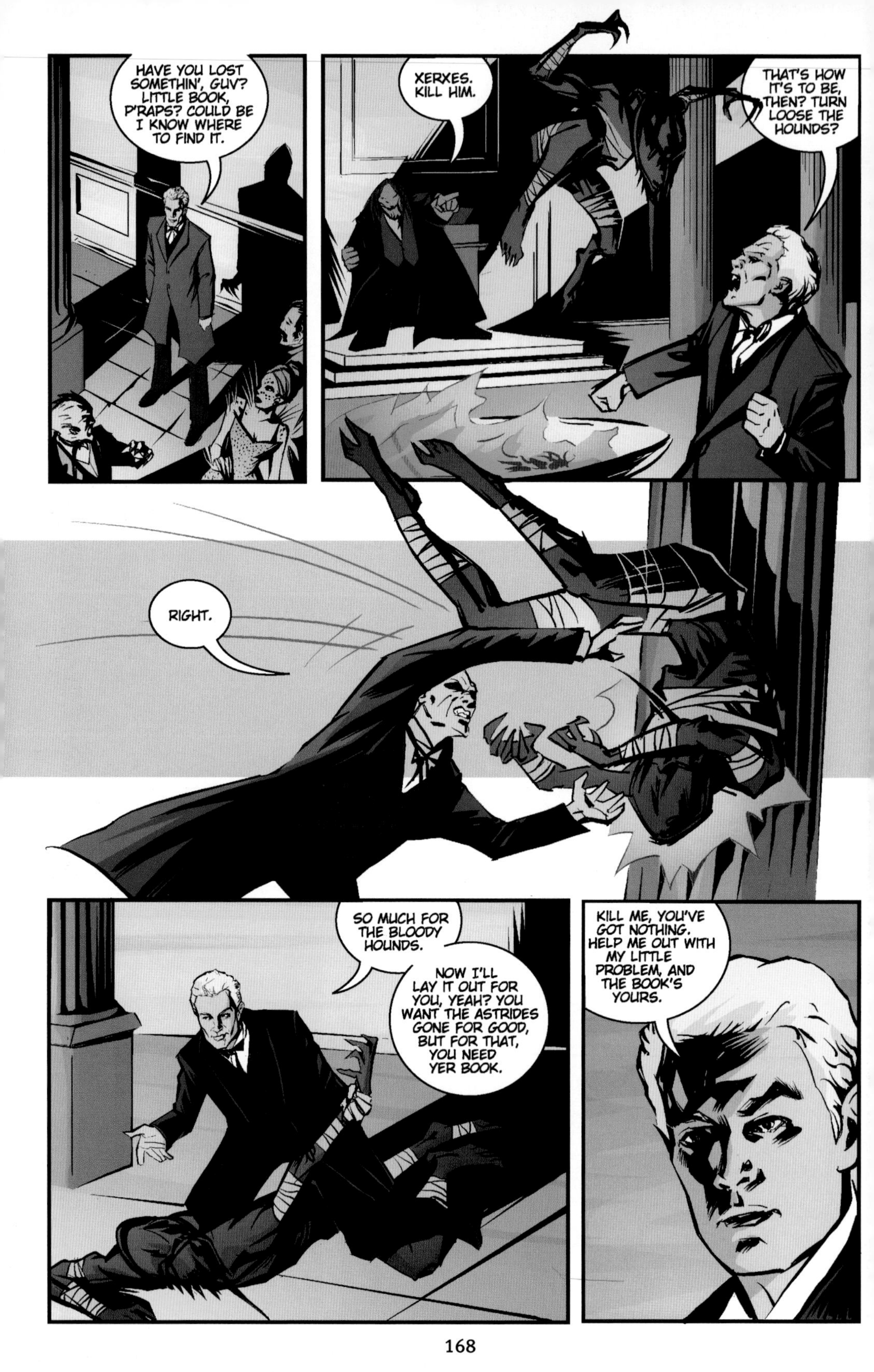

HAVE YOU LOST SOMETHIN', GUV? LITTLE BOOK, P'RAPS? COULD BE I KNOW WHERE TO FIND IT.
XERXES. KILL HIM.
THAT'S HOW IT'S TO BE, THEN? TURN LOOSE THE HOUNDS?
RIGHT.
SO MUCH FOR THE BLOODY HOUNDS.
NOW I'LL LAY IT OUT FOR YOU, YEAH? YOU WANT THE ASTRIDES GONE FOR GOOD, BUT FOR THAT, YOU NEED YER BOOK.
KILL ME, YOU'VE GOT NOTHING. HELP ME OUT WITH MY LITTLE PROBLEM, AND THE BOOK'S YOURS.

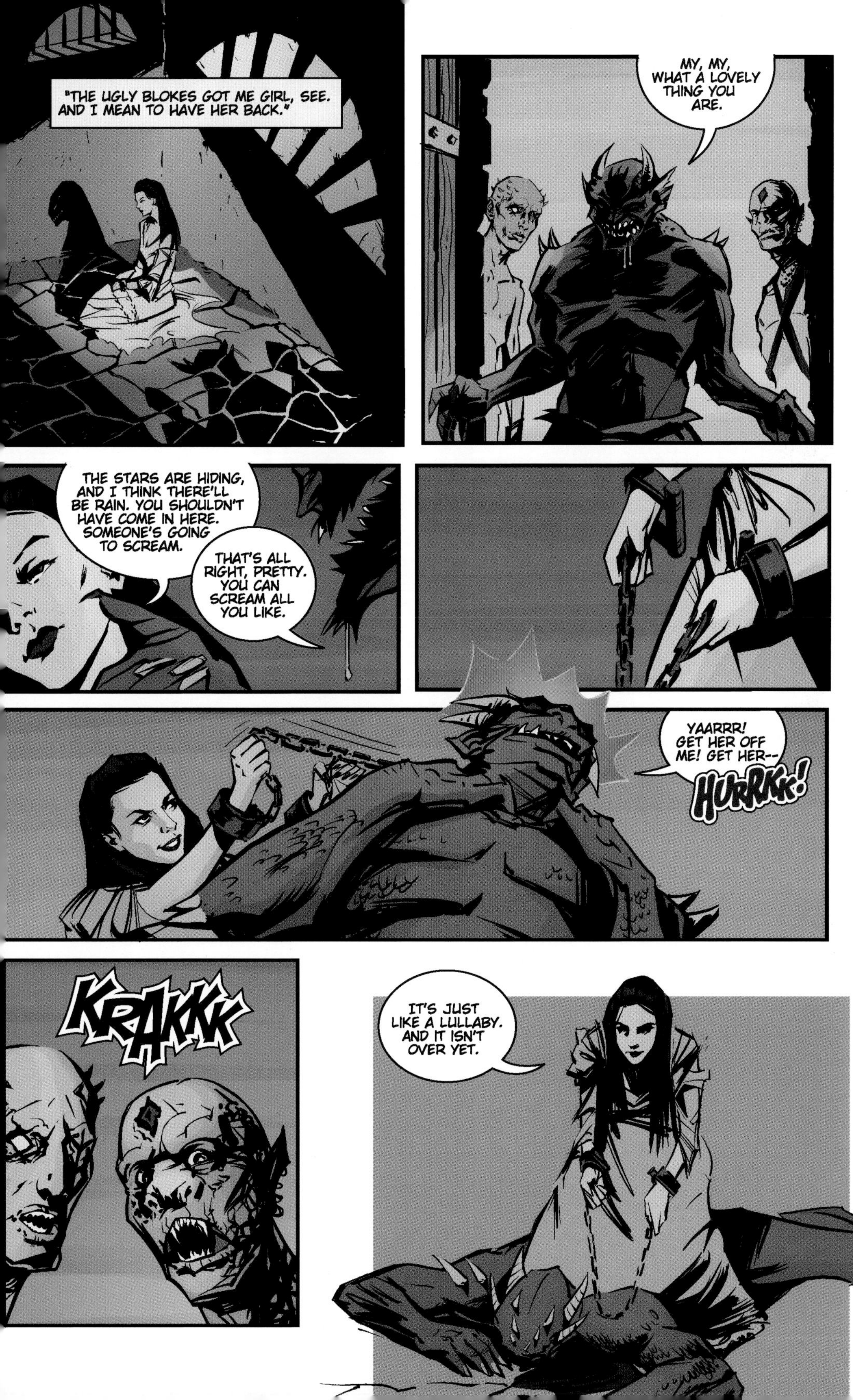
"THE UGLY BLOKES GOT ME GIRL, SEE. AND I MEAN TO HAVE HER BACK."
MY, MY, WHAT A LOVELY THING YOU ARE.
THE STARS ARE HIDING, AND I THINK THERE'LL BE RAIN. YOU SHOULDN'T HAVE COME IN HERE. SOMEONE'S GOING TO SCREAM.
THAT'S ALL RIGHT, PRETTY. YOU CAN SCREAM ALL YOU LIKE.
YAARRR! GET HER OFF ME! GET HER--
HURRKK!
KRAKKK
IT'S JUST LIKE A LULLABY. AND IT ISN'T OVER YET.

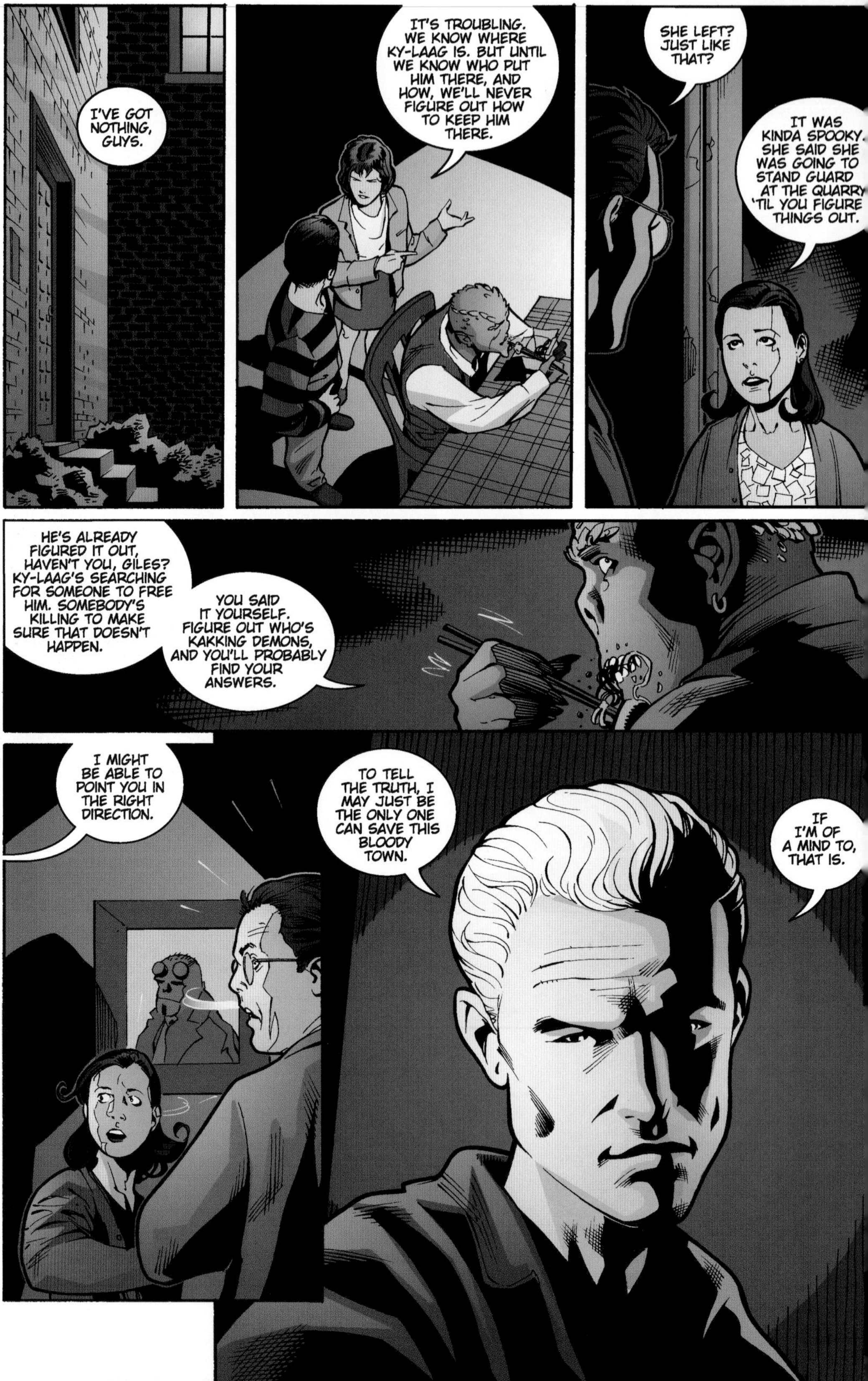
I'VE GOT NOTHING, GUYS.
IT'S TROUBLING. WE KNOW WHERE KY-LAAG IS. BUT UNTIL WE KNOW WHO PUT HIM THERE, AND HOW, WE'LL NEVER FIGURE OUT HOW TO KEEP HIM THERE.
SHE LEFT? JUST LIKE THAT?
IT WAS KINDA SPOOKY. SHE SAID SHE WAS GOING TO STAND GUARD AT THE QUARRY 'TIL YOU FIGURE THINGS OUT.
HE'S ALREADY FIGURED IT OUT, HAVEN'T YOU, GILES? KY-LAAG'S SEARCHING FOR SOMEONE TO FREE HIM. SOMEBODY'S KILLING TO MAKE SURE THAT DOESN'T HAPPEN.
YOU SAID IT YOURSELF. FIGURE OUT WHO'S KAKKING DEMONS, AND YOU'LL PROBABLY FIND YOUR ANSWERS.
I MIGHT BE ABLE TO POINT YOU IN THE RIGHT DIRECTION.
TO TELL THE TRUTH, I MAY JUST BE THE ONLY ONE CAN SAVE THIS BLOODY TOWN.
IF I'M OF A MIND TO, THAT IS.

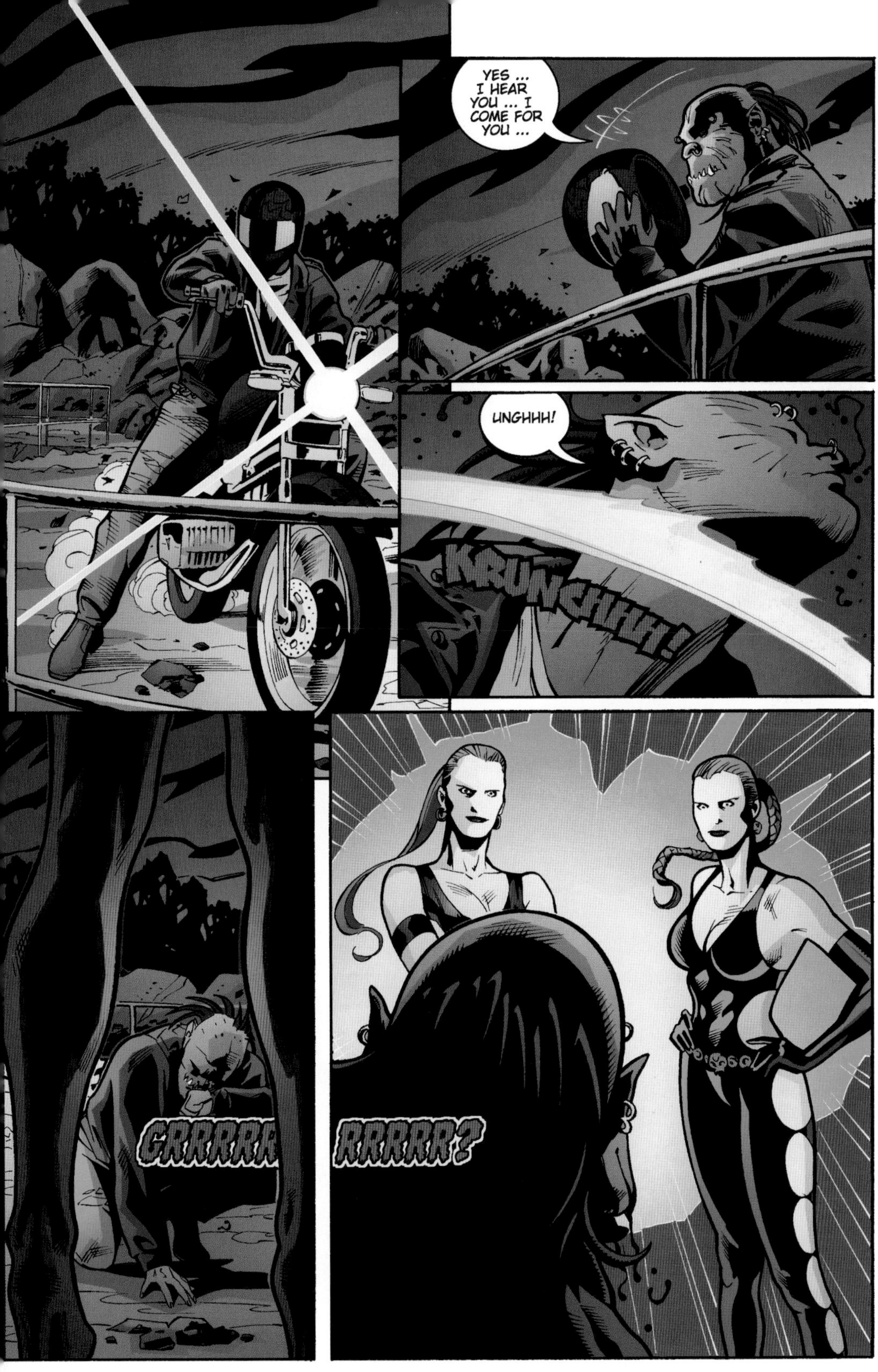
YES ... I HEAR YOU ... I COME FOR YOU ...
UNGHHH!
KRUNCHHH!
GRRRRRR RRRRR?

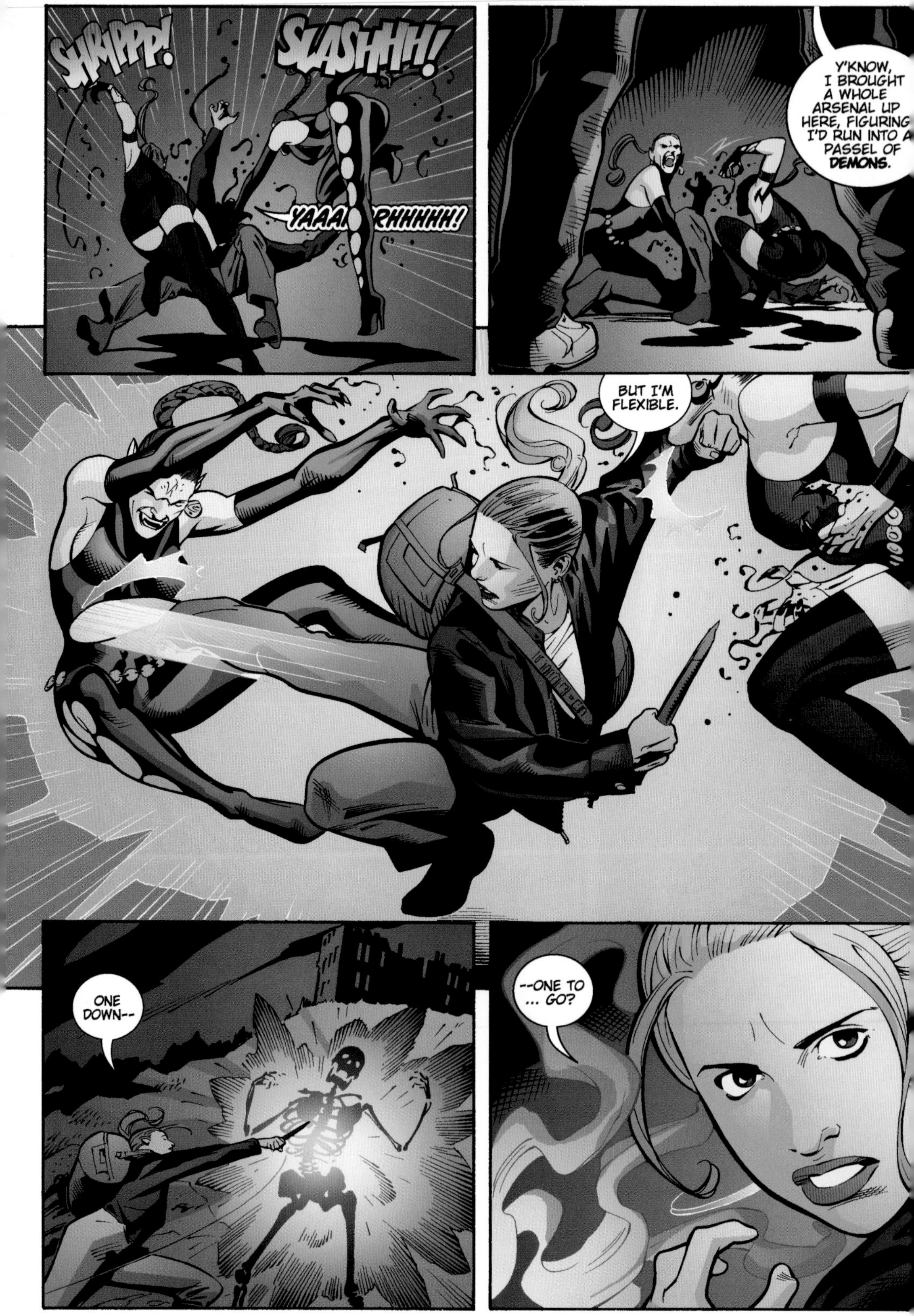
SHRIPPP!
SLASHHH!
YAAAARHHHHH!
Y'KNOW, I BROUGHT A WHOLE ARSENAL UP HERE, FIGURING I'D RUN INTO A PASSEL OF DEMONS.
BUT I'M FLEXIBLE.
ONE DOWN--
--ONE TO ... GO?

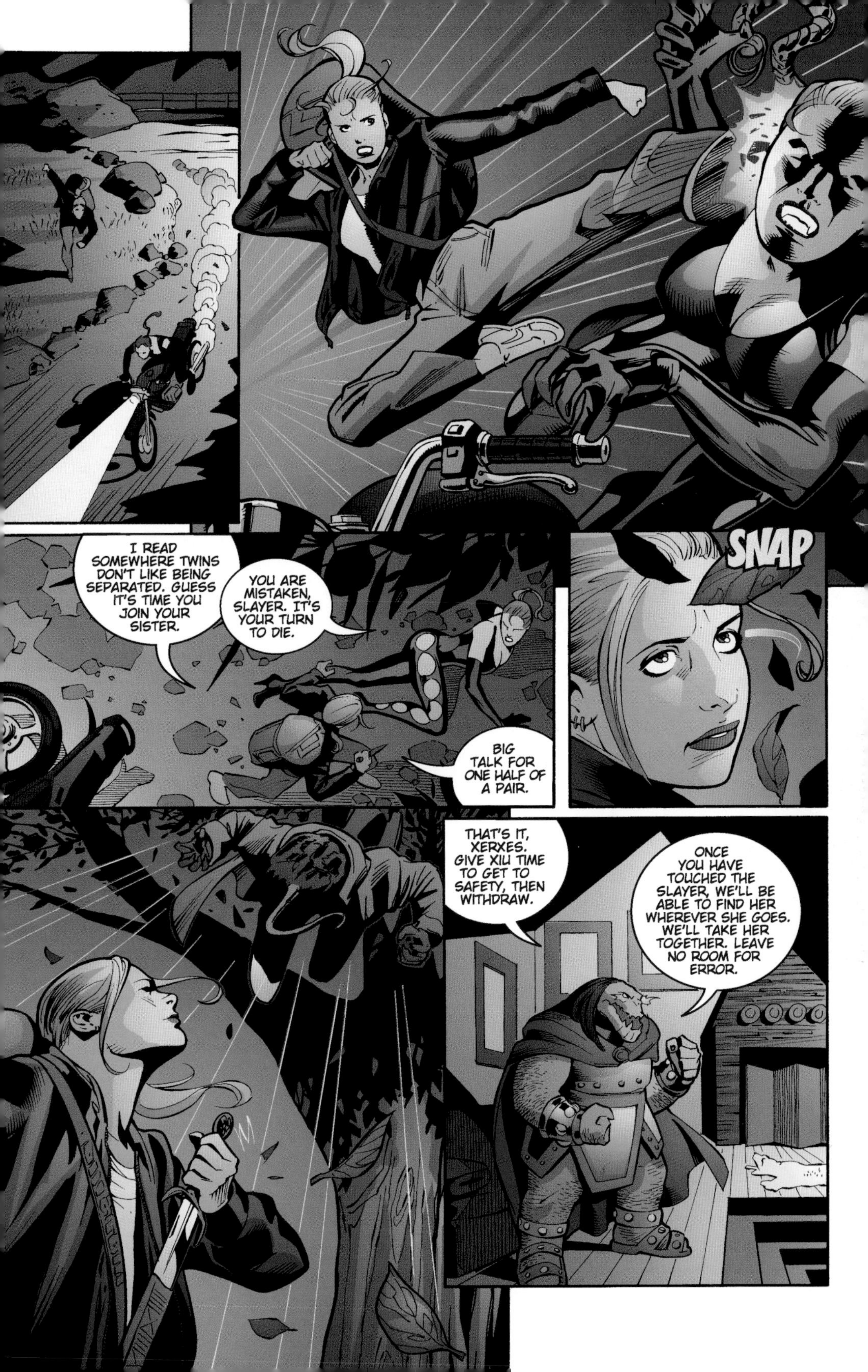

I READ SOMEWHERE TWINS DON'T LIKE BEING SEPARATED. GUESS IT'S TIME YOU JOIN YOUR SISTER.
YOU ARE MISTAKEN, SLAYER. IT'S YOUR TURN TO DIE.
BIG TALK FOR ONE HALF OF A PAIR.
SNAP
THAT'S IT, XERXES. GIVE XIU TIME TO GET TO SAFETY, THEN WITHDRAW.
ONCE YOU HAVE TOUCHED THE SLAYER, WE'LL BE ABLE TO FIND HER WHEREVER SHE GOES. WE'LL TAKE HER TOGETHER. LEAVE NO ROOM FOR ERROR.

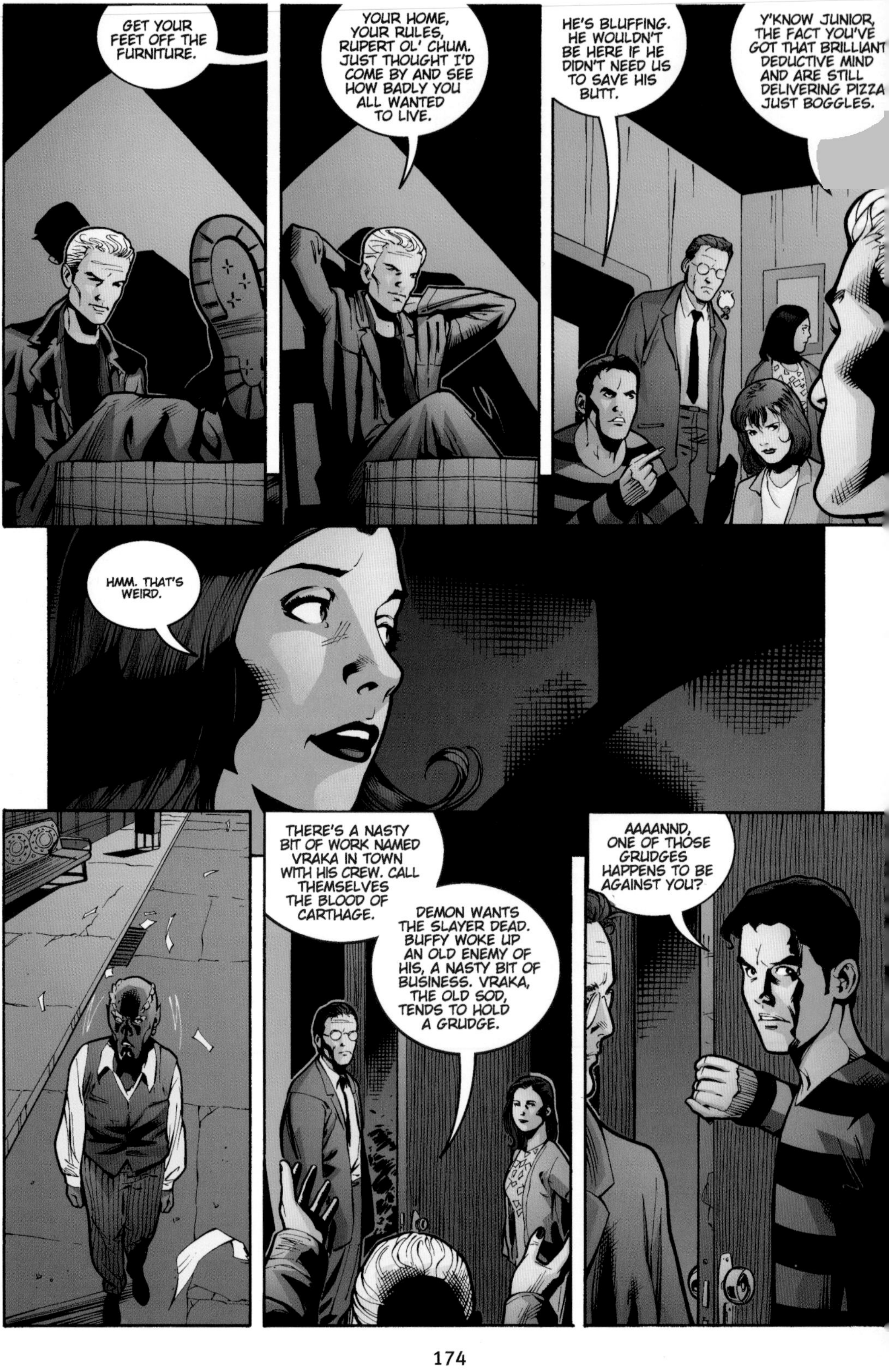
GET YOUR FEET OFF THE FURNITURE.
YOUR HOME, YOUR RULES, RUPERT OL' CHUM. JUST THOUGHT I'D COME BY AND SEE HOW BADLY YOU ALL WANTED TO LIVE.
HE'S BLUFFING. HE WOULDN'T BE HERE IF HE DIDN'T NEED US TO SAVE HIS BUTT.
Y'KNOW JUNIOR, THE FACT YOU'VE GOT THAT BRILLIANT DEDUCTIVE MIND AND ARE STILL DELIVERING PIZZA JUST BOGGLES.
HMM. THAT'S WEIRD.
THERE'S A NASTY BIT OF WORK NAMED VRAKA IN TOWN WITH HIS CREW. CALL THEMSELVES THE BLOOD OF CARTHAGE.
DEMON WANTS THE SLAYER DEAD. BUFFY WOKE UP AN OLD ENEMY OF HIS, A NASTY BIT OF BUSINESS. VRAKA, THE OLD SOD, TENDS TO HOLD A GRUDGE.
AAAANND, ONE OF THOSE GRUDGES HAPPENS TO BE AGAINST YOU?

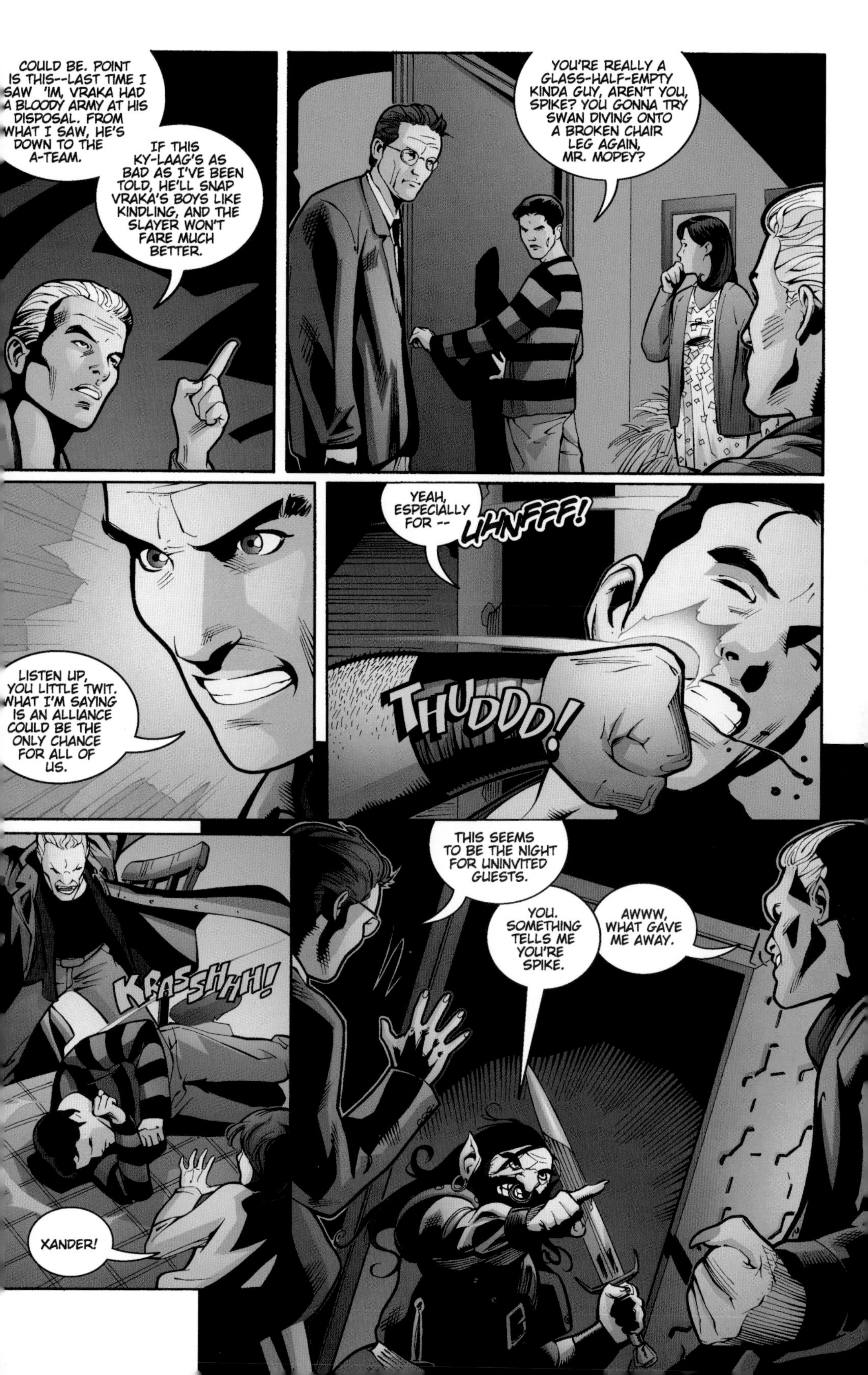
COULD BE. POINT IS THIS--LAST TIME I SAW 'IM, VRAKA HAD A BLOODY ARMY AT HIS DISPOSAL. FROM WHAT I SAW, HE'S DOWN TO THE A-TEAM.
IF THIS KY-LAAG'S AS BAD AS I'VE BEEN TOLD, HE'LL SNAP VRAKA'S BOYS LIKE KINDLING, AND THE SLAYER WON'T FARE MUCH BETTER.
YOU'RE REALLY A GLASS-HALF-EMPTY KINDA GUY, AREN'T YOU, SPIKE? YOU GONNA TRY SWAN DIVING ONTO A BROKEN CHAIR LEG AGAIN, MR. MOPEY?
LISTEN UP, YOU LITTLE TWIT. WHAT I'M SAYING IS AN ALLIANCE COULD BE THE ONLY CHANCE FOR ALL OF US.
YEAH, ESPECIALLY FOR --
UHNFFF!
THUDDD!
KRASSHHH!
XANDER!
THIS SEEMS TO BE THE NIGHT FOR UNINVITED GUESTS.
YOU. SOMETHING TELLS ME YOU'RE SPIKE.
AWWW, WHAT GAVE ME AWAY.

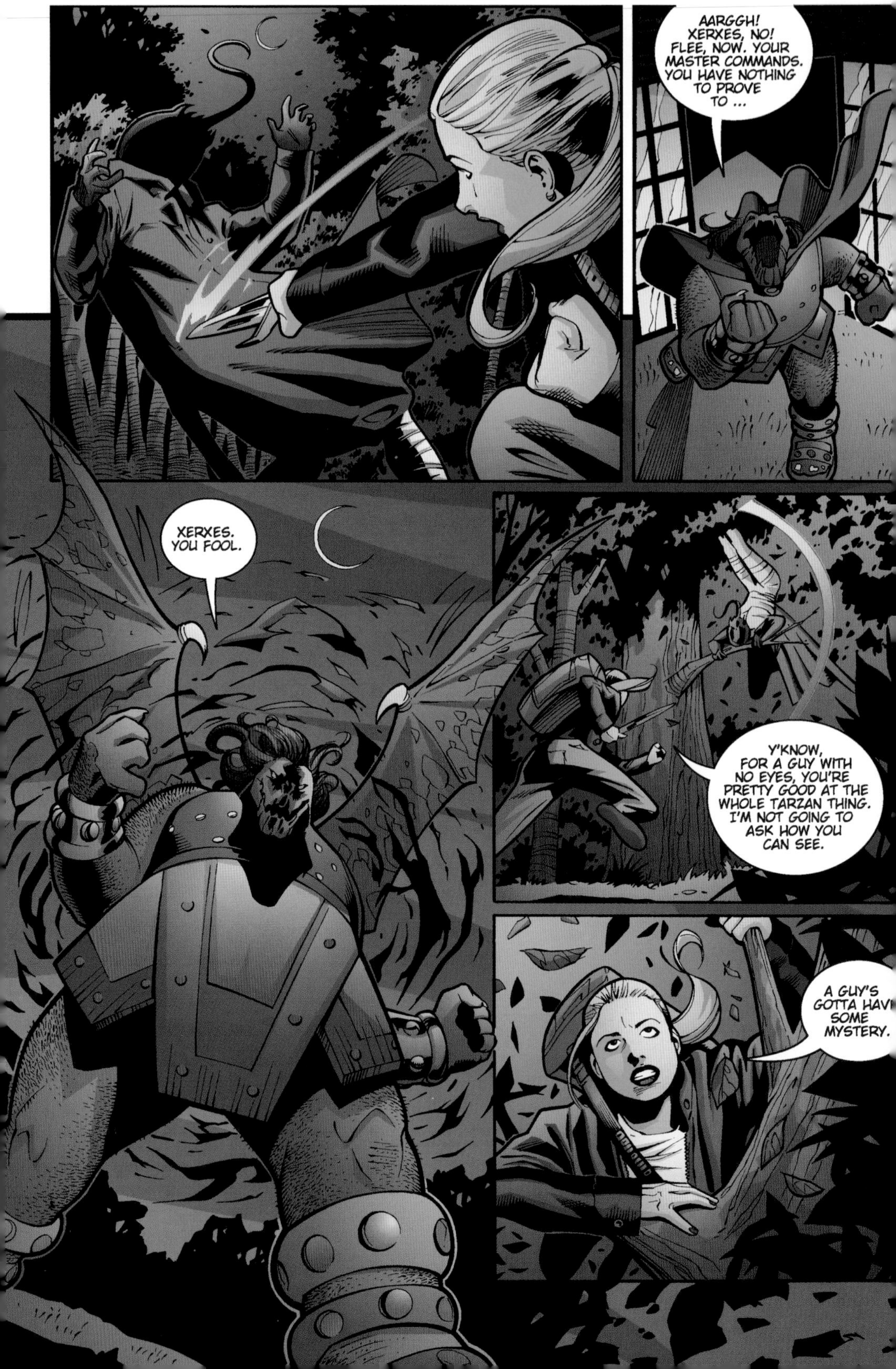

AARGGH! XERXES, NO! FLEE, NOW. YOUR MASTER COMMANDS. YOU HAVE NOTHING TO PROVE TO ...
XERXES. YOU FOOL.
Y'KNOW, FOR A GUY WITH NO EYES, YOU'RE PRETTY GOOD AT THE WHOLE TARZAN THING. I'M NOT GOING TO ASK HOW YOU CAN SEE.
A GUY'S GOTTA HAVE SOME MYSTERY.

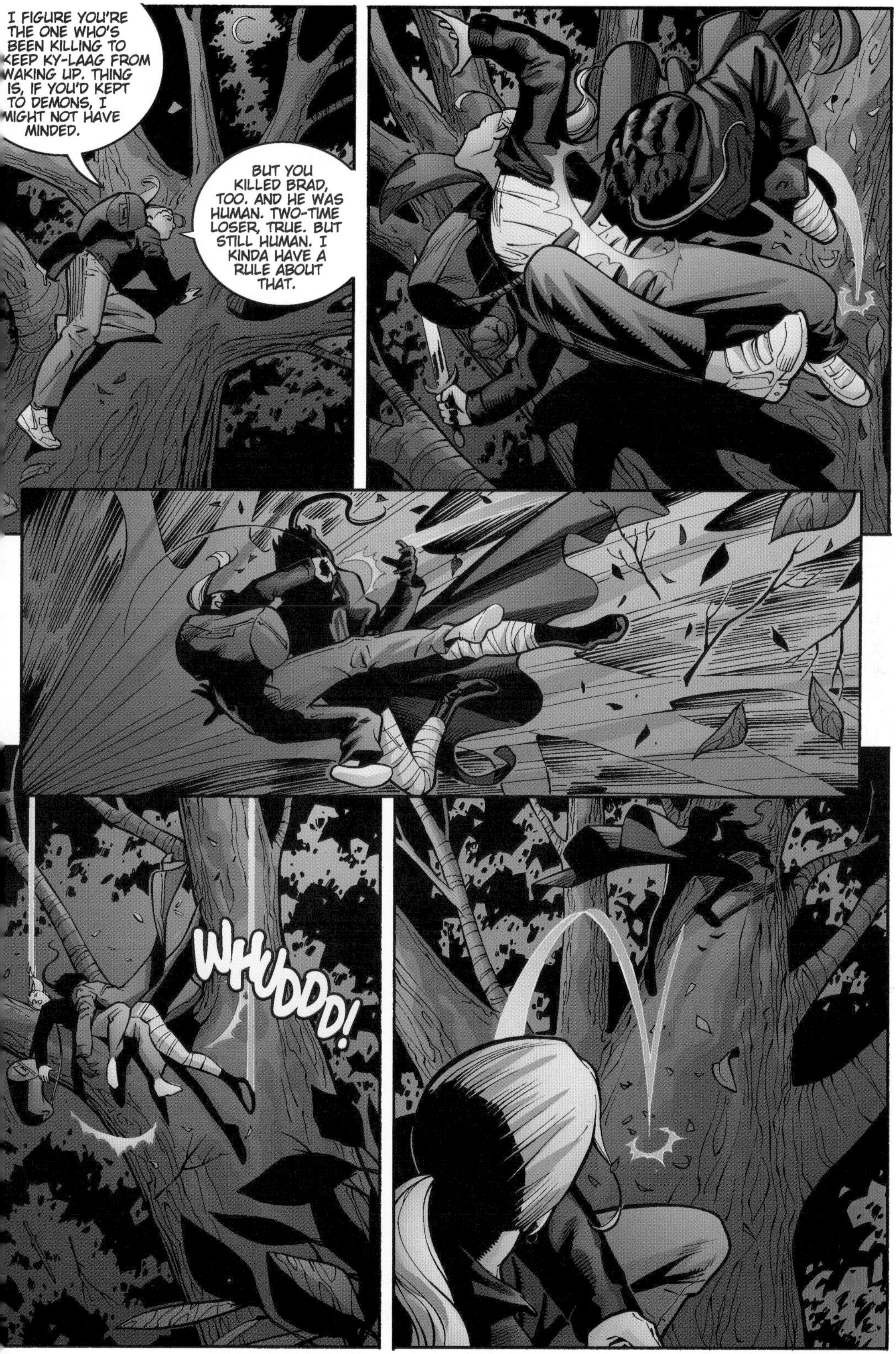
I FIGURE YOU'RE THE ONE WHO'S BEEN KILLING TO KEEP KY-LAAG FROM WAKING UP. THING IS, IF YOU'D KEPT TO DEMONS, I MIGHT NOT HAVE MINDED.
BUT YOU KILLED BRAD, TOO. AND HE WAS HUMAN. TWO-TIME LOSER, TRUE. BUT STILL HUMAN. I KINDA HAVE A RULE ABOUT THAT.
WHUDDD!

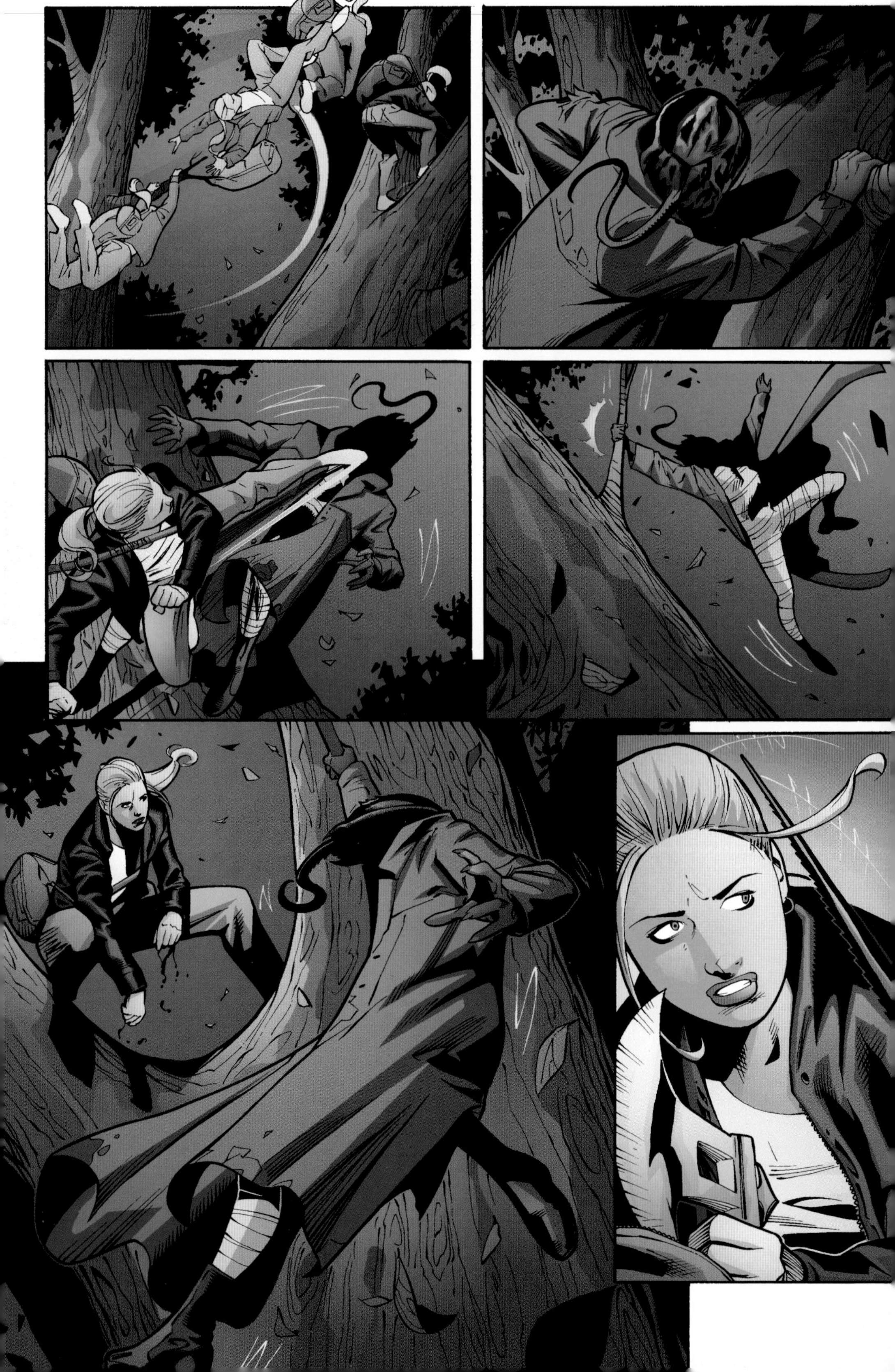

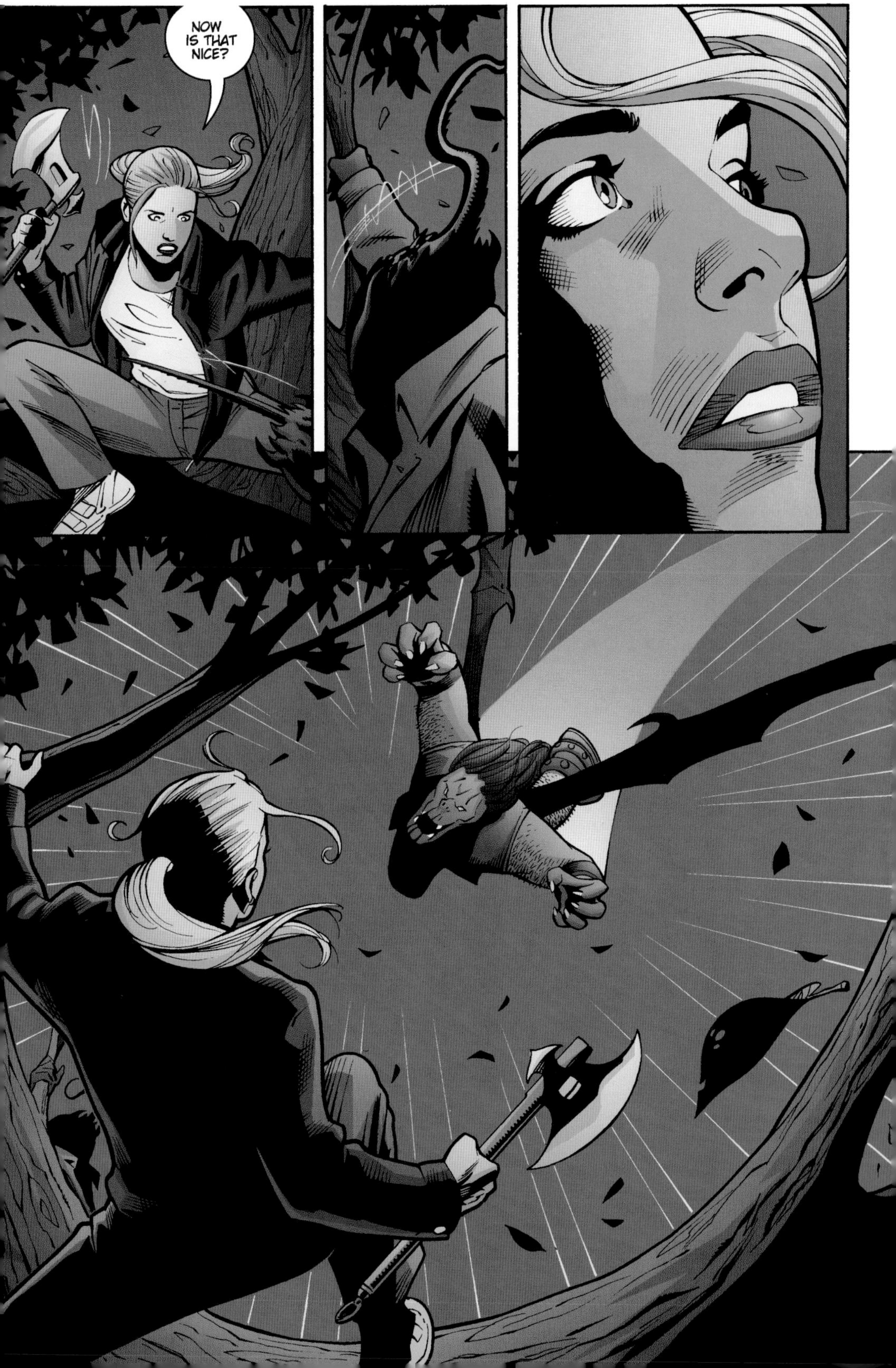
NOW IS THAT NICE?

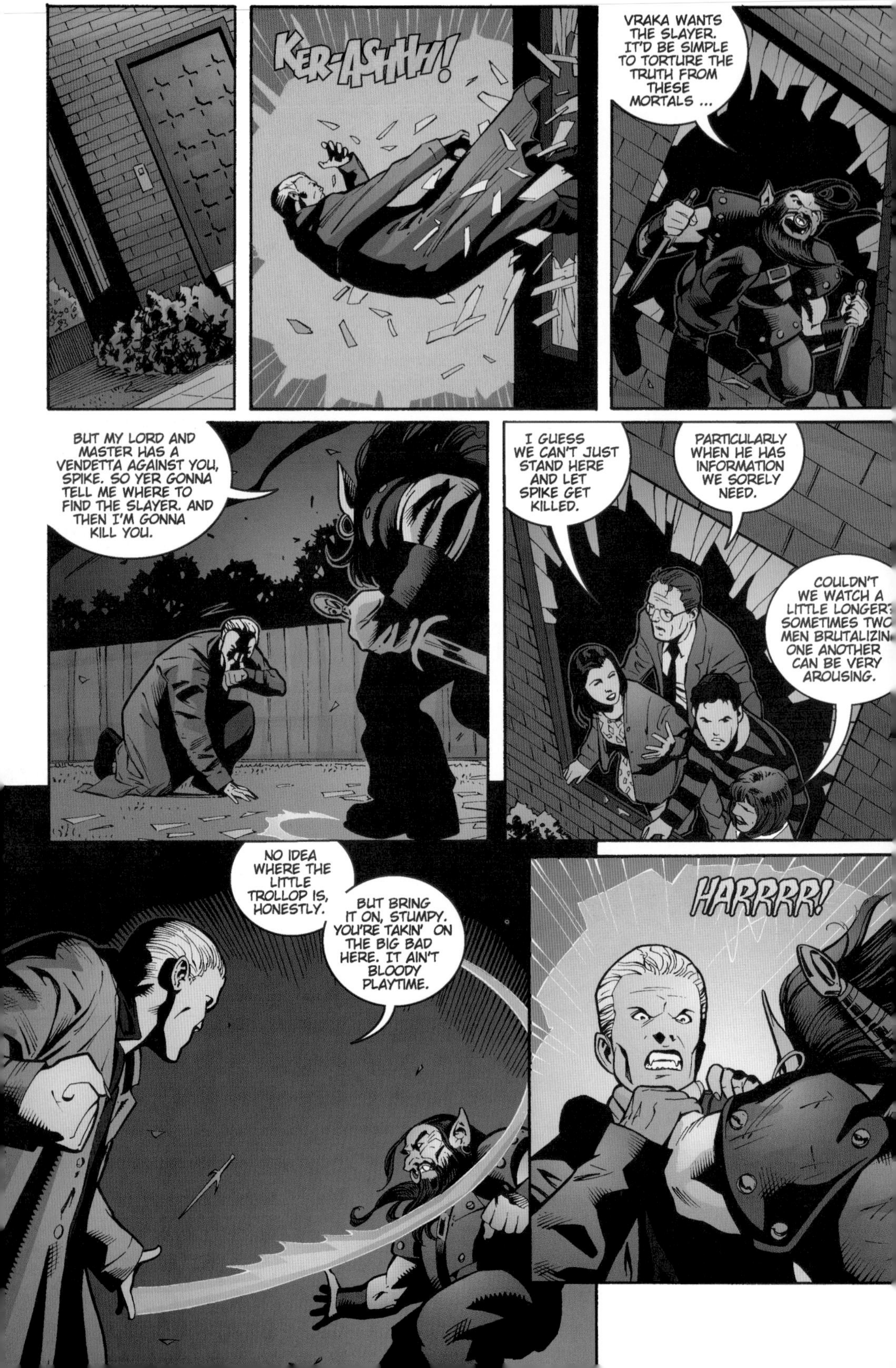
KER-ASHHH!
VRAKA WANTS THE SLAYER. IT'D BE SIMPLE TO TORTURE THE TRUTH FROM THESE MORTALS ...
BUT MY LORD AND MASTER HAS A VENDETTA AGAINST YOU, SPIKE. SO YER GONNA TELL ME WHERE TO FIND THE SLAYER. AND THEN I'M GONNA KILL YOU.
I GUESS WE CAN'T JUST STAND HERE AND LET SPIKE GET KILLED.
PARTICULARLY WHEN HE HAS INFORMATION WE SORELY NEED.
COULDN'T WE WATCH A LITTLE LONGER? SOMETIMES TWO MEN BRUTALIZING ONE ANOTHER CAN BE VERY AROUSING.
NO IDEA WHERE THE LITTLE TROLLOP IS, HONESTLY.
BUT BRING IT ON, STUMPY. YOU'RE TAKIN' ON THE BIG BAD HERE. IT AIN'T BLOODY PLAYTIME.
HARRRR!

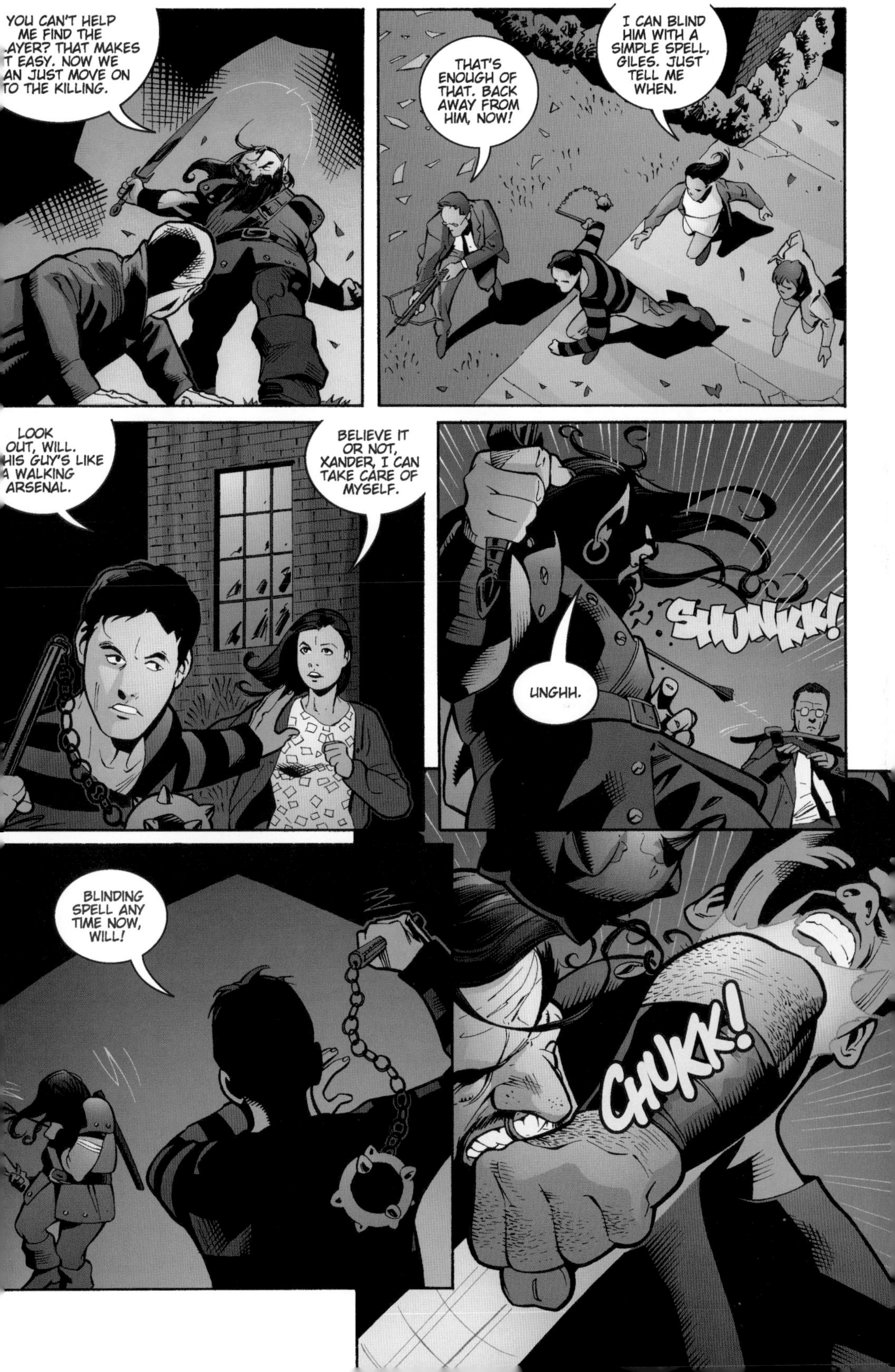
YOU CAN'T HELP ME FIND THE LAYER? THAT MAKES IT EASY. NOW WE CAN JUST MOVE ON TO THE KILLING.
THAT'S ENOUGH OF THAT. BACK AWAY FROM HIM, NOW!
I CAN BLIND HIM WITH A SIMPLE SPELL, GILES. JUST TELL ME WHEN.
LOOK OUT, WILL. THIS GUY'S LIKE A WALKING ARSENAL.
BELIEVE IT OR NOT, XANDER, I CAN TAKE CARE OF MYSELF.
SHUNKK!
UNGHH.
BLINDING SPELL ANY TIME NOW, WILL!
CHUKK!

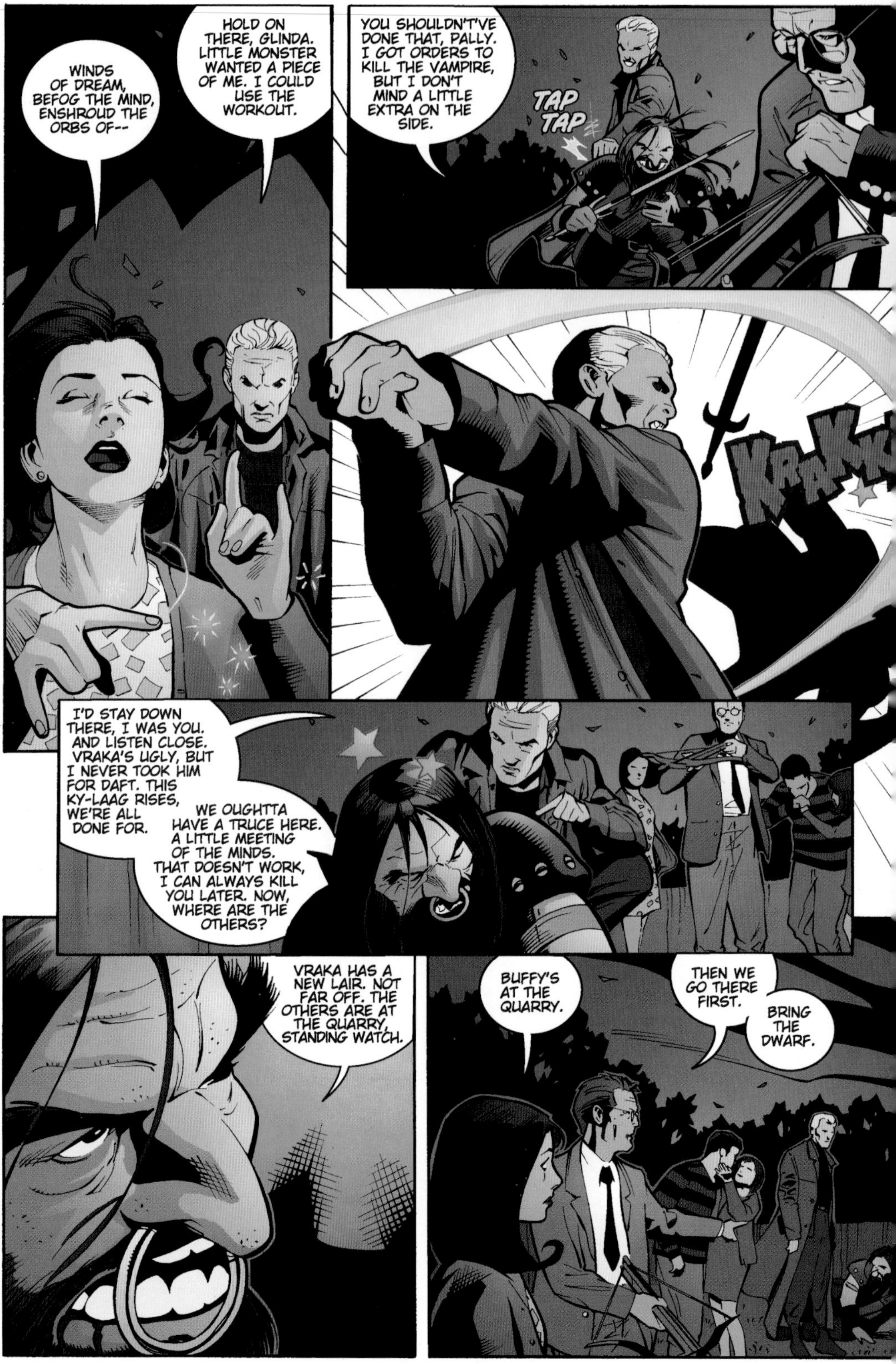
WINDS OF DREAM, BEFOG THE MIND, ENSHROUD THE ORBS OF--
HOLD ON THERE, GLINDA. LITTLE MONSTER WANTED A PIECE OF ME. I COULD USE THE WORKOUT.
YOU SHOULDN'T'VE DONE THAT, PALLY. I GOT ORDERS TO KILL THE VAMPIRE, BUT I DON'T MIND A LITTLE EXTRA ON THE SIDE.
TAP TAP
I'D STAY DOWN THERE, I WAS YOU. AND LISTEN CLOSE. VRAKA'S UGLY, BUT I NEVER TOOK HIM FOR DAFT. THIS KY-LAAG RISES, WE'RE ALL DONE FOR.
WE OUGHTTA HAVE A TRUCE HERE. A LITTLE MEETING OF THE MINDS. THAT DOESN'T WORK, I CAN ALWAYS KILL YOU LATER. NOW, WHERE ARE THE OTHERS?
VRAKA HAS A NEW LAIR. NOT FAR OFF. THE OTHERS ARE AT THE QUARRY, STANDING WATCH.
BUFFY'S AT THE QUARRY.
THEN WE GO THERE FIRST.
BRING THE DWARF.

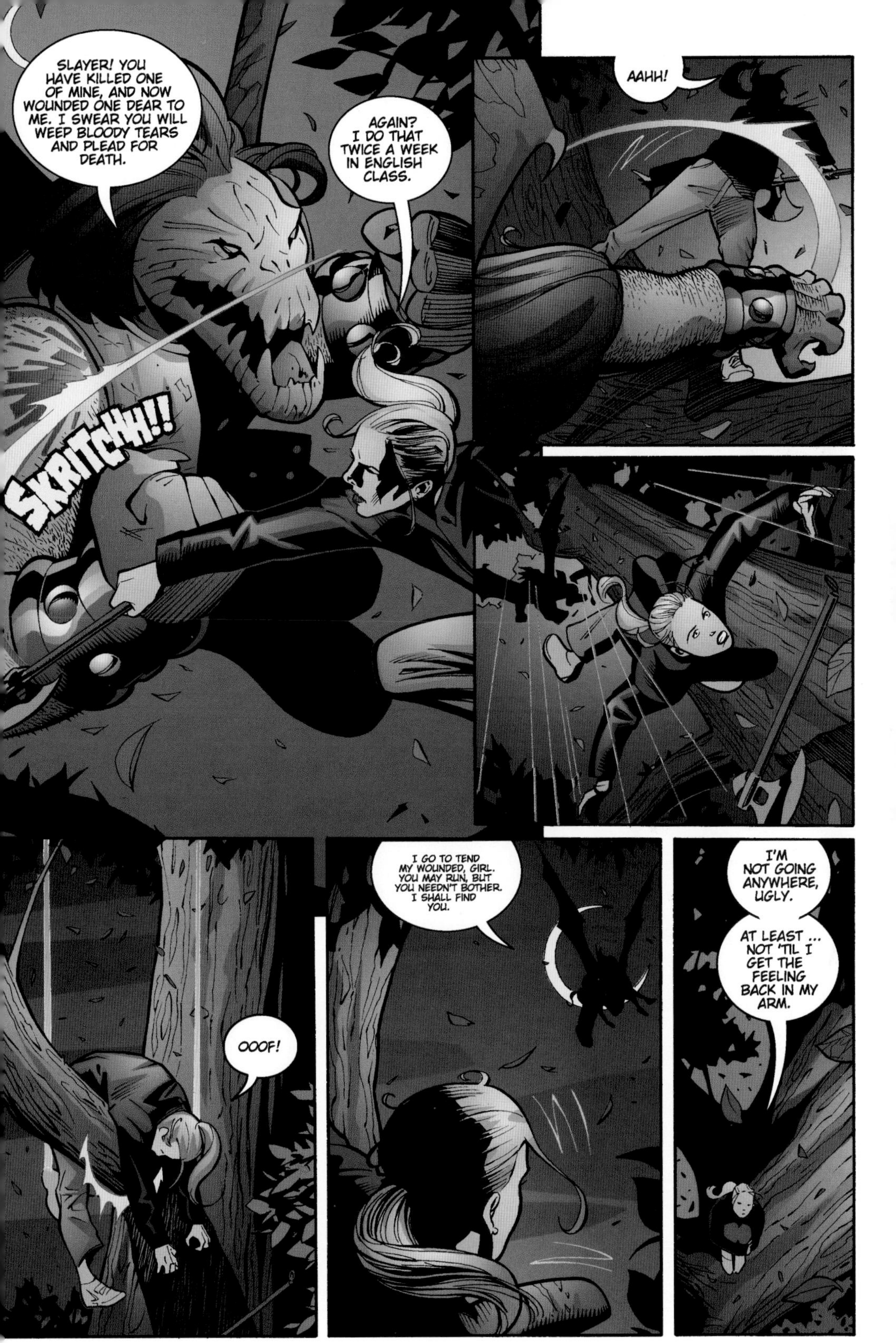
SLAYER! YOU HAVE KILLED ONE OF MINE, AND NOW WOUNDED ONE DEAR TO ME. I SWEAR YOU WILL WEEP BLOODY TEARS AND PLEAD FOR DEATH.
AGAIN? I DO THAT TWICE A WEEK IN ENGLISH CLASS.
SKRITCHH!!
AAHH!
OOOF!
I GO TO TEND MY WOUNDED, GIRL. YOU MAY RUN, BUT YOU NEEDN'T BOTHER. I SHALL FIND YOU.
I'M NOT GOING ANYWHERE, UGLY.
AT LEAST ... NOT 'TIL I GET THE FEELING BACK IN MY ARM.

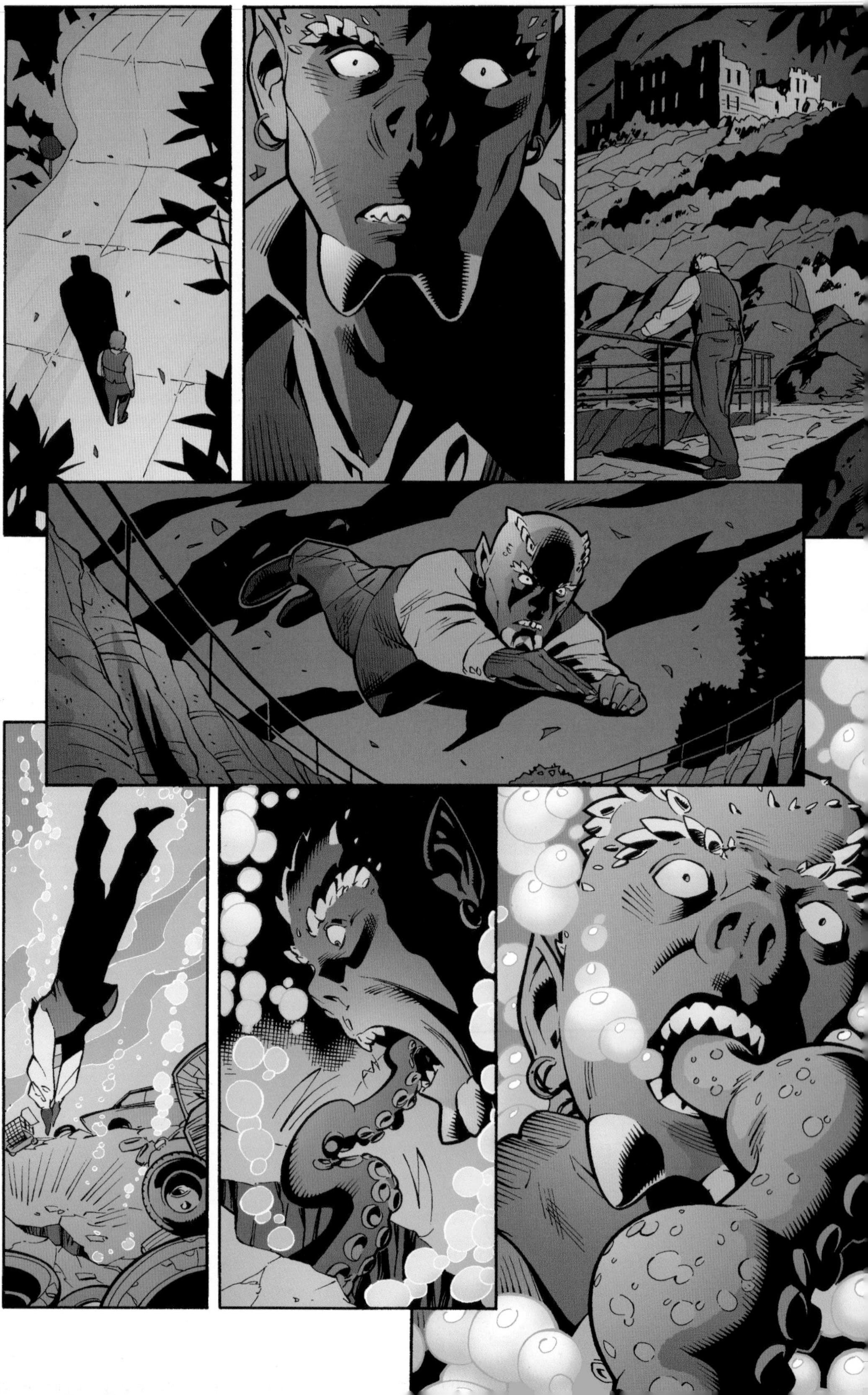

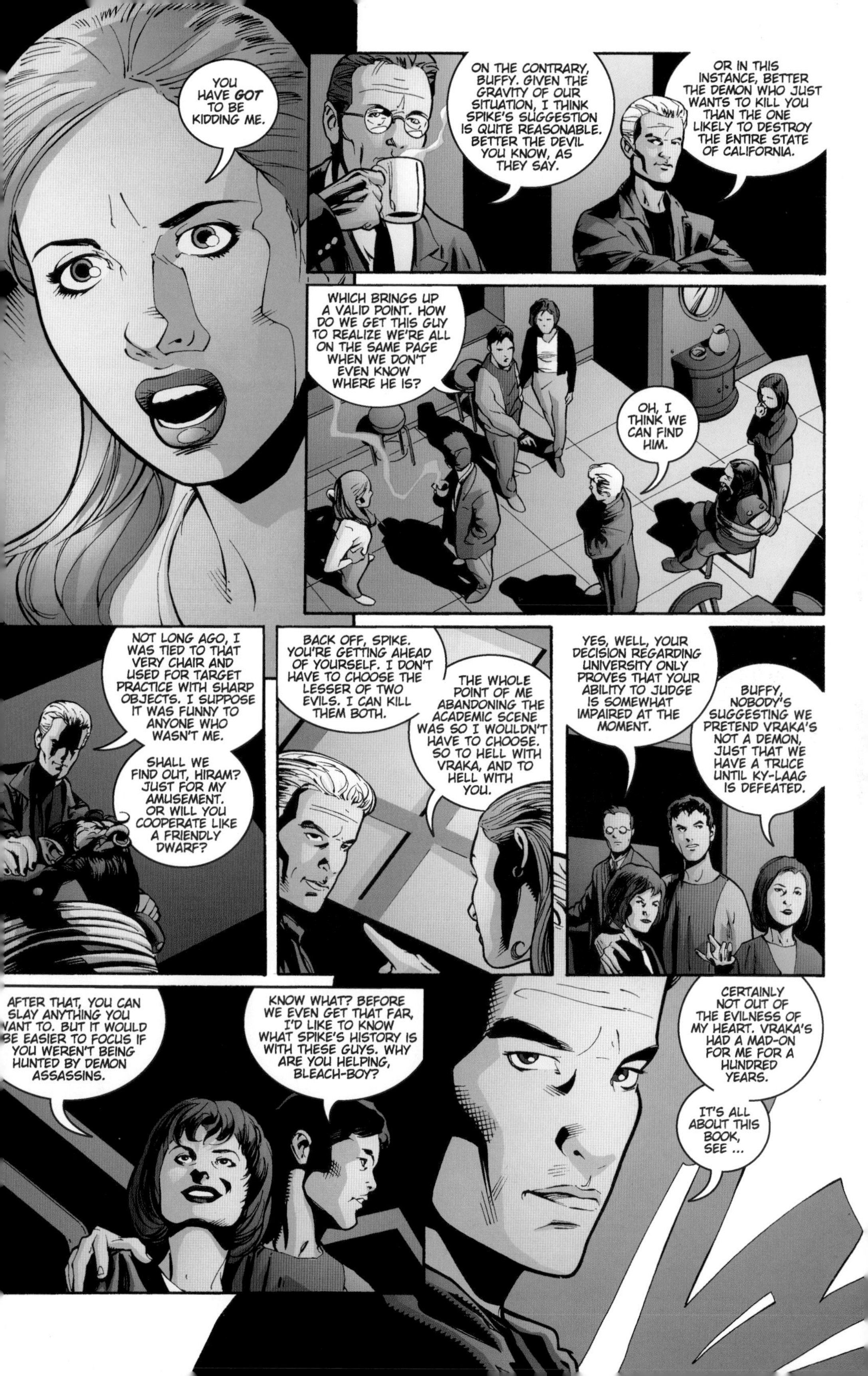
YOU HAVE GOT TO BE KIDDING ME.
ON THE CONTRARY, BUFFY. GIVEN THE GRAVITY OF OUR SITUATION, I THINK SPIKE'S SUGGESTION IS QUITE REASONABLE. BETTER THE DEVIL YOU KNOW, AS THEY SAY.
OR IN THIS INSTANCE, BETTER THE DEMON WHO JUST WANTS TO KILL YOU THAN THE ONE LIKELY TO DESTROY THE ENTIRE STATE OF CALIFORNIA.
WHICH BRINGS UP A VALID POINT. HOW DO WE GET THIS GUY TO REALIZE WE'RE ALL ON THE SAME PAGE WHEN WE DON'T EVEN KNOW WHERE HE IS?
OH, I THINK WE CAN FIND HIM.
NOT LONG AGO, I WAS TIED TO THAT VERY CHAIR AND USED FOR TARGET PRACTICE WITH SHARP OBJECTS. I SUPPOSE IT WAS FUNNY TO ANYONE WHO WASN'T ME.
SHALL WE FIND OUT, HIRAM? JUST FOR MY AMUSEMENT. OR WILL YOU COOPERATE LIKE A FRIENDLY DWARF?
BACK OFF, SPIKE. YOU'RE GETTING AHEAD OF YOURSELF. I DON'T HAVE TO CHOOSE THE LESSER OF TWO EVILS. I CAN KILL THEM BOTH.
THE WHOLE POINT OF ME ABANDONING THE ACADEMIC SCENE WAS SO I WOULDN'T HAVE TO CHOOSE. SO TO HELL WITH VRAKA, AND TO HELL WITH YOU.
YES, WELL, YOUR DECISION REGARDING UNIVERSITY ONLY PROVES THAT YOUR ABILITY TO JUDGE IS SOMEWHAT IMPAIRED AT THE MOMENT.
BUFFY, NOBODY'S SUGGESTING WE PRETEND VRAKA'S NOT A DEMON, JUST THAT WE HAVE A TRUCE UNTIL KY-LAAG IS DEFEATED.
AFTER THAT, YOU CAN SLAY ANYTHING YOU WANT TO. BUT IT WOULD BE EASIER TO FOCUS IF YOU WEREN'T BEING HUNTED BY DEMON ASSASSINS.
KNOW WHAT? BEFORE WE EVEN GET THAT FAR, I'D LIKE TO KNOW WHAT SPIKE'S HISTORY IS WITH THESE GUYS. WHY ARE YOU HELPING, BLEACH-BOY?
CERTAINLY NOT OUT OF THE EVILNESS OF MY HEART. VRAKA'S HAD A MAD-ON FOR ME FOR A HUNDRED YEARS.
IT'S ALL ABOUT THIS BOOK, SEE ...

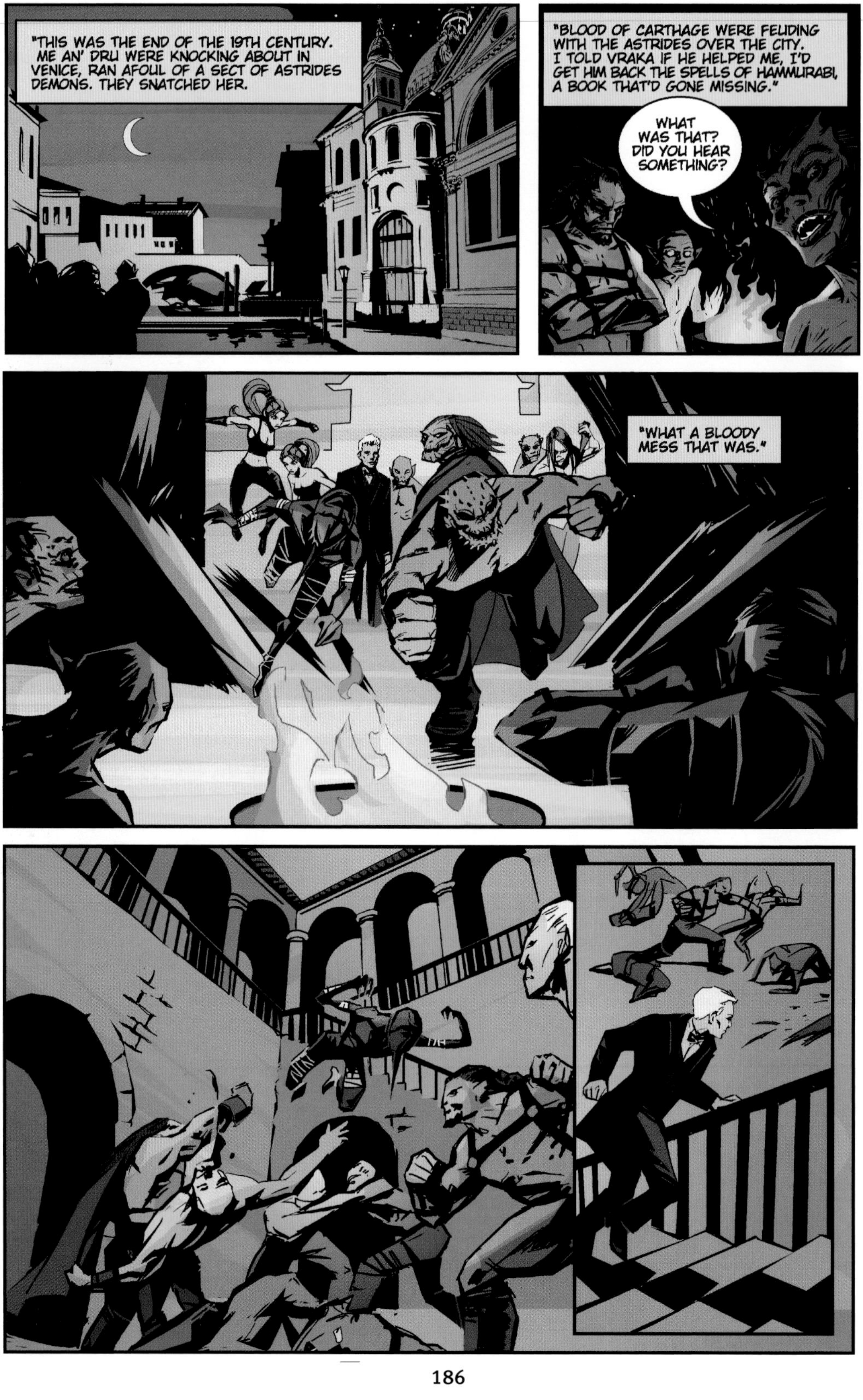
"THIS WAS THE END OF THE 19TH CENTURY. ME AN' DRU WERE KNOCKING ABOUT IN VENICE, RAN AFOUL OF A SECT OF ASTRIDES DEMONS. THEY SNATCHED HER.
"BLOOD OF CARTHAGE WERE FEUDING WITH THE ASTRIDES OVER THE CITY. I TOLD VRAKA IF HE HELPED ME, I'D GET HIM BACK THE SPELLS OF HAMMURABI, A BOOK THAT'D GONE MISSING."
WHAT WAS THAT? DID YOU HEAR SOMETHING?
"WHAT A BLOODY MESS THAT WAS."

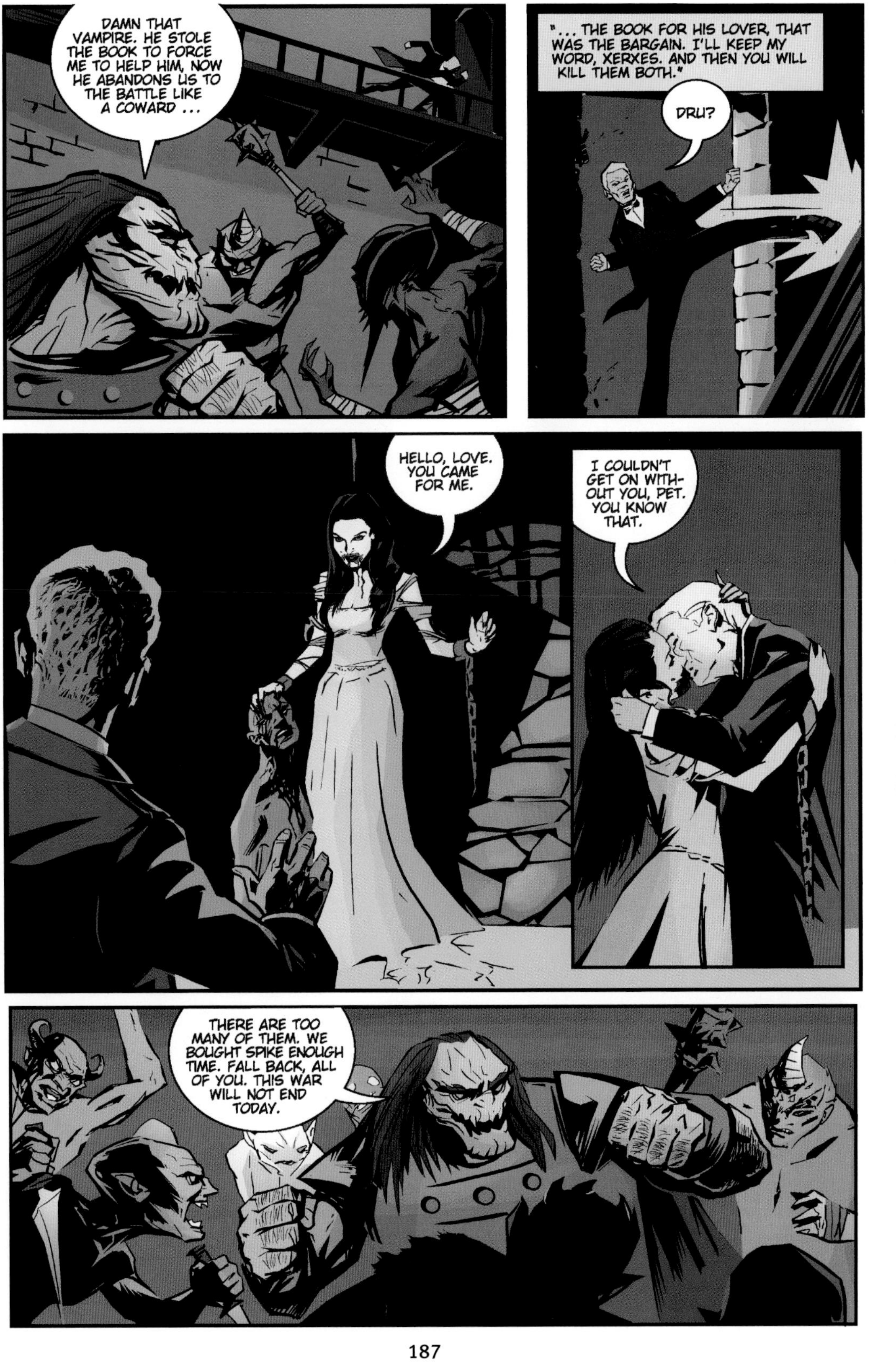
DAMN THAT VAMPIRE. HE STOLE THE BOOK TO FORCE ME TO HELP HIM, NOW HE ABANDONS US TO THE BATTLE LIKE A COWARD ...
"... THE BOOK FOR HIS LOVER, THAT WAS THE BARGAIN. I'LL KEEP MY WORD, XERXES. AND THEN YOU WILL KILL THEM BOTH."
DRU?
HELLO, LOVE. YOU CAME FOR ME.
I COULDN'T GET ON WITH-OUT YOU, PET. YOU KNOW THAT.
THERE ARE TOO MANY OF THEM. WE BOUGHT SPIKE ENOUGH TIME. FALL BACK, ALL OF YOU. THIS WAR WILL NOT END TODAY.

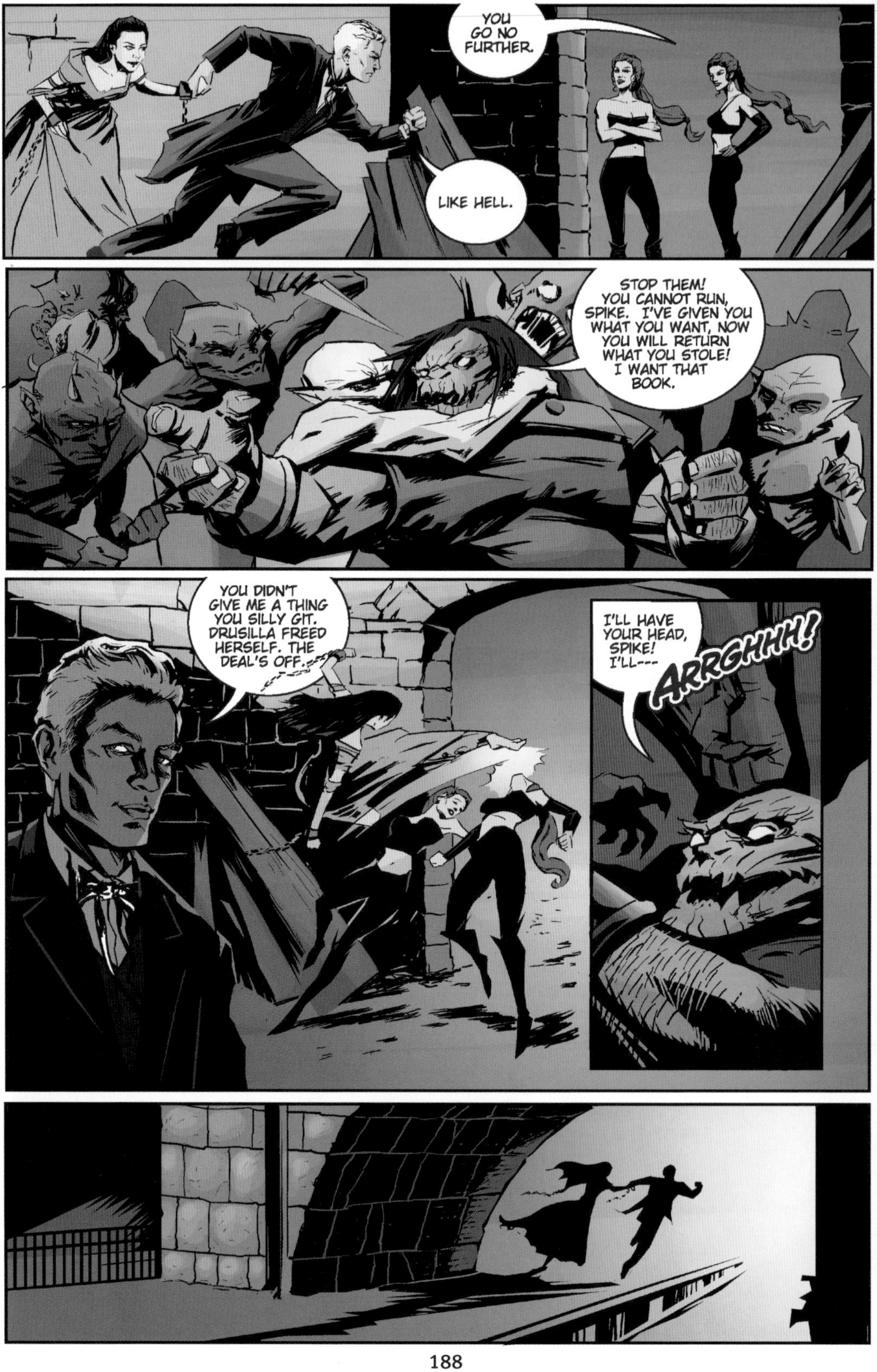
YOU GO NO FURTHER.
LIKE HELL.
STOP THEM! YOU CANNOT RUN, SPIKE. I'VE GIVEN YOU WHAT YOU WANT, NOW YOU WILL RETURN WHAT YOU STOLE! I WANT THAT BOOK.
YOU DIDN'T GIVE ME A THING YOU SILLY GIT. DRUSILLA FREED HERSELF. THE DEAL'S OFF.
I'LL HAVE YOUR HEAD, SPIKE! I'LL---
ARRGHHH!

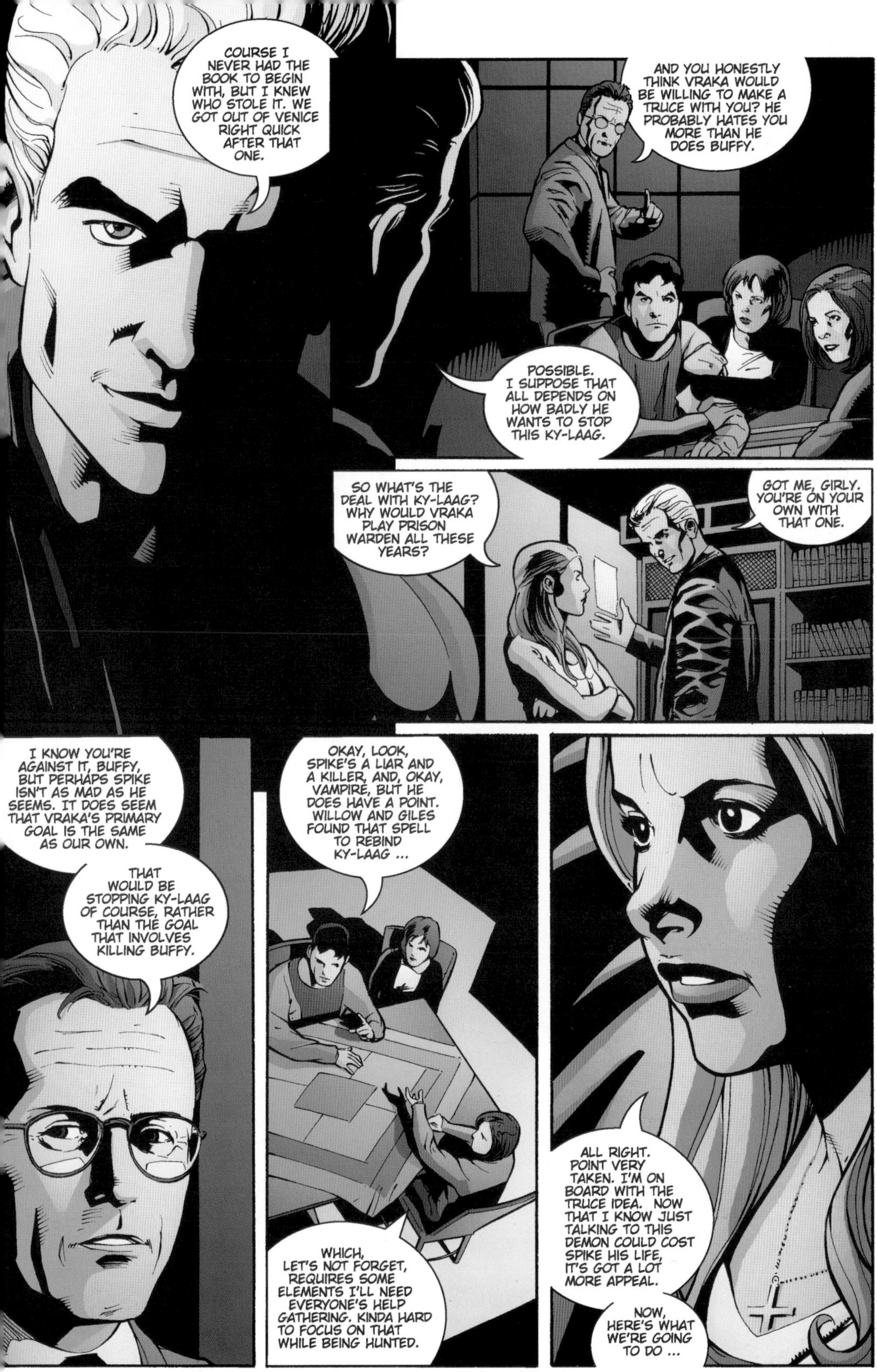
COURSE I NEVER HAD THE BOOK TO BEGIN WITH, BUT I KNEW WHO STOLE IT. WE GOT OUT OF VENICE RIGHT QUICK AFTER THAT ONE.
AND YOU HONESTLY THINK VRAKA WOULD BE WILLING TO MAKE A TRUCE WITH YOU? HE PROBABLY HATES YOU MORE THAN HE DOES BUFFY.
POSSIBLE. I SUPPOSE THAT ALL DEPENDS ON HOW BADLY HE WANTS TO STOP THIS KY-LAAG.
SO WHAT'S THE DEAL WITH KY-LAAG? WHY WOULD VRAKA PLAY PRISON WARDEN ALL THESE YEARS?
GOT ME, GIRLY. YOU'RE ON YOUR OWN WITH THAT ONE.
I KNOW YOU'RE AGAINST IT, BUFFY, BUT PERHAPS SPIKE ISN'T AS MAD AS HE SEEMS. IT DOES SEEM THAT VRAKA'S PRIMARY GOAL IS THE SAME AS OUR OWN.
THAT WOULD BE STOPPING KY-LAAG OF COURSE, RATHER THAN THE GOAL THAT INVOLVES KILLING BUFFY.
OKAY, LOOK, SPIKE'S A LIAR AND A KILLER, AND, OKAY, VAMPIRE, BUT HE DOES HAVE A POINT. WILLOW AND GILES FOUND THAT SPELL TO REBIND KY-LAAG ...
WHICH, LET'S NOT FORGET, REQUIRES SOME ELEMENTS I'LL NEED EVERYONE'S HELP GATHERING. KINDA HARD TO FOCUS ON THAT WHILE BEING HUNTED.
ALL RIGHT. POINT VERY TAKEN. I'M ON BOARD WITH THE TRUCE IDEA. NOW THAT I KNOW JUST TALKING TO THIS DEMON COULD COST SPIKE HIS LIFE, IT'S GOT A LOT MORE APPEAL.
NOW, HERE'S WHAT WE'RE GOING TO DO ...

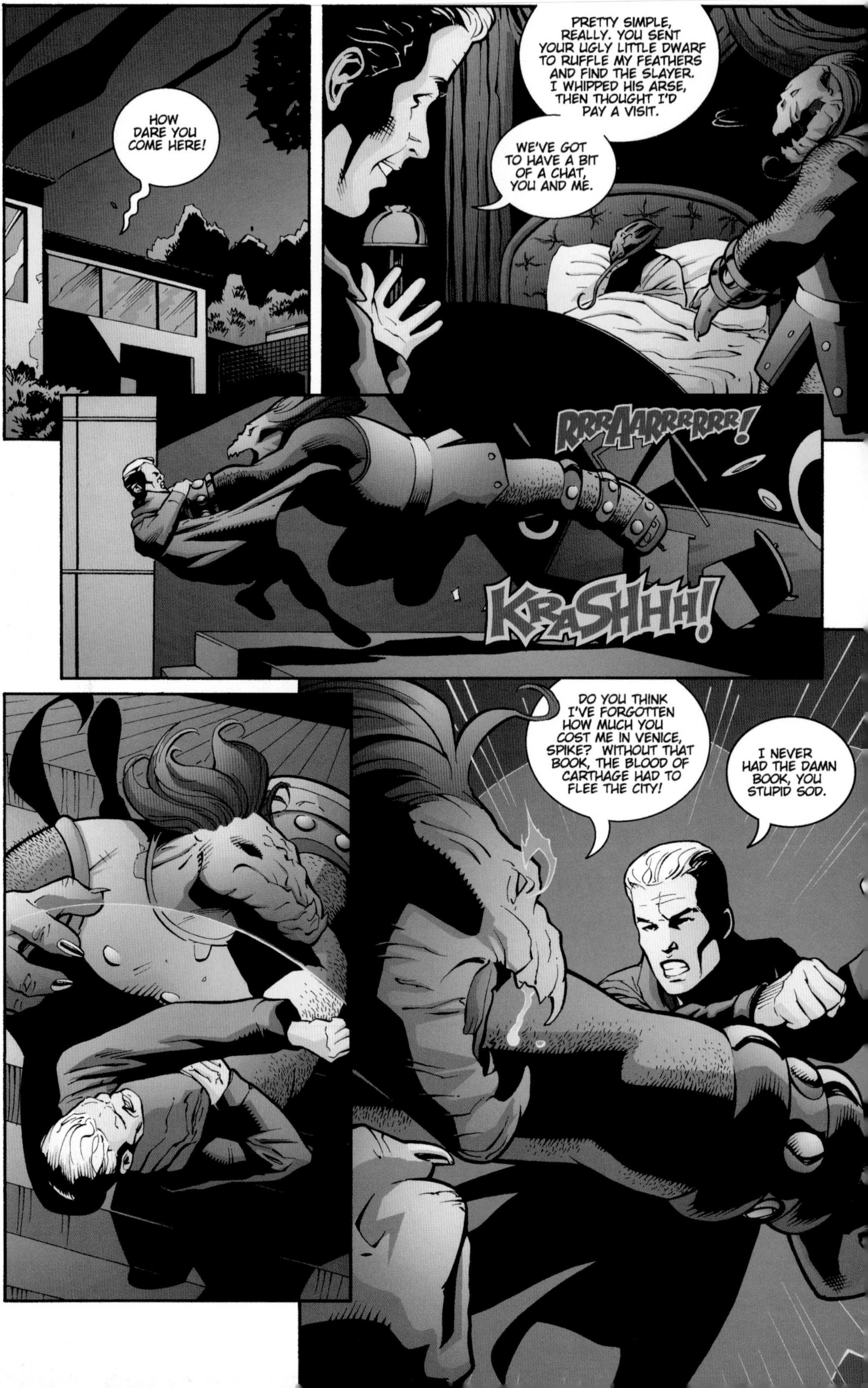
HOW DARE YOU COME HERE!
PRETTY SIMPLE, REALLY. YOU SENT YOUR UGLY LITTLE DWARF TO RUFFLE MY FEATHERS AND FIND THE SLAYER. I WHIPPED HIS ARSE, THEN THOUGHT I'D PAY A VISIT.
WE'VE GOT TO HAVE A BIT OF A CHAT, YOU AND ME.
RRRAARRRRRR!
KRASHHH!
DO YOU THINK I'VE FORGOTTEN HOW MUCH YOU COST ME IN VENICE, SPIKE? WITHOUT THAT BOOK, THE BLOOD OF CARTHAGE HAD TO FLEE THE CITY!
I NEVER HAD THE DAMN BOOK, YOU STUPID SOD.

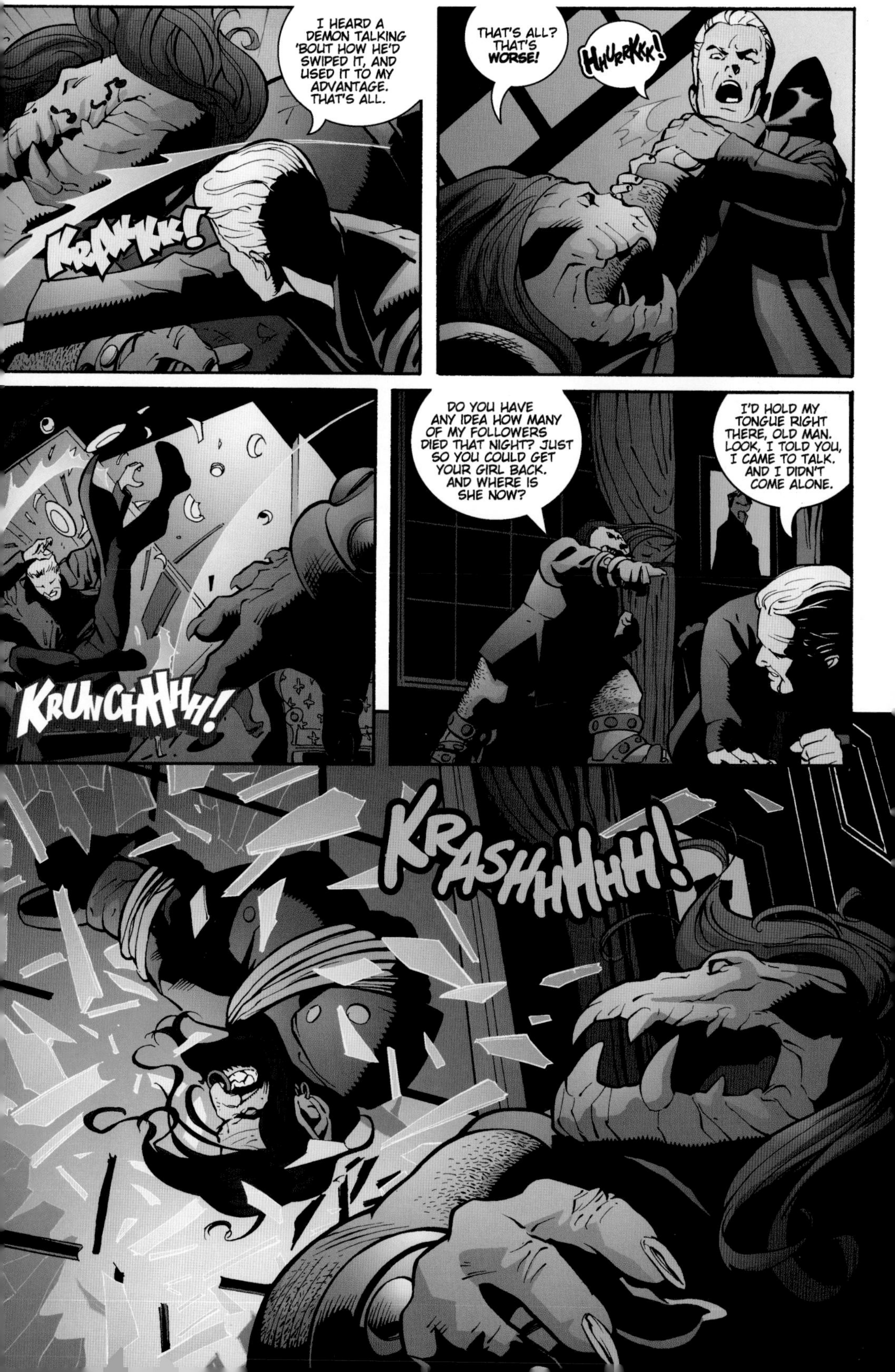
I HEARD A DEMON TALKING 'BOUT HOW HE'D SWIPED IT, AND USED IT TO MY ADVANTAGE. THAT'S ALL.
KRAKKKK!
THAT'S ALL? THAT'S WORSE!
HHURRKKK!
KRUNCHHHHH!
DO YOU HAVE ANY IDEA HOW MANY OF MY FOLLOWERS DIED THAT NIGHT? JUST SO YOU COULD GET YOUR GIRL BACK. AND WHERE IS SHE NOW?
I'D HOLD MY TONGUE RIGHT THERE, OLD MAN. LOOK, I TOLD YOU, I CAME TO TALK. AND I DIDN'T COME ALONE.
KRASHHHHHH!

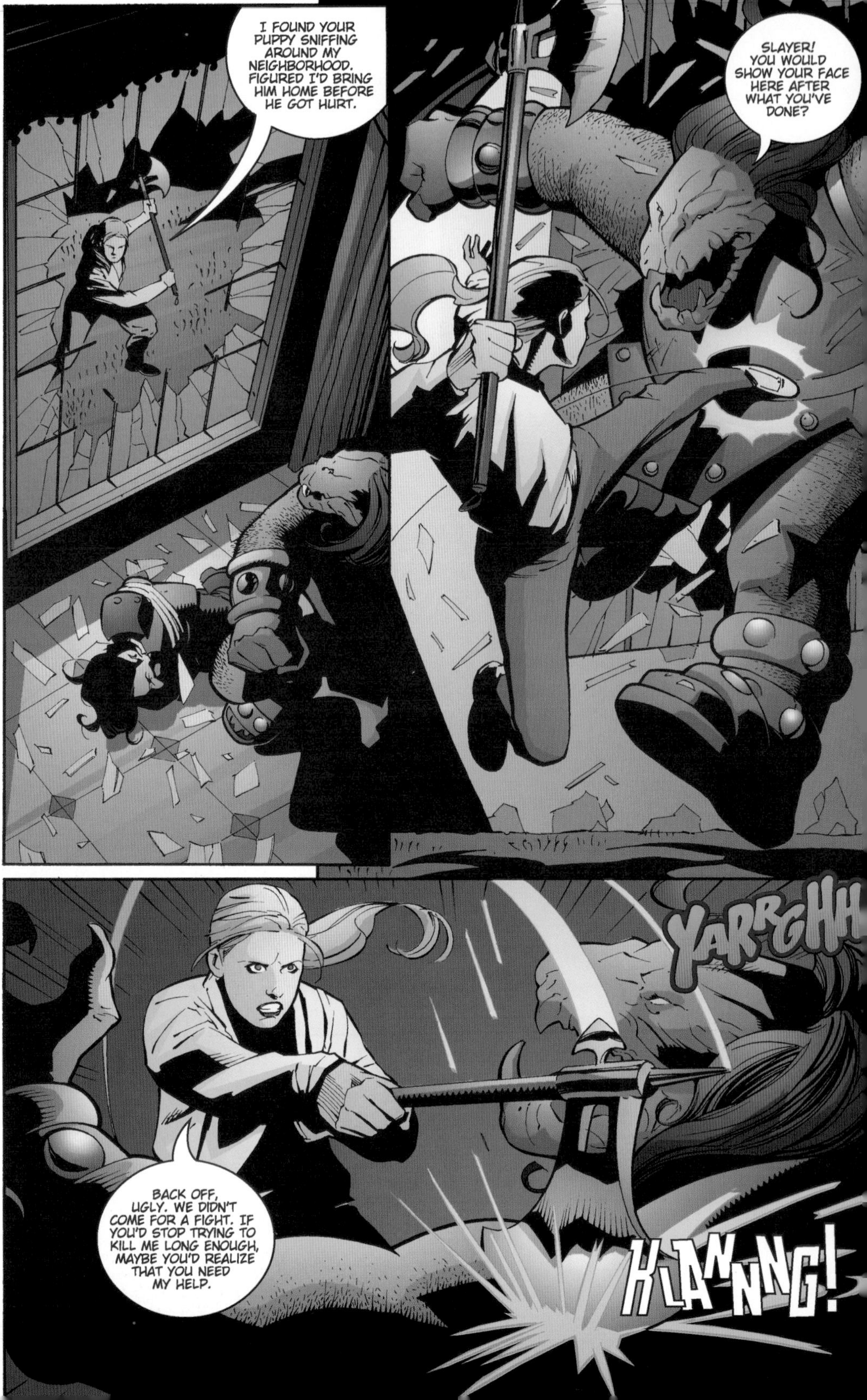
I FOUND YOUR PUPPY SNIFFING AROUND MY NEIGHBORHOOD. FIGURED I'D BRING HIM HOME BEFORE HE GOT HURT.
SLAYER! YOU WOULD SHOW YOUR FACE HERE AFTER WHAT YOU'VE DONE?
YARRGHH
BACK OFF, UGLY. WE DIDN'T COME FOR A FIGHT. IF YOU'D STOP TRYING TO KILL ME LONG ENOUGH, MAYBE YOU'D REALIZE THAT YOU NEED MY HELP.
KLANNNG!

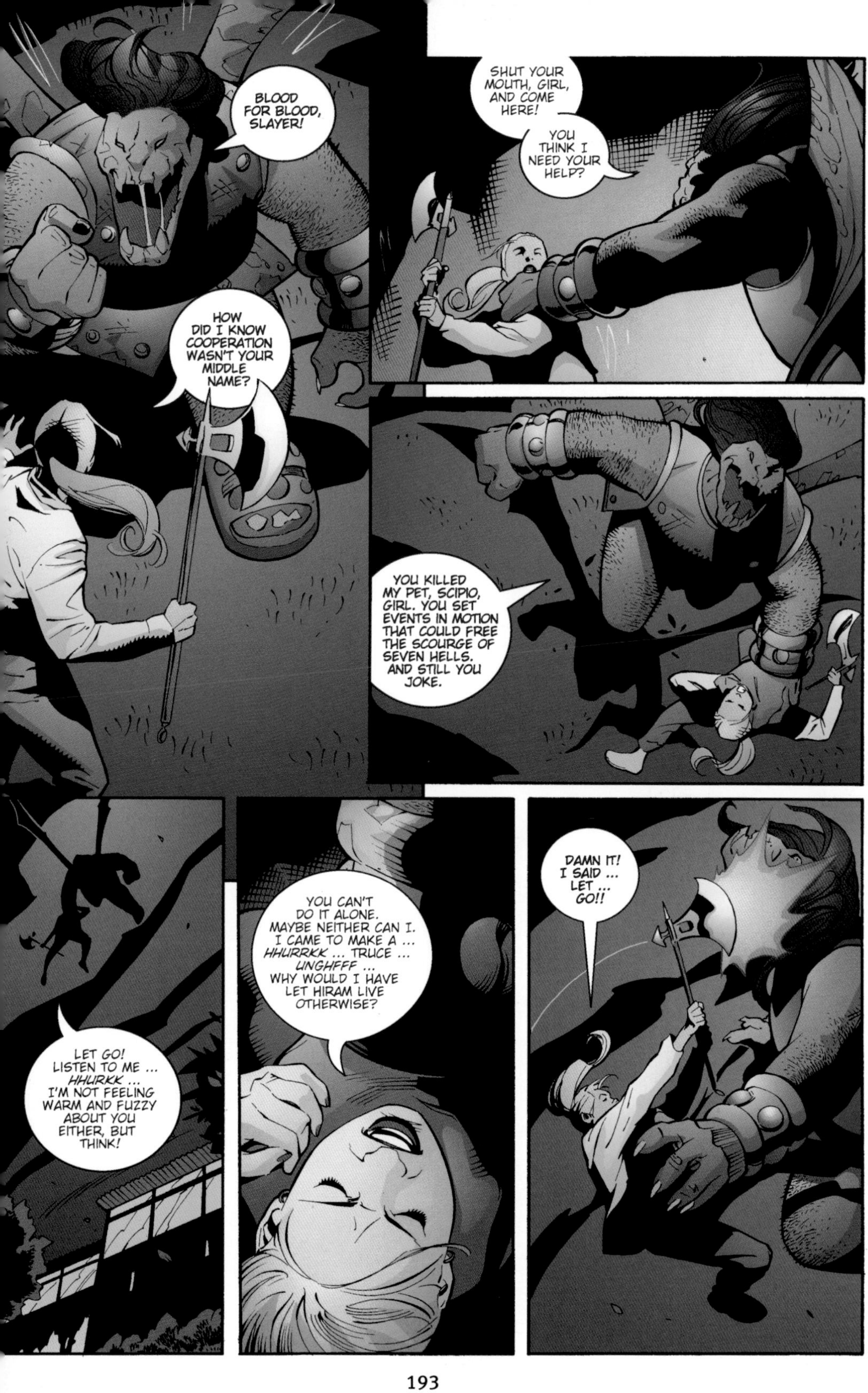
BLOOD FOR BLOOD, SLAYER!
SHUT YOUR MOUTH, GIRL, AND COME HERE!
YOU THINK I NEED YOUR HELP?
HOW DID I KNOW COOPERATION WASN'T YOUR MIDDLE NAME?
YOU KILLED MY PET, SCIPIO, GIRL. YOU SET EVENTS IN MOTION THAT COULD FREE THE SCOURGE OF SEVEN HELLS. AND STILL YOU JOKE.
LET GO! LISTEN TO ME ... HHURKK ... I'M NOT FEELING WARM AND FUZZY ABOUT YOU EITHER, BUT THINK!
YOU CAN'T DO IT ALONE. MAYBE NEITHER CAN I. I CAME TO MAKE A ... HHURRKK ... TRUCE ... UNGHFFF ... WHY WOULD I HAVE LET HIRAM LIVE OTHERWISE?
DAMN IT! I SAID ... LET ... GO!!

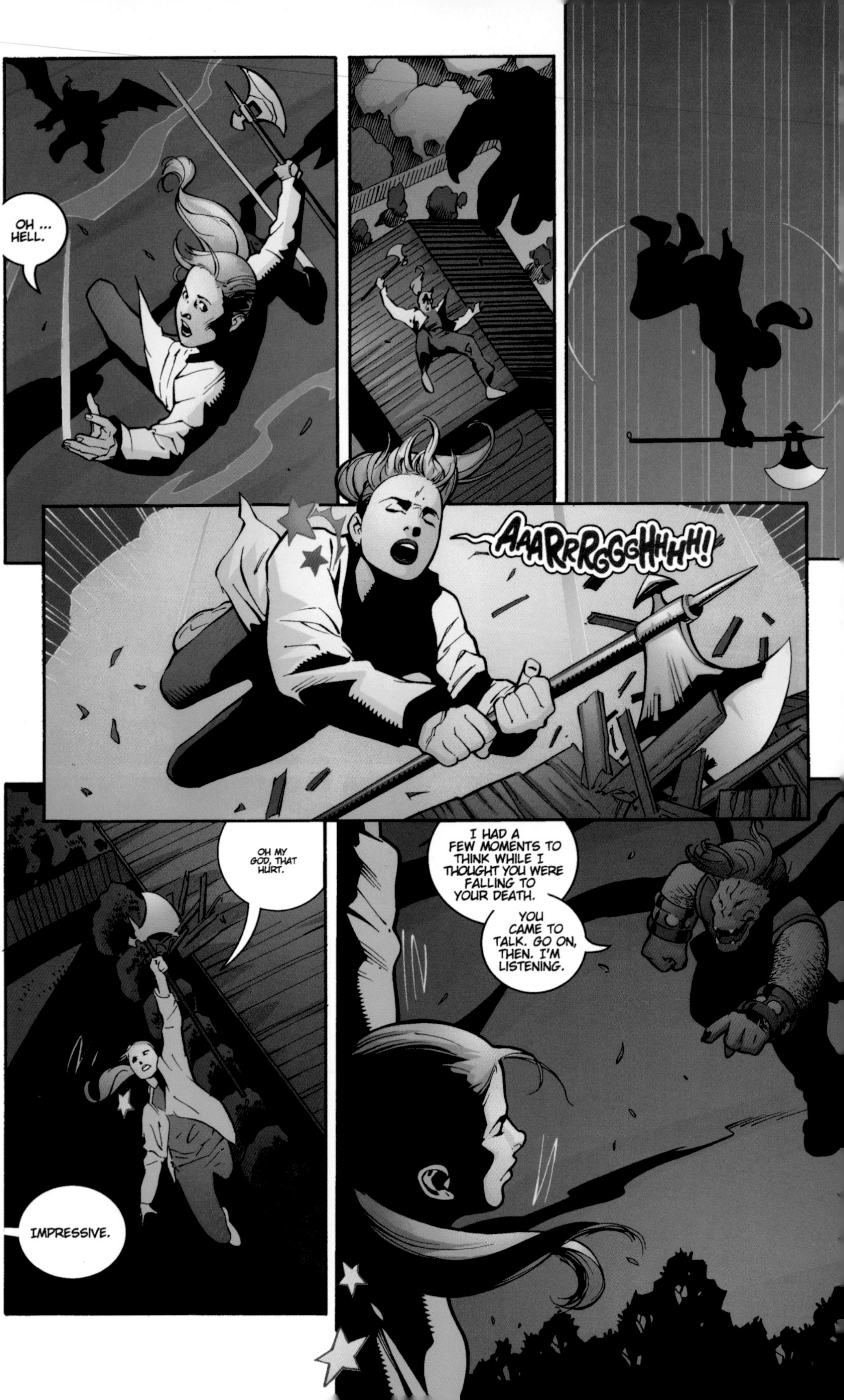
OH ... HELL.
AAARRRGGGHHHH!
OH MY GOD, THAT HURT.
IMPRESSIVE.
I HAD A FEW MOMENTS TO THINK WHILE I THOUGHT YOU WERE FALLING TO YOUR DEATH.
YOU CAME TO TALK. GO ON, THEN. I'M LISTENING.

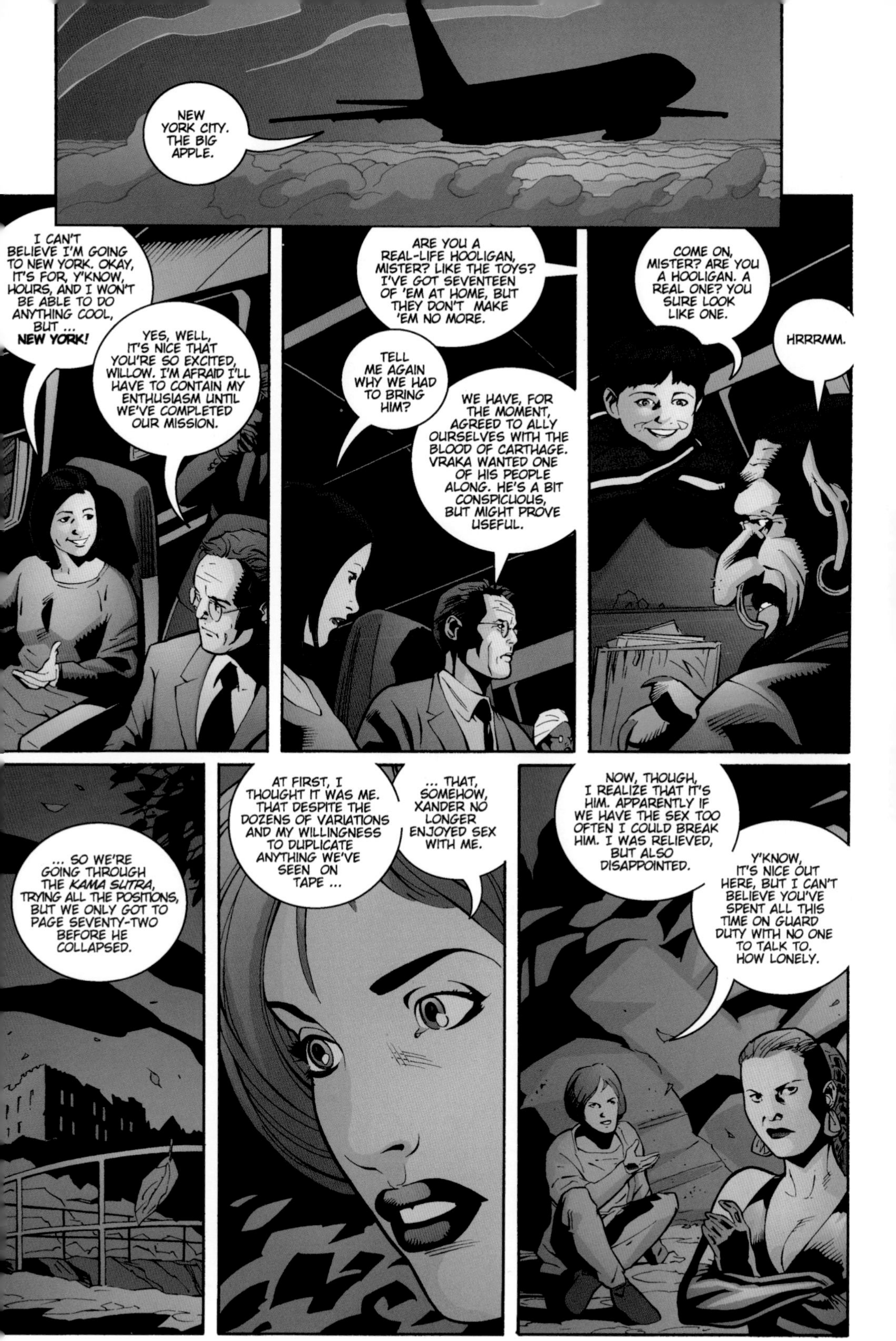
NEW YORK CITY. THE BIG APPLE.
I CAN'T BELIEVE I'M GOING TO NEW YORK. OKAY, IT'S FOR, Y'KNOW, HOURS, AND I WON'T BE ABLE TO DO ANYTHING COOL, BUT ... **NEW YORK!**
YES, WELL, IT'S NICE THAT YOU'RE SO EXCITED, WILLOW. I'M AFRAID I'LL HAVE TO CONTAIN MY ENTHUSIASM UNTIL WE'VE COMPLETED OUR MISSION.
ARE YOU A REAL-LIFE HOOLIGAN, MISTER? LIKE THE TOYS? I'VE GOT SEVENTEEN OF 'EM AT HOME, BUT THEY DON'T MAKE 'EM NO MORE.
TELL ME AGAIN WHY WE HAD TO BRING HIM?
WE HAVE, FOR THE MOMENT, AGREED TO ALLY OURSELVES WITH THE BLOOD OF CARTHAGE. VRAKA WANTED ONE OF HIS PEOPLE ALONG. HE'S A BIT CONSPICUOUS, BUT MIGHT PROVE USEFUL.
COME ON, MISTER? ARE YOU A HOOLIGAN. A REAL ONE? YOU SURE LOOK LIKE ONE.
HRRRMM.
... SO WE'RE GOING THROUGH THE *KAMA SUTRA*, TRYING ALL THE POSITIONS, BUT WE ONLY GOT TO PAGE SEVENTY-TWO BEFORE HE COLLAPSED.
AT FIRST, I THOUGHT IT WAS ME. THAT DESPITE THE DOZENS OF VARIATIONS AND MY WILLINGNESS TO DUPLICATE ANYTHING WE'VE SEEN ON TAPE ...
... THAT, SOMEHOW, XANDER NO LONGER ENJOYED SEX WITH ME.
NOW, THOUGH, I REALIZE THAT IT'S HIM. APPARENTLY IF WE HAVE THE SEX TOO OFTEN I COULD BREAK HIM. I WAS RELIEVED, BUT ALSO DISAPPOINTED.
Y'KNOW, IT'S NICE OUT HERE, BUT I CAN'T BELIEVE YOU'VE SPENT ALL THIS TIME ON GUARD DUTY WITH NO ONE TO TALK TO. HOW LONELY.

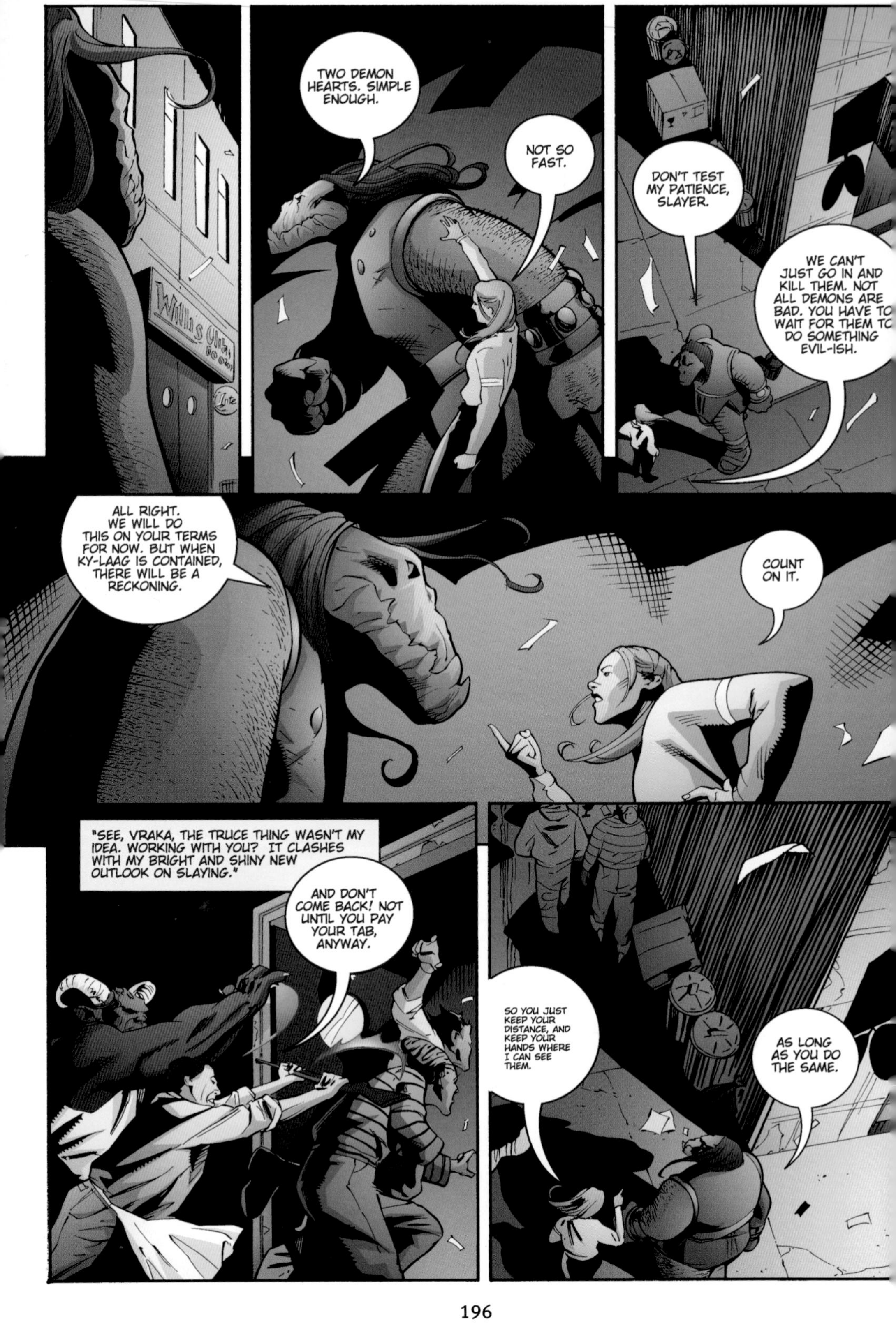

TWO DEMON HEARTS. SIMPLE ENOUGH.
NOT SO FAST.
DON'T TEST MY PATIENCE, SLAYER.
WE CAN'T JUST GO IN AND KILL THEM. NOT ALL DEMONS ARE BAD. YOU HAVE TO WAIT FOR THEM TO DO SOMETHING EVIL-ISH.
ALL RIGHT. WE WILL DO THIS ON YOUR TERMS FOR NOW. BUT WHEN KY-LAAG IS CONTAINED, THERE WILL BE A RECKONING.
COUNT ON IT.
"SEE, VRAKA, THE TRUCE THING WASN'T MY IDEA. WORKING WITH YOU? IT CLASHES WITH MY BRIGHT AND SHINY NEW OUTLOOK ON SLAYING."
AND DON'T COME BACK! NOT UNTIL YOU PAY YOUR TAB, ANYWAY.
SO YOU JUST KEEP YOUR DISTANCE, AND KEEP YOUR HANDS WHERE I CAN SEE THEM.
AS LONG AS YOU DO THE SAME.

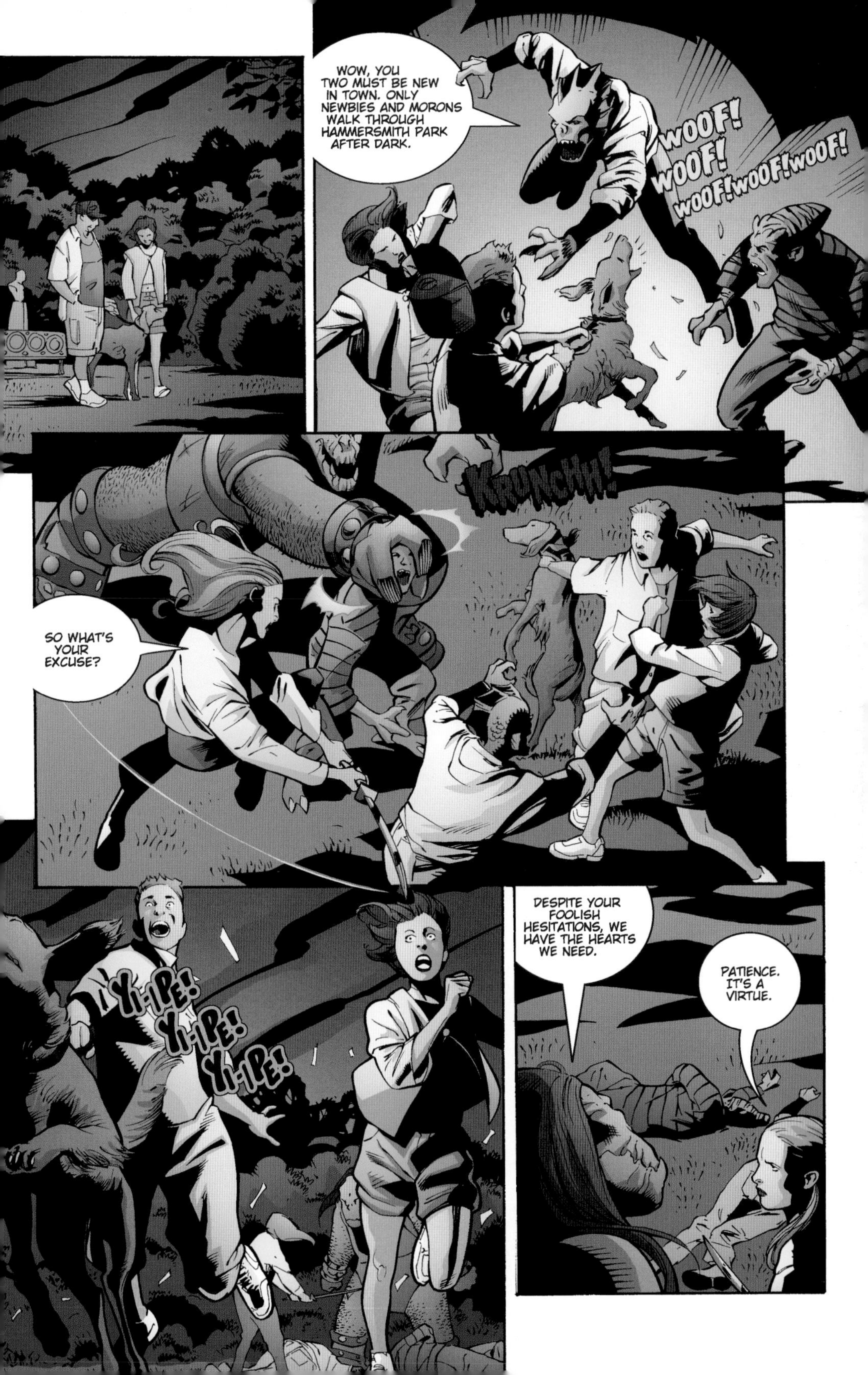
WOW, YOU TWO MUST BE NEW IN TOWN. ONLY NEWBIES AND MORONS WALK THROUGH HAMMERSMITH PARK AFTER DARK.
WOOF! WOOF! WOOF! WOOF! WOOF!
KRUNCHH!
SO WHAT'S YOUR EXCUSE?
YI-IPE! YI-IPE! YI-IPE!
DESPITE YOUR FOOLISH HESITATIONS, WE HAVE THE HEARTS WE NEED.
PATIENCE. IT'S A VIRTUE.

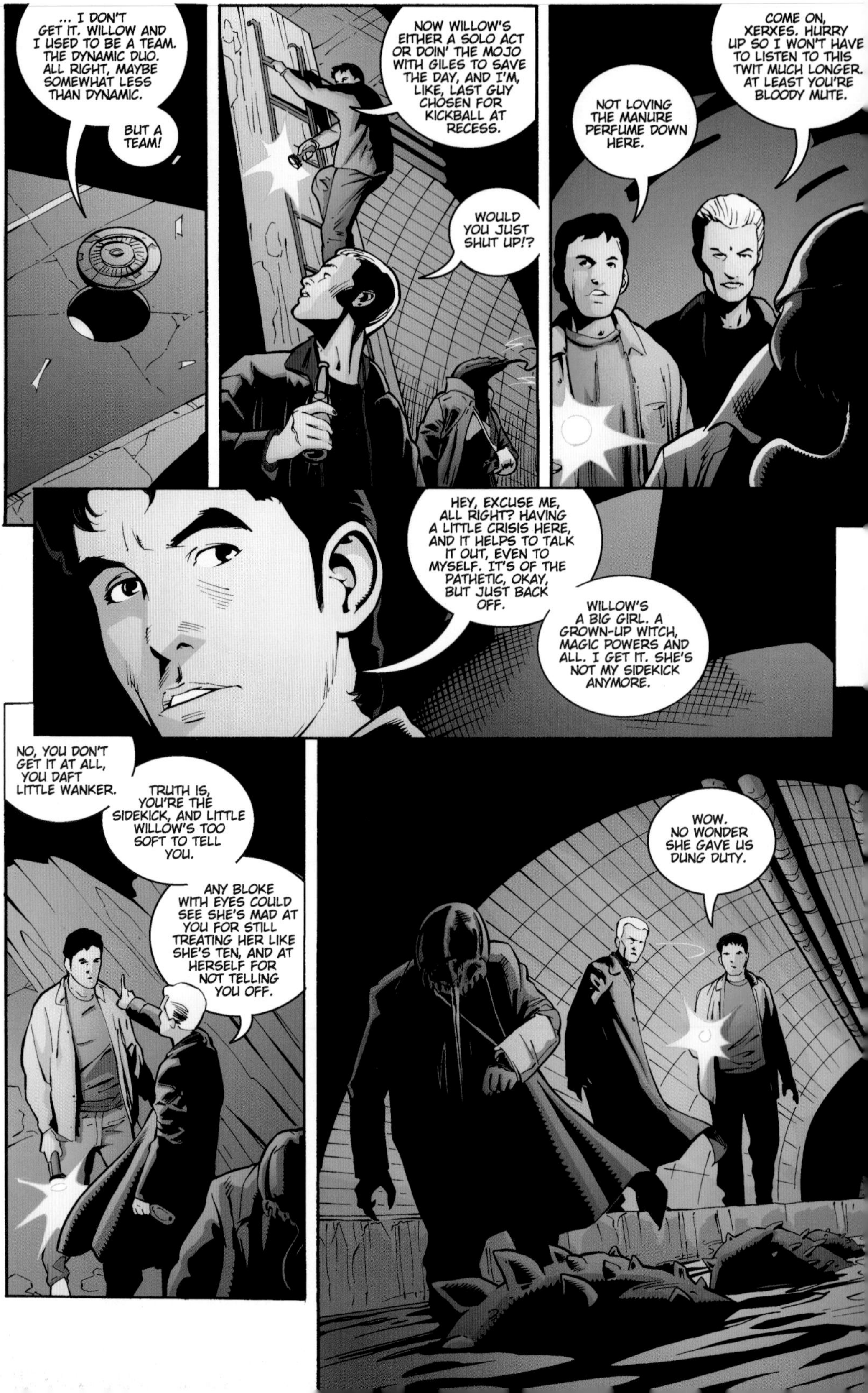
... I DON'T GET IT. WILLOW AND I USED TO BE A TEAM. THE DYNAMIC DUO. ALL RIGHT, MAYBE SOMEWHAT LESS THAN DYNAMIC.
BUT A TEAM!
NOW WILLOW'S EITHER A SOLO ACT OR DOIN' THE MOJO WITH GILES TO SAVE THE DAY, AND I'M, LIKE, LAST GUY CHOSEN FOR KICKBALL AT RECESS.
WOULD YOU JUST SHUT UP!?
NOT LOVING THE MANURE PERFUME DOWN HERE.
COME ON, XERXES. HURRY UP SO I WON'T HAVE TO LISTEN TO THIS TWIT MUCH LONGER. AT LEAST YOU'RE BLOODY MUTE.
HEY, EXCUSE ME, ALL RIGHT? HAVING A LITTLE CRISIS HERE, AND IT HELPS TO TALK IT OUT, EVEN TO MYSELF. IT'S OF THE PATHETIC, OKAY, BUT JUST BACK OFF.
WILLOW'S A BIG GIRL. A GROWN-UP WITCH, MAGIC POWERS AND ALL. I GET IT. SHE'S NOT MY SIDEKICK ANYMORE.
NO, YOU DON'T GET IT AT ALL, YOU DAFT LITTLE WANKER.
TRUTH IS, YOU'RE THE SIDEKICK, AND LITTLE WILLOW'S TOO SOFT TO TELL YOU.
ANY BLOKE WITH EYES COULD SEE SHE'S MAD AT YOU FOR STILL TREATING HER LIKE SHE'S TEN, AND AT HERSELF FOR NOT TELLING YOU OFF.
WOW. NO WONDER SHE GAVE US DUNG DUTY.

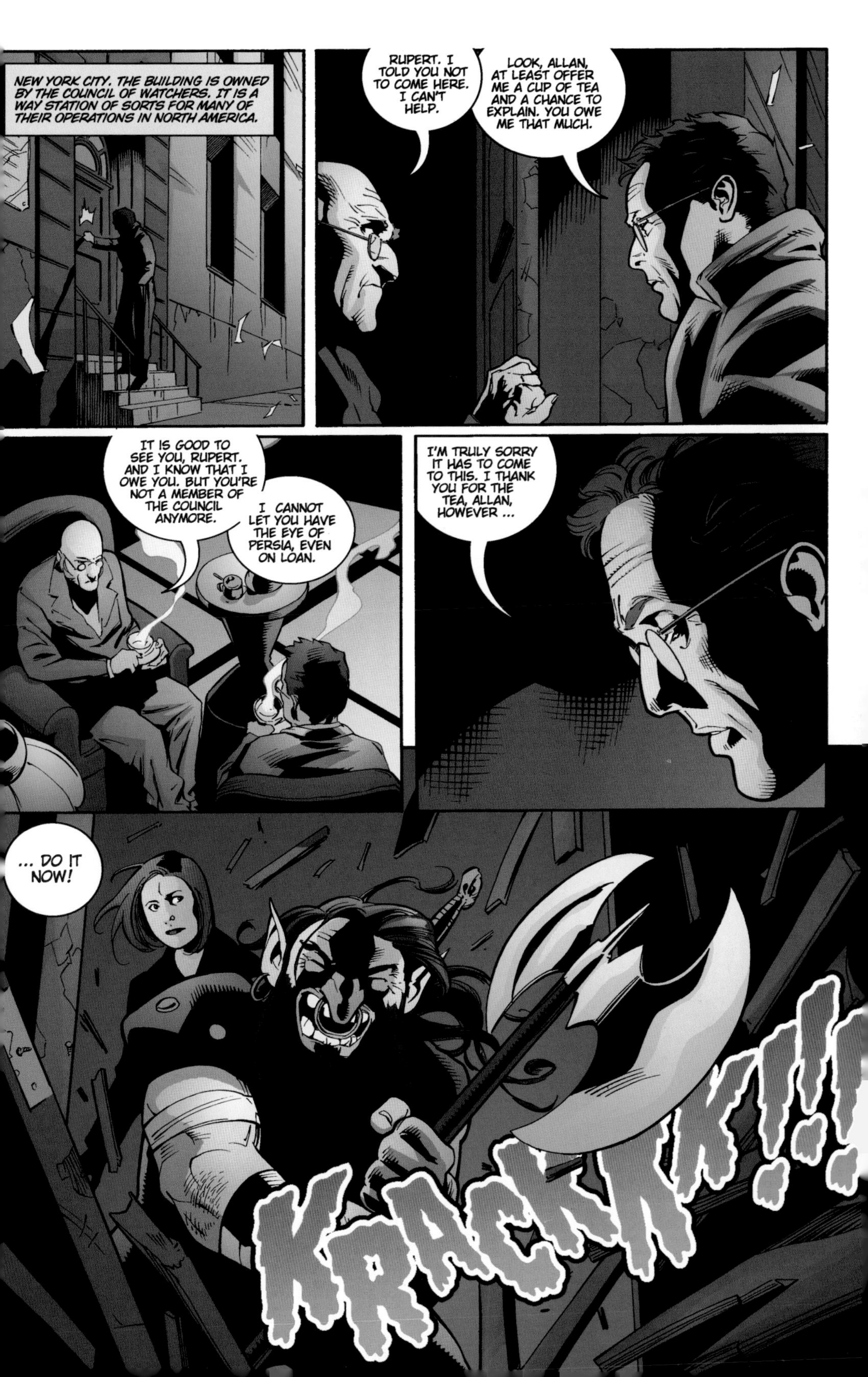
NEW YORK CITY. THE BUILDING IS OWNED BY THE COUNCIL OF WATCHERS. IT IS A WAY STATION OF SORTS FOR MANY OF THEIR OPERATIONS IN NORTH AMERICA.
RUPERT. I TOLD YOU NOT TO COME HERE. I CAN'T HELP.
LOOK, ALLAN, AT LEAST OFFER ME A CUP OF TEA AND A CHANCE TO EXPLAIN. YOU OWE ME THAT MUCH.
IT IS GOOD TO SEE YOU, RUPERT. AND I KNOW THAT I OWE YOU. BUT YOU'RE NOT A MEMBER OF THE COUNCIL ANYMORE.
I CANNOT LET YOU HAVE THE EYE OF PERSIA, EVEN ON LOAN.
I'M TRULY SORRY IT HAS TO COME TO THIS. I THANK YOU FOR THE TEA, ALLAN, HOWEVER ...
... DO IT NOW!
KRACKKK!!!

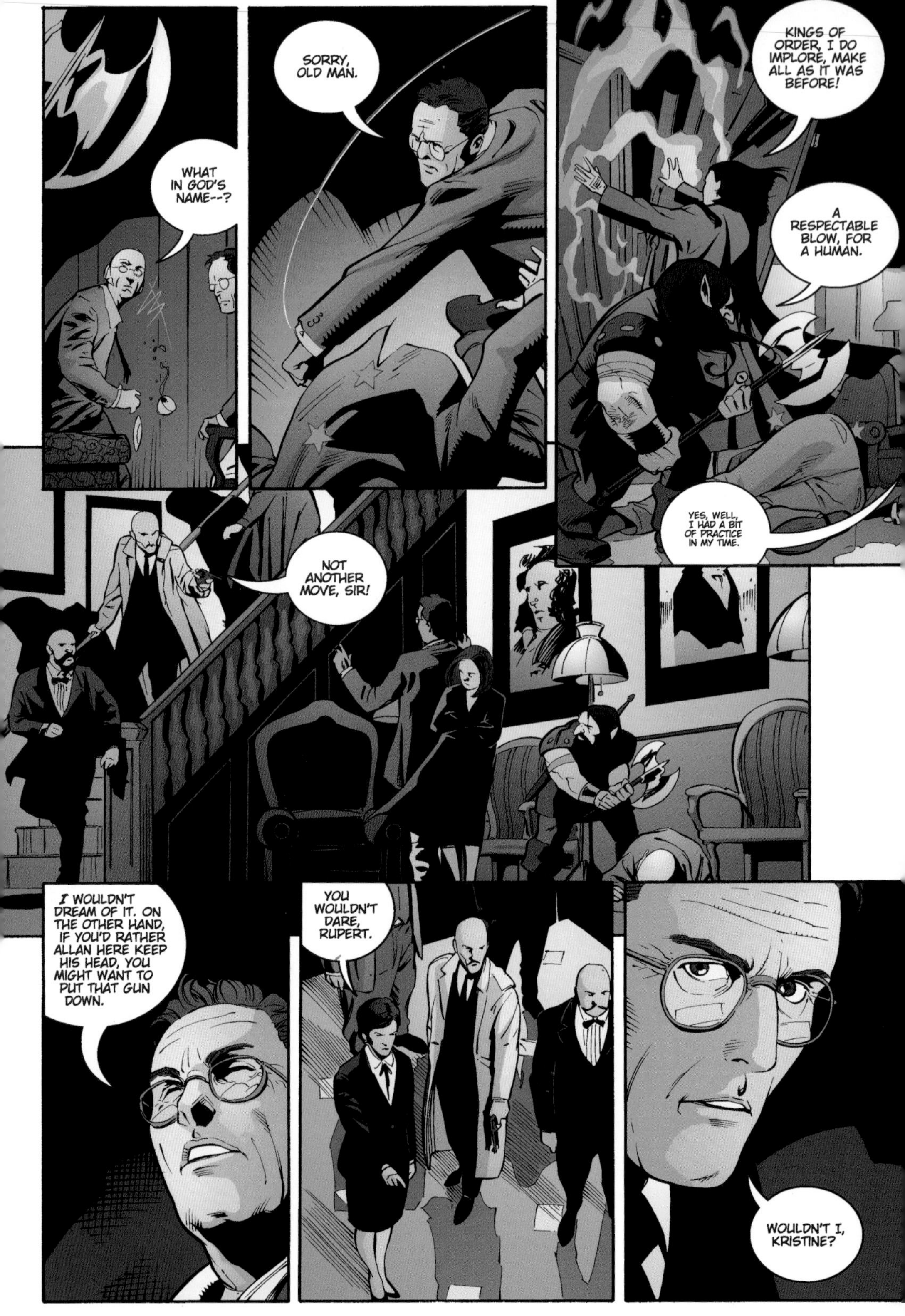
WHAT IN GOD'S NAME--?
SORRY, OLD MAN.
KINGS OF ORDER, I DO IMPLORE, MAKE ALL AS IT WAS BEFORE!
A RESPECTABLE BLOW, FOR A HUMAN.
YES, WELL, I HAD A BIT OF PRACTICE IN MY TIME.
NOT ANOTHER MOVE, SIR!
I WOULDN'T DREAM OF IT. ON THE OTHER HAND, IF YOU'D RATHER ALLAN HERE KEEP HIS HEAD, YOU MIGHT WANT TO PUT THAT GUN DOWN.
YOU WOULDN'T DARE, RUPERT.
WOULDN'T I, KRISTINE?

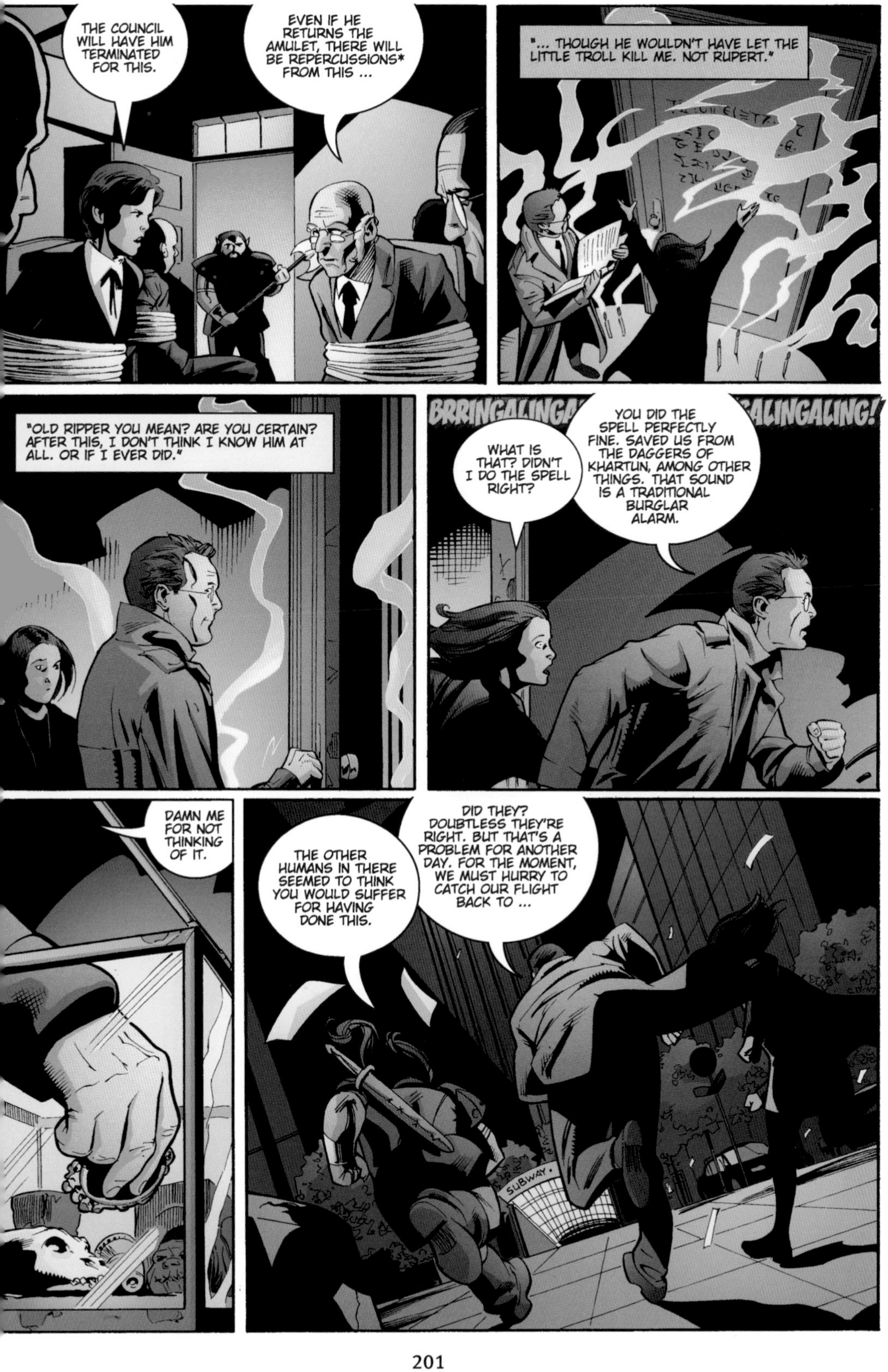
THE COUNCIL WILL HAVE HIM TERMINATED FOR THIS.
EVEN IF HE RETURNS THE AMULET, THERE WILL BE REPERCUSSIONS* FROM THIS ...
"... THOUGH HE WOULDN'T HAVE LET THE LITTLE TROLL KILL ME. NOT RUPERT."
"OLD RIPPER YOU MEAN? ARE YOU CERTAIN? AFTER THIS, I DON'T THINK I KNOW HIM AT ALL. OR IF I EVER DID."
BRRINGALINGA ... GALINGALING!
WHAT IS THAT? DIDN'T I DO THE SPELL RIGHT?
YOU DID THE SPELL PERFECTLY FINE. SAVED US FROM THE DAGGERS OF KHARTUN, AMONG OTHER THINGS. THAT SOUND IS A TRADITIONAL BURGLAR ALARM.
DAMN ME FOR NOT THINKING OF IT.
THE OTHER HUMANS IN THERE SEEMED TO THINK YOU WOULD SUFFER FOR HAVING DONE THIS.
DID THEY? DOUBTLESS THEY'RE RIGHT. BUT THAT'S A PROBLEM FOR ANOTHER DAY. FOR THE MOMENT, WE MUST HURRY TO CATCH OUR FLIGHT BACK TO ...
SUBWAY

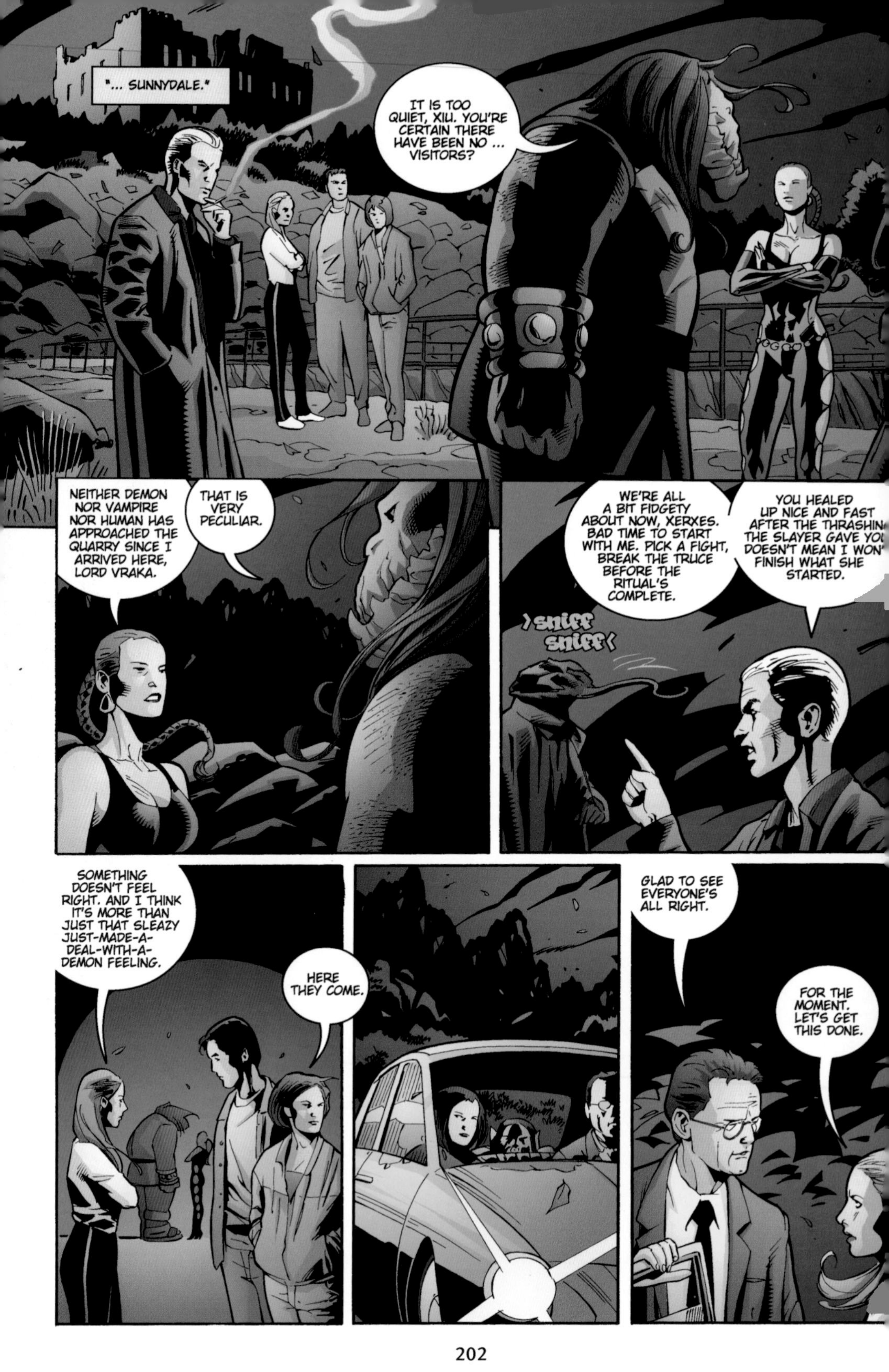
"... SUNNYDALE."
IT IS TOO QUIET, XIU. YOU'RE CERTAIN THERE HAVE BEEN NO ... VISITORS?
NEITHER DEMON NOR VAMPIRE NOR HUMAN HAS APPROACHED THE QUARRY SINCE I ARRIVED HERE, LORD VRAKA.
THAT IS VERY PECULIAR.
›SNIFF SNIFF‹
WE'RE ALL A BIT FIDGETY ABOUT NOW, XERXES. BAD TIME TO START WITH ME. PICK A FIGHT, BREAK THE TRUCE BEFORE THE RITUAL'S COMPLETE.
YOU HEALED UP NICE AND FAST AFTER THE THRASHIN THE SLAYER GAVE YO DOESN'T MEAN I WON' FINISH WHAT SHE STARTED.
SOMETHING DOESN'T FEEL RIGHT. AND I THINK IT'S MORE THAN JUST THAT SLEAZY JUST-MADE-A-DEAL-WITH-A-DEMON FEELING.
HERE THEY COME.
GLAD TO SEE EVERYONE'S ALL RIGHT.
FOR THE MOMENT. LET'S GET THIS DONE.

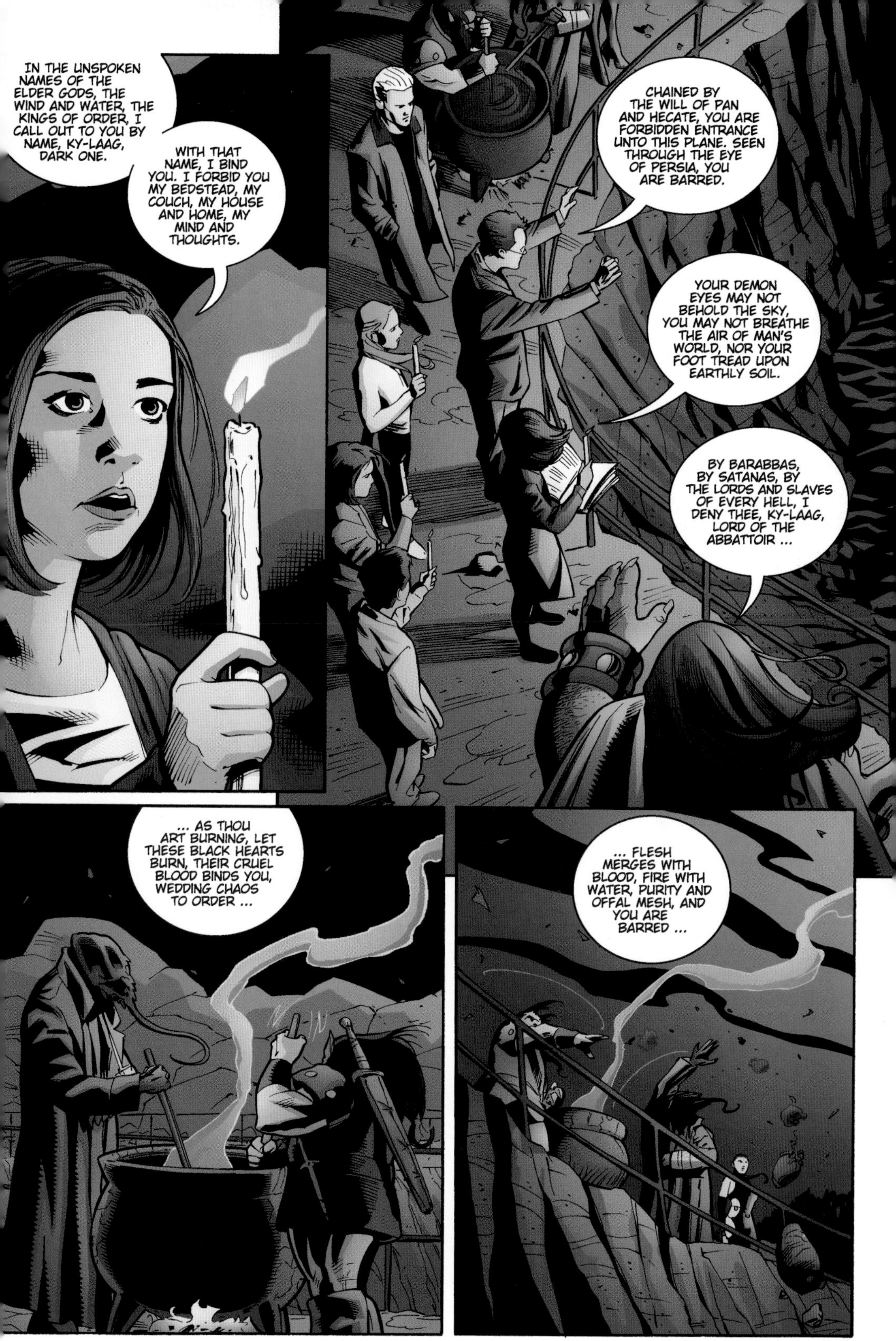
IN THE UNSPOKEN NAMES OF THE ELDER GODS, THE WIND AND WATER, THE KINGS OF ORDER, I CALL OUT TO YOU BY NAME, KY-LAAG, DARK ONE.
WITH THAT NAME, I BIND YOU. I FORBID YOU MY BEDSTEAD, MY COUCH, MY HOUSE AND HOME, MY MIND AND THOUGHTS.
CHAINED BY THE WILL OF PAN AND HECATE, YOU ARE FORBIDDEN ENTRANCE UNTO THIS PLANE. SEEN THROUGH THE EYE OF PERSIA, YOU ARE BARRED.
YOUR DEMON EYES MAY NOT BEHOLD THE SKY, YOU MAY NOT BREATHE THE AIR OF MAN'S WORLD, NOR YOUR FOOT TREAD UPON EARTHLY SOIL.
BY BARABBAS, BY SATANAS, BY THE LORDS AND SLAVES OF EVERY HELL, I DENY THEE, KY-LAAG, LORD OF THE ABBATTOIR ...
... AS THOU ART BURNING, LET THESE BLACK HEARTS BURN, THEIR CRUEL BLOOD BINDS YOU, WEDDING CHAOS TO ORDER ...
... FLESH MERGES WITH BLOOD, FIRE WITH WATER, PURITY AND OFFAL MESH, AND YOU ARE BARRED ...

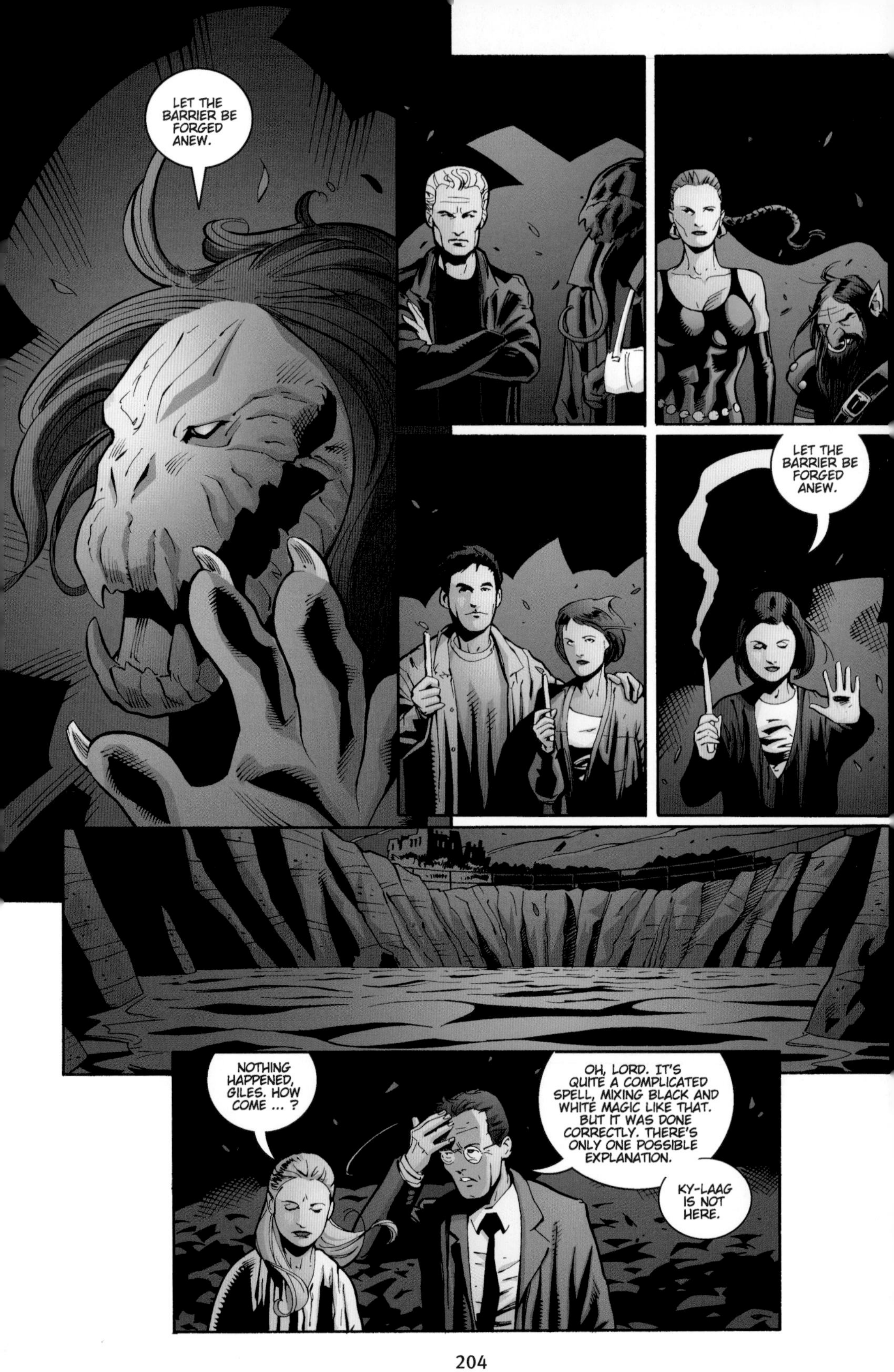
LET THE BARRIER BE FORGED ANEW.
LET THE BARRIER BE FORGED ANEW.
NOTHING HAPPENED, GILES. HOW COME ... ?
OH, LORD. IT'S QUITE A COMPLICATED SPELL, MIXING BLACK AND WHITE MAGIC LIKE THAT. BUT IT WAS DONE CORRECTLY. THERE'S ONLY ONE POSSIBLE EXPLANATION.
KY-LAAG IS NOT HERE.

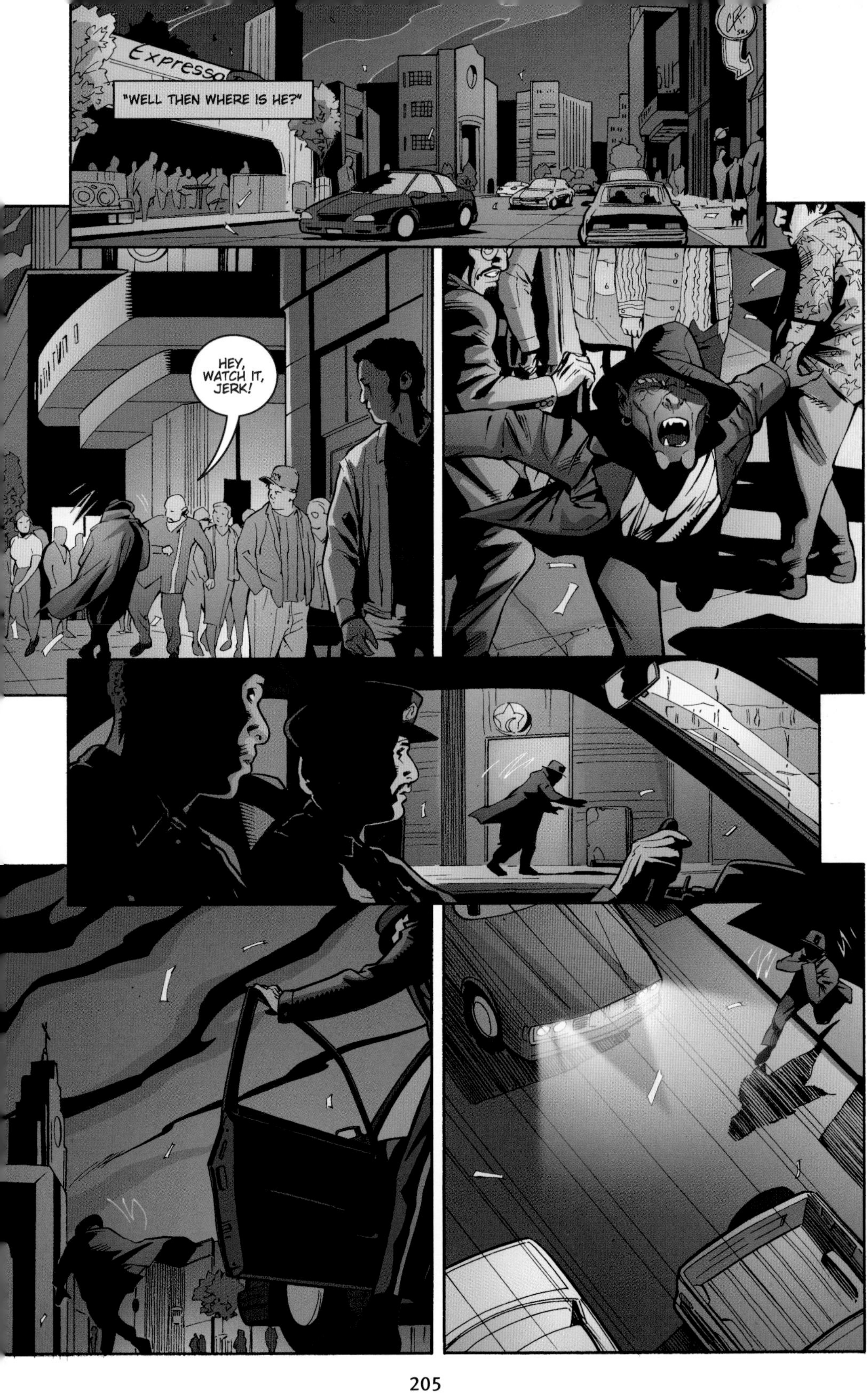
Expresso
"WELL THEN WHERE IS HE?"
HEY, WATCH IT, JERK!

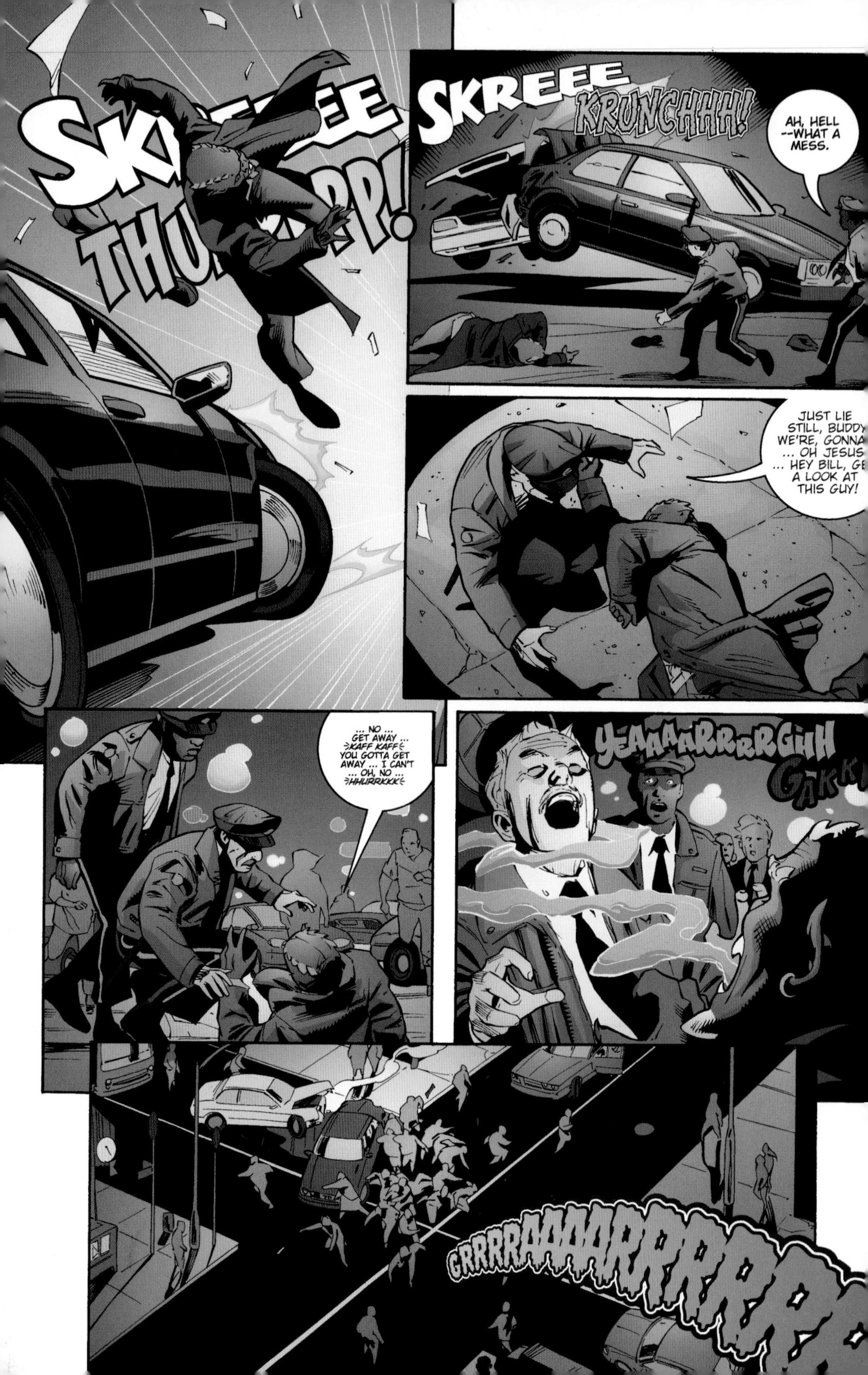
SKREEEE
THUMPP!
SKREEE
KRUNCHHH!
AH, HELL --WHAT A MESS.
JUST LIE STILL, BUDDY WE'RE, GONNA ... OH JESUS ... HEY BILL, GE A LOOK AT THIS GUY!
... NO ... GET AWAY ... KAFF KAFF YOU GOTTA GET AWAY ... I CAN'T ... OH, NO ... HHURRKKK
YEAAAARRRRGHH
GRRRRAAAARRRRRR

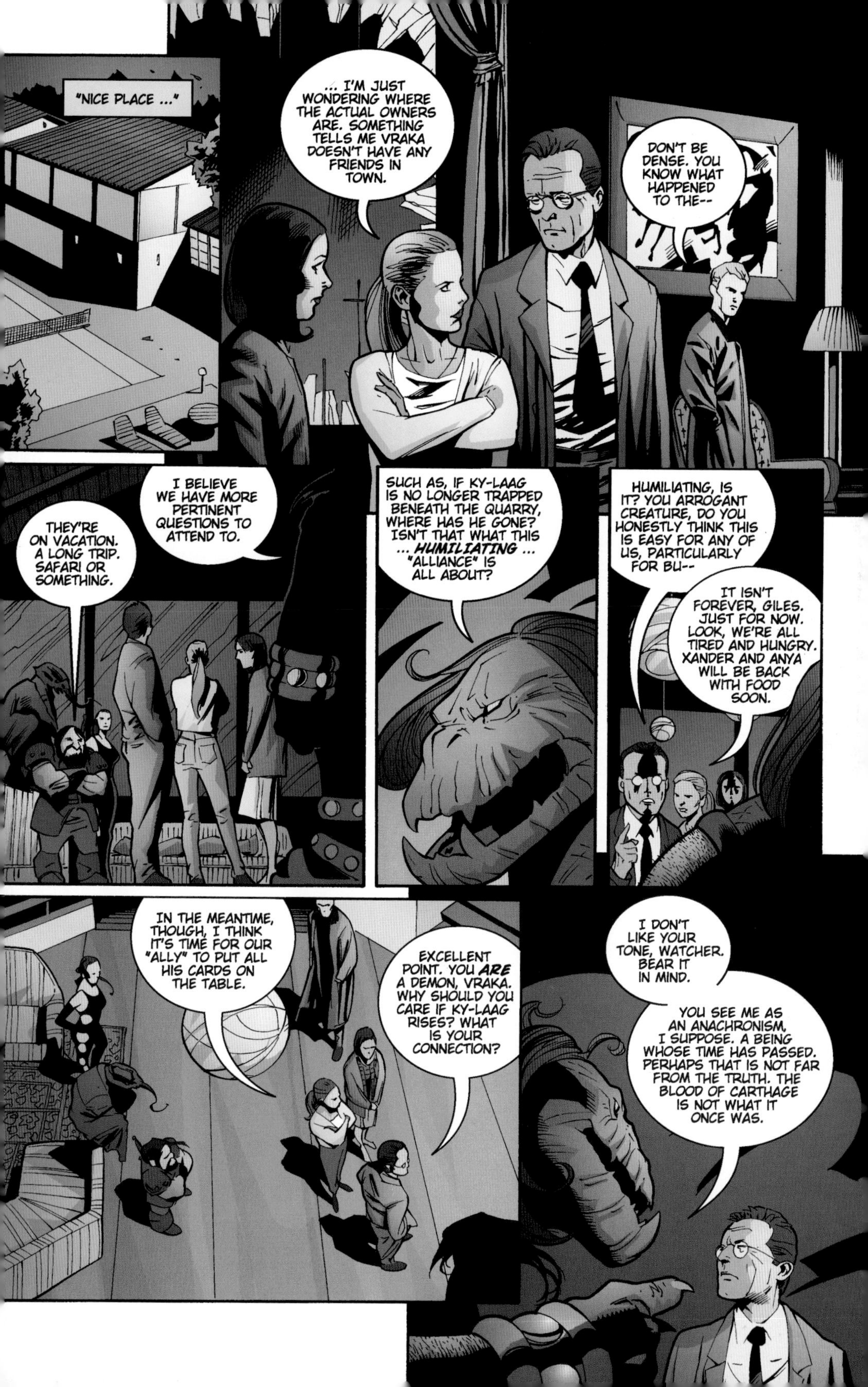
"NICE PLACE ..."
... I'M JUST WONDERING WHERE THE ACTUAL OWNERS ARE. SOMETHING TELLS ME VRAKA DOESN'T HAVE ANY FRIENDS IN TOWN.
DON'T BE DENSE. YOU KNOW WHAT HAPPENED TO THE--
THEY'RE ON VACATION. A LONG TRIP. SAFARI OR SOMETHING.
I BELIEVE WE HAVE MORE PERTINENT QUESTIONS TO ATTEND TO.
SUCH AS, IF KY-LAAG IS NO LONGER TRAPPED BENEATH THE QUARRY, WHERE HAS HE GONE? ISN'T THAT WHAT THIS ... HUMILIATING ... "ALLIANCE" IS ALL ABOUT?
HUMILIATING, IS IT? YOU ARROGANT CREATURE, DO YOU HONESTLY THINK THIS IS EASY FOR ANY OF US, PARTICULARLY FOR BU--
IT ISN'T FOREVER, GILES. JUST FOR NOW. LOOK, WE'RE ALL TIRED AND HUNGRY. XANDER AND ANYA WILL BE BACK WITH FOOD SOON.
IN THE MEANTIME, THOUGH, I THINK IT'S TIME FOR OUR "ALLY" TO PUT ALL HIS CARDS ON THE TABLE.
EXCELLENT POINT. YOU ARE A DEMON, VRAKA. WHY SHOULD YOU CARE IF KY-LAAG RISES? WHAT IS YOUR CONNECTION?
I DON'T LIKE YOUR TONE, WATCHER. BEAR IT IN MIND.
YOU SEE ME AS AN ANACHRONISM, I SUPPOSE. A BEING WHOSE TIME HAS PASSED. PERHAPS THAT IS NOT FAR FROM THE TRUTH. THE BLOOD OF CARTHAGE IS NOT WHAT IT ONCE WAS.

"BUT, OH, THERE WAS A TIME WHEN I WAS WORSHIPPED AND THE BLOOD OF CARTHAGE THREATENED THE WORLD LIKE NO OTHER FORCE OF DARKNESS EVER HAD.

"IT WAS 149 B.C. AND WE WERE BUILDING AN EMPIRE, TO RE-PLACE THE CURRENT HUMAN EMPIRE.

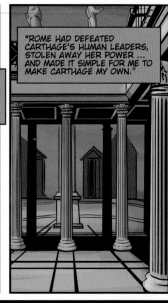

"ROME HAD DEFEATED CARTHAGE'S HUMAN LEADERS, STOLEN AWAY HER POWER ... AND MADE IT SIMPLE FOR ME TO MAKE CARTHAGE MY OWN."

YOU'RE CERTAIN, GENERAL? IT SEEMS ALMOST TOO FANTASTIC, CARTHAGE RULED BY ... MONSTERS.

QUITE CERTAIN, CATO. YOUR SENATE MUST ACT BEFORE THE DEMONS' POWER SPREADS.

AGREED, GENERAL. I WILL SEE TO IT. CARTHAGE MUST BE DESTROYED.

IT WILL BE DONE, SENATOR. I SWEAR IT.

HOW CAN THIS BE? HOW HAVE THE ROMANS DISCOVERED OUR PRESENCE SO QUICKLY?

WE DO NOT KNOW, LORD VRAKA. THE SENATE IS SENDING GENERAL SCIPIO AEMILIANUS WITH ORDERS TO RAZE THE CITY, TO EXPUNGE THE ... YOU, MY LORD.

WE SHALL SEE ABOUT THAT.

208

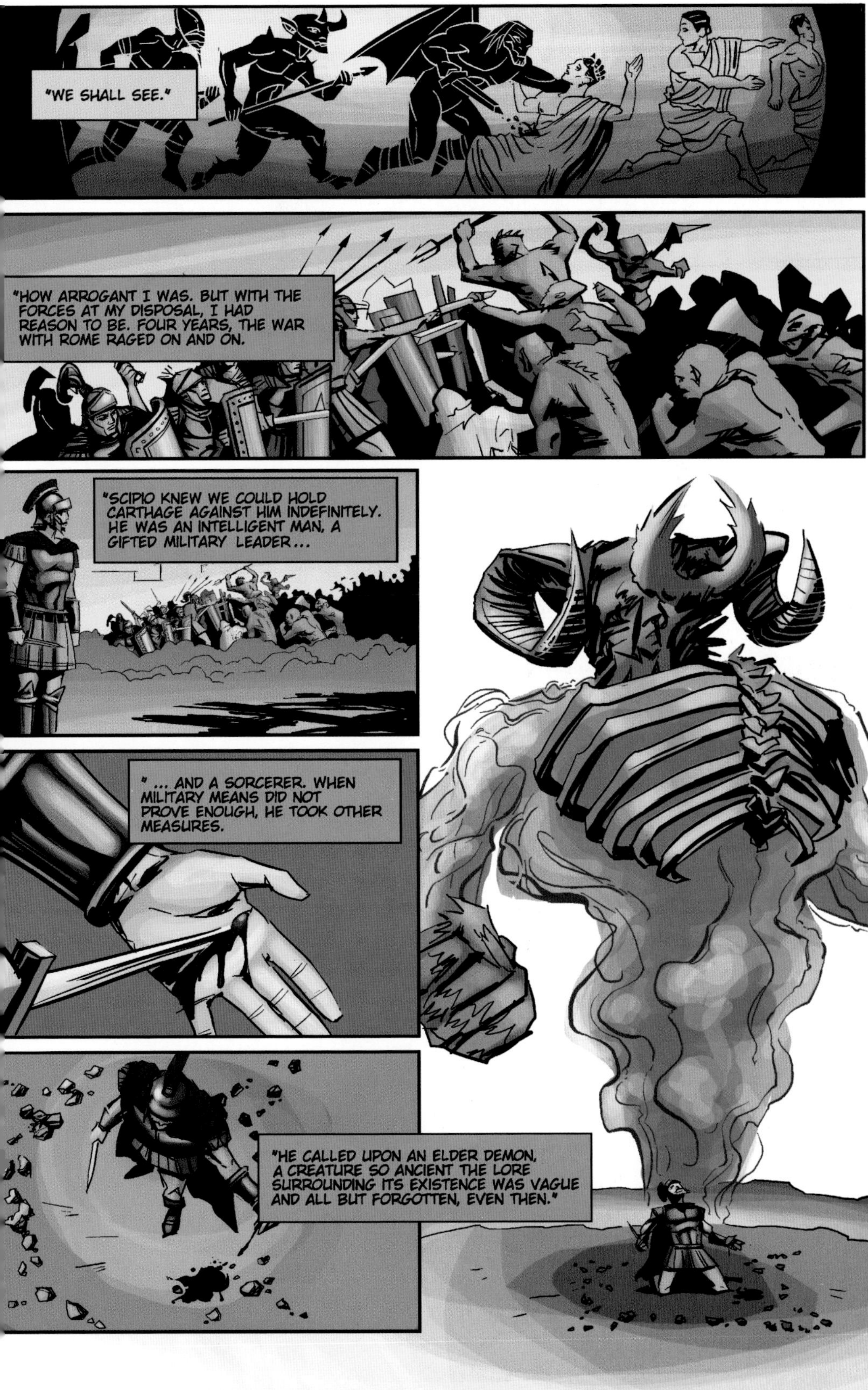
"WE SHALL SEE."
"HOW ARROGANT I WAS. BUT WITH THE FORCES AT MY DISPOSAL, I HAD REASON TO BE. FOUR YEARS, THE WAR WITH ROME RAGED ON AND ON.
"SCIPIO KNEW WE COULD HOLD CARTHAGE AGAINST HIM INDEFINITELY. HE WAS AN INTELLIGENT MAN, A GIFTED MILITARY LEADER...
" ... AND A SORCERER. WHEN MILITARY MEANS DID NOT PROVE ENOUGH, HE TOOK OTHER MEASURES.
"HE CALLED UPON AN ELDER DEMON, A CREATURE SO ANCIENT THE LORE SURROUNDING ITS EXISTENCE WAS VAGUE AND ALL BUT FORGOTTEN, EVEN THEN."

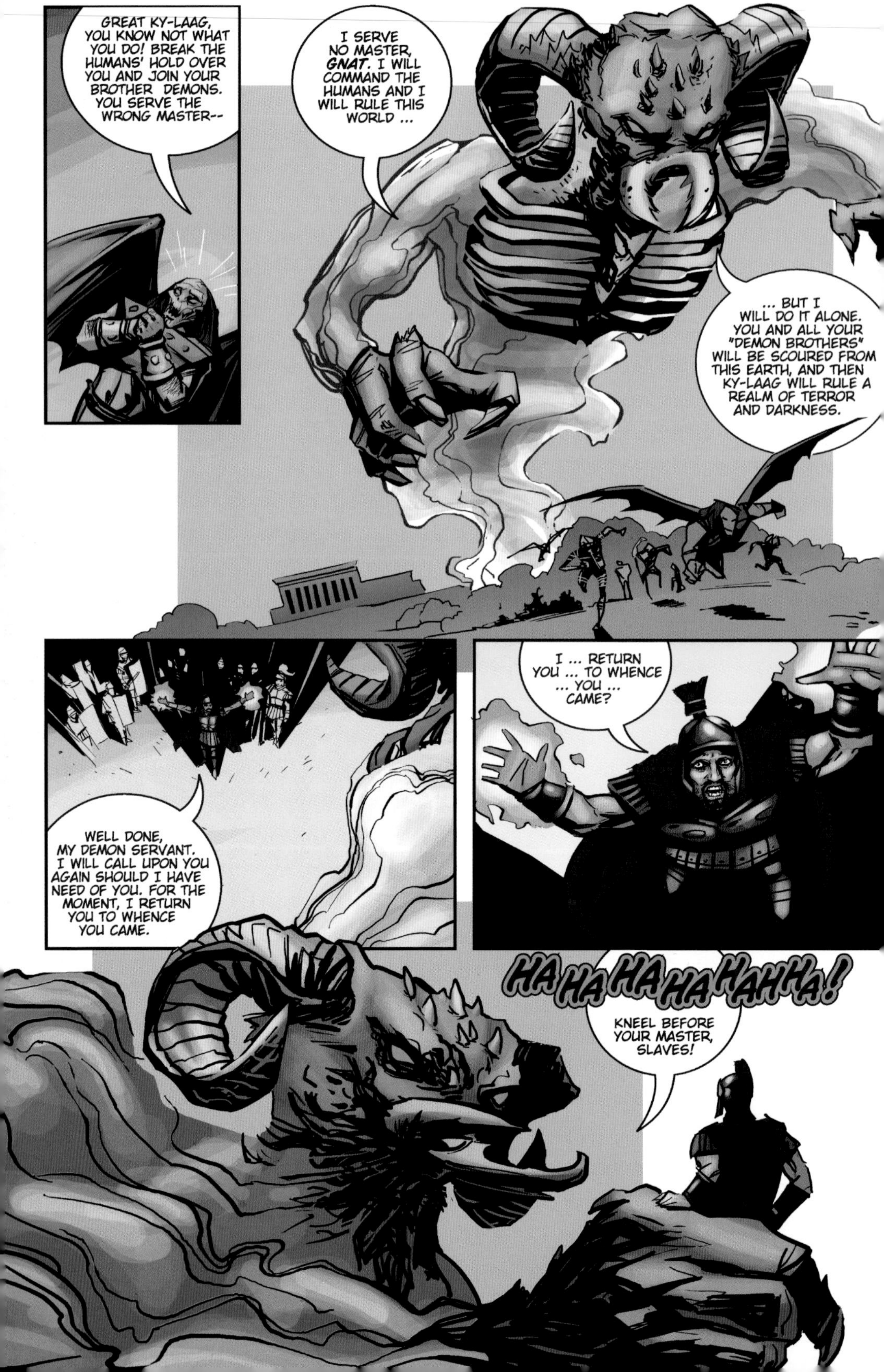
GREAT KY-LAAG, YOU KNOW NOT WHAT YOU DO! BREAK THE HUMANS' HOLD OVER YOU AND JOIN YOUR BROTHER DEMONS. YOU SERVE THE WRONG MASTER--
I SERVE NO MASTER, GNAT. I WILL COMMAND THE HUMANS AND I WILL RULE THIS WORLD ...
... BUT I WILL DO IT ALONE. YOU AND ALL YOUR "DEMON BROTHERS" WILL BE SCOURED FROM THIS EARTH, AND THEN KY-LAAG WILL RULE A REALM OF TERROR AND DARKNESS.
WELL DONE, MY DEMON SERVANT. I WILL CALL UPON YOU AGAIN SHOULD I HAVE NEED OF YOU. FOR THE MOMENT, I RETURN YOU TO WHENCE YOU CAME.
I ... RETURN YOU ... TO WHENCE ... YOU ... CAME?
HA HA HA HA HAHHA!
KNEEL BEFORE YOUR MASTER, SLAVES!

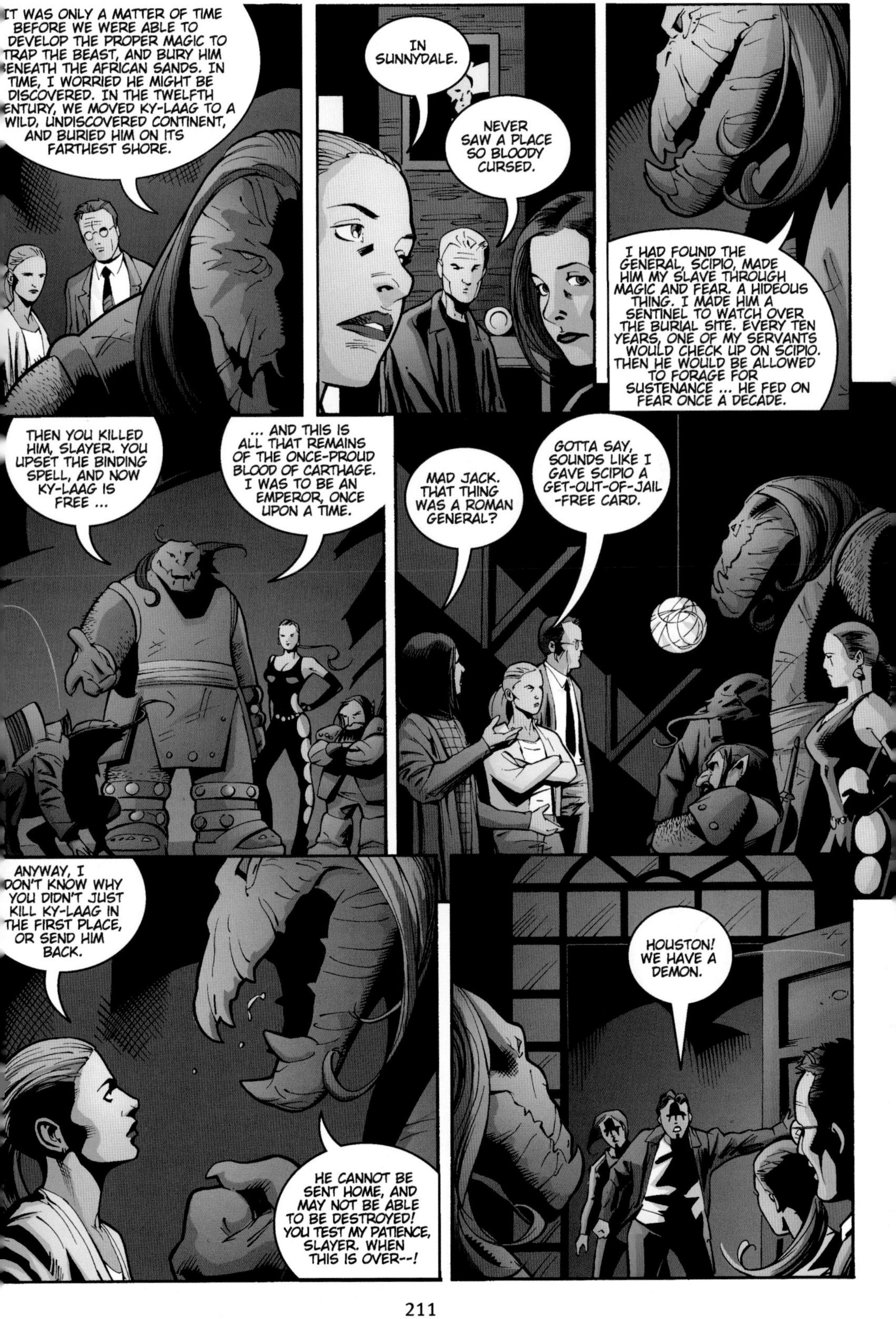
IT WAS ONLY A MATTER OF TIME BEFORE WE WERE ABLE TO DEVELOP THE PROPER MAGIC TO TRAP THE BEAST, AND BURY HIM BENEATH THE AFRICAN SANDS. IN TIME, I WORRIED HE MIGHT BE DISCOVERED. IN THE TWELFTH CENTURY, WE MOVED KY-LAAG TO A WILD, UNDISCOVERED CONTINENT, AND BURIED HIM ON ITS FARTHEST SHORE.
IN SUNNYDALE.
NEVER SAW A PLACE SO BLOODY CURSED.
I HAD FOUND THE GENERAL, SCIPIO, MADE HIM MY SLAVE THROUGH MAGIC AND FEAR. A HIDEOUS THING. I MADE HIM A SENTINEL TO WATCH OVER THE BURIAL SITE. EVERY TEN YEARS, ONE OF MY SERVANTS WOULD CHECK UP ON SCIPIO. THEN HE WOULD BE ALLOWED TO FORAGE FOR SUSTENANCE ... HE FED ON FEAR ONCE A DECADE.
THEN YOU KILLED HIM, SLAYER. YOU UPSET THE BINDING SPELL, AND NOW KY-LAAG IS FREE ...
... AND THIS IS ALL THAT REMAINS OF THE ONCE-PROUD BLOOD OF CARTHAGE. I WAS TO BE AN EMPEROR, ONCE UPON A TIME.
MAD JACK. THAT THING WAS A ROMAN GENERAL?
GOTTA SAY, SOUNDS LIKE I GAVE SCIPIO A GET-OUT-OF-JAIL -FREE CARD.
ANYWAY, I DON'T KNOW WHY YOU DIDN'T JUST KILL KY-LAAG IN THE FIRST PLACE, OR SEND HIM BACK.
HE CANNOT BE SENT HOME, AND MAY NOT BE ABLE TO BE DESTROYED! YOU TEST MY PATIENCE, SLAYER. WHEN THIS IS OVER--!
HOUSTON! WE HAVE A DEMON.

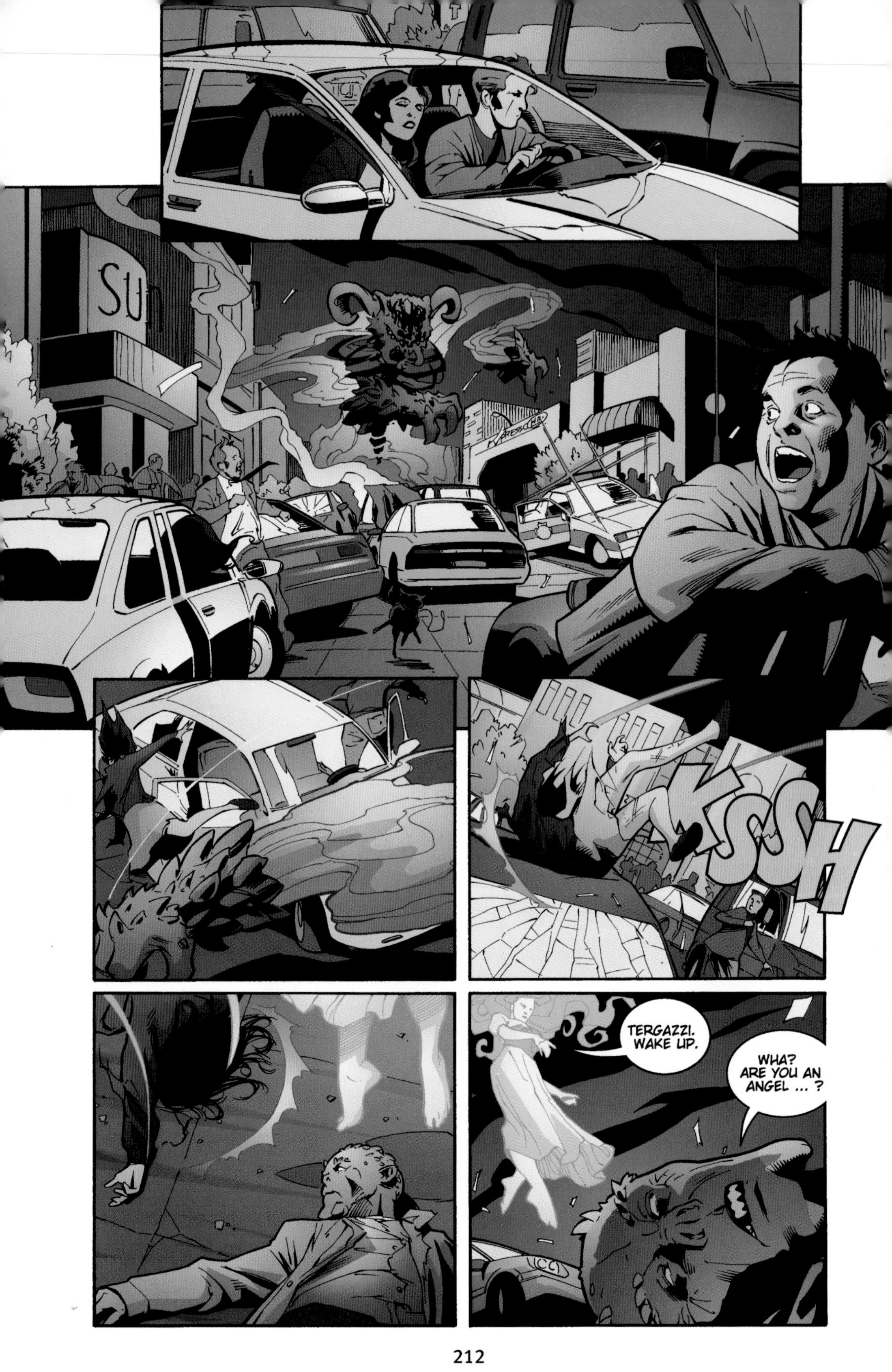

KSSH
TERGAZZI. WAKE UP.
WHA? ARE YOU AN ANGEL ... ?

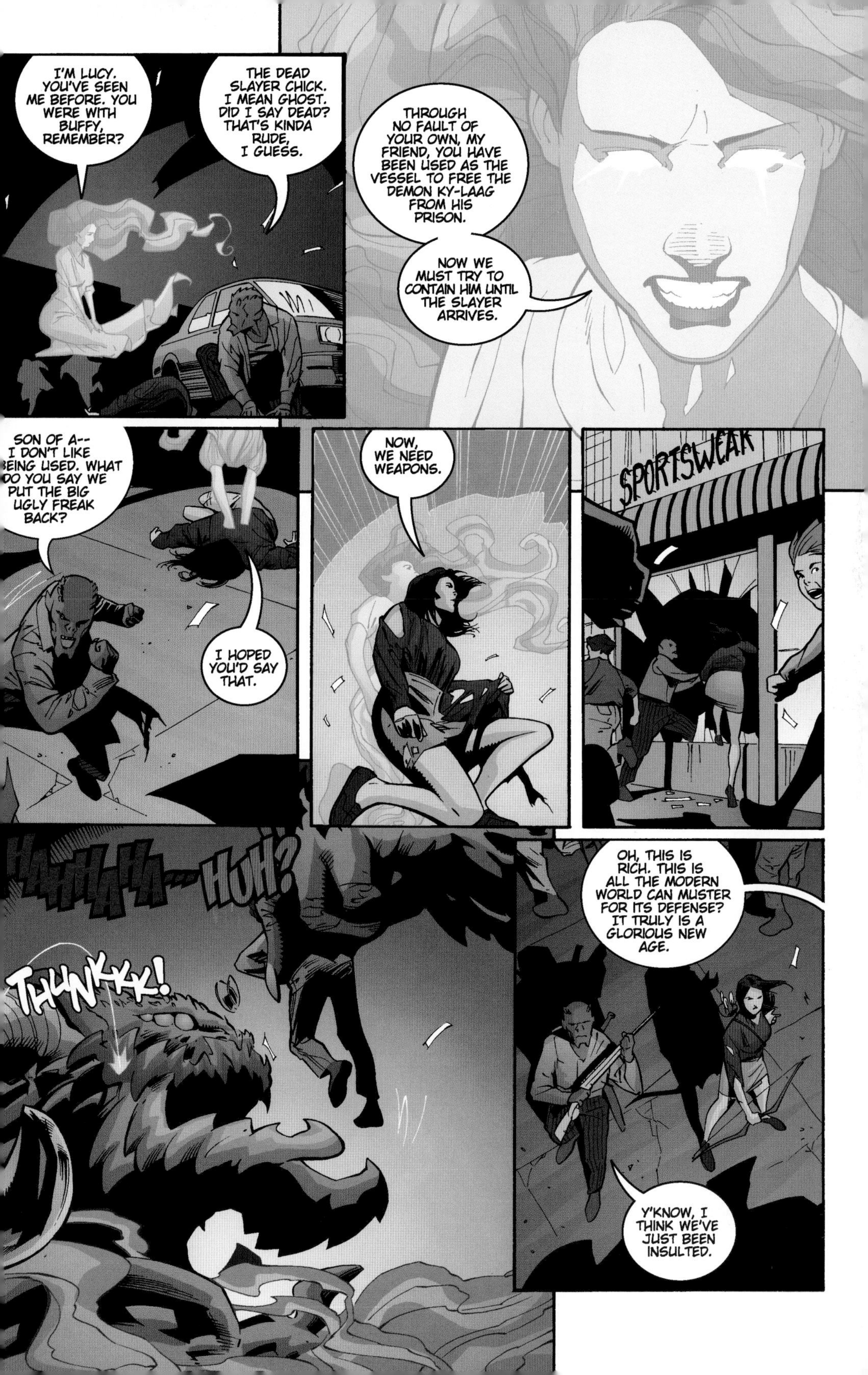
I'M LUCY. YOU'VE SEEN ME BEFORE. YOU WERE WITH BUFFY, REMEMBER?
THE DEAD SLAYER CHICK. I MEAN GHOST. DID I SAY DEAD? THAT'S KINDA RUDE, I GUESS.
THROUGH NO FAULT OF YOUR OWN, MY FRIEND, YOU HAVE BEEN USED AS THE VESSEL TO FREE THE DEMON KY-LAAG FROM HIS PRISON.
NOW WE MUST TRY TO CONTAIN HIM UNTIL THE SLAYER ARRIVES.
SON OF A-- I DON'T LIKE BEING USED. WHAT DO YOU SAY WE PUT THE BIG UGLY FREAK BACK?
I HOPED YOU'D SAY THAT.
NOW, WE NEED WEAPONS.
SPORTSWEAR
HAHHAHA--HUH?
THUNKKK!
OH, THIS IS RICH. THIS IS ALL THE MODERN WORLD CAN MUSTER FOR ITS DEFENSE? IT TRULY IS A GLORIOUS NEW AGE.
Y'KNOW, I THINK WE'VE JUST BEEN INSULTED.

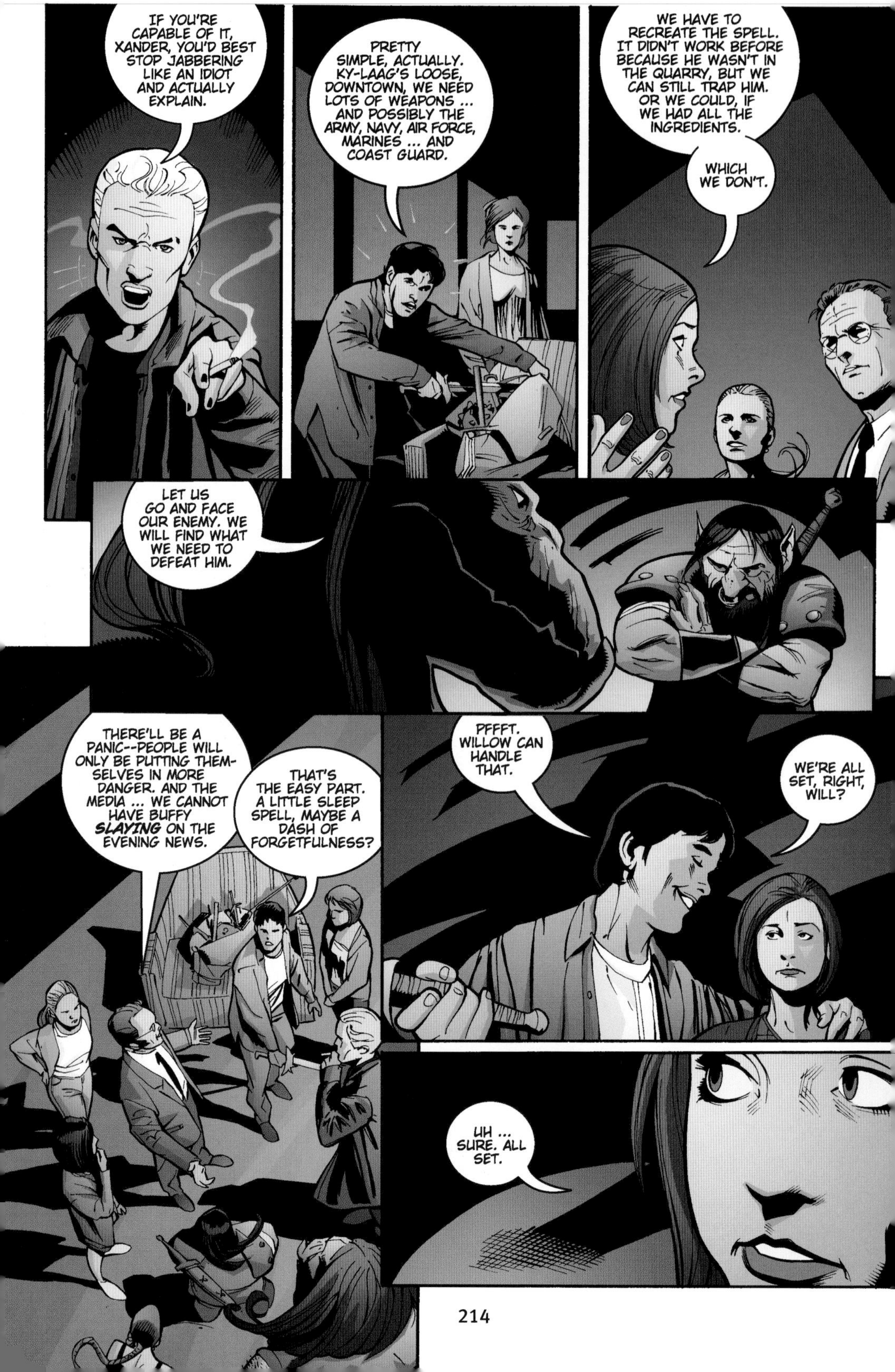
IF YOU'RE CAPABLE OF IT, XANDER, YOU'D BEST STOP JABBERING LIKE AN IDIOT AND ACTUALLY EXPLAIN.
PRETTY SIMPLE, ACTUALLY. KY-LAAG'S LOOSE, DOWNTOWN, WE NEED LOTS OF WEAPONS ... AND POSSIBLY THE ARMY, NAVY, AIR FORCE, MARINES ... AND COAST GUARD.
WE HAVE TO RECREATE THE SPELL. IT DIDN'T WORK BEFORE BECAUSE HE WASN'T IN THE QUARRY, BUT WE CAN STILL TRAP HIM. OR WE COULD, IF WE HAD ALL THE INGREDIENTS.
WHICH WE DON'T.
LET US GO AND FACE OUR ENEMY. WE WILL FIND WHAT WE NEED TO DEFEAT HIM.
THERE'LL BE A PANIC--PEOPLE WILL ONLY BE PUTTING THEMSELVES IN MORE DANGER. AND THE MEDIA ... WE CANNOT HAVE BUFFY SLAYING ON THE EVENING NEWS.
THAT'S THE EASY PART. A LITTLE SLEEP SPELL, MAYBE A DASH OF FORGETFULNESS?
PFFFT. WILLOW CAN HANDLE THAT.
WE'RE ALL SET, RIGHT, WILL?
UH ... SURE. ALL SET.

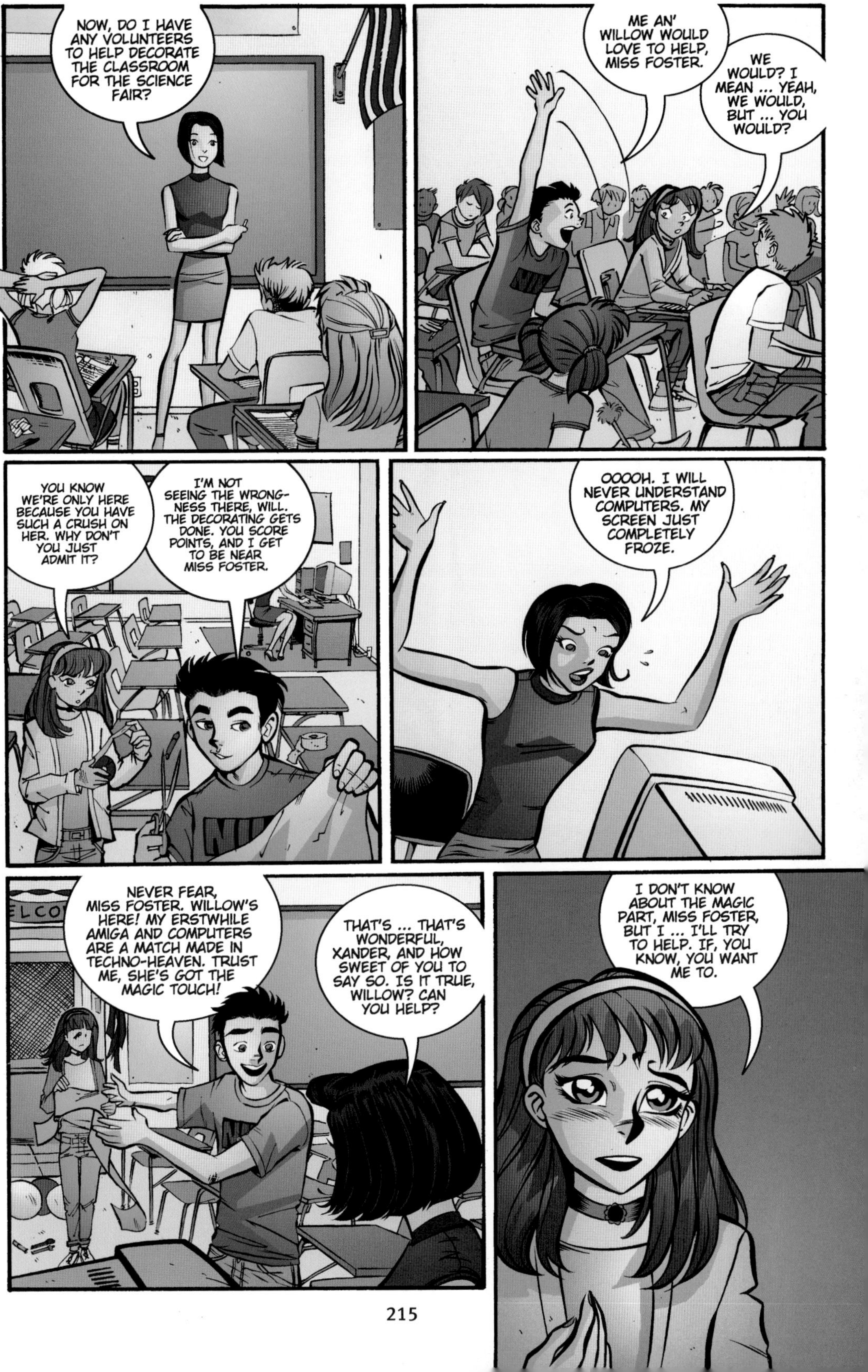
NOW, DO I HAVE ANY VOLUNTEERS TO HELP DECORATE THE CLASSROOM FOR THE SCIENCE FAIR?
ME AN' WILLOW WOULD LOVE TO HELP, MISS FOSTER.
WE WOULD? I MEAN ... YEAH, WE WOULD, BUT ... YOU WOULD?
YOU KNOW WE'RE ONLY HERE BECAUSE YOU HAVE SUCH A CRUSH ON HER. WHY DON'T YOU JUST ADMIT IT?
I'M NOT SEEING THE WRONGNESS THERE, WILL. THE DECORATING GETS DONE. YOU SCORE POINTS, AND I GET TO BE NEAR MISS FOSTER.
OOOOH. I WILL NEVER UNDERSTAND COMPUTERS. MY SCREEN JUST COMPLETELY FROZE.
NEVER FEAR, MISS FOSTER. WILLOW'S HERE! MY ERSTWHILE AMIGA AND COMPUTERS ARE A MATCH MADE IN TECHNO-HEAVEN. TRUST ME, SHE'S GOT THE MAGIC TOUCH!
THAT'S ... THAT'S WONDERFUL, XANDER, AND HOW SWEET OF YOU TO SAY SO. IS IT TRUE, WILLOW? CAN YOU HELP?
I DON'T KNOW ABOUT THE MAGIC PART, MISS FOSTER, BUT I ... I'LL TRY TO HELP. IF, YOU KNOW, YOU WANT ME TO.

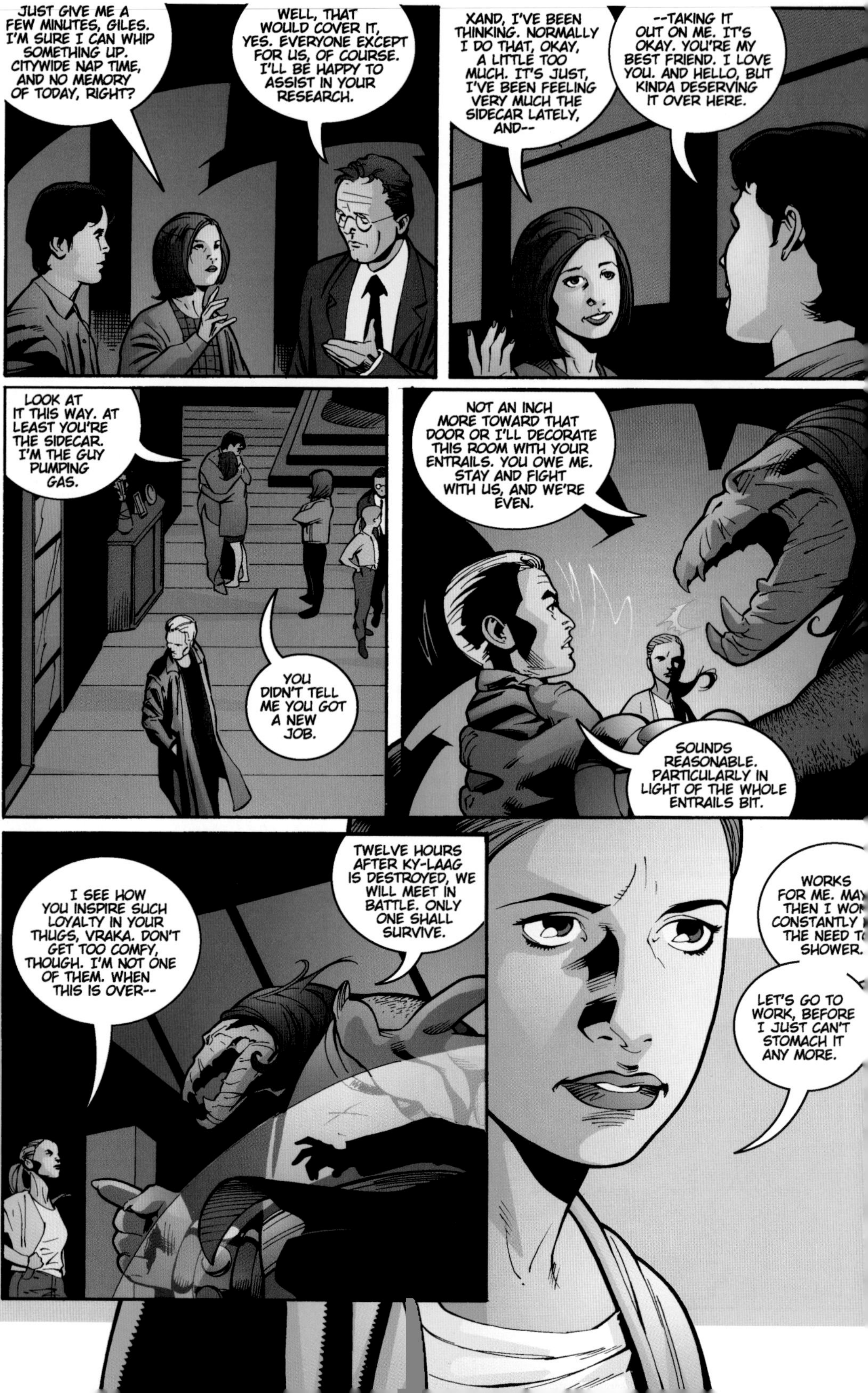
JUST GIVE ME A FEW MINUTES, GILES. I'M SURE I CAN WHIP SOMETHING UP. CITYWIDE NAP TIME, AND NO MEMORY OF TODAY, RIGHT?
WELL, THAT WOULD COVER IT, YES. EVERYONE EXCEPT FOR US, OF COURSE. I'LL BE HAPPY TO ASSIST IN YOUR RESEARCH.
XAND, I'VE BEEN THINKING. NORMALLY I DO THAT, OKAY, A LITTLE TOO MUCH. IT'S JUST, I'VE BEEN FEELING VERY MUCH THE SIDECAR LATELY, AND--
--TAKING IT OUT ON ME. IT'S OKAY. YOU'RE MY BEST FRIEND. I LOVE YOU. AND HELLO, BUT KINDA DESERVING IT OVER HERE.
LOOK AT IT THIS WAY. AT LEAST YOU'RE THE SIDECAR. I'M THE GUY PUMPING GAS.
YOU DIDN'T TELL ME YOU GOT A NEW JOB.
NOT AN INCH MORE TOWARD THAT DOOR OR I'LL DECORATE THIS ROOM WITH YOUR ENTRAILS. YOU OWE ME. STAY AND FIGHT WITH US, AND WE'RE EVEN.
SOUNDS REASONABLE. PARTICULARLY IN LIGHT OF THE WHOLE ENTRAILS BIT.
I SEE HOW YOU INSPIRE SUCH LOYALTY IN YOUR THUGS, VRAKA. DON'T GET TOO COMFY, THOUGH. I'M NOT ONE OF THEM. WHEN THIS IS OVER--
TWELVE HOURS AFTER KY-LAAG IS DESTROYED, WE WILL MEET IN BATTLE. ONLY ONE SHALL SURVIVE.
WORKS FOR ME. MA THEN I WO CONSTANTLY THE NEED T SHOWER.
LET'S GO TO WORK, BEFORE I JUST CAN'T STOMACH IT ANY MORE.

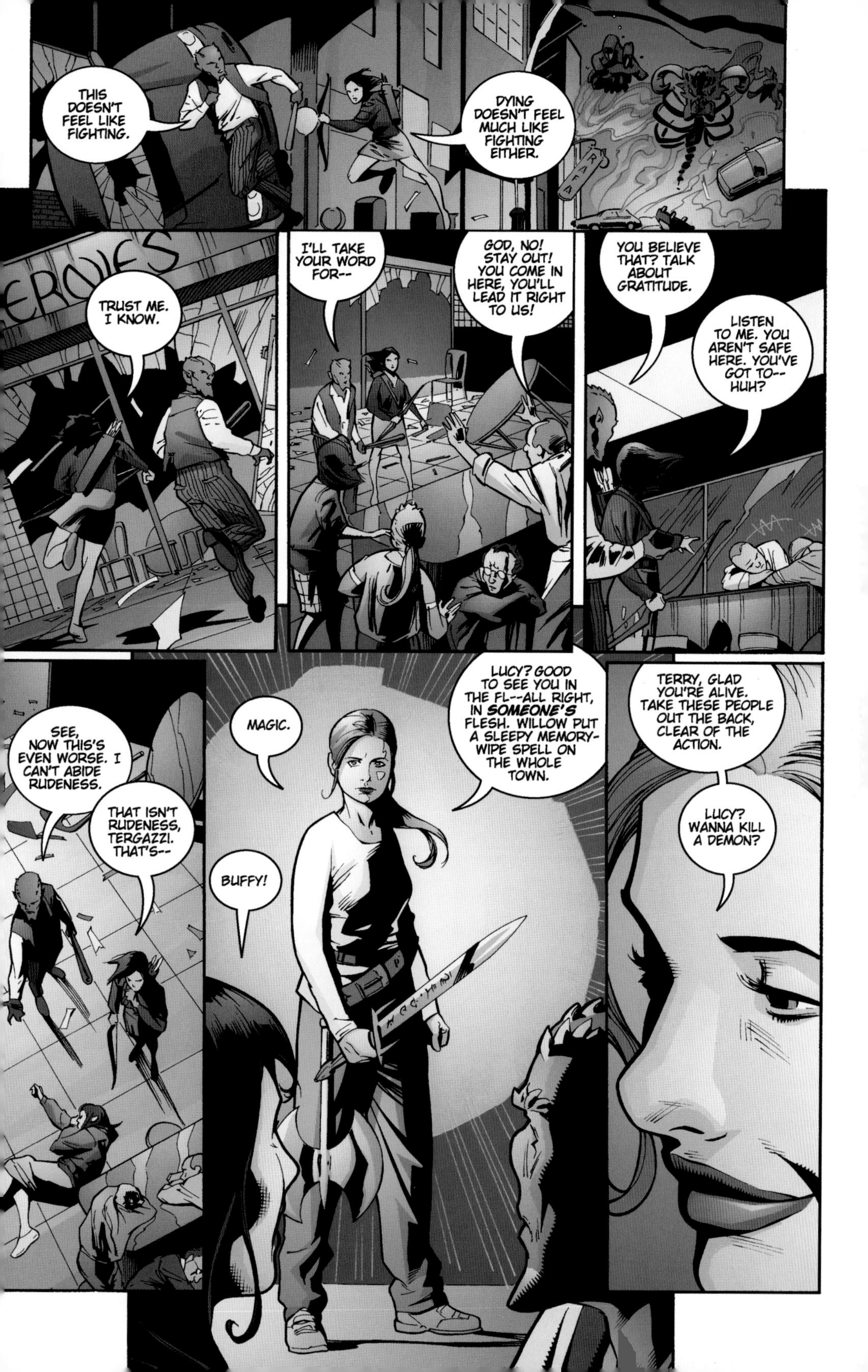
THIS DOESN'T FEEL LIKE FIGHTING.
DYING DOESN'T FEEL MUCH LIKE FIGHTING EITHER.
TRUST ME. I KNOW.
I'LL TAKE YOUR WORD FOR--
GOD, NO! STAY OUT! YOU COME IN HERE, YOU'LL LEAD IT RIGHT TO US!
YOU BELIEVE THAT? TALK ABOUT GRATITUDE.
LISTEN TO ME. YOU AREN'T SAFE HERE. YOU'VE GOT TO-- HUH?
SEE, NOW THIS'S EVEN WORSE. I CAN'T ABIDE RUDENESS.
THAT ISN'T RUDENESS, TERGAZZI. THAT'S--
MAGIC.
BUFFY!
LUCY? GOOD TO SEE YOU IN THE FL--ALL RIGHT, IN SOMEONE'S FLESH. WILLOW PUT A SLEEPY MEMORY-WIPE SPELL ON THE WHOLE TOWN.
TERRY, GLAD YOU'RE ALIVE. TAKE THESE PEOPLE OUT THE BACK, CLEAR OF THE ACTION.
LUCY? WANNA KILL A DEMON?

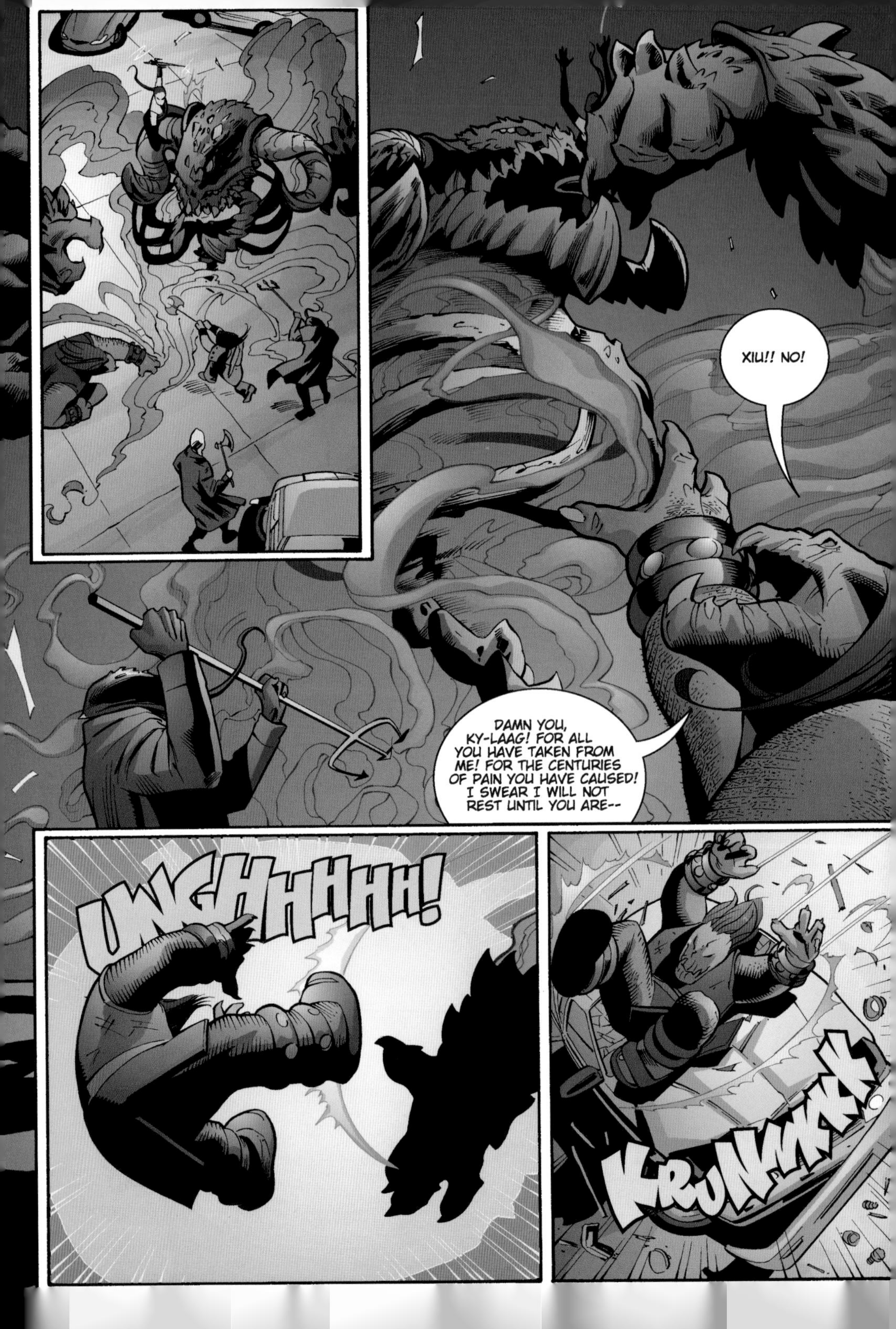
XIU!! NO!
DAMN YOU, KY-LAAG! FOR ALL YOU HAVE TAKEN FROM ME! FOR THE CENTURIES OF PAIN YOU HAVE CAUSED! I SWEAR I WILL NOT REST UNTIL YOU ARE--
UNGHHHHH!
KRUNKKK

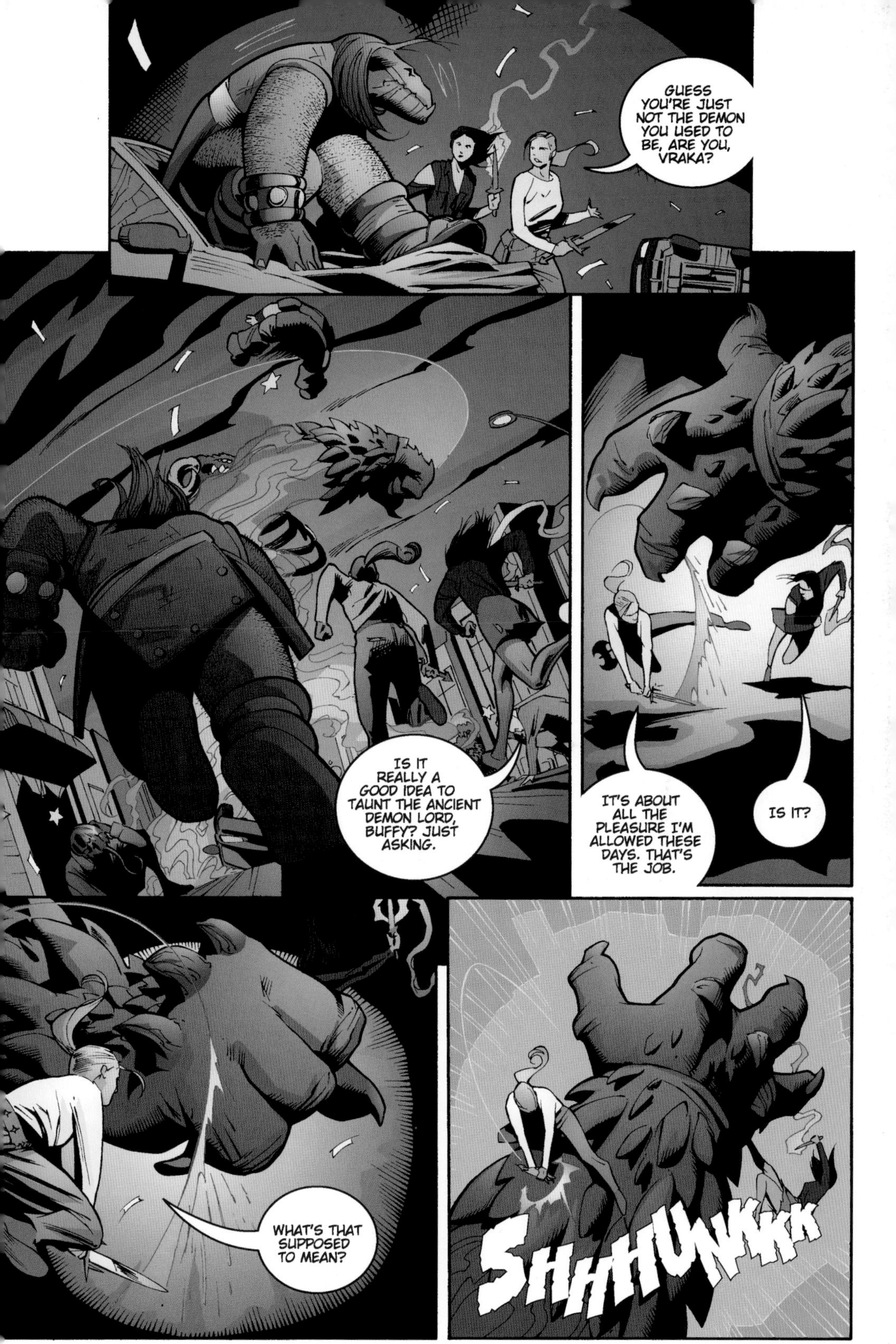

GUESS YOU'RE JUST NOT THE DEMON YOU USED TO BE, ARE YOU, VRAKA?
IS IT REALLY A GOOD IDEA TO TAUNT THE ANCIENT DEMON LORD, BUFFY? JUST ASKING.
IT'S ABOUT ALL THE PLEASURE I'M ALLOWED THESE DAYS. THAT'S THE JOB.
IS IT?
WHAT'S THAT SUPPOSED TO MEAN?
SHHHUNKKK

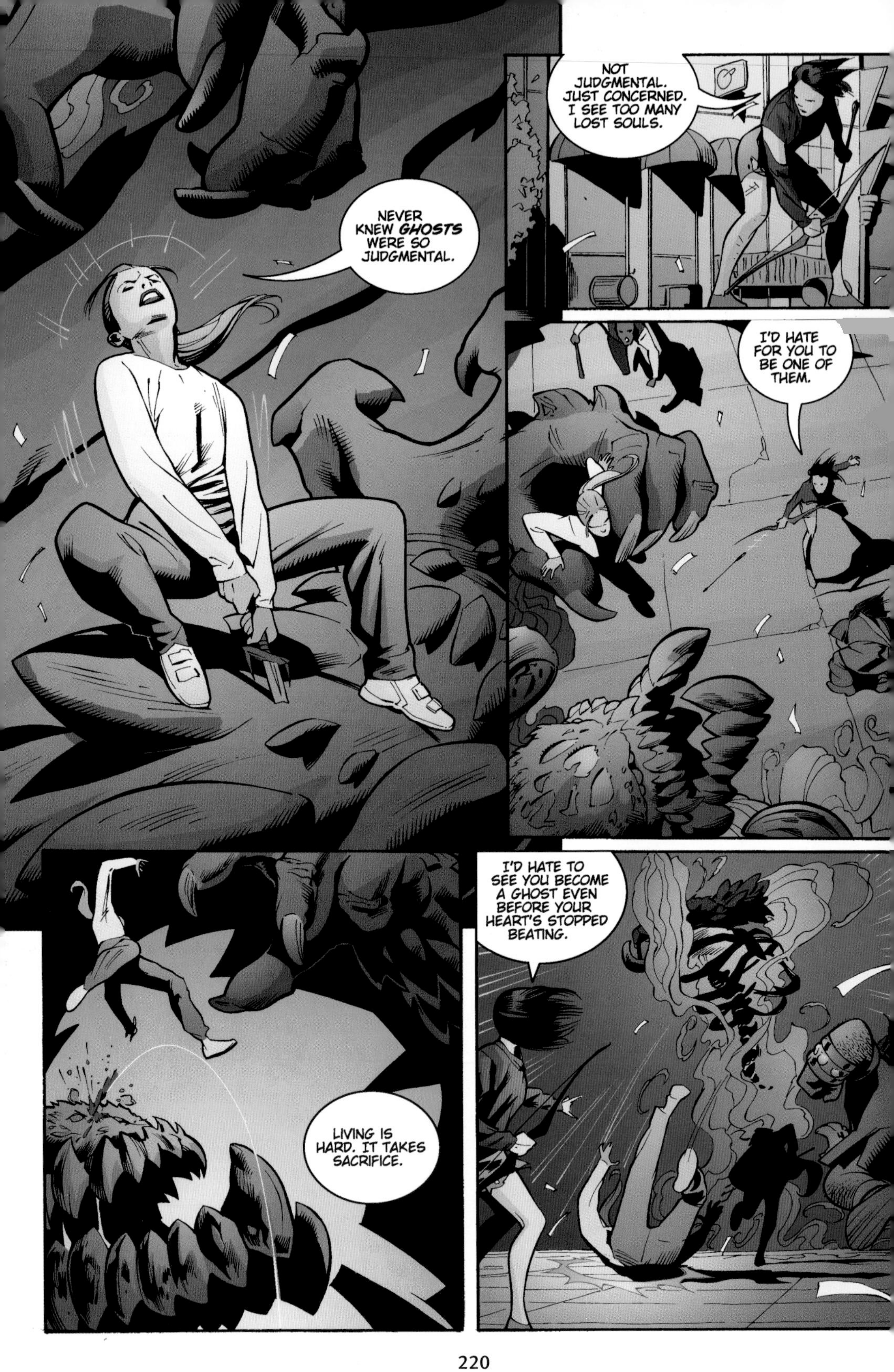
NEVER KNEW GHOSTS WERE SO JUDGMENTAL.
NOT JUDGMENTAL. JUST CONCERNED. I SEE TOO MANY LOST SOULS.
I'D HATE FOR YOU TO BE ONE OF THEM.
LIVING IS HARD. IT TAKES SACRIFICE.
I'D HATE TO SEE YOU BECOME A GHOST EVEN BEFORE YOUR HEART'S STOPPED BEATING.

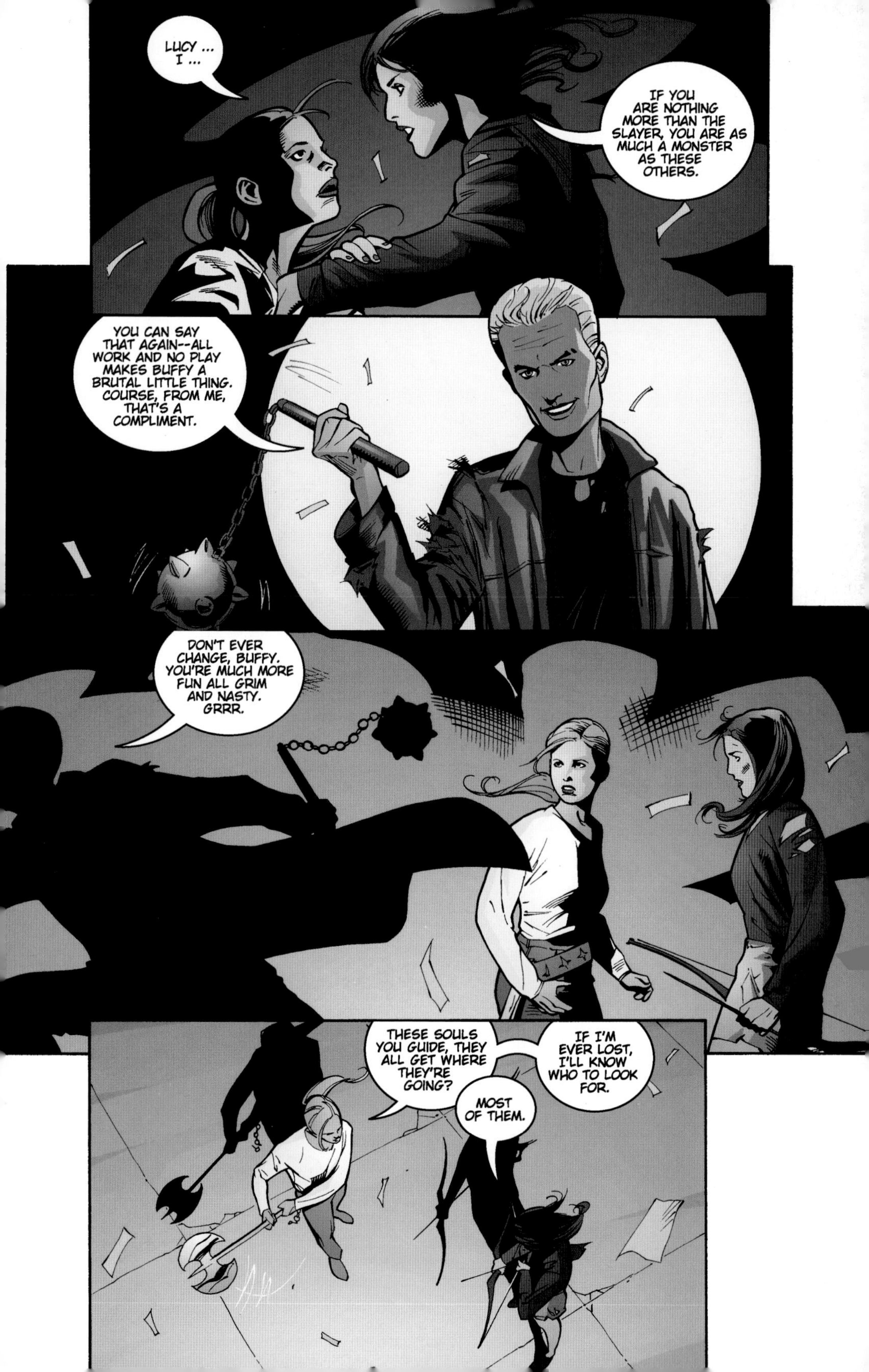
LUCY ... I ...
IF YOU ARE NOTHING MORE THAN THE SLAYER, YOU ARE AS MUCH A MONSTER AS THESE OTHERS.
YOU CAN SAY THAT AGAIN--ALL WORK AND NO PLAY MAKES BUFFY A BRUTAL LITTLE THING. COURSE, FROM ME, THAT'S A COMPLIMENT.
DON'T EVER CHANGE, BUFFY. YOU'RE MUCH MORE FUN ALL GRIM AND NASTY. GRRR.
THESE SOULS YOU GUIDE, THEY ALL GET WHERE THEY'RE GOING?
MOST OF THEM.
IF I'M EVER LOST, I'LL KNOW WHO TO LOOK FOR.

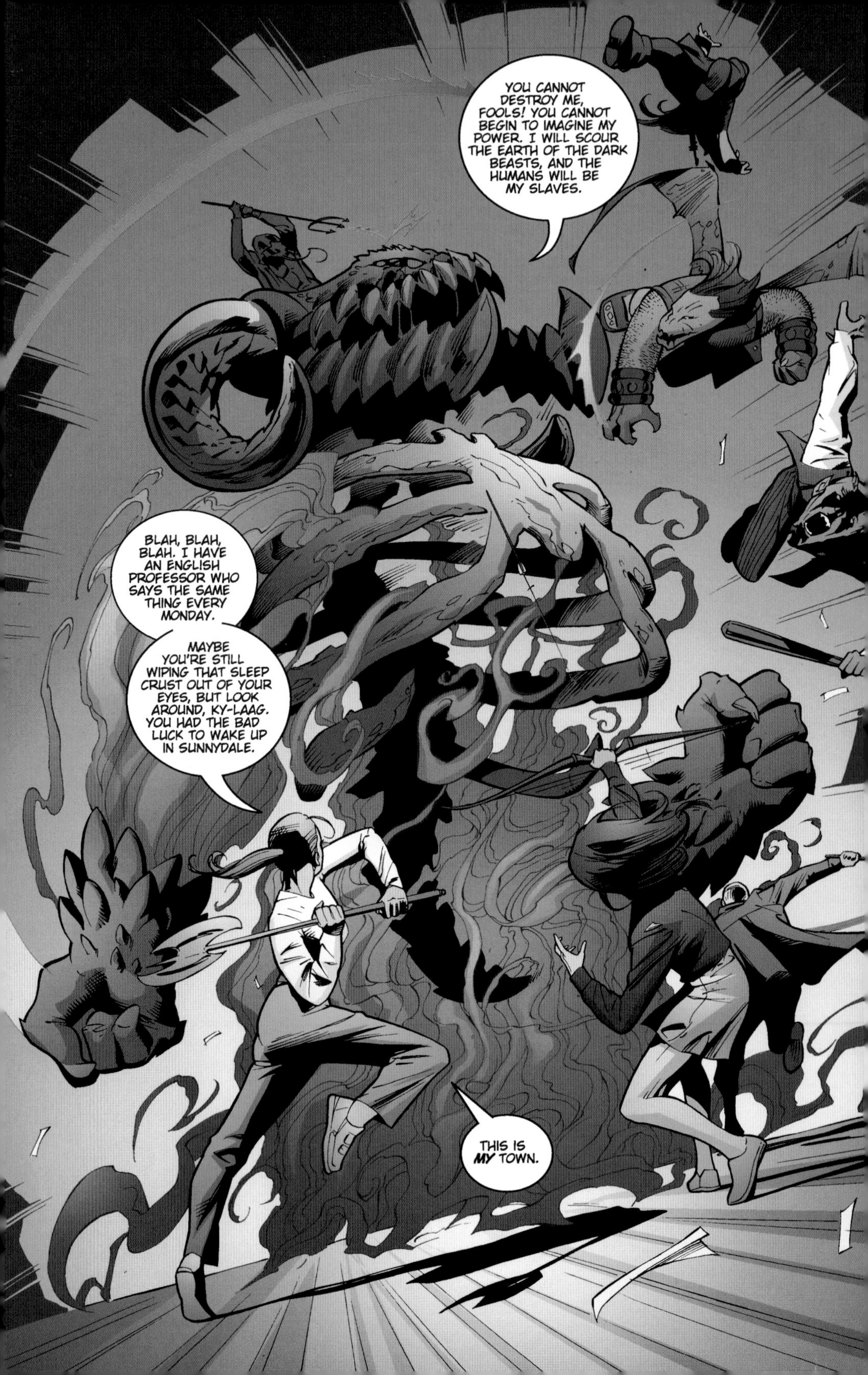
YOU CANNOT DESTROY ME, FOOLS! YOU CANNOT BEGIN TO IMAGINE MY POWER. I WILL SCOUR THE EARTH OF THE DARK BEASTS, AND THE HUMANS WILL BE MY SLAVES.
BLAH, BLAH, BLAH. I HAVE AN ENGLISH PROFESSOR WHO SAYS THE SAME THING EVERY MONDAY.
MAYBE YOU'RE STILL WIPING THAT SLEEP CRUST OUT OF YOUR EYES, BUT LOOK AROUND, KY-LAAG. YOU HAD THE BAD LUCK TO WAKE UP IN SUNNYDALE.
THIS IS *MY* TOWN.

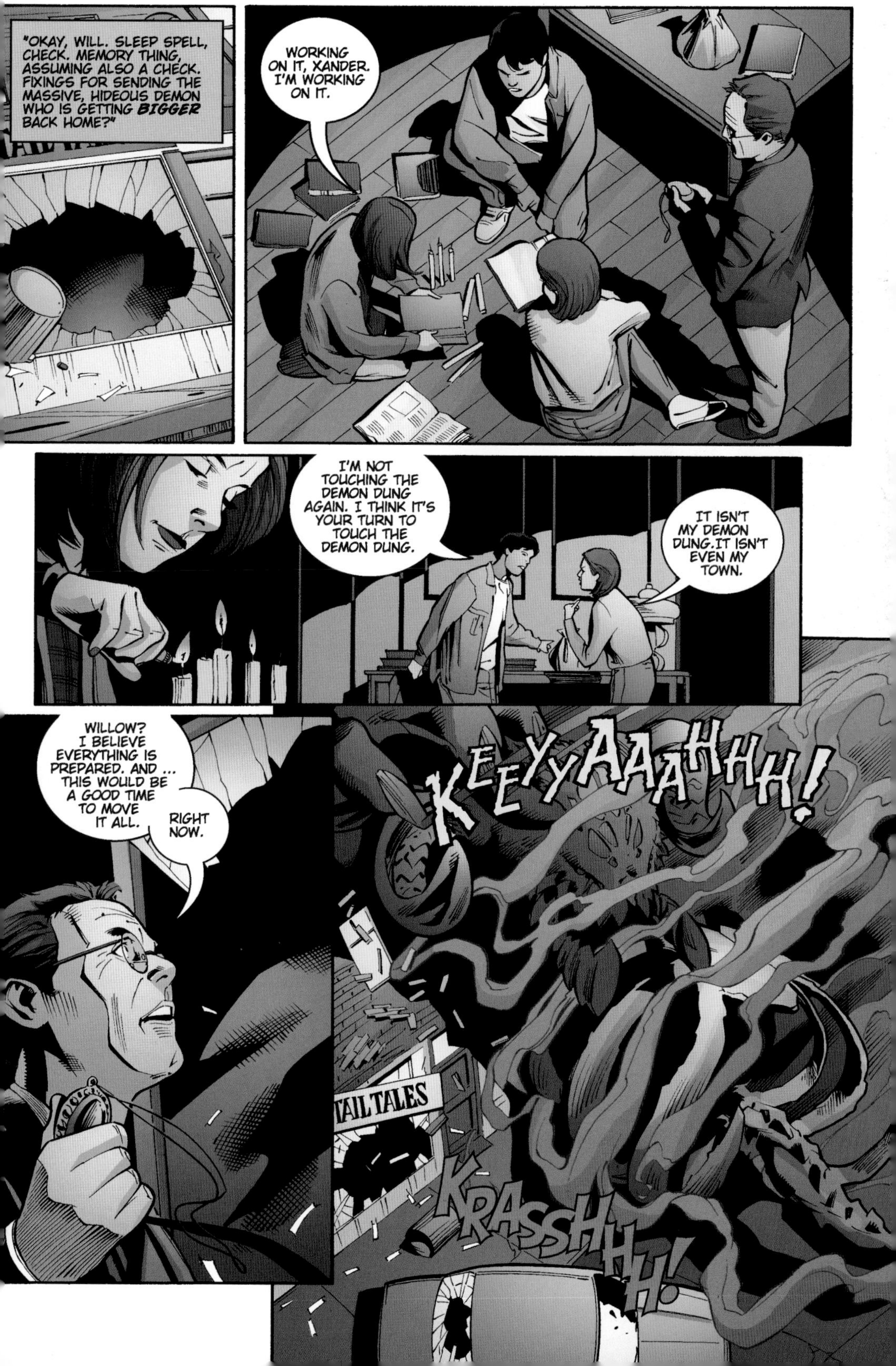
"OKAY, WILL. SLEEP SPELL, CHECK. MEMORY THING, ASSUMING ALSO A CHECK. FIXINGS FOR SENDING THE MASSIVE, HIDEOUS DEMON WHO IS GETTING **BIGGER** BACK HOME?"
WORKING ON IT, XANDER. I'M WORKING ON IT.
I'M NOT TOUCHING THE DEMON DUNG AGAIN. I THINK IT'S YOUR TURN TO TOUCH THE DEMON DUNG.
IT ISN'T MY DEMON DUNG. IT ISN'T EVEN MY TOWN.
WILLOW? I BELIEVE EVERYTHING IS PREPARED. AND ... THIS WOULD BE A GOOD TIME TO MOVE IT ALL.
RIGHT NOW.
KEEYYAAAHHHH!
TAIL TALES
KRASSHHH!

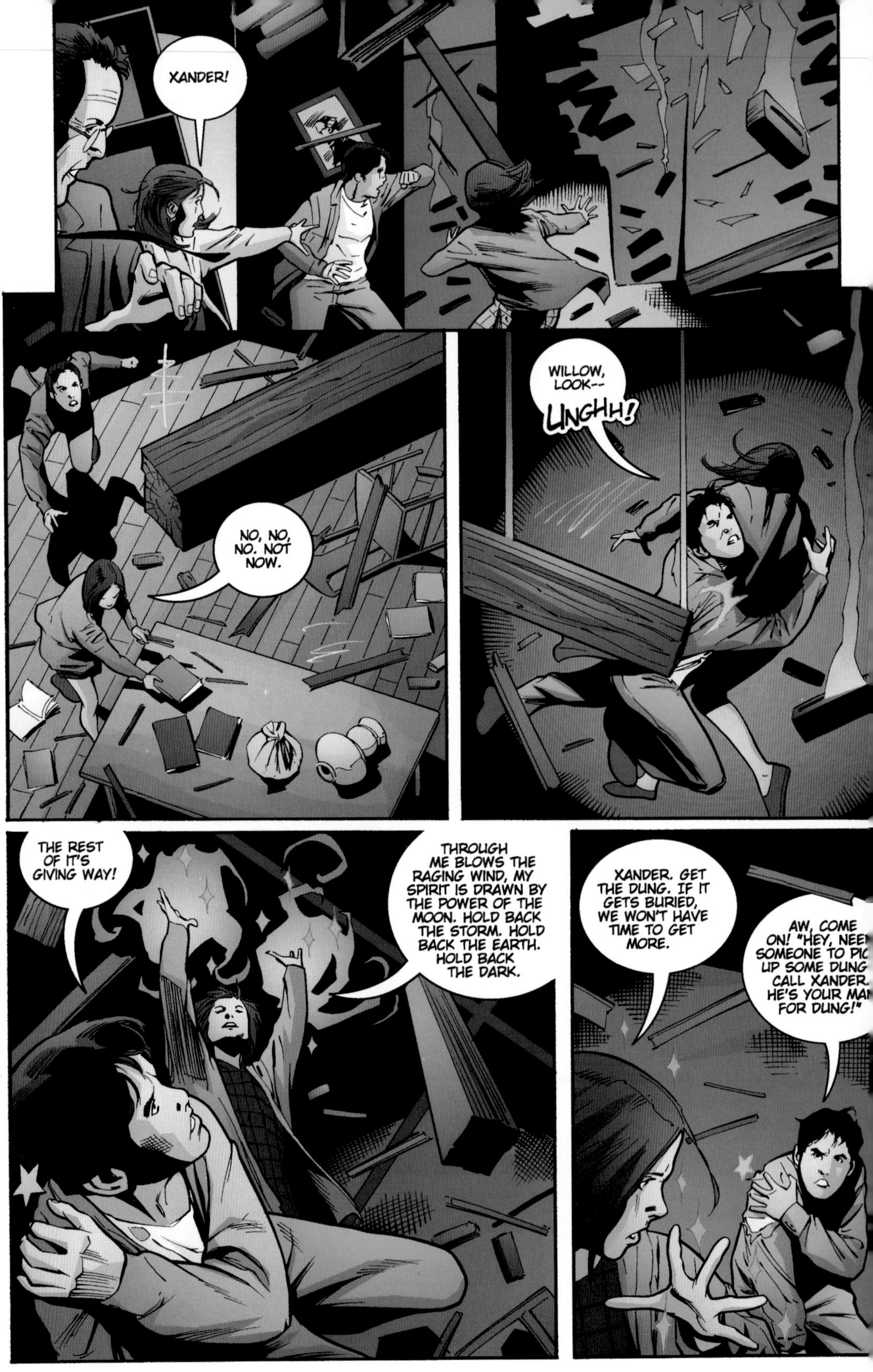
XANDER!
WILLOW, LOOK--
UNGHH!
NO, NO, NO. NOT NOW.
THE REST OF IT'S GIVING WAY!
THROUGH ME BLOWS THE RAGING WIND, MY SPIRIT IS DRAWN BY THE POWER OF THE MOON. HOLD BACK THE STORM. HOLD BACK THE EARTH. HOLD BACK THE DARK.
XANDER. GET THE DUNG. IF IT GETS BURIED, WE WON'T HAVE TIME TO GET MORE.
AW, COME ON! "HEY, NEE SOMEONE TO PI UP SOME DUNG CALL XANDER HE'S YOUR MA FOR DUNG!"

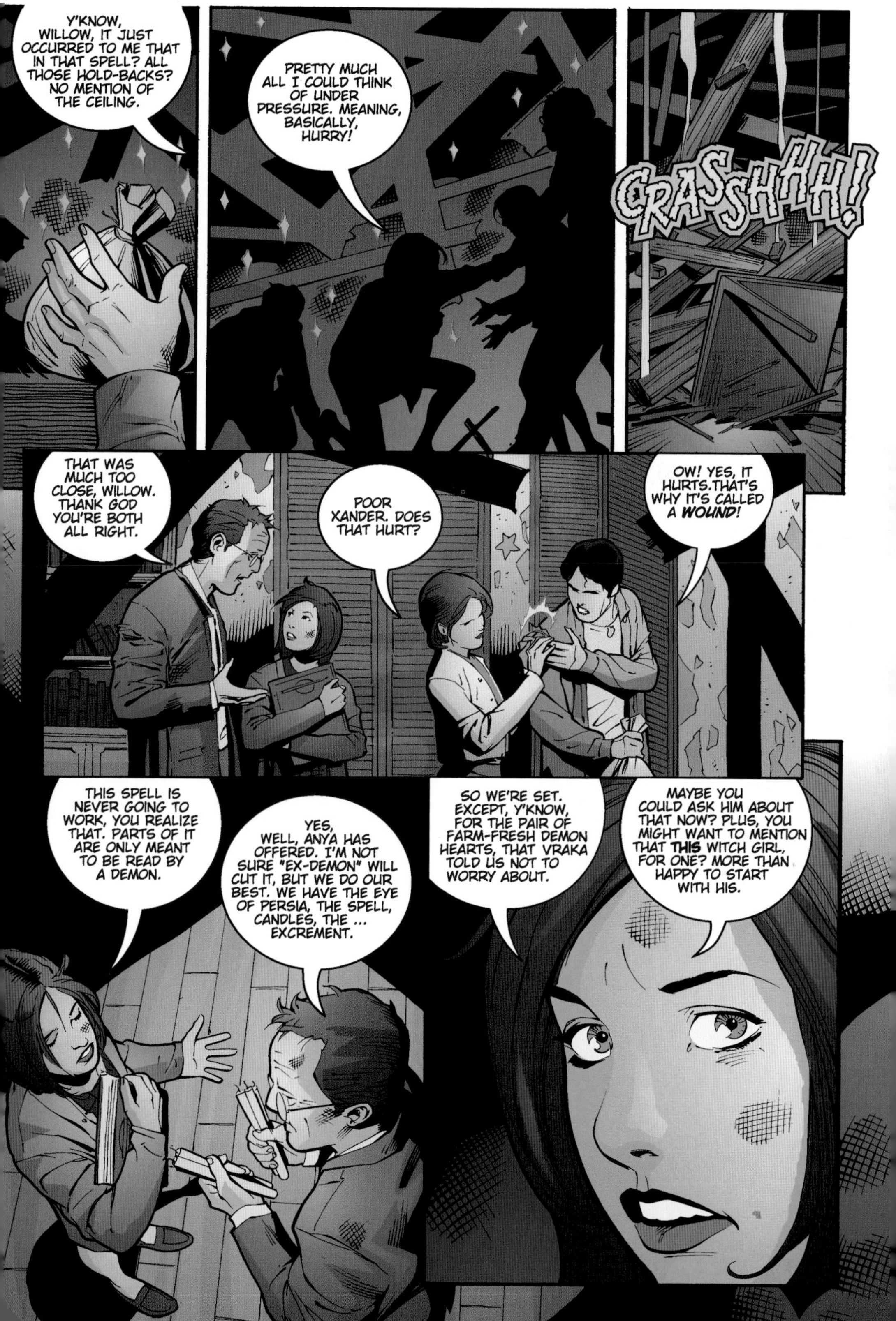

Y'KNOW, WILLOW, IT JUST OCCURRED TO ME THAT IN THAT SPELL? ALL THOSE HOLD-BACKS? NO MENTION OF THE CEILING.
PRETTY MUCH ALL I COULD THINK OF UNDER PRESSURE. MEANING, BASICALLY, HURRY!
CRASSHHH!
THAT WAS MUCH TOO CLOSE, WILLOW. THANK GOD YOU'RE BOTH ALL RIGHT.
POOR XANDER. DOES THAT HURT?
OW! YES, IT HURTS. THAT'S WHY IT'S CALLED A ***WOUND!***
THIS SPELL IS NEVER GOING TO WORK, YOU REALIZE THAT. PARTS OF IT ARE ONLY MEANT TO BE READ BY A DEMON.
YES, WELL, ANYA HAS OFFERED. I'M NOT SURE "EX-DEMON" WILL CUT IT, BUT WE DO OUR BEST. WE HAVE THE EYE OF PERSIA, THE SPELL, CANDLES, THE ... EXCREMENT.
SO WE'RE SET. EXCEPT, Y'KNOW, FOR THE PAIR OF FARM-FRESH DEMON HEARTS, THAT VRAKA TOLD US NOT TO WORRY ABOUT.
MAYBE YOU COULD ASK HIM ABOUT THAT NOW? PLUS, YOU MIGHT WANT TO MENTION THAT **THIS** WITCH GIRL, FOR ONE? MORE THAN HAPPY TO START WITH HIS.

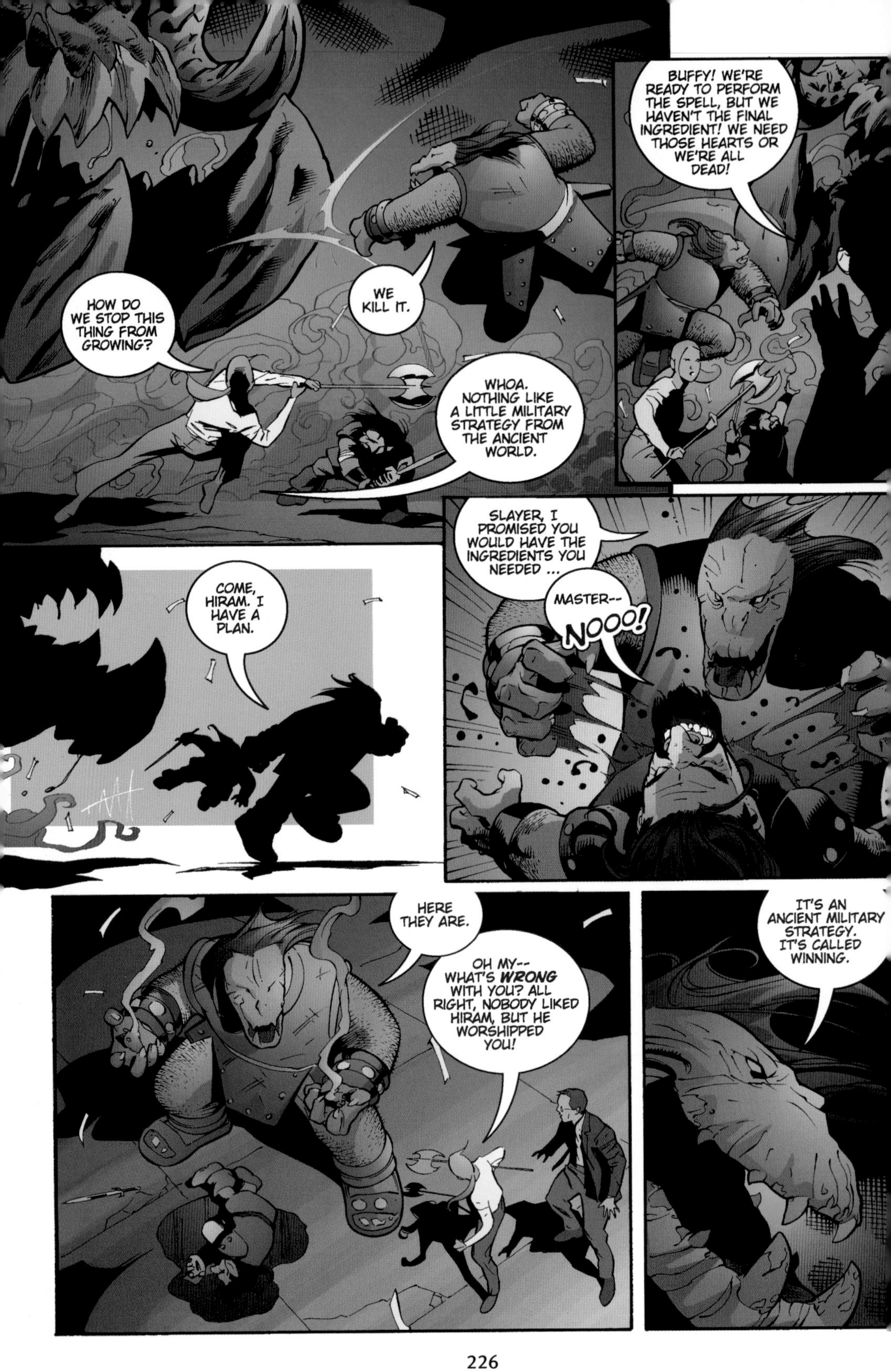
BUFFY! WE'RE READY TO PERFORM THE SPELL, BUT WE HAVEN'T THE FINAL INGREDIENT! WE NEED THOSE HEARTS OR WE'RE ALL DEAD!
HOW DO WE STOP THIS THING FROM GROWING?
WE KILL IT.
WHOA. NOTHING LIKE A LITTLE MILITARY STRATEGY FROM THE ANCIENT WORLD.
COME, HIRAM. I HAVE A PLAN.
SLAYER, I PROMISED YOU WOULD HAVE THE INGREDIENTS YOU NEEDED ...
MASTER--
NOOO!
HERE THEY ARE.
OH MY-- WHAT'S WRONG WITH YOU? ALL RIGHT, NOBODY LIKED HIRAM, BUT HE WORSHIPPED YOU!
IT'S AN ANCIENT MILITARY STRATEGY. IT'S CALLED WINNING.

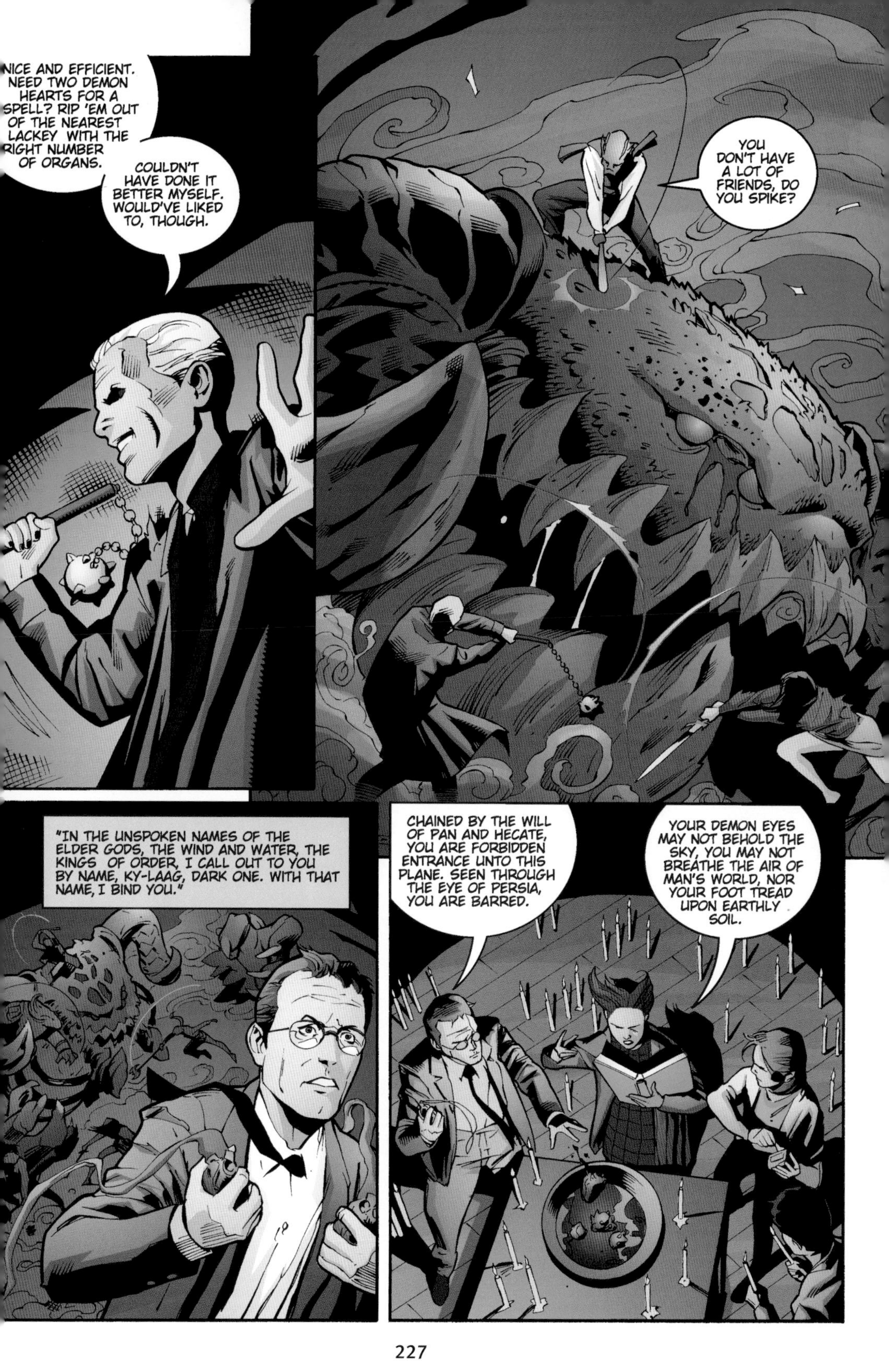
NICE AND EFFICIENT. NEED TWO DEMON HEARTS FOR A SPELL? RIP 'EM OUT OF THE NEAREST LACKEY WITH THE RIGHT NUMBER OF ORGANS.
COULDN'T HAVE DONE IT BETTER MYSELF. WOULD'VE LIKED TO, THOUGH.
YOU DON'T HAVE A LOT OF FRIENDS, DO YOU SPIKE?
"IN THE UNSPOKEN NAMES OF THE ELDER GODS, THE WIND AND WATER, THE KINGS OF ORDER, I CALL OUT TO YOU BY NAME, KY-LAAG, DARK ONE. WITH THAT NAME, I BIND YOU."
CHAINED BY THE WILL OF PAN AND HECATE, YOU ARE FORBIDDEN ENTRANCE UNTO THIS PLANE. SEEN THROUGH THE EYE OF PERSIA, YOU ARE BARRED.
YOUR DEMON EYES MAY NOT BEHOLD THE SKY, YOU MAY NOT BREATHE THE AIR OF MAN'S WORLD, NOR YOUR FOOT TREAD UPON EARTHLY SOIL.

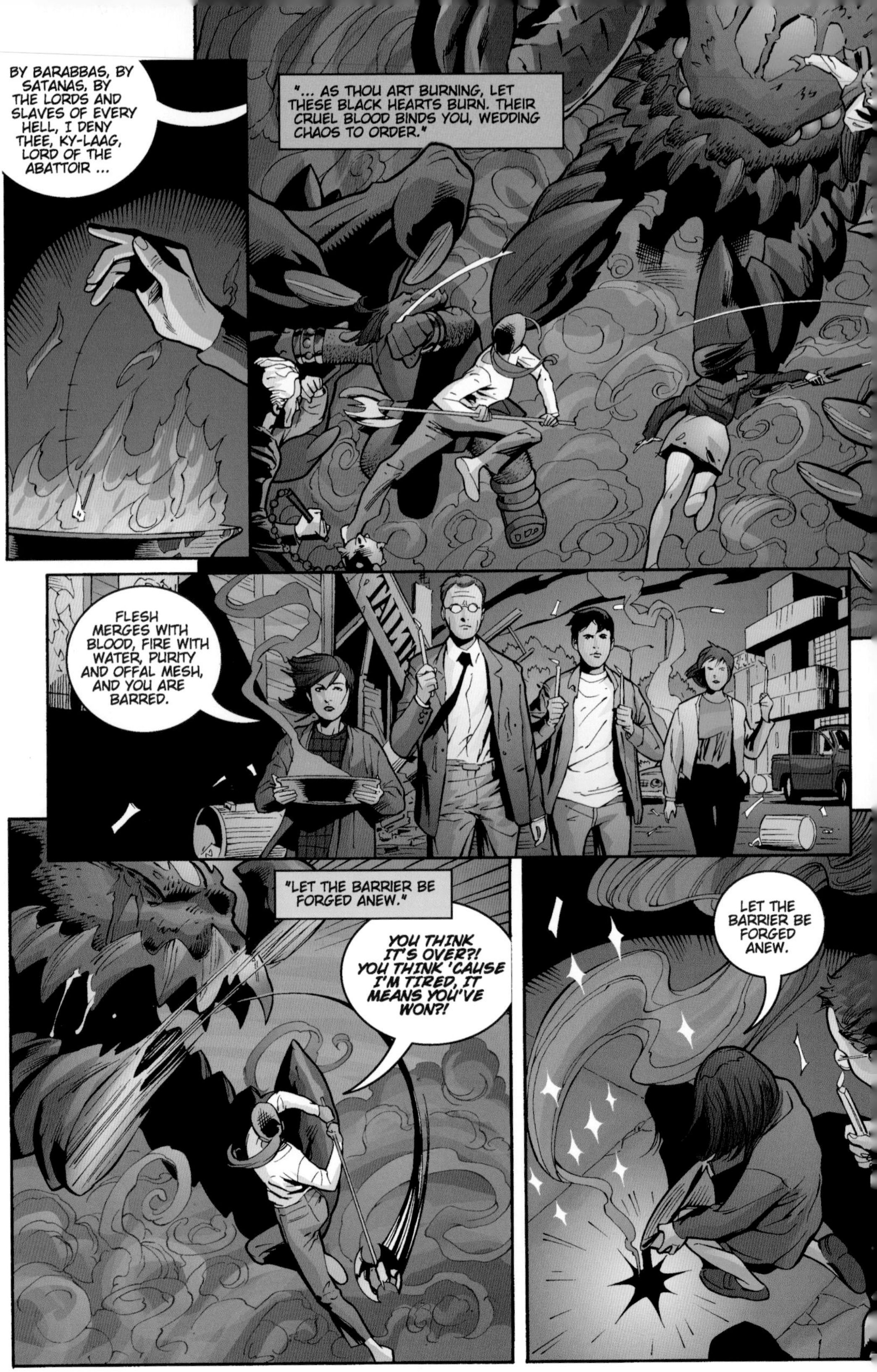
BY BARABBAS, BY SATANAS, BY THE LORDS AND SLAVES OF EVERY HELL, I DENY THEE, KY-LAAG, LORD OF THE ABATTOIR ...
"... AS THOU ART BURNING, LET THESE BLACK HEARTS BURN. THEIR CRUEL BLOOD BINDS YOU, WEDDING CHAOS TO ORDER."
FLESH MERGES WITH BLOOD, FIRE WITH WATER, PURITY AND OFFAL MESH, AND YOU ARE BARRED.
"LET THE BARRIER BE FORGED ANEW."
YOU THINK IT'S OVER?! YOU THINK 'CAUSE I'M TIRED, IT MEANS YOU'VE WON?!
LET THE BARRIER BE FORGED ANEW.

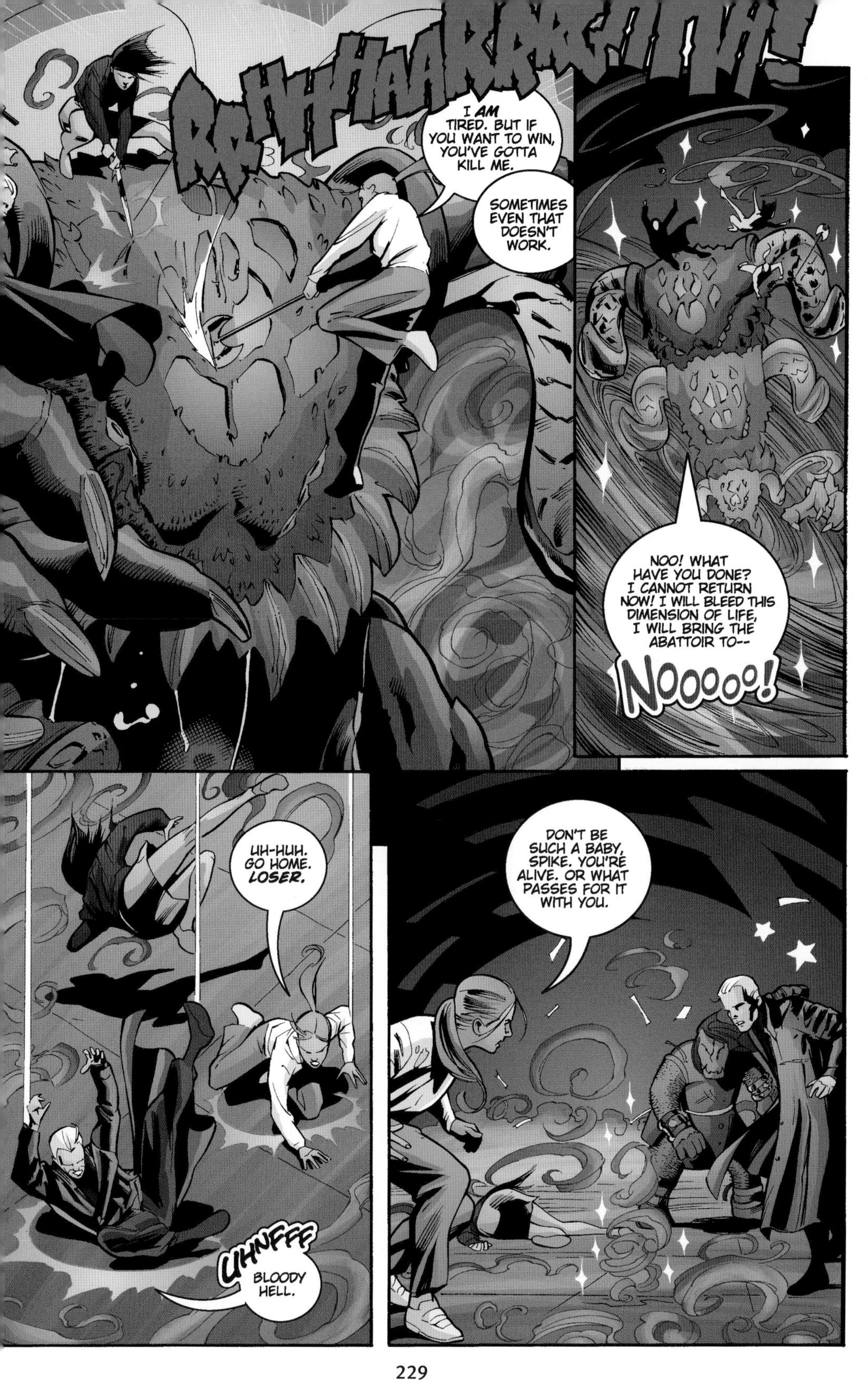
RAHHHAARRRGHHH!
I AM TIRED. BUT IF YOU WANT TO WIN, YOU'VE GOTTA KILL ME.
SOMETIMES EVEN THAT DOESN'T WORK.
NOO! WHAT HAVE YOU DONE? I CANNOT RETURN NOW! I WILL BLEED THIS DIMENSION OF LIFE, I WILL BRING THE ABATTOIR TO--
NOOOOO!
UH-HUH. GO HOME. LOSER.
UHNFFF
BLOODY HELL.
DON'T BE SUCH A BABY, SPIKE. YOU'RE ALIVE. OR WHAT PASSES FOR IT WITH YOU.

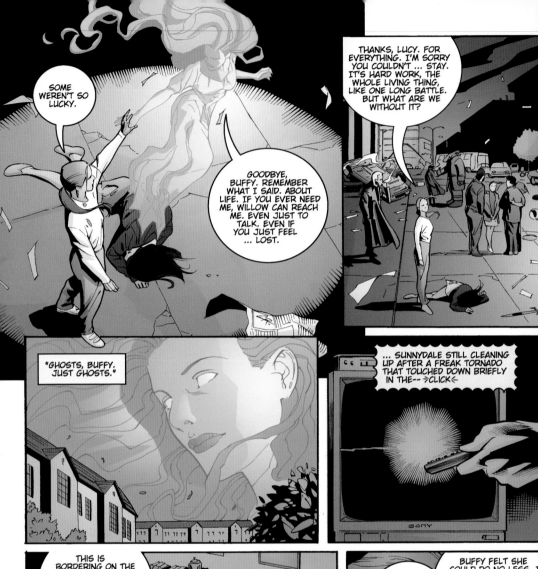

SOME WEREN'T SO LUCKY.

GOODBYE, BUFFY. REMEMBER WHAT I SAID. ABOUT LIFE. IF YOU EVER NEED ME, WILLOW CAN REACH ME. EVEN JUST TO TALK. EVEN IF YOU JUST FEEL ... LOST.

THANKS, LUCY. FOR EVERYTHING. I'M SORRY YOU COULDN'T ... STAY. IT'S HARD WORK, THE WHOLE LIVING THING, LIKE ONE LONG BATTLE. BUT WHAT ARE WE WITHOUT IT?

"GHOSTS, BUFFY. JUST GHOSTS."

... SUNNYDALE STILL CLEANING UP AFTER A FREAK TORNADO THAT TOUCHED DOWN BRIEFLY IN THE-- >CLICK<-

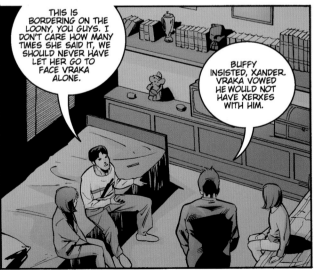

THIS IS BORDERING ON THE LOONY, YOU GUYS. I DON'T CARE HOW MANY TIMES SHE SAID IT, WE SHOULD NEVER HAVE LET HER GO TO FACE VRAKA ALONE.

BUFFY INSISTED, XANDER. VRAKA VOWED HE WOULD NOT HAVE XERXES WITH HIM.

SHE BELIEVES HIM NOBLE ENOUGH TO KEEP HIS WORD.

BUFFY FELT SHE COULD DO NO LESS. BELIEVE SHE ALSO WANTED TO ... CLOSE THIS CHAPTER OF HER LIFE THE WAY SHE BEGAN IT. ON HER OWN. MUCH AS IT PAINS US ...

"... WE MUST RESPECT HER WISHES."

I'M HERE.

IT'S TIME.

IT'S FINALLY OVER FOR YOU.

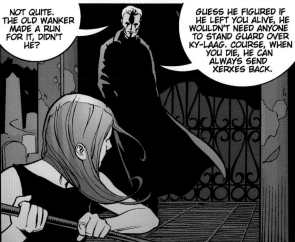

NOT QUITE. THE OLD WANKER MADE A RUN FOR IT, DIDN'T HE?

GUESS HE FIGURED IF HE LEFT YOU ALIVE, HE WOULDN'T NEED ANYONE TO STAND GUARD OVER KY-LAAG. COURSE, WHEN YOU DIE, HE CAN ALWAYS SEND XERXES BACK.

HE'S GONE?

DON'T GET ALL MISTY. WOULDN'T HAVE BEEN MUCH OF A CHALLENGE FOR YOU, NOW WOULD HE? VRAKA'S LONG PAST HIS PRIME, INTO HIS TWILIGHT CENTURIES AND ALL.

NOT THAT WATCHING YOU KILL HIM WOULDN'T HAVE BEEN A HOWL, MIND. BUT I'M GLAD TO BE QUIT OF THE BUZZARD. THERE'S NOTHING TO BE GAINED FROM LIVING IN THE PAST ...

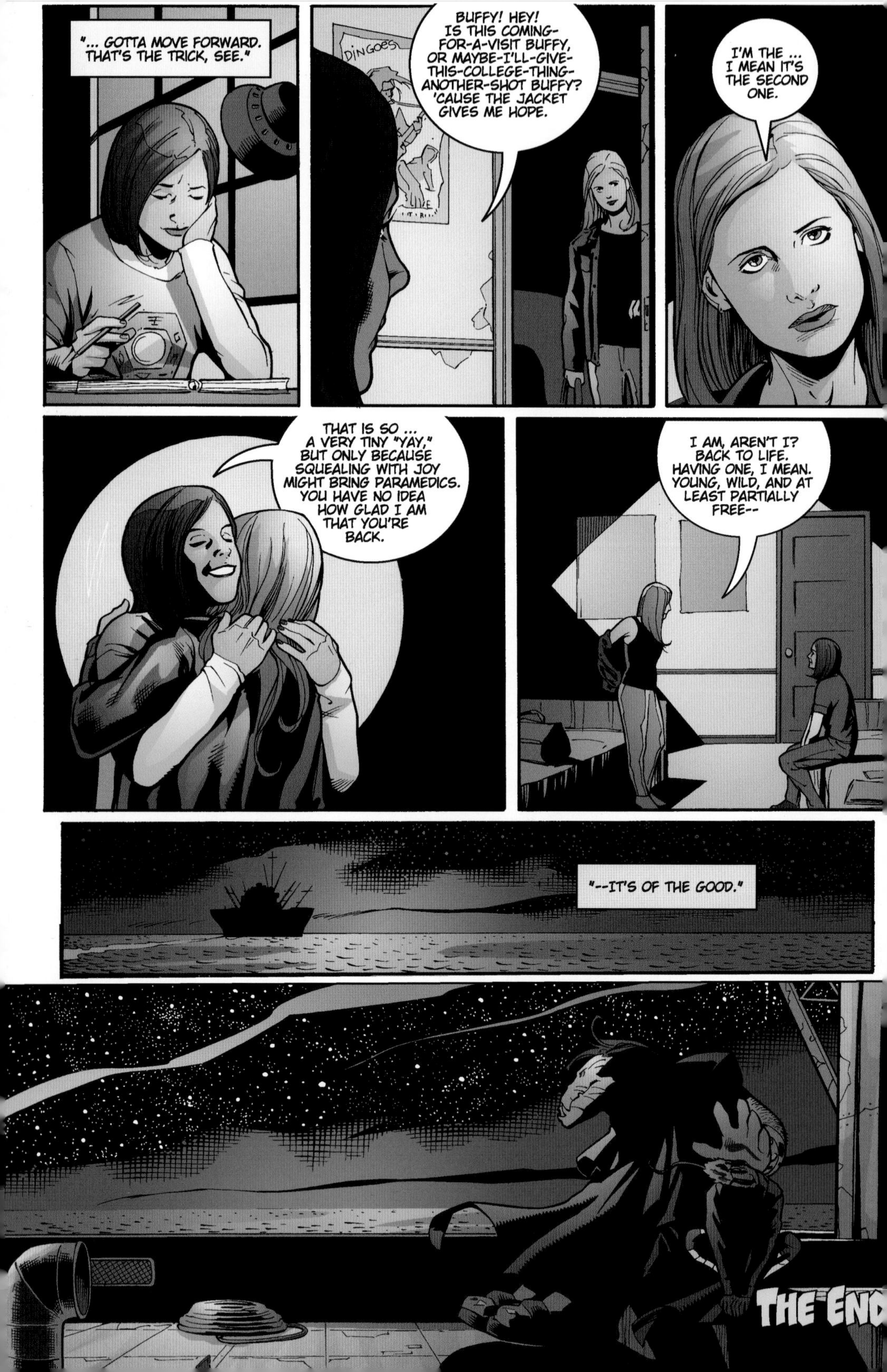
"... GOTTA MOVE FORWARD. THAT'S THE TRICK, SEE."
DINGOES
BUFFY! HEY! IS THIS COMING-FOR-A-VISIT BUFFY, OR MAYBE-I'LL-GIVE-THIS-COLLEGE-THING-ANOTHER-SHOT BUFFY? 'CAUSE THE JACKET GIVES ME HOPE.
I'M THE ... I MEAN IT'S THE SECOND ONE.
THAT IS SO ... A VERY TINY "YAY," BUT ONLY BECAUSE SQUEALING WITH JOY MIGHT BRING PARAMEDICS. YOU HAVE NO IDEA HOW GLAD I AM THAT YOU'RE BACK.
I AM, AREN'T I? BACK TO LIFE. HAVING ONE, I MEAN. YOUNG, WILD, AND AT LEAST PARTIALLY FREE--
"--IT'S OF THE GOOD."
THE END

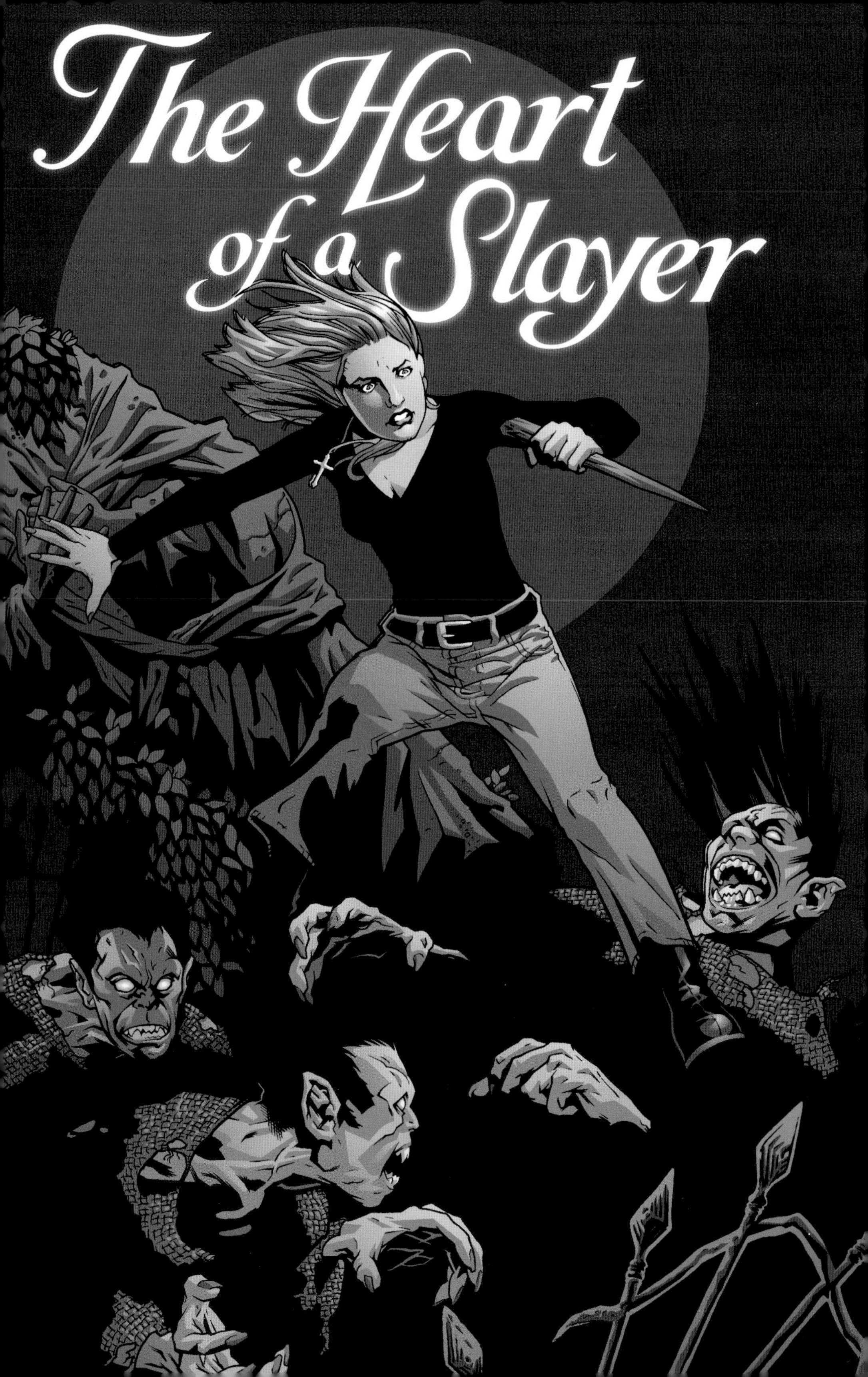
The Heart of a Slayer

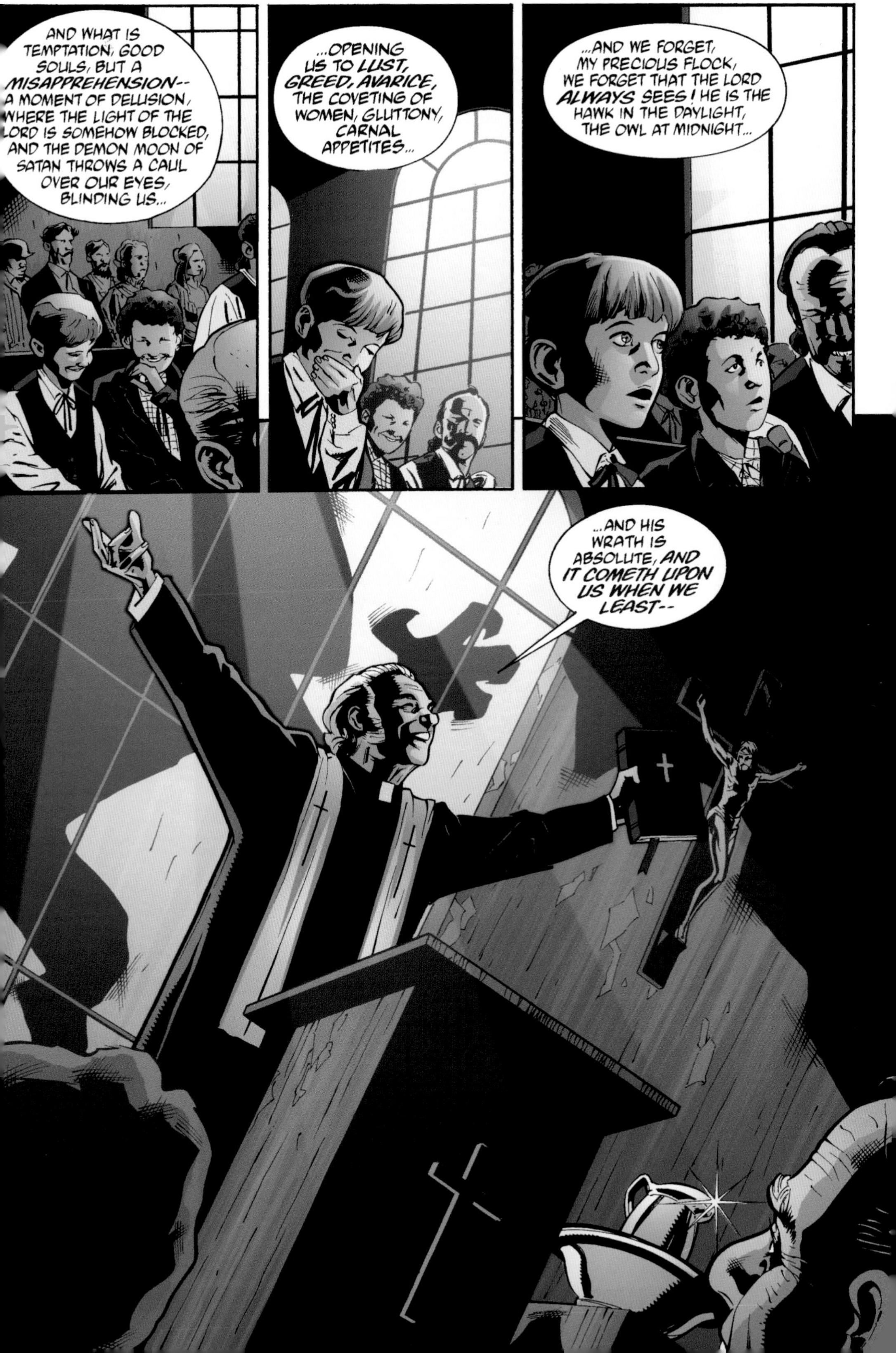
AND WHAT IS TEMPTATION, GOOD SOULS, BUT A MISAPPREHENSION-- A MOMENT OF DELUSION, WHERE THE LIGHT OF THE LORD IS SOMEHOW BLOCKED, AND THE DEMON MOON OF SATAN THROWS A CAUL OVER OUR EYES, BLINDING US...
...OPENING US TO LUST, GREED, AVARICE, THE COVETING OF WOMEN, GLUTTONY, CARNAL APPETITES...
...AND WE FORGET, MY PRECIOUS FLOCK, WE FORGET THAT THE LORD ALWAYS SEES! HE IS THE HAWK IN THE DAYLIGHT, THE OWL AT MIDNIGHT...
...AND HIS WRATH IS ABSOLUTE, AND IT COMETH UPON US WHEN WE LEAST--

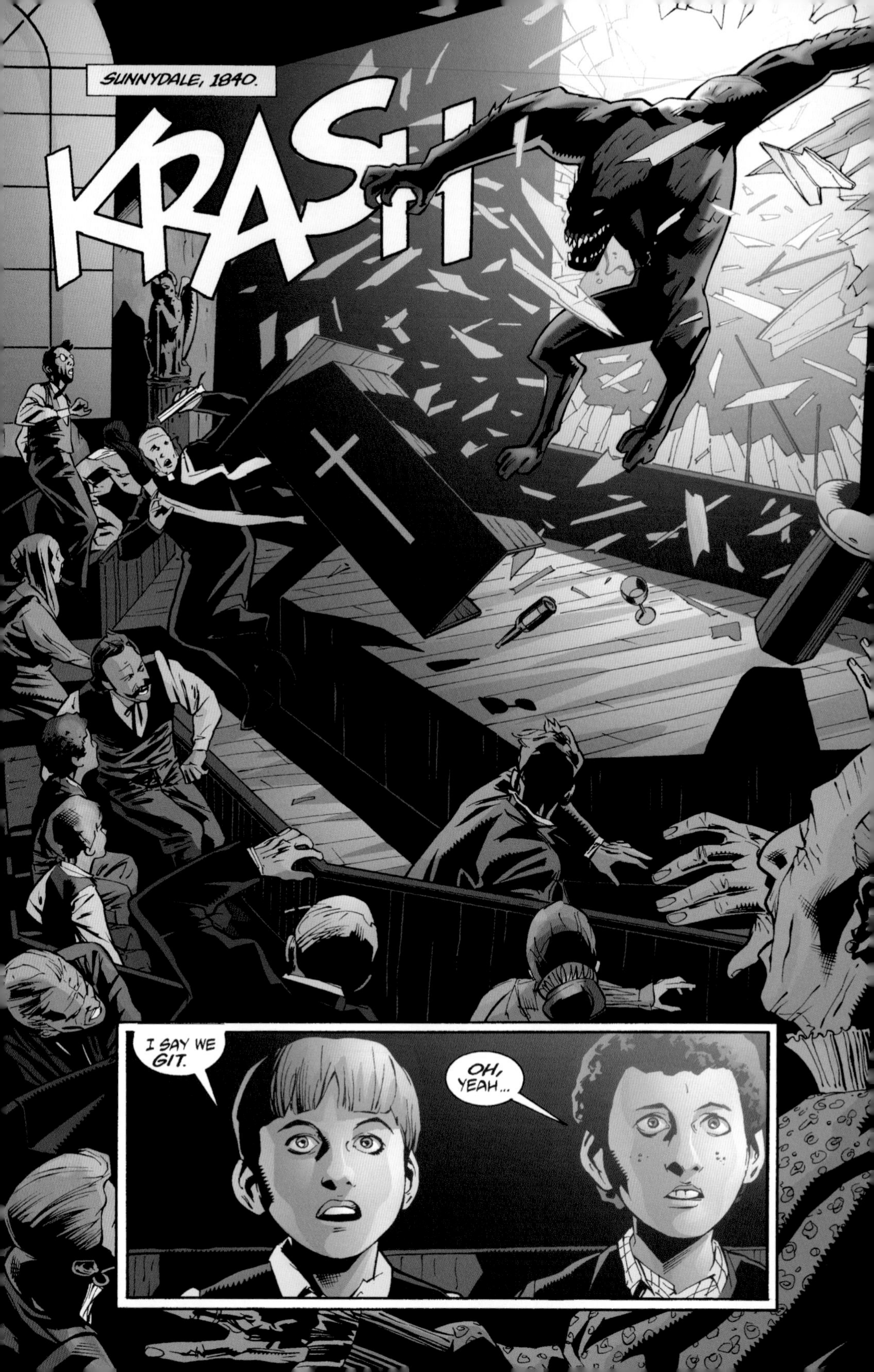
SUNNYDALE, 1840.
KRASH
I SAY WE GIT.
OH, YEAH...

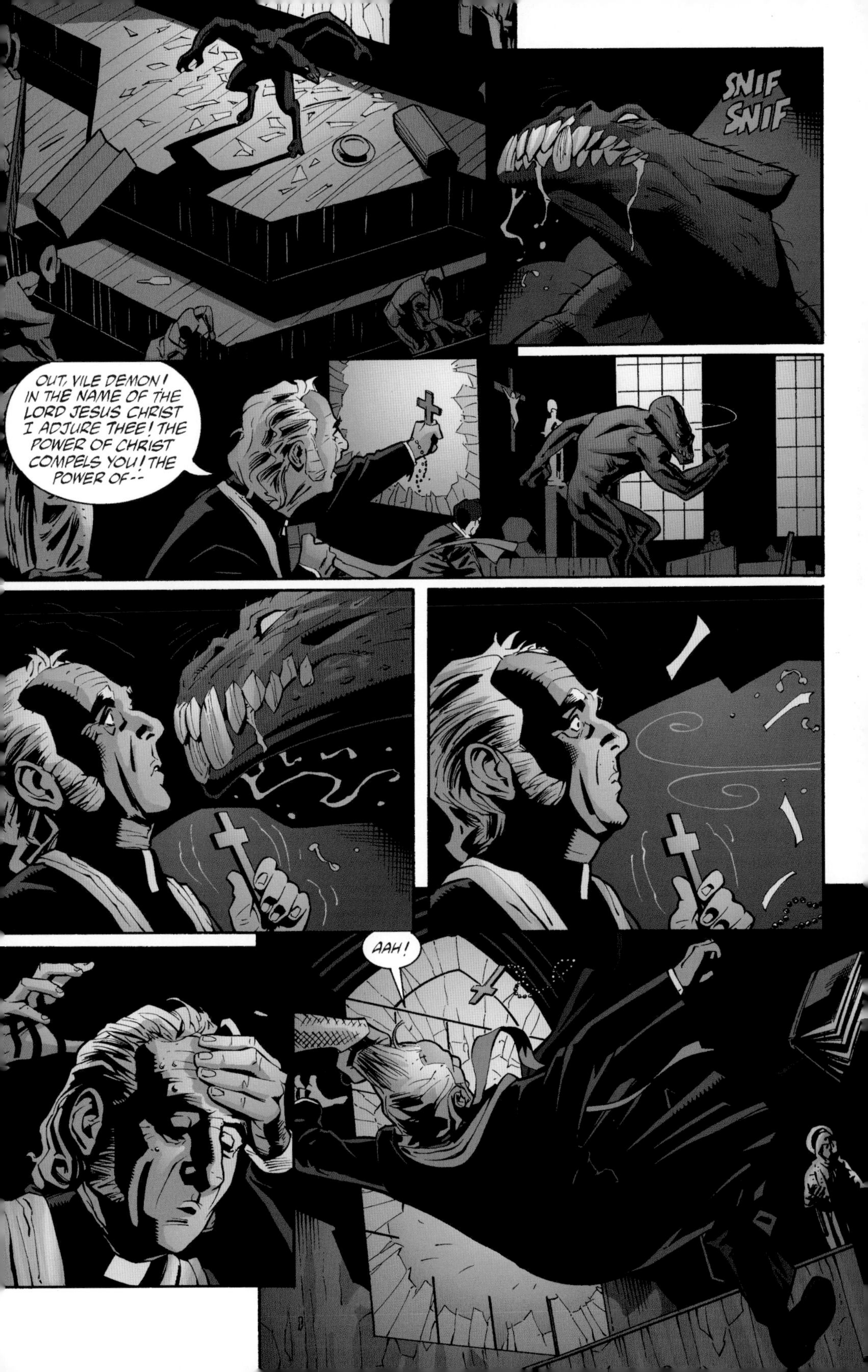
SNIF
SNIF
OUT, VILE DEMON! IN THE NAME OF THE LORD JESUS CHRIST I ADJURE THEE! THE POWER OF CHRIST COMPELS YOU! THE POWER OF--
AAH!

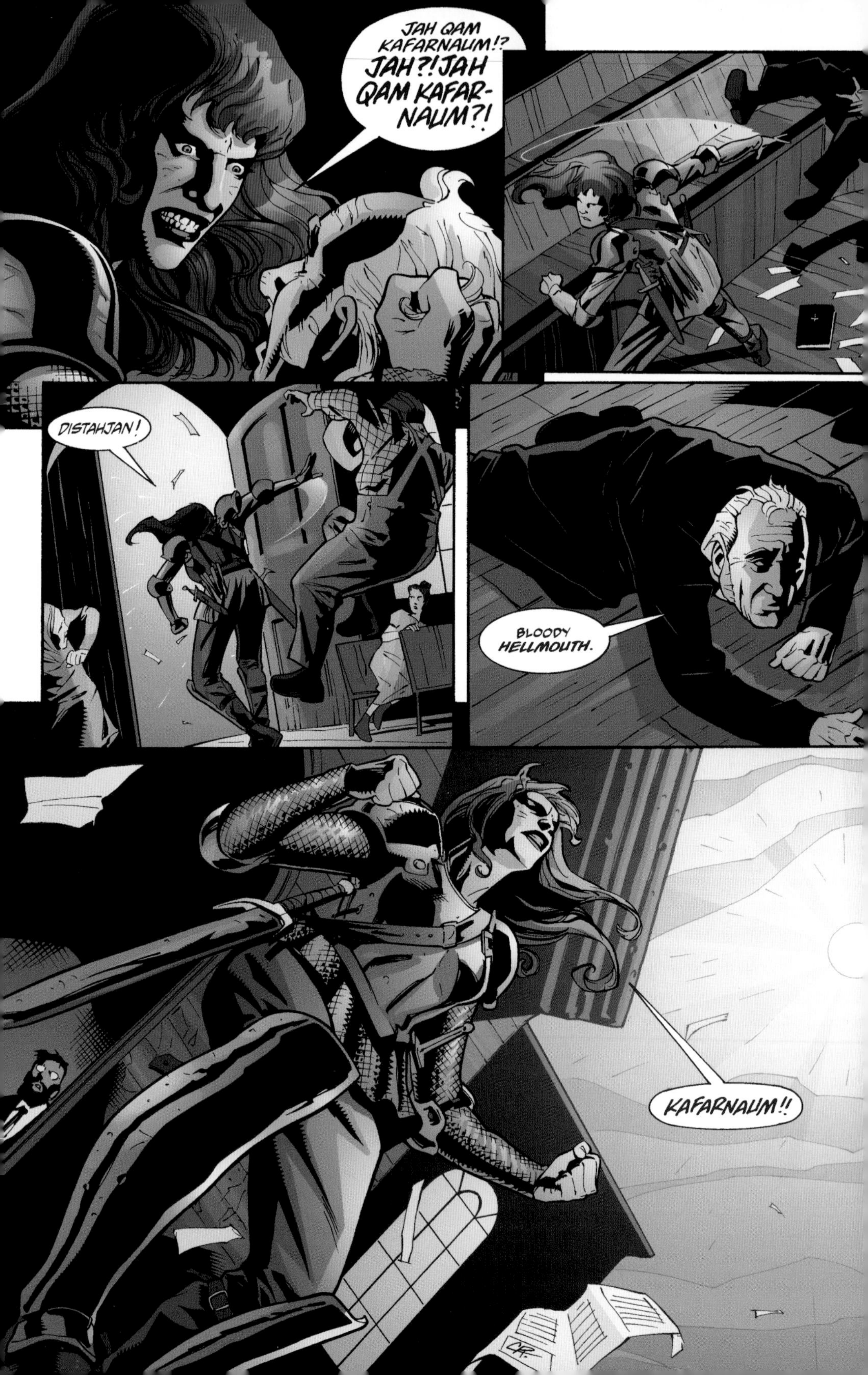

JAH QAM KAFARNAUM!? JAH?! JAH QAM KAFARNAUM?!
DISTAHJAN!
BLOODY HELLMOUTH.
KAFARNAUM!!

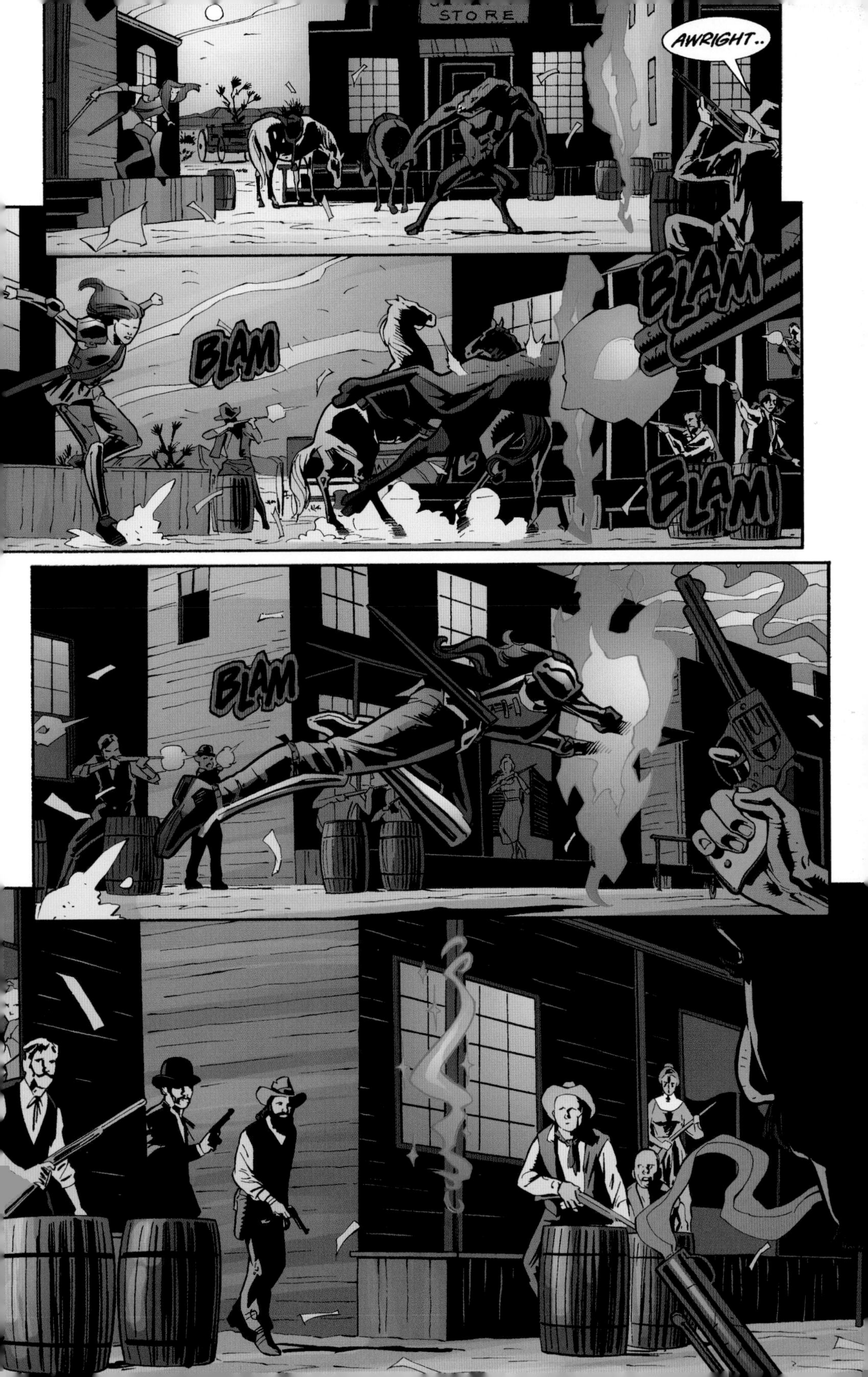
STORE
AWRIGHT..
BLAM
BLAM
BLAM
BLAM

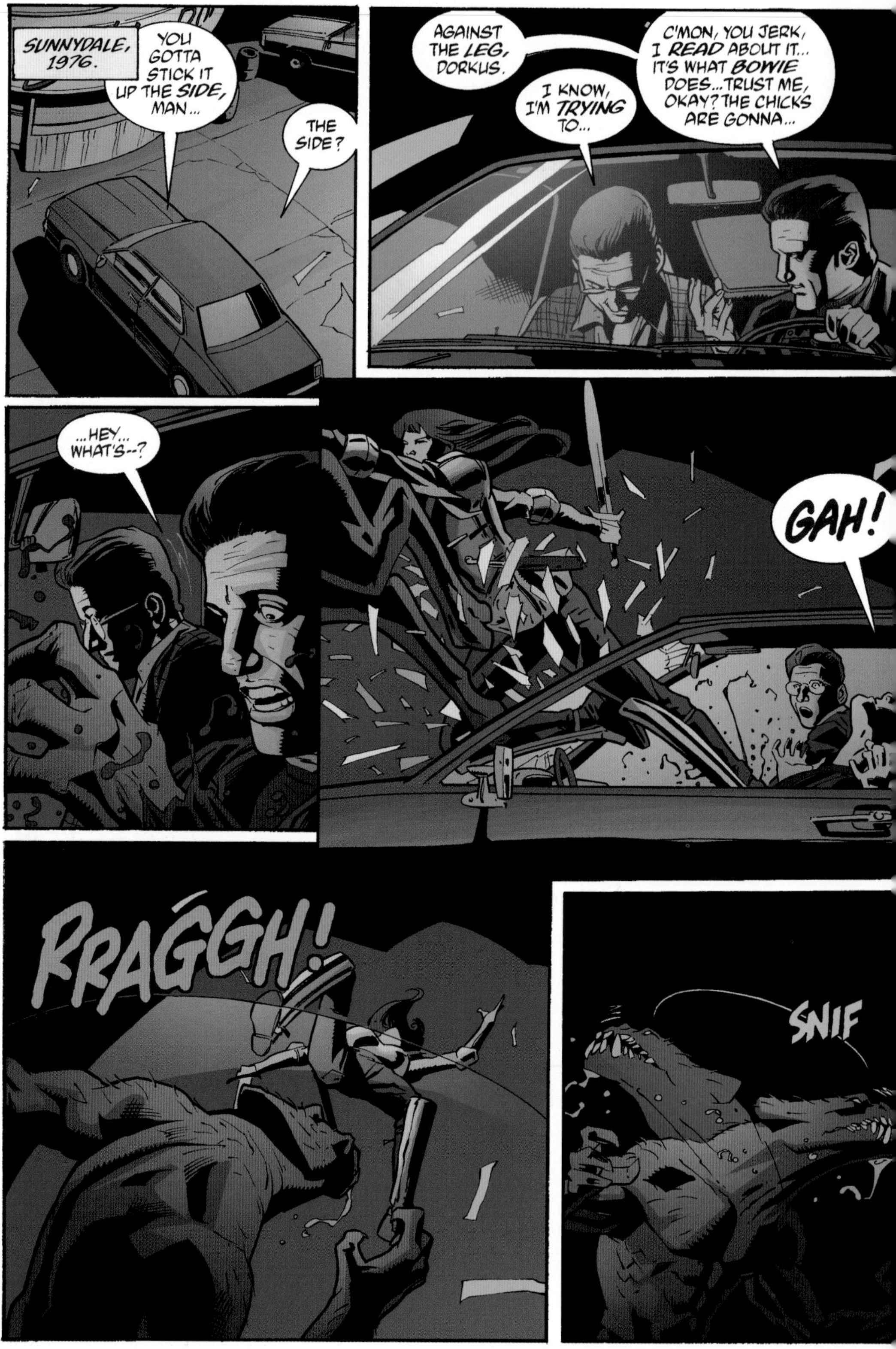
SUNNYDALE, 1976.
YOU GOTTA STICK IT UP THE SIDE, MAN...
THE SIDE?
AGAINST THE LEG, DORKUS.
I KNOW, I'M TRYING TO...
C'MON, YOU JERK, I READ ABOUT IT... IT'S WHAT BOWIE DOES...TRUST ME, OKAY? THE CHICKS ARE GONNA...
...HEY... WHAT'S--?
GAH!
RRAGGH!
SNIF

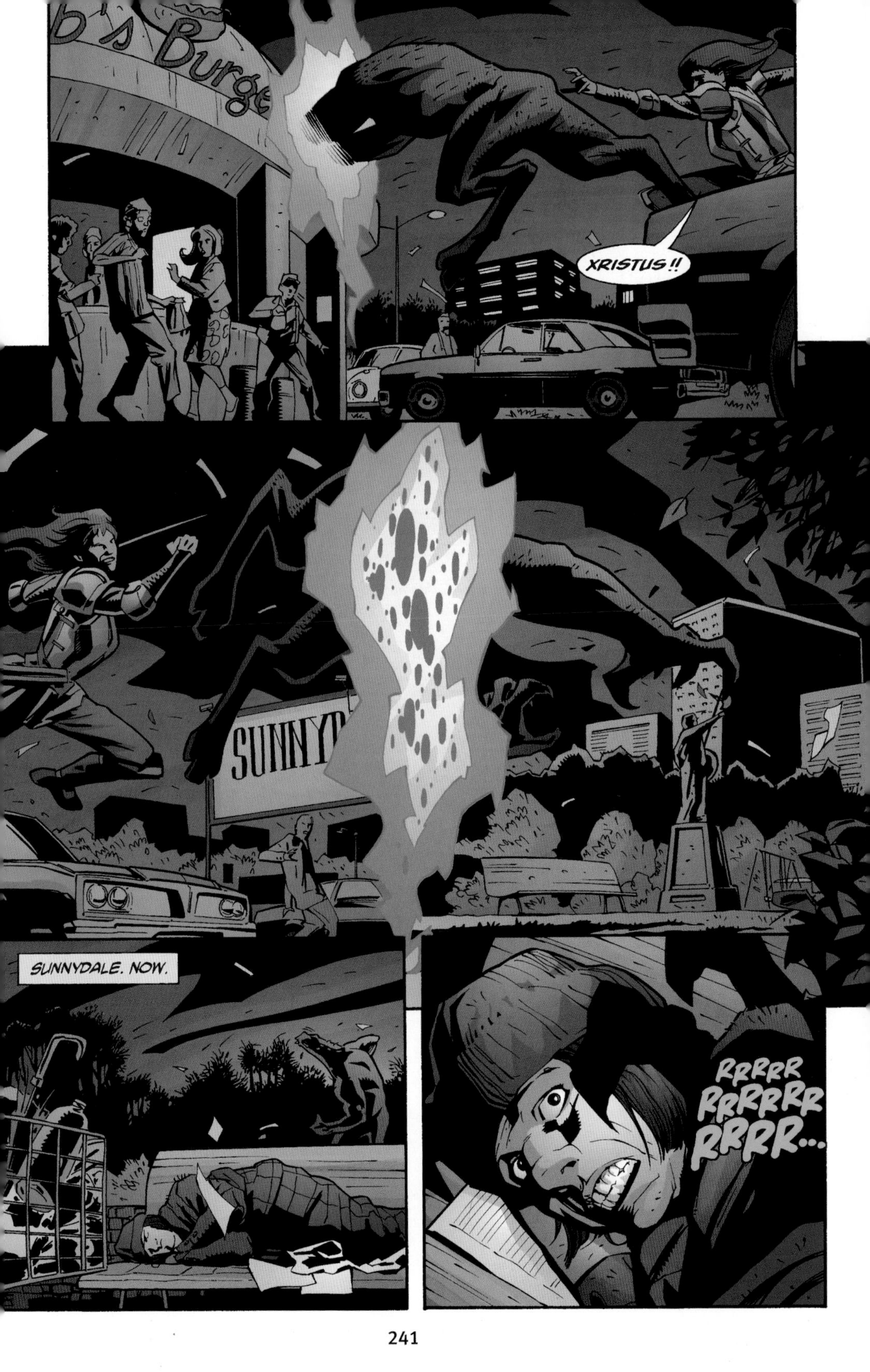
b's Burge
XRISTUS !!
SUNNYD
SUNNYDALE. NOW.
RRRRR RRRRRR RRRR...

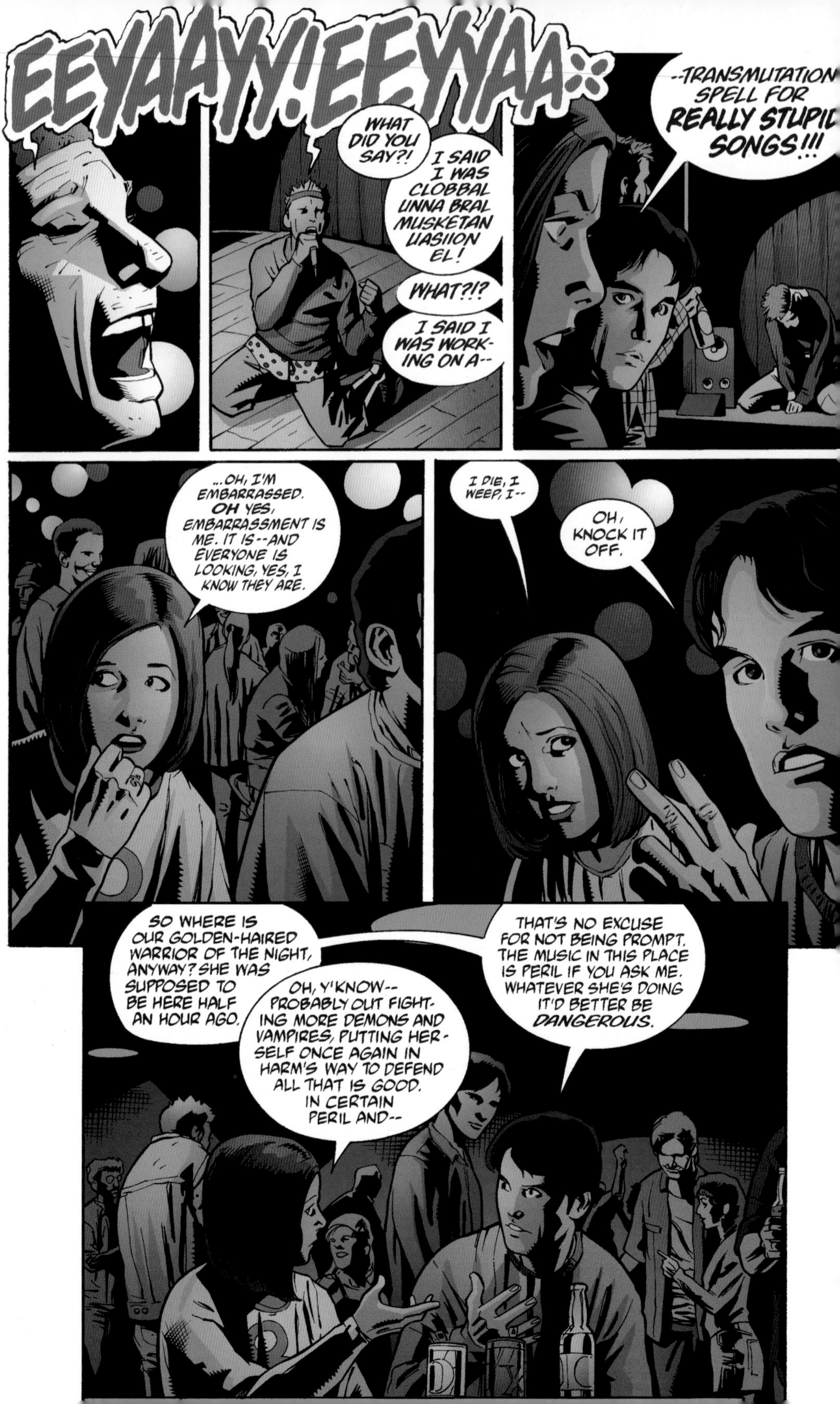
EEYAAYY! EEYYAA:
WHAT DID YOU SAY?!
I SAID I WAS CLOBBAL UNNA BRAL MUSKETAN UASIION EL!
WHAT?!?
I SAID I WAS WORKING ON A--
--TRANSMUTATION SPELL FOR REALLY STUPID SONGS!!!
...OH, I'M EMBARRASSED. OH YES, EMBARRASSMENT IS ME. IT IS--AND EVERYONE IS LOOKING, YES, I KNOW THEY ARE.
I DIE, I WEEP, I--
OH, KNOCK IT OFF.
SO WHERE IS OUR GOLDEN-HAIRED WARRIOR OF THE NIGHT, ANYWAY? SHE WAS SUPPOSED TO BE HERE HALF AN HOUR AGO.
OH, Y'KNOW--PROBABLY OUT FIGHTING MORE DEMONS AND VAMPIRES, PUTTING HERSELF ONCE AGAIN IN HARM'S WAY TO DEFEND ALL THAT IS GOOD. IN CERTAIN PERIL AND--
THAT'S NO EXCUSE FOR NOT BEING PROMPT. THE MUSIC IN THIS PLACE IS PERIL IF YOU ASK ME. WHATEVER SHE'S DOING IT'D BETTER BE DANGEROUS.

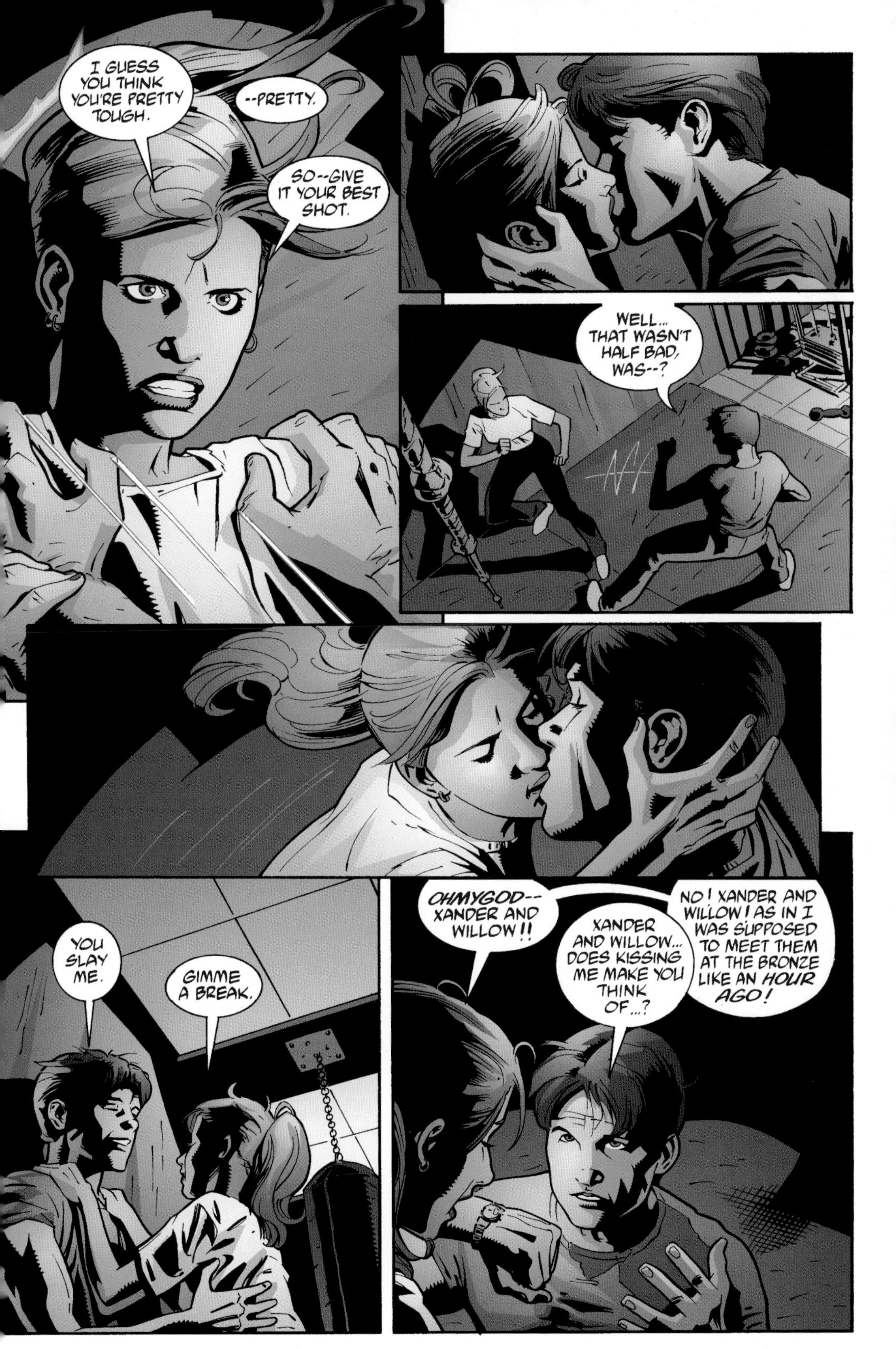
I GUESS YOU THINK YOU'RE PRETTY TOUGH.
--PRETTY.
SO--GIVE IT YOUR BEST SHOT.
WELL... THAT WASN'T HALF BAD, WAS--?
YOU SLAY ME.
GIMME A BREAK.
OHMYGOD-- XANDER AND WILLOW!!
XANDER AND WILLOW... DOES KISSING ME MAKE YOU THINK OF...?
NO! XANDER AND WILLOW! AS IN I WAS SUPPOSED TO MEET THEM AT THE BRONZE LIKE AN HOUR AGO!

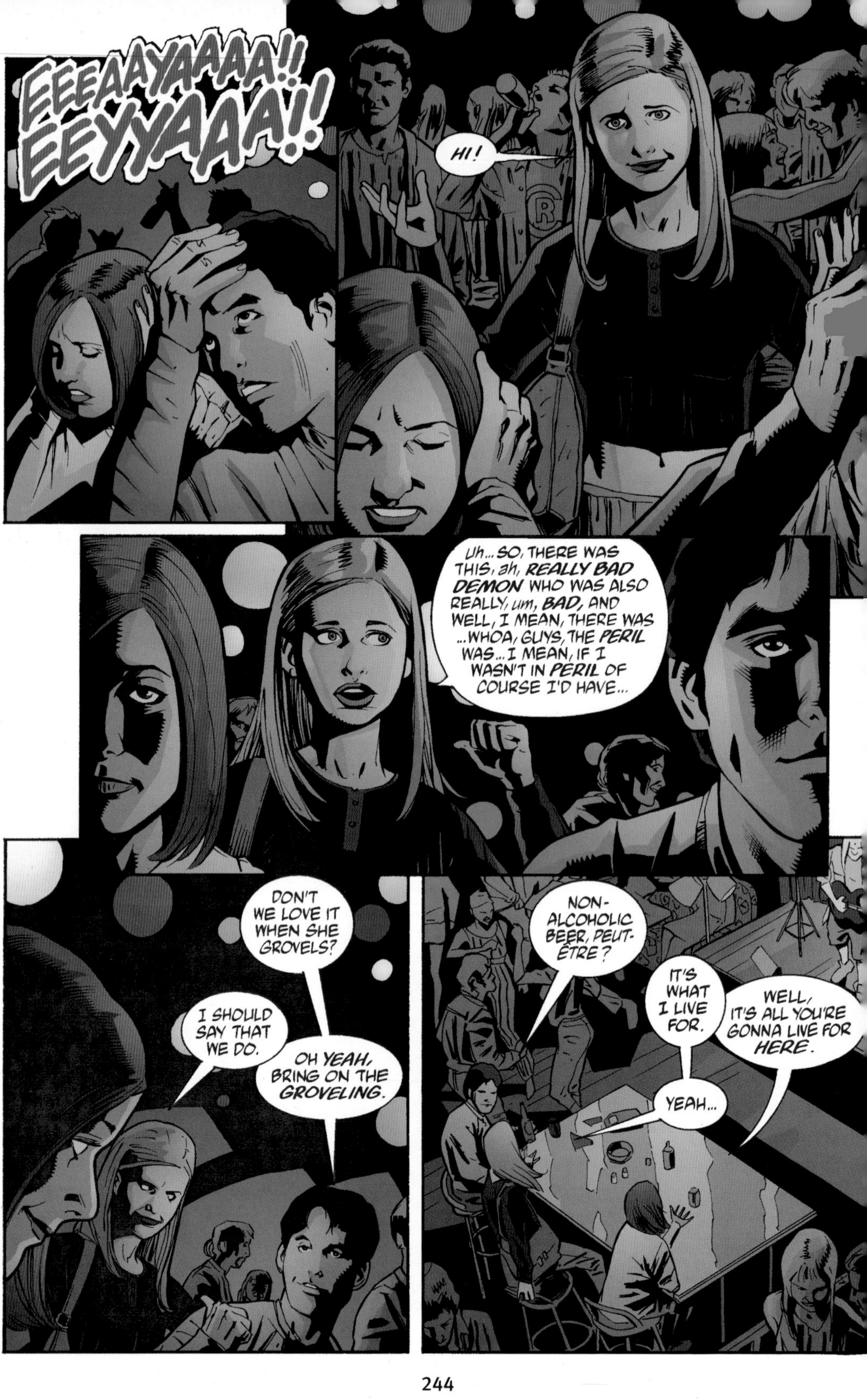
EEEAAYAAAA!! EEYYAAA!!
HI!
Uh... SO, THERE WAS THIS, ah, REALLY BAD DEMON WHO WAS ALSO REALLY, um, BAD, AND WELL, I MEAN, THERE WAS ...WHOA, GUYS, THE PERIL WAS... I MEAN, IF I WASN'T IN PERIL OF COURSE I'D HAVE...
DON'T WE LOVE IT WHEN SHE GROVELS?
I SHOULD SAY THAT WE DO.
OH YEAH, BRING ON THE GROVELING.
NON-ALCOHOLIC BEER, PEUT-ÊTRE?
IT'S WHAT I LIVE FOR.
WELL, IT'S ALL YOU'RE GONNA LIVE FOR HERE.
YEAH...

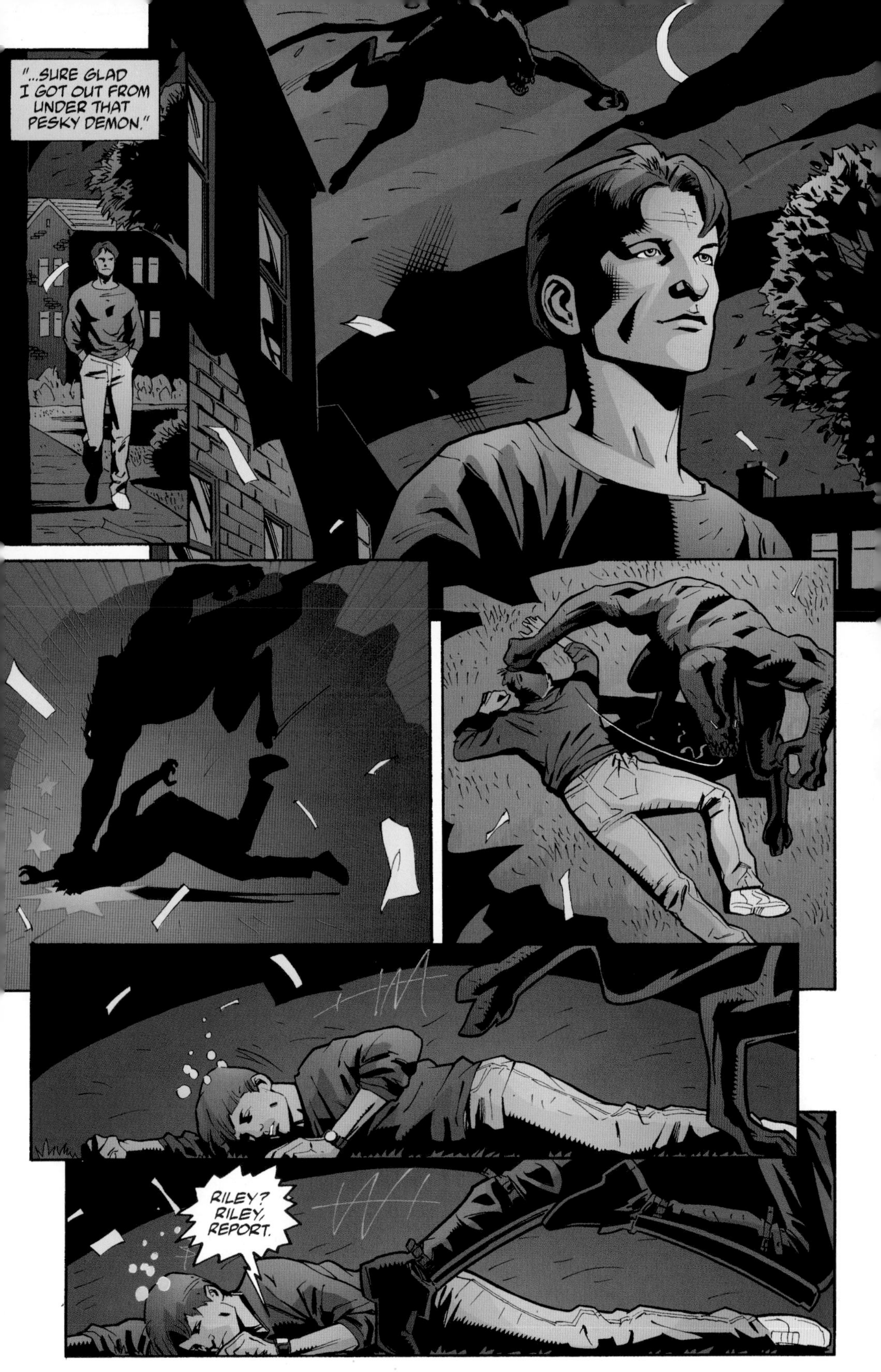
"...SURE GLAD I GOT OUT FROM UNDER THAT PESKY DEMON."
RILEY? RILEY, REPORT.

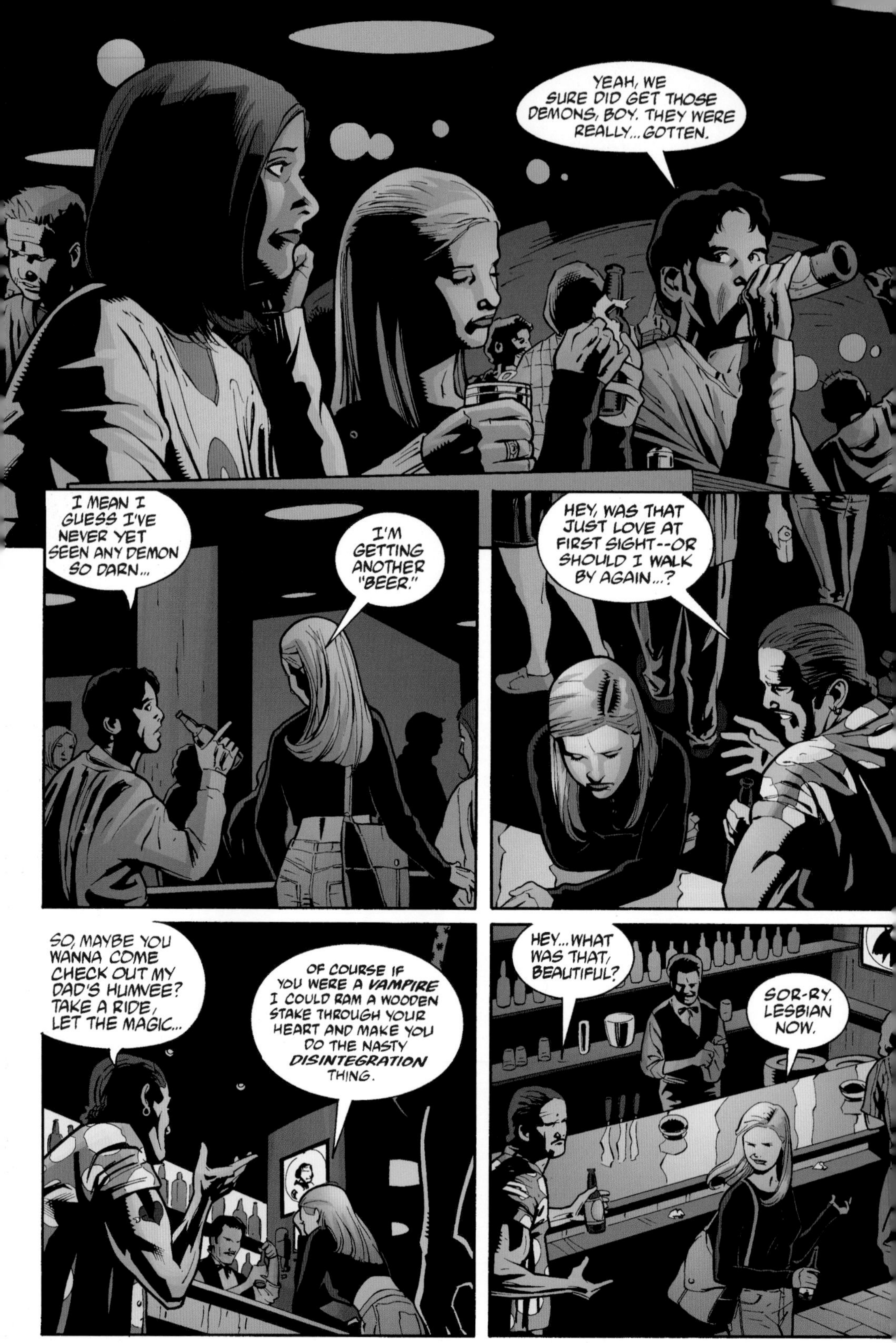
YEAH, WE SURE DID GET THOSE DEMONS, BOY. THEY WERE REALLY... GOTTEN.
I MEAN I GUESS I'VE NEVER YET SEEN ANY DEMON SO DARN...
I'M GETTING ANOTHER "BEER."
HEY, WAS THAT JUST LOVE AT FIRST SIGHT--OR SHOULD I WALK BY AGAIN...?
SO, MAYBE YOU WANNA COME CHECK OUT MY DAD'S HUMVEE? TAKE A RIDE, LET THE MAGIC...
OF COURSE IF YOU WERE A VAMPIRE I COULD RAM A WOODEN STAKE THROUGH YOUR HEART AND MAKE YOU DO THE NASTY DISINTEGRATION THING.
HEY... WHAT WAS THAT, BEAUTIFUL?
SOR-RY. LESBIAN NOW.

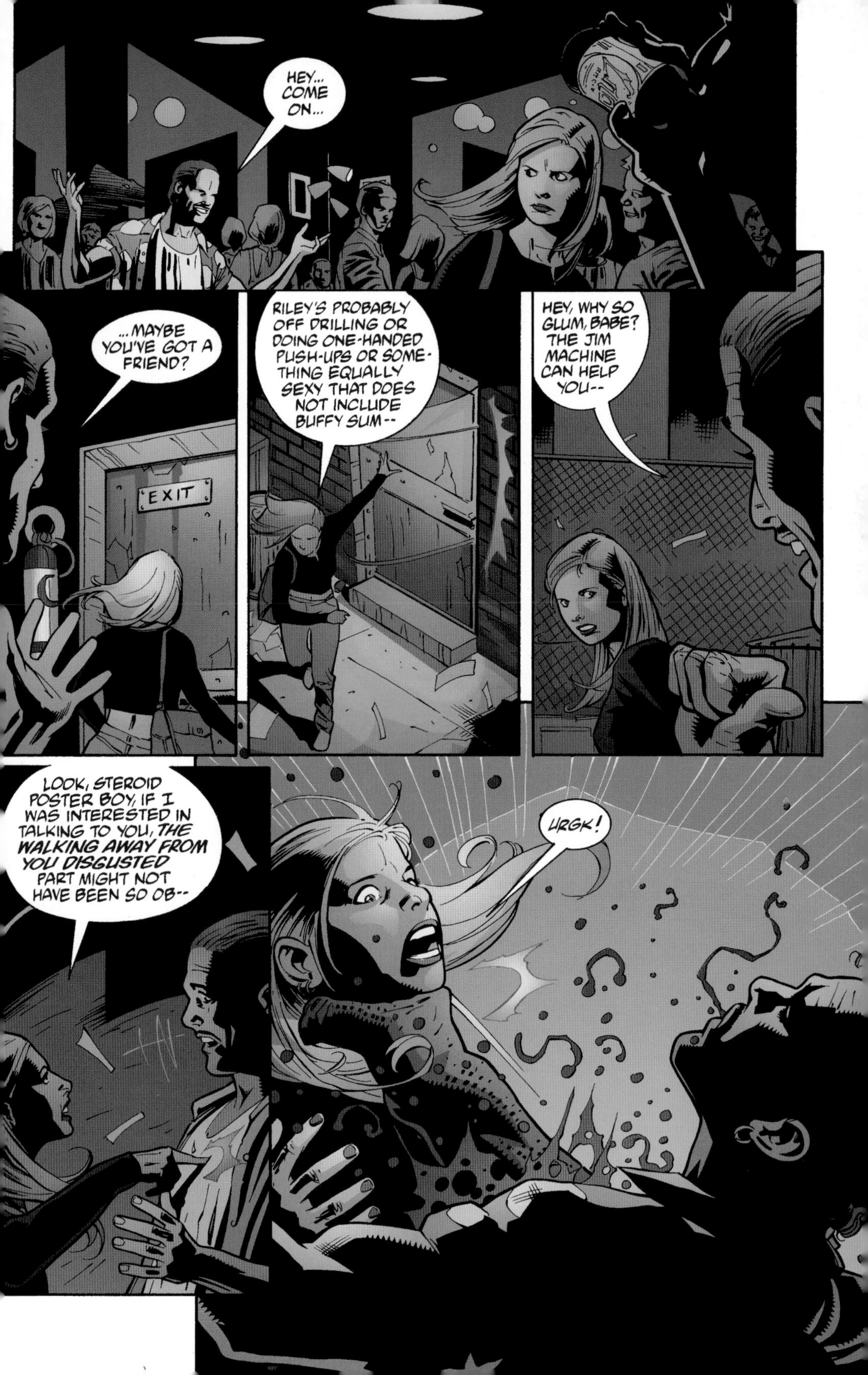
HEY... COME ON...
...MAYBE YOU'VE GOT A FRIEND?
RILEY'S PROBABLY OFF DRILLING OR DOING ONE-HANDED PUSH-UPS OR SOMETHING EQUALLY SEXY THAT DOES NOT INCLUDE BUFFY SUM--
EXIT
HEY, WHY SO GLUM, BABE? THE JIM MACHINE CAN HELP YOU--
LOOK, STEROID POSTER BOY, IF I WAS INTERESTED IN TALKING TO YOU, *THE WALKING AWAY FROM YOU DISGUSTED* PART MIGHT NOT HAVE BEEN SO OB--
URGK!

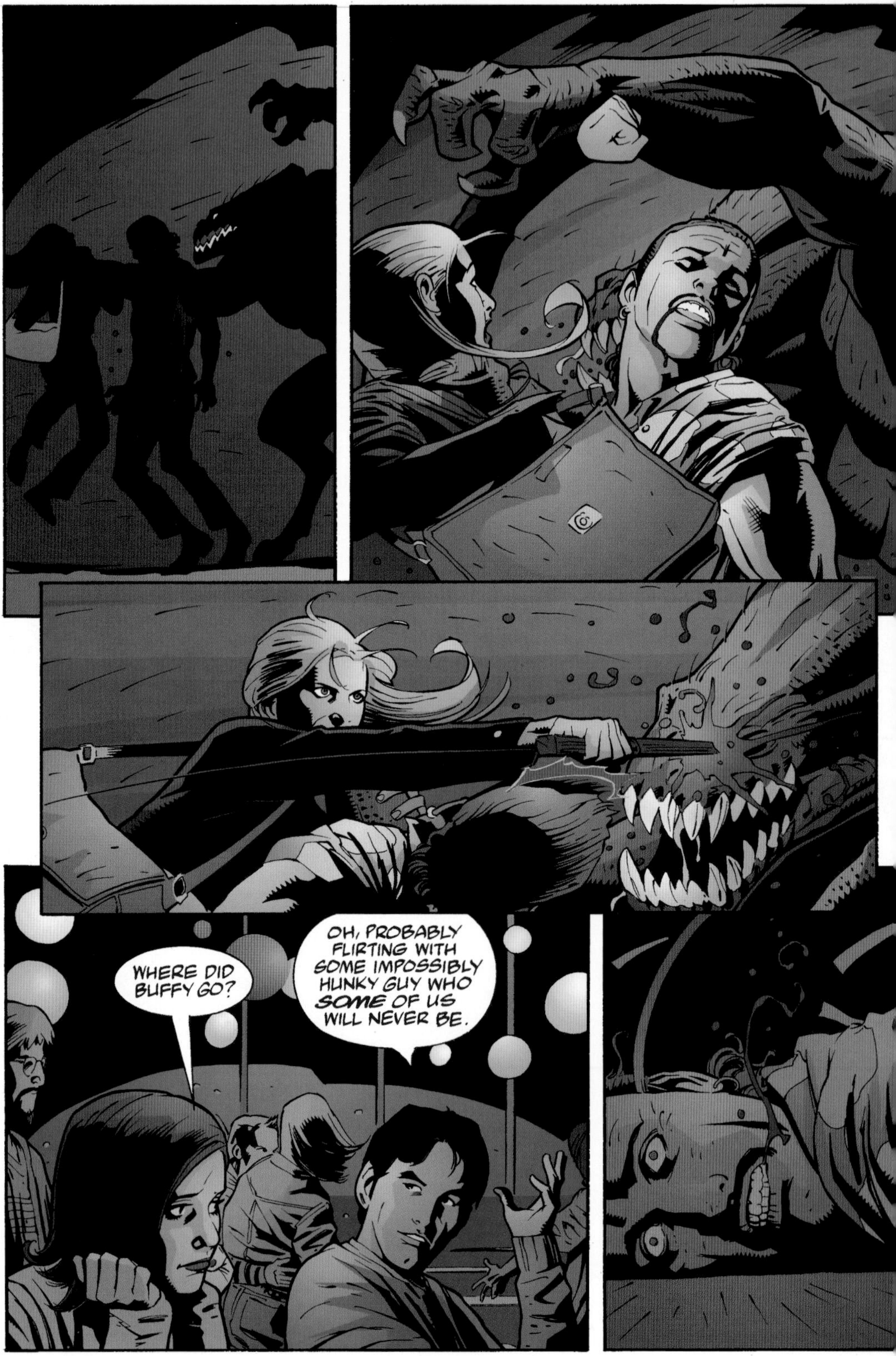
WHERE DID BUFFY GO?
OH, PROBABLY FLIRTING WITH SOME IMPOSSIBLY HUNKY GUY WHO SOME OF US WILL NEVER BE.

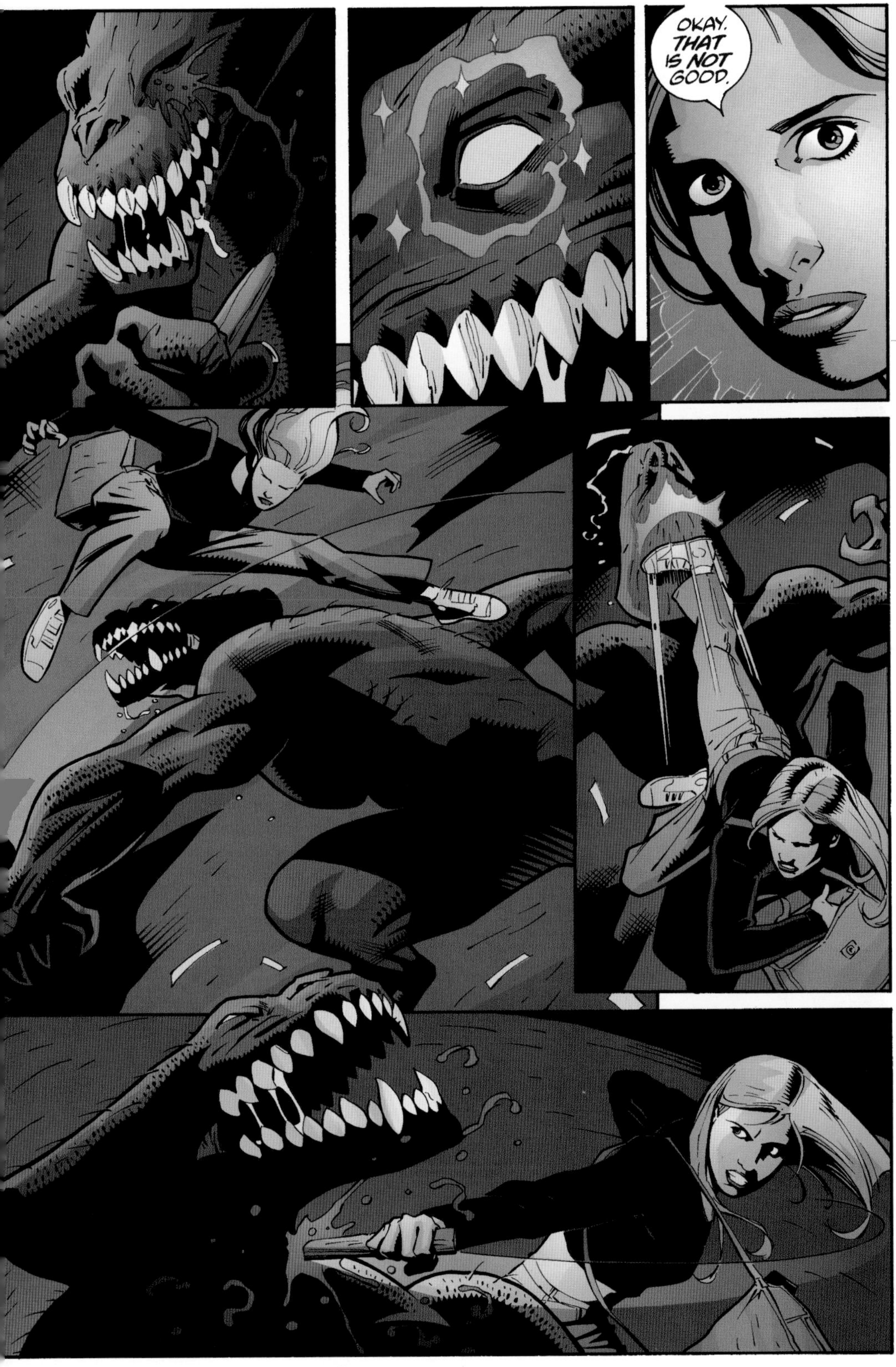
OKAY. THAT IS NOT GOOD.

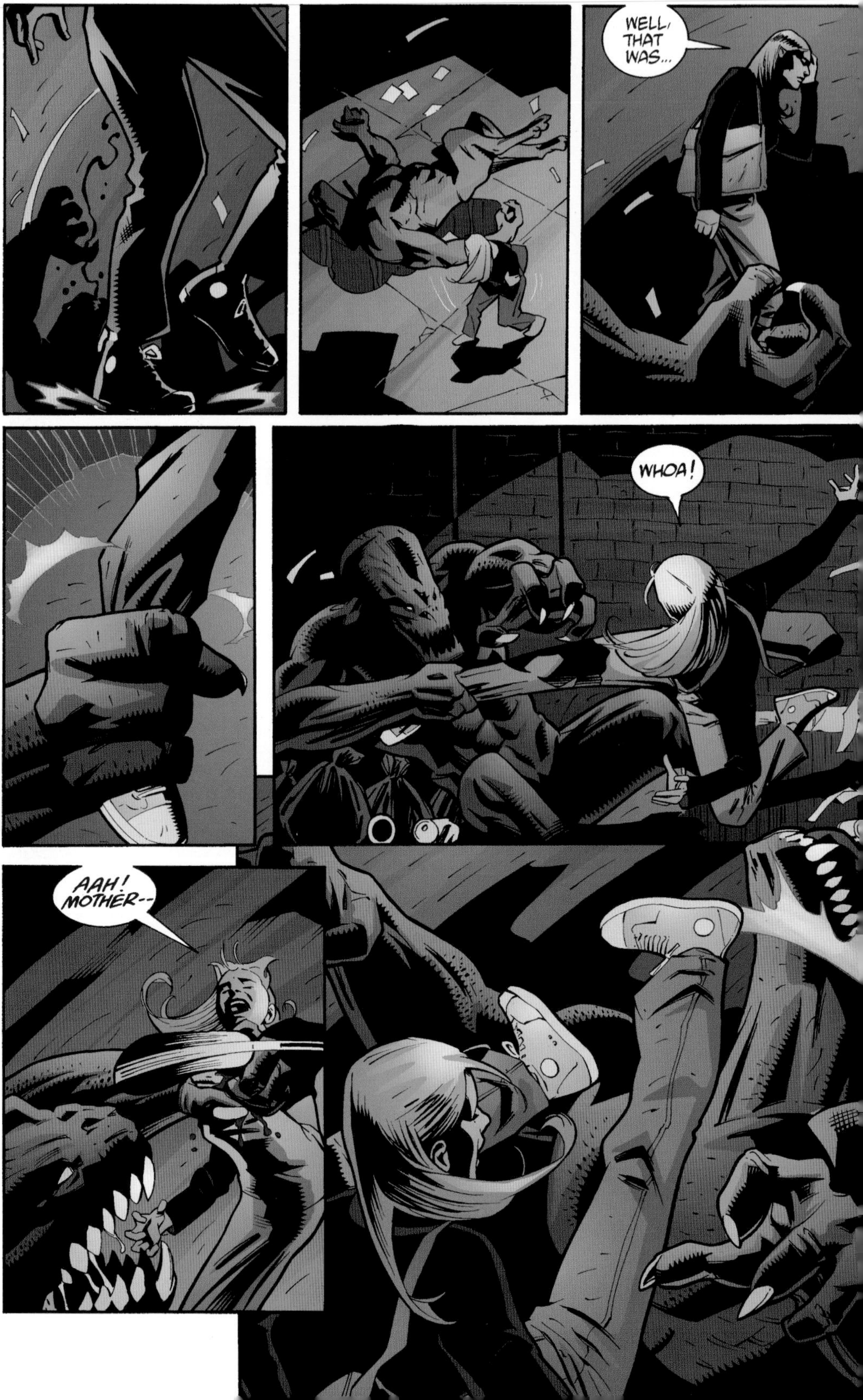
WELL, THAT WAS...
WHOA!
AAH! MOTHER--

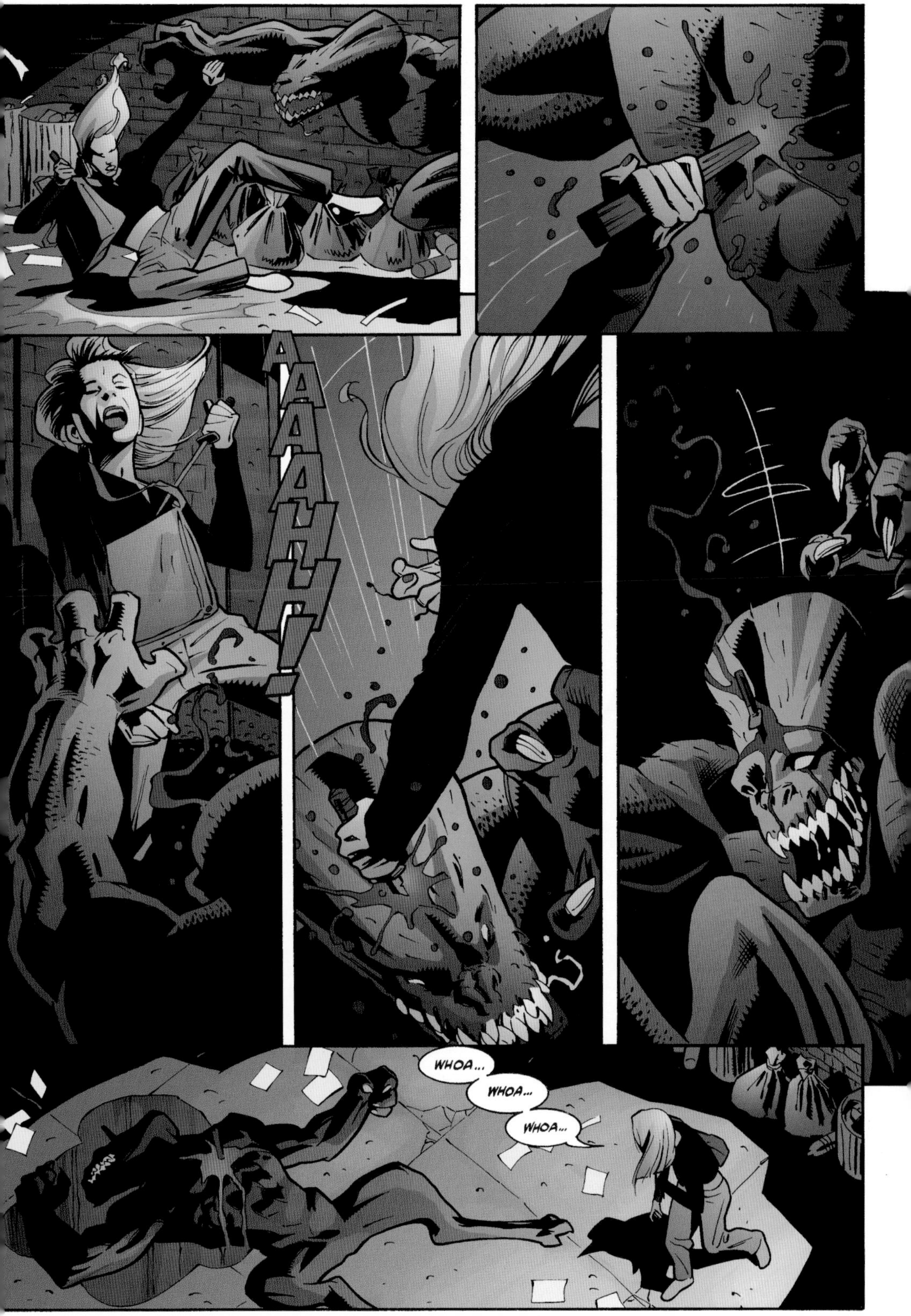
AAAAAHH!
WHOA...
WHOA...
WHOA...

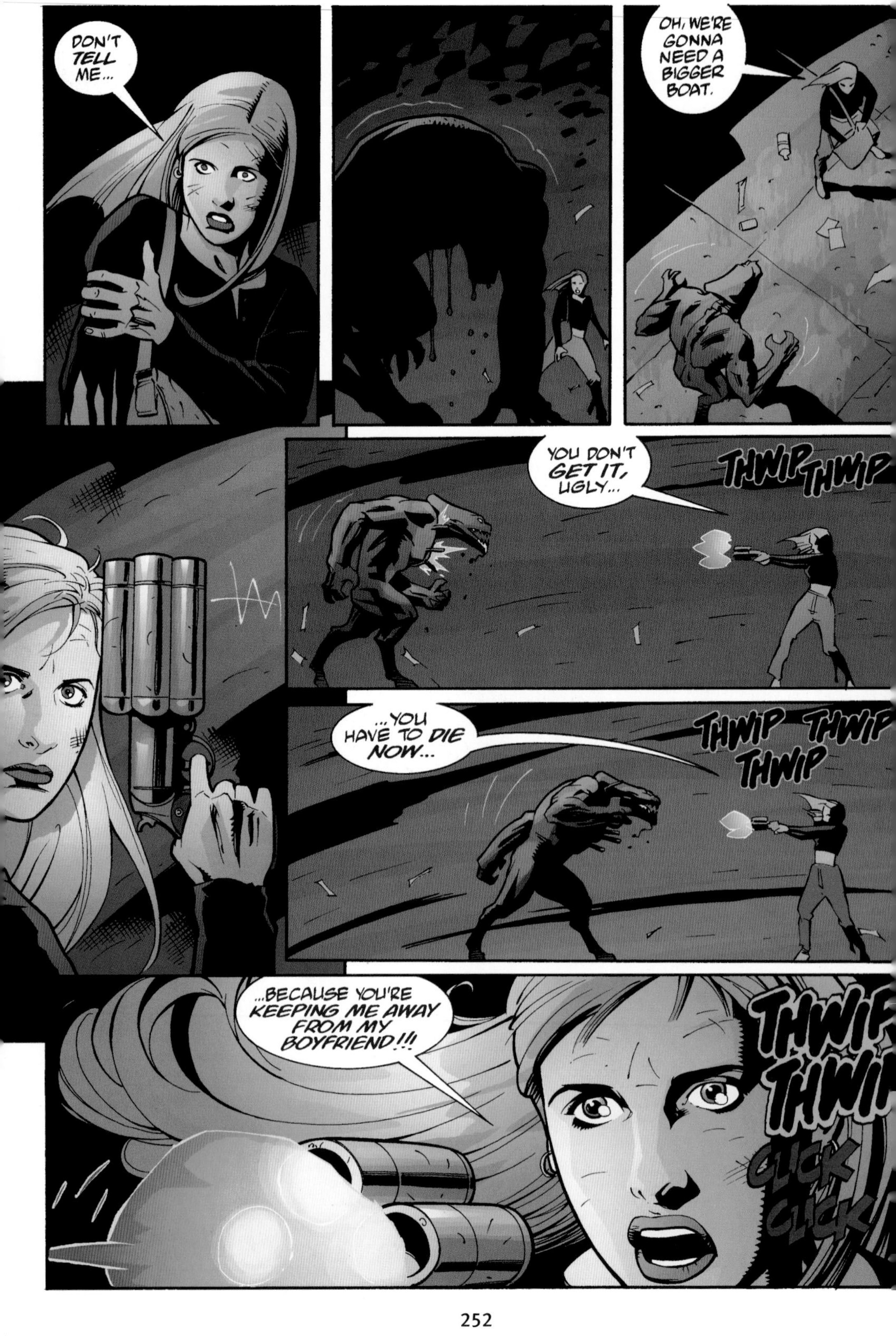
DON'T TELL ME...
OH, WE'RE GONNA NEED A BIGGER BOAT.
YOU DON'T GET IT, UGLY...
THWIP THWIP
...YOU HAVE TO DIE NOW...
THWIP THWIP THWIP
...BECAUSE YOU'RE KEEPING ME AWAY FROM MY BOYFRIEND!!!
CLICK CLICK

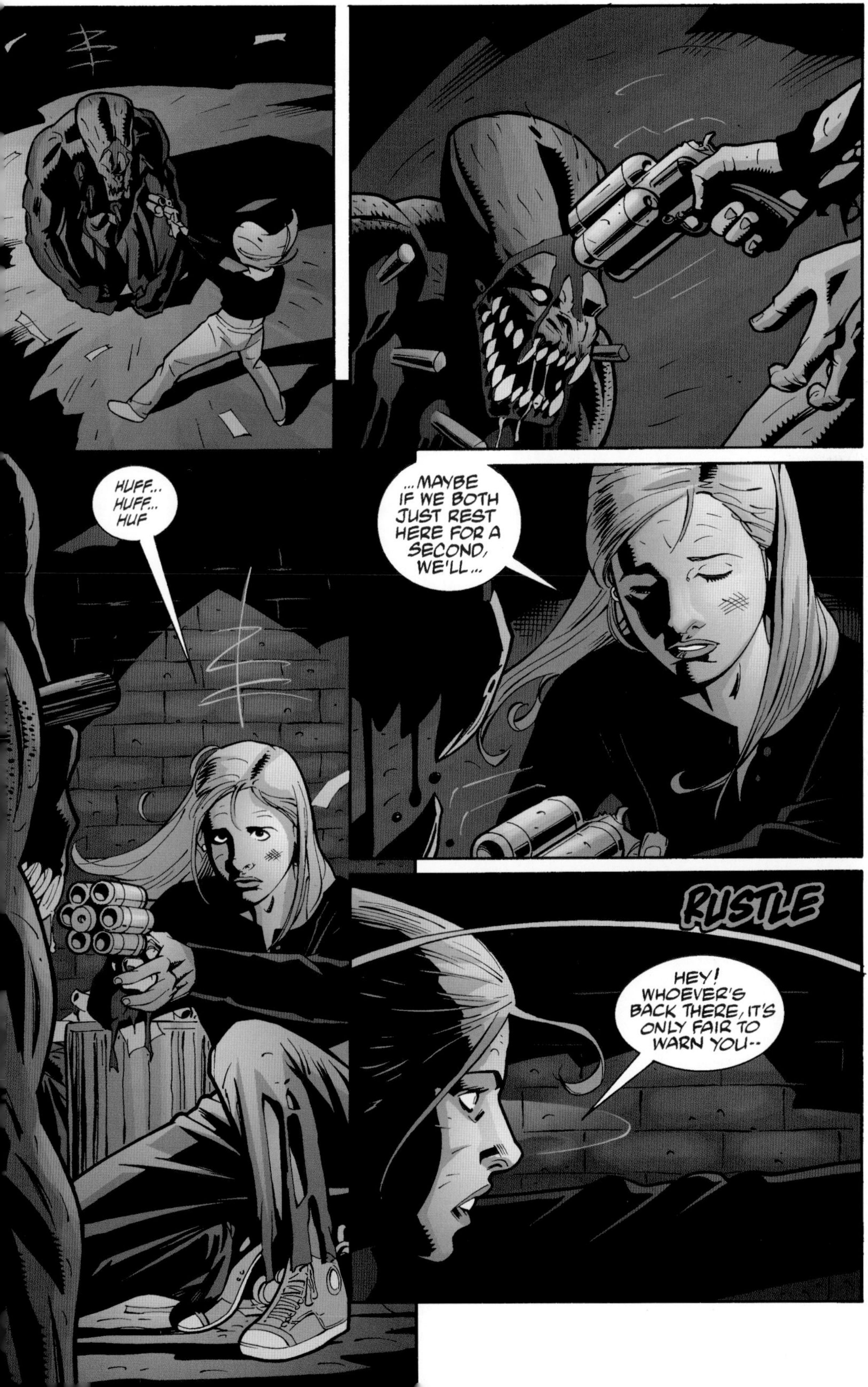
HUFF...
HUFF...
HUF
...MAYBE IF WE BOTH JUST REST HERE FOR A SECOND, WE'LL...
RUSTLE
HEY! WHOEVER'S BACK THERE, IT'S ONLY FAIR TO WARN YOU--

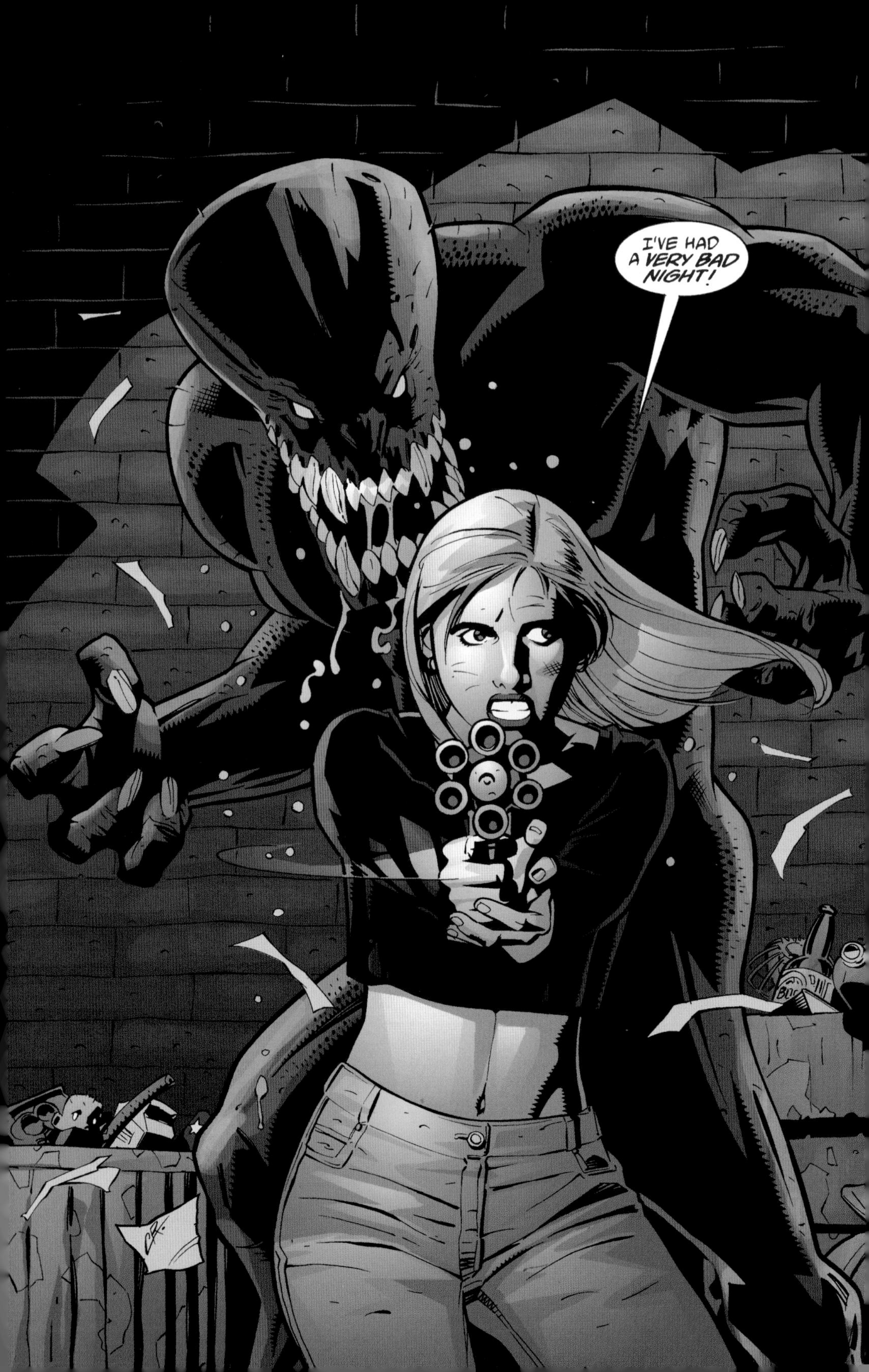
I'VE HAD A VERY BAD NIGHT!

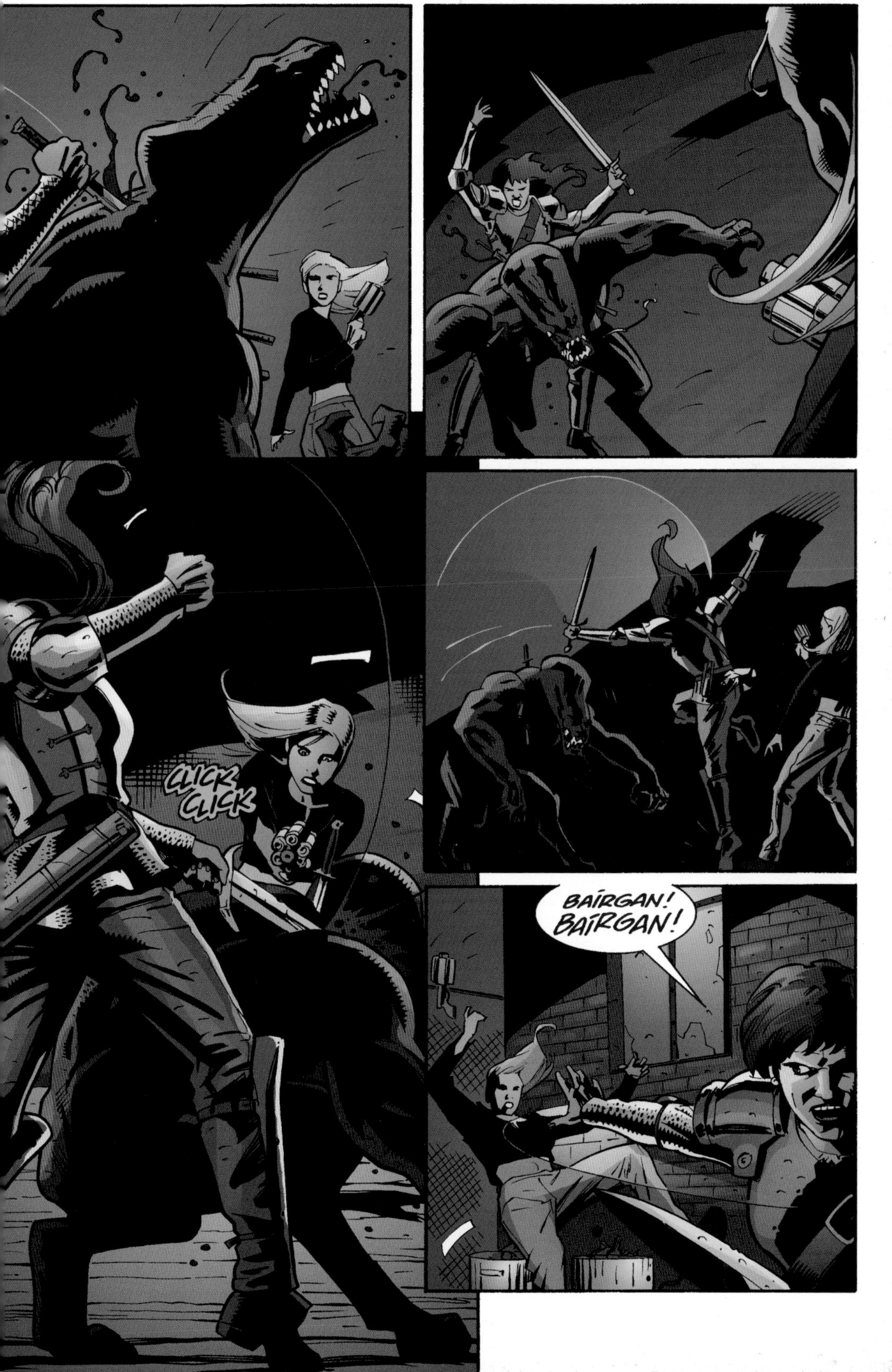
CLICK CLICK
BAÍRGAN! BAÍRGAN!

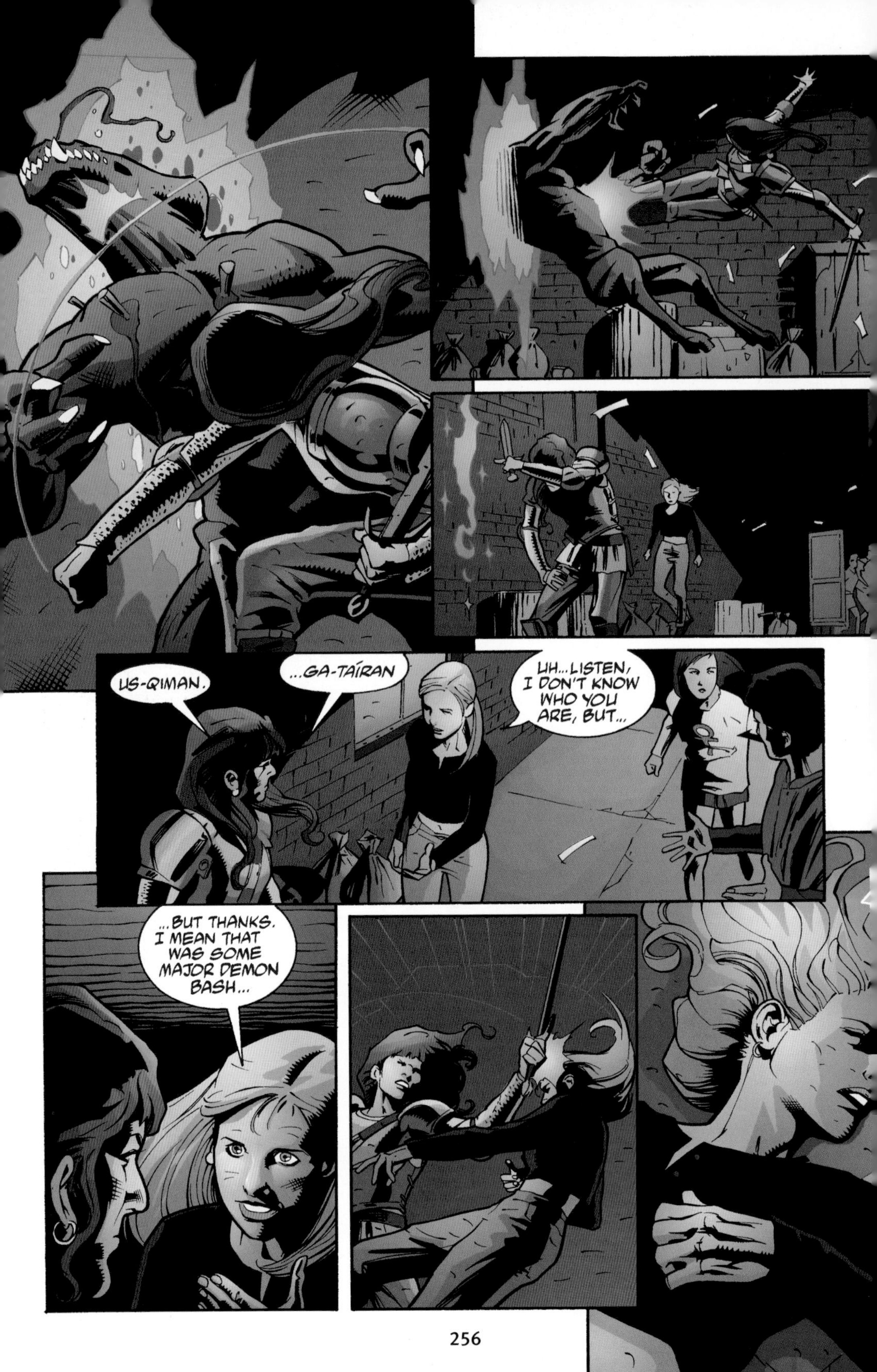
US-QIMAN.
...GA-TAÍRAN
UH...LISTEN, I DON'T KNOW WHO YOU ARE, BUT...
...BUT THANKS. I MEAN THAT WAS SOME MAJOR DEMON BASH...

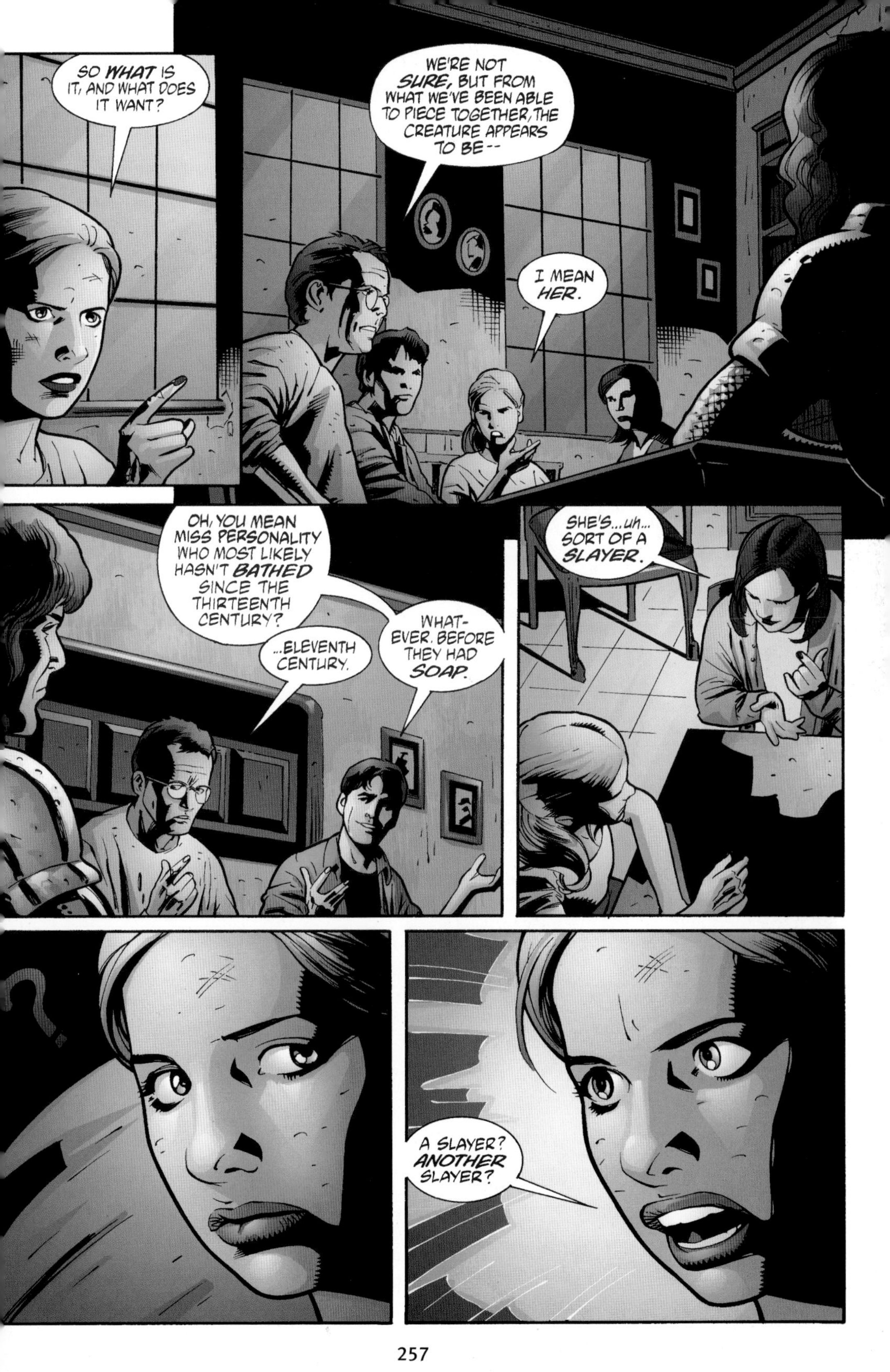
SO WHAT IS IT, AND WHAT DOES IT WANT?
WE'RE NOT SURE, BUT FROM WHAT WE'VE BEEN ABLE TO PIECE TOGETHER, THE CREATURE APPEARS TO BE--
I MEAN HER.
OH, YOU MEAN MISS PERSONALITY WHO MOST LIKELY HASN'T BATHED SINCE THE THIRTEENTH CENTURY?
...ELEVENTH CENTURY.
WHAT-EVER. BEFORE THEY HAD SOAP.
SHE'S...uh... SORT OF A SLAYER.
A SLAYER? ANOTHER SLAYER?

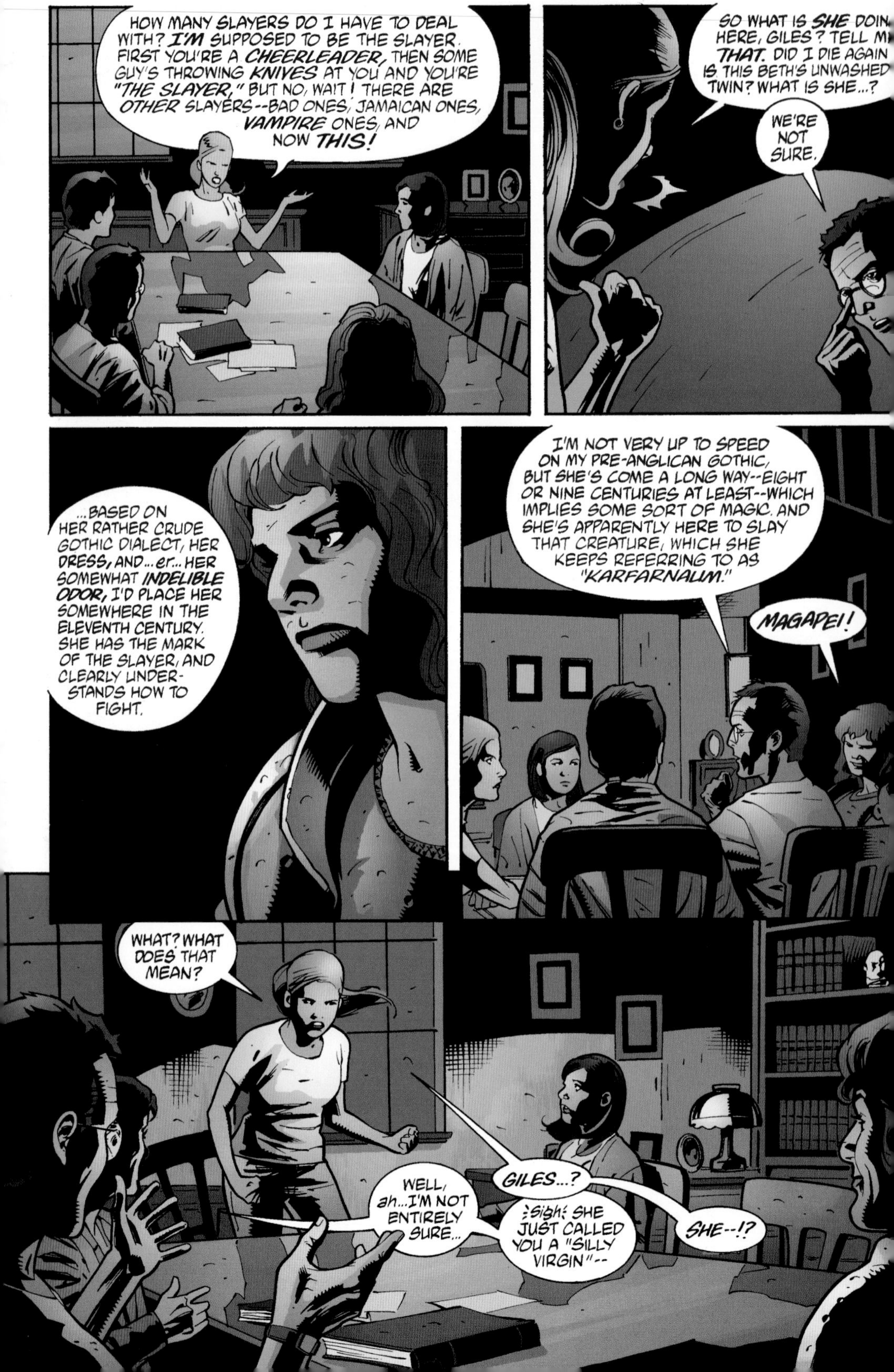
HOW MANY SLAYERS DO I HAVE TO DEAL WITH? I'M SUPPOSED TO BE THE SLAYER. FIRST YOU'RE A CHEERLEADER, THEN SOME GUY'S THROWING KNIVES AT YOU AND YOU'RE "THE SLAYER," BUT NO, WAIT! THERE ARE OTHER SLAYERS--BAD ONES, JAMAICAN ONES, VAMPIRE ONES, AND NOW THIS!
SO WHAT IS SHE DOIN HERE, GILES? TELL M THAT. DID I DIE AGAIN IS THIS BETH'S UNWASHED TWIN? WHAT IS SHE...?
WE'RE NOT SURE.
...BASED ON HER RATHER CRUDE GOTHIC DIALECT, HER DRESS, AND...er...HER SOMEWHAT INDELIBLE ODOR, I'D PLACE HER SOMEWHERE IN THE ELEVENTH CENTURY. SHE HAS THE MARK OF THE SLAYER, AND CLEARLY UNDER-STANDS HOW TO FIGHT.
I'M NOT VERY UP TO SPEED ON MY PRE-ANGLICAN GOTHIC, BUT SHE'S COME A LONG WAY--EIGHT OR NINE CENTURIES AT LEAST--WHICH IMPLIES SOME SORT OF MAGIC. AND SHE'S APPARENTLY HERE TO SLAY THAT CREATURE, WHICH SHE KEEPS REFERRING TO AS "KARFARNAUM."
MAGAPEI!
WHAT? WHAT DOES THAT MEAN?
GILES...?
WELL, ah...I'M NOT ENTIRELY SURE...
:sigh: SHE JUST CALLED YOU A "SILLY VIRGIN"--
SHE--!?

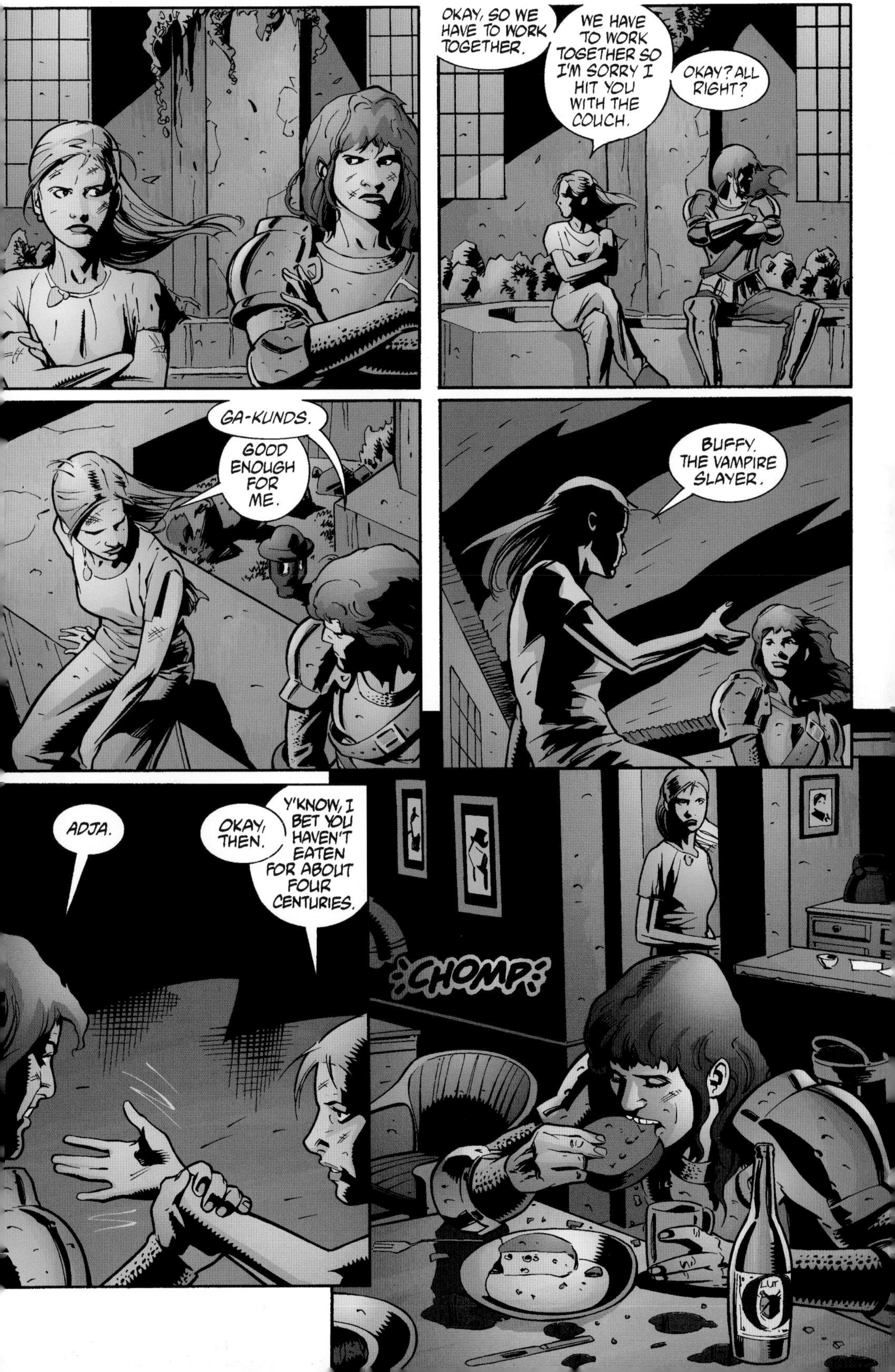
OKAY, SO WE HAVE TO WORK TOGETHER.
WE HAVE TO WORK TOGETHER SO I'M SORRY I HIT YOU WITH THE COUCH.
OKAY? ALL RIGHT?
GA-KUNDS.
GOOD ENOUGH FOR ME.
BUFFY. THE VAMPIRE SLAYER.
ADJA.
OKAY, THEN.
Y'KNOW, I BET YOU HAVEN'T EATEN FOR ABOUT FOUR CENTURIES.
CHOMP

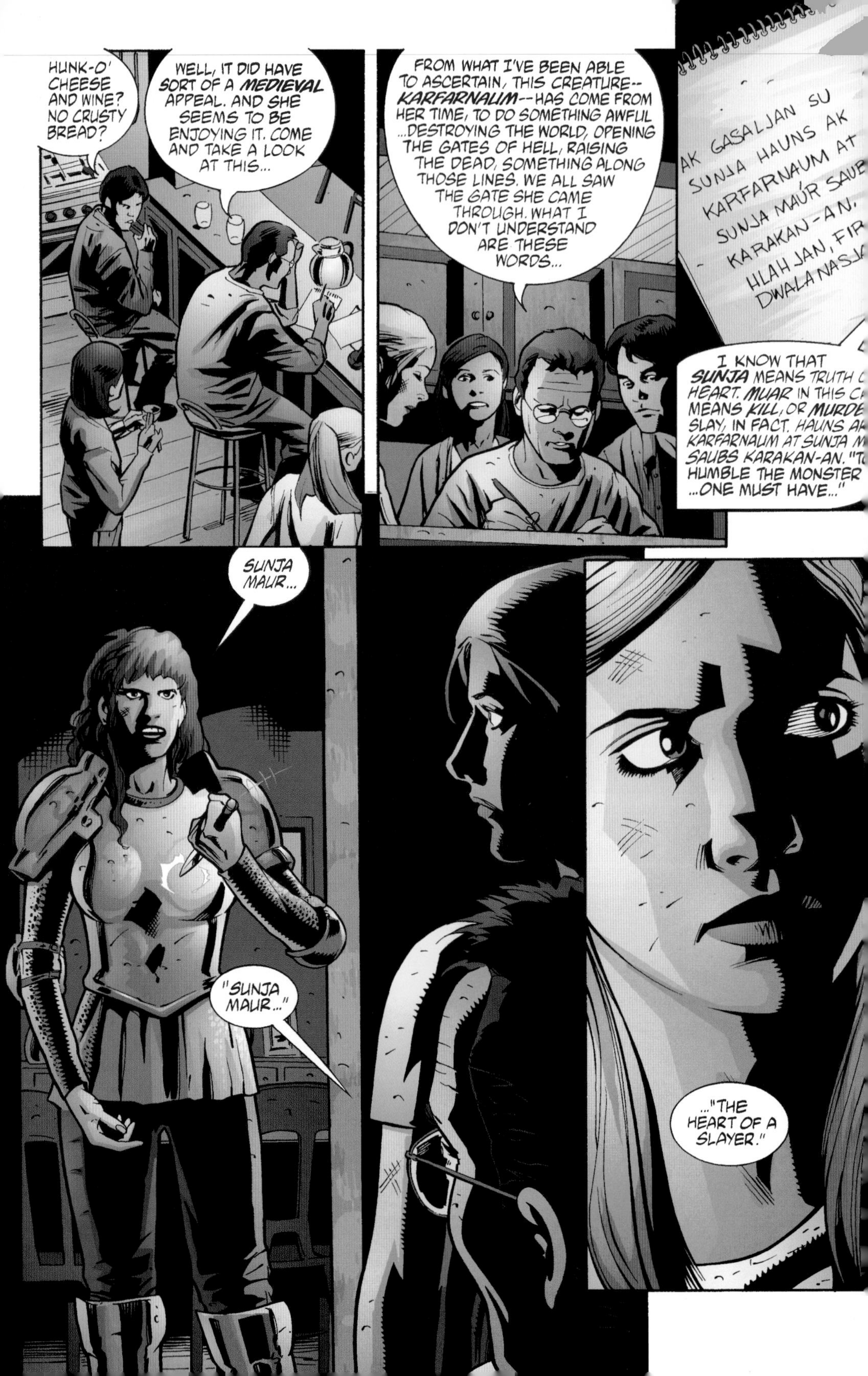
HUNK-O' CHEESE AND WINE? NO CRUSTY BREAD?
WELL, IT DID HAVE SORT OF A MEDIEVAL APPEAL. AND SHE SEEMS TO BE ENJOYING IT. COME AND TAKE A LOOK AT THIS...
FROM WHAT I'VE BEEN ABLE TO ASCERTAIN, THIS CREATURE-- KARFARNAUM--HAS COME FROM HER TIME, TO DO SOMETHING AWFUL ...DESTROYING THE WORLD, OPENING THE GATES OF HELL, RAISING THE DEAD, SOMETHING ALONG THOSE LINES. WE ALL SAW THE GATE SHE CAME THROUGH. WHAT I DON'T UNDERSTAND ARE THESE WORDS...
AK GASALJAN SU
SUNJA HAUNS AK
KARFARNAUM AT
SUNJA MAÚR SAUB
KARAKAN-AN,
HLAH JAN, FIR
DWALANASJA
I KNOW THAT SUNJA MEANS TRUTH O HEART. MUAR IN THIS CA MEANS KILL, OR MURDE SLAY, IN FACT. HAUNS AK KARFARNAUM AT SUNJA M SAUBS KARAKAN-AN. "TO HUMBLE THE MONSTER ...ONE MUST HAVE..."
SUNJA MAUR...
"SUNJA MAUR..."
..."THE HEART OF A SLAYER."

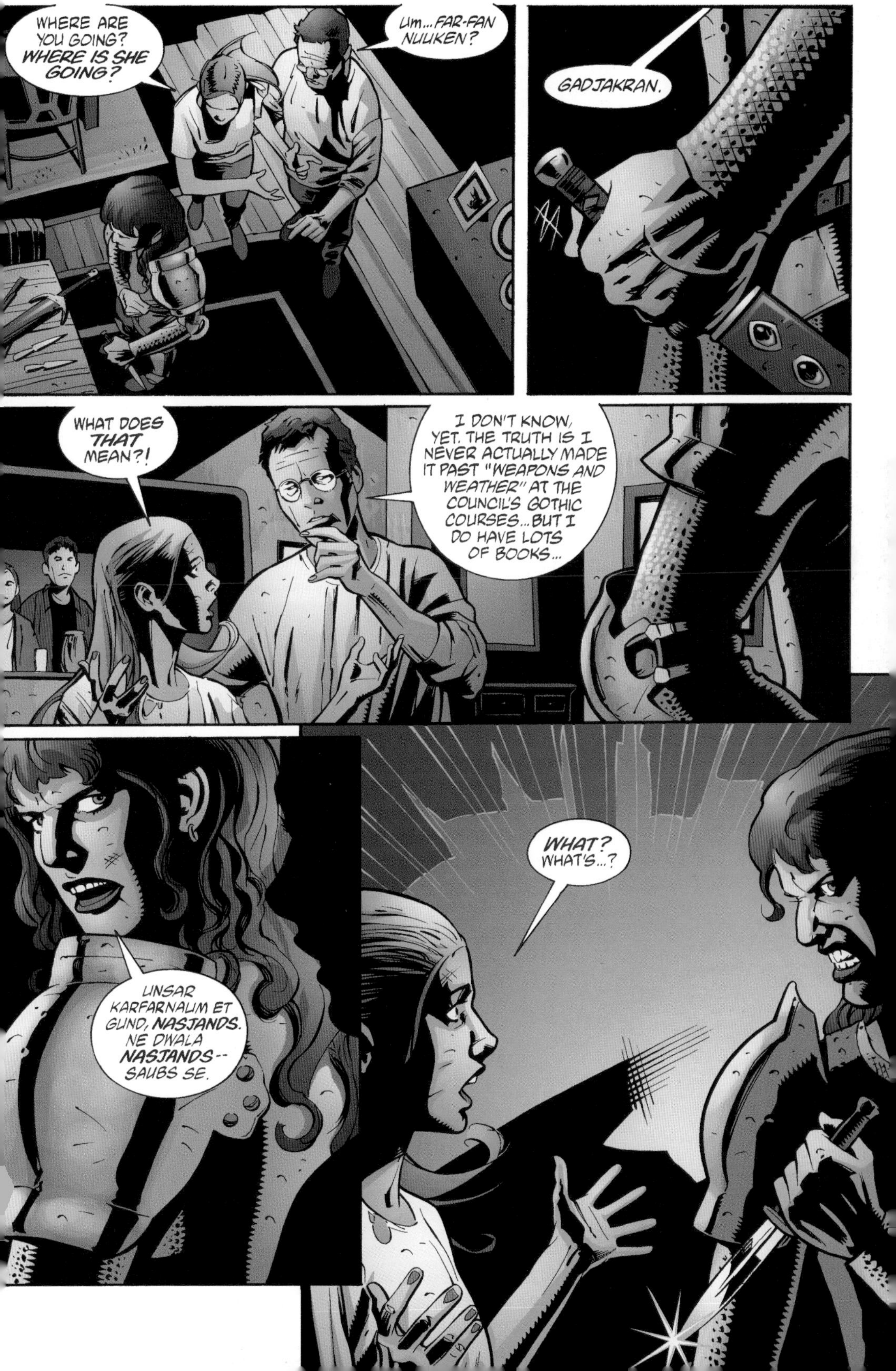
WHERE ARE YOU GOING? WHERE IS SHE GOING?
Um... FAR-FAN NUUKEN?
GADJAKRAN.
WHAT DOES THAT MEAN?!
I DON'T KNOW, YET. THE TRUTH IS I NEVER ACTUALLY MADE IT PAST "WEAPONS AND WEATHER" AT THE COUNCIL'S GOTHIC COURSES... BUT I DO HAVE LOTS OF BOOKS...
UNSAR KARFARNAUM ET GUND, NASJANDS. NE DWALA NASJANDS-- SAUBS SE.
WHAT? WHAT'S...?

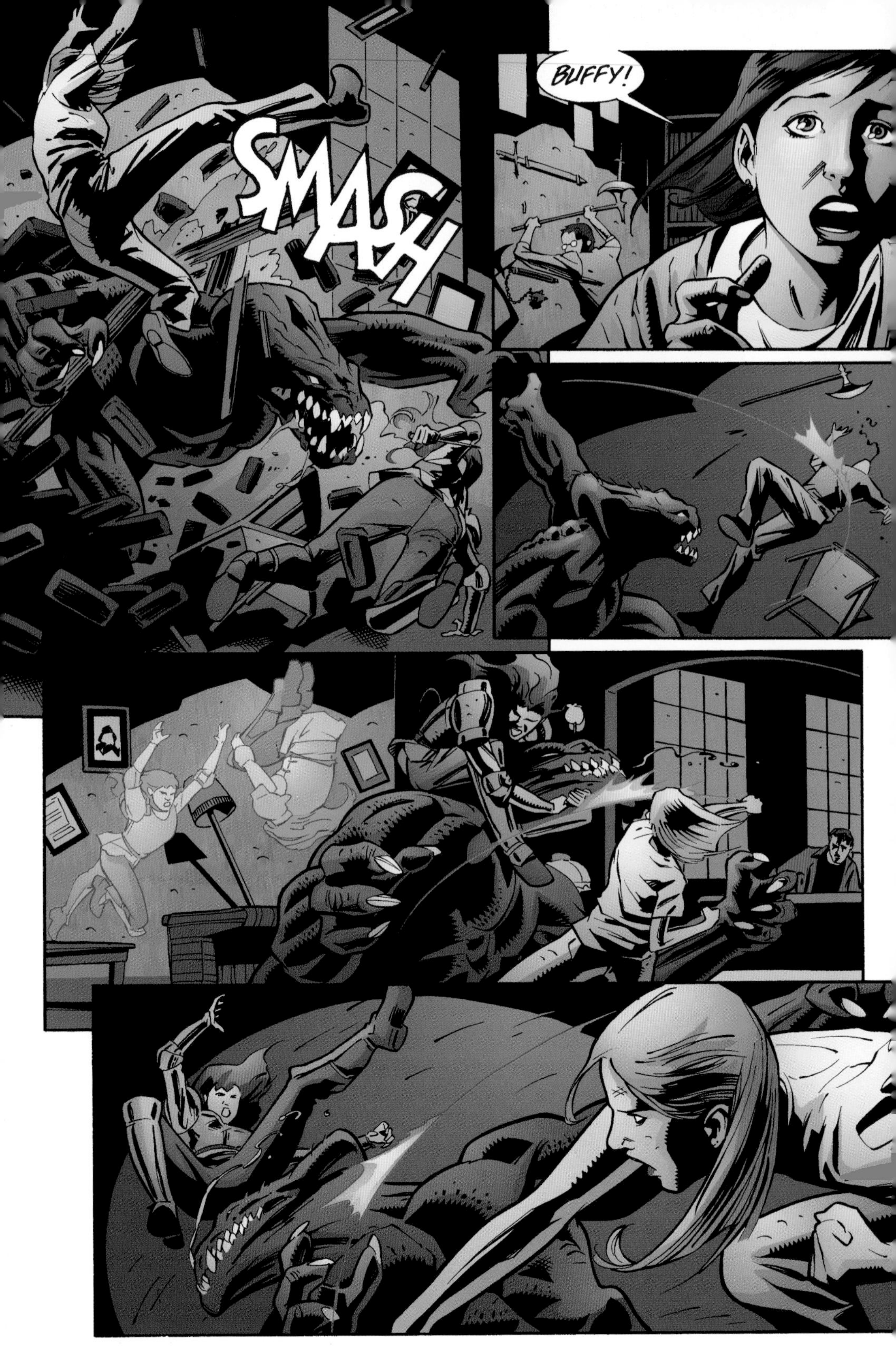
SMASH
BUFFY!

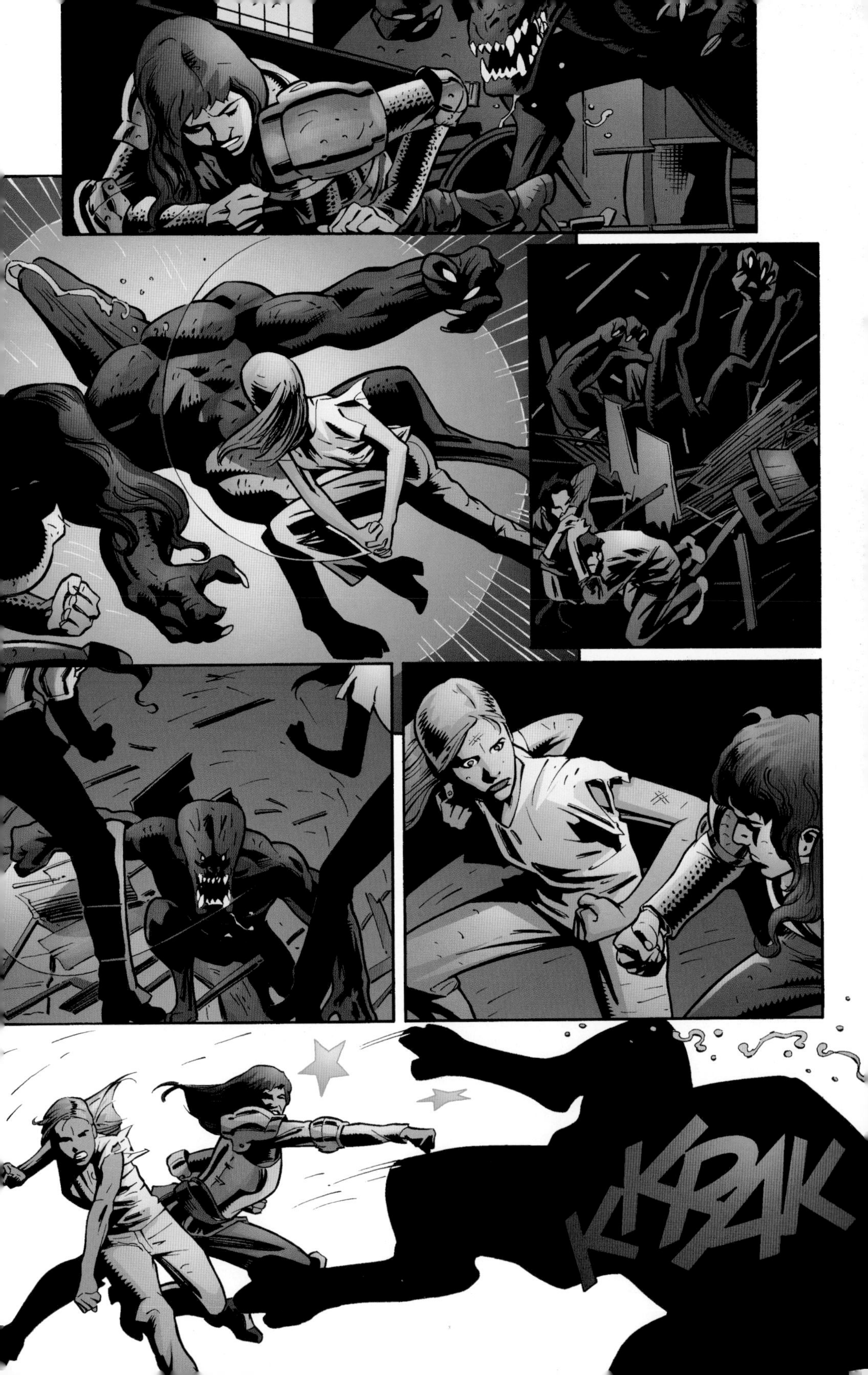
KKRAK

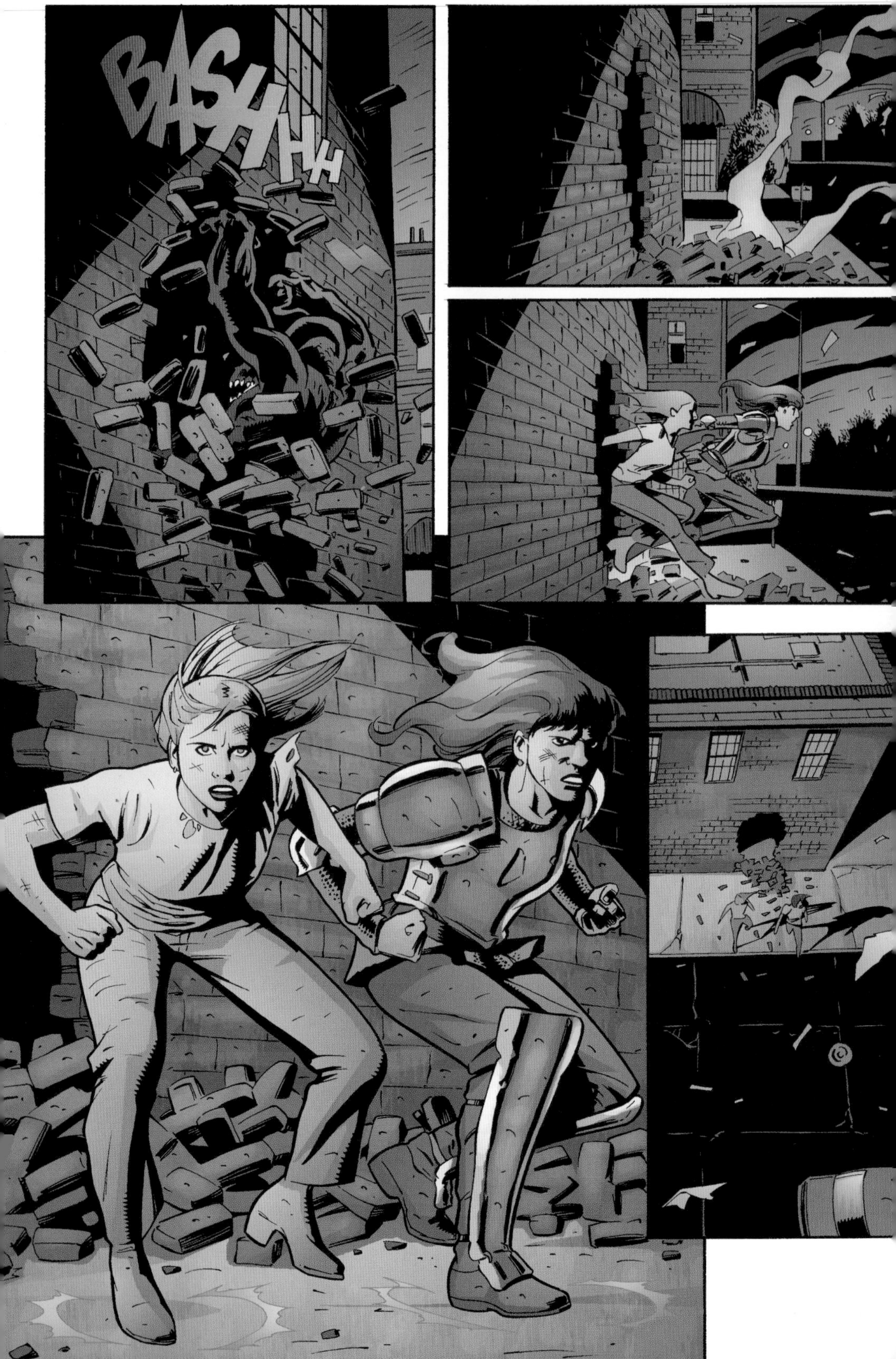
BASHHH

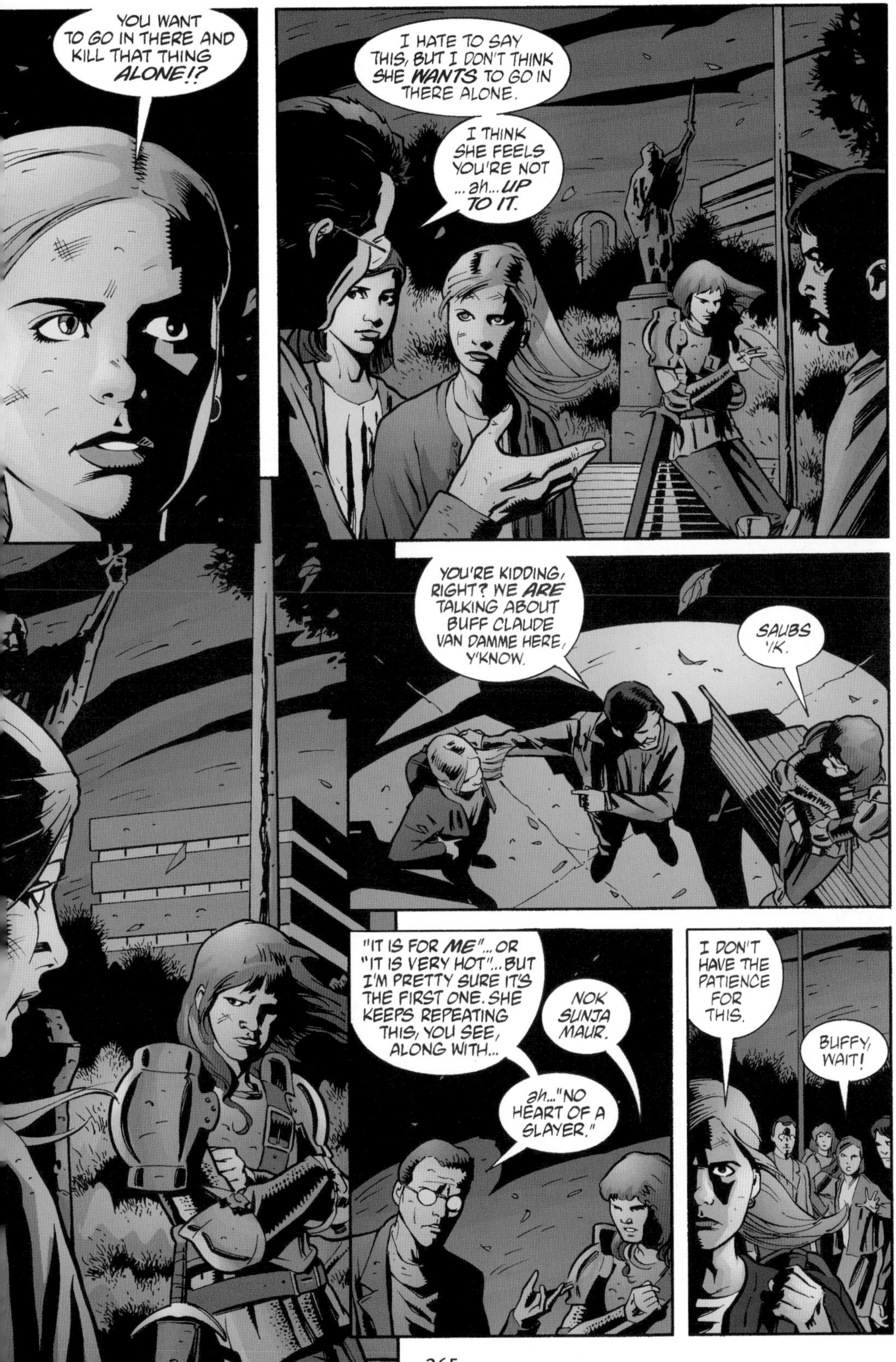
YOU WANT TO GO IN THERE AND KILL THAT THING ALONE!?
I HATE TO SAY THIS, BUT I DON'T THINK SHE WANTS TO GO IN THERE ALONE.
I THINK SHE FEELS YOU'RE NOT ...ah... UP TO IT.
YOU'RE KIDDING, RIGHT? WE ARE TALKING ABOUT BUFF CLAUDE VAN DAMME HERE, Y'KNOW.
SAUBS 'IK.
"IT IS FOR ME"... OR "IT IS VERY HOT"... BUT I'M PRETTY SURE IT'S THE FIRST ONE. SHE KEEPS REPEATING THIS, YOU SEE, ALONG WITH...
NOK SUNJA MAUR.
ah..."NO HEART OF A SLAYER."
I DON'T HAVE THE PATIENCE FOR THIS.
BUFFY, WAIT!

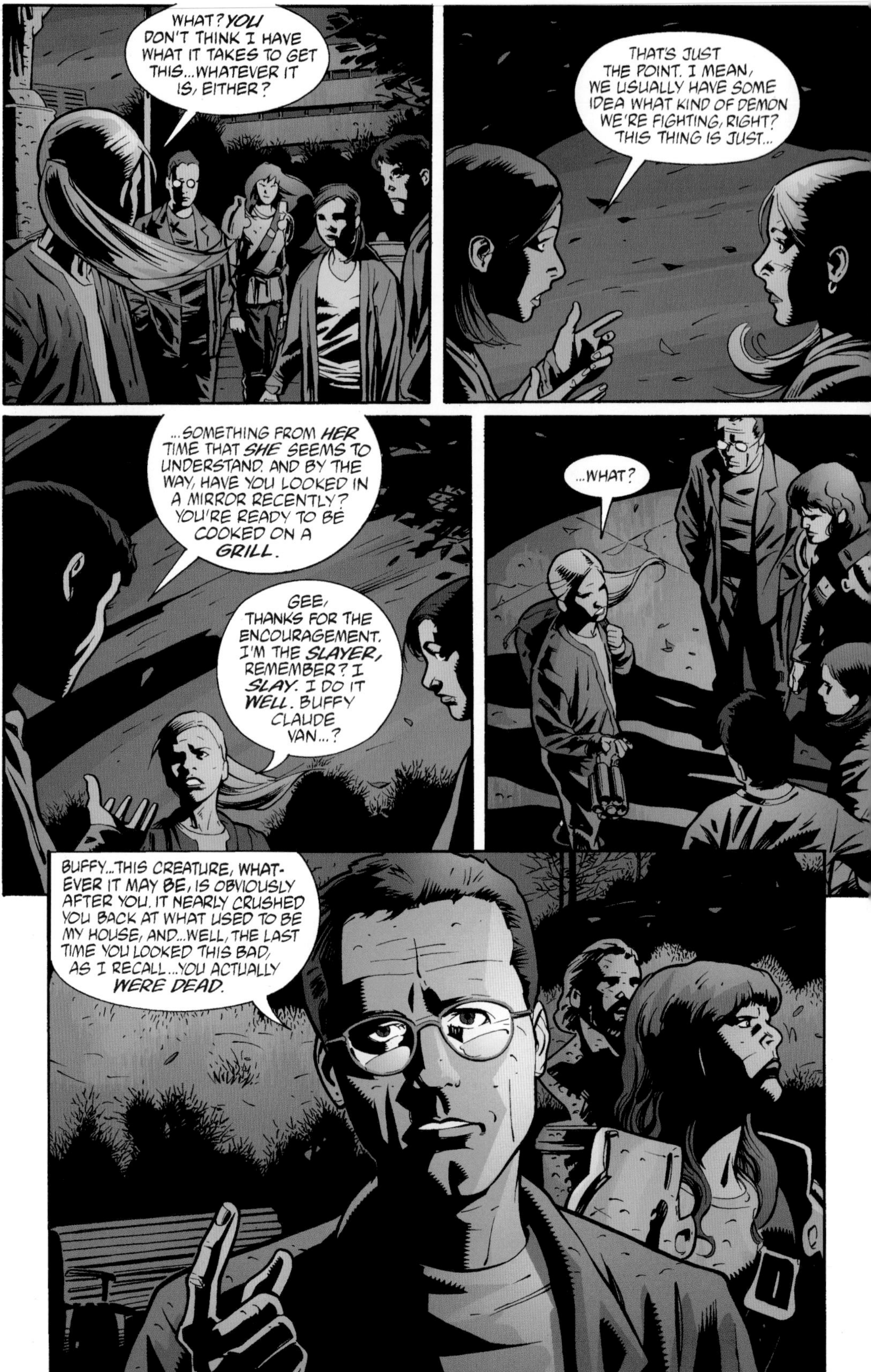
WHAT? YOU DON'T THINK I HAVE WHAT IT TAKES TO GET THIS...WHATEVER IT IS, EITHER?
THAT'S JUST THE POINT. I MEAN, WE USUALLY HAVE SOME IDEA WHAT KIND OF DEMON WE'RE FIGHTING, RIGHT? THIS THING IS JUST...
...SOMETHING FROM HER TIME THAT SHE SEEMS TO UNDERSTAND. AND BY THE WAY, HAVE YOU LOOKED IN A MIRROR RECENTLY? YOU'RE READY TO BE COOKED ON A GRILL.
GEE, THANKS FOR THE ENCOURAGEMENT. I'M THE SLAYER, REMEMBER? I SLAY. I DO IT WELL. BUFFY CLAUDE VAN...?
...WHAT?
BUFFY...THIS CREATURE, WHATEVER IT MAY BE, IS OBVIOUSLY AFTER YOU. IT NEARLY CRUSHED YOU BACK AT WHAT USED TO BE MY HOUSE, AND...WELL, THE LAST TIME YOU LOOKED THIS BAD, AS I RECALL...YOU ACTUALLY WERE DEAD.

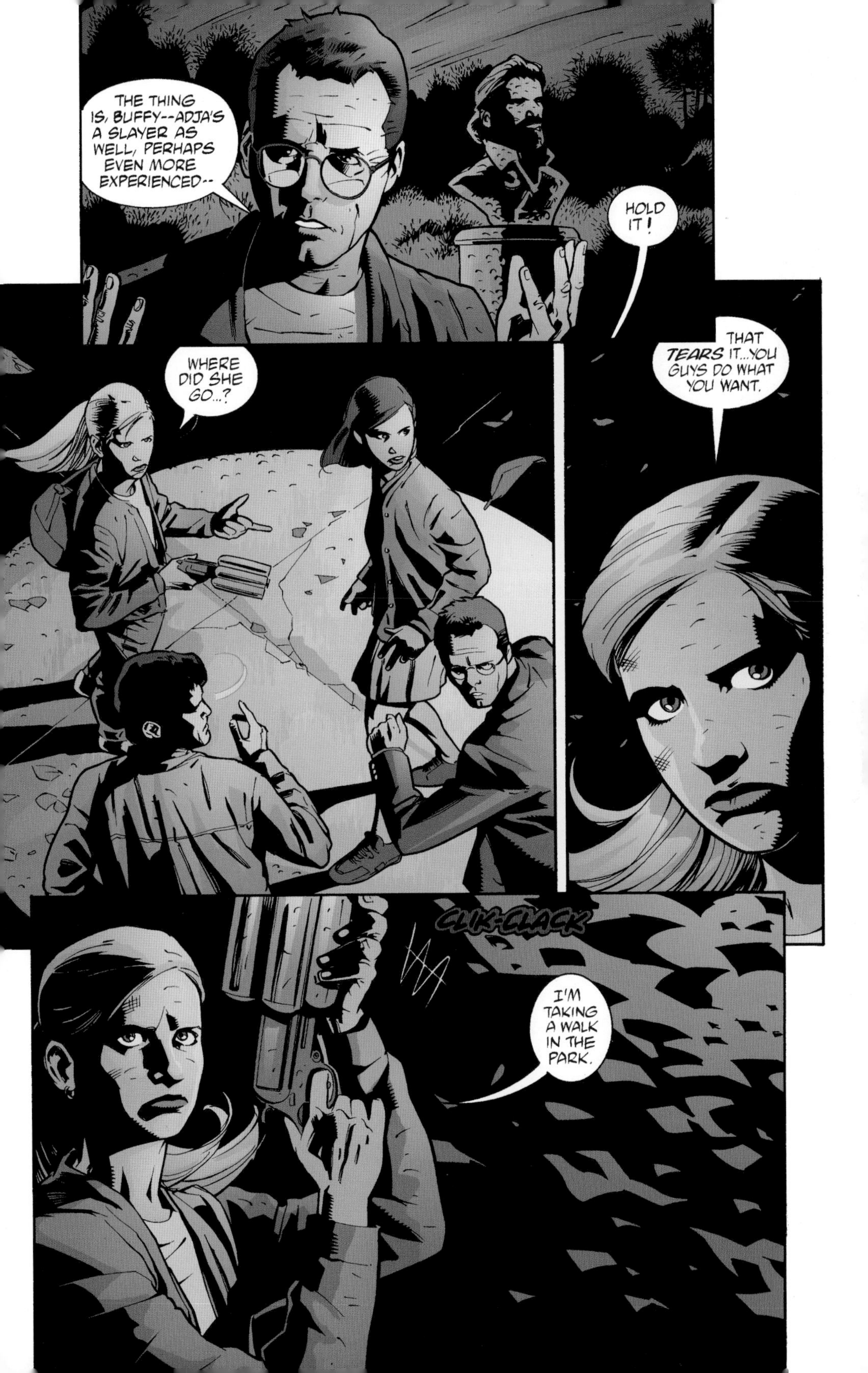
THE THING IS, BUFFY--ADJA'S A SLAYER AS WELL, PERHAPS EVEN MORE EXPERIENCED--
HOLD IT!
WHERE DID SHE GO...?
THAT *TEARS* IT...YOU GUYS DO WHAT YOU WANT.
CLIK-CLACK
I'M TAKING A WALK IN THE PARK.

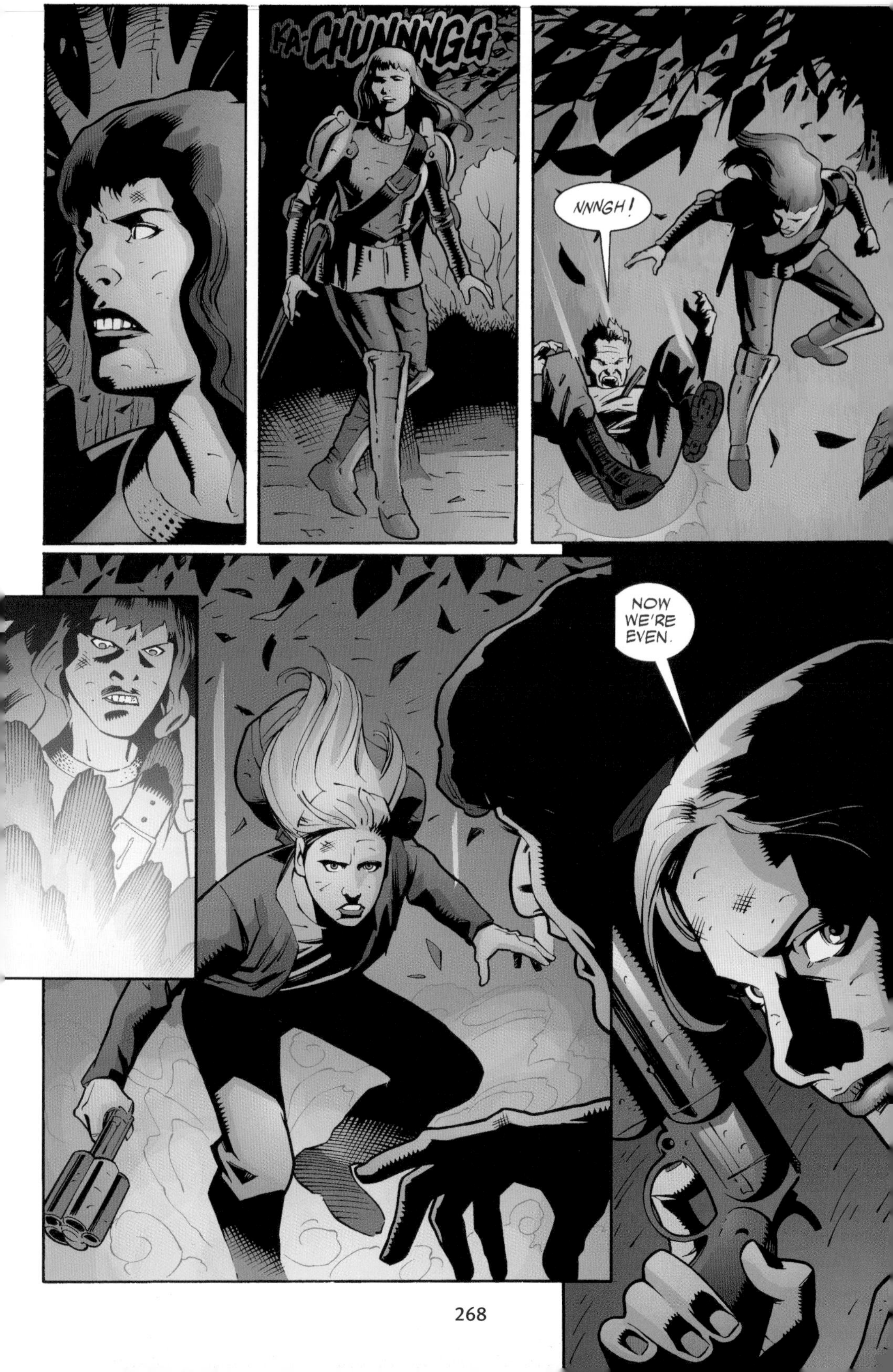
KA-CHUNNNGG
NNNGH!
NOW WE'RE EVEN.

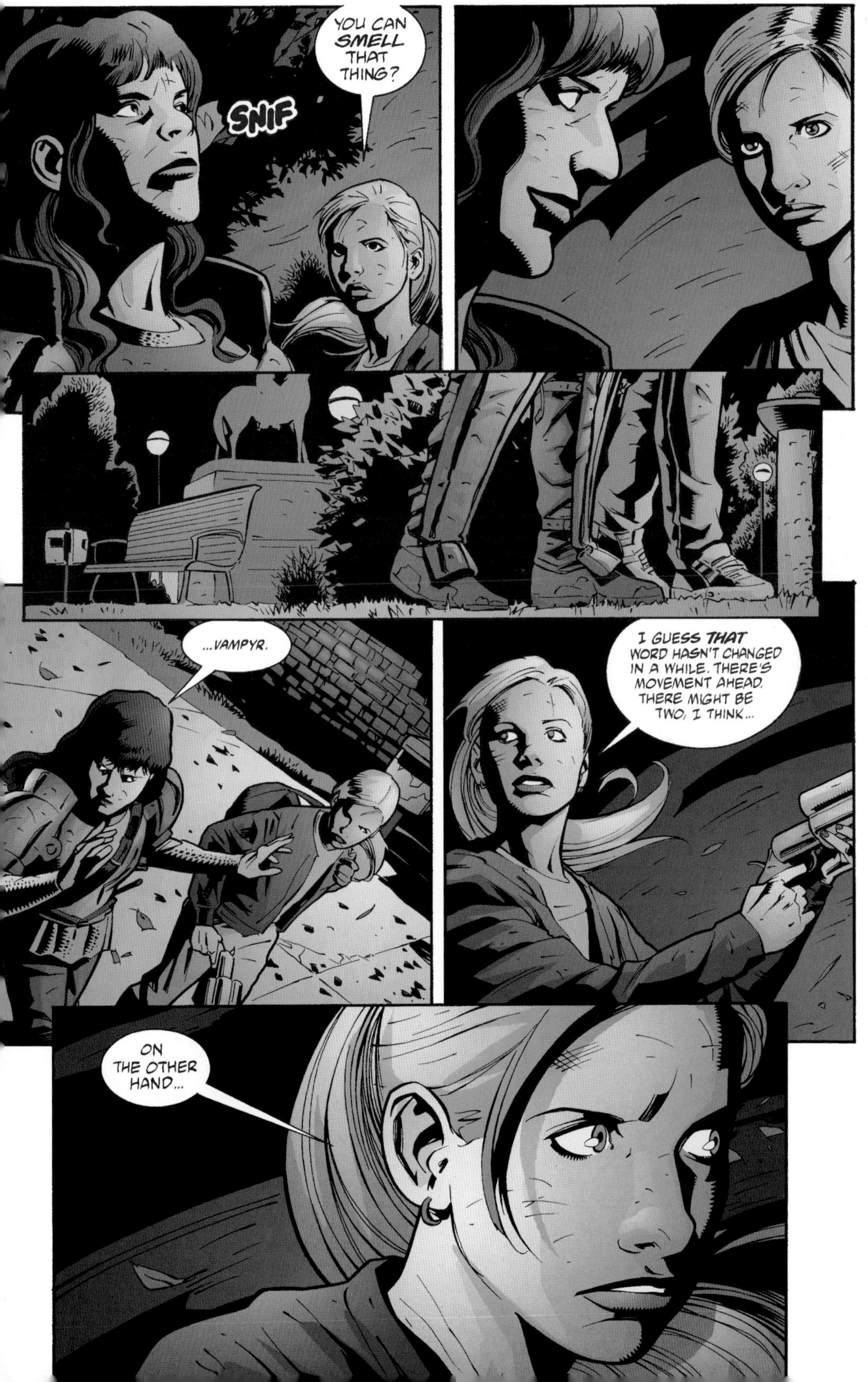

SNIF
YOU CAN SMELL THAT THING?
...VAMPYR.
I GUESS THAT WORD HASN'T CHANGED IN A WHILE. THERE'S MOVEMENT AHEAD. THERE MIGHT BE TWO, I THINK...
ON THE OTHER HAND...

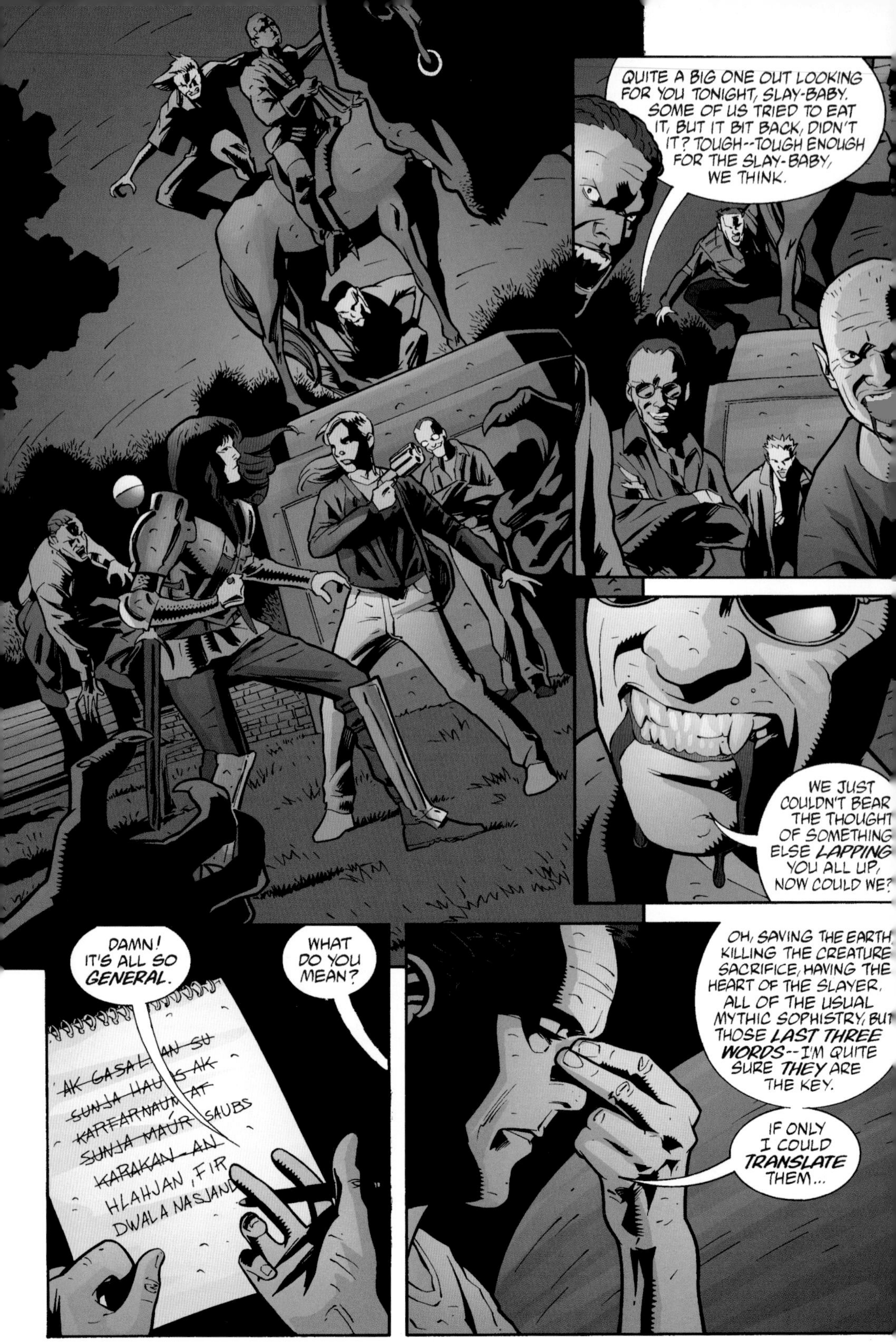

QUITE A BIG ONE OUT LOOKING FOR YOU TONIGHT, SLAY-BABY. SOME OF US TRIED TO EAT IT, BUT IT BIT BACK, DIDN'T IT? TOUGH--TOUGH ENOUGH FOR THE SLAY-BABY, WE THINK.
WE JUST COULDN'T BEAR THE THOUGHT OF SOMETHING ELSE LAPPING YOU ALL UP, NOW COULD WE?
DAMN! IT'S ALL SO GENERAL.
WHAT DO YOU MEAN?
AK GASAL-AN SU
SUNJA HAUBS AK
KARFARNAUM AF
SUNJA MAUR SAUBS
KARAKAN-AN
HLAHJAN, FIR
DWALA NASJAND
OH, SAVING THE EARTH, KILLING THE CREATURE, SACRIFICE, HAVING THE HEART OF THE SLAYER, ALL OF THE USUAL MYTHIC SOPHISTRY, BUT THOSE LAST THREE WORDS--I'M QUITE SURE THEY ARE THE KEY.
IF ONLY I COULD TRANSLATE THEM...

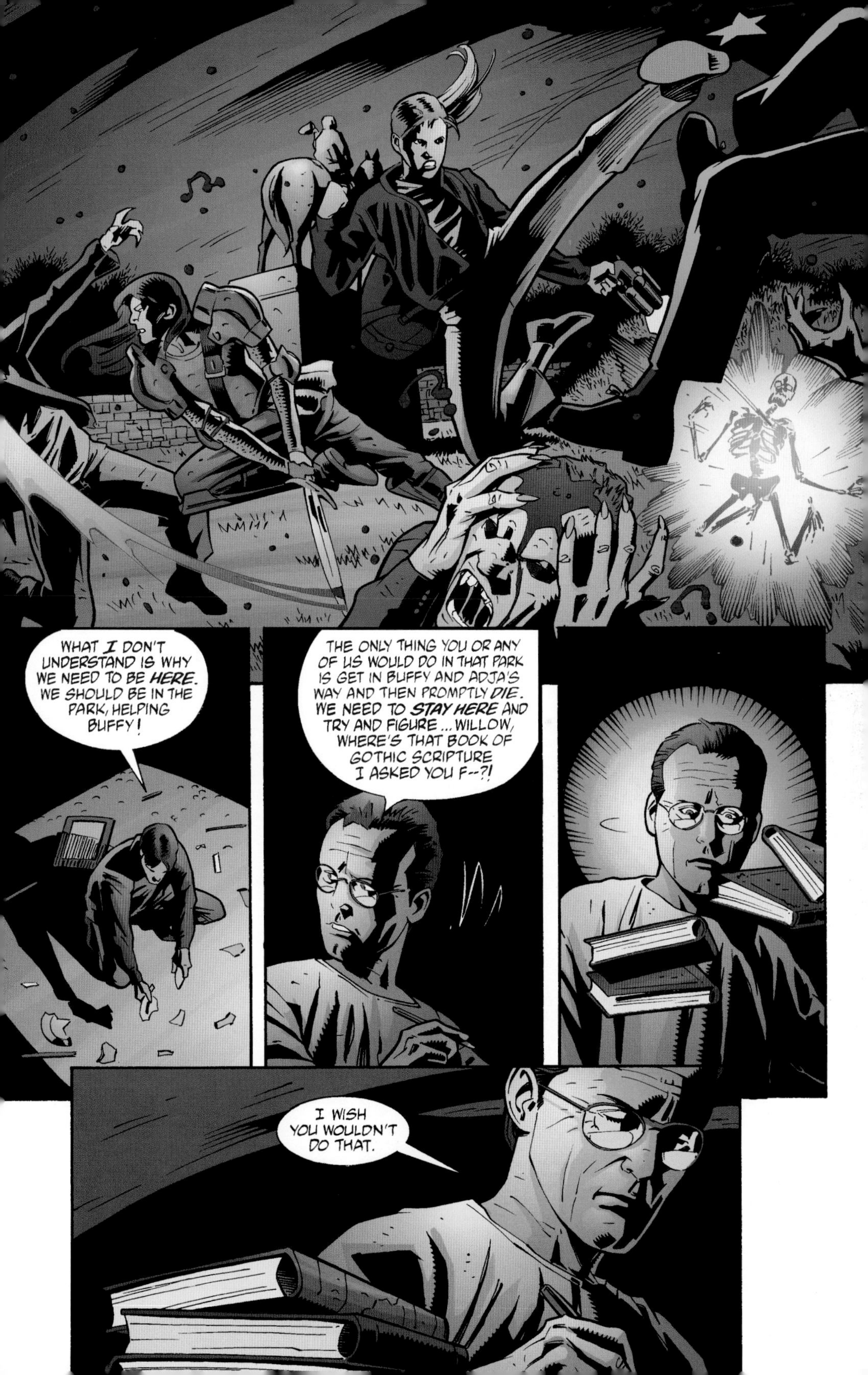
WHAT *I* DON'T UNDERSTAND IS WHY WE NEED TO BE *HERE*. WE SHOULD BE IN THE PARK, HELPING BUFFY!
THE ONLY THING YOU OR ANY OF US WOULD DO IN THAT PARK IS GET IN BUFFY AND ADJA'S WAY AND THEN PROMPTLY *DIE*. WE NEED TO *STAY HERE* AND TRY AND FIGURE ... WILLOW, WHERE'S THAT BOOK OF GOTHIC SCRIPTURE I ASKED YOU F--?!
I WISH YOU WOULDN'T DO THAT.

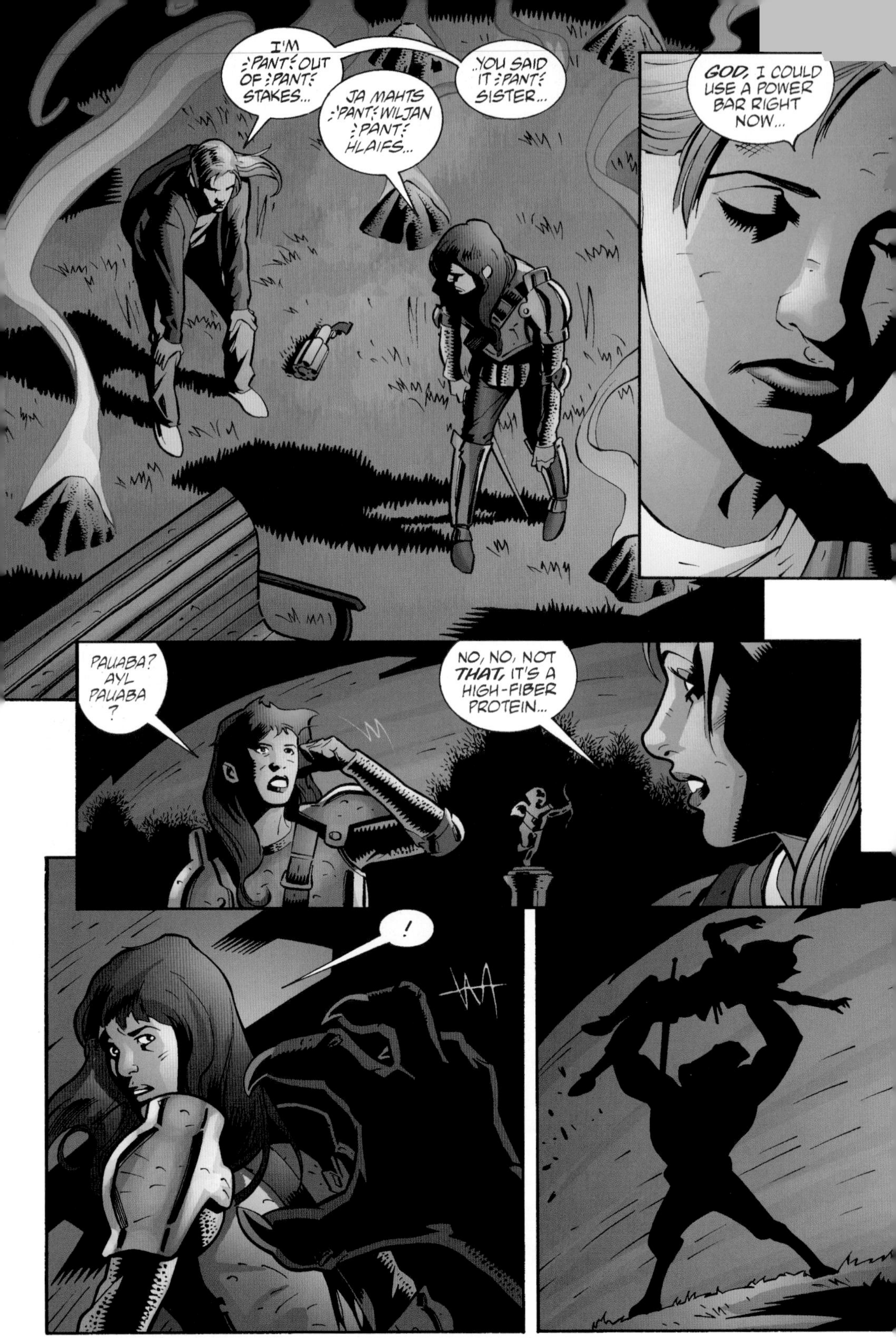
I'M :PANT: OUT OF :PANT: STAKES...
JA MAHTS :PANT: WILJAN :PANT: HLAIFS...
...YOU SAID IT :PANT: SISTER...
GOD, I COULD USE A POWER BAR RIGHT NOW...
PAUABA? AYL PAUABA ?
NO, NO, NOT THAT, IT'S A HIGH-FIBER PROTEIN...
!

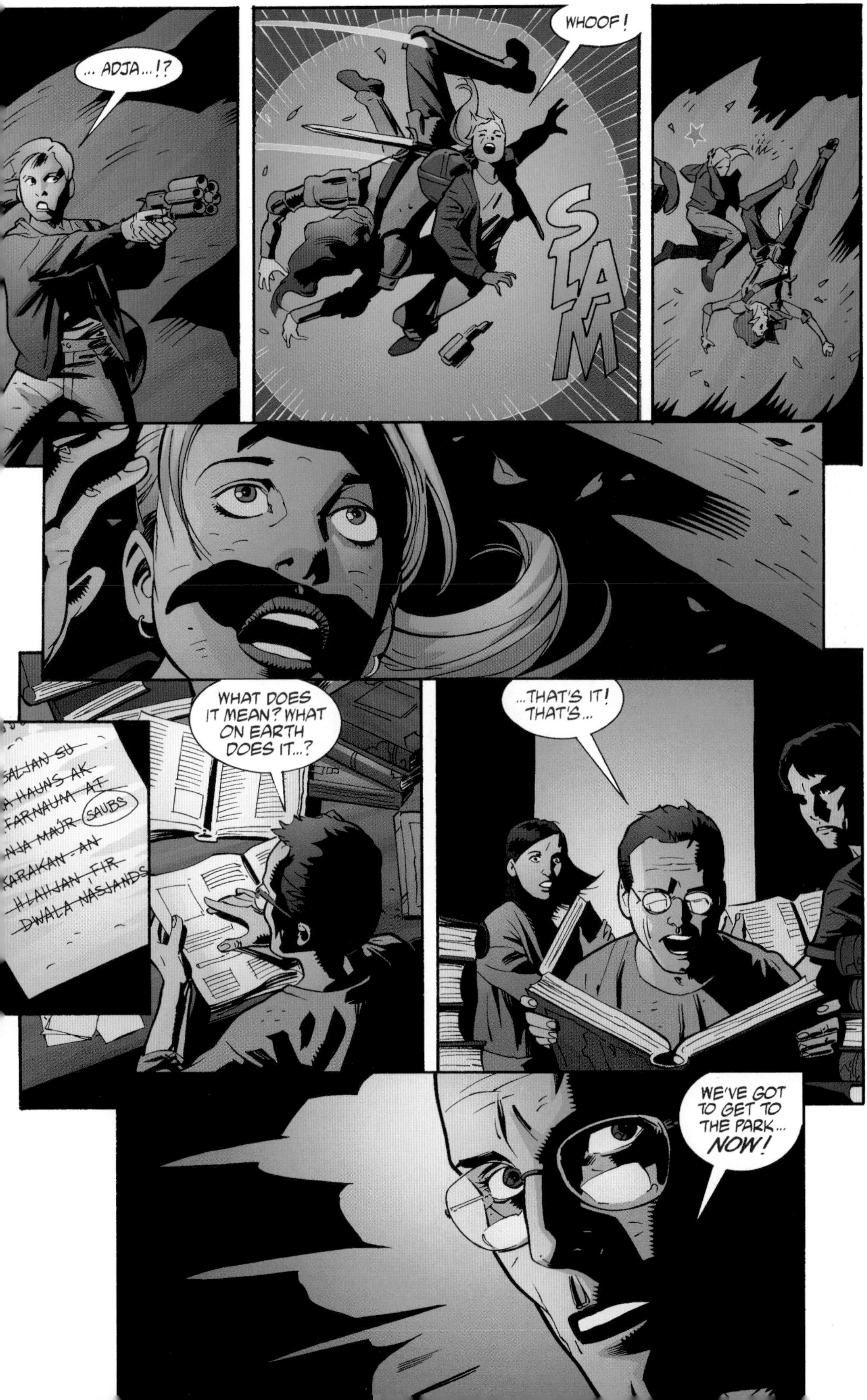

... ADJA...!?
WHOOF!
SLAM
ALJAN SU
A HAUNS AK
FARNAUM AF
NJA MAÚR
SAUBS
KARAKAN AN
HLAIHJAN FIR
DWALA NASJANDS
WHAT DOES IT MEAN? WHAT ON EARTH DOES IT...?
...THAT'S IT! THAT'S...
WE'VE GOT TO GET TO THE PARK... NOW!

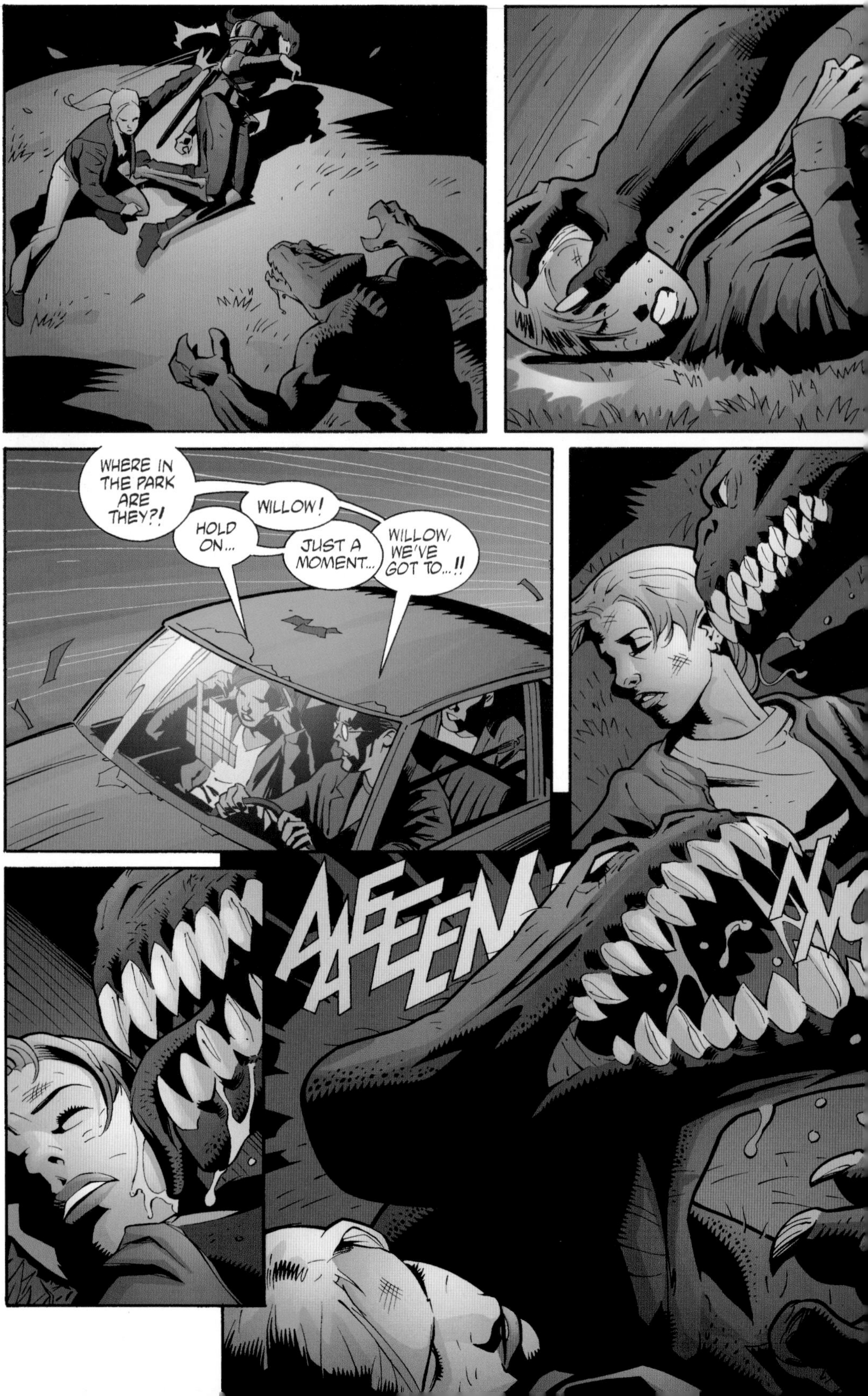
WHERE IN THE PARK ARE THEY?!
WILLOW!
HOLD ON...
JUST A MOMENT...
WILLOW, WE'VE GOT TO...!!

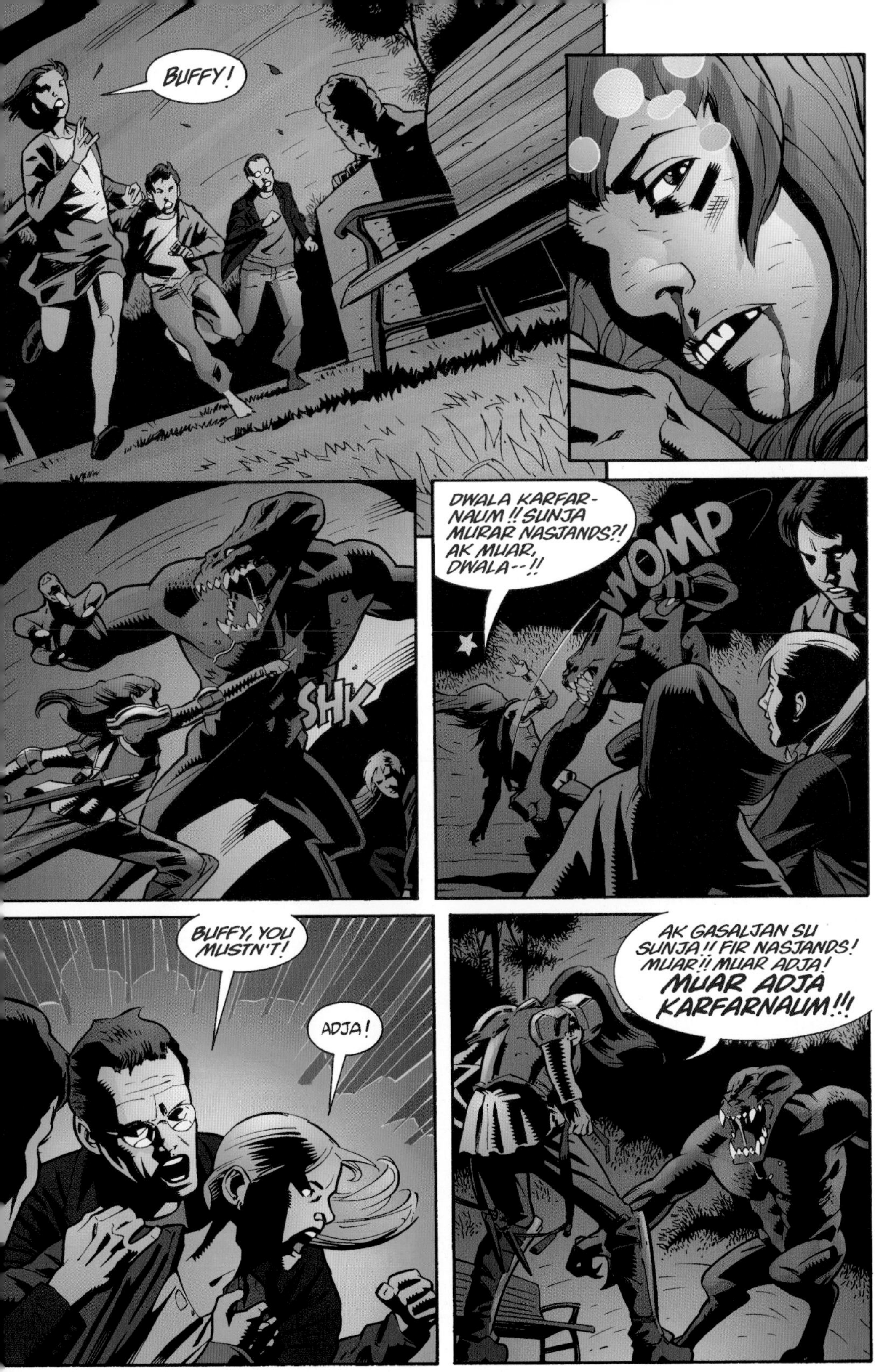
BUFFY!
DWALA KARFAR-NAUM!! SUNJA MURAR NASJANDS?! AK MUAR, DWALA--!!
WOMP
SHK
BUFFY, YOU MUSTN'T!
ADJA!
AK GASALJAN SU SUNJA!! FIR NASJANDS! MUAR!! MUAR ADJA! MUAR ADJA KARFARNAUM!!!

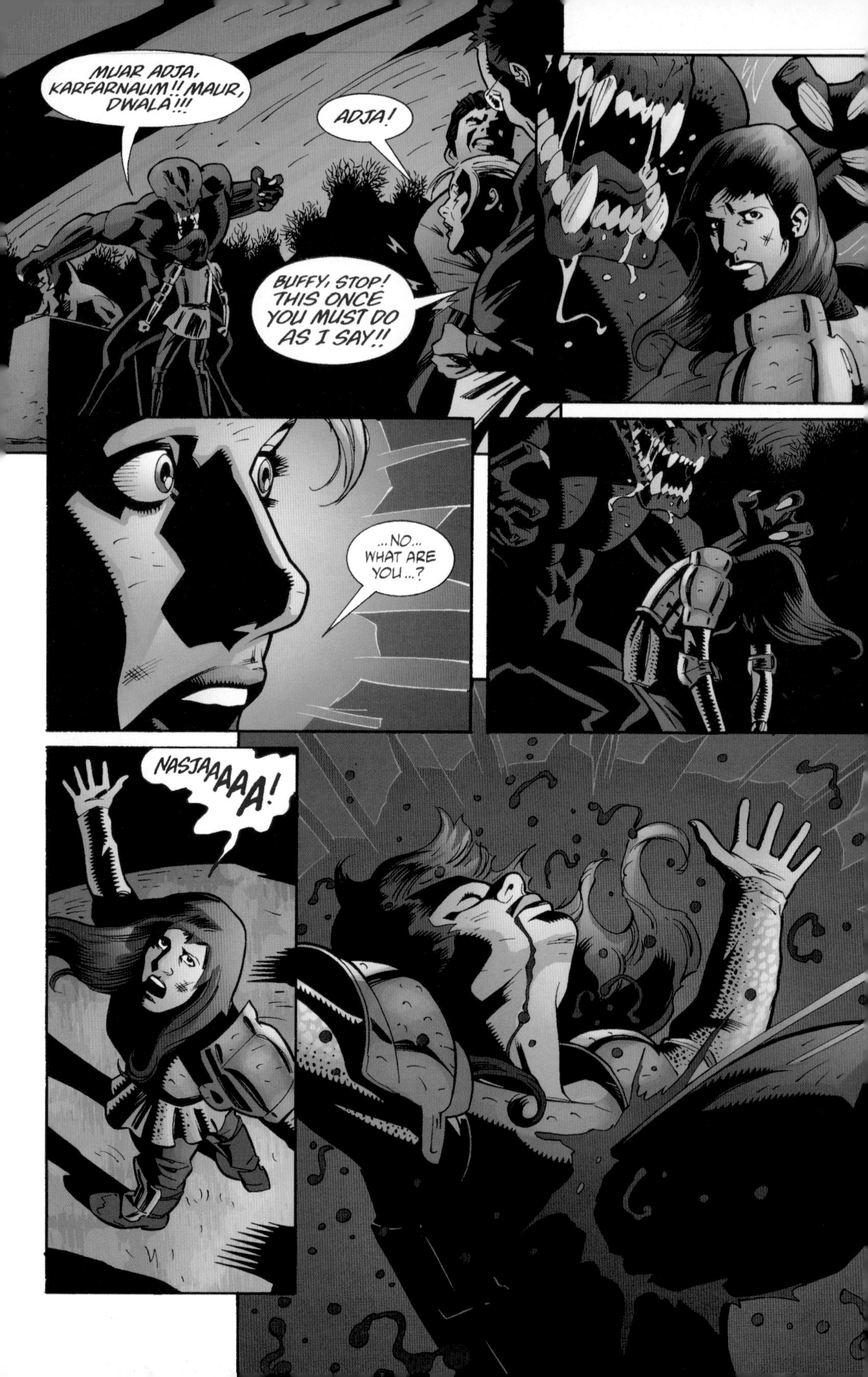
MUAR ADJA, KARFARNAUM!! MAUR, DWALA!!!
ADJA!
BUFFY, STOP! THIS ONCE YOU MUST DO AS I SAY!!
...NO... WHAT ARE YOU...?
NASJAAAAA!

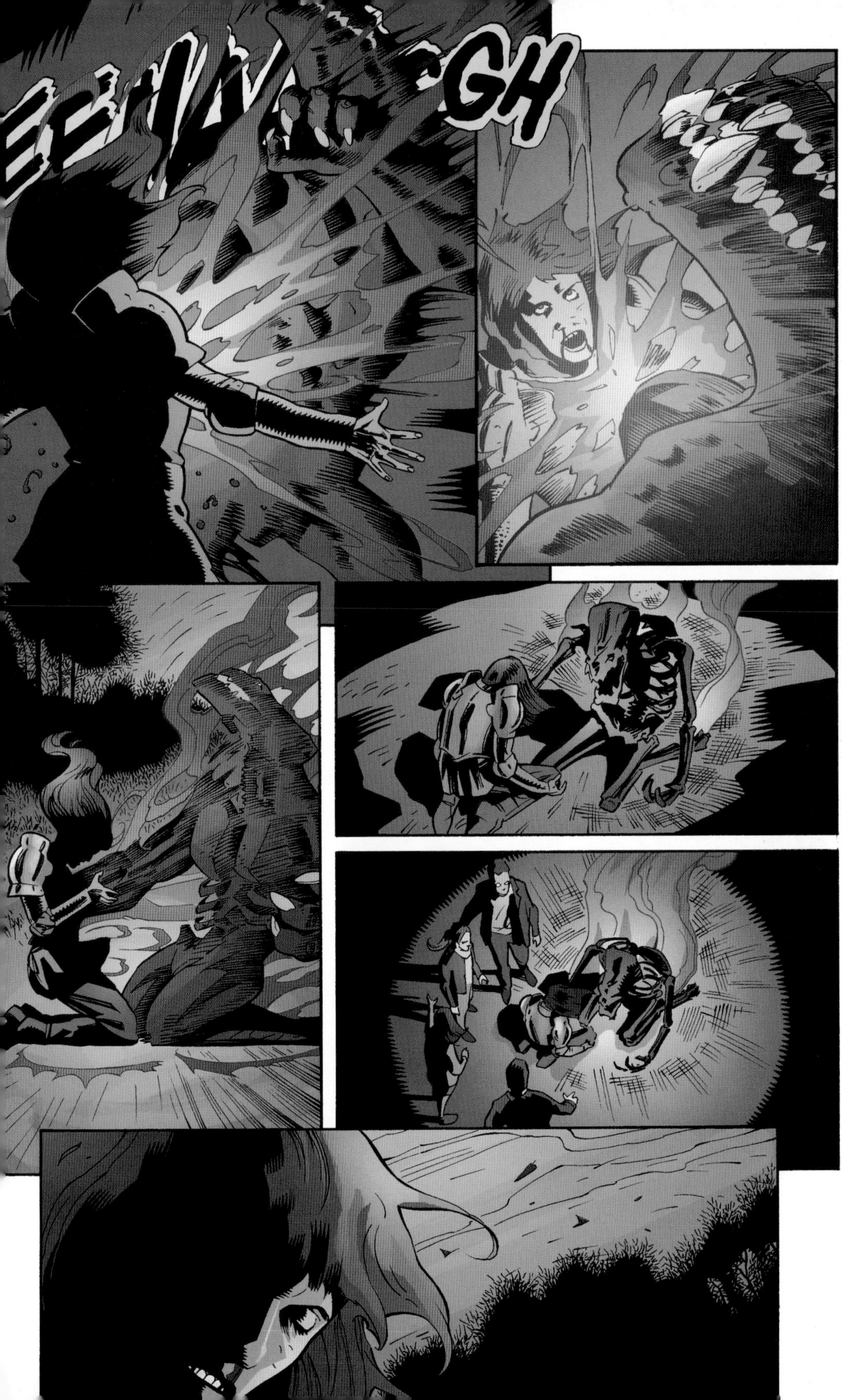
GH

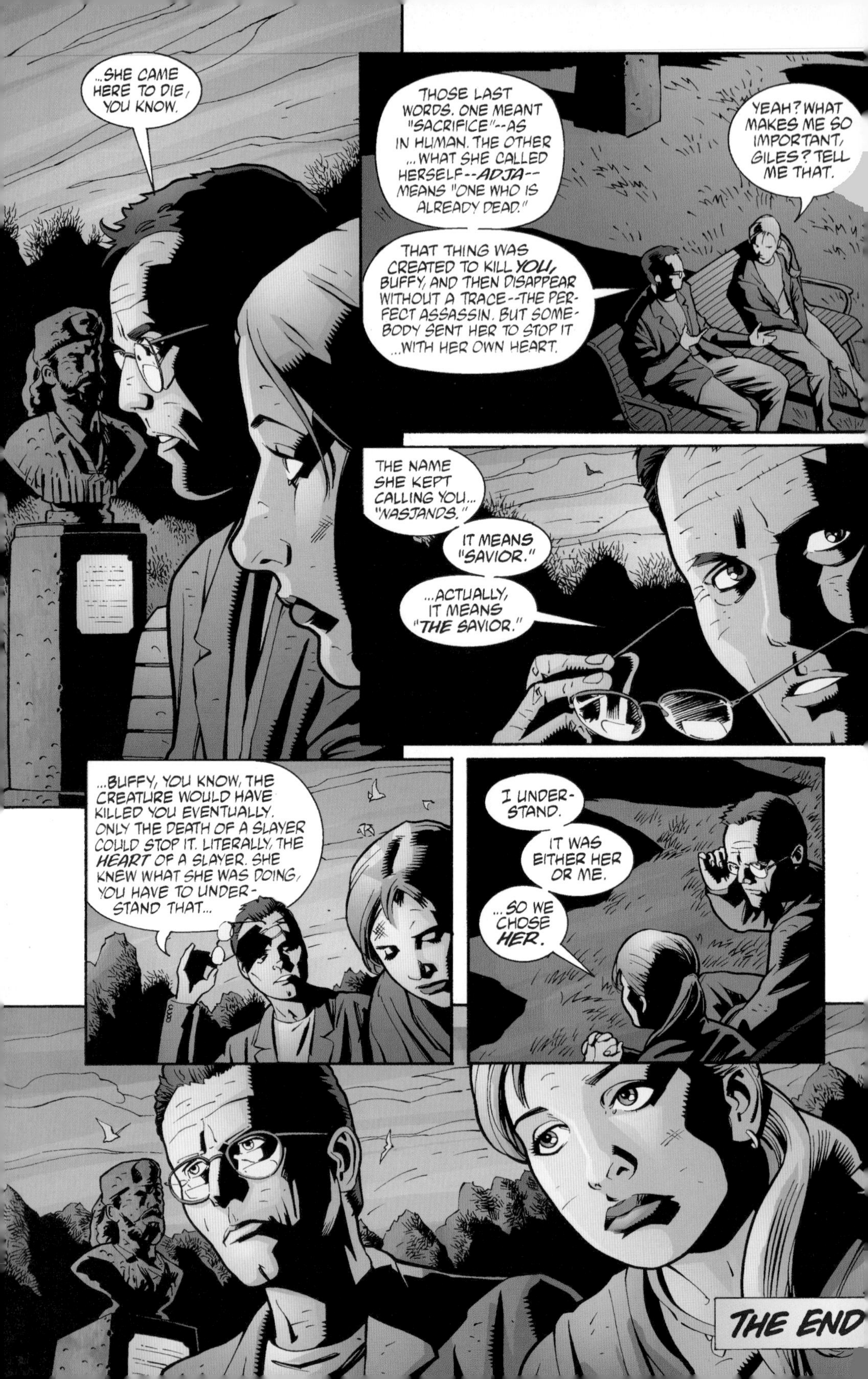
...SHE CAME HERE TO DIE, YOU KNOW.
THOSE LAST WORDS. ONE MEANT "SACRIFICE"--AS IN HUMAN. THE OTHER ...WHAT SHE CALLED HERSELF--ADJA--MEANS "ONE WHO IS ALREADY DEAD."
THAT THING WAS CREATED TO KILL YOU, BUFFY, AND THEN DISAPPEAR WITHOUT A TRACE--THE PERFECT ASSASSIN. BUT SOMEBODY SENT HER TO STOP IT ...WITH HER OWN HEART.
YEAH? WHAT MAKES ME SO IMPORTANT, GILES? TELL ME THAT.
THE NAME SHE KEPT CALLING YOU... "NASJANDS."
IT MEANS "SAVIOR."
...ACTUALLY, IT MEANS "THE SAVIOR."
...BUFFY, YOU KNOW, THE CREATURE WOULD HAVE KILLED YOU EVENTUALLY. ONLY THE DEATH OF A SLAYER COULD STOP IT. LITERALLY, THE HEART OF A SLAYER. SHE KNEW WHAT SHE WAS DOING, YOU HAVE TO UNDERSTAND THAT...
I UNDERSTAND.
IT WAS EITHER HER OR ME.
...SO WE CHOSE HER.
THE END

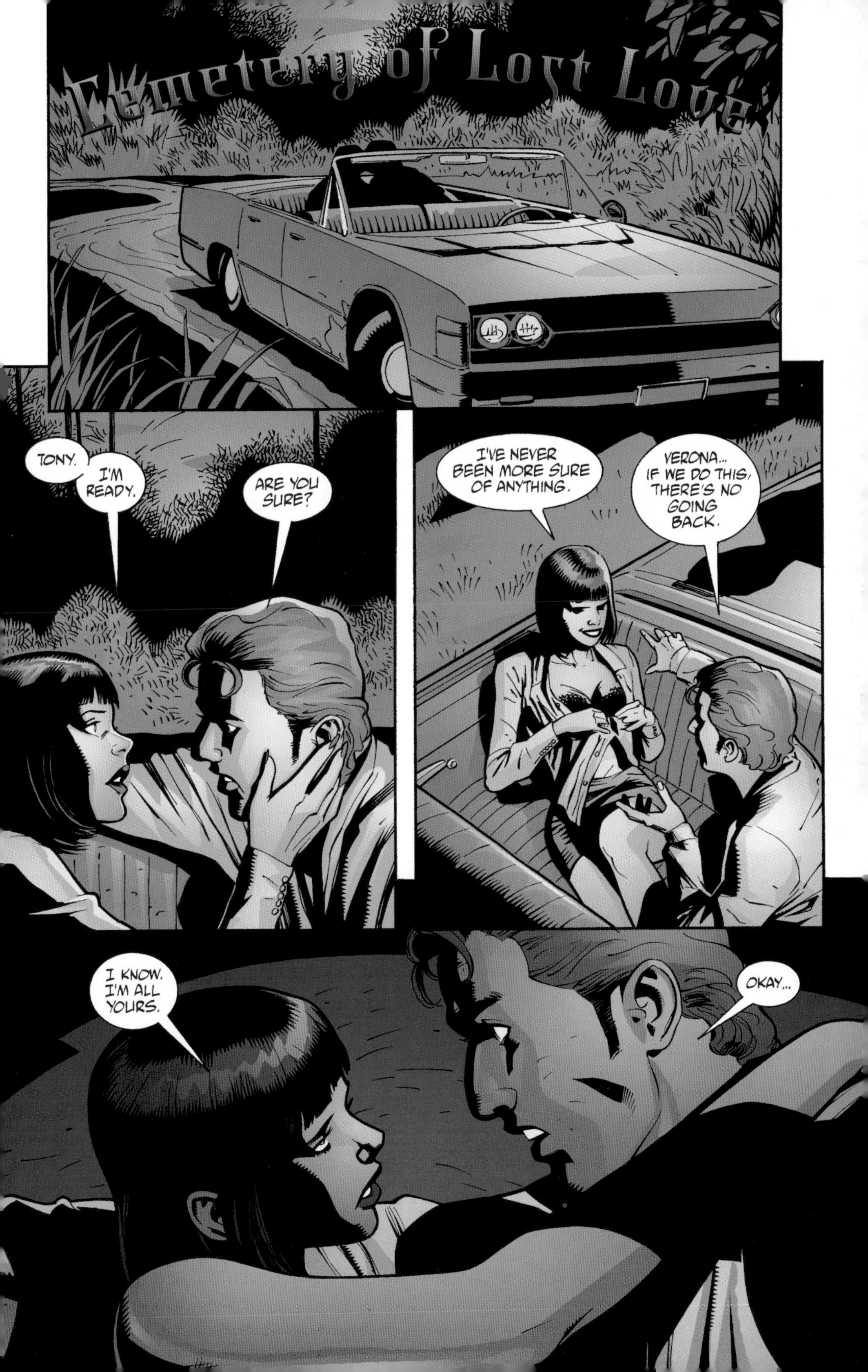
Cemetery of Lost Love
TONY.
I'M READY.
ARE YOU SURE?
I'VE NEVER BEEN MORE SURE OF ANYTHING.
VERONA... IF WE DO THIS, THERE'S NO GOING BACK.
I KNOW. I'M ALL YOURS.
OKAY...

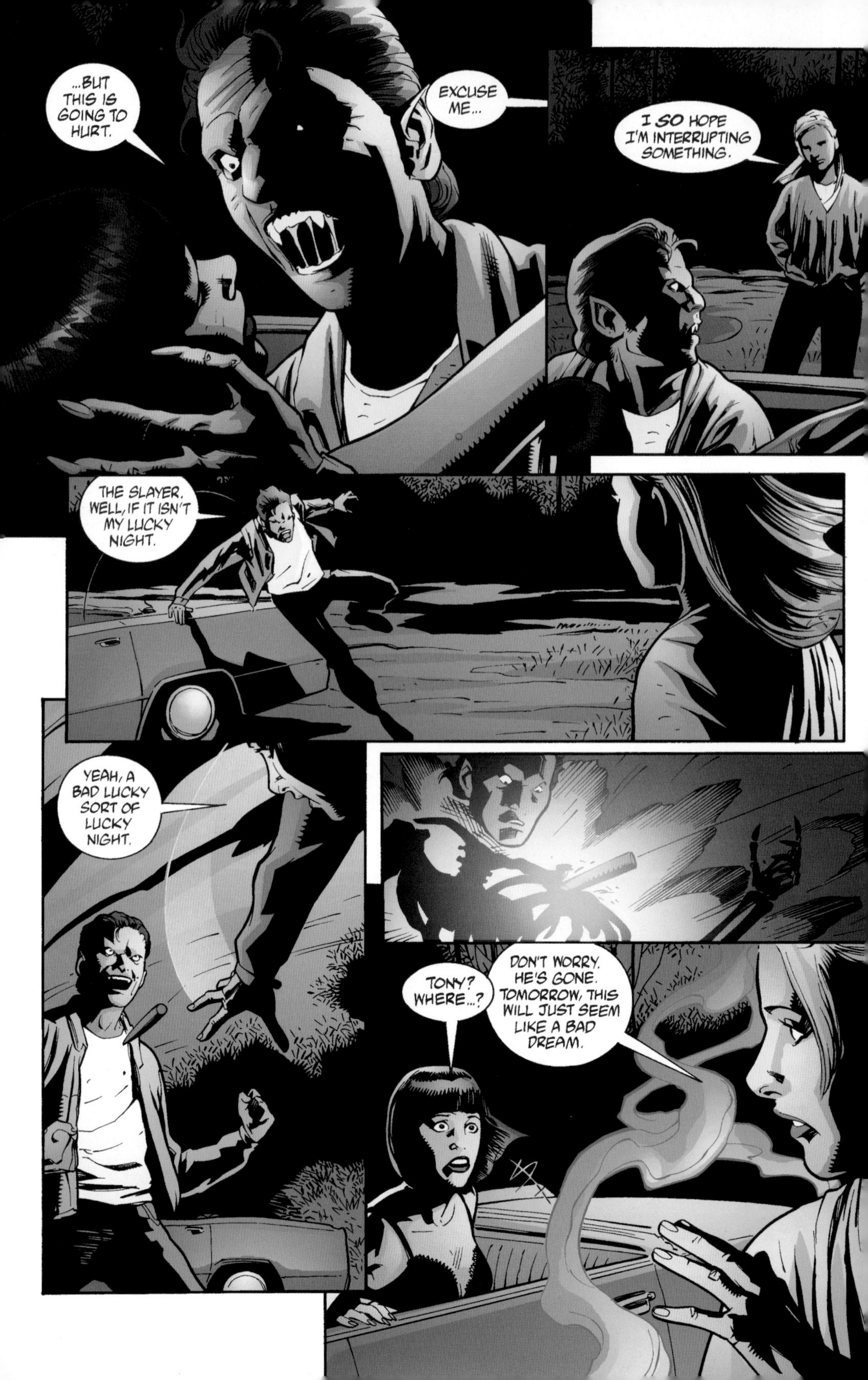
...BUT THIS IS GOING TO HURT.
EXCUSE ME...
I SO HOPE I'M INTERRUPTING SOMETHING.
THE SLAYER. WELL, IF IT ISN'T MY LUCKY NIGHT.
YEAH, A BAD LUCKY SORT OF LUCKY NIGHT.
TONY? WHERE...?
DON'T WORRY. HE'S GONE. TOMORROW, THIS WILL JUST SEEM LIKE A BAD DREAM.

YOU OKAY, WILL?

...WHAT?

I WAS JUST TELLING YOU ABOUT MY ADVENTURE LAST NIGHT. BUT IT'S NO BIG DEAL.

SORRY, I GUESS I'M A LITTLE DISTRACTED.

MISSING OZ, HUH?

IS IT THAT OBVIOUS?

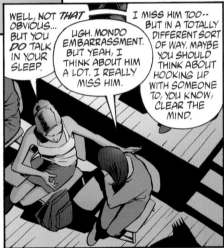

WELL, NOT *THAT* OBVIOUS... BUT YOU *DO* TALK IN YOUR SLEEP.

UGH. MONDO EMBARRASSMENT. BUT YEAH, I THINK ABOUT HIM A LOT. I REALLY MISS HIM.

I MISS HIM TOO-- BUT IN A TOTALLY DIFFERENT SORT OF WAY. MAYBE YOU SHOULD THINK ABOUT HOOKING UP WITH SOMEONE TO, YOU KNOW, CLEAR THE MIND.

OH SURE, THAT'S EASY FOR YOU TO SAY NOW THAT YOU AND RILEY ARE GIVING EACH OTHER WARM FUZZIES.

ALL WE'VE DONE IS KISS...

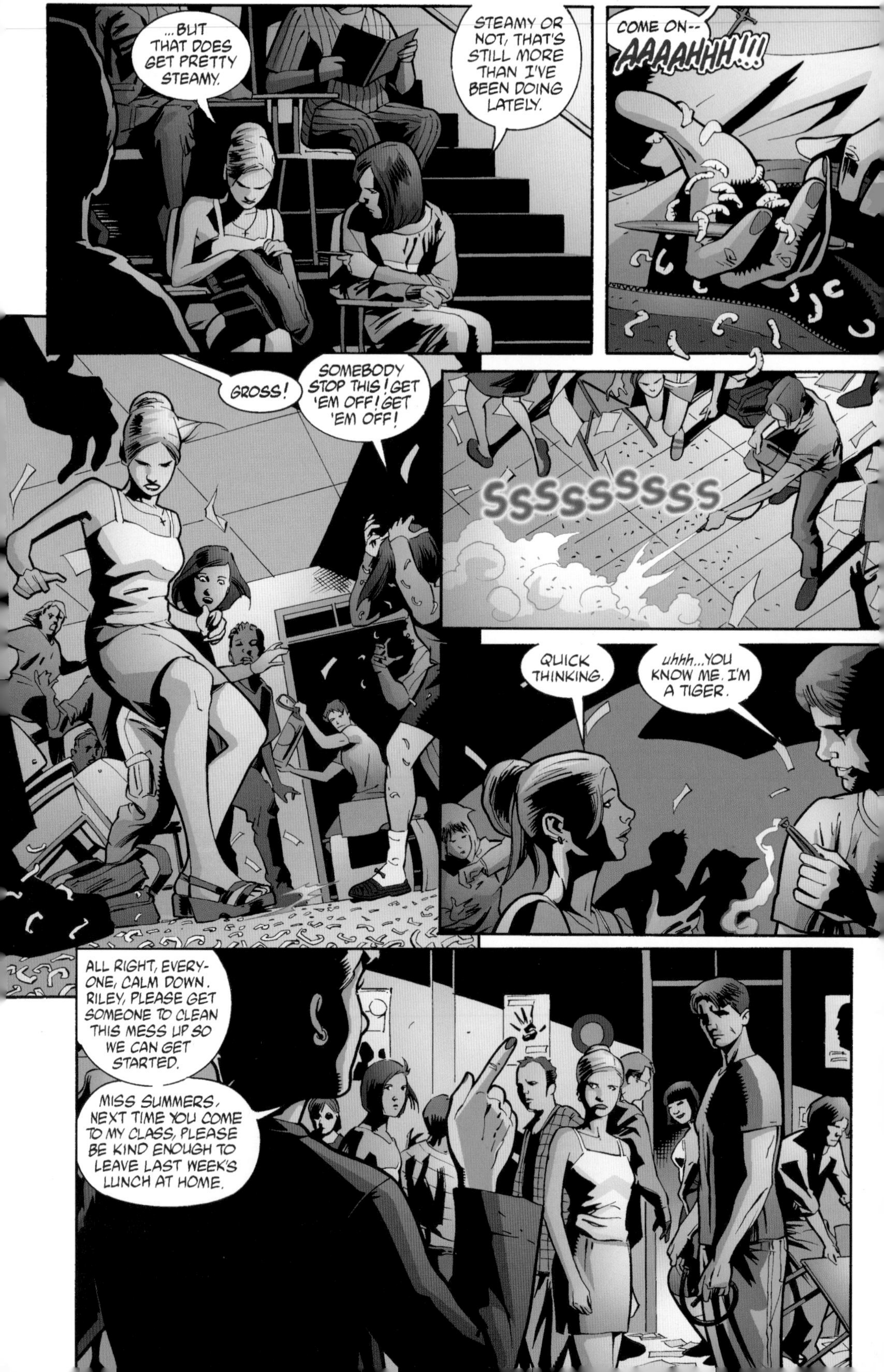
...BUT THAT DOES GET PRETTY STEAMY.
STEAMY OR NOT, THAT'S STILL MORE THAN I'VE BEEN DOING LATELY.
COME ON--
AAAAHHH!!!
GROSS!
SOMEBODY STOP THIS! GET 'EM OFF! GET 'EM OFF!
SSSSSSSSS
QUICK THINKING.
uhhh...YOU KNOW ME. I'M A TIGER.
ALL RIGHT, EVERYONE, CALM DOWN. RILEY, PLEASE GET SOMEONE TO CLEAN THIS MESS UP SO WE CAN GET STARTED.
MISS SUMMERS, NEXT TIME YOU COME TO MY CLASS, PLEASE BE KIND ENOUGH TO LEAVE LAST WEEK'S LUNCH AT HOME.

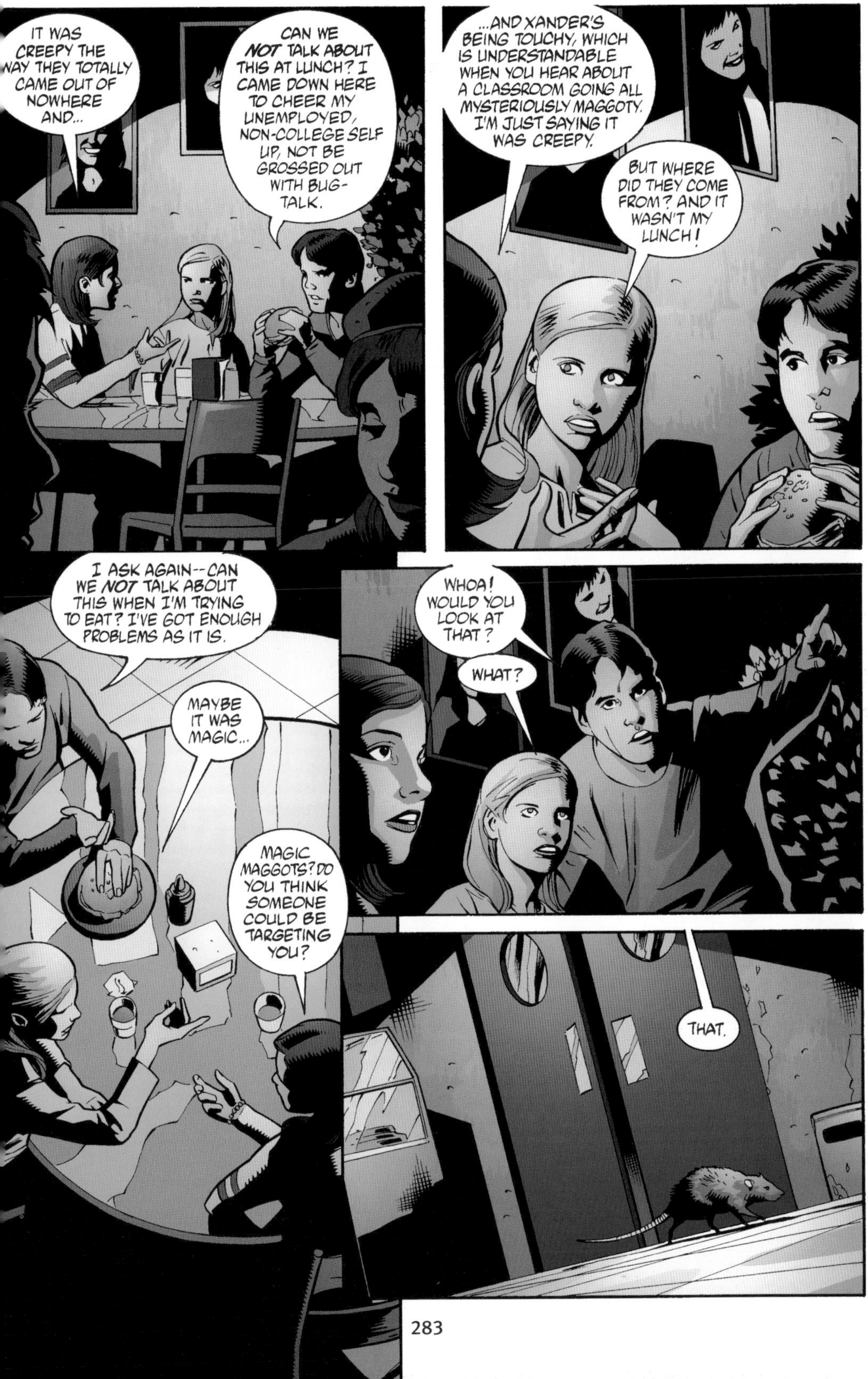
IT WAS CREEPY THE WAY THEY TOTALLY CAME OUT OF NOWHERE AND...
CAN WE NOT TALK ABOUT THIS AT LUNCH? I CAME DOWN HERE TO CHEER MY UNEMPLOYED, NON-COLLEGE SELF UP, NOT BE GROSSED OUT WITH BUG-TALK.
...AND XANDER'S BEING TOUCHY, WHICH IS UNDERSTANDABLE WHEN YOU HEAR ABOUT A CLASSROOM GOING ALL MYSTERIOUSLY MAGGOTY. I'M JUST SAYING IT WAS CREEPY.
BUT WHERE DID THEY COME FROM? AND IT WASN'T MY LUNCH!
I ASK AGAIN--CAN WE NOT TALK ABOUT THIS WHEN I'M TRYING TO EAT? I'VE GOT ENOUGH PROBLEMS AS IT IS.
MAYBE IT WAS MAGIC...
MAGIC MAGGOTS? DO YOU THINK SOMEONE COULD BE TARGETING YOU?
WHOA! WOULD YOU LOOK AT THAT?
WHAT?
THAT.

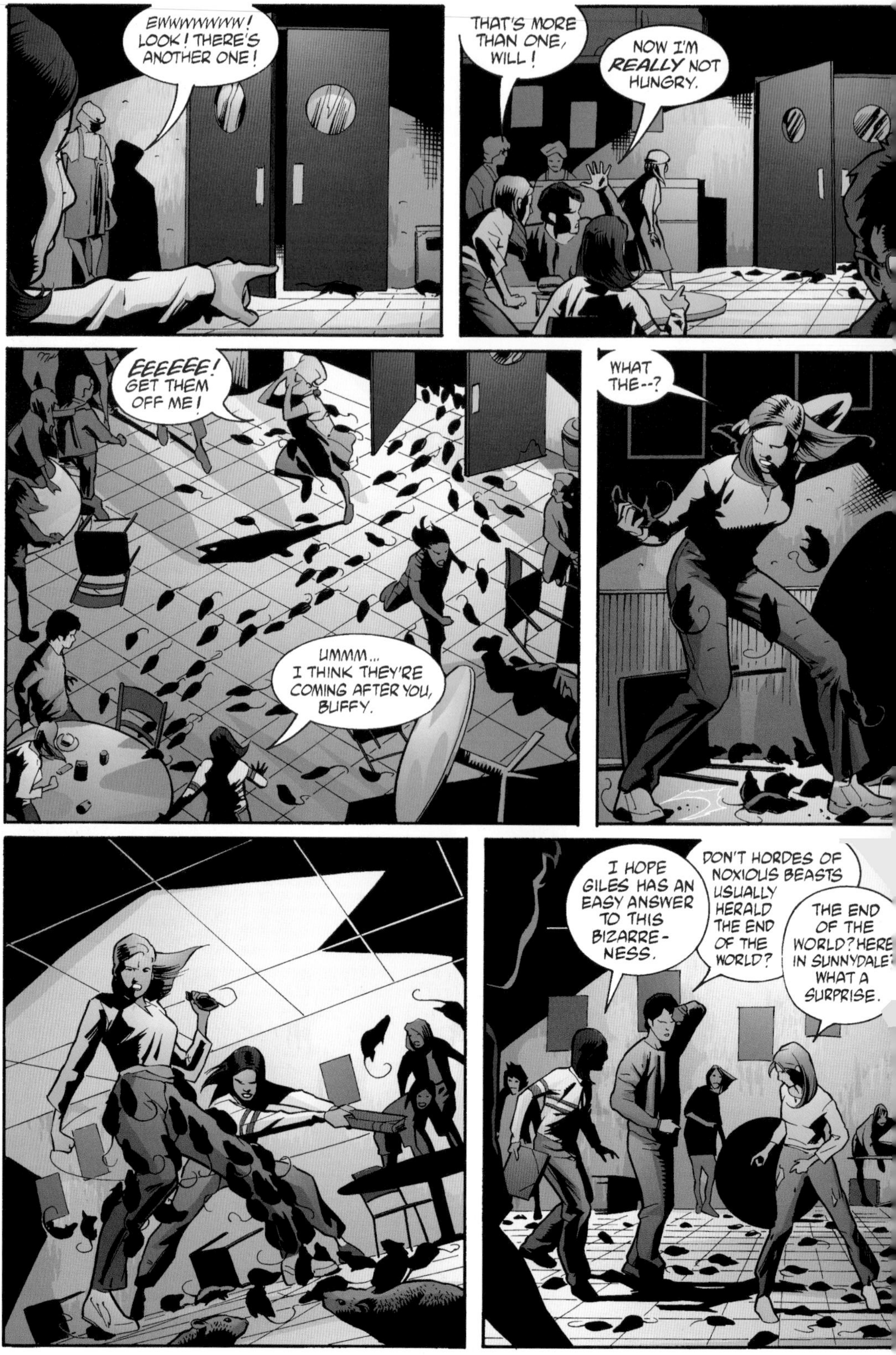
EWWWWWWW! LOOK! THERE'S ANOTHER ONE!
THAT'S MORE THAN ONE, WILL!
NOW I'M REALLY NOT HUNGRY.
EEEEEE! GET THEM OFF ME!
UMMM... I THINK THEY'RE COMING AFTER YOU, BUFFY.
WHAT THE--?
I HOPE GILES HAS AN EASY ANSWER TO THIS BIZARRE-NESS.
DON'T HORDES OF NOXIOUS BEASTS USUALLY HERALD THE END OF THE WORLD?
THE END OF THE WORLD? HERE IN SUNNYDALE? WHAT A SURPRISE.

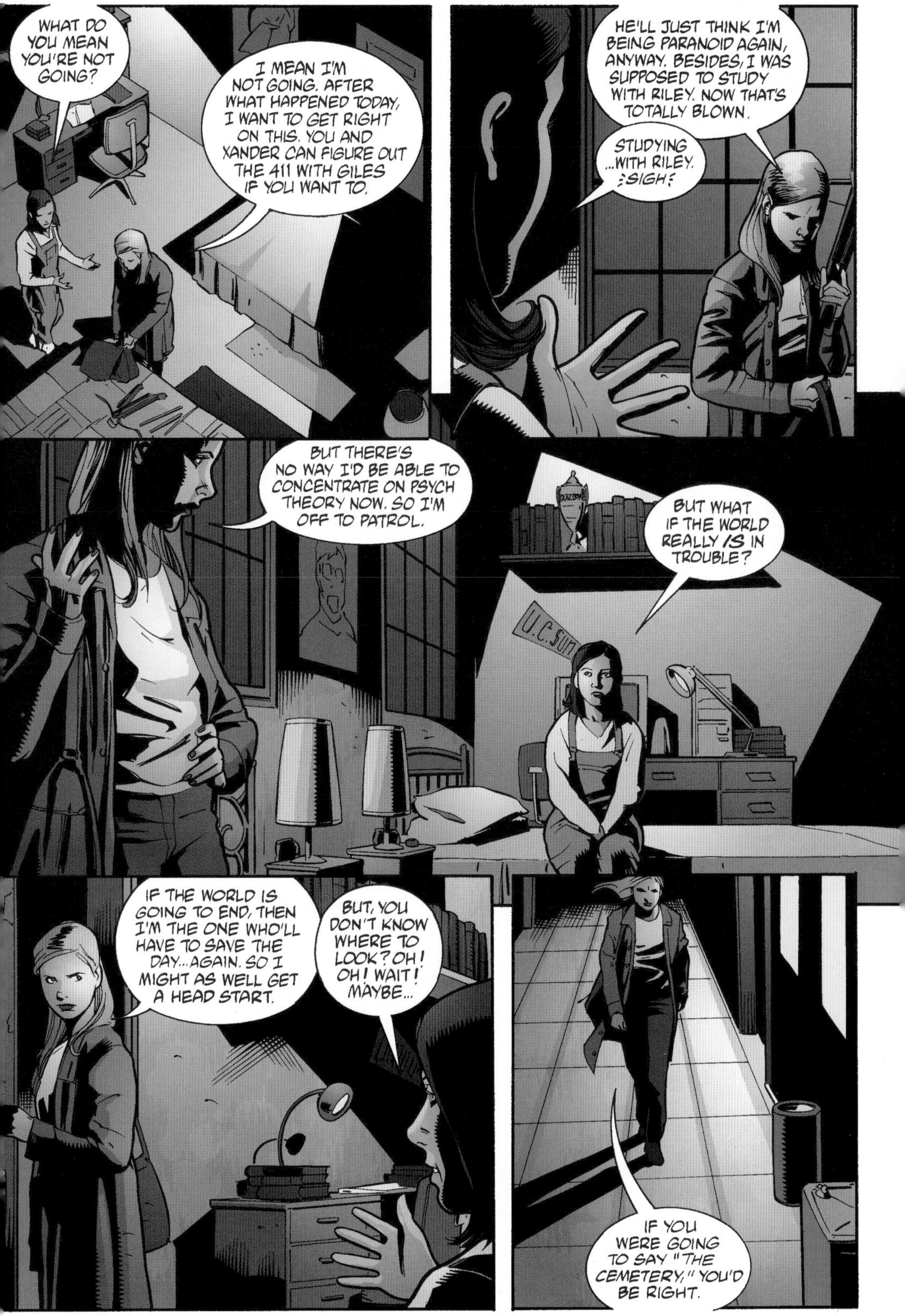
WHAT DO YOU MEAN YOU'RE NOT GOING?
I MEAN I'M NOT GOING. AFTER WHAT HAPPENED TODAY, I WANT TO GET RIGHT ON THIS. YOU AND XANDER CAN FIGURE OUT THE 411 WITH GILES IF YOU WANT TO.
HE'LL JUST THINK I'M BEING PARANOID AGAIN, ANYWAY. BESIDES, I WAS SUPPOSED TO STUDY WITH RILEY. NOW THAT'S TOTALLY BLOWN.
STUDYING ...WITH RILEY. :SIGH:
BUT THERE'S NO WAY I'D BE ABLE TO CONCENTRATE ON PSYCH THEORY NOW. SO I'M OFF TO PATROL.
BUT WHAT IF THE WORLD REALLY IS IN TROUBLE?
IF THE WORLD IS GOING TO END, THEN I'M THE ONE WHO'LL HAVE TO SAVE THE DAY...AGAIN. SO I MIGHT AS WELL GET A HEAD START.
BUT, YOU DON'T KNOW WHERE TO LOOK? OH! OH! WAIT! MAYBE...
IF YOU WERE GOING TO SAY "THE CEMETERY," YOU'D BE RIGHT.

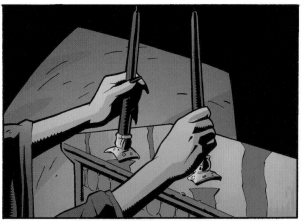

... NOW YOU KNOW AS MUCH AS WE DO.

A CON-UNDRUM INDEED.

SO WHAT DO WE DO?

EVERYONE GRAB A BOOK. WE'VE GOT A LOT OF WORK TO DO.

HOW DID I KNOW YOU WERE GOING TO SAY THAT?

RUSTLE
RUSTLE

GREAT, NOW THE CATS ARE GOING ALL WES CRAVEN.

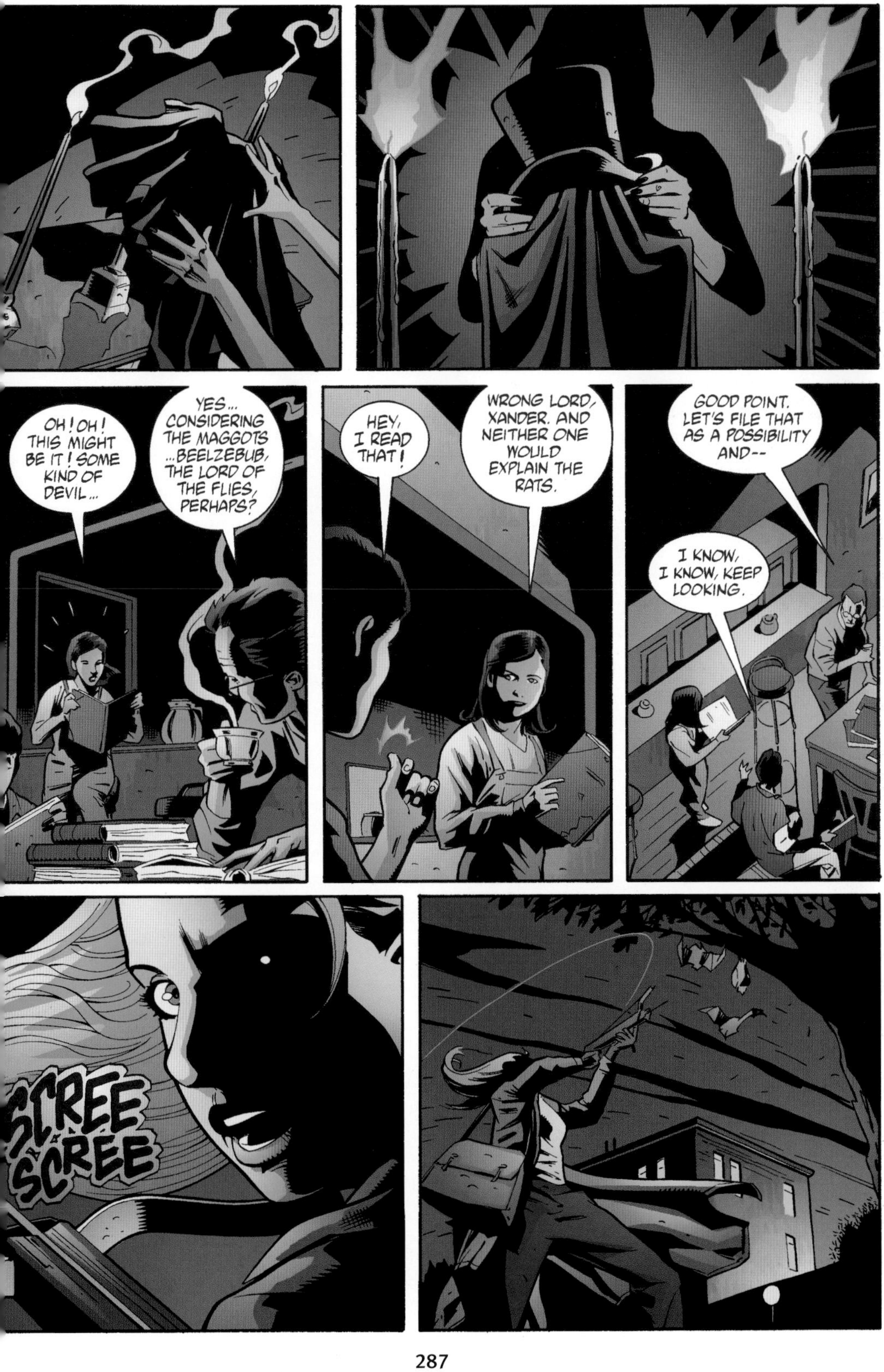
OH! OH! THIS MIGHT BE IT! SOME KIND OF DEVIL...
YES... CONSIDERING THE MAGGOTS ...BEELZEBUB, THE LORD OF THE FLIES, PERHAPS?
HEY, I READ THAT!
WRONG LORD, XANDER. AND NEITHER ONE WOULD EXPLAIN THE RATS.
GOOD POINT. LET'S FILE THAT AS A POSSIBILITY AND--
I KNOW, I KNOW, KEEP LOOKING.
SCREE SCREE

RATS, RATS, RATS...

WILL YOU QUIT FOOLING AROUND? THIS IS SERIOUS!

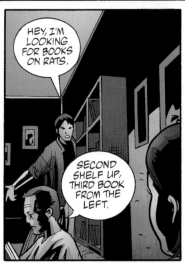

HEY, I'M LOOKING FOR BOOKS ON RATS.

SECOND SHELF UP, THIRD BOOK FROM THE LEFT.

CEREMONIAL APPLICATIONS OF MURIDAE?

THAT'S THE ONE.

BINGO.

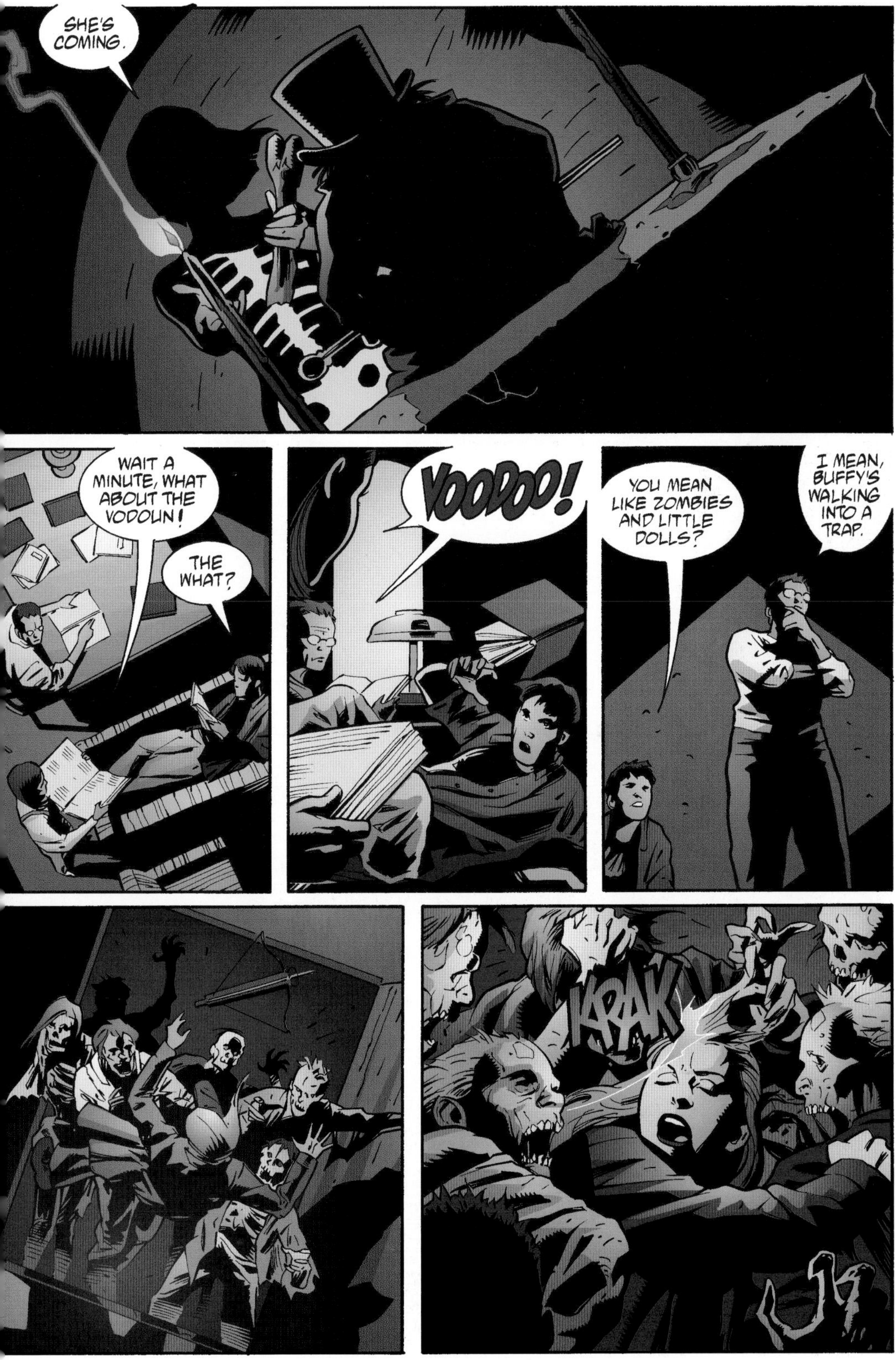
SHE'S COMING.
WAIT A MINUTE, WHAT ABOUT THE VODOUN!
THE WHAT?
VOODOO!
YOU MEAN LIKE ZOMBIES AND LITTLE DOLLS?
I MEAN, BUFFY'S WALKING INTO A TRAP.
KRAK

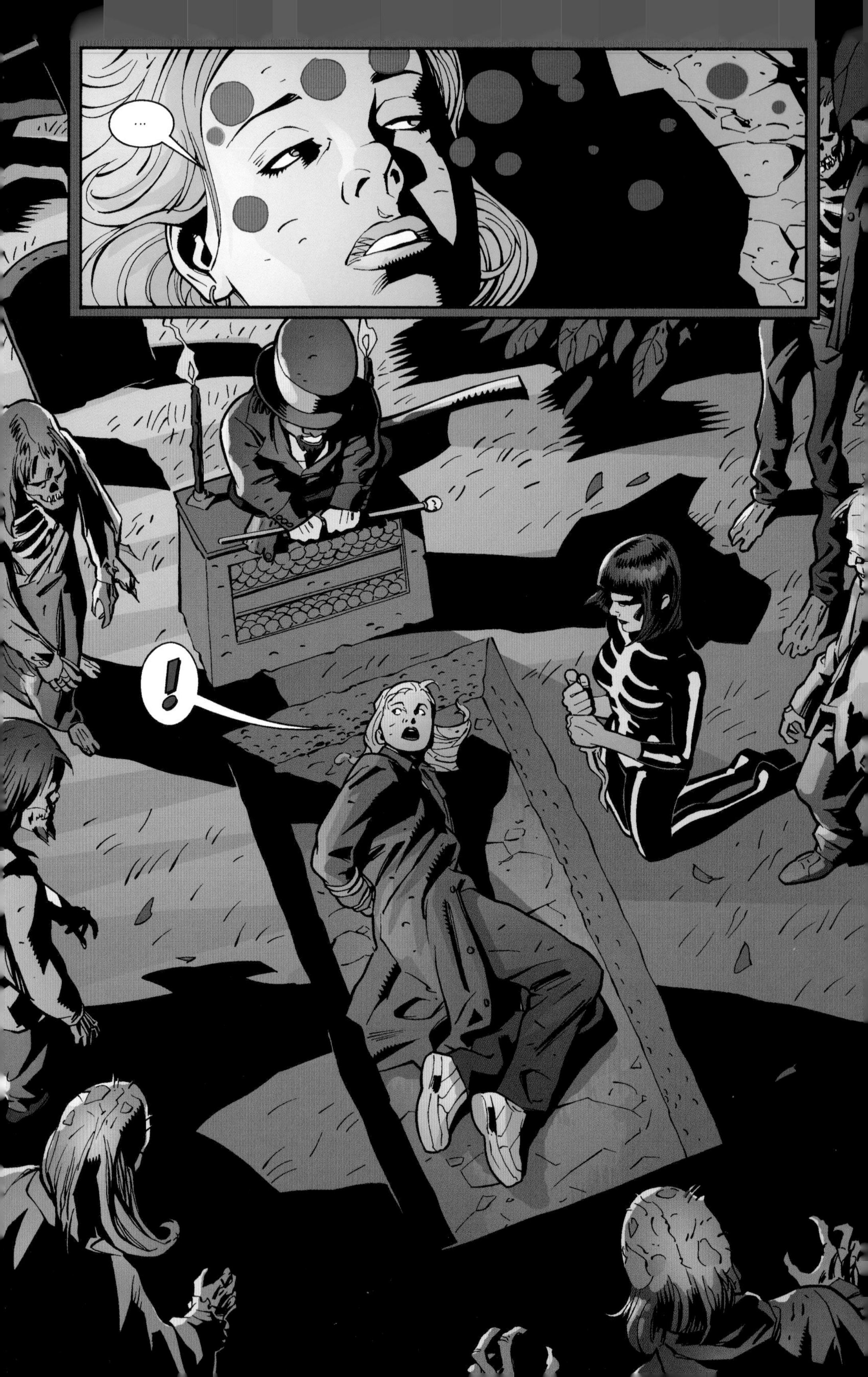
...
!

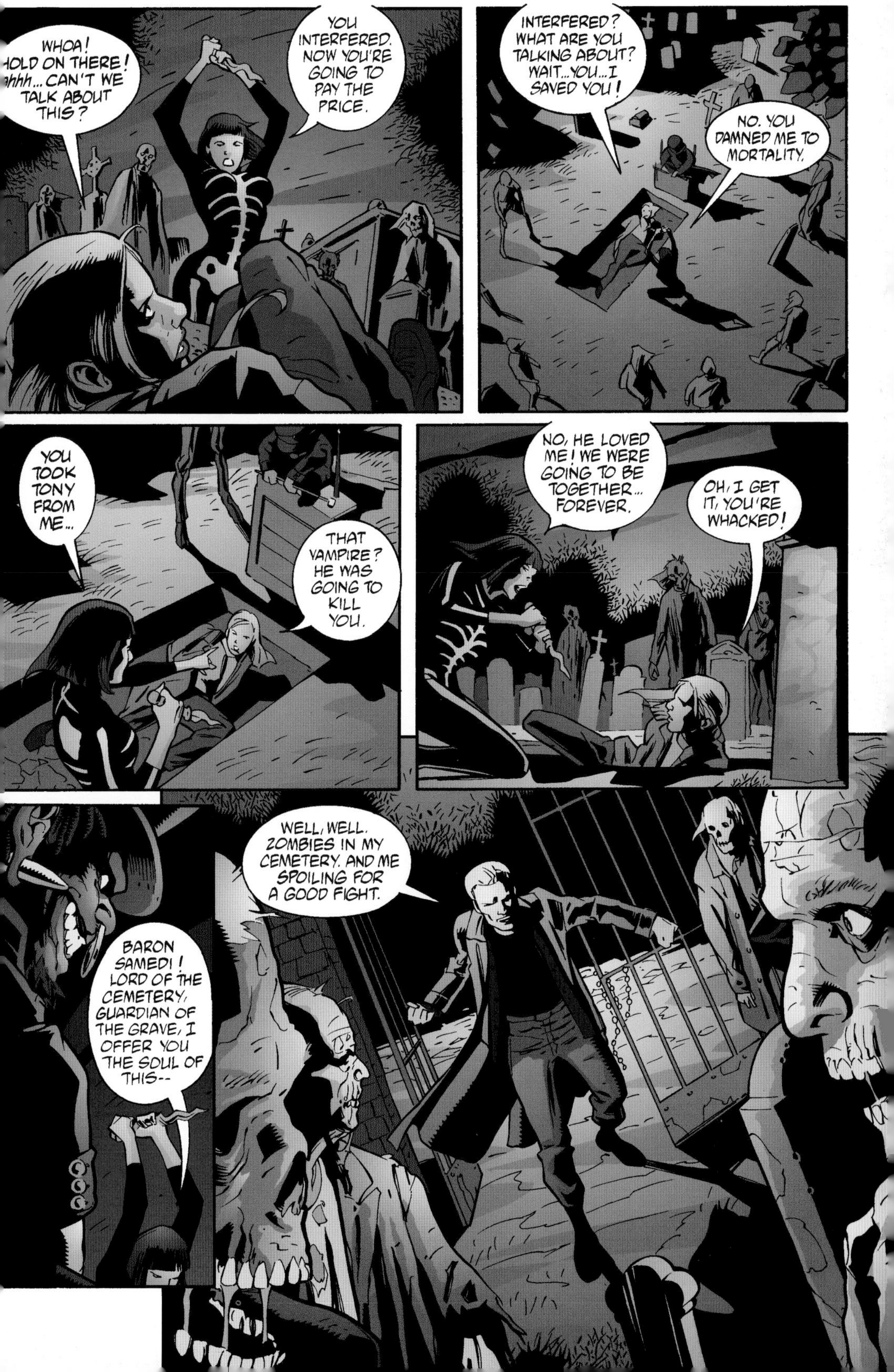
WHOA! HOLD ON THERE! ahhh... CAN'T WE TALK ABOUT THIS?
YOU INTERFERED. NOW YOU'RE GOING TO PAY THE PRICE.
INTERFERED? WHAT ARE YOU TALKING ABOUT? WAIT... YOU... I SAVED YOU!
NO. YOU DAMNED ME TO MORTALITY.
YOU TOOK TONY FROM ME...
THAT VAMPIRE? HE WAS GOING TO KILL YOU.
NO, HE LOVED ME! WE WERE GOING TO BE TOGETHER... FOREVER.
OH, I GET IT, YOU'RE WHACKED!
BARON SAMEDI! LORD OF THE CEMETERY, GUARDIAN OF THE GRAVE, I OFFER YOU THE SOUL OF THIS--
WELL, WELL. ZOMBIES IN MY CEMETERY. AND ME SPOILING FOR A GOOD FIGHT.

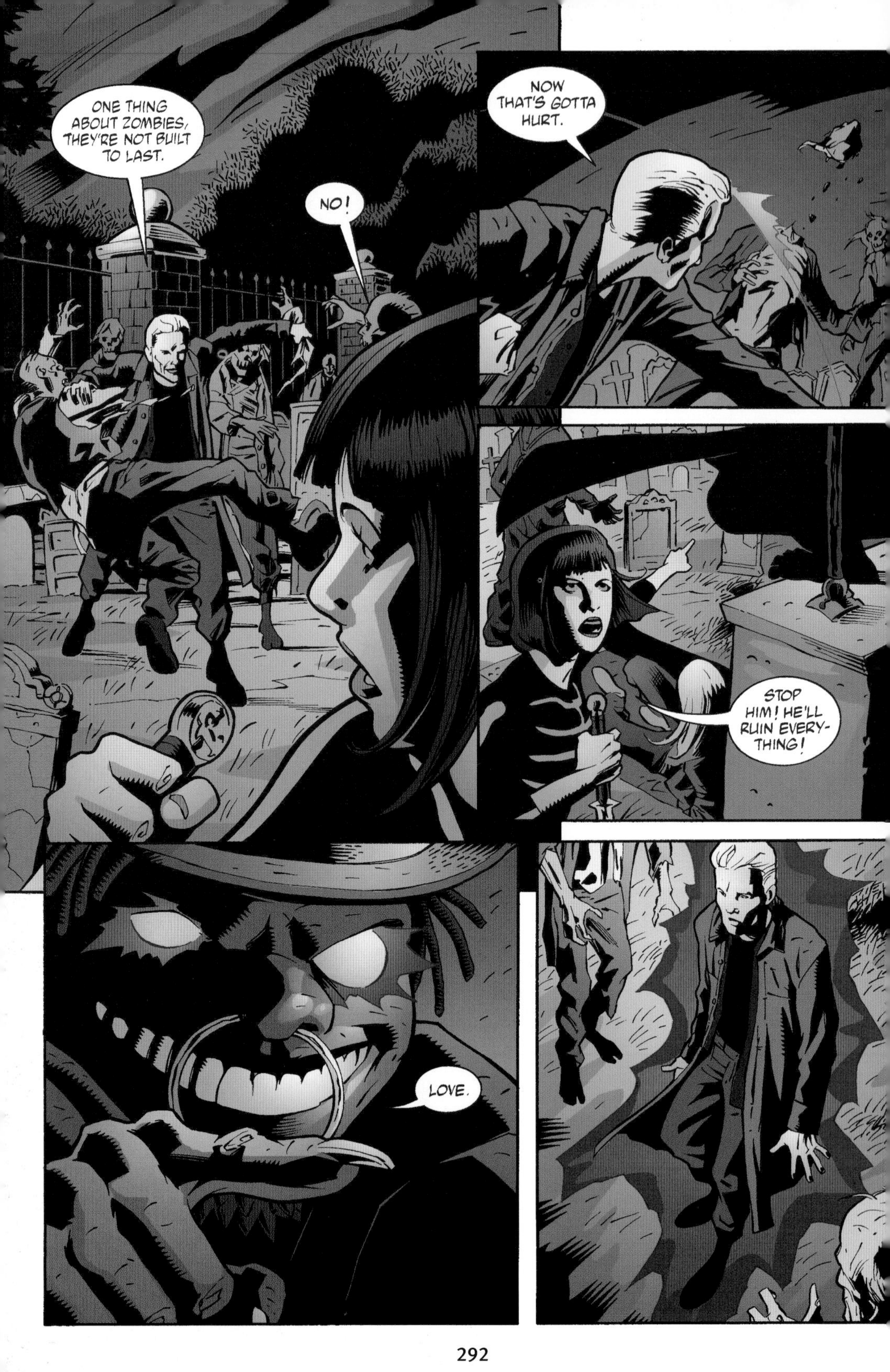
ONE THING ABOUT ZOMBIES, THEY'RE NOT BUILT TO LAST.
NO!
NOW THAT'S GOTTA HURT.
STOP HIM! HE'LL RUIN EVERY-THING!
LOVE.

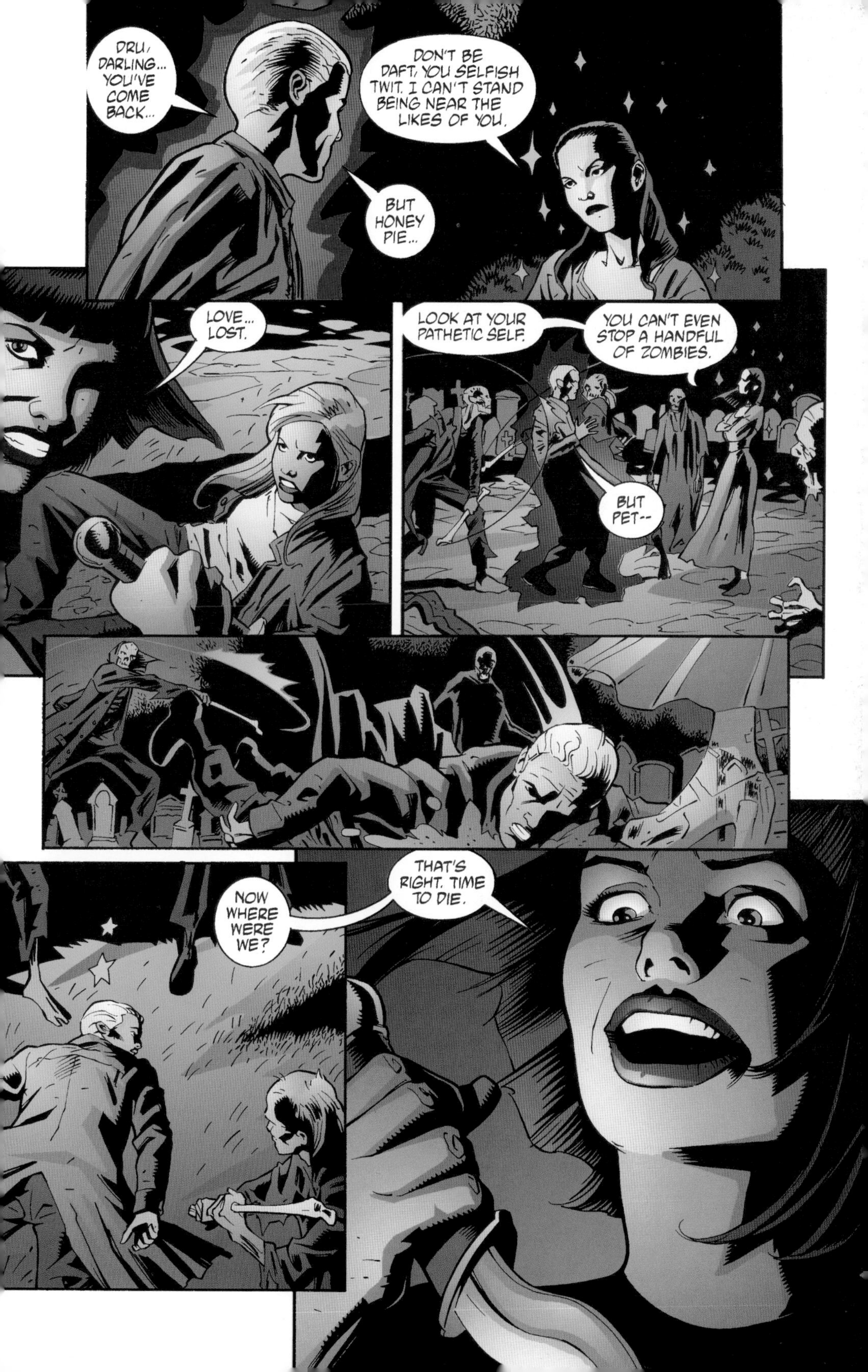
DRU, DARLING... YOU'VE COME BACK...
DON'T BE DAFT, YOU SELFISH TWIT. I CAN'T STAND BEING NEAR THE LIKES OF YOU.
BUT HONEY PIE...
LOVE... LOST.
LOOK AT YOUR PATHETIC SELF.
YOU CAN'T EVEN STOP A HANDFUL OF ZOMBIES.
BUT PET--
NOW WHERE WERE WE?
THAT'S RIGHT. TIME TO DIE.

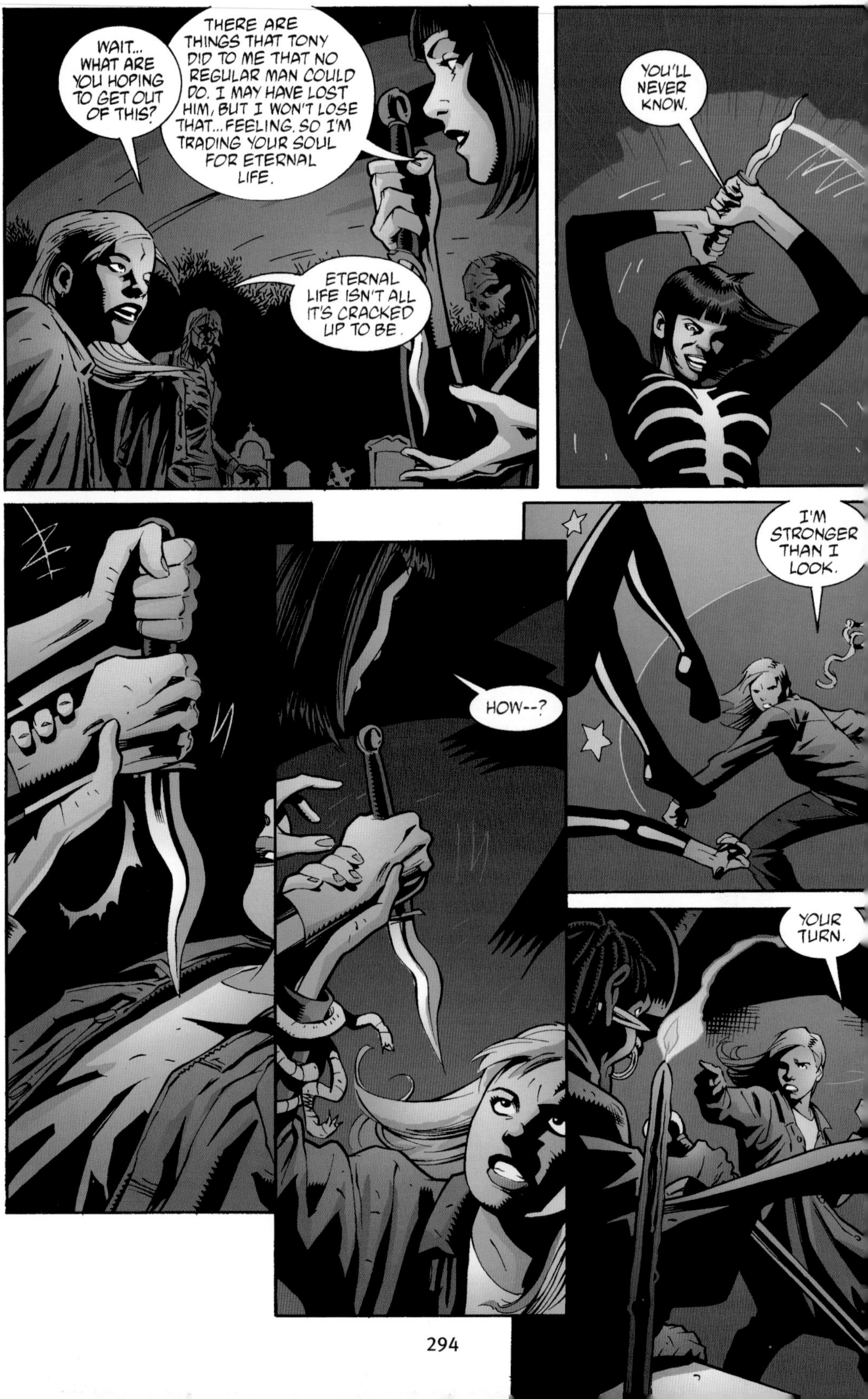
WAIT... WHAT ARE YOU HOPING TO GET OUT OF THIS?
THERE ARE THINGS THAT TONY DID TO ME THAT NO REGULAR MAN COULD DO. I MAY HAVE LOST HIM, BUT I WON'T LOSE THAT...FEELING. SO I'M TRADING YOUR SOUL FOR ETERNAL LIFE.
ETERNAL LIFE ISN'T ALL IT'S CRACKED UP TO BE.
YOU'LL NEVER KNOW.
HOW--?
I'M STRONGER THAN I LOOK.
YOUR TURN.

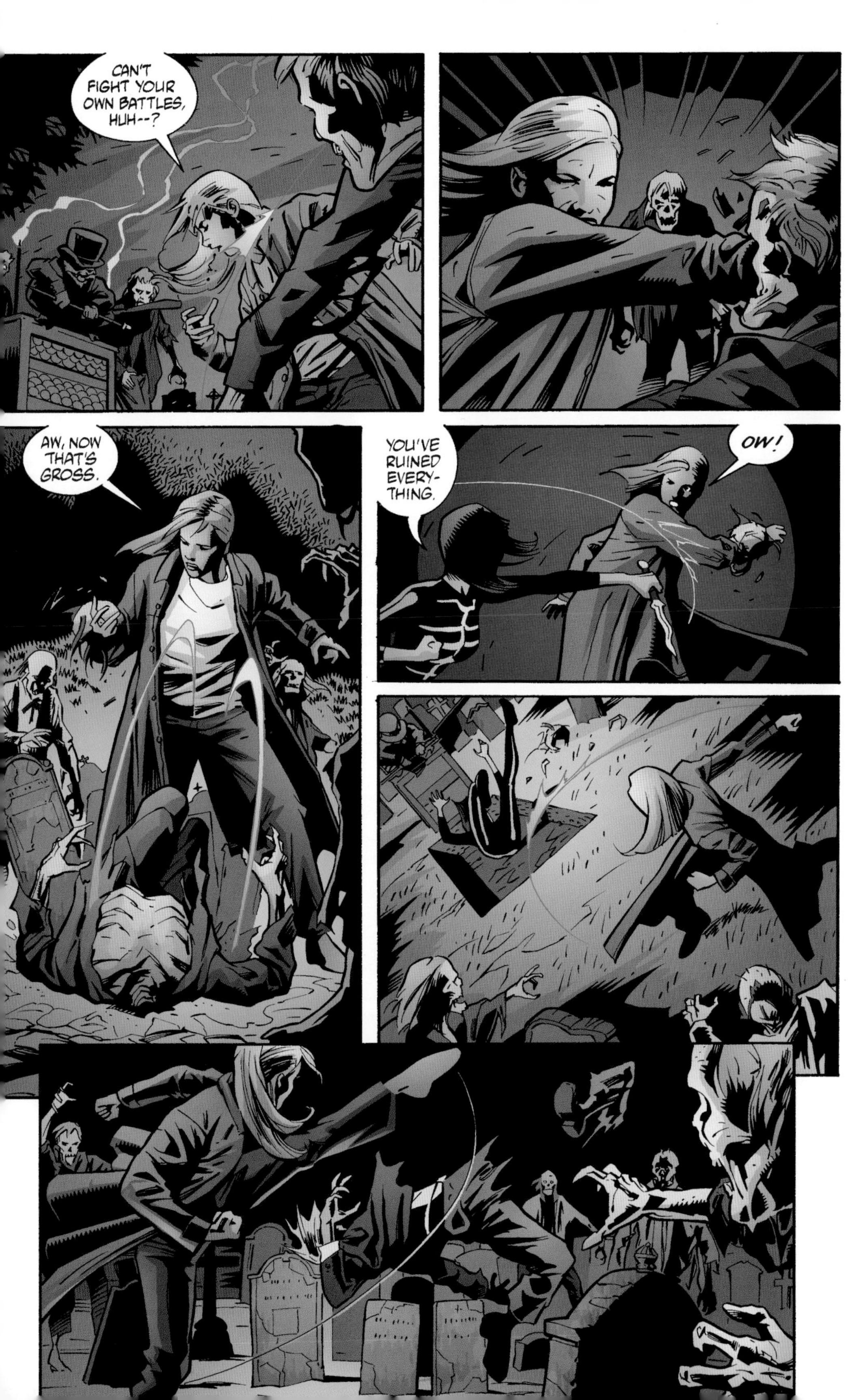
CAN'T FIGHT YOUR OWN BATTLES, HUH--?
AW, NOW THAT'S GROSS.
YOU'VE RUINED EVERY-THING.
OW!

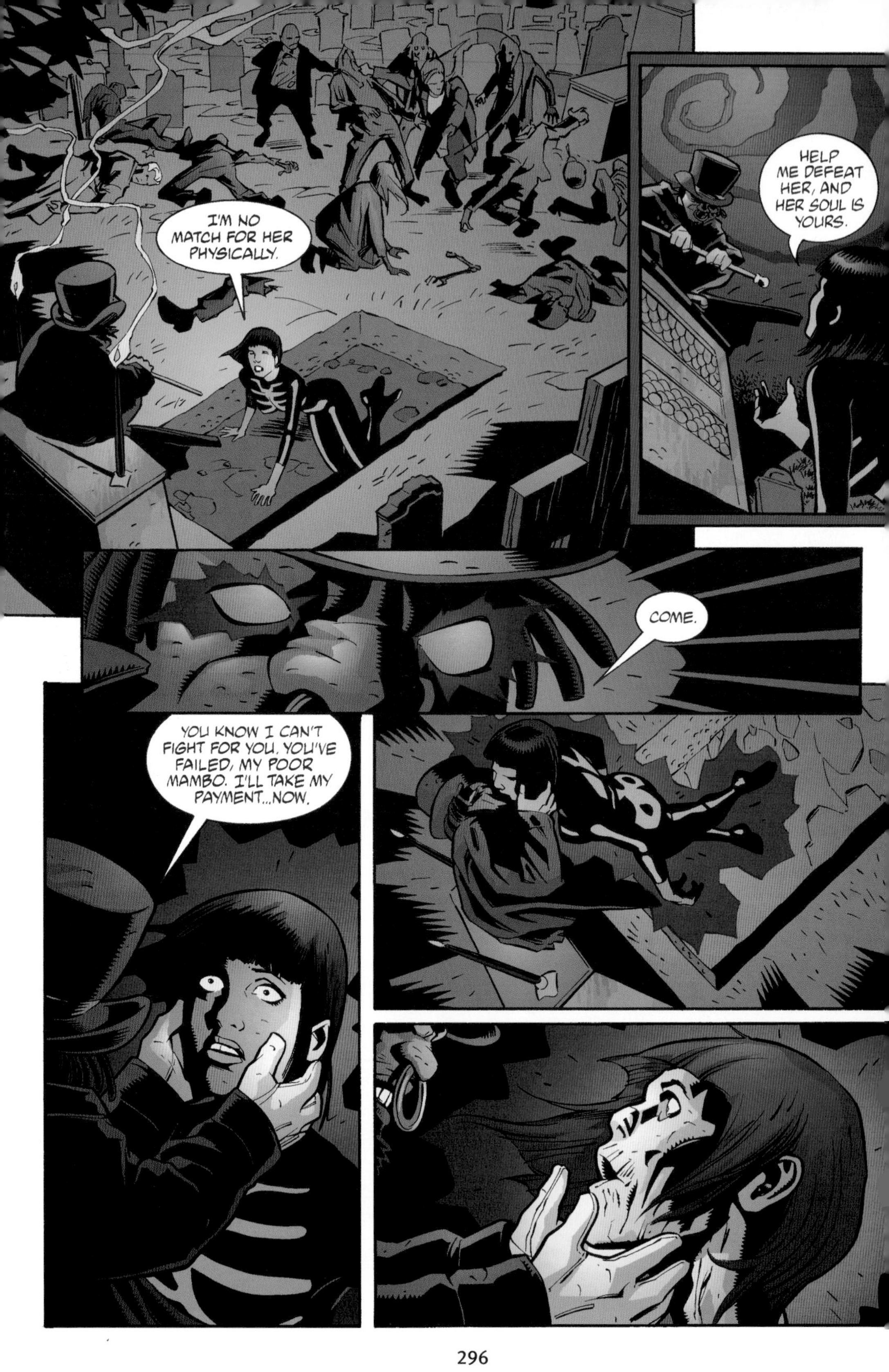
I'M NO MATCH FOR HER PHYSICALLY.
HELP ME DEFEAT HER, AND HER SOUL IS YOURS.
COME.
YOU KNOW I CAN'T FIGHT FOR YOU. YOU'VE FAILED, MY POOR MAMBO. I'LL TAKE MY PAYMENT...NOW.

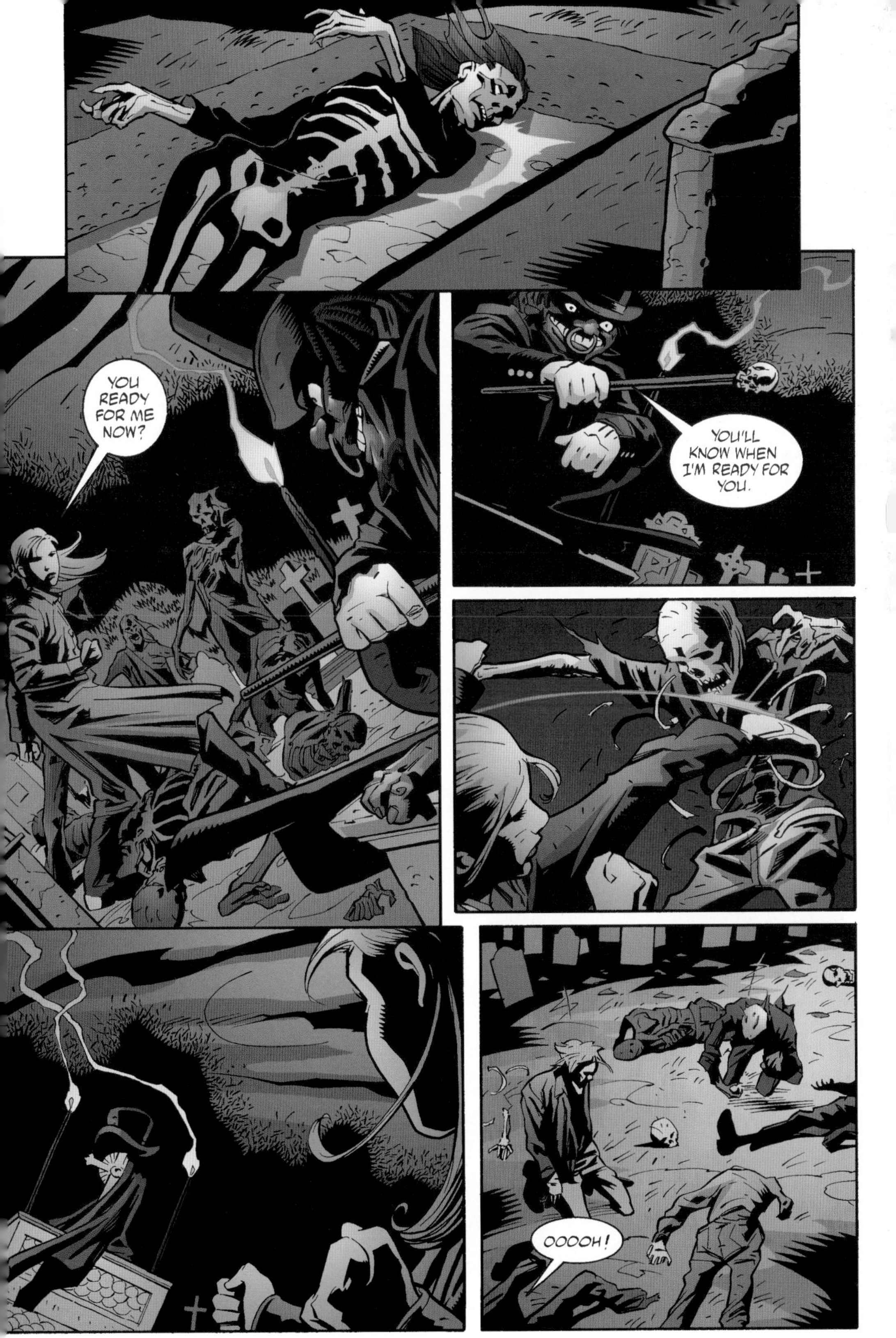
YOU READY FOR ME NOW?
YOU'LL KNOW WHEN I'M READY FOR YOU.
OOOOH!

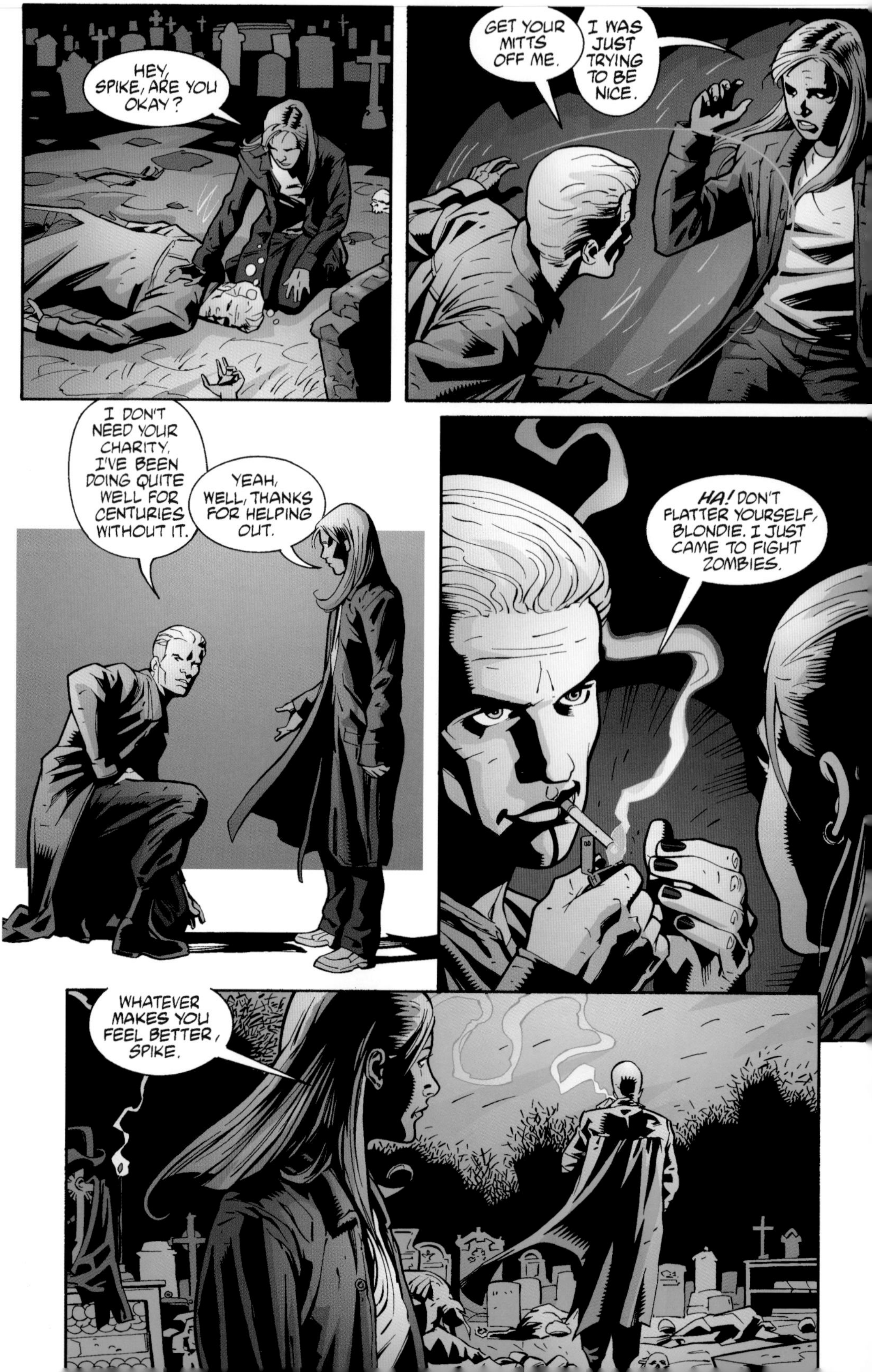
HEY, SPIKE, ARE YOU OKAY?
GET YOUR MITTS OFF ME.
I WAS JUST TRYING TO BE NICE.
I DON'T NEED YOUR CHARITY. I'VE BEEN DOING QUITE WELL FOR CENTURIES WITHOUT IT.
YEAH, WELL, THANKS FOR HELPING OUT.
HA! DON'T FLATTER YOURSELF, BLONDIE. I JUST CAME TO FIGHT ZOMBIES.
WHATEVER MAKES YOU FEEL BETTER, SPIKE.

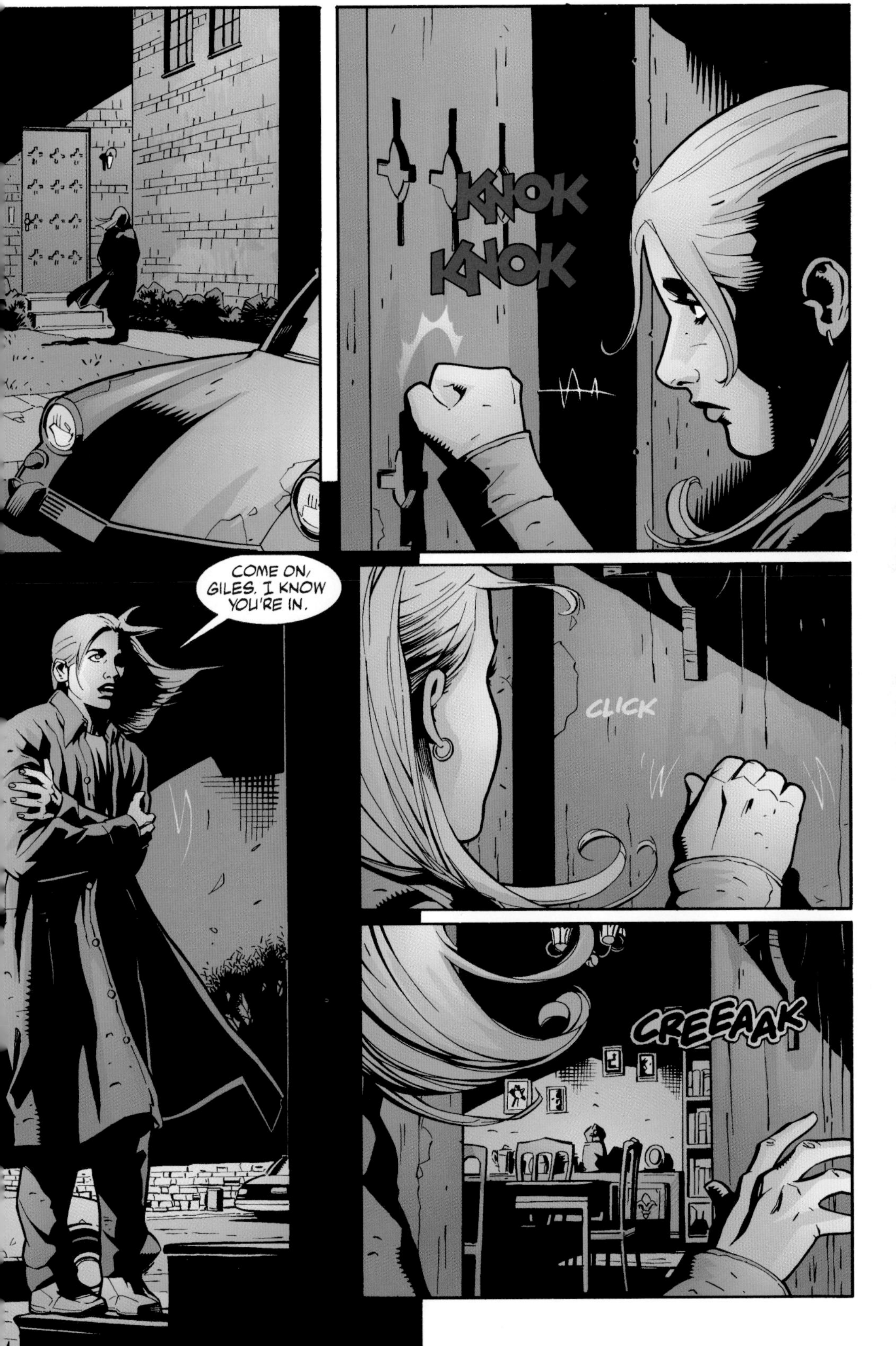
KNOK
KNOK
COME ON, GILES. I KNOW YOU'RE IN.
CLICK
CREEAAK

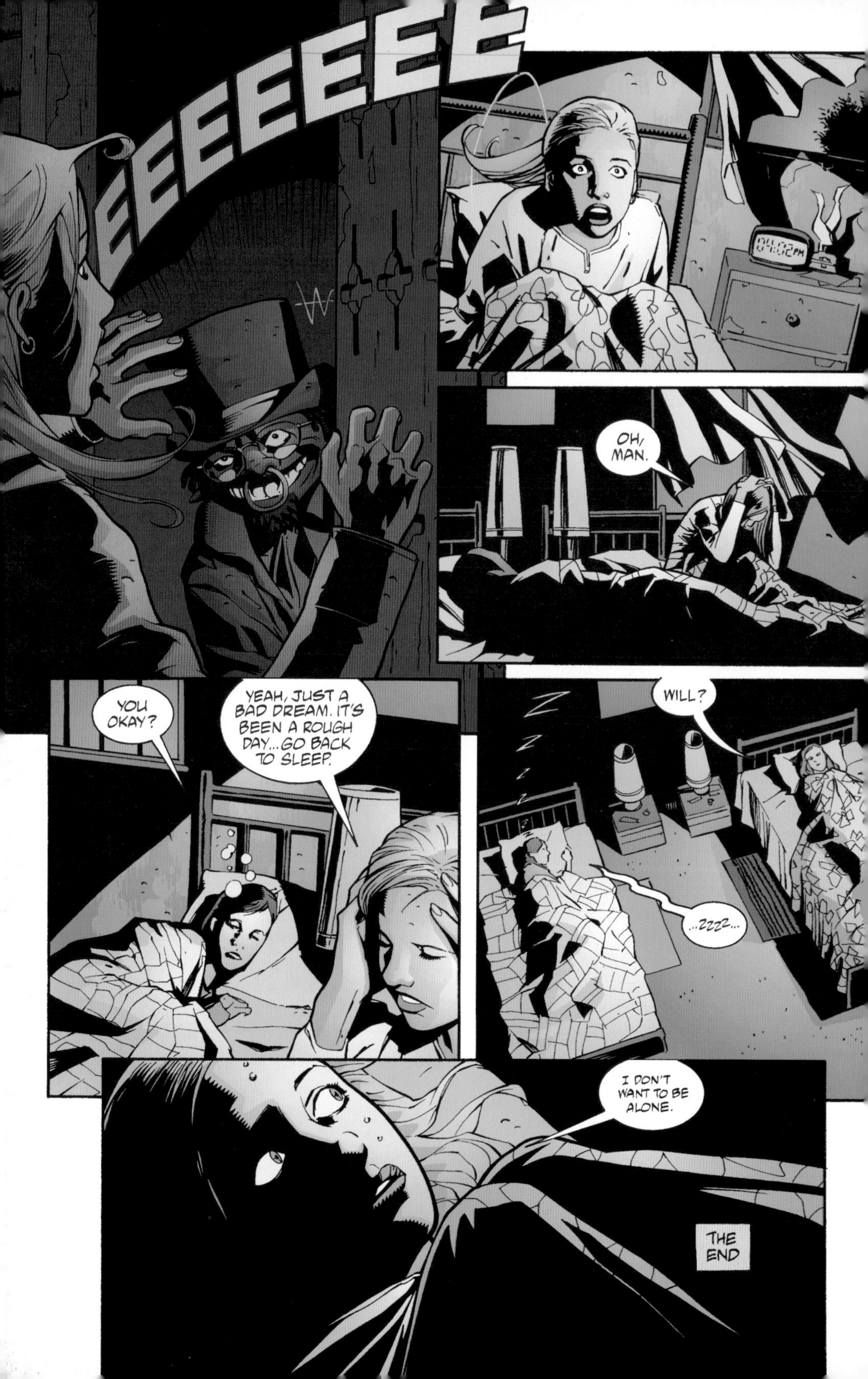
EEEEEEEE
04:02PM
OH, MAN.
YOU OKAY?
YEAH, JUST A BAD DREAM. IT'S BEEN A ROUGH DAY...GO BACK TO SLEEP.
Z Z Z Z
WILL?
...ZZZZ...
I DON'T WANT TO BE ALONE.
THE END

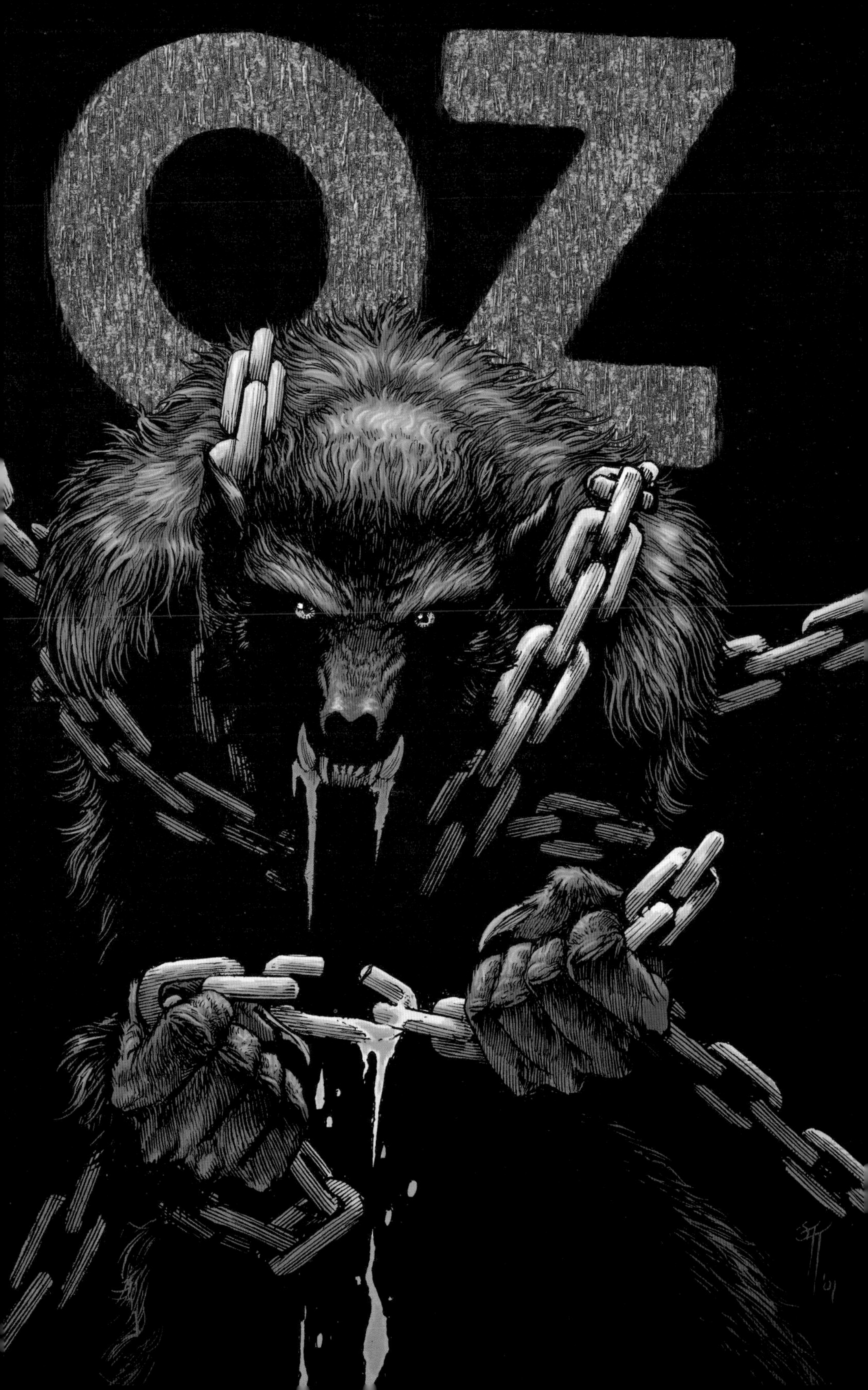
OZ

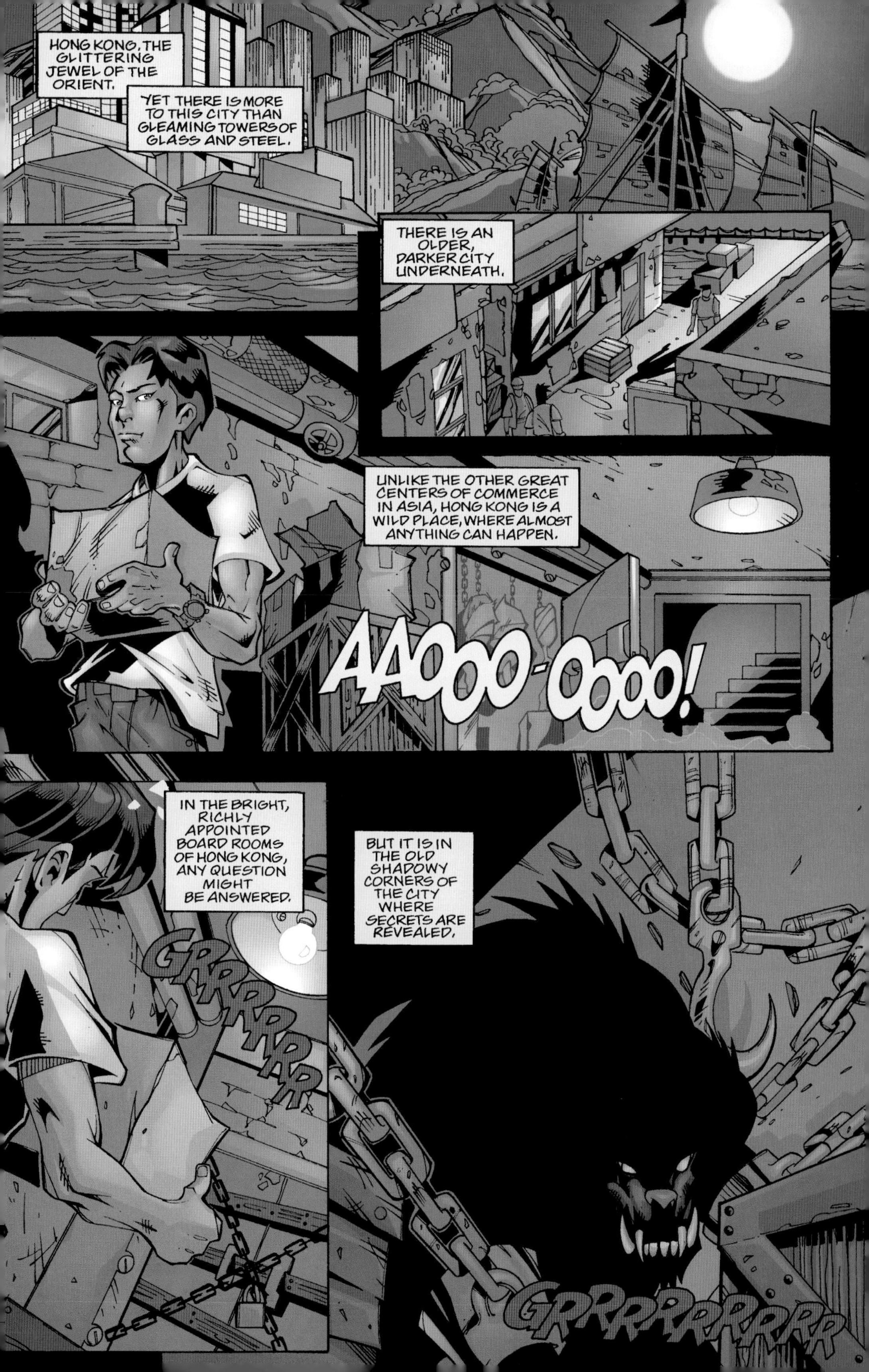
HONG KONG, THE GLITTERING JEWEL OF THE ORIENT.
YET THERE IS MORE TO THIS CITY THAN GLEAMING TOWERS OF GLASS AND STEEL.
THERE IS AN OLDER, DARKER CITY UNDERNEATH.
UNLIKE THE OTHER GREAT CENTERS OF COMMERCE IN ASIA, HONG KONG IS A WILD PLACE, WHERE ALMOST ANYTHING CAN HAPPEN.
AAOOO-OOOO!
IN THE BRIGHT, RICHLY APPOINTED BOARD ROOMS OF HONG KONG, ANY QUESTION MIGHT BE ANSWERED.
GRRRRRR
BUT IT IS IN THE OLD SHADOWY CORNERS OF THE CITY WHERE SECRETS ARE REVEALED.
GRRRRRRRRR

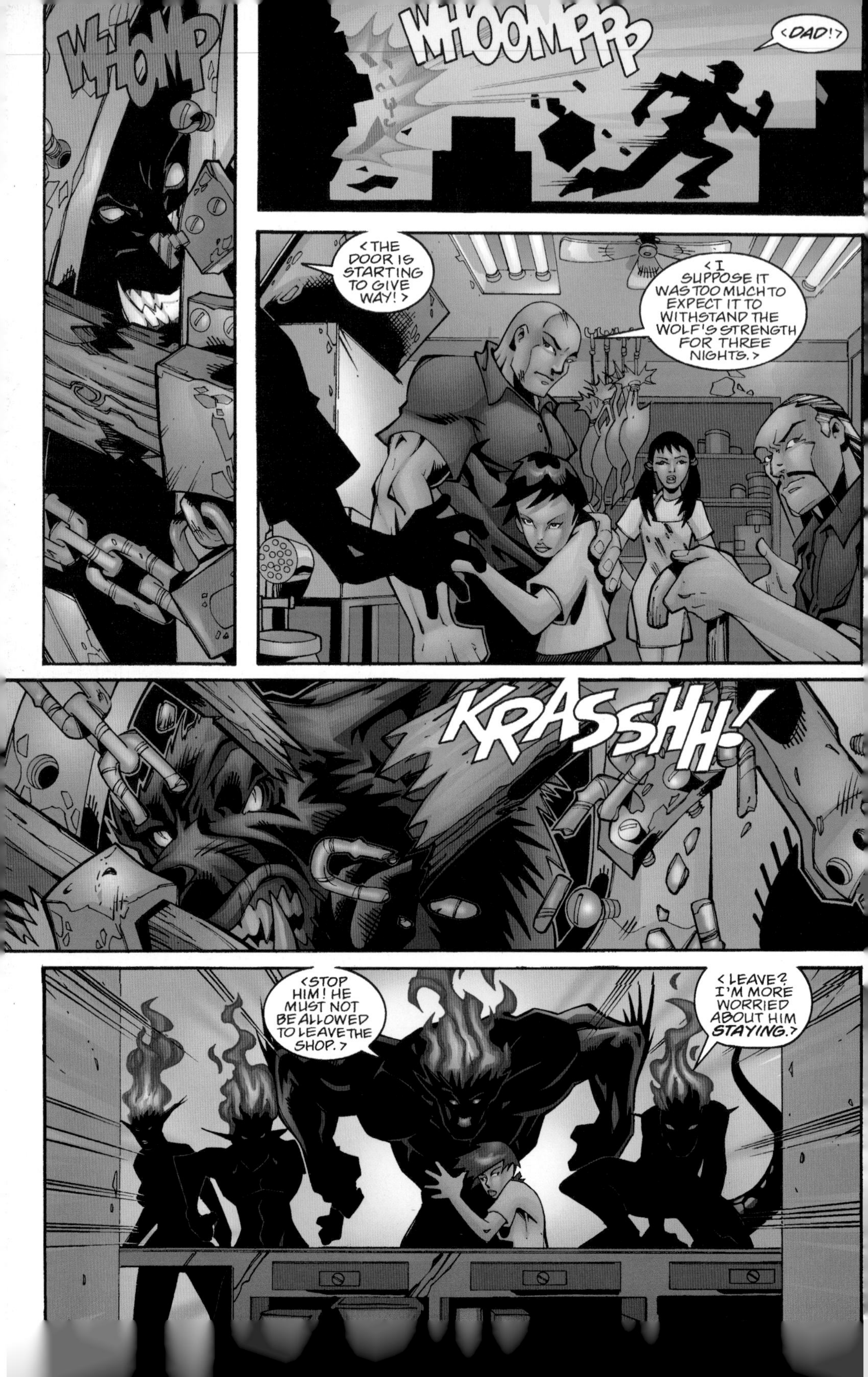
WHOMP
WHOOMPPP
<DAD!>
<THE DOOR IS STARTING TO GIVE WAY!>
<I SUPPOSE IT WAS TOO MUCH TO EXPECT IT TO WITHSTAND THE WOLF'S STRENGTH FOR THREE NIGHTS.>
KRASSHH!
<STOP HIM! HE MUST NOT BE ALLOWED TO LEAVE THE SHOP.>
<LEAVE? I'M MORE WORRIED ABOUT HIM STAYING.>

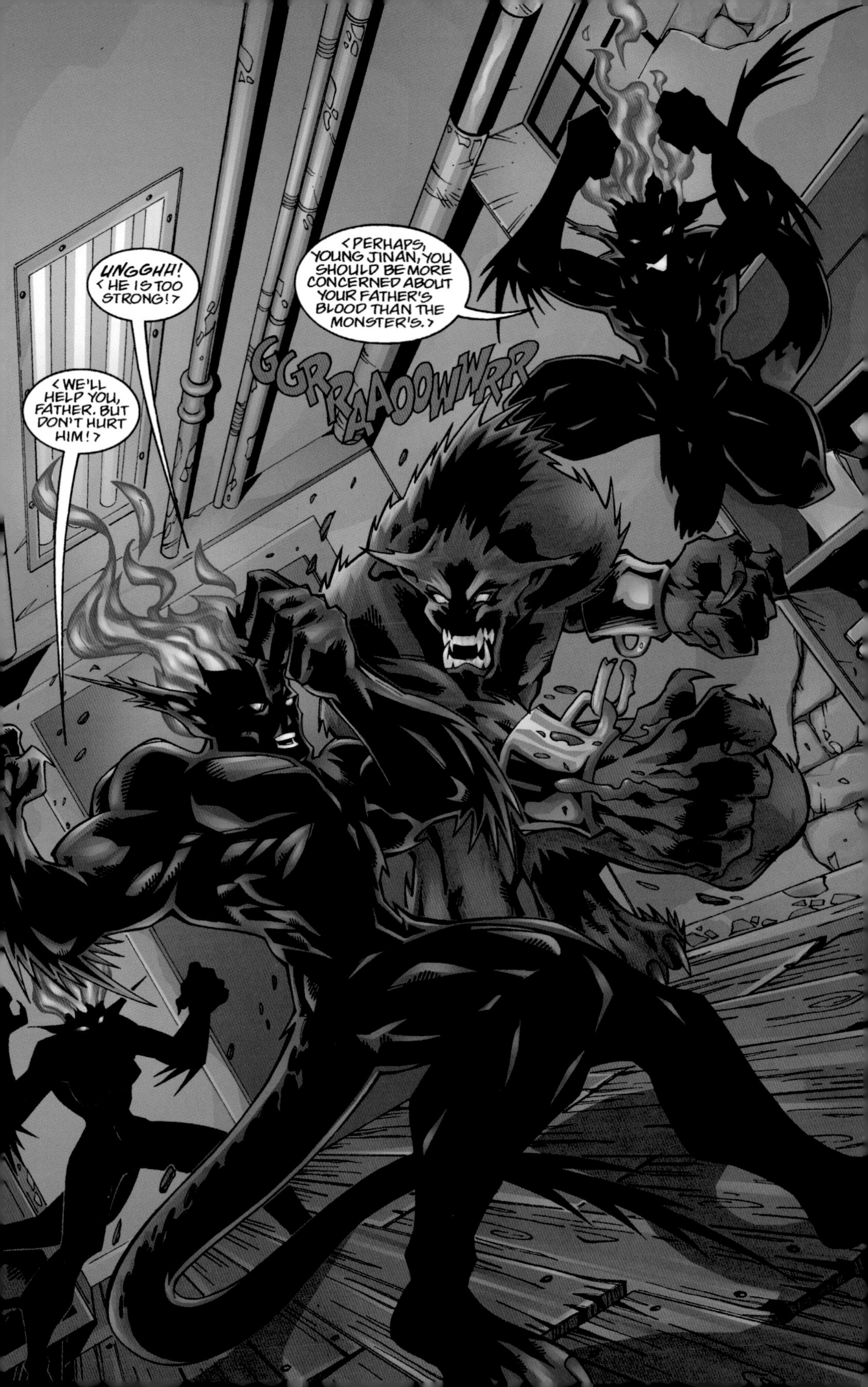
UNGGHH! < HE IS TOO STRONG! >
< WE'LL HELP YOU, FATHER. BUT DON'T HURT HIM! >
< PERHAPS, YOUNG JINAN, YOU SHOULD BE MORE CONCERNED ABOUT YOUR FATHER'S BLOOD THAN THE MONSTER'S. >
GGRRAAOOWWRR

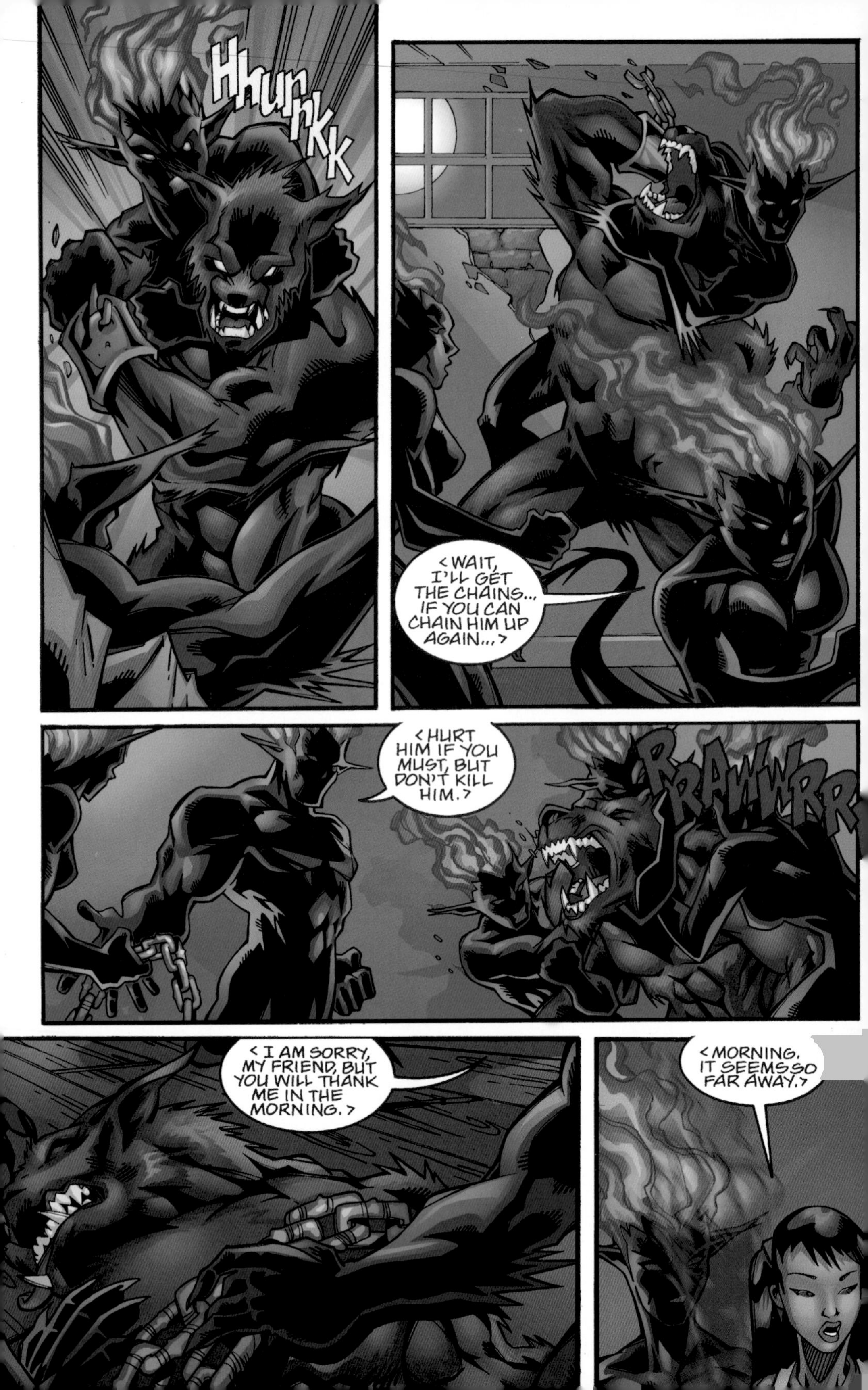
HHURNKK
<WAIT, I'LL GET THE CHAINS... IF YOU CAN CHAIN HIM UP AGAIN...>
<HURT HIM IF YOU MUST, BUT DON'T KILL HIM.>
RRAWWRR
<I AM SORRY, MY FRIEND, BUT YOU WILL THANK ME IN THE MORNING.>
<MORNING. IT SEEMS SO FAR AWAY.>

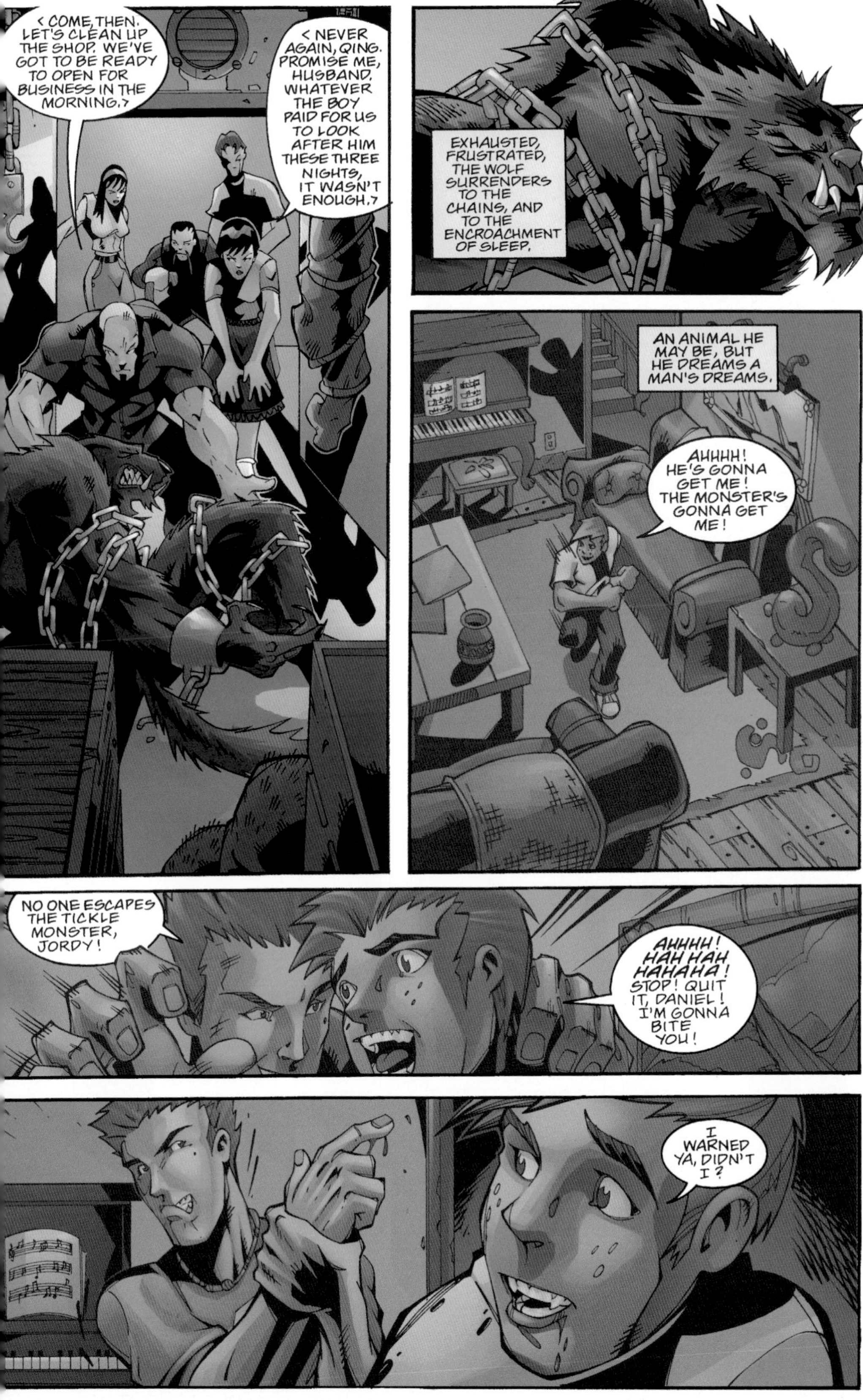
< COME, THEN. LET'S CLEAN UP THE SHOP. WE'VE GOT TO BE READY TO OPEN FOR BUSINESS IN THE MORNING. >
< NEVER AGAIN, QING. PROMISE ME, HUSBAND. WHATEVER THE BOY PAID FOR US TO LOOK AFTER HIM THESE THREE NIGHTS, IT WASN'T ENOUGH. >
EXHAUSTED, FRUSTRATED, THE WOLF SURRENDERS TO THE CHAINS, AND TO THE ENCROACHMENT OF SLEEP.
AN ANIMAL HE MAY BE, BUT HE DREAMS A MAN'S DREAMS.
AHHHH! HE'S GONNA GET ME! THE MONSTER'S GONNA GET ME!
NO ONE ESCAPES THE TICKLE MONSTER, JORDY!
AHHHH! HAH HAH HAHAHA! STOP! QUIT IT, DANIEL! I'M GONNA BITE YOU!
I WARNED YA, DIDN'T I?

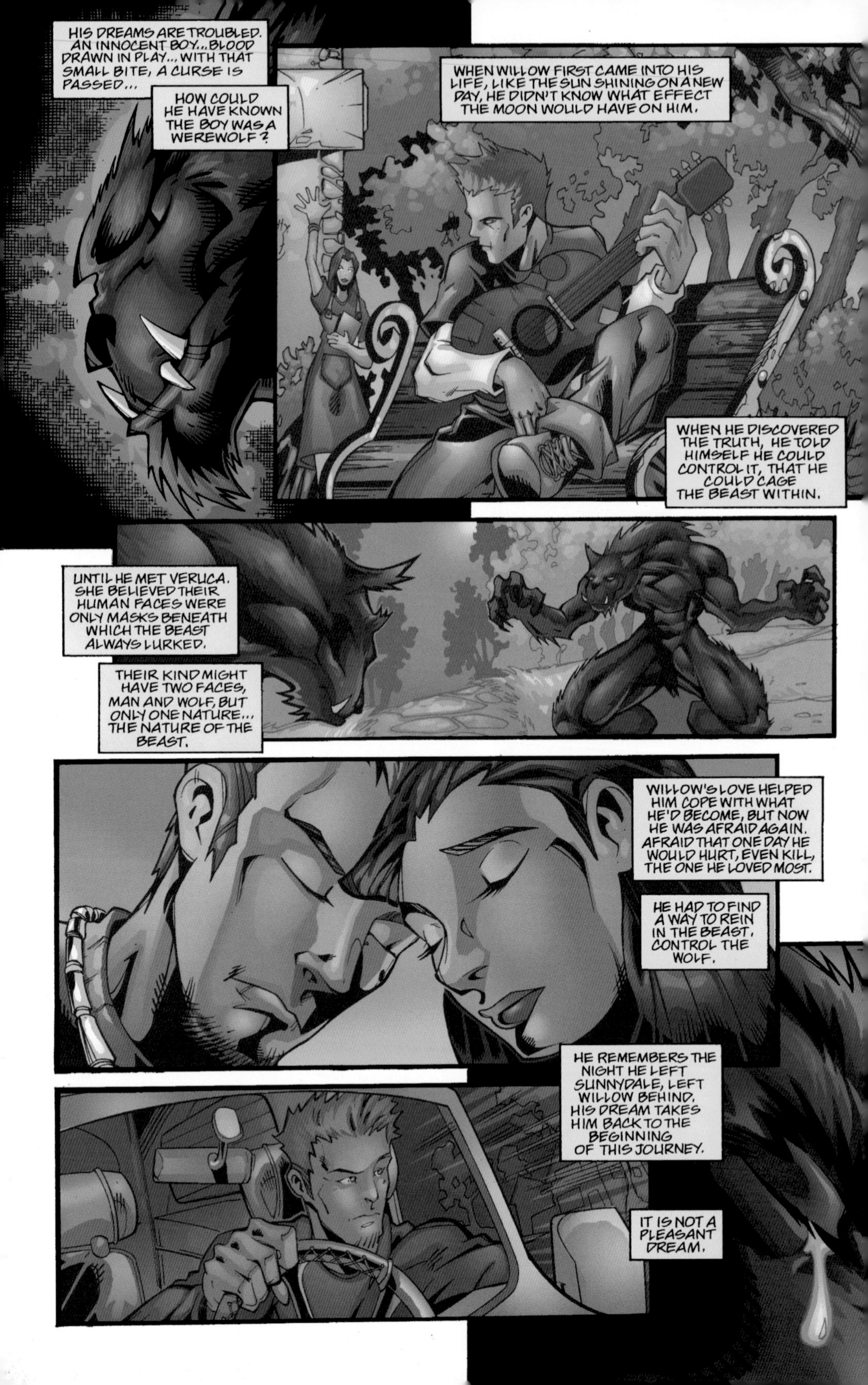
HIS DREAMS ARE TROUBLED. AN INNOCENT BOY... BLOOD DRAWN IN PLAY... WITH THAT SMALL BITE, A CURSE IS PASSED...
HOW COULD HE HAVE KNOWN THE BOY WAS A WEREWOLF?
WHEN WILLOW FIRST CAME INTO HIS LIFE, LIKE THE SUN SHINING ON A NEW DAY, HE DIDN'T KNOW WHAT EFFECT THE MOON WOULD HAVE ON HIM.
WHEN HE DISCOVERED THE TRUTH, HE TOLD HIMSELF HE COULD CONTROL IT, THAT HE COULD CAGE THE BEAST WITHIN.
UNTIL HE MET VERUCA. SHE BELIEVED THEIR HUMAN FACES WERE ONLY MASKS BENEATH WHICH THE BEAST ALWAYS LURKED.
THEIR KIND MIGHT HAVE TWO FACES, MAN AND WOLF, BUT ONLY ONE NATURE... THE NATURE OF THE BEAST.
WILLOW'S LOVE HELPED HIM COPE WITH WHAT HE'D BECOME, BUT NOW HE WAS AFRAID AGAIN. AFRAID THAT ONE DAY HE WOULD HURT, EVEN KILL, THE ONE HE LOVED MOST.
HE HAD TO FIND A WAY TO REIN IN THE BEAST, CONTROL THE WOLF.
HE REMEMBERS THE NIGHT HE LEFT SUNNYDALE, LEFT WILLOW BEHIND. HIS DREAM TAKES HIM BACK TO THE BEGINNING OF THIS JOURNEY.
IT IS NOT A PLEASANT DREAM.

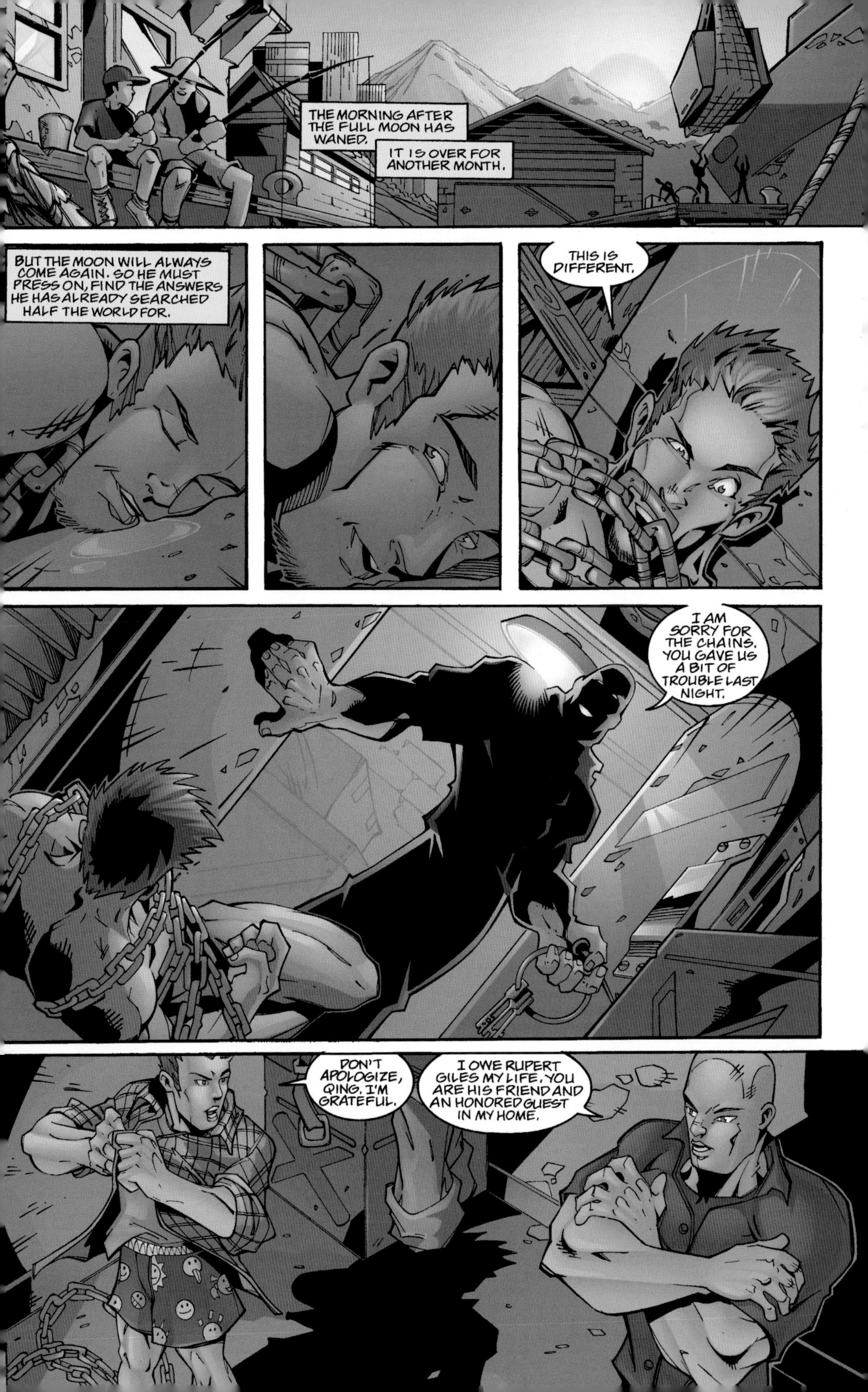

THE MORNING AFTER THE FULL MOON HAS WANED.
IT IS OVER FOR ANOTHER MONTH.
BUT THE MOON WILL ALWAYS COME AGAIN. SO HE MUST PRESS ON, FIND THE ANSWERS HE HAS ALREADY SEARCHED HALF THE WORLD FOR.
THIS IS DIFFERENT.
I AM SORRY FOR THE CHAINS. YOU GAVE US A BIT OF TROUBLE LAST NIGHT.
DON'T APOLOGIZE, QING. I'M GRATEFUL.
I OWE RUPERT GILES MY LIFE. YOU ARE HIS FRIEND AND AN HONORED GUEST IN MY HOME.

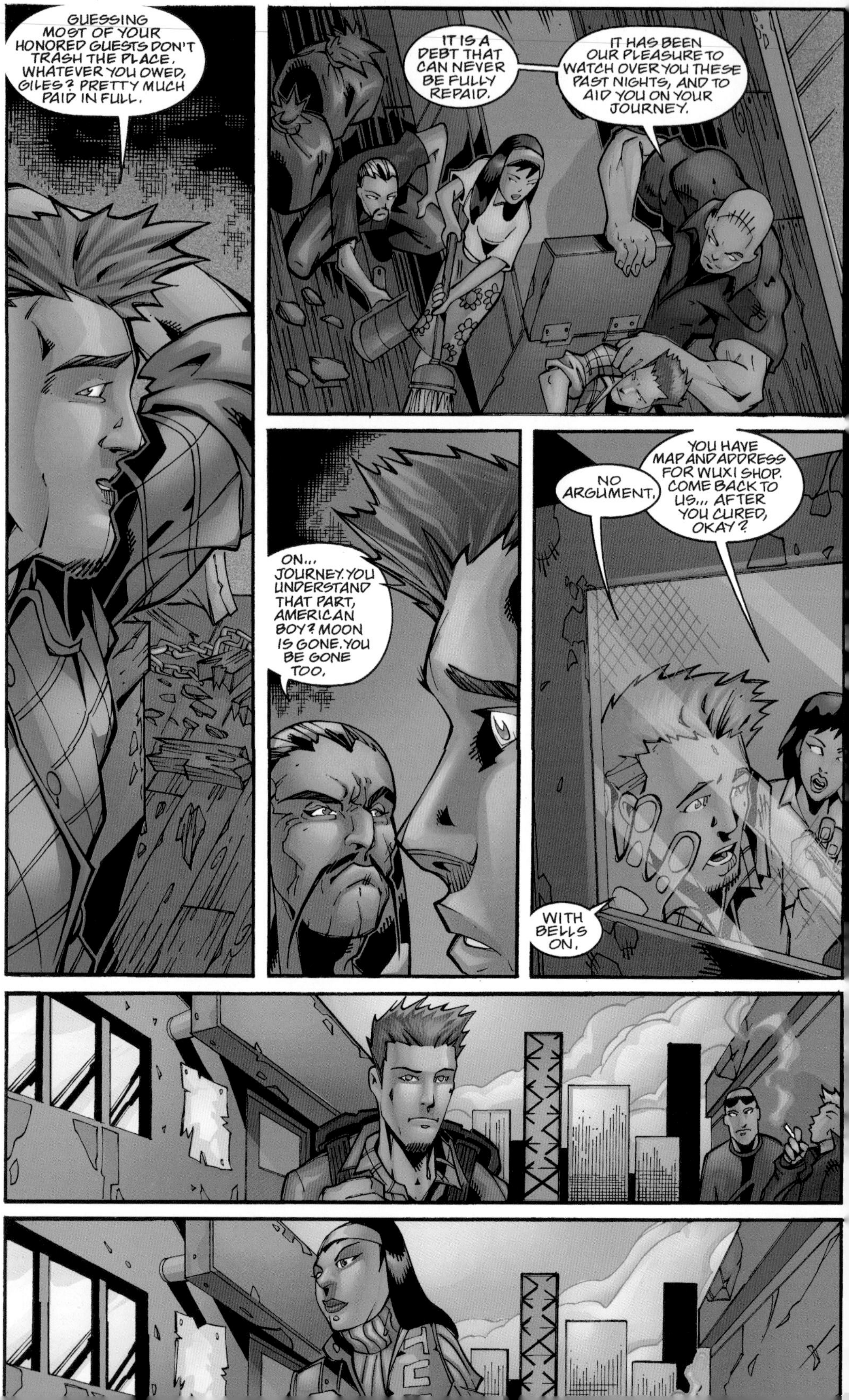
GUESSING MOST OF YOUR HONORED GUESTS DON'T TRASH THE PLACE. WHATEVER YOU OWED, GILES? PRETTY MUCH PAID IN FULL.
IT IS A DEBT THAT CAN NEVER BE FULLY REPAID.
IT HAS BEEN OUR PLEASURE TO WATCH OVER YOU THESE PAST NIGHTS, AND TO AID YOU ON YOUR JOURNEY.
ON... JOURNEY. YOU UNDERSTAND THAT PART, AMERICAN BOY? MOON IS GONE. YOU BE GONE TOO.
YOU HAVE MAP AND ADDRESS FOR WUXI SHOP. COME BACK TO US... AFTER YOU CURED, OKAY?
NO ARGUMENT.
WITH BELLS ON.

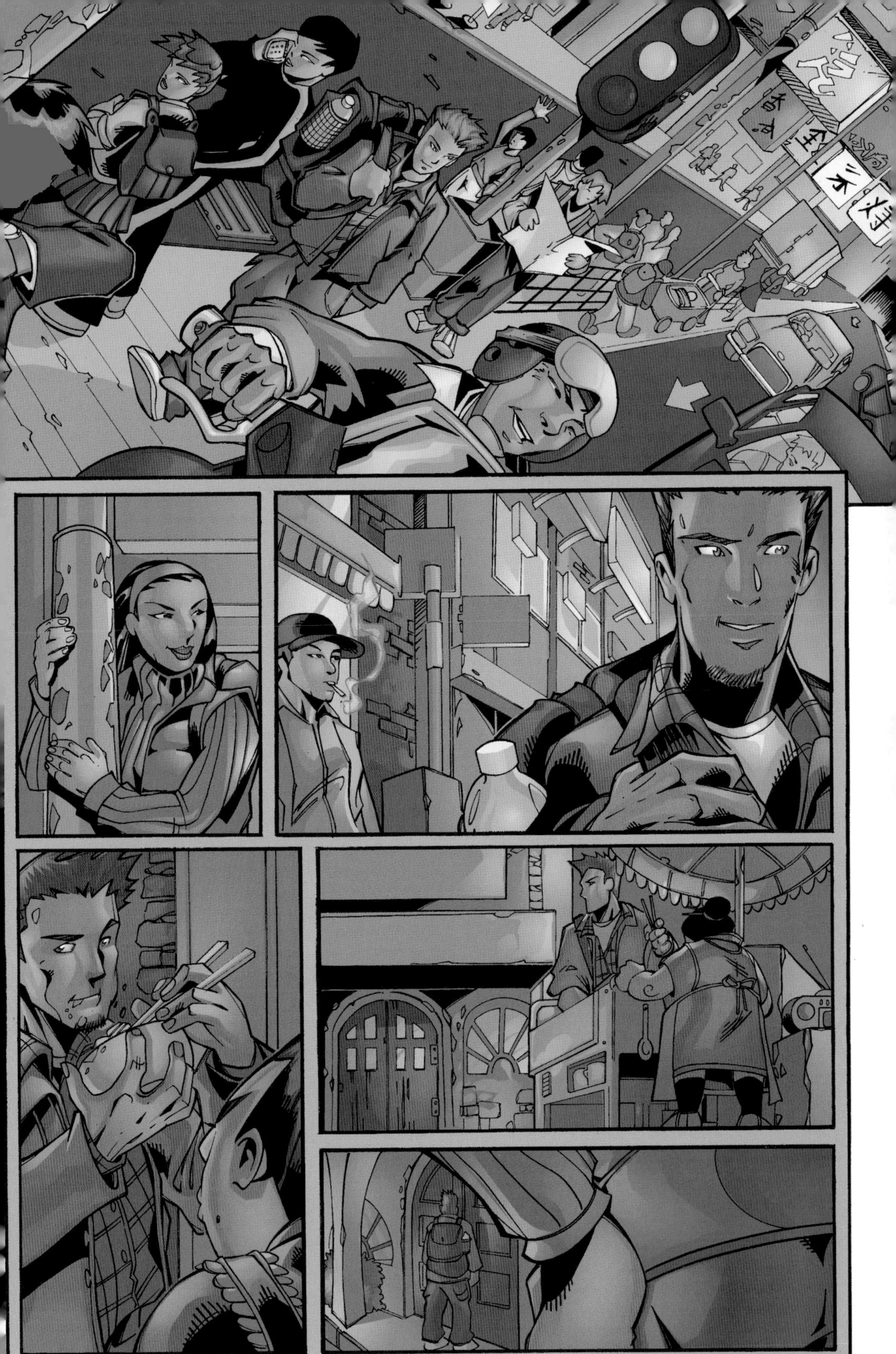

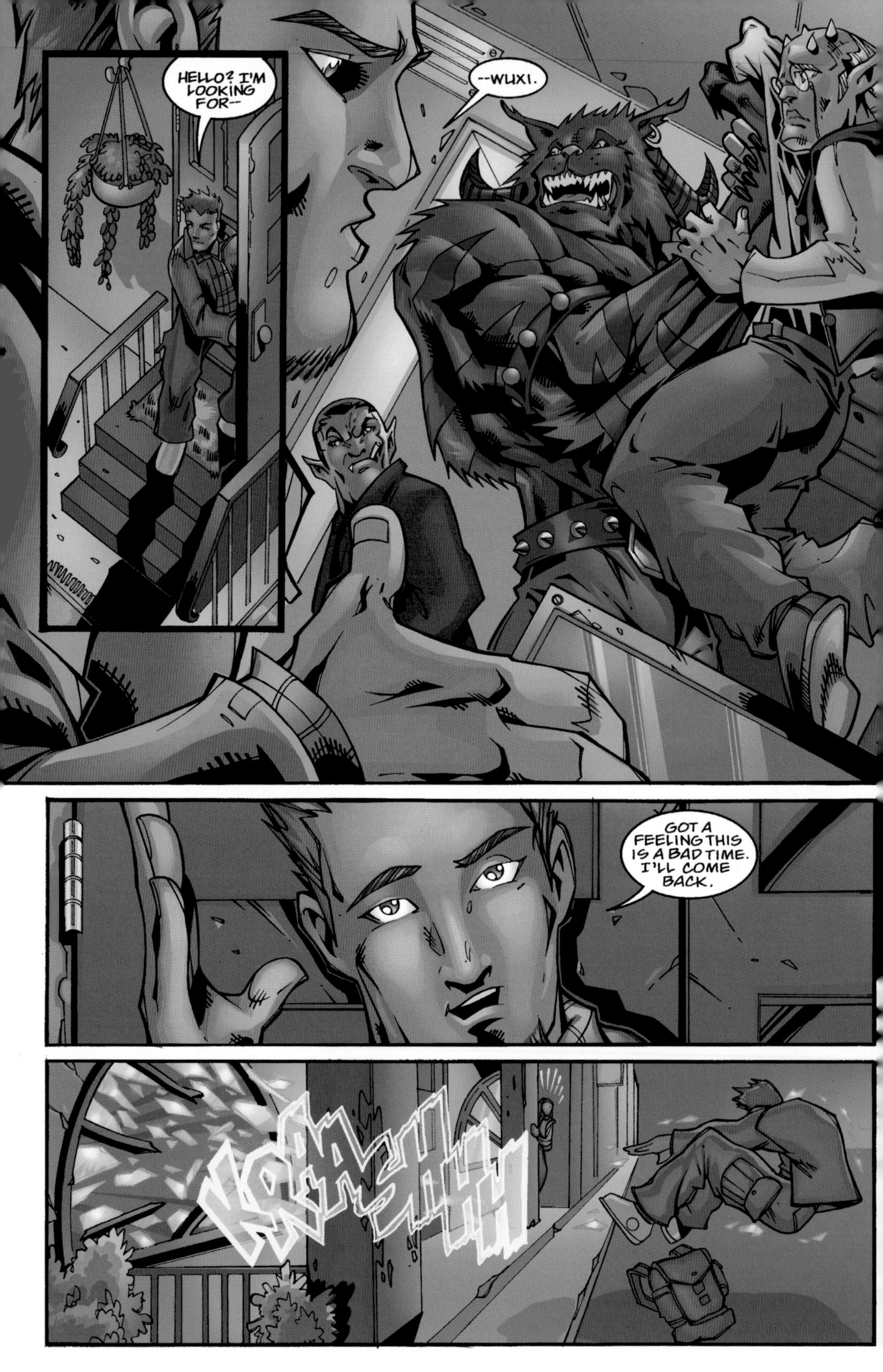
HELLO? I'M LOOKING FOR--
--WUXI.
GOT A FEELING THIS IS A BAD TIME. I'LL COME BACK.
KRASHHH

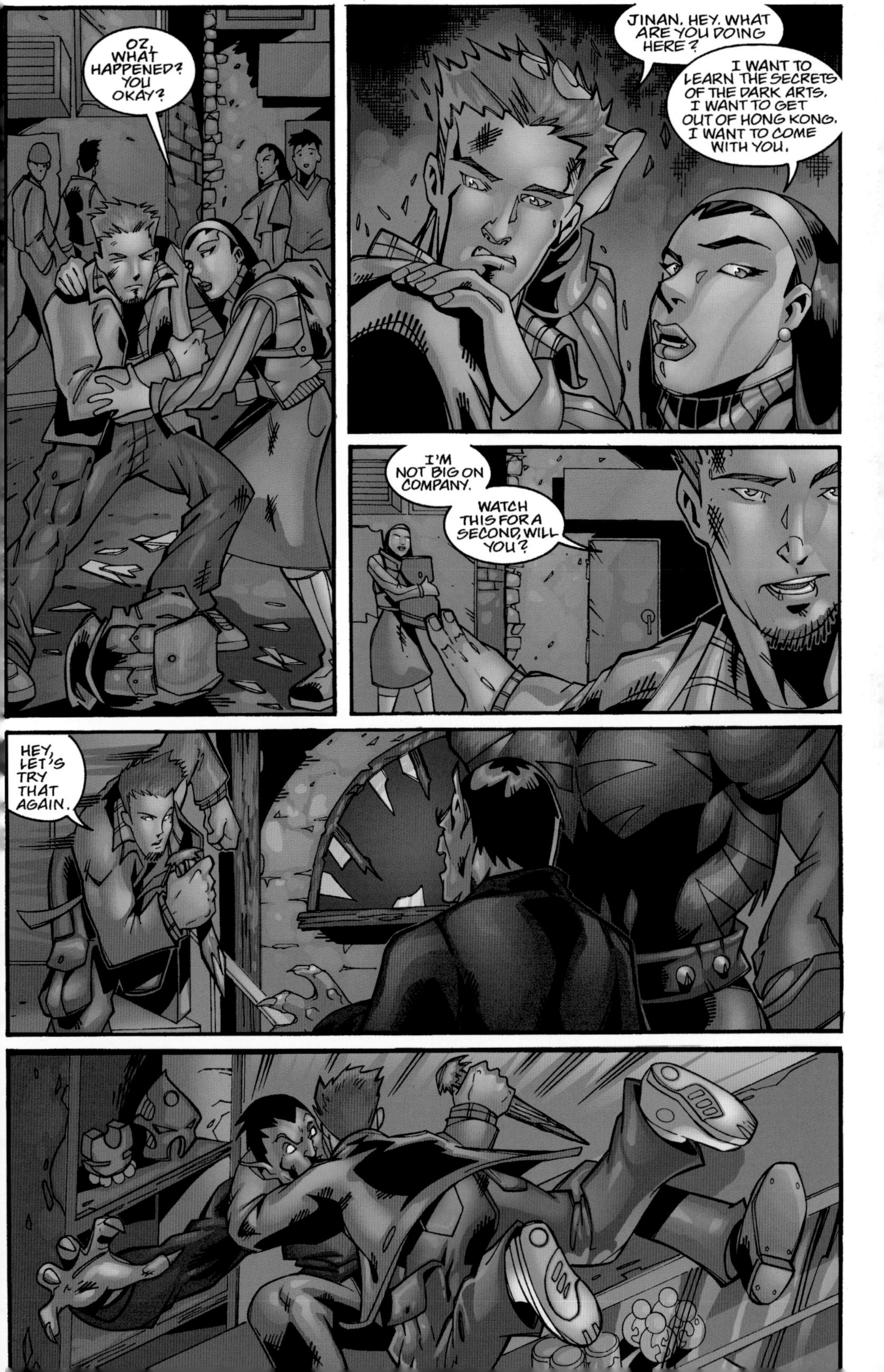

OZ, WHAT HAPPENED? YOU OKAY?
JINAN. HEY. WHAT ARE YOU DOING HERE?
I WANT TO LEARN THE SECRETS OF THE DARK ARTS. I WANT TO GET OUT OF HONG KONG. I WANT TO COME WITH YOU.
I'M NOT BIG ON COMPANY.
WATCH THIS FOR A SECOND, WILL YOU?
HEY, LET'S TRY THAT AGAIN.

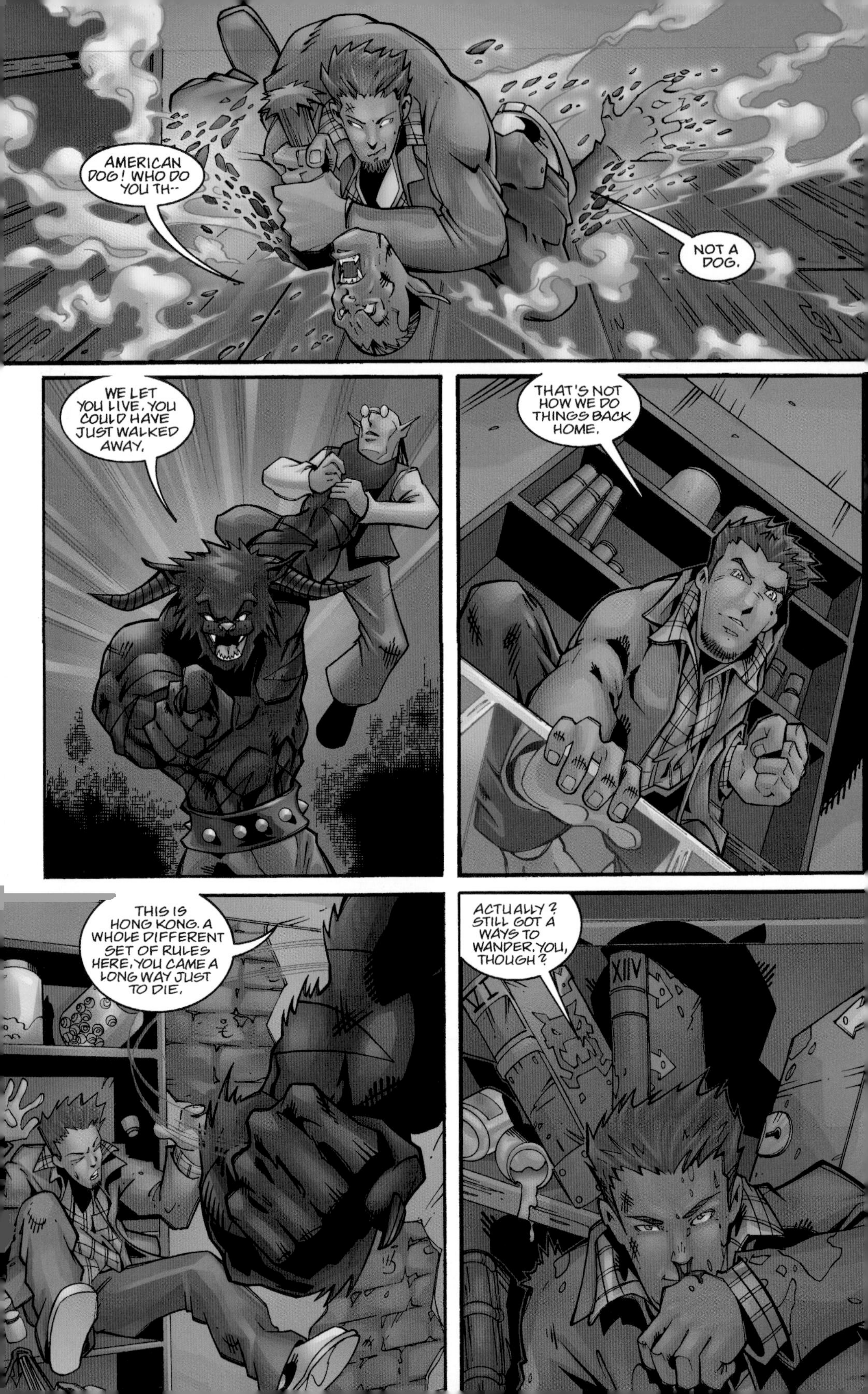
AMERICAN DOG! WHO DO YOU TH--
NOT A DOG.
WE LET YOU LIVE. YOU COULD HAVE JUST WALKED AWAY.
THAT'S NOT HOW WE DO THINGS BACK HOME.
THIS IS HONG KONG. A WHOLE DIFFERENT SET OF RULES HERE. YOU CAME A LONG WAY JUST TO DIE.
ACTUALLY? STILL GOT A WAYS TO WANDER. YOU, THOUGH?

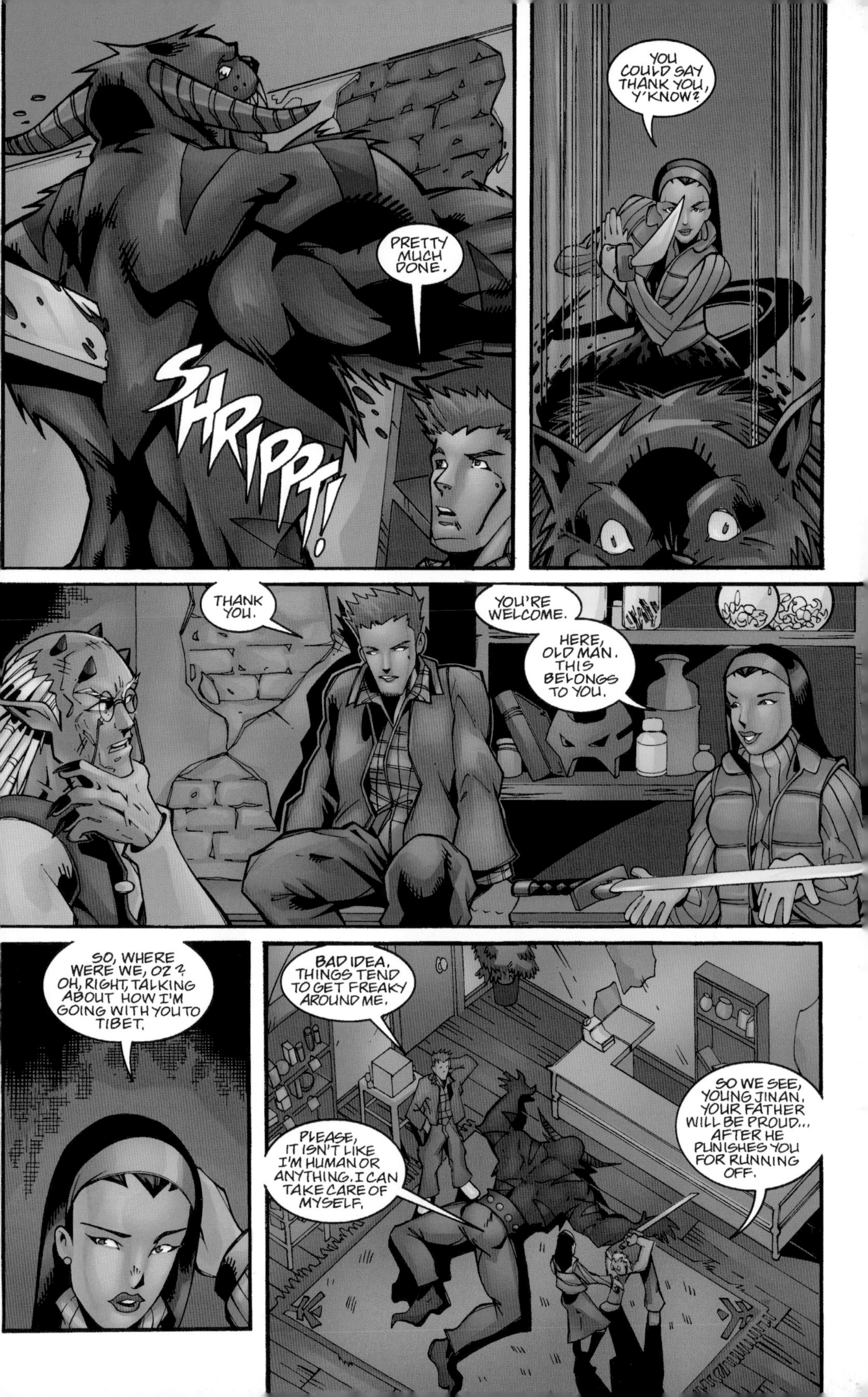
PRETTY MUCH DONE.
SHRIPPT!
YOU COULD SAY THANK YOU, Y'KNOW?
THANK YOU.
YOU'RE WELCOME.
HERE, OLD MAN. THIS BELONGS TO YOU.
SO, WHERE WERE WE, OZ? OH, RIGHT, TALKING ABOUT HOW I'M GOING WITH YOU TO TIBET.
BAD IDEA. THINGS TEND TO GET FREAKY AROUND ME.
PLEASE, IT ISN'T LIKE I'M HUMAN OR ANYTHING. I CAN TAKE CARE OF MYSELF.
SO WE SEE, YOUNG JINAN, YOUR FATHER WILL BE PROUD... AFTER HE PUNISHES YOU FOR RUNNING OFF.

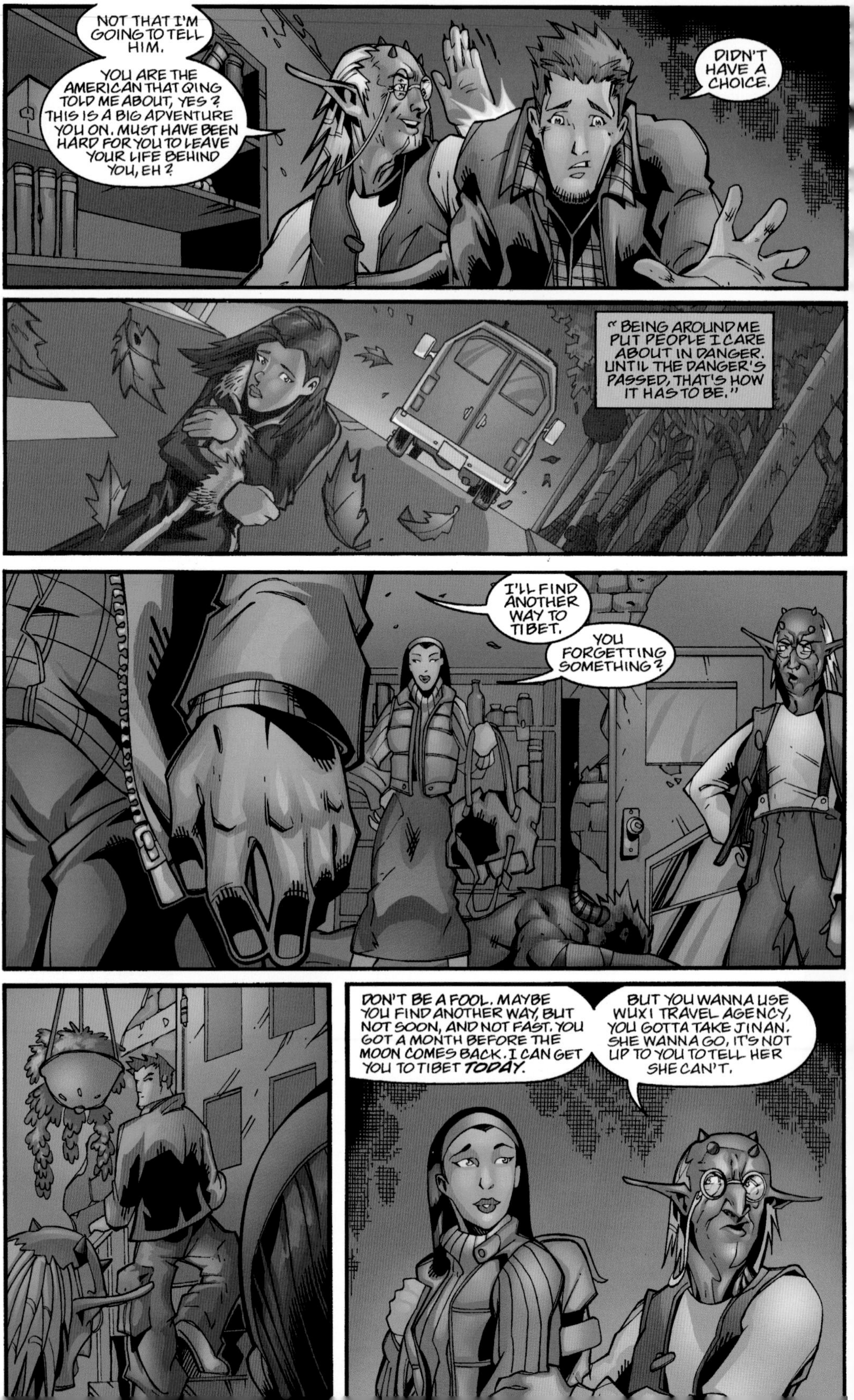
NOT THAT I'M GOING TO TELL HIM.
YOU ARE THE AMERICAN THAT QING TOLD ME ABOUT, YES? THIS IS A BIG ADVENTURE YOU ON. MUST HAVE BEEN HARD FOR YOU TO LEAVE YOUR LIFE BEHIND YOU, EH?
DIDN'T HAVE A CHOICE.
"BEING AROUND ME PUT PEOPLE I CARE ABOUT IN DANGER. UNTIL THE DANGER'S PASSED, THAT'S HOW IT HAS TO BE."
I'LL FIND ANOTHER WAY TO TIBET.
YOU FORGETTING SOMETHING?
DON'T BE A FOOL. MAYBE YOU FIND ANOTHER WAY, BUT NOT SOON, AND NOT FAST. YOU GOT A MONTH BEFORE THE MOON COMES BACK. I CAN GET YOU TO TIBET TODAY.
BUT YOU WANNA USE WUXI TRAVEL AGENCY, YOU GOTTA TAKE JINAN. SHE WANNA GO, IT'S NOT UP TO YOU TO TELL HER SHE CAN'T.

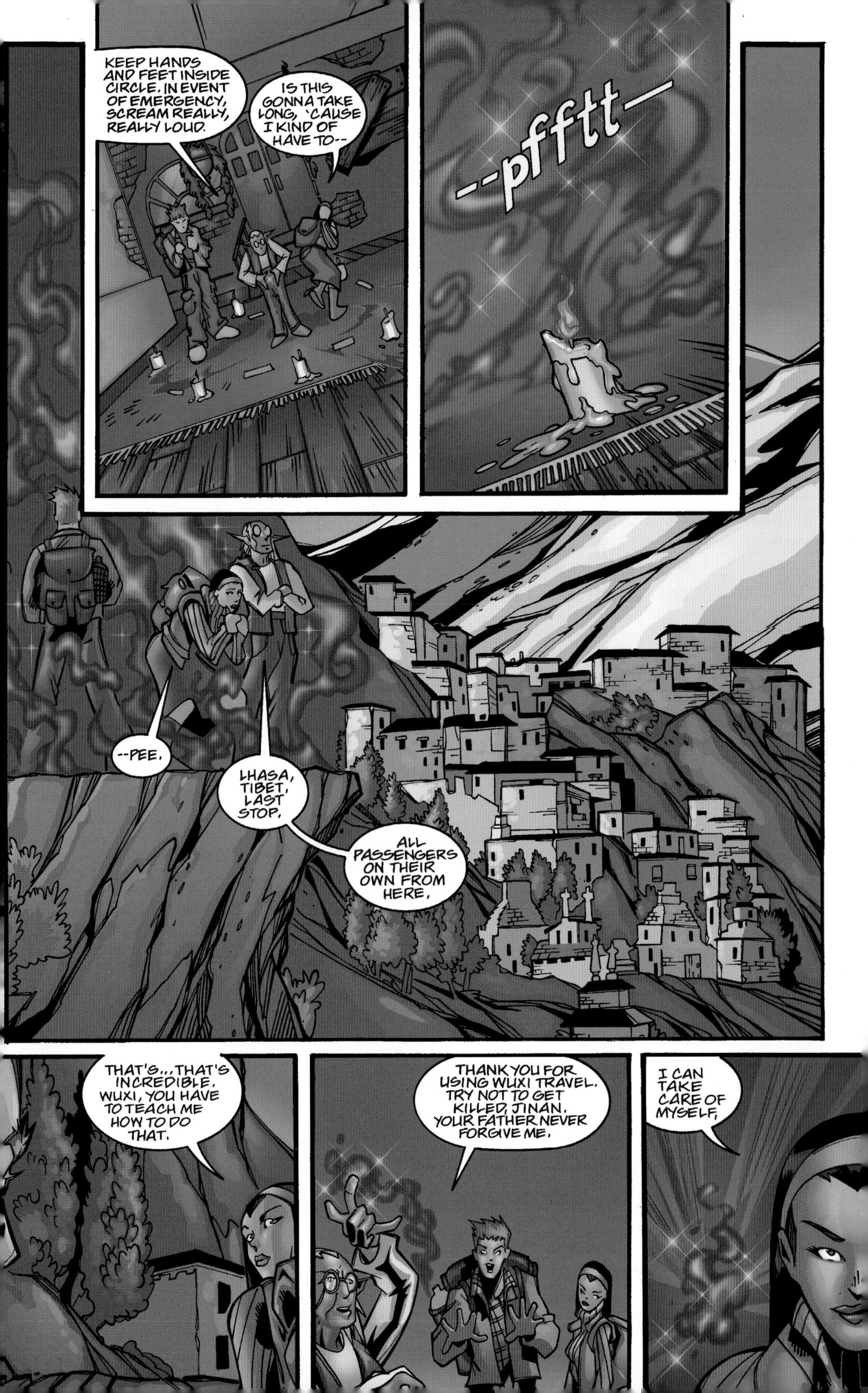
KEEP HANDS AND FEET INSIDE CIRCLE. IN EVENT OF EMERGENCY, SCREAM REALLY, REALLY LOUD.
IS THIS GONNA TAKE LONG, 'CAUSE I KIND OF HAVE TO--
--pfftt--
--PEE.
LHASA, TIBET. LAST STOP.
ALL PASSENGERS ON THEIR OWN FROM HERE.
THAT'S... THAT'S INCREDIBLE. WUXI, YOU HAVE TO TEACH ME HOW TO DO THAT.
THANK YOU FOR USING WUXI TRAVEL. TRY NOT TO GET KILLED, JINAN. YOUR FATHER NEVER FORGIVE ME.
I CAN TAKE CARE OF MYSELF.

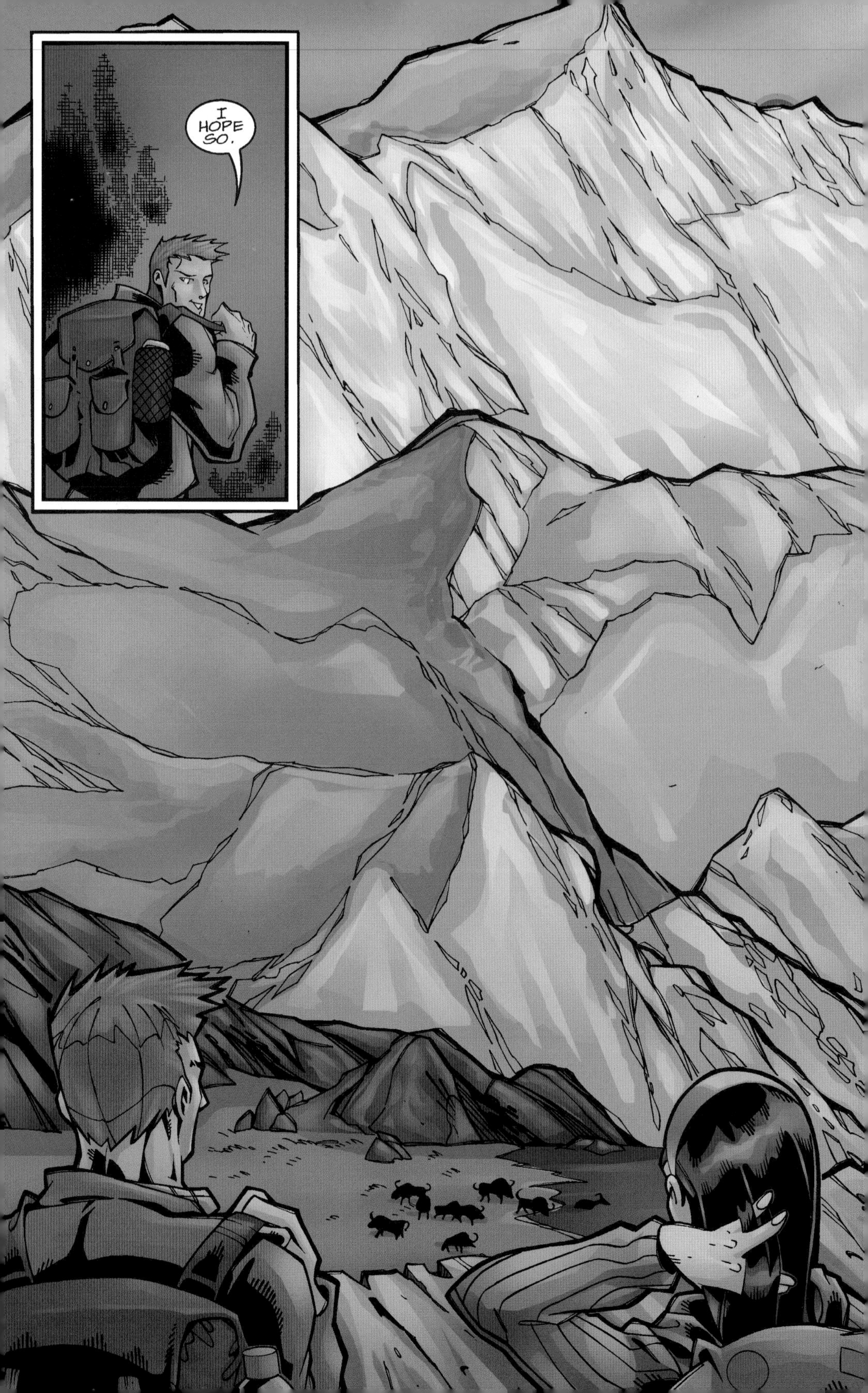
I HOPE SO.

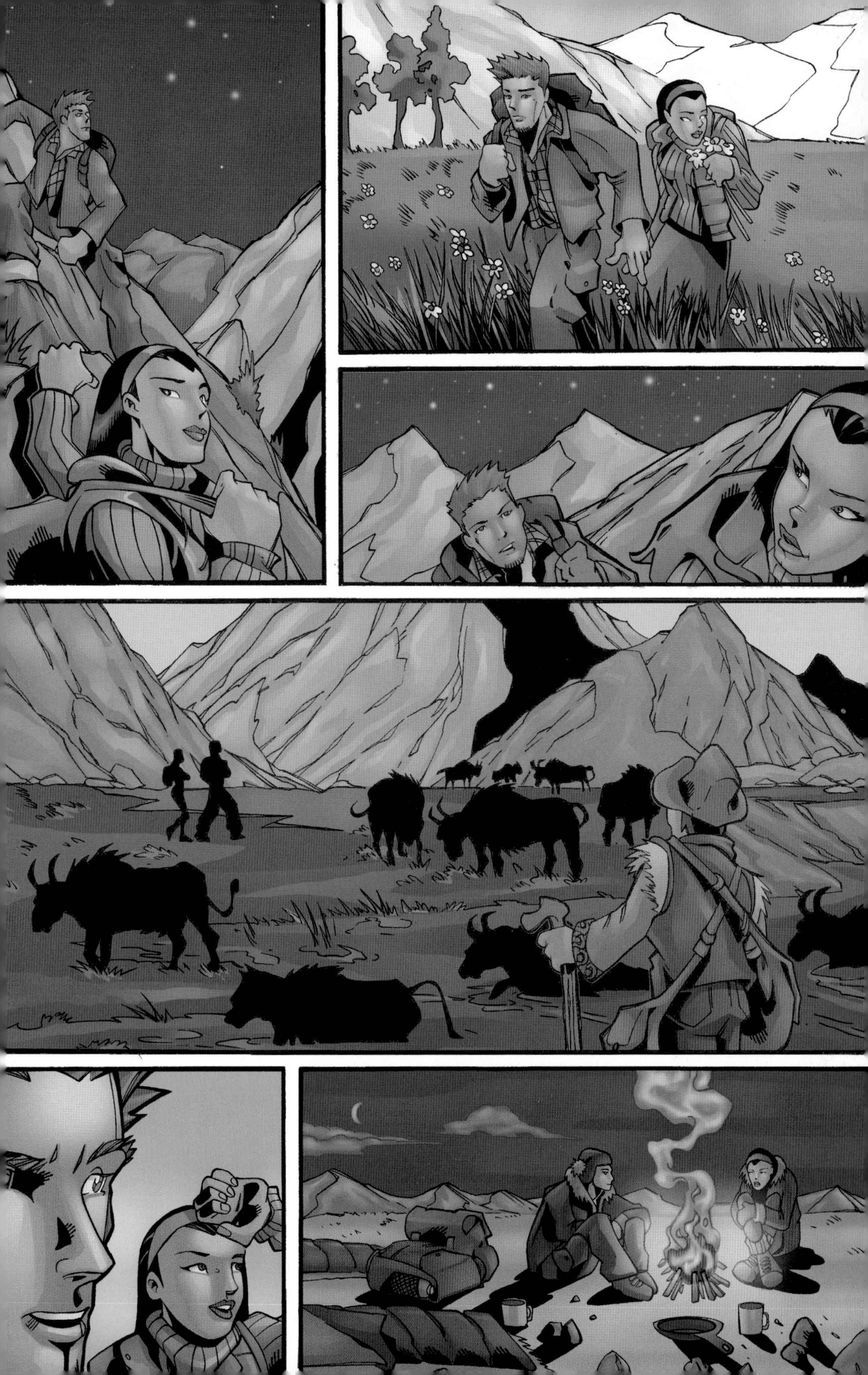

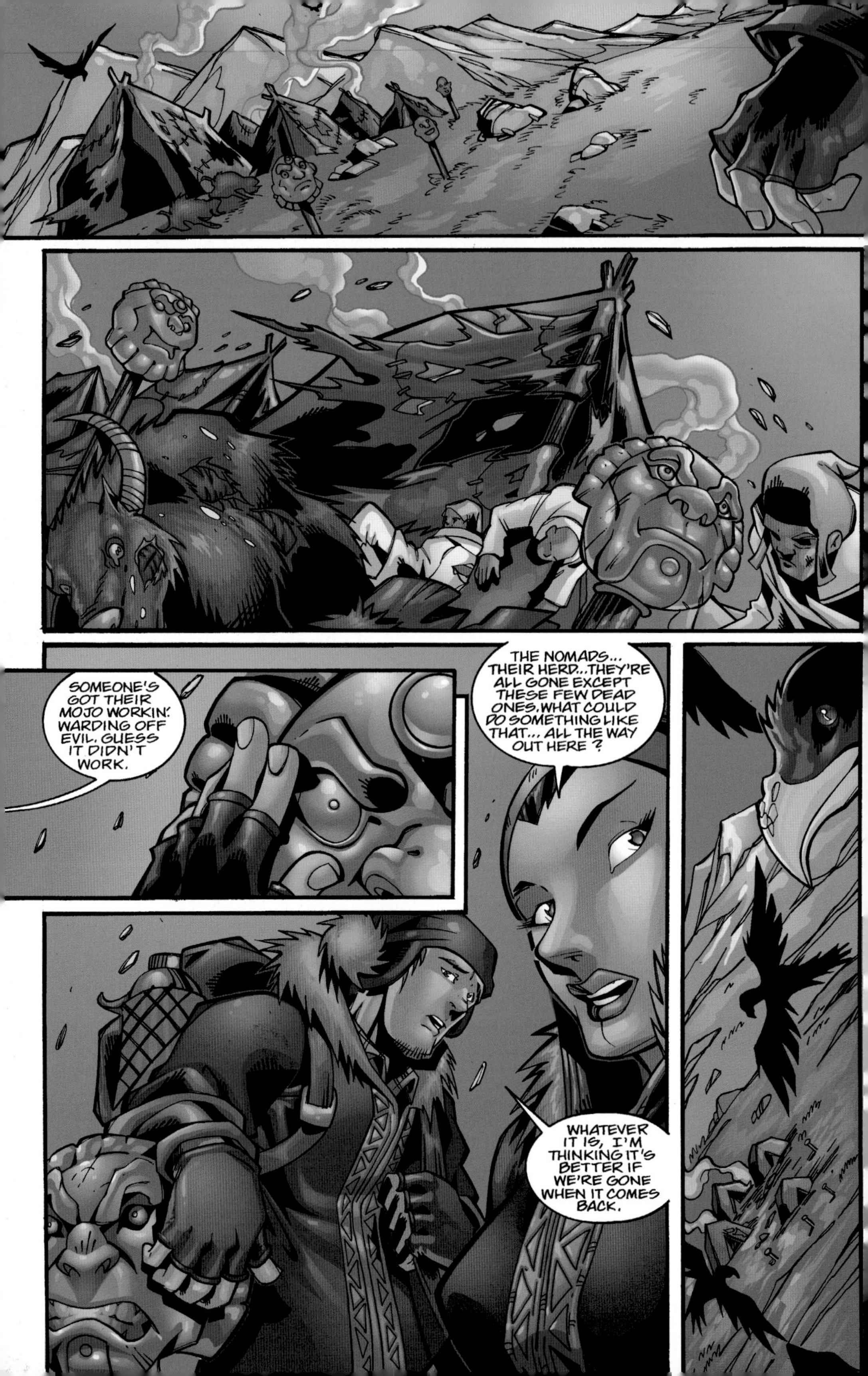
SOMEONE'S GOT THEIR MOJO WORKIN'. WARDING OFF EVIL. GUESS IT DIDN'T WORK.
THE NOMADS... THEIR HERD... THEY'RE ALL GONE EXCEPT THESE FEW DEAD ONES. WHAT COULD DO SOMETHING LIKE THAT... ALL THE WAY OUT HERE ?
WHATEVER IT IS, I'M THINKING IT'S BETTER IF WE'RE GONE WHEN IT COMES BACK.

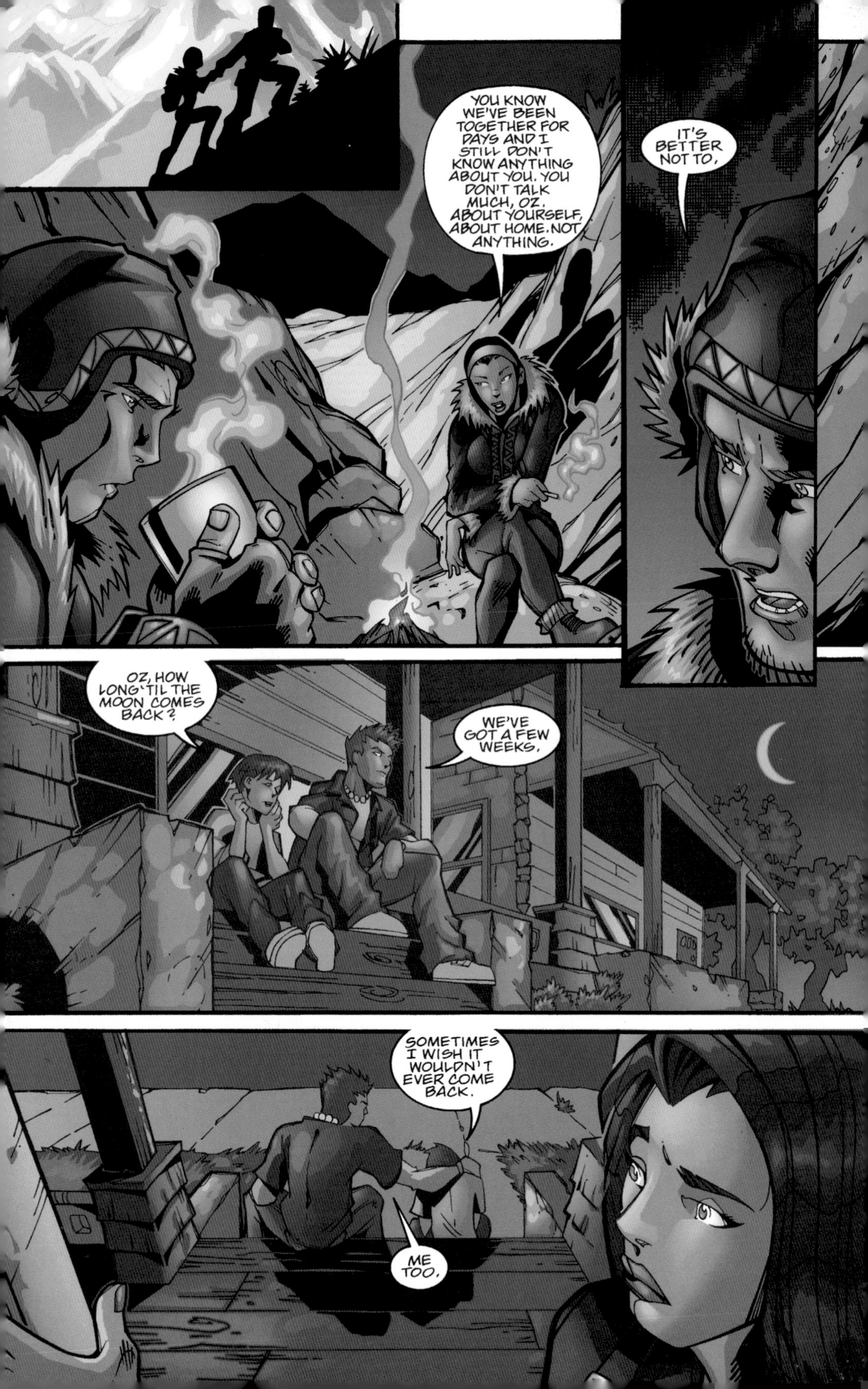
YOU KNOW WE'VE BEEN TOGETHER FOR DAYS AND I STILL DON'T KNOW ANYTHING ABOUT YOU. YOU DON'T TALK MUCH, OZ. ABOUT YOURSELF, ABOUT HOME. NOT ANYTHING.
IT'S BETTER NOT TO.
OZ, HOW LONG 'TIL THE MOON COMES BACK?
WE'VE GOT A FEW WEEKS.
SOMETIMES I WISH IT WOULDN'T EVER COME BACK.
ME TOO.

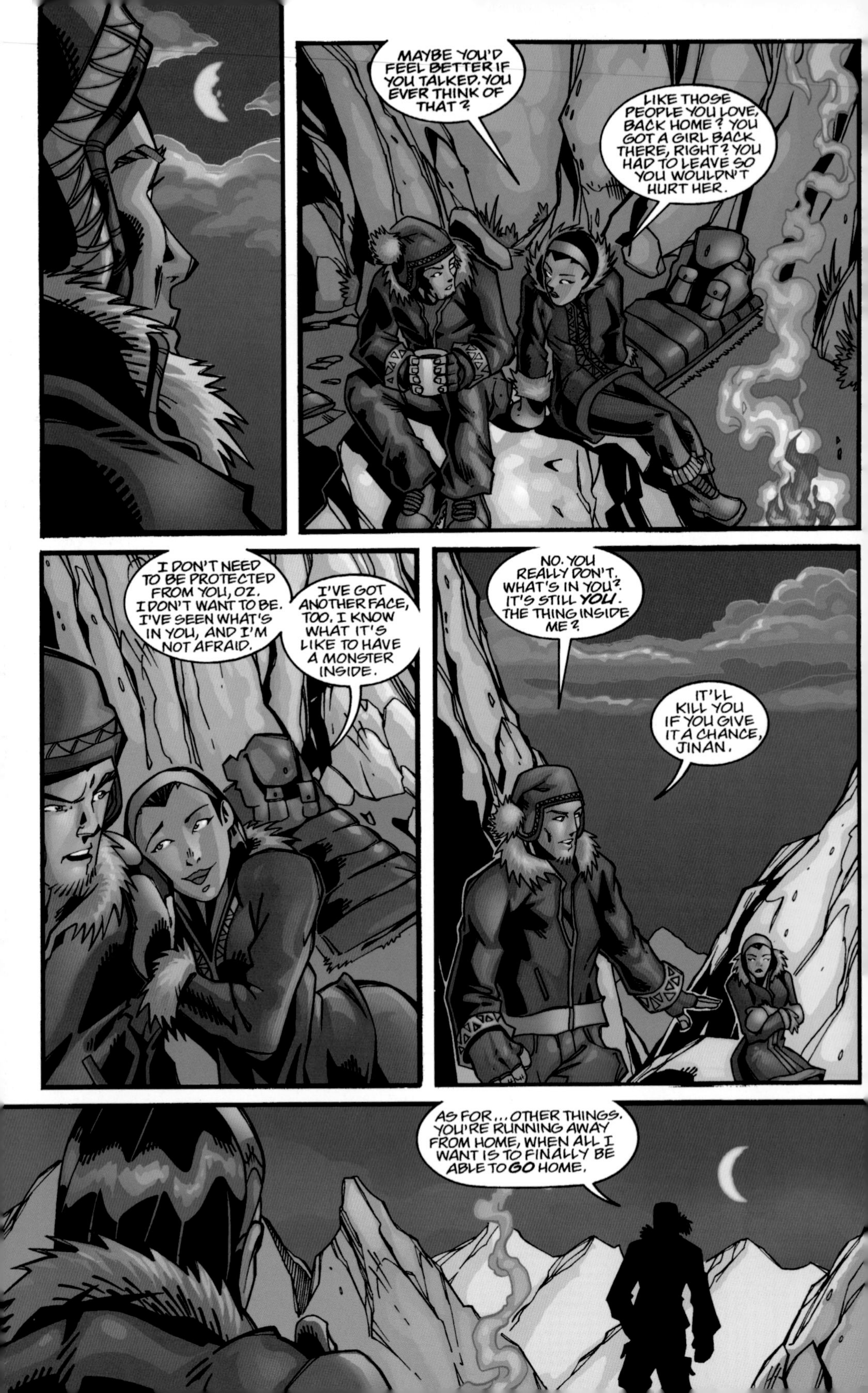
MAYBE YOU'D FEEL BETTER IF YOU TALKED. YOU EVER THINK OF THAT?
LIKE THOSE PEOPLE YOU LOVE, BACK HOME? YOU GOT A GIRL BACK THERE, RIGHT? YOU HAD TO LEAVE SO YOU WOULDN'T HURT HER.
I DON'T NEED TO BE PROTECTED FROM YOU, OZ. I DON'T WANT TO BE. I'VE SEEN WHAT'S IN YOU, AND I'M NOT AFRAID.
I'VE GOT ANOTHER FACE, TOO. I KNOW WHAT IT'S LIKE TO HAVE A MONSTER INSIDE.
NO. YOU REALLY DON'T. WHAT'S IN YOU? IT'S STILL YOU. THE THING INSIDE ME?
IT'LL KILL YOU IF YOU GIVE IT A CHANCE, JINAN.
AS FOR... OTHER THINGS, YOU'RE RUNNING AWAY FROM HOME, WHEN ALL I WANT IS TO FINALLY BE ABLE TO GO HOME.

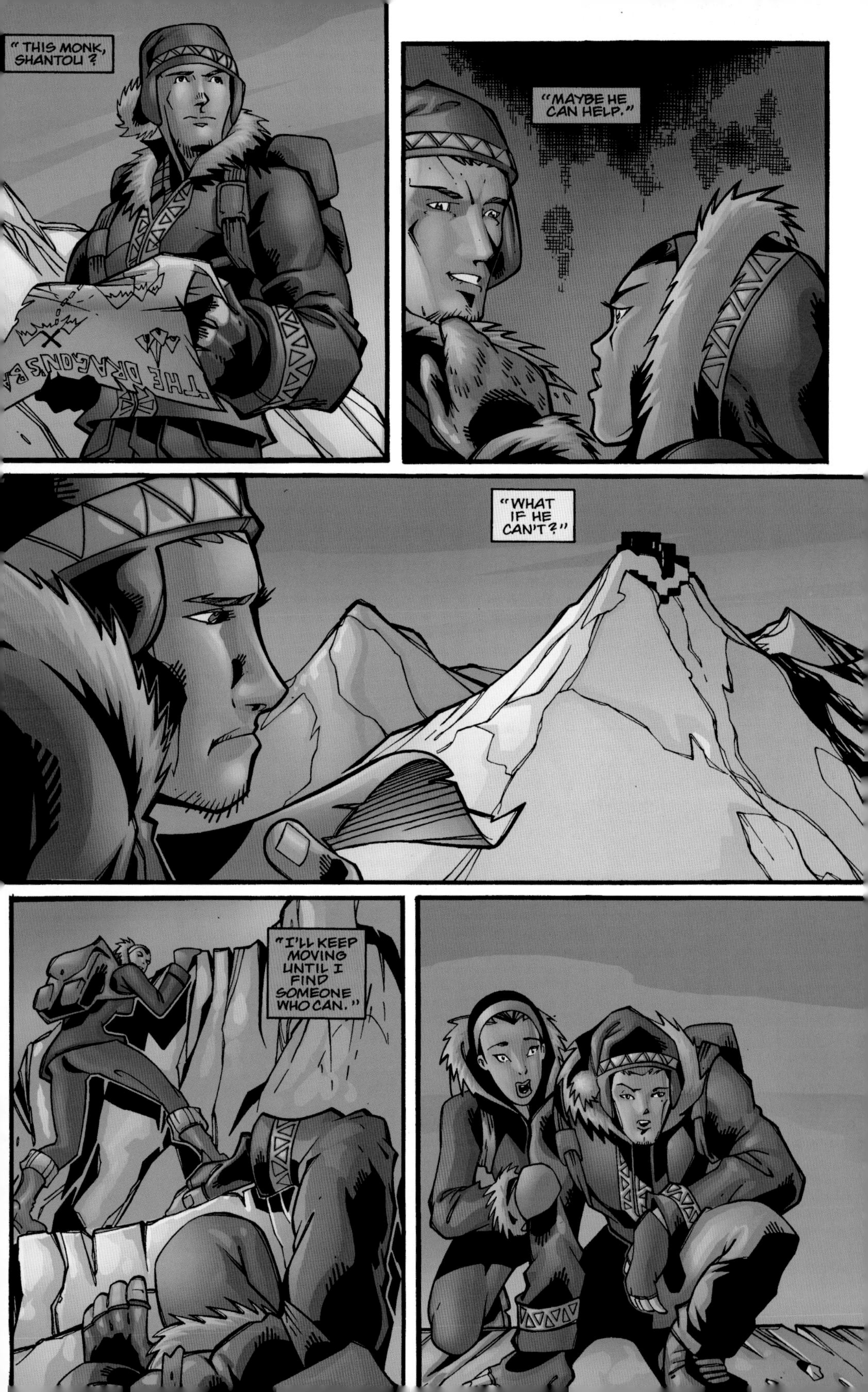
"THIS MONK, SHANTOU?
THE DRAGONS
"MAYBE HE CAN HELP."
"WHAT IF HE CAN'T?"
"I'LL KEEP MOVING UNTIL I FIND SOMEONE WHO CAN."

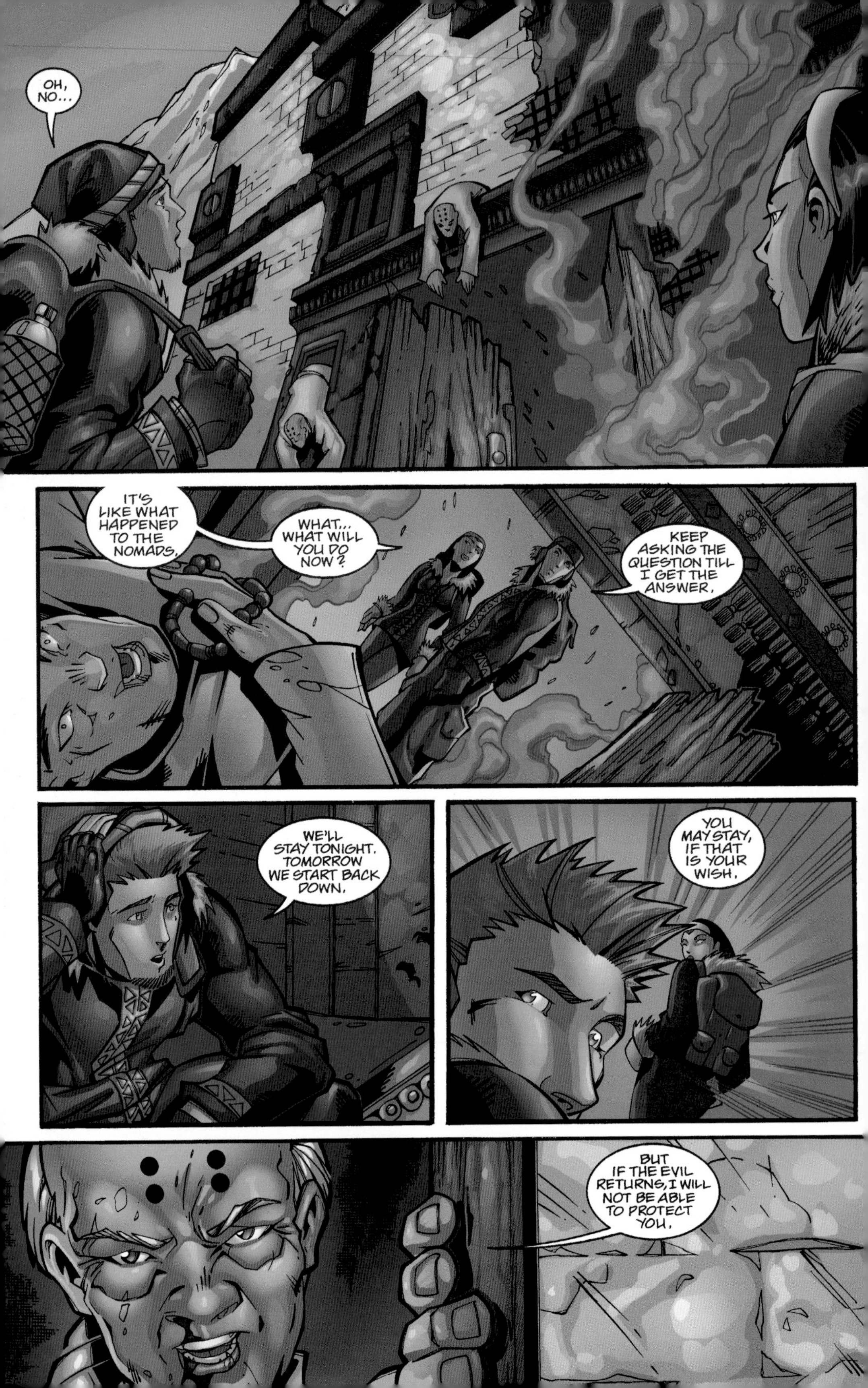
OH, NO...
IT'S LIKE WHAT HAPPENED TO THE NOMADS.
WHAT... WHAT WILL YOU DO NOW?
KEEP ASKING THE QUESTION TILL I GET THE ANSWER.
WE'LL STAY TONIGHT. TOMORROW WE START BACK DOWN.
YOU MAY STAY, IF THAT IS YOUR WISH.
BUT IF THE EVIL RETURNS, I WILL NOT BE ABLE TO PROTECT YOU.

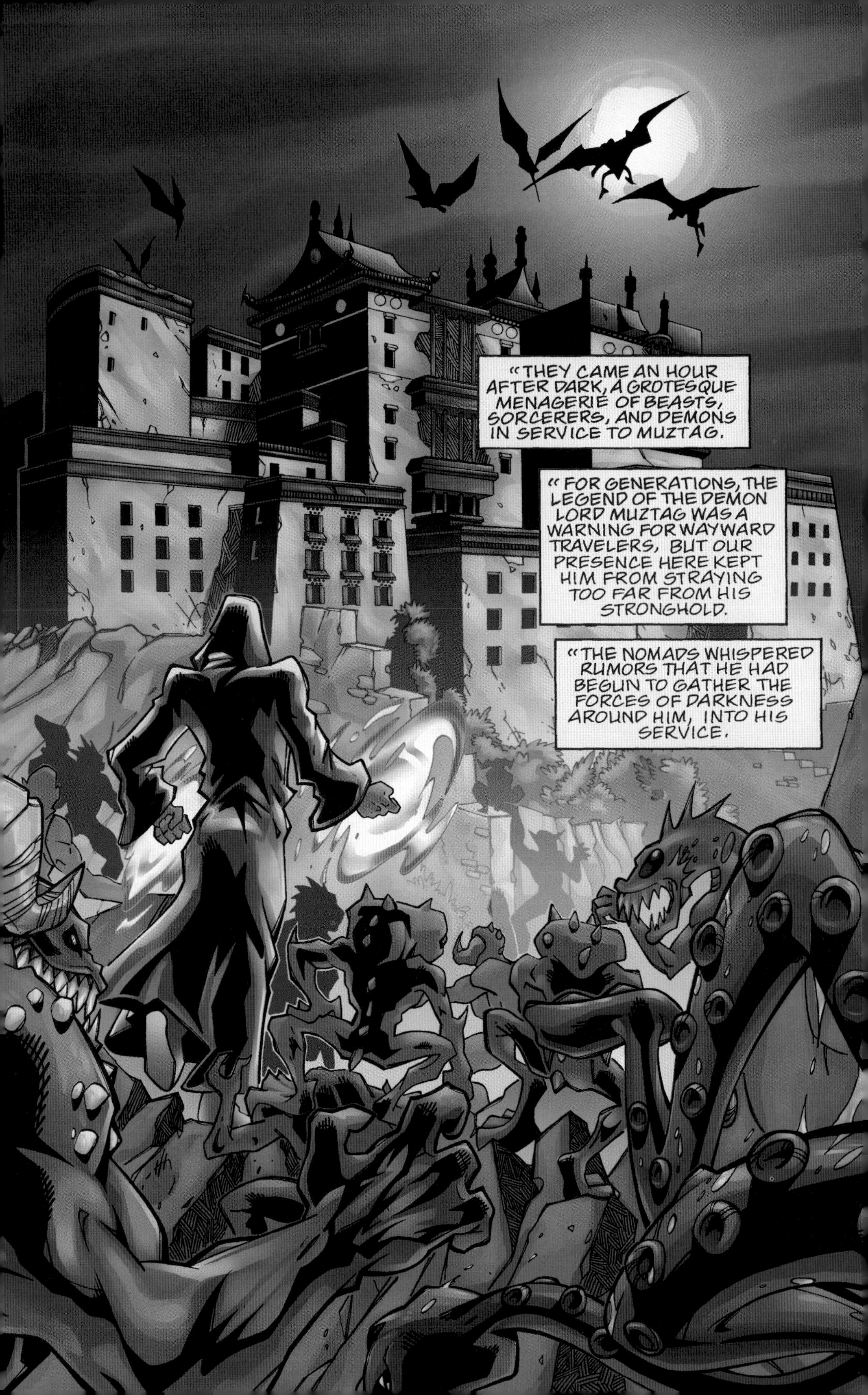
"THEY CAME AN HOUR AFTER DARK, A GROTESQUE MENAGERIE OF BEASTS, SORCERERS, AND DEMONS IN SERVICE TO MUZTAG.
"FOR GENERATIONS, THE LEGEND OF THE DEMON LORD MUZTAG WAS A WARNING FOR WAYWARD TRAVELERS, BUT OUR PRESENCE HERE KEPT HIM FROM STRAYING TOO FAR FROM HIS STRONGHOLD.
"THE NOMADS WHISPERED RUMORS THAT HE HAD BEGUN TO GATHER THE FORCES OF DARKNESS AROUND HIM, INTO HIS SERVICE.

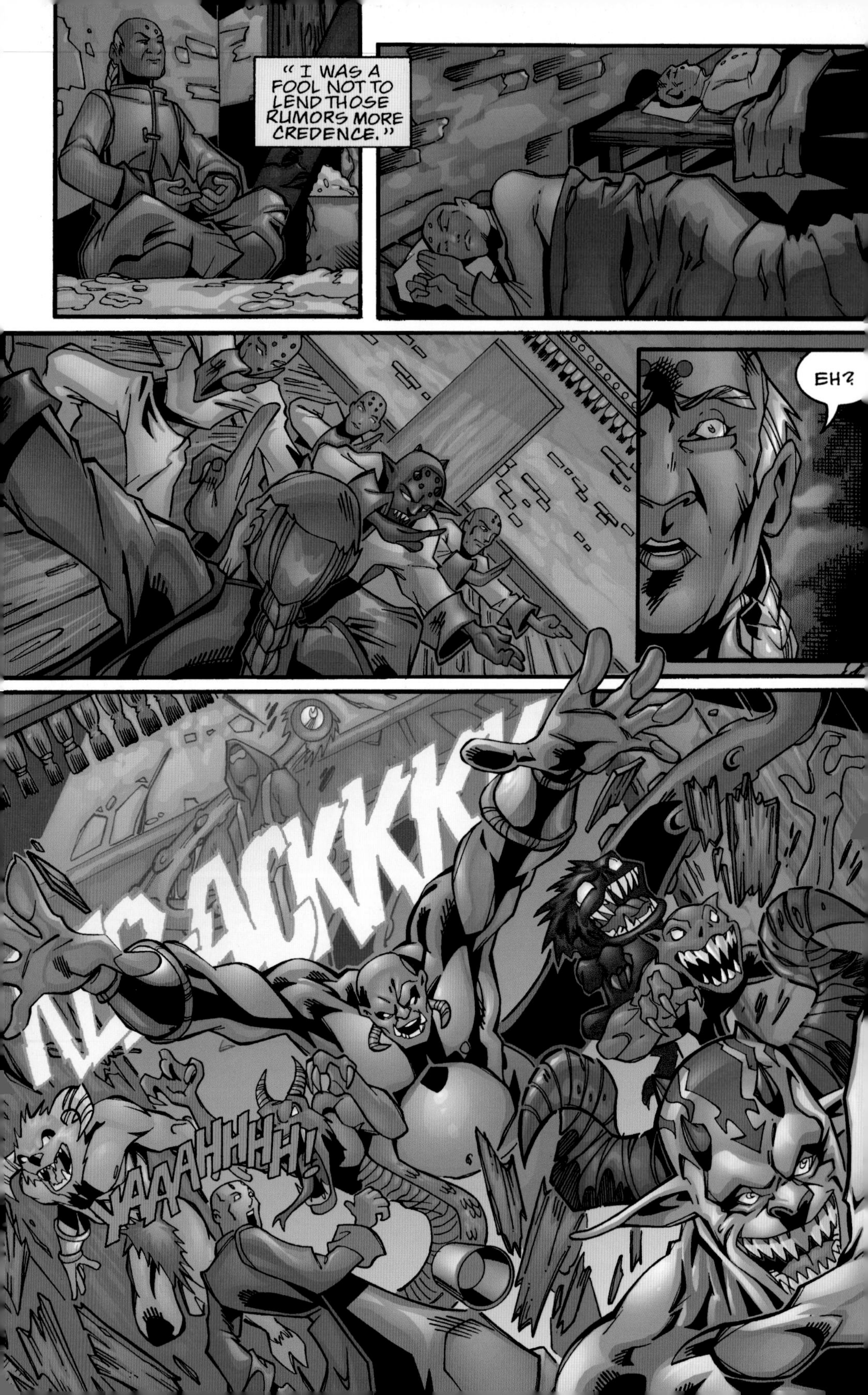
"I WAS A FOOL NOT TO LEND THOSE RUMORS MORE CREDENCE."
EH?
YAAAHHHHH!

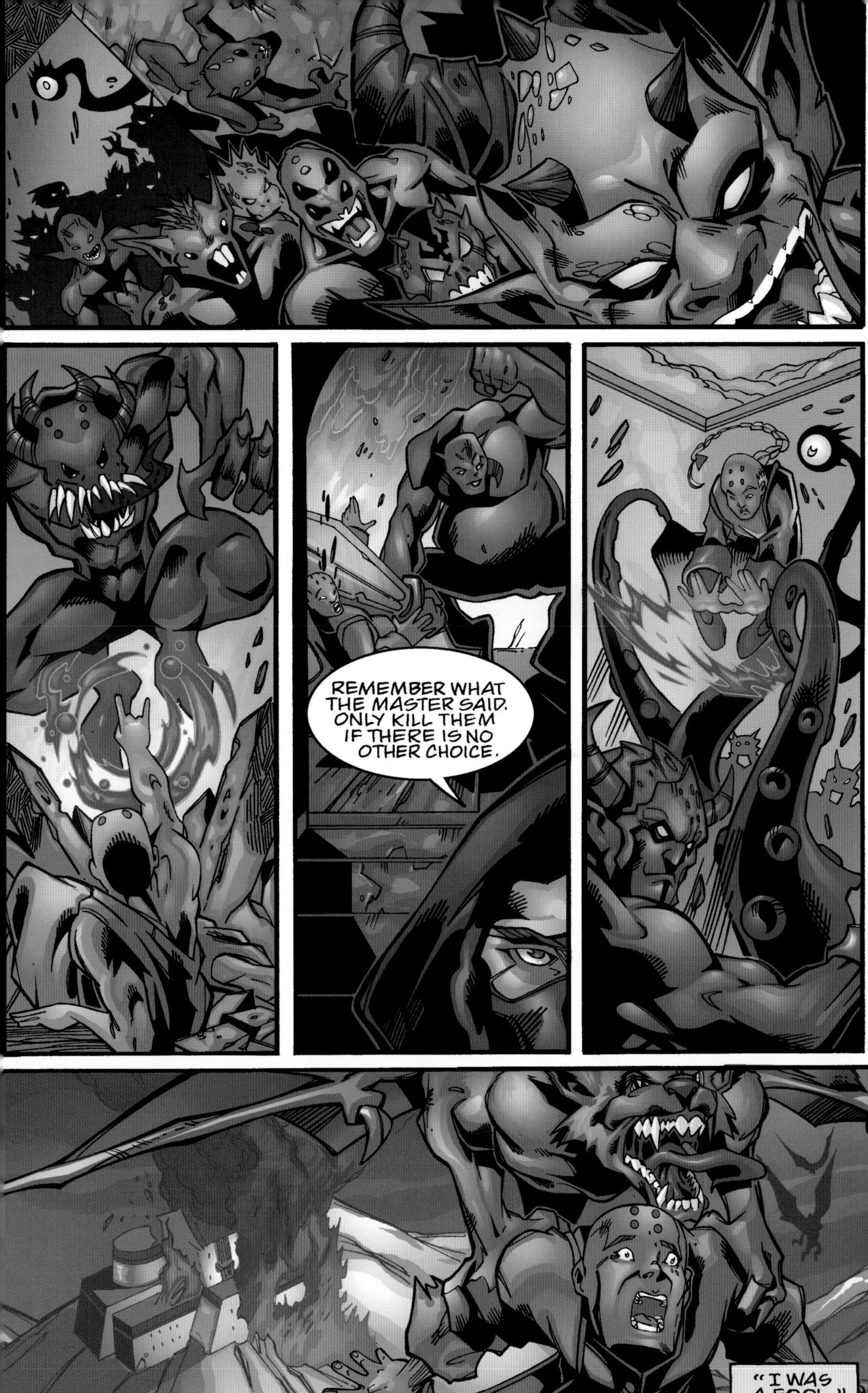
REMEMBER WHAT THE MASTER SAID. ONLY KILL THEM IF THERE IS NO OTHER CHOICE.
"I WAS A FOOL."

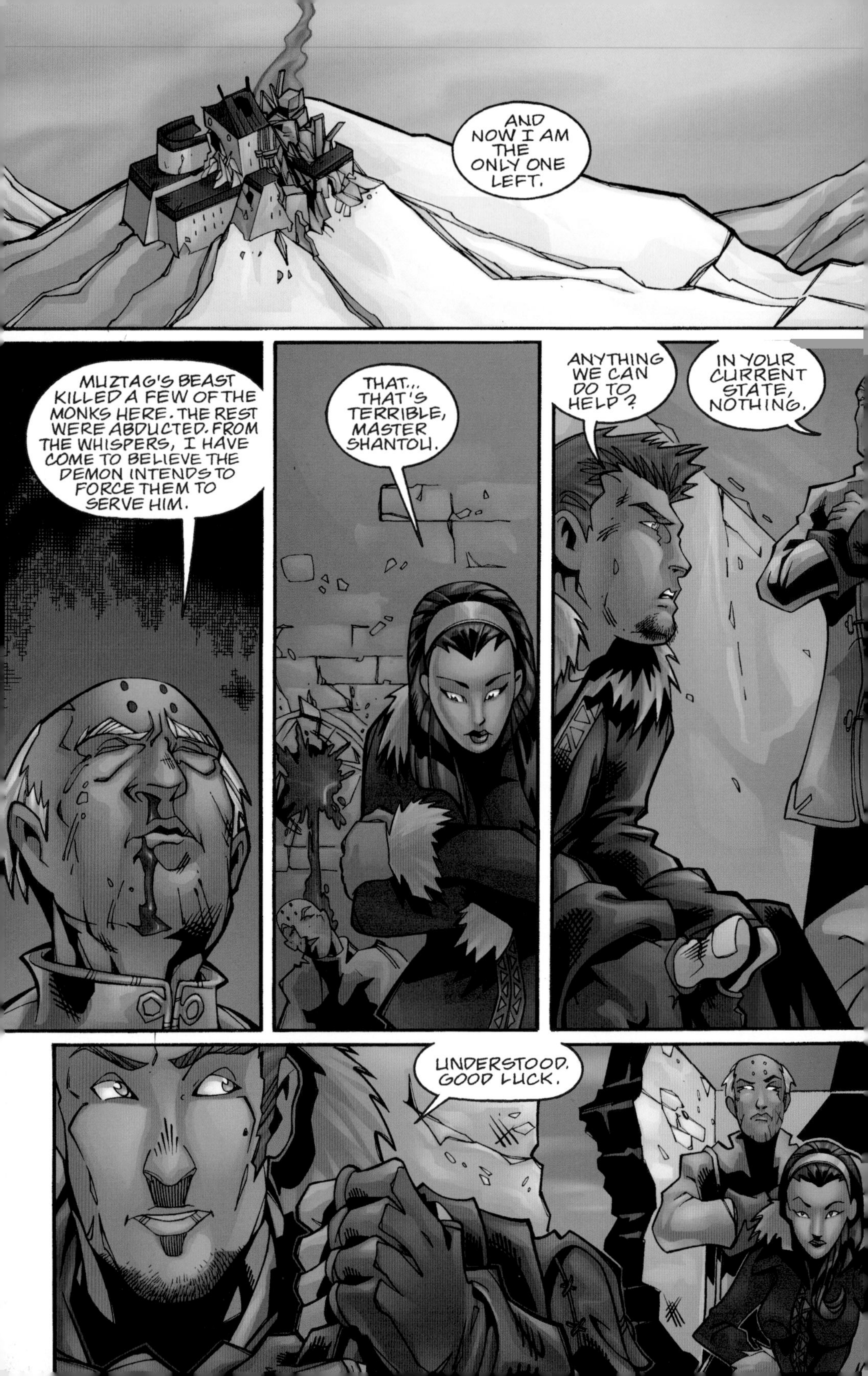
AND NOW I AM THE ONLY ONE LEFT.
MUZTAG'S BEAST KILLED A FEW OF THE MONKS HERE. THE REST WERE ABDUCTED. FROM THE WHISPERS, I HAVE COME TO BELIEVE THE DEMON INTENDS TO FORCE THEM TO SERVE HIM.
THAT... THAT'S TERRIBLE, MASTER SHANTOU.
ANYTHING WE CAN DO TO HELP?
IN YOUR CURRENT STATE, NOTHING.
UNDERSTOOD. GOOD LUCK.

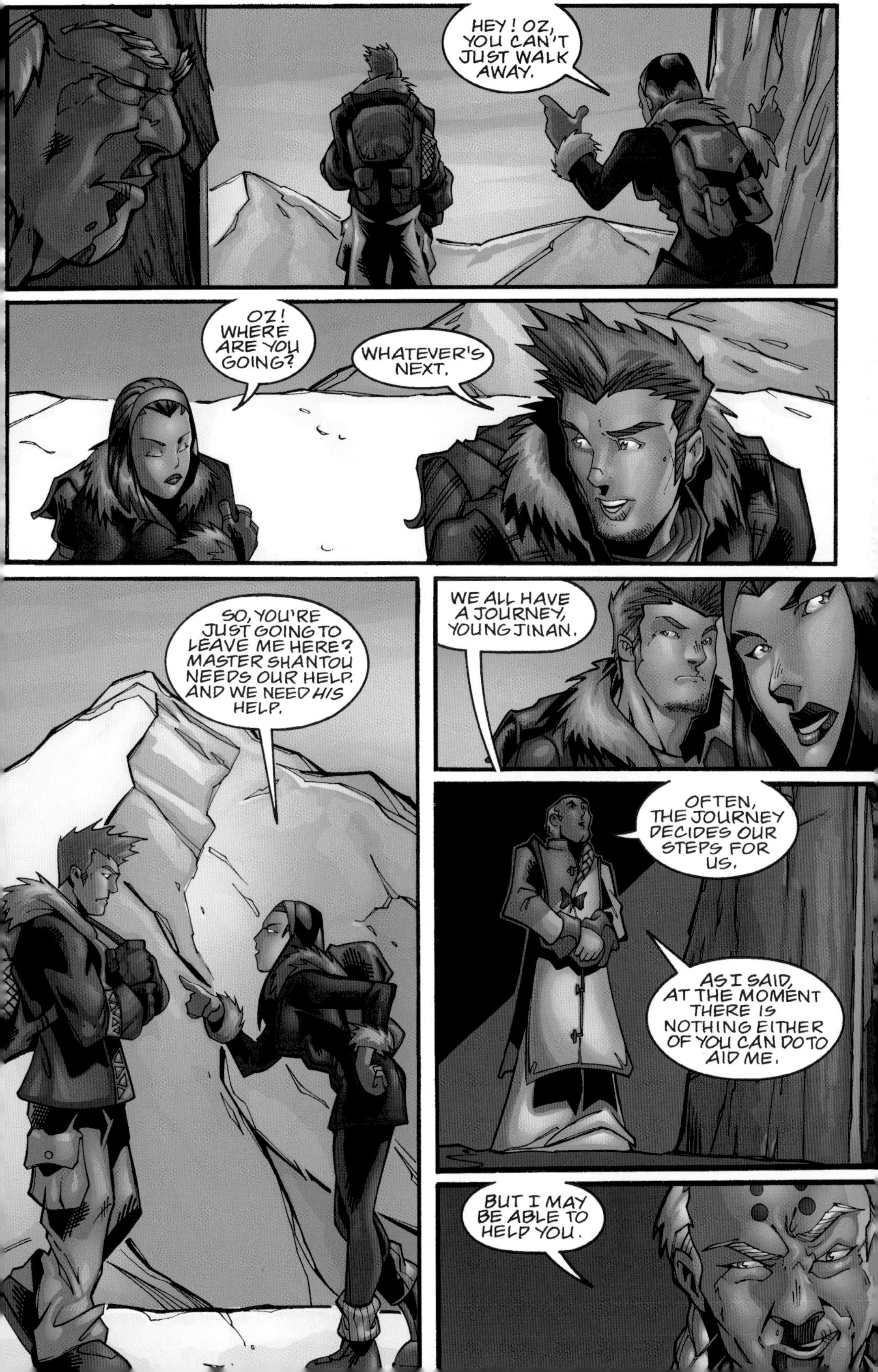
HEY! OZ, YOU CAN'T JUST WALK AWAY.
OZ! WHERE ARE YOU GOING?
WHATEVER'S NEXT.
SO, YOU'RE JUST GOING TO LEAVE ME HERE? MASTER SHANTOU NEEDS OUR HELP. AND WE NEED HIS HELP.
WE ALL HAVE A JOURNEY, YOUNG JINAN.
OFTEN, THE JOURNEY DECIDES OUR STEPS FOR US.
AS I SAID, AT THE MOMENT THERE IS NOTHING EITHER OF YOU CAN DO TO AID ME.
BUT I MAY BE ABLE TO HELP YOU.

YOU HAVE COME TO ME TO FIND A WAY TO CONFRONT THE BEAST, I SENSE THE CONFLICT WITHIN YOU, WOLF.

DON'T CALL ME THAT.

LET YOUR JOURNEY LEAD YOU, MY FRIEND.

BUT, IF YOU WISH TO REMAIN, I MAY BE ABLE TO HELP YOU CONTROL THE BEAST.

I'D BE IN YOUR DEBT.

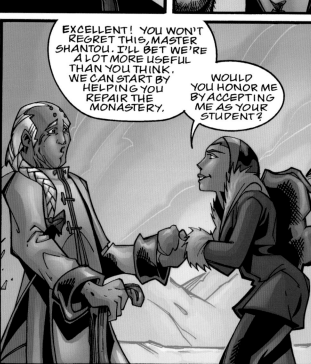

EXCELLENT! YOU WON'T REGRET THIS, MASTER SHANTOU. I'LL BET WE'RE A LOT MORE USEFUL THAN YOU THINK. WE CAN START BY HELPING YOU REPAIR THE MONASTERY.

WOULD YOU HONOR ME BY ACCEPTING ME AS YOUR STUDENT?

ALL DEMONS SHOULD HAVE AT LEAST SOME UNDERSTANDING OF MAGIC, JINAN. ENTER AND BE WELCOME IN MY HOME. BOTH OF YOU.

LET US SPEAK FURTHER, AWAY FROM THE EYES OF THE MOUNTAIN.

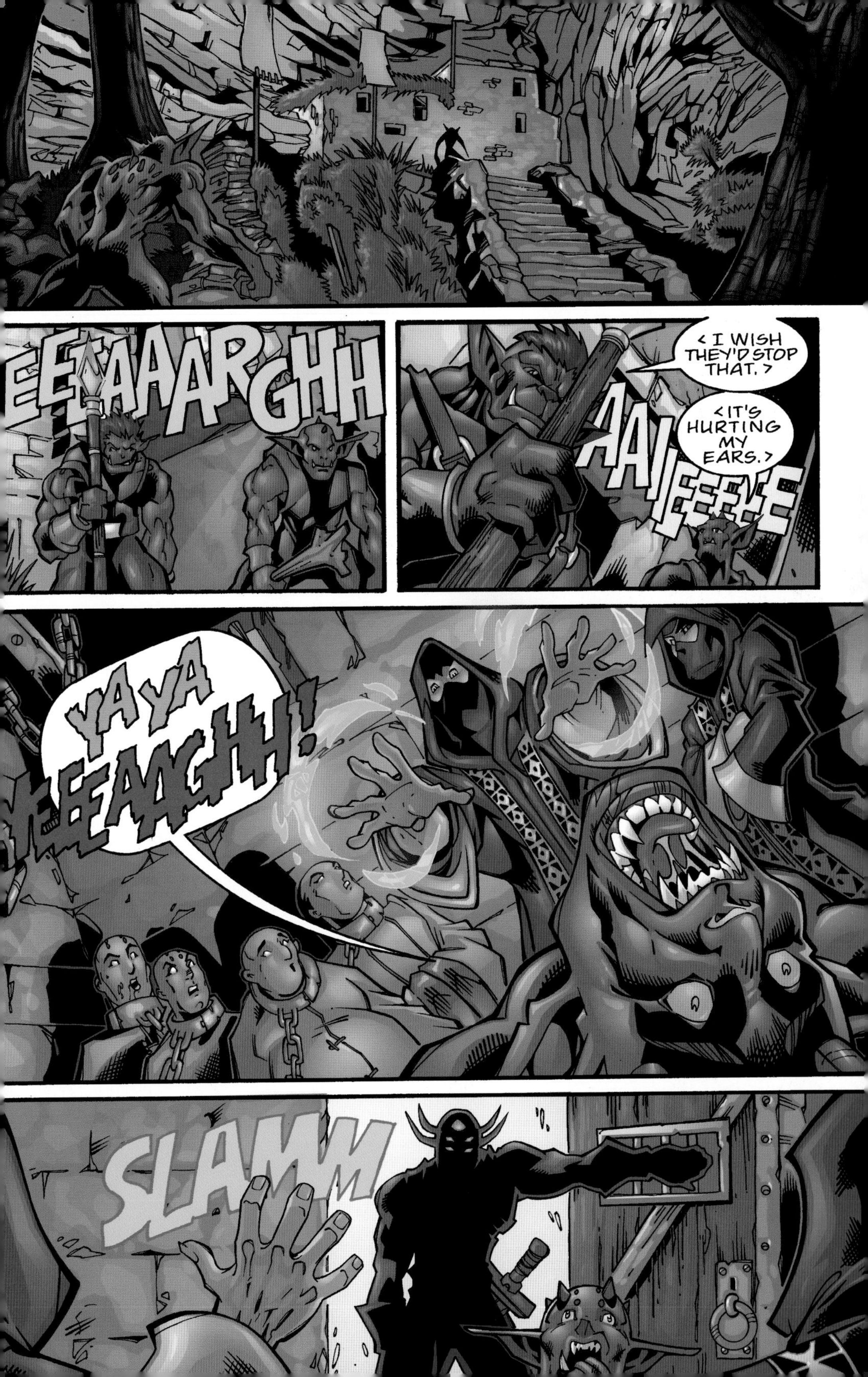
EEEAAARGHH
< I WISH THEY'D STOP THAT. >
AAIEEEEE
< IT'S HURTING MY EARS. >
YA YA YEEEAAGHH!
SLAMM

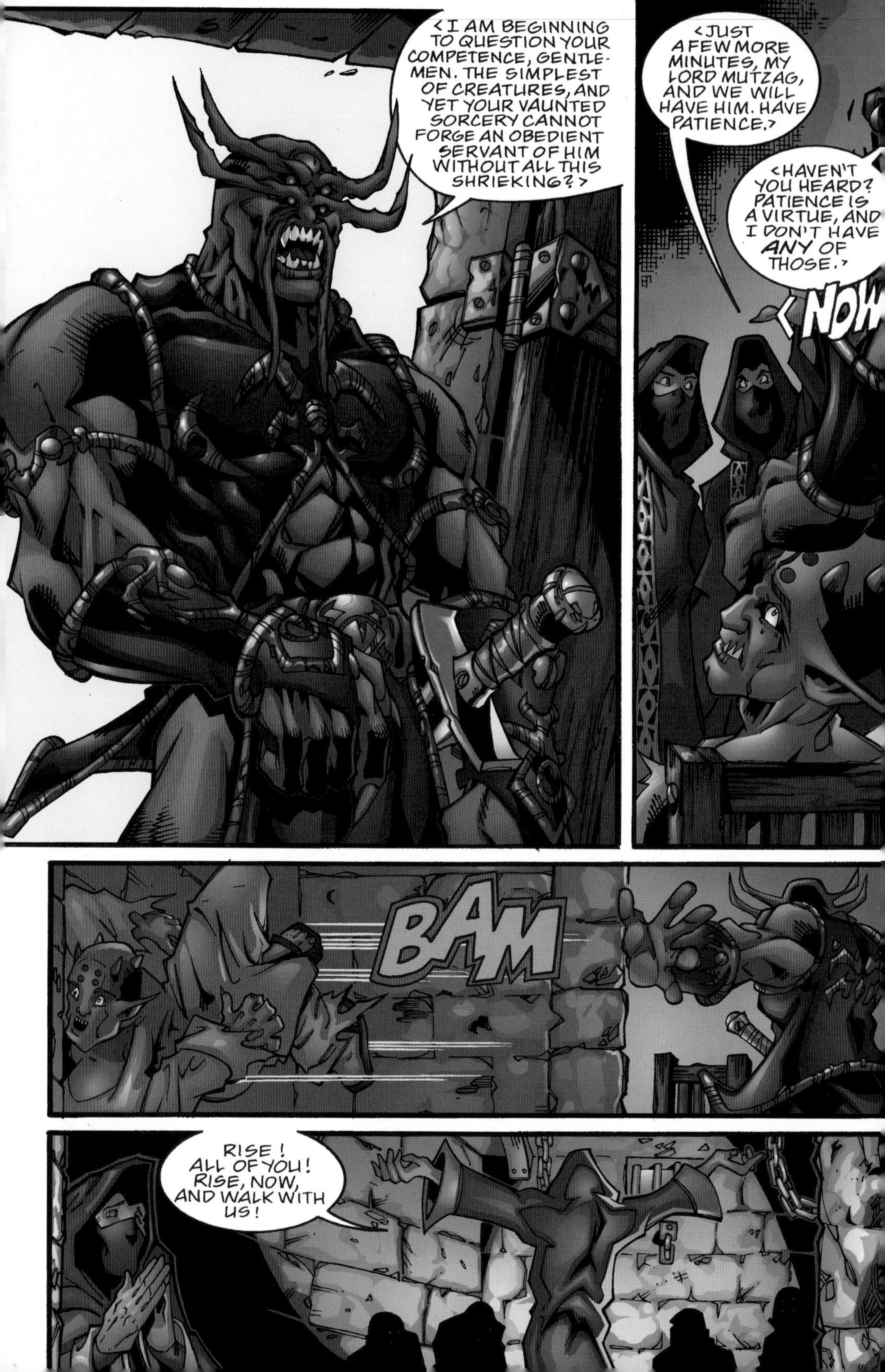
<I AM BEGINNING TO QUESTION YOUR COMPETENCE, GENTLE-MEN. THE SIMPLEST OF CREATURES, AND YET YOUR VAUNTED SORCERY CANNOT FORGE AN OBEDIENT SERVANT OF HIM WITHOUT ALL THIS SHRIEKING?>
<JUST A FEW MORE MINUTES, MY LORD MUTZAG, AND WE WILL HAVE HIM. HAVE PATIENCE.>
<HAVEN'T YOU HEARD? PATIENCE IS A VIRTUE, AND I DON'T HAVE ANY OF THOSE.>
<NOW
BAM
RISE! ALL OF YOU! RISE, NOW, AND WALK WITH US!

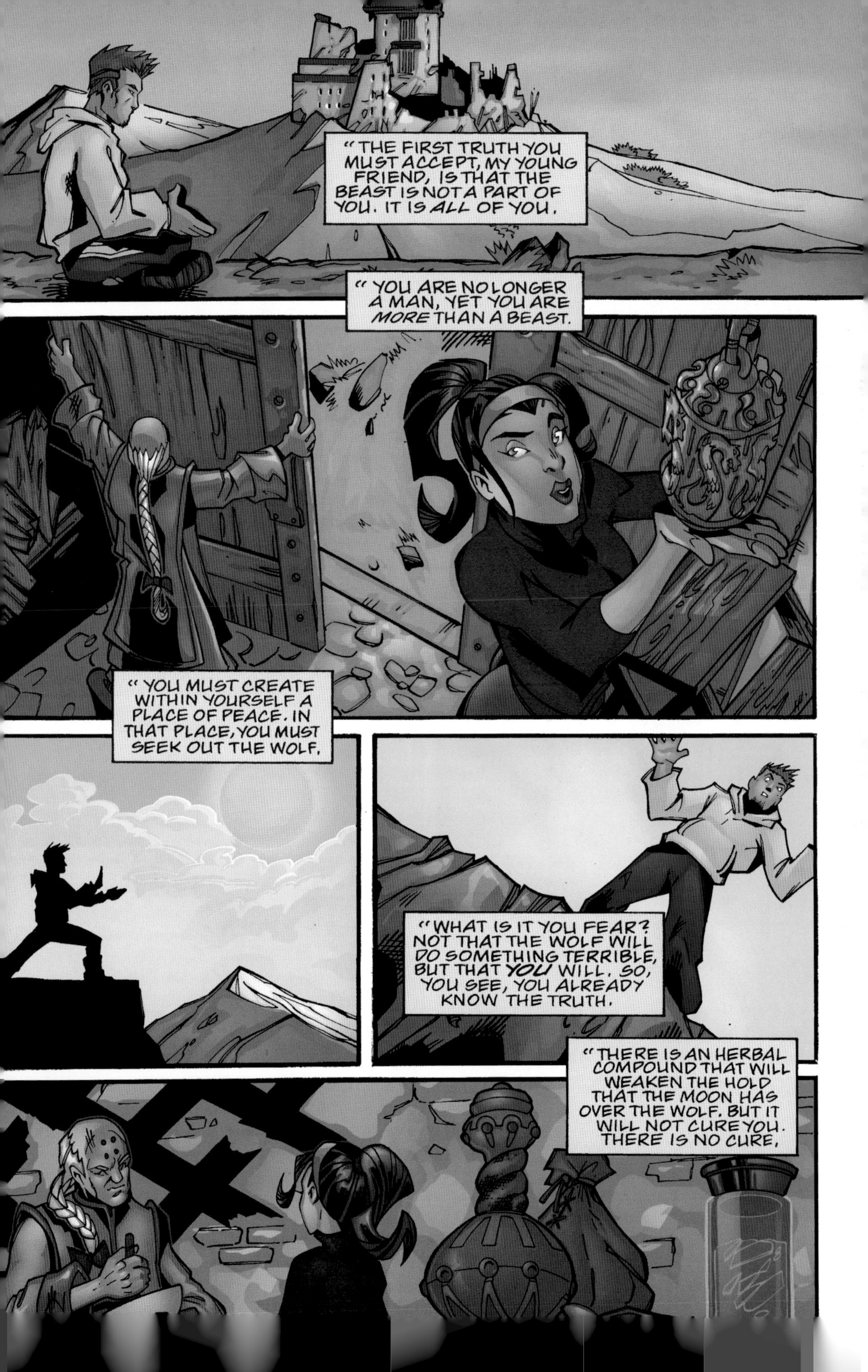
"THE FIRST TRUTH YOU MUST ACCEPT, MY YOUNG FRIEND, IS THAT THE BEAST IS NOT A PART OF YOU. IT IS *ALL* OF YOU.
"YOU ARE NO LONGER A MAN, YET YOU ARE *MORE* THAN A BEAST.
"YOU MUST CREATE WITHIN YOURSELF A PLACE OF PEACE. IN THAT PLACE, YOU MUST SEEK OUT THE WOLF.
"WHAT IS IT YOU FEAR? NOT THAT THE WOLF WILL DO SOMETHING TERRIBLE, BUT THAT *YOU* WILL. SO, YOU SEE, YOU ALREADY KNOW THE TRUTH.
"THERE IS AN HERBAL COMPOUND THAT WILL WEAKEN THE HOLD THAT THE MOON HAS OVER THE WOLF. BUT IT WILL NOT CURE YOU. THERE IS NO CURE,

"YOU MUST FIND A BALANCE BETWEEN THE TWIN ASPECTS OF YOUR NATURE. YOU MUST STOP THINKING LIKE A MAN, AND ALLOW YOURSELF TO EVOLVE, TO BECOME WHAT YOU ARE.

"IN THE END, MAGIC AND HERBS AND MEDITATION CAN ONLY SMOOTH YOUR WAY, BUT AS ALWAYS, THE JOURNEY IS YOURS ALONE.

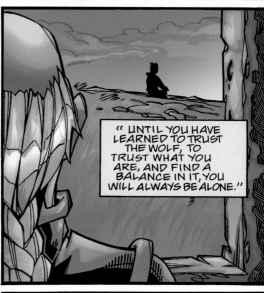

"UNTIL YOU HAVE LEARNED TO TRUST THE WOLF, TO TRUST WHAT YOU ARE, AND FIND A BALANCE IN IT, YOU WILL ALWAYS BE ALONE."

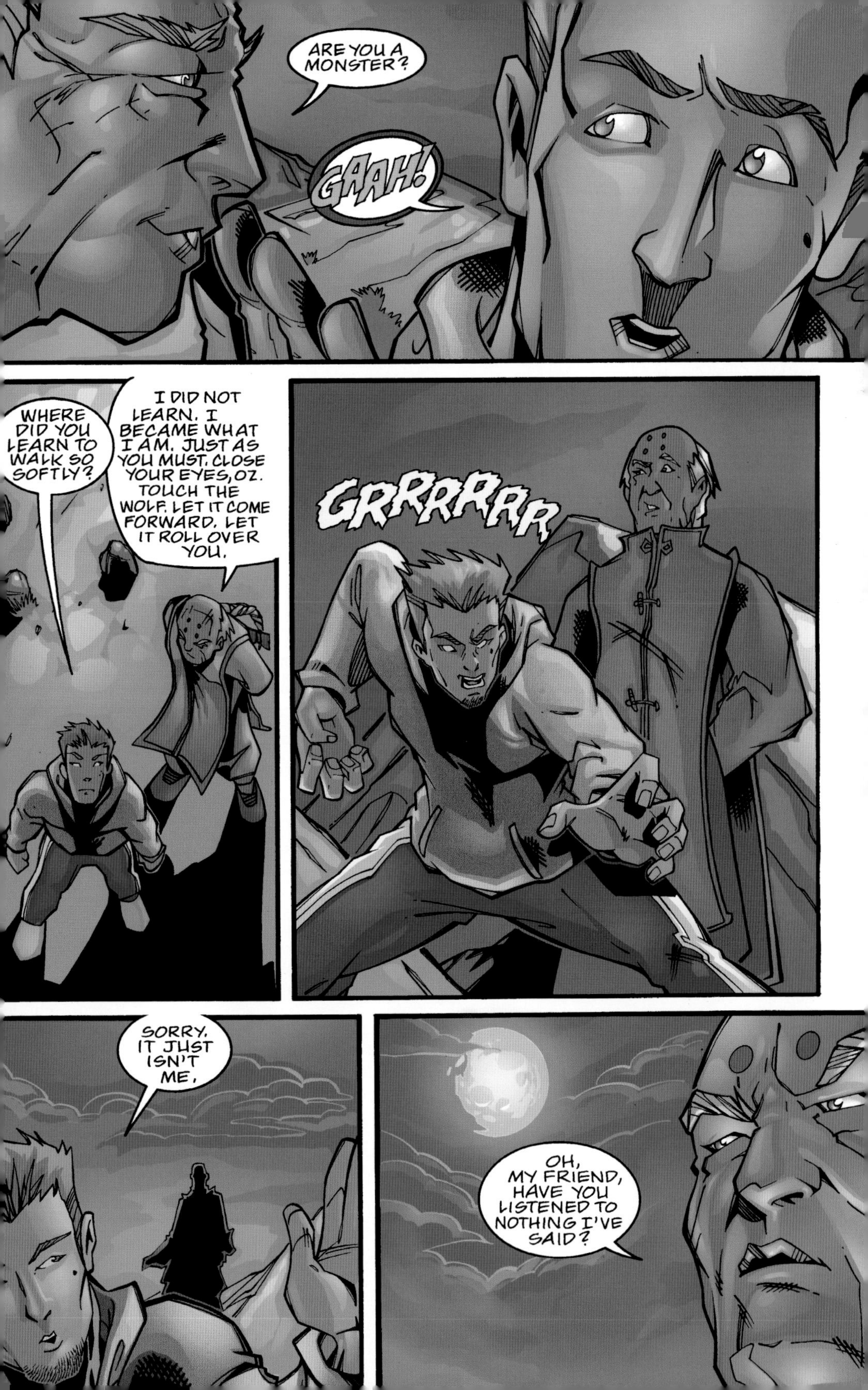
ARE YOU A MONSTER?
GAAH!
WHERE DID YOU LEARN TO WALK SO SOFTLY?
I DID NOT LEARN. I BECAME WHAT I AM. JUST AS YOU MUST. CLOSE YOUR EYES, OZ. TOUCH THE WOLF. LET IT COME FORWARD. LET IT ROLL OVER YOU.
GRRRRRRR
SORRY. IT JUST ISN'T ME.
OH, MY FRIEND, HAVE YOU LISTENED TO NOTHING I'VE SAID?

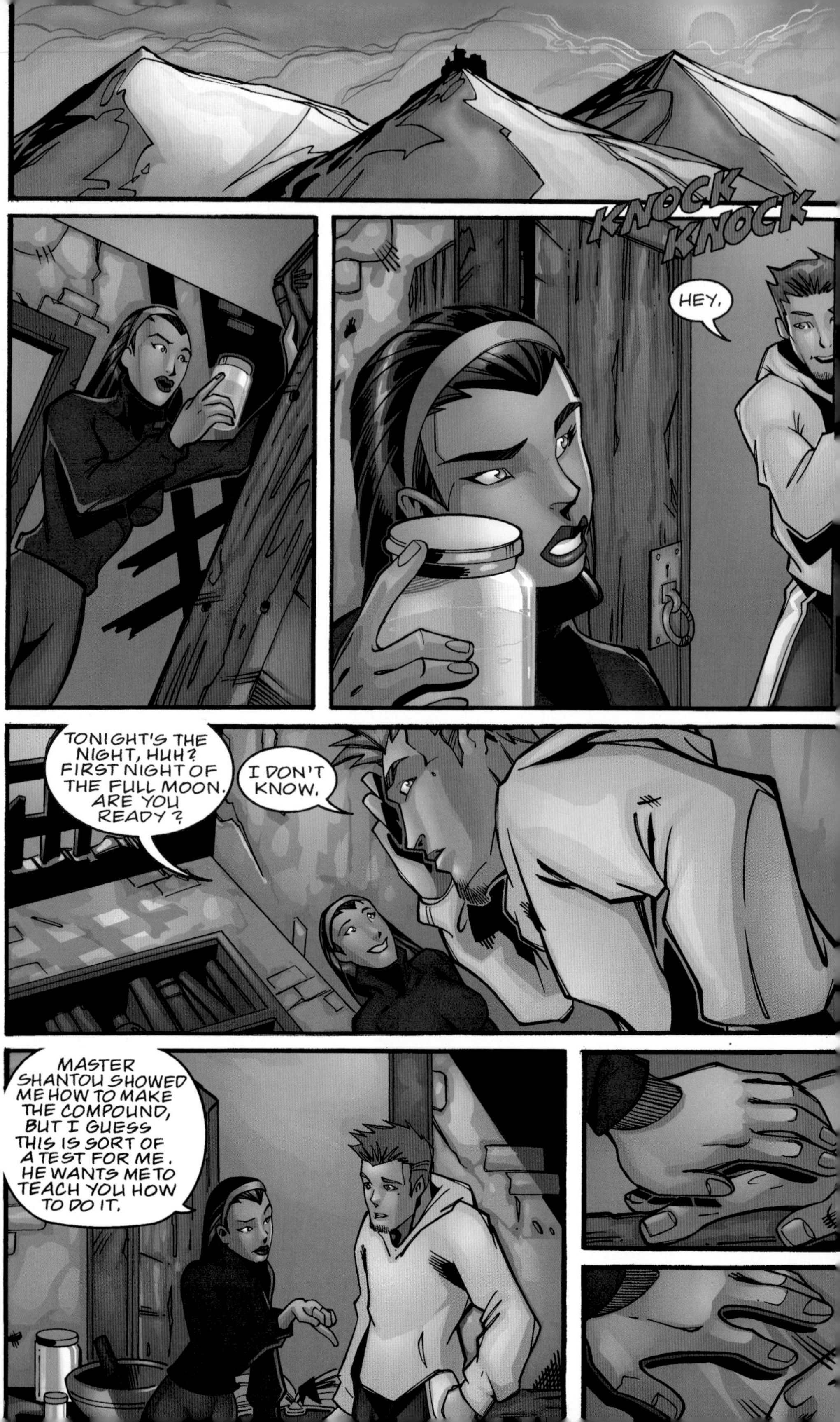

KNOCK KNOCK
HEY.
TONIGHT'S THE NIGHT, HUH? FIRST NIGHT OF THE FULL MOON. ARE YOU READY?
I DON'T KNOW.
MASTER SHANTOU SHOWED ME HOW TO MAKE THE COMPOUND, BUT I GUESS THIS IS SORT OF A TEST FOR ME. HE WANTS ME TO TEACH YOU HOW TO DO IT.

THE NIGHT APPROCHES.

AFTER I'M GONE, BAR THE DOORS.

WE CANNOT BAR THE DOORS IF WE ARE OUTSIDE WITH YOU.

NOW, FINISH PREPARING THE COMPOUND. JINAN WILL INSTRUCT YOU, BUT YOU MUST DO IT YOURSELF. AND QUICKLY. THERE IS LITTLE TIME.

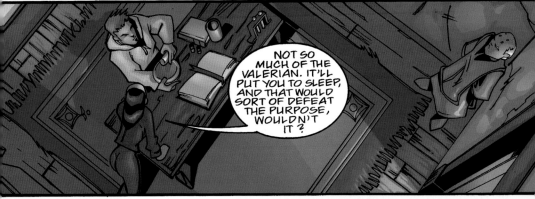

NOT SO MUCH OF THE VALERIAN. IT'LL PUT YOU TO SLEEP, AND THAT WOULD SORT OF DEFEAT THE PURPOSE, WOULDN'T IT?

NOBODY THOUGHT TO MAKE A PILL FOR THIS. WEIRD.

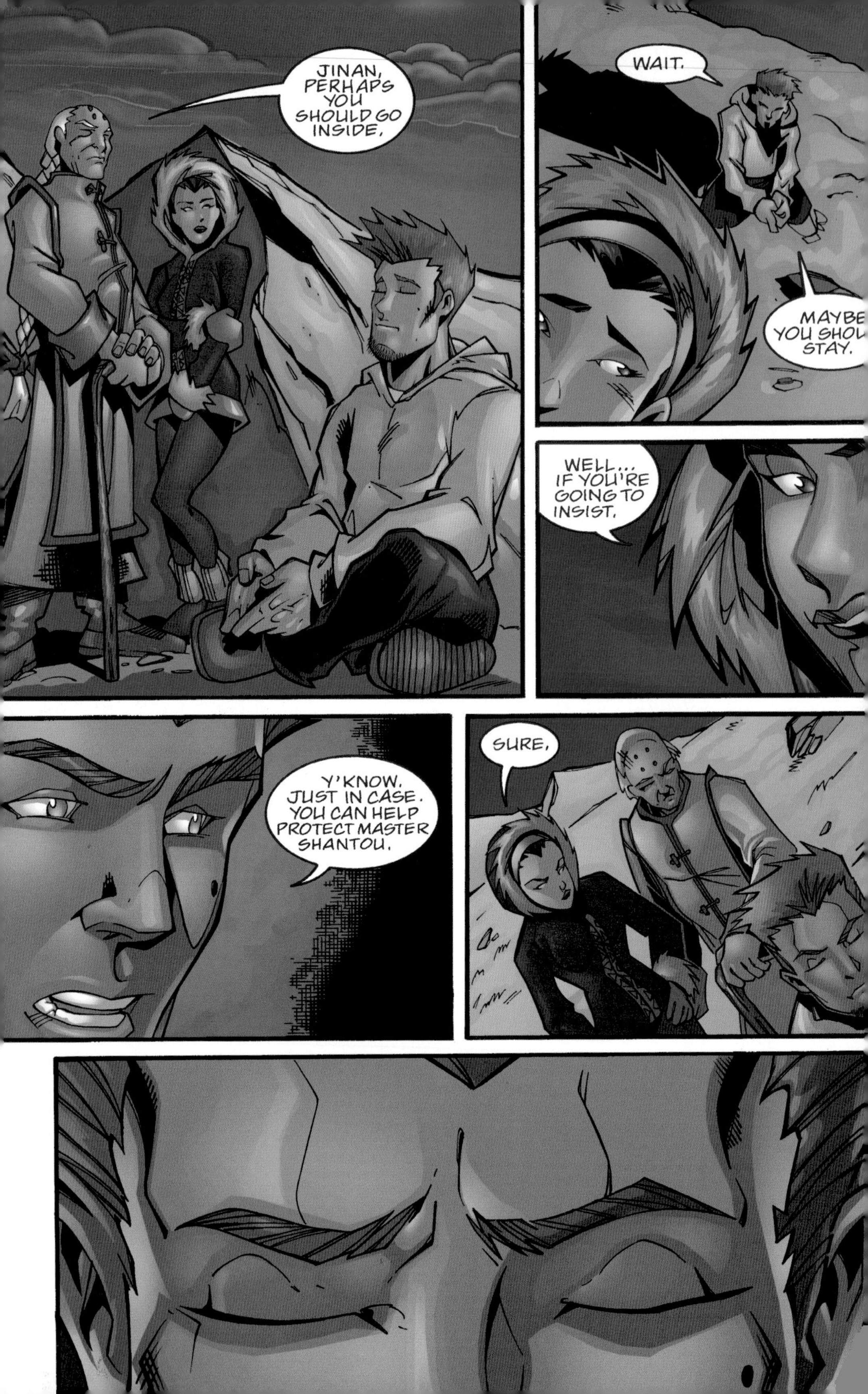
JINAN, PERHAPS YOU SHOULD GO INSIDE.
WAIT.
MAYBE YOU SHOU STAY.
WELL... IF YOU'RE GOING TO INSIST.
Y'KNOW. JUST IN CASE. YOU CAN HELP PROTECT MASTER SHANTOU.
SURE.

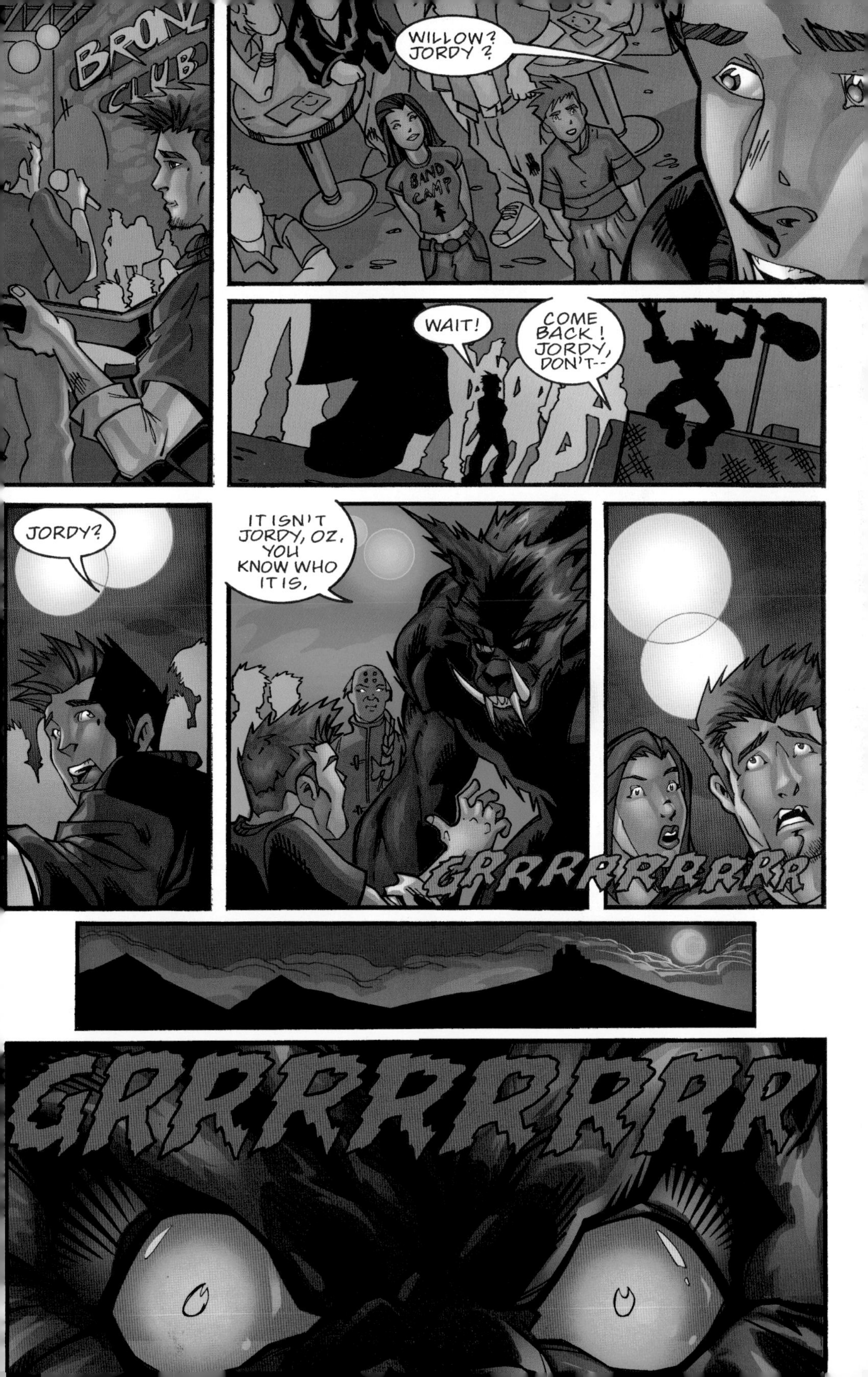
BRONZE CLUB
WILLOW? JORDY?
BAND CAMP
WAIT!
COME BACK! JORDY, DON'T--
JORDY?
IT ISN'T JORDY, OZ. YOU KNOW WHO IT IS.
GRRRRRRRRRR
GRRRRRRRRRR

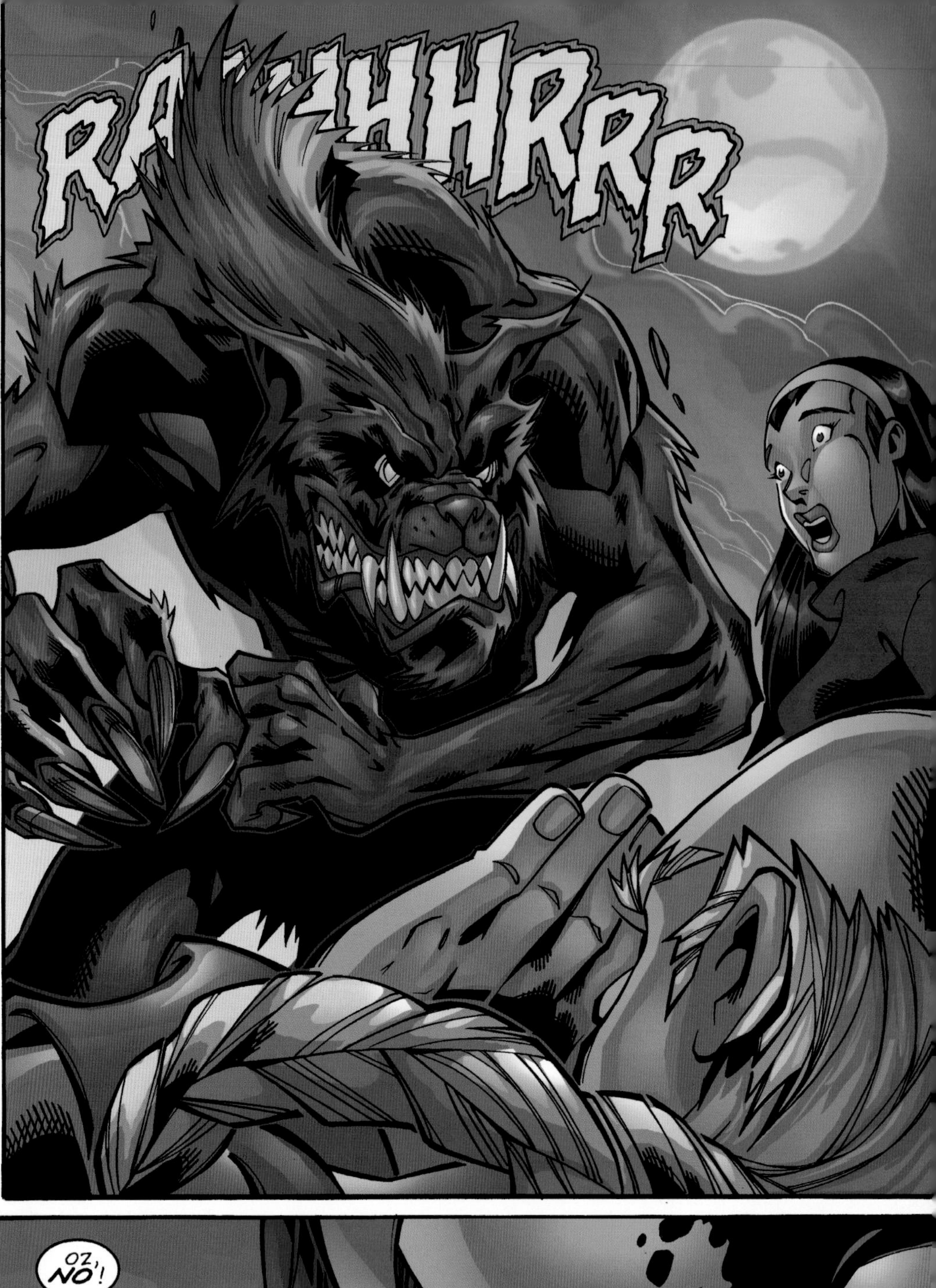
RA HHRRRR

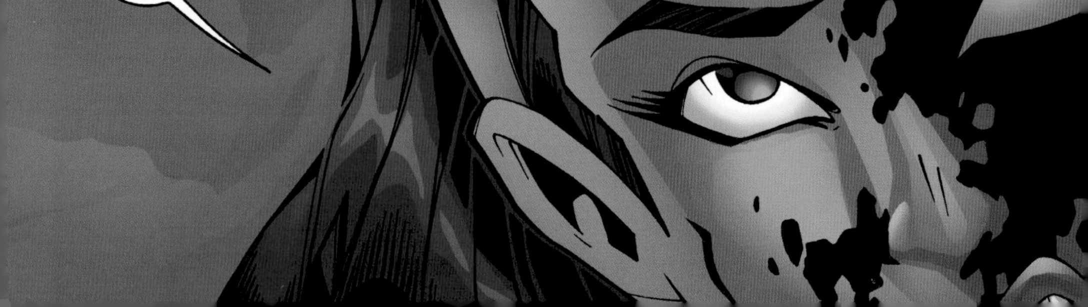
OZ, NO!

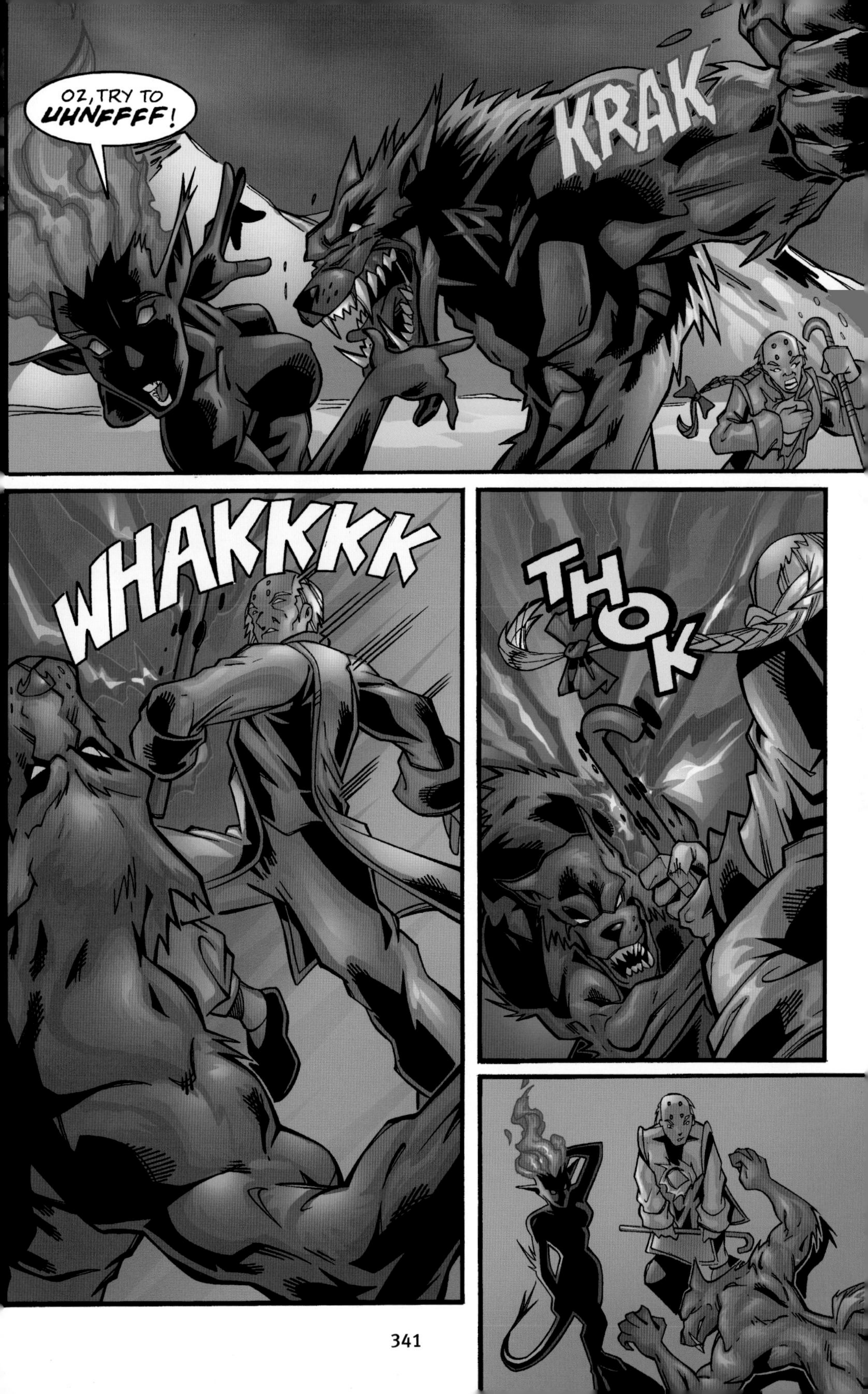
OZ, TRY TO UHNFFFF!
KRAK
WHAKKKK
THOK

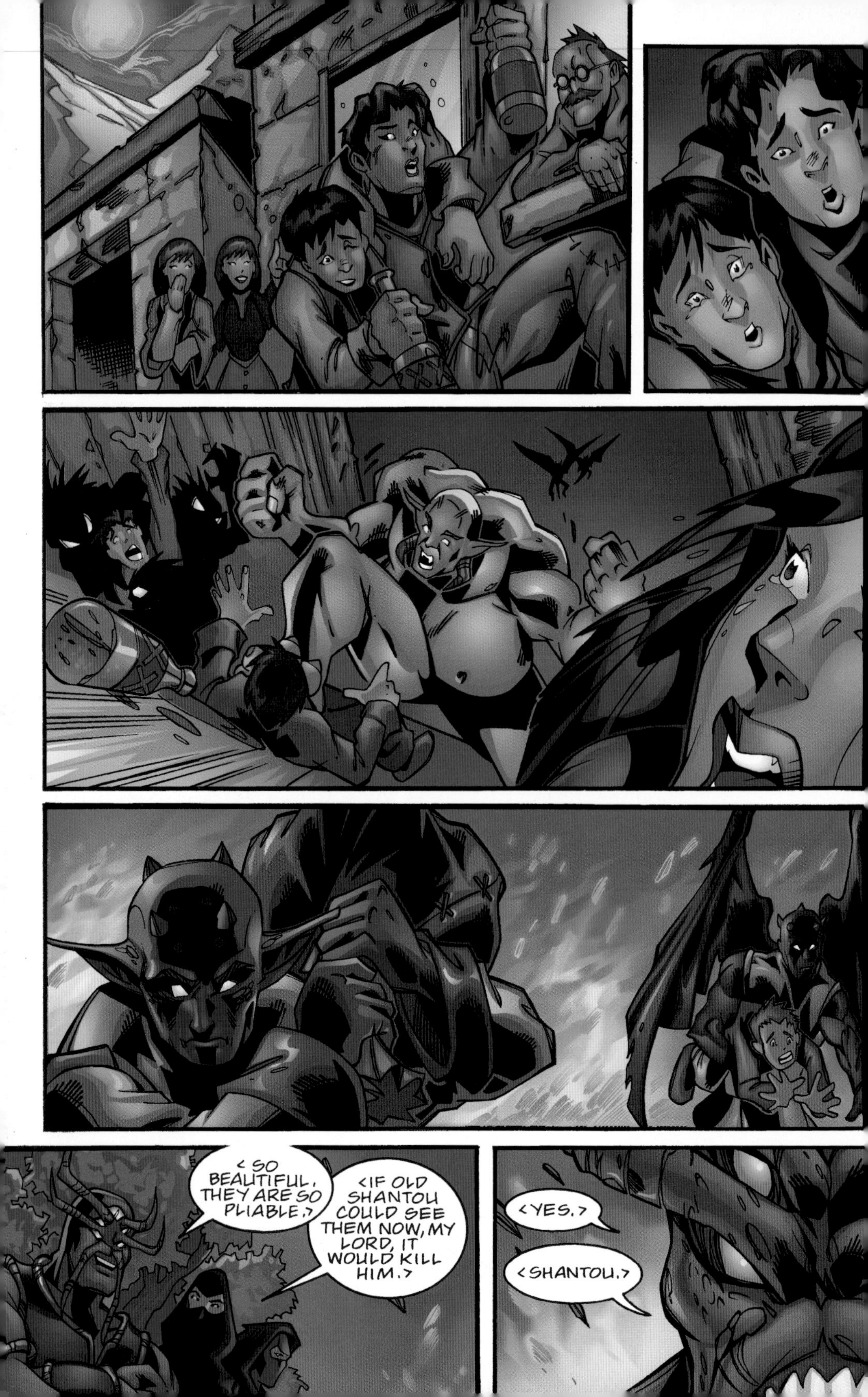
< SO BEAUTIFUL, THEY ARE SO PLIABLE.>
<IF OLD SHANTOU COULD SEE THEM NOW, MY LORD, IT WOULD KILL HIM.>
<YES.>
<SHANTOU.>

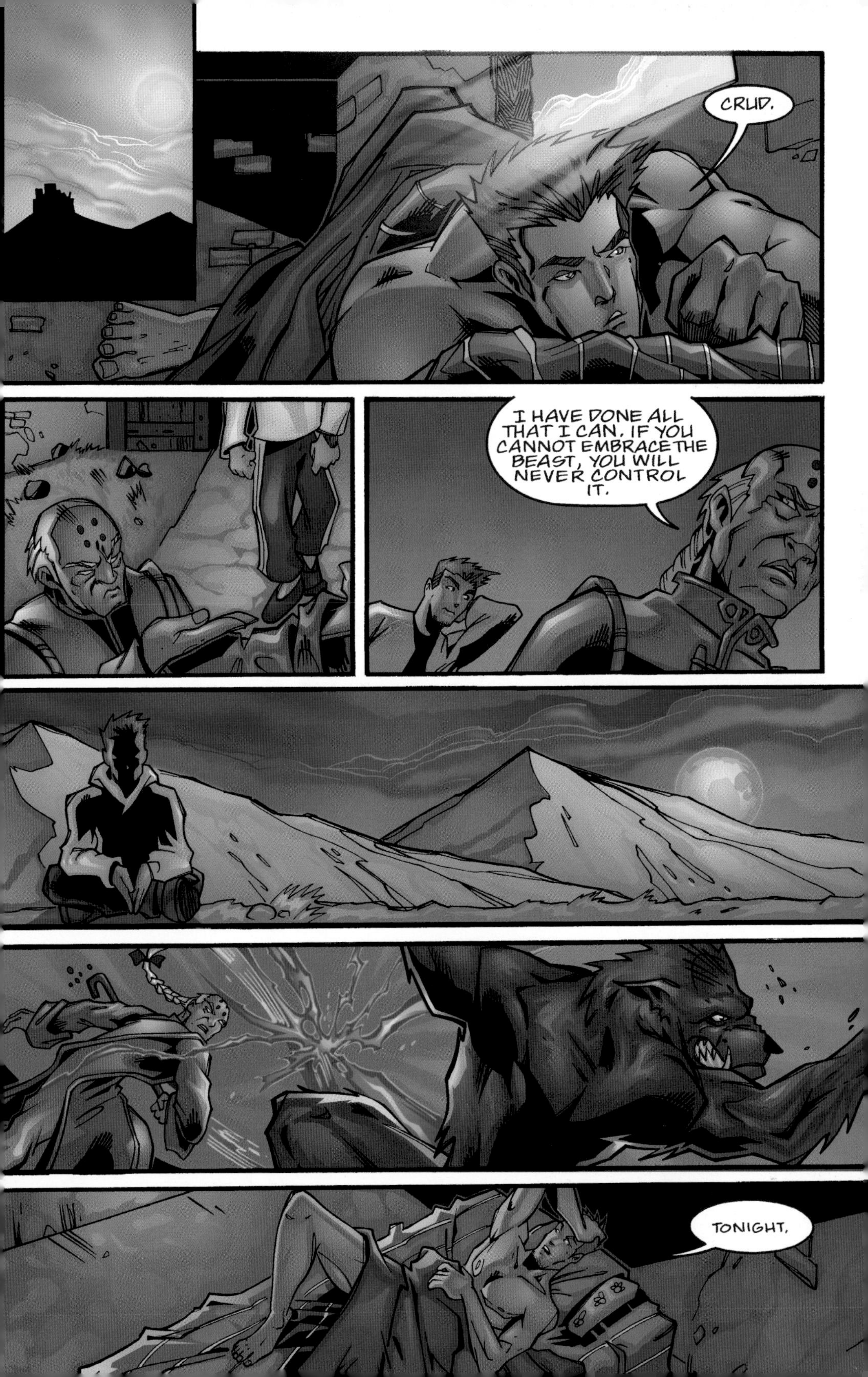
CRUD.
I HAVE DONE ALL THAT I CAN. IF YOU CANNOT EMBRACE THE BEAST, YOU WILL NEVER CONTROL IT.
TONIGHT,

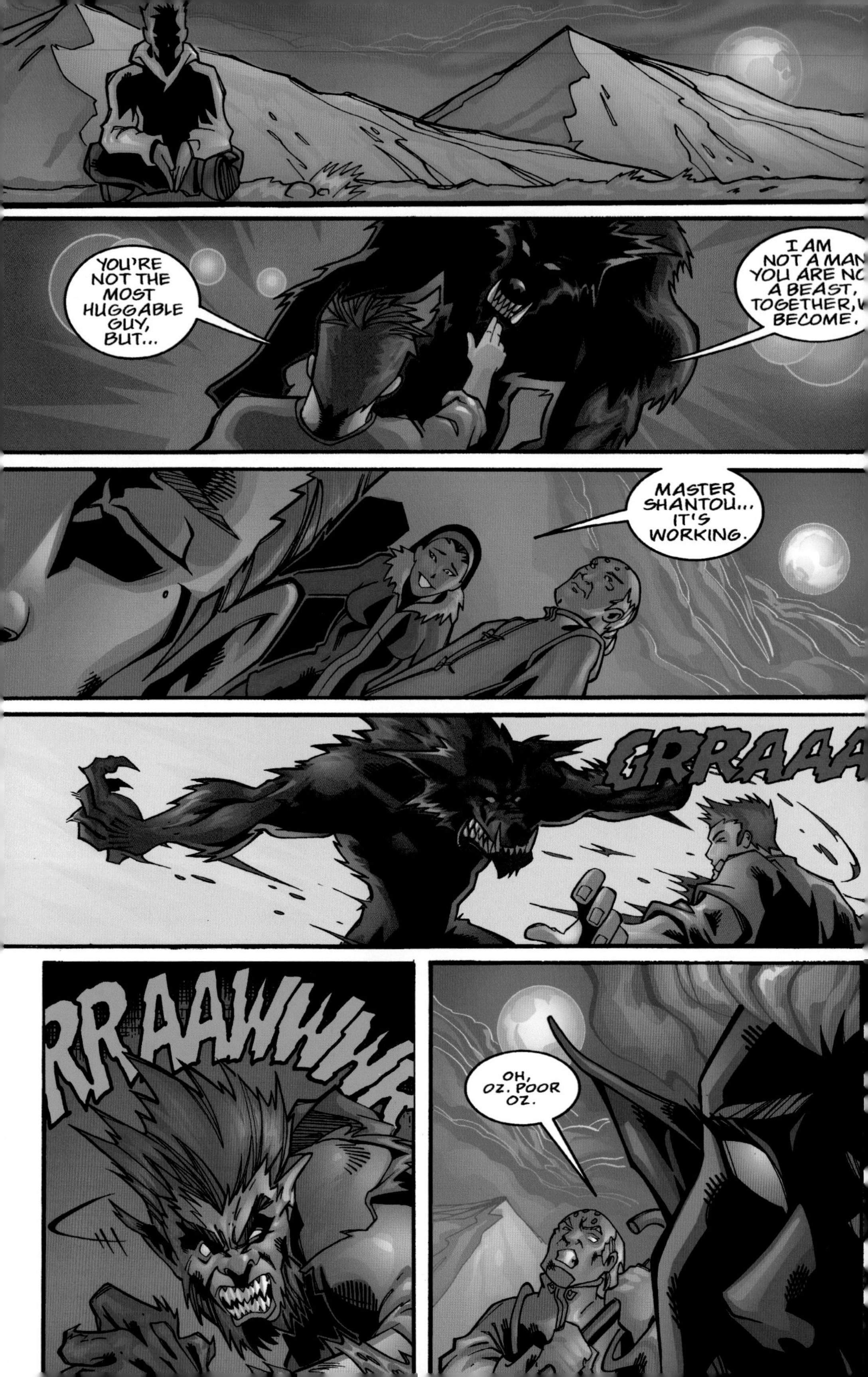
YOU'RE NOT THE MOST HUGGABLE GUY, BUT...
I AM NOT A MAN YOU ARE NO A BEAST, TOGETHER, W BECOME.
MASTER SHANTOU... IT'S WORKING.
GRRAAA
RRAAWWR
OH, OZ. POOR OZ.

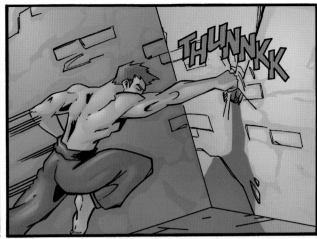

THUNNKK

NEXT MONTH, OZ, YOU WERE SO CLOSE, I KNOW YOU'LL GET IT.

I KNOW WHAT MASTER SHANTOU SAID, ABOUT YOU BEING ALONE? BUT YOU'RE NOT ALONE, NOT REALLY.

THANKS, BUT NOTHING'S CHANGED, JINAN.

TRUTH IS, I AM ALONE NOW, BUT THERE'S SOME-ONE I WANT TO GET BACK TO.

OZ...?

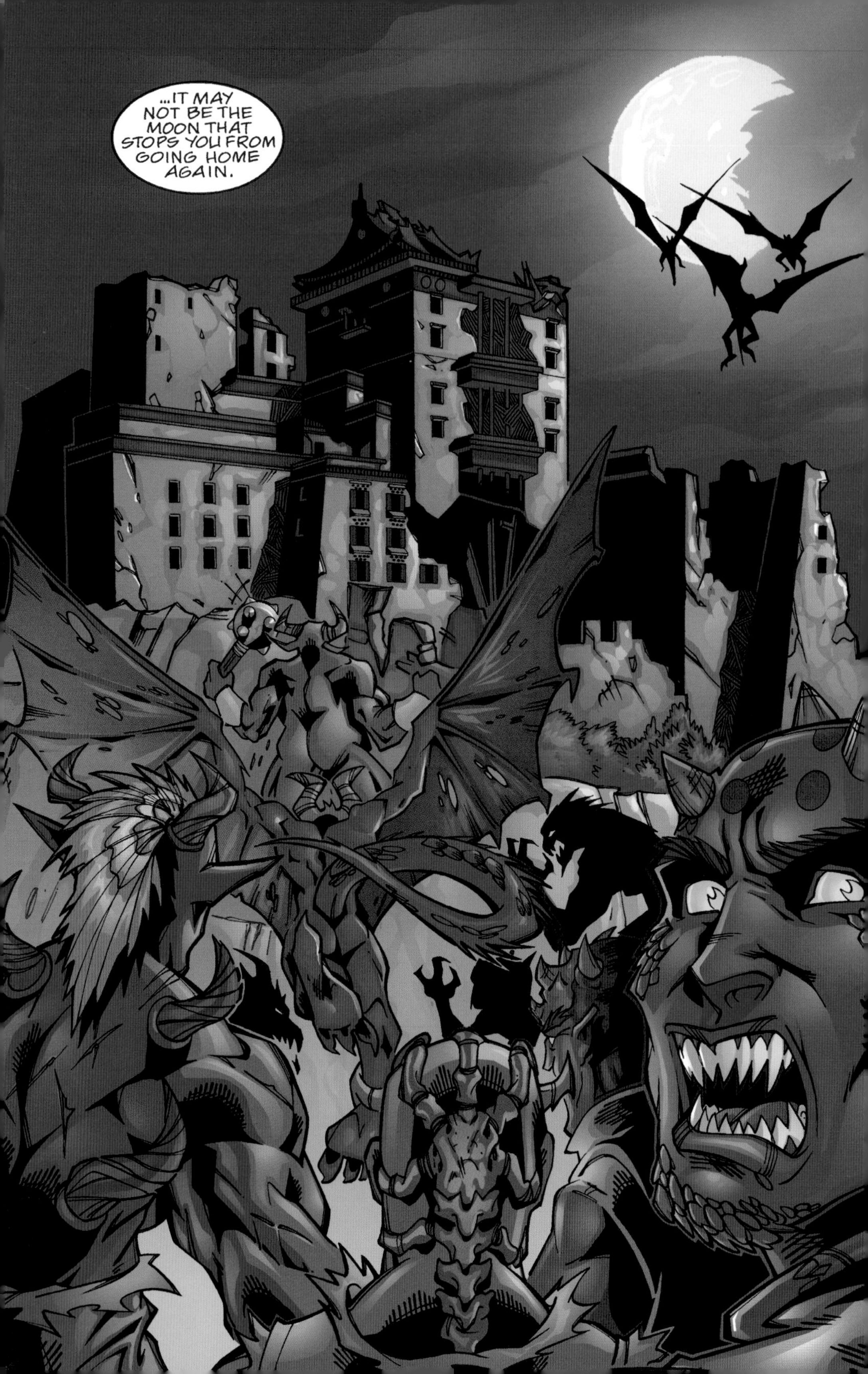
...IT MAY NOT BE THE MOON THAT STOPS YOU FROM GOING HOME AGAIN.

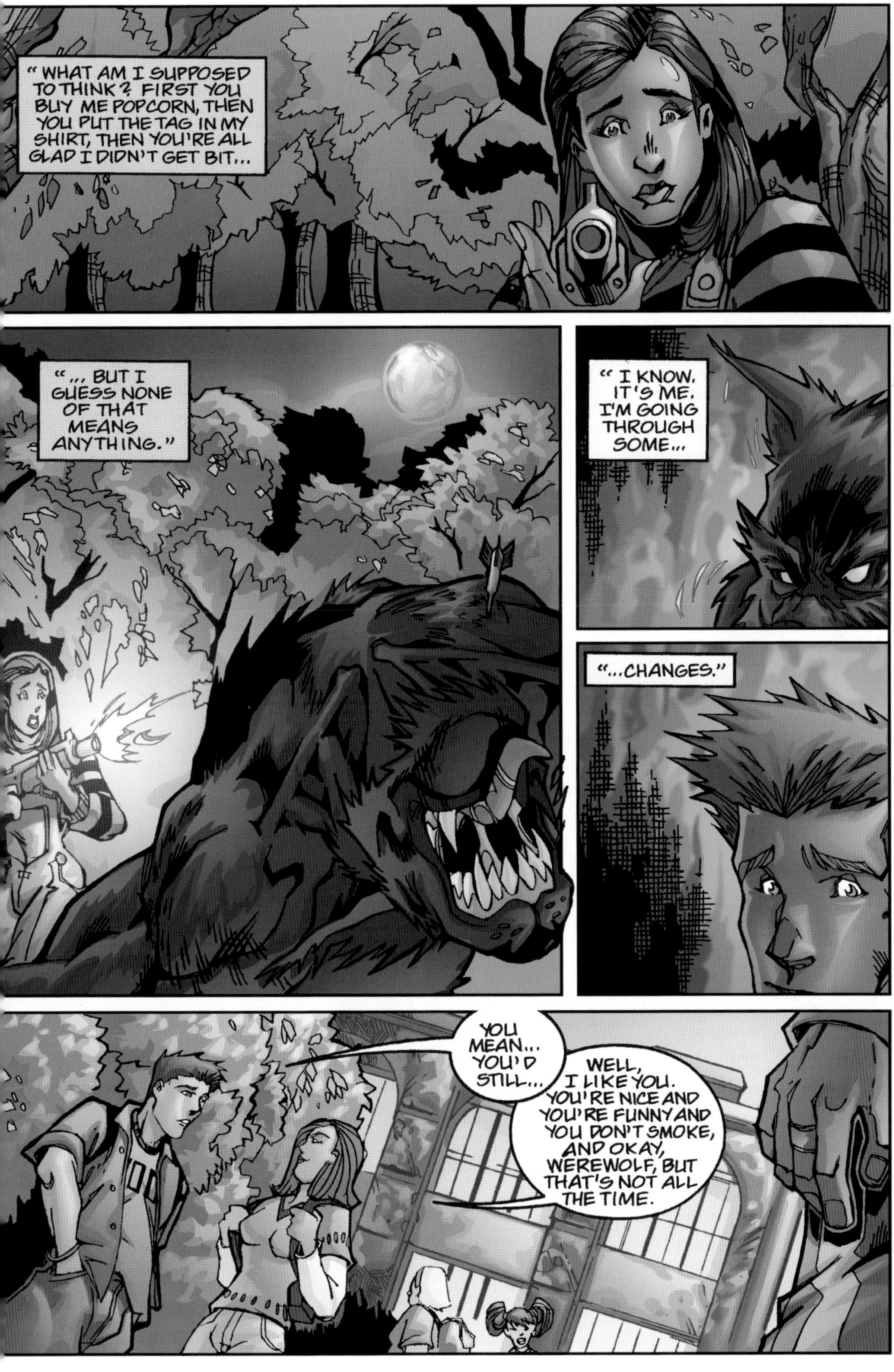
"WHAT AM I SUPPOSED TO THINK? FIRST YOU BUY ME POPCORN, THEN YOU PUT THE TAG IN MY SHIRT, THEN YOU'RE ALL GLAD I DIDN'T GET BIT...
"... BUT I GUESS NONE OF THAT MEANS ANYTHING."
"I KNOW. IT'S ME. I'M GOING THROUGH SOME...
"...CHANGES."
YOU MEAN... YOU'D STILL...
WELL, I LIKE YOU. YOU'RE NICE AND YOU'RE FUNNY AND YOU DON'T SMOKE, AND OKAY, WEREWOLF, BUT THAT'S NOT ALL THE TIME.

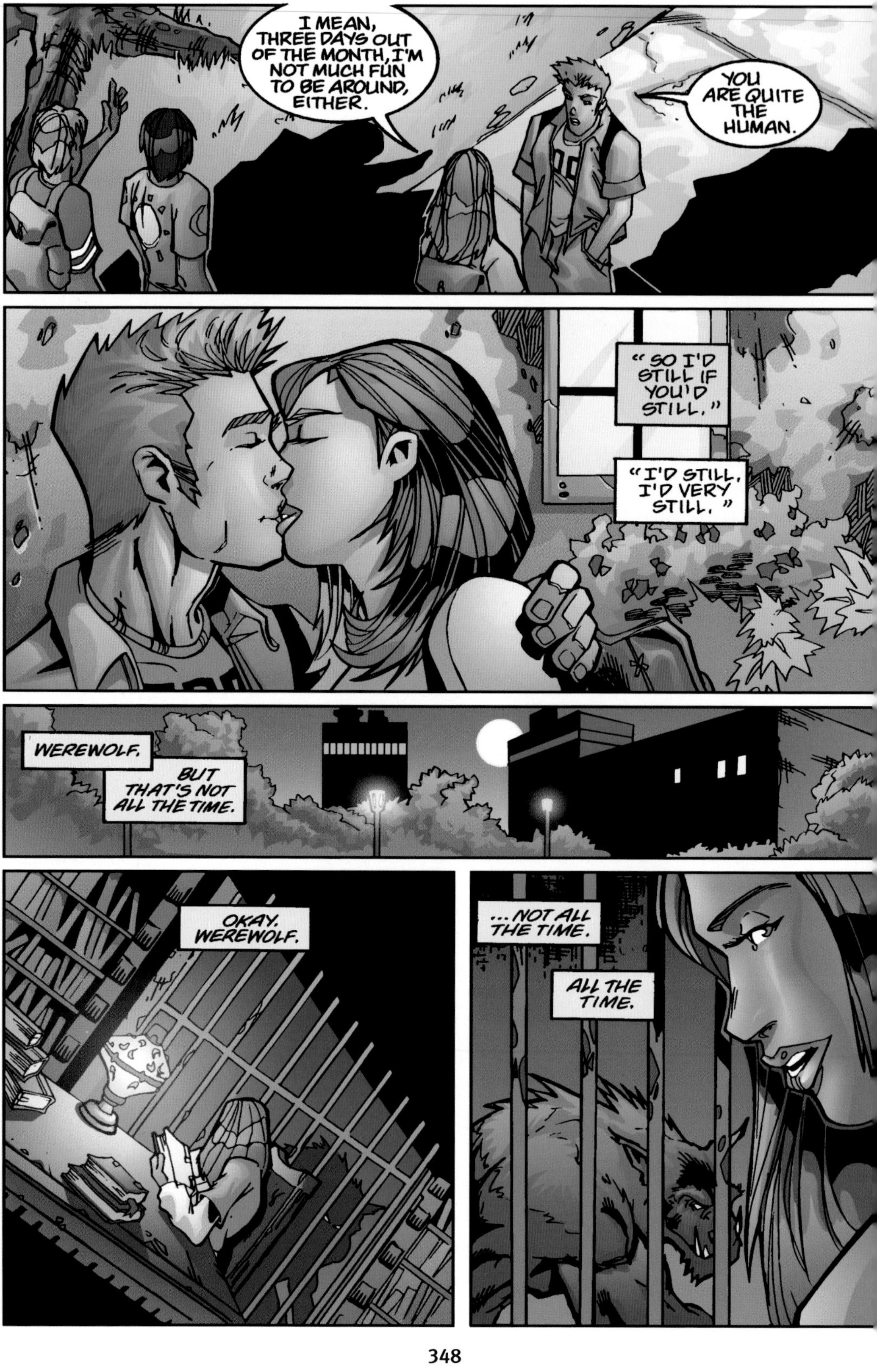
I MEAN, THREE DAYS OUT OF THE MONTH, I'M NOT MUCH FUN TO BE AROUND, EITHER.
YOU ARE QUITE THE HUMAN.
"SO I'D STILL IF YOU'D STILL."
"I'D STILL. I'D VERY STILL."
WEREWOLF.
BUT THAT'S NOT ALL THE TIME.
OKAY. WEREWOLF.
...NOT ALL THE TIME.
ALL THE TIME.

OZ, WAIT! MAYBE YOU SHOULD LET ME--

THEY'RE ATTACKING MASTER SHANTOU, JINAN.

I'M NOT JUST GOING TO WATCH.

BUT WHAT CAN YOU DO? LIKE THIS, I MEAN?

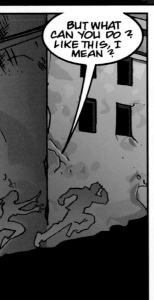

I DON'T KNOW. MAYBE NOTHING.

BUT MAYBE SOMETHING.

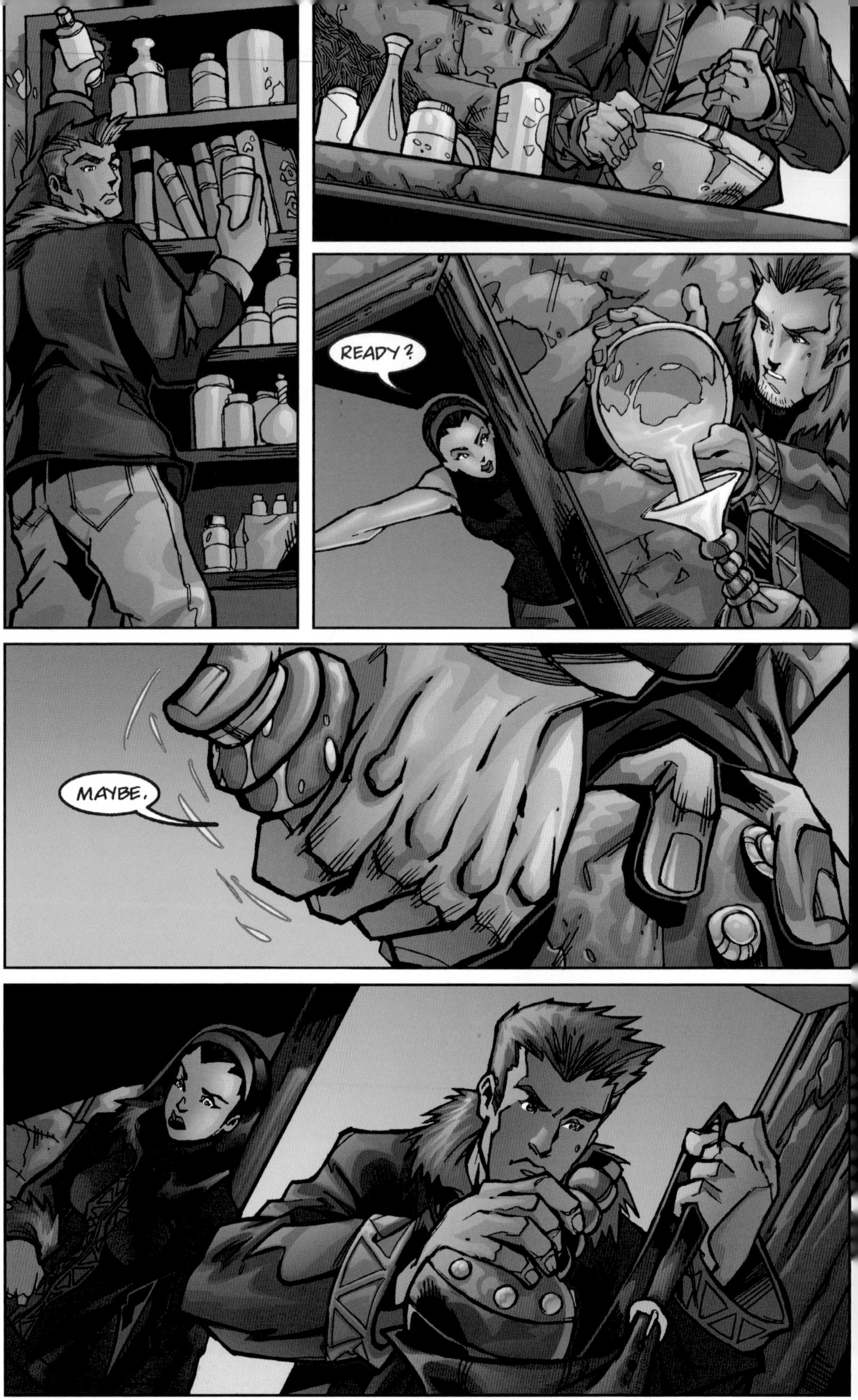
READY?
MAYBE.

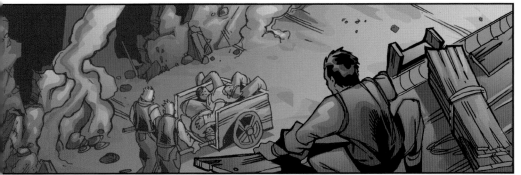

I DON'T THINK WE'RE GOING TO FIND MUCH HELP HERE.

< EXCUSE ME, BUT WHAT HAPPENED HERE?>

< PLEASE DO NOT SPEAK OF IT. THE DEMONS HEAR THE SMALLEST WHISPER. >

<LET THEM HEAR! WICE IN MY LIFETIME THEY HAVE BROUGHT HEIR WRATH ON THIS ILLAGE. MY SONS SAID HEY WERE ONLY LEGENDS, WOULD NOT LISTEN TO ME!>

< NOW MY SONS ARE DEAD. I HOPE THE DEMONS RETURN FOR ME, SO THAT I CAN SPILL THEIR BLOOD AS I DIE!>

< PLEASE GO AWAY. HE DOES NOT KNOW WHAT HE'S SAYING. WE ARE TRYING TO SALVAGE WHAT WE CAN. >

351

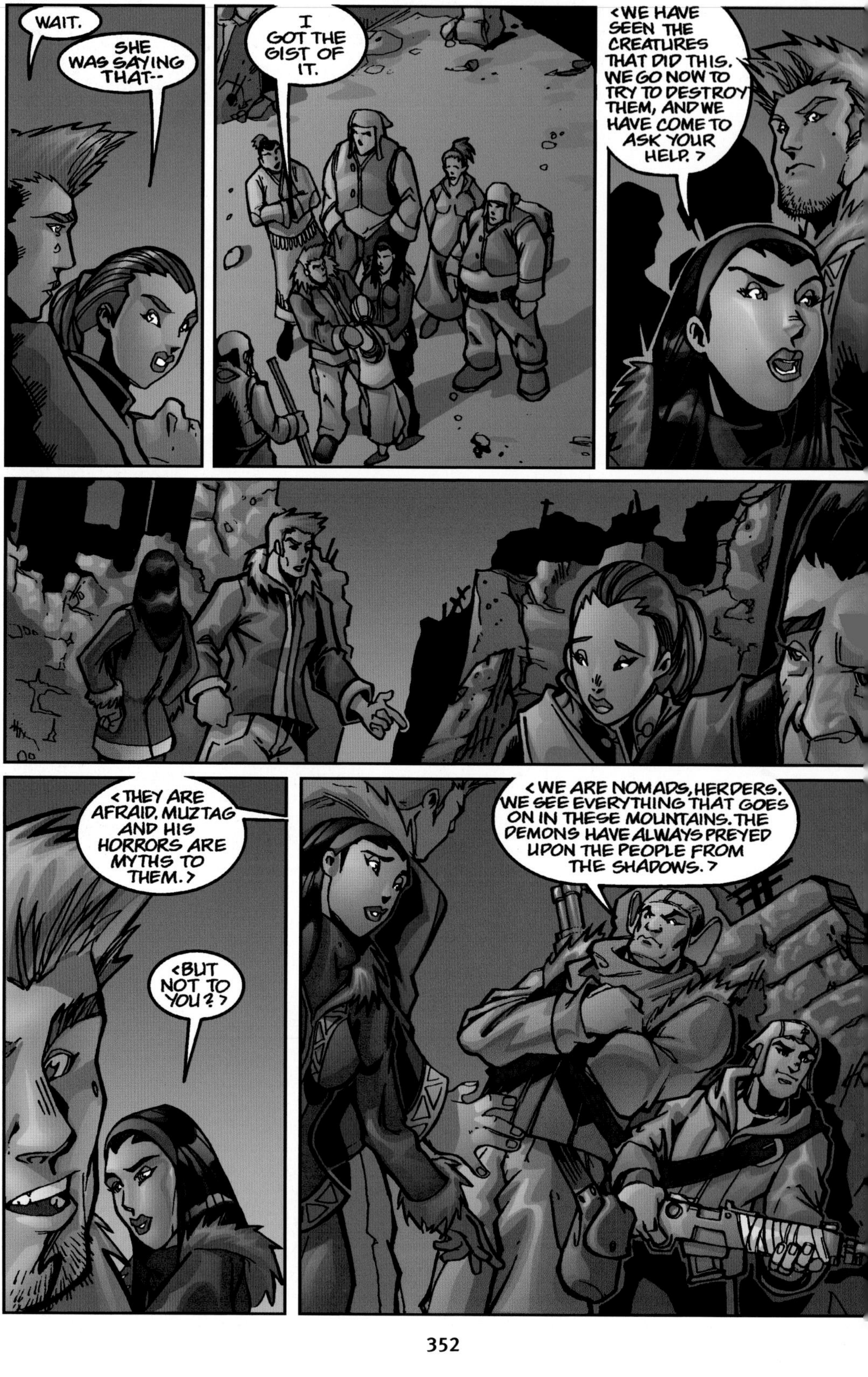
WAIT.
SHE WAS SAYING THAT--
I GOT THE GIST OF IT.
<WE HAVE SEEN THE CREATURES THAT DID THIS. WE GO NOW TO TRY TO DESTROY THEM, AND WE HAVE COME TO ASK YOUR HELP.>
<THEY ARE AFRAID, MUZTAG AND HIS HORRORS ARE MYTHS TO THEM.>
<BUT NOT TO YOU?>
<WE ARE NOMADS, HERDERS. WE SEE EVERYTHING THAT GOES ON IN THESE MOUNTAINS. THE DEMONS HAVE ALWAYS PREYED UPON THE PEOPLE FROM THE SHADOWS.>

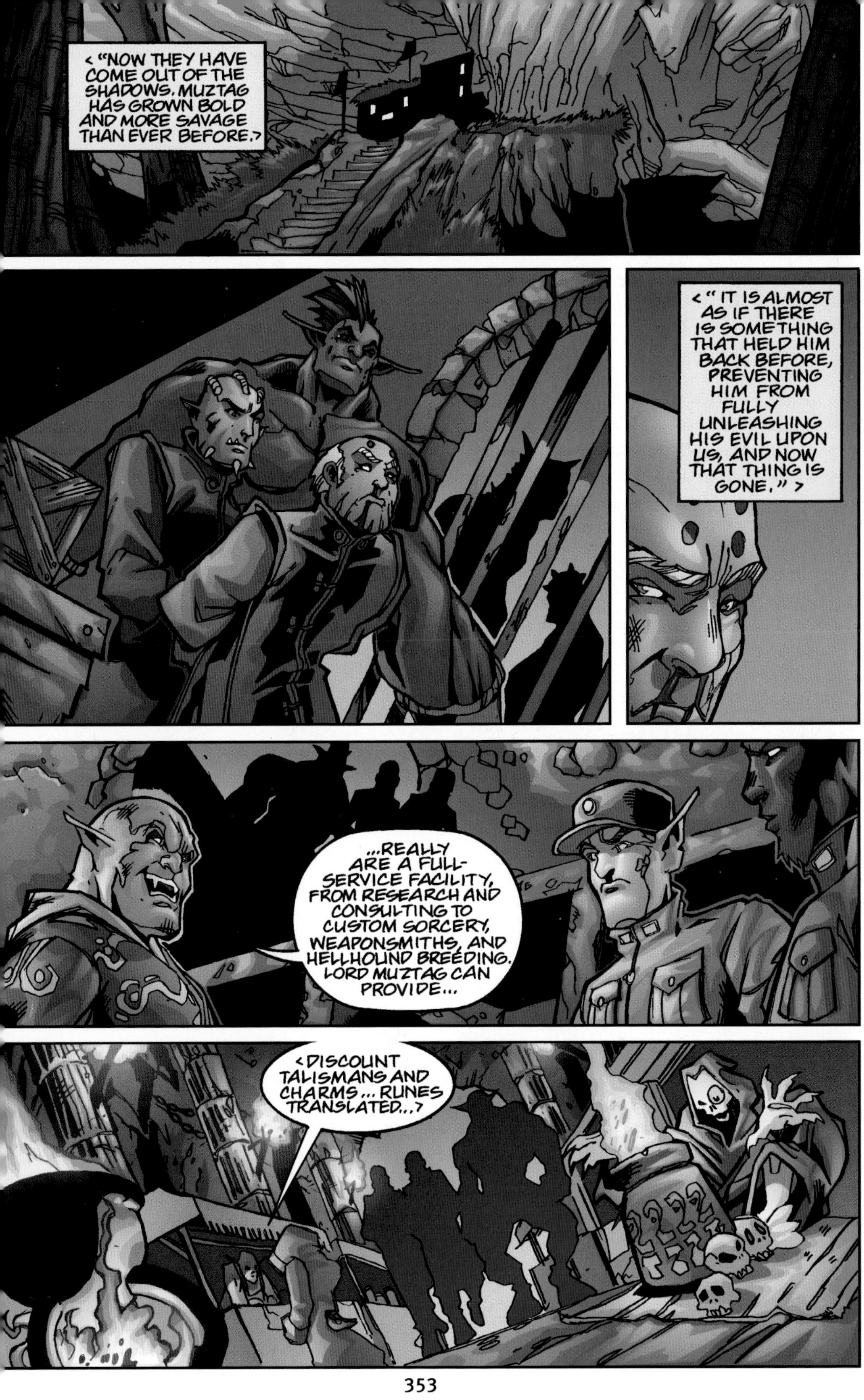

< "NOW THEY HAVE COME OUT OF THE SHADOWS. MUZTAG HAS GROWN BOLD AND MORE SAVAGE THAN EVER BEFORE.>
< " IT IS ALMOST AS IF THERE IS SOMETHING THAT HELD HIM BACK BEFORE, PREVENTING HIM FROM FULLY UNLEASHING HIS EVIL UPON US, AND NOW THAT THING IS GONE." >
...REALLY ARE A FULL-SERVICE FACILITY, FROM RESEARCH AND CONSULTING TO CUSTOM SORCERY, WEAPONSMITHS, AND HELLHOUND BREEDING. LORD MUZTAG CAN PROVIDE...
<DISCOUNT TALISMANS AND CHARMS... RUNES TRANSLATED...>

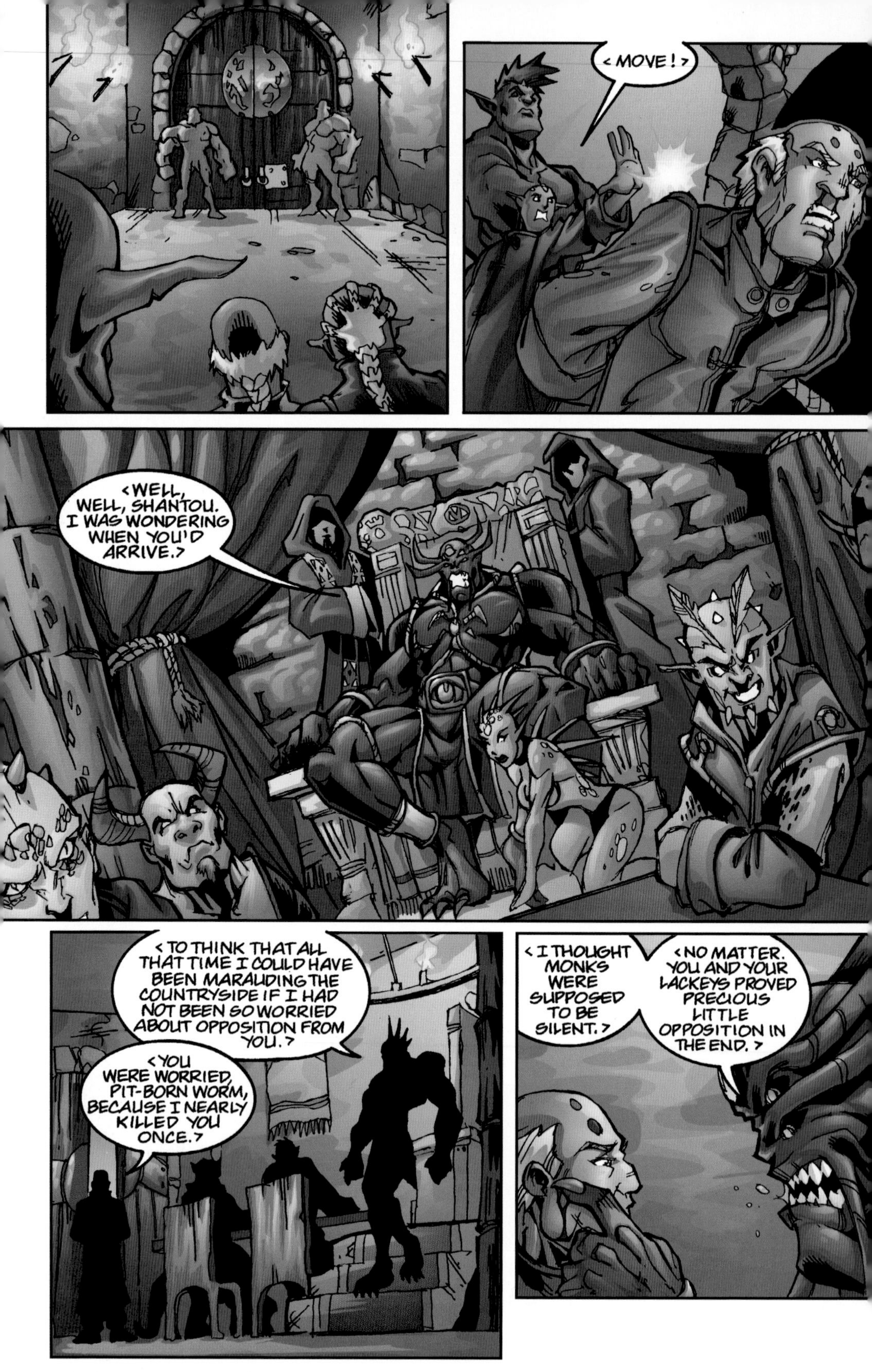
< MOVE! >
<WELL, WELL, SHANTOU. I WAS WONDERING WHEN YOU'D ARRIVE.>
< TO THINK THAT ALL THAT TIME I COULD HAVE BEEN MARAUDING THE COUNTRYSIDE IF I HAD NOT BEEN SO WORRIED ABOUT OPPOSITION FROM YOU. >
<YOU WERE WORRIED, PIT-BORN WORM, BECAUSE I NEARLY KILLED YOU ONCE.>
< I THOUGHT MONKS WERE SUPPOSED TO BE SILENT. >
<NO MATTER. YOU AND YOUR LACKEYS PROVED PRECIOUS LITTLE OPPOSITION IN THE END. >

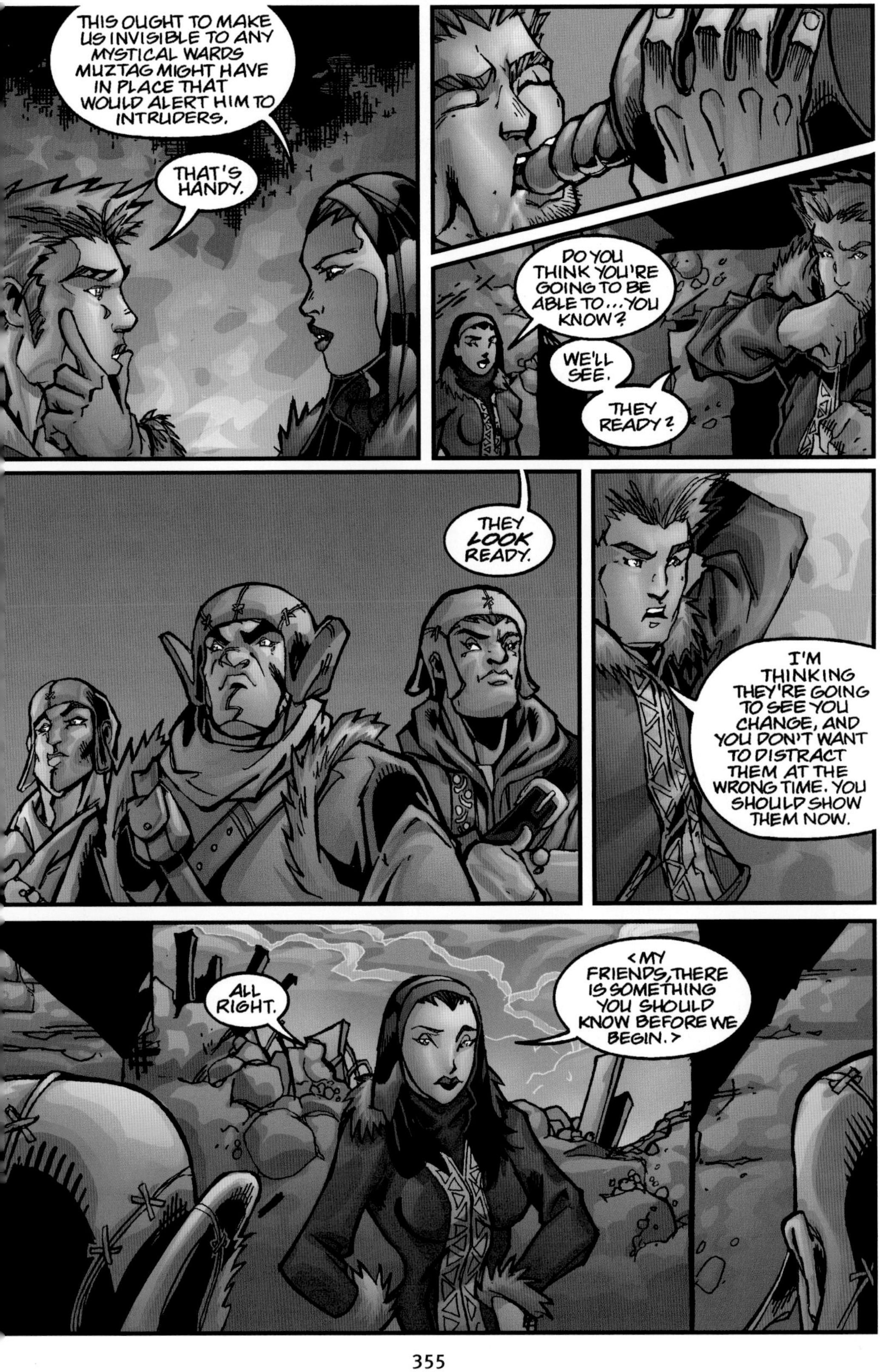
THIS OUGHT TO MAKE US INVISIBLE TO ANY MYSTICAL WARDS MUZTAG MIGHT HAVE IN PLACE THAT WOULD ALERT HIM TO INTRUDERS.
THAT'S HANDY.
DO YOU THINK YOU'RE GOING TO BE ABLE TO... YOU KNOW?
WE'LL SEE.
THEY READY?
THEY LOOK READY.
I'M THINKING THEY'RE GOING TO SEE YOU CHANGE, AND YOU DON'T WANT TO DISTRACT THEM AT THE WRONG TIME. YOU SHOULD SHOW THEM NOW.
ALL RIGHT.
<MY FRIENDS, THERE IS SOMETHING YOU SHOULD KNOW BEFORE WE BEGIN.>

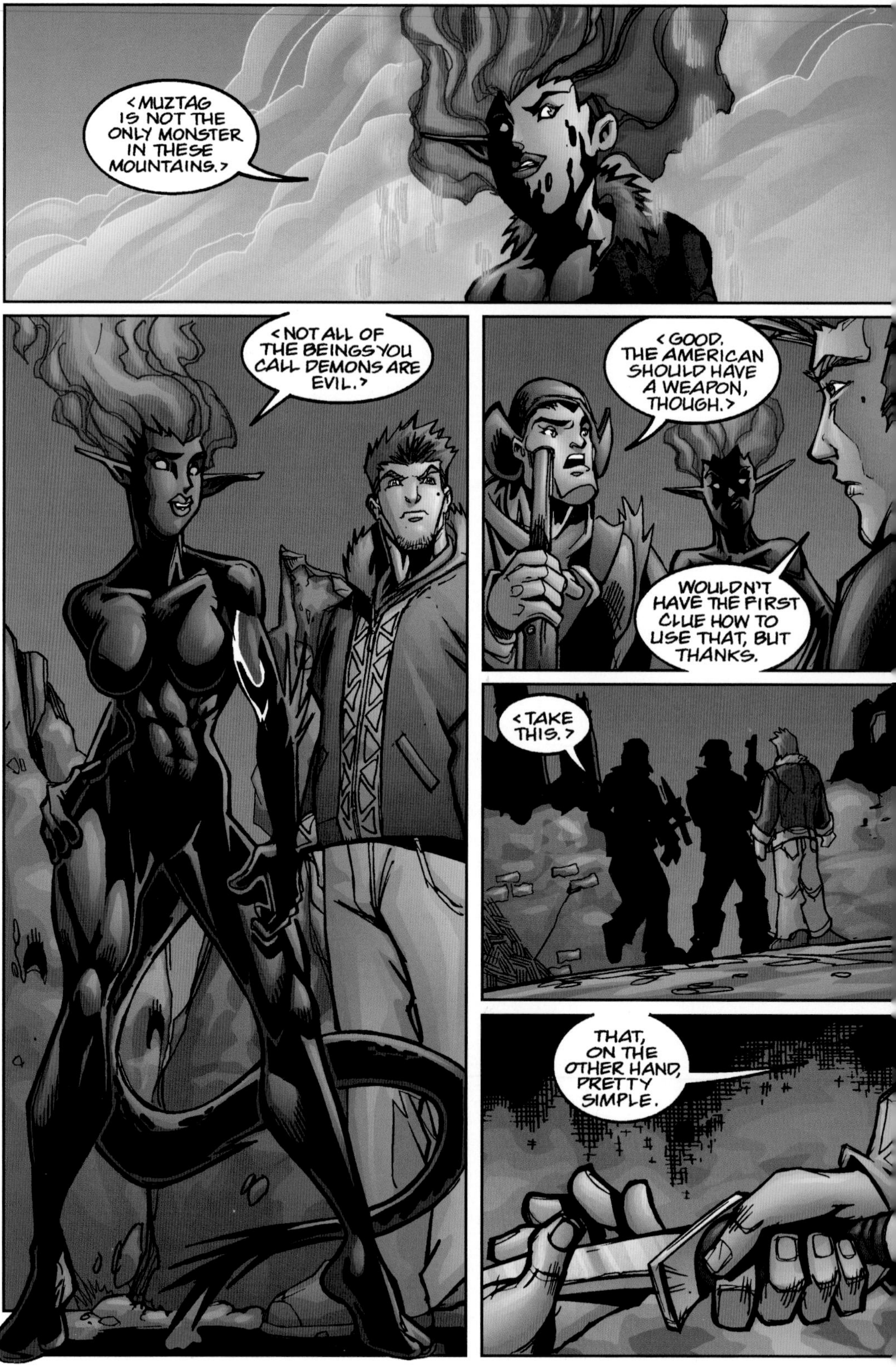
<MUZTAG IS NOT THE ONLY MONSTER IN THESE MOUNTAINS.>
<NOT ALL OF THE BEINGS YOU CALL DEMONS ARE EVIL.>
<GOOD. THE AMERICAN SHOULD HAVE A WEAPON, THOUGH.>
WOULDN'T HAVE THE FIRST CLUE HOW TO USE THAT, BUT THANKS.
<TAKE THIS.>
THAT, ON THE OTHER HAND, PRETTY SIMPLE.

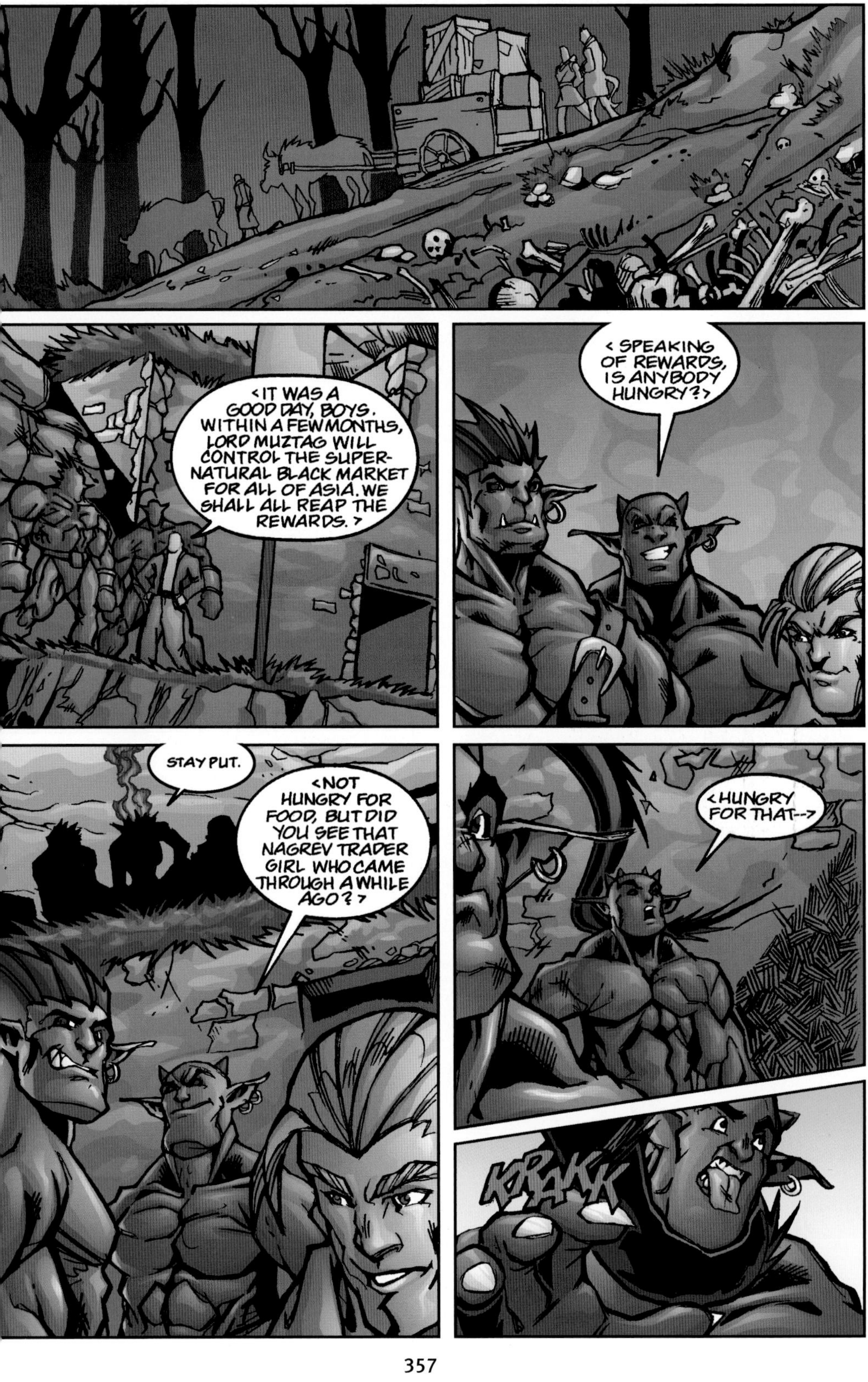
<IT WAS A GOOD DAY, BOYS. WITHIN A FEW MONTHS, LORD MUZTAG WILL CONTROL THE SUPER-NATURAL BLACK MARKET FOR ALL OF ASIA. WE SHALL ALL REAP THE REWARDS.>
<SPEAKING OF REWARDS, IS ANYBODY HUNGRY?>
STAY PUT.
<NOT HUNGRY FOR FOOD, BUT DID YOU SEE THAT NAGREV TRADER GIRL WHO CAME THROUGH A WHILE AGO?>
<HUNGRY FOR THAT-->
KRAKK

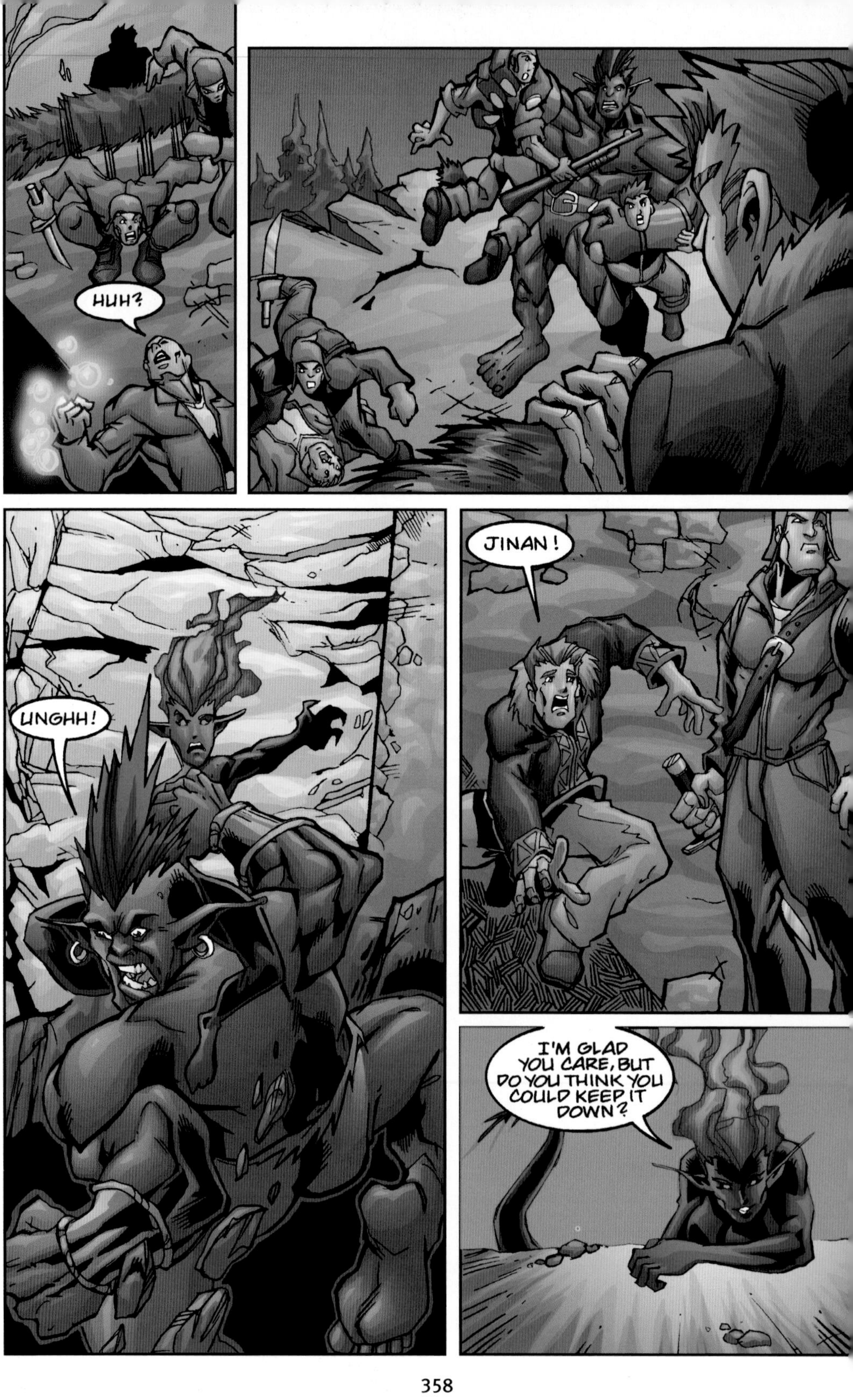
HUH?
UNGHH!
JINAN!
I'M GLAD YOU CARE, BUT DO YOU THINK YOU COULD KEEP IT DOWN?

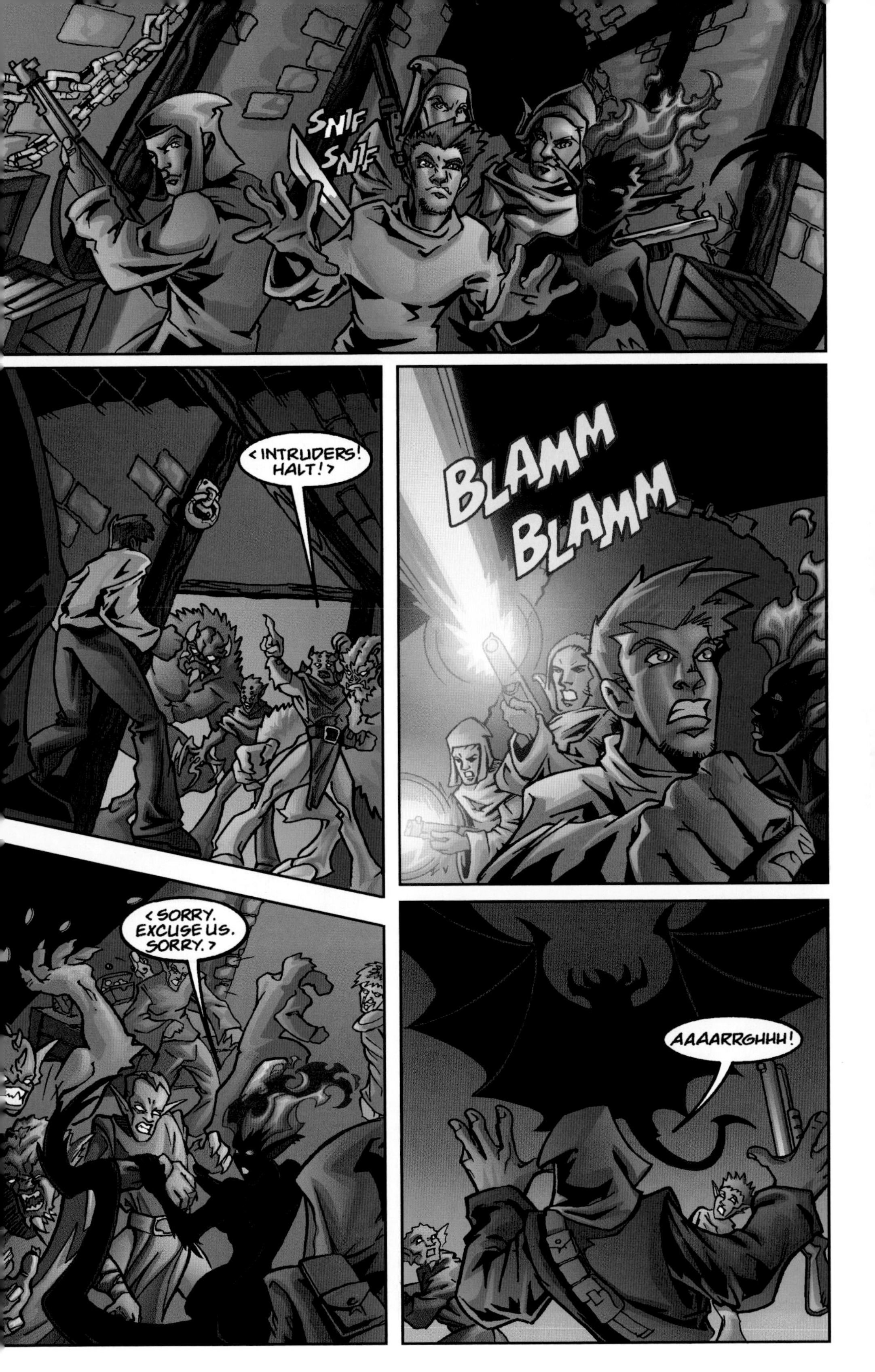
SNIF
SNIF
< INTRUDERS! HALT! >
BLAMM
BLAMM
< SORRY. EXCUSE US. SORRY. >
AAAARRGHHH!

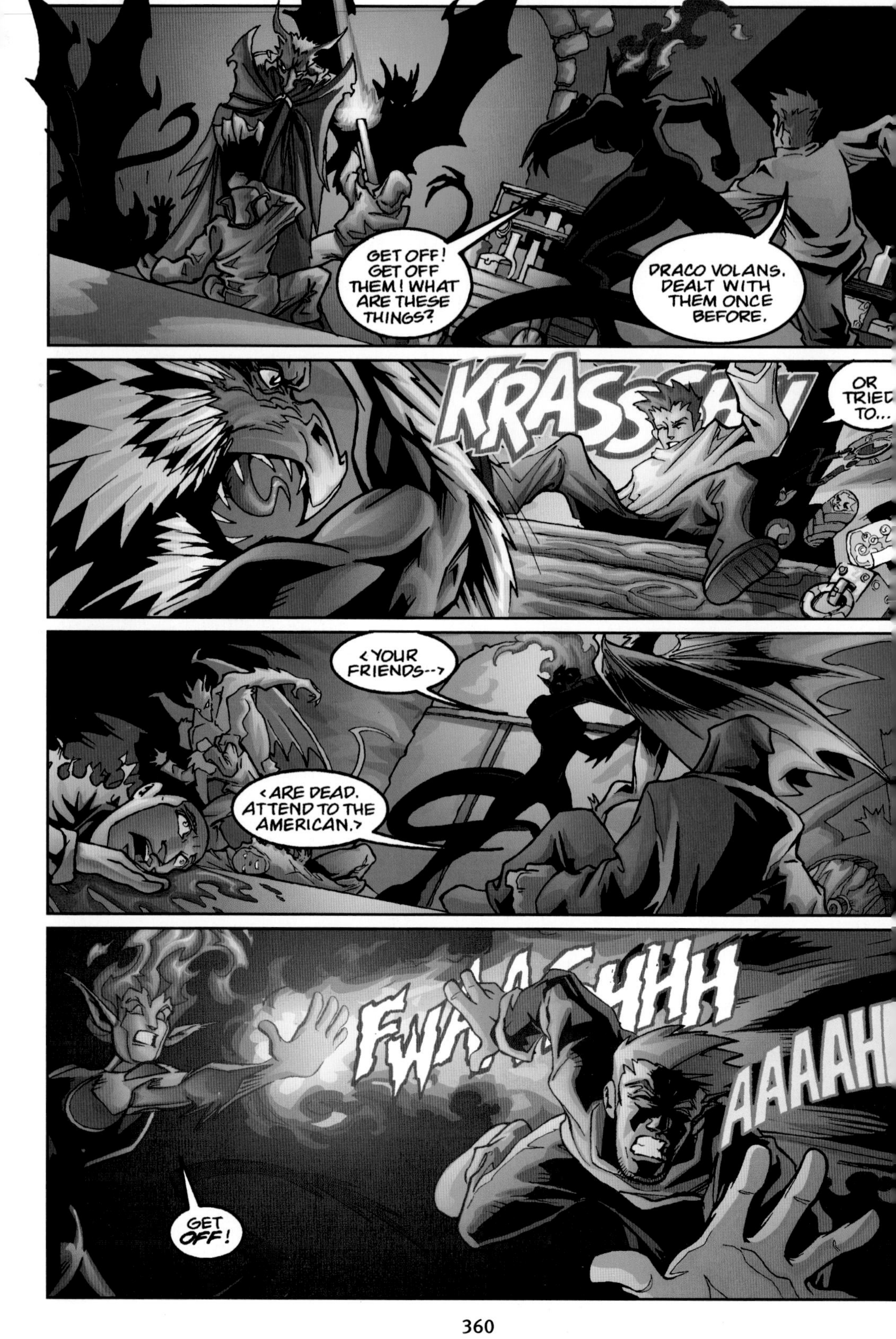
GET OFF! GET OFF THEM! WHAT ARE THESE THINGS?
DRACO VOLANS. DEALT WITH THEM ONCE BEFORE.
KRASS
OR TRIED TO...
<YOUR FRIENDS-->
<ARE DEAD. ATTEND TO THE AMERICAN.>
HH
GET OFF!

I'M SORRY. SO SORRY. I'M ALWAYS SO CAREFUL WITH MY FLAMES, SO AFRAID... ARE YOU ALL RIGHT?

ALIVE, FOR AT LEAST A LITTLE WHILE LONGER.

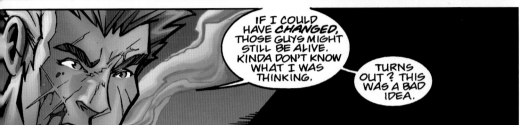

IF I COULD HAVE *CHANGED*, THOSE GUYS MIGHT STILL BE ALIVE. KINDA DON'T KNOW WHAT I WAS THINKING.

TURNS OUT? THIS WAS A BAD IDEA.

I I WOULDN'T SAY THAT.

ANYTHING THAT WILL ADD TO THE DAMNABLE MONK'S PAIN AND HUMILIATION IS WORTHWHILE.

I HAVE TAKEN HIS STUDENTS FROM HIM AND TWISTED THEIR SOULS. I HAVE MADE HIM MY CAPTIVE, DRIVEN HIM TO HIS KNEES,

AND NOW I SHALL DESTROY HIS LAST HOPE. THOSE WHO WOULD RESCUE SHANTOU WILL DIE AT THE HANDS OF HIS FORMER STUDENTS.

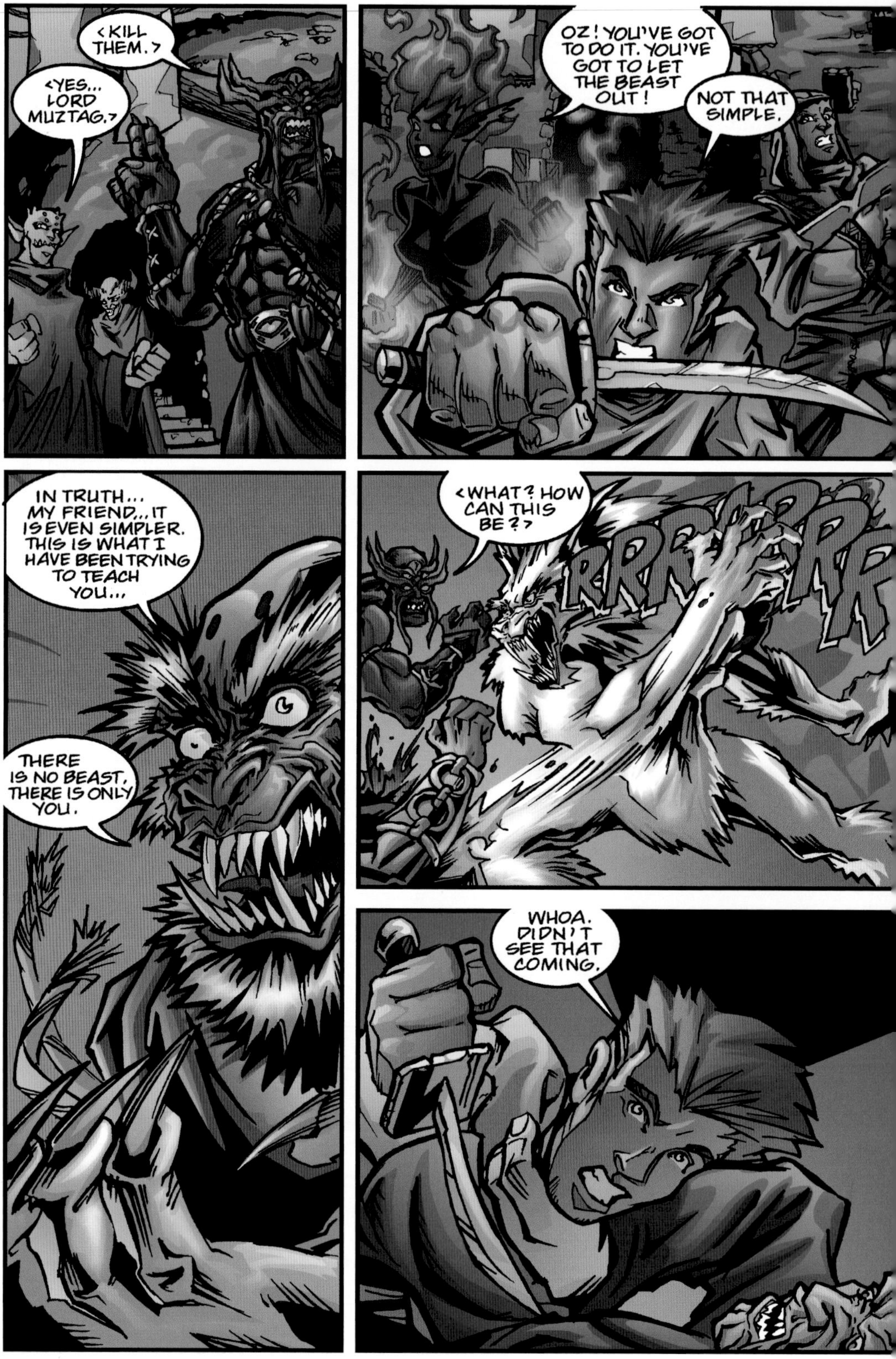
<KILL THEM.>
<YES... LORD MUZTAG.>
OZ! YOU'VE GOT TO DO IT. YOU'VE GOT TO LET THE BEAST OUT!
NOT THAT SIMPLE.
IN TRUTH... MY FRIEND... IT IS EVEN SIMPLER. THIS IS WHAT I HAVE BEEN TRYING TO TEACH YOU...
THERE IS NO BEAST, THERE IS ONLY YOU.
<WHAT? HOW CAN THIS BE?>
RRRAARRRR
WHOA. DIDN'T SEE THAT COMING.

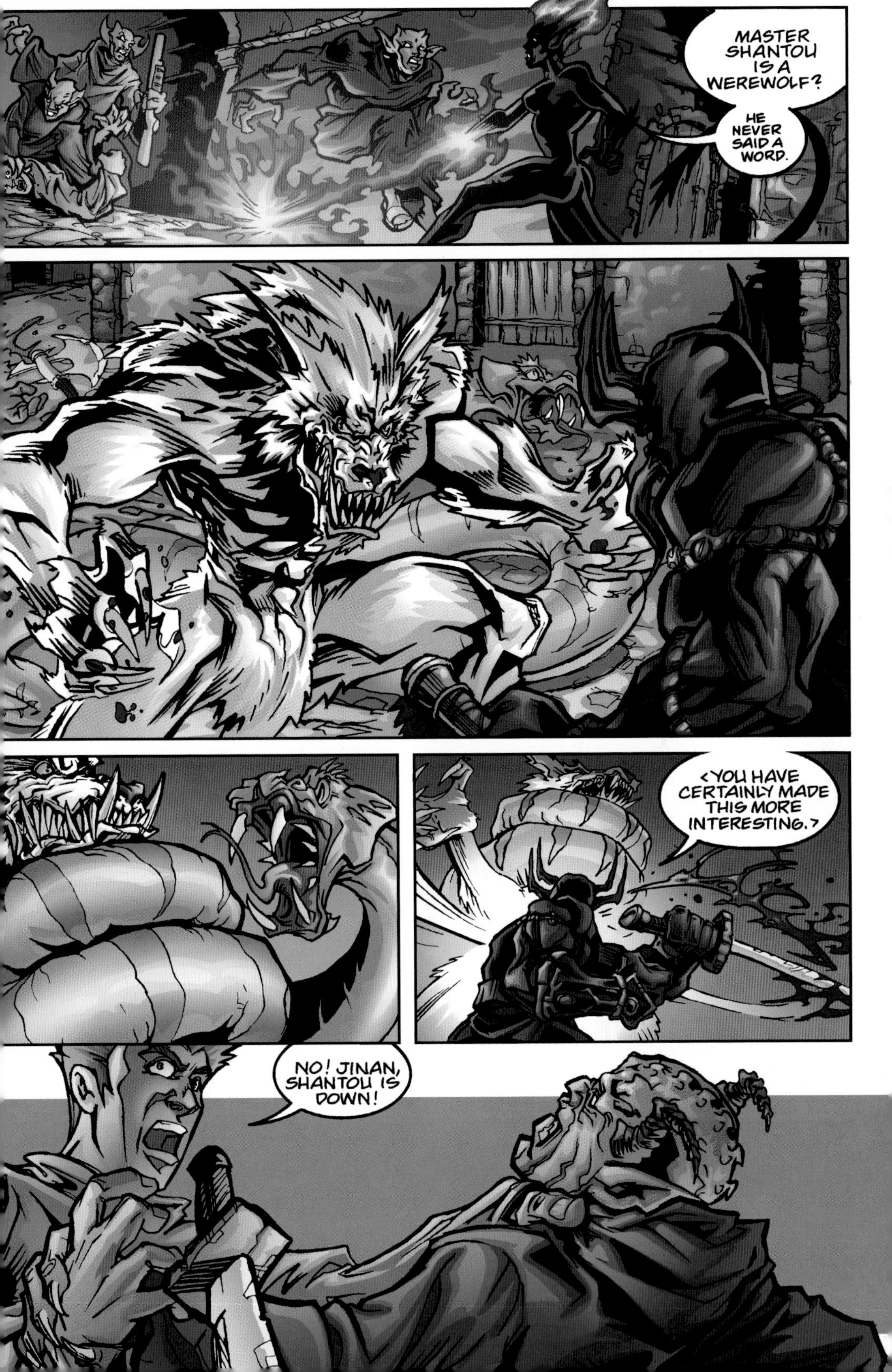
MASTER SHANTOU IS A WEREWOLF?
HE NEVER SAID A WORD.
<YOU HAVE CERTAINLY MADE THIS MORE INTERESTING.>
NO! JINAN, SHANTOU IS DOWN!

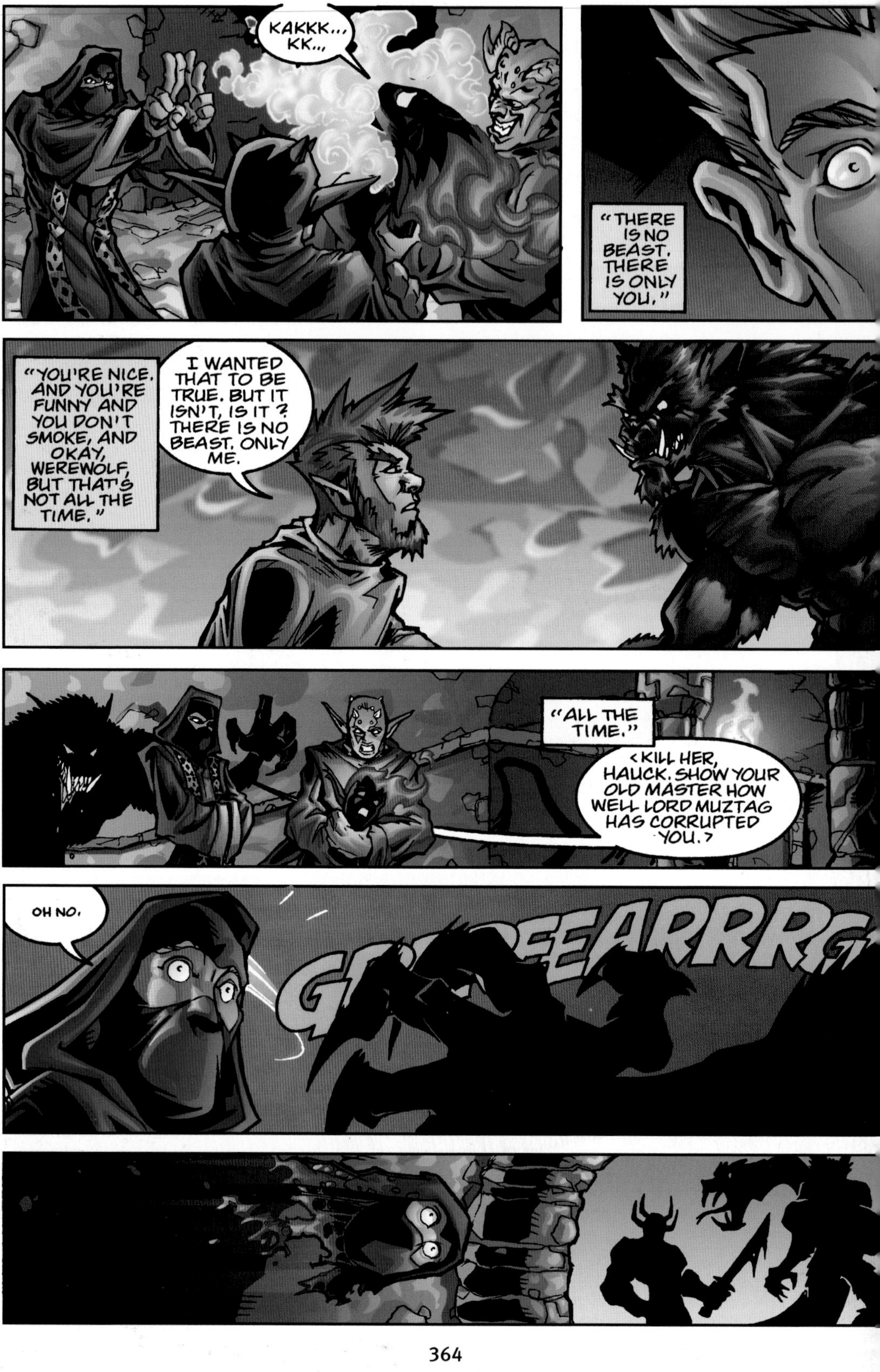
KAKKK..., KK...
"THERE IS NO BEAST. THERE IS ONLY YOU."
"YOU'RE NICE. AND YOU'RE FUNNY AND YOU DON'T SMOKE, AND OKAY, WEREWOLF, BUT THAT'S NOT ALL THE TIME."
I WANTED THAT TO BE TRUE. BUT IT ISN'T, IS IT? THERE IS NO BEAST. ONLY ME.
"ALL THE TIME."
<KILL HER, HAUCK. SHOW YOUR OLD MASTER HOW WELL LORD MUZTAG HAS CORRUPTED YOU.>
OH NO.

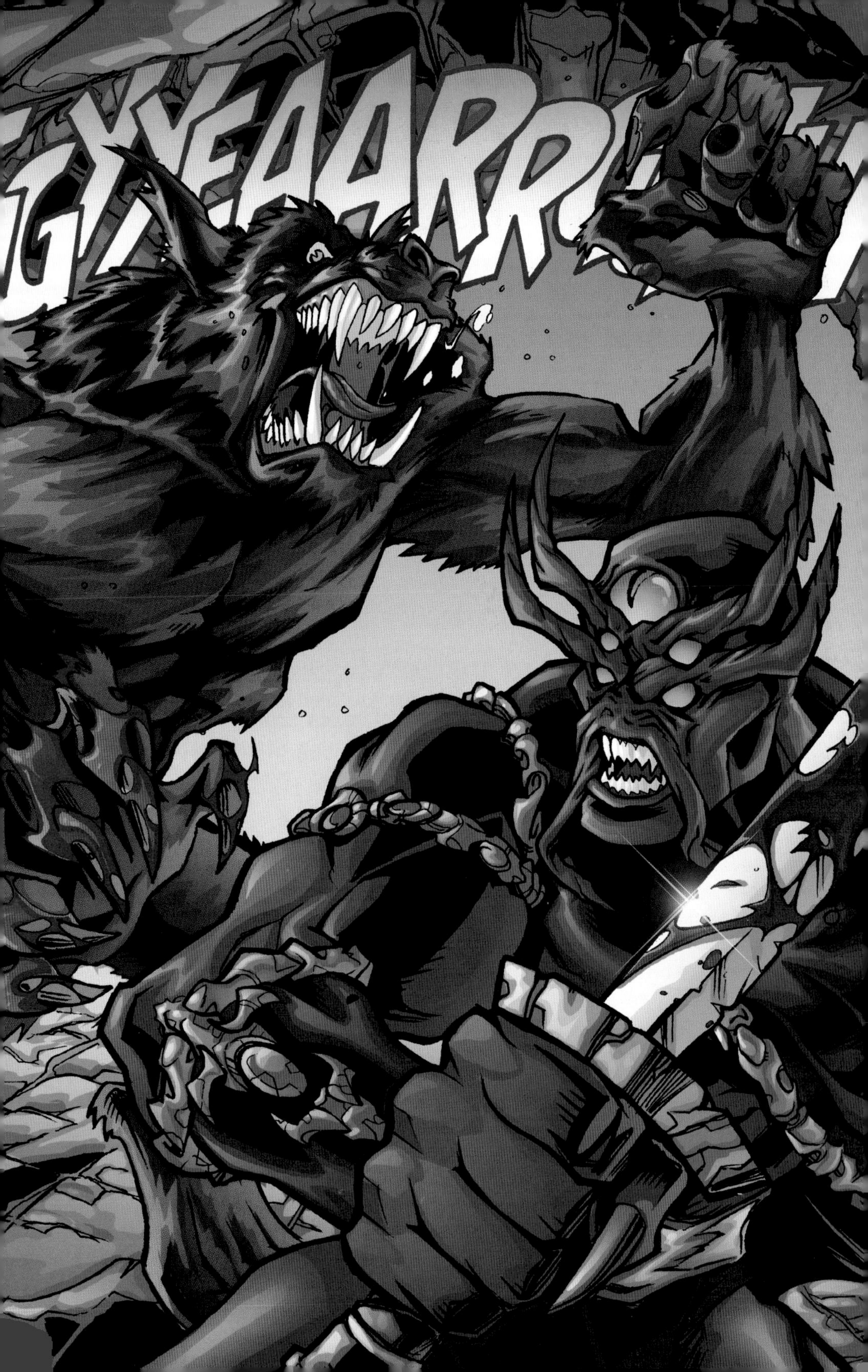
GYEAARR

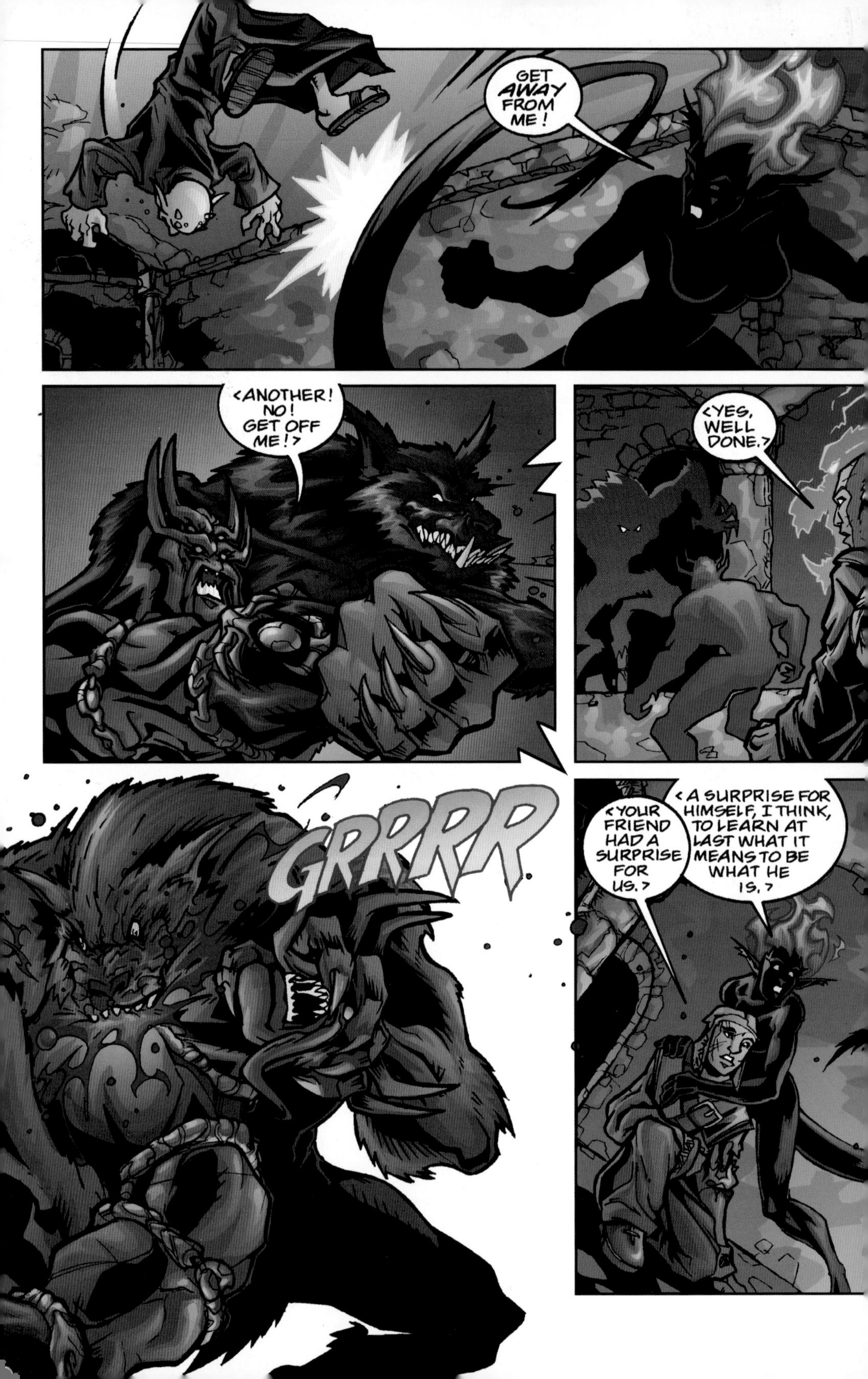
GET AWAY FROM ME!
<ANOTHER! NO! GET OFF ME!>
<YES, WELL DONE.>
GRRRR
<YOUR FRIEND HAD A SURPRISE FOR US.>
<A SURPRISE FOR HIMSELF, I THINK, TO LEARN AT LAST WHAT IT MEANS TO BE WHAT HE IS.>

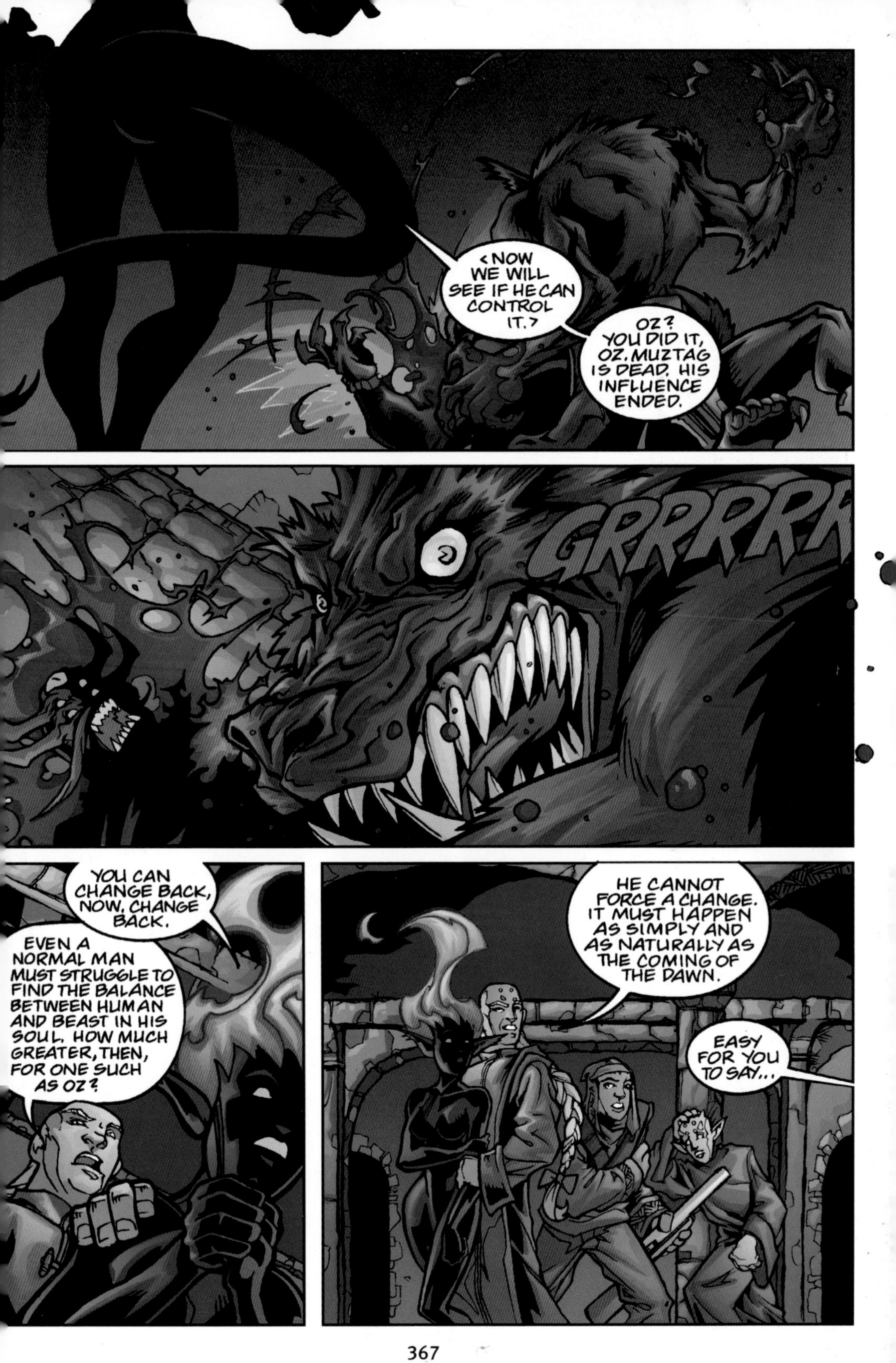
<NOW WE WILL SEE IF HE CAN CONTROL IT.>
OZ? YOU DID IT, OZ. MUZTAG IS DEAD. HIS INFLUENCE ENDED.
GRRRRR
YOU CAN CHANGE BACK, NOW. CHANGE BACK.
EVEN A NORMAL MAN MUST STRUGGLE TO FIND THE BALANCE BETWEEN HUMAN AND BEAST IN HIS SOUL. HOW MUCH GREATER, THEN, FOR ONE SUCH AS OZ?
HE CANNOT FORCE A CHANGE. IT MUST HAPPEN AS SIMPLY AND AS NATURALLY AS THE COMING OF THE DAWN.
EASY FOR YOU TO SAY...

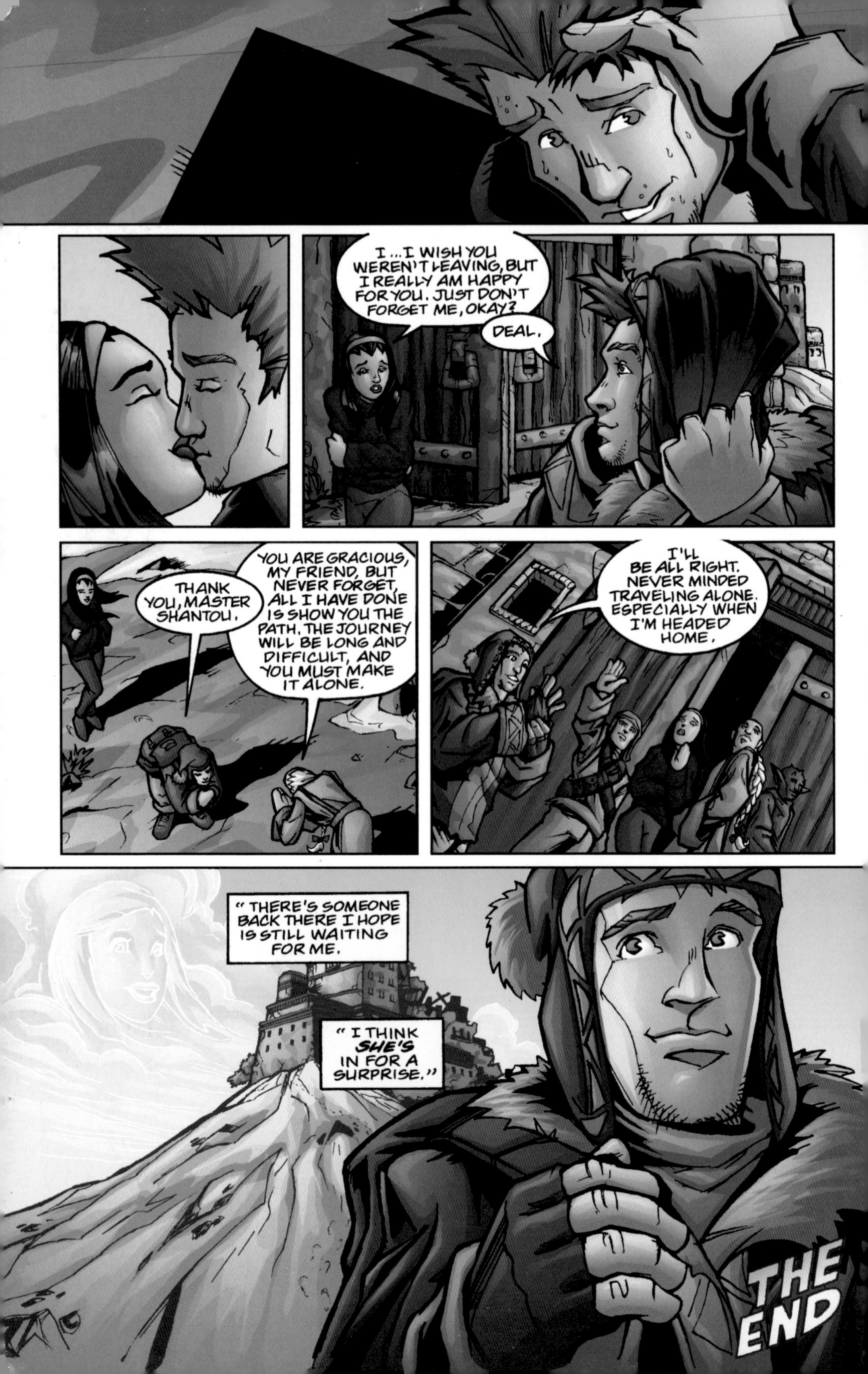
I ... I WISH YOU WEREN'T LEAVING, BUT I REALLY AM HAPPY FOR YOU. JUST DON'T FORGET ME, OKAY?
DEAL.
THANK YOU, MASTER SHANTOU.
YOU ARE GRACIOUS, MY FRIEND, BUT NEVER FORGET, ALL I HAVE DONE IS SHOW YOU THE PATH. THE JOURNEY WILL BE LONG AND DIFFICULT, AND YOU MUST MAKE IT ALONE.
I'LL BE ALL RIGHT. NEVER MINDED TRAVELING ALONE. ESPECIALLY WHEN I'M HEADED HOME.
"THERE'S SOMEONE BACK THERE I HOPE IS STILL WAITING FOR ME.
"I THINK SHE'S IN FOR A SURPRISE."
THE END